YEAR
OF THE
WICKED

YEAR
OF THE
WICKED

SUMMER · FALL · WINTER · SPRING
Previously titled *Dark Vengeance Vol. 1* and *Vol. 2*

JEFF MARIOTTE

SIMON PULSE
NEW YORK LONDON TORONTO SYDNEY NEW DELHI

SIMON PULSE

An imprint of Simon & Schuster Children's Publishing Division

1230 Avenue of the Americas, New York, New York 10020

This Simon Pulse paperback edition September 2019

Summer and *Fall* copyright © 2004 by Jeff Mariotte

Winter and *Spring* copyright © 2005 by Jeff Mariotte

Previously titled *Dark Vengeance Vol. 1* and *Vol. 2*

Cover illustration copyright © 2019 by Helen Crawford-White

For information about special discounts for bulk purchases, please contact Simon & Schuster Special Sales at 1-866-506-1949 or business@simonandschuster.com.

The Simon & Schuster Speakers Bureau can bring authors to your live event. For more information or to book an event contact the Simon & Schuster Speakers Bureau at 1-866-248-3049 or visit our website at www.simonspeakers.com.

Cover designed by Tiara Iandiorio

Interior designed by Mike Rosamilia

The text of this book was set in Adobe Garamond Pro.

Manufactured in the United States of America

2 4 6 8 10 9 7 5 3 1

Library of Congress Control Number 2019931883

ISBN 978-1-5344-4482-9 (pbk)

ISBN 978-1-4424-3625-1 (*Dark Vengeance Vol. 1* eBook)

ISBN 978-1-4424-3626-8 (*Dark Vengeance Vol. 2* eBook)

These titles were previously published individually.

FOR MARCY, WITH ALL MY LOVE,
AND FOR ALL YOU WITCHES OUT THERE

† † †

CONTENTS

SUMMER

Kerry Profitt's diary, August 11

Once again I woke up screaming. Drenched in sweat, wet sheets tangled around my legs as if I'd been flailing them for hours. Brandy even came into our room and told me she could tell the instant I snapped out of it. My mouth was open like a gasping fish, she said, and then it closed, and my eyes opened. And I had let out a real ear-piercer, because, after all, there was this face in front of me, looking at me like I was some kind of sideshow freak.

Which, you know, if the shoe fits . . .

When my heart stopped trying to tear through my rib cage, and I could breathe again, she asked me what I'd been dreaming about. Hell if I know, I told her. Whenever I wake up, I can never remember anything more than an overpowering sense of dread. Doom on wheels.

Maybe it's the weird hours I've been keeping. I worked till eleven last night, same as the night before, but had the breakfast-and-lunch shift for three days before that. Today it's the late shift again, so I slept in probably longer than I should have. My head is throbbing so hard I can barely see the computer screen, and who knows if I'll be able to read this later?

But that's why Einstein invented ibuprofen, right? And spell check. And Scott's brewing fresh coffee. Nectar of the gods.

More later.
K.

1

She couldn't see the ocean from where she stood on a grease-caked cement step just outside the kitchen's back door. A row of bungalows—identical dark boxes, some with glowing windows—blocked her view. She could hear the water, though—the steady, dull thunder of the surf reminding her that it was close, at the edge of both the Seaside Resort and the continent. And she could smell it, a sharp tang that battled for supremacy over the smells of steak, seafood, and smoke that blew out from the kitchen. Towering above the bungalows, underlit by the resort's floodlights, incredibly tall palm trees swayed on their skinny trunks in the evening breeze, looking like skyrocket bursts frozen in time at the ends of their own contrails. A sliver of crescent moon dangled above them, high and distant.

Kerry Profitt was a daughter of the Great Plains, born and raised near the confluence of two great rivers in Cairo, Illinois. But the Mississippi and Ohio, powerful as they were, had nothing on the Pacific Ocean. The ocean was magical to her, its depths and mysteries were boundless, its call irresistible. She had made a point, since hitting La Jolla, California, for her summer job, of keeping it in sight whenever possible. Bad for the skin, all that sun and salt air, and she, with her complexion like fresh snow ("whitest white girl I've ever seen" was what Brandy said) knew better. But she couldn't deny the ocean's magnetic pull.

Lost in thought, she didn't see the shadowed figure slip into the alley, didn't know she wasn't alone until the voice startled her. "Hey, Kerr, where is it the swallows go back to?"

Startled, she managed to keep her cool, and she smiled when she recognized the voice. She knew it belonged to Josh Quinn, one of her housemates, but it took her a moment to refocus her gaze and pick him out in the dark alley. His skin was every bit as pale as hers, but by choice, not genetics, and the black of his hair came from a bottle, unlike hers. He looked as out-of-place in the valet's uniform—white shirt, maroon vest, black pants—as a lion on a kindergarten playground.

"Umm . . . Capistrano, I think," Kerry replied after a moment's consideration. She was used to this kind of thing from Josh, king of the non sequitur. *If his middle name isn't Random, it should be.*

"Yeah, that's right," he agreed.

Since it didn't seem like he was going to take the discussion any further, she decided to press the point. "Why?"

He struck a match in the darkness and shielded it with cupped hands to a cigarette held between his lips. "These tourists, man," he said around the butt. Then, blowing out a plume of smoke—away from Kerry, because she would have killed him if he hadn't—he continued with an exasperated tone. "They're like those swallows."

"The ones in Capistrano?"

"Yeah, those."

"In what way?" *You had to ask,* she immediately chastised herself, bracing for the answer.

"Some of them seem to come here every summer, like clockwork."

She had noticed the same thing, though without the bird metaphor. "Good for business, I guess," she pointed out.

"I guess. But this one guy—you know the kind, enormous gut, Texas accent, gold watch that cost more than everything I've owned in my life put together—yelled at me just now because I didn't turn on the heat in his Mercedes."

"The heat?" Kerry asked with surprise. It was a fairly cool night. They all were here, close to the water, and balmy eves, she had learned, were not so much a southern California thing. Once the sun went down, the day's heat fled fast. But even so, far from wintry cold.

"That's what I said. Only it was more like, 'Dude, are you freaking crazy? It's August!' And he was like, 'I told you last year, if it's after dark, I like the heat on when you bring the car around. It takes time to warm up.'"

"But you didn't work here last year," Kerry pointed out.

Josh jabbed the glowing end of his cigarette at her to emphasize his point. "Exactly," he said. "But you think reality matters to this guy? Like I'm the first Goth valet in California history or something, so it couldn't have been someone else he told last year. He's so convinced it was me, he stiffed me on the tip."

Kerry pushed aside the hand that held the cigarette. She had made clear, plenty of times, what she thought of that habit and couldn't understand how he managed to reconcile it with his vegan lifestyle. "Hey," he had said when she'd raised the question once, "who said life was free of contradiction? Anyway, it's a vegetable. If tobacco had a face, I wouldn't smoke it." Sympathetically, in spite of the noxious weed, she rubbed Josh's bony shoulder. "There are always a few pains," she said. "But most of the guests are pretty nice."

"Maybe to you," Josh countered. "You can spit in their food. All I can do is adjust their seat backs wrong, and the potential threat level just isn't the same."

Kerry laughed then and punched the shoulder she had just been rubbing. "I'll tell you what," she offered. "I'll trade places with you for a day. You deal with complaints about food being too hot or too cold or too spicy or too bland, and guys grabbing your ass and winking at you like you're going to go, 'Oh, you're just so handsome. I'll put this tray of food down and meet you in the alley.'"

"I guess it depends on the guy," Josh suggested with a smile she could see in the glow of his cigarette embers as he inhaled. "Hey, my principles are nothing if not situational. And believe me, I'm not under any illusions that you have an easy job either."

"Summer jobs aren't supposed to be easy," Kerry replied, ignoring his jokes. "They're supposed to be brutal and demeaning and ill-paying. Toughens you up for the rest of your life."

Josh nodded. "I guess you're right." He flipped his smoke to the sidewalk and crushed it out with his shoe. "So, you ready to jet? Waiting on Mace?"

"Waiting on Mace," Kerry confirmed. It had become a house motto over the summer. Mace Winston was never ready on time for anything—he was the only person she had ever known who was perpetually late *leaving* work. She was more than ready to go—her headache from that morning had never really gone away, and working in the noise of the crowded dining room had just made it worse.

Before Josh could reply, Mace came through the kitchen door. He was a dishwasher, and the hairs on his muscular forearms were plastered to his skin by the water that had leaked into his rubber gloves. Even the sleeves of his T-shirt were wet. His broad, handsome face was flushed from the hot water he'd been working in, a line of sweat sitting on his upper lip.

He tossed Kerry a lopsided grin, as if something hurt in a place too embarrassing to mention. "You've got to start encouraging those folks to eat less," he told her. "Fewer side dishes. Better for their hearts, and better for me."

"I'll see what I can do," she said with a laugh. Neither of these guys were people she'd have been likely to hang out with under other circumstances, but over the course of the summer, they'd become close friends. Whenever she was talking with them, Kerry felt an easy, pleasant sense of comfort envelop her like a warm blanket on a cold night. It almost—but not quite—overwhelmed the sense of impending disaster her dreams had left her with and the headache that accompanied them. "Now can we go home?"

The others offered consent, as if either of them would be likely to argue in favor of staying and working awhile longer. Kerry took one last glimpse toward the water she couldn't see, breathed in a final lungful of ocean air, and headed for the parking lot with the others.

The Seaside Resort at La Jolla, to use its full name, was as soulless and impersonal as most large corporations. But it was also a corporation that recognized the fact that its business was largely seasonal, and to help it through the busy summer season, it hired a lot of temporary workers. Summer help came from all over the world—Prague, Sydney, Heidelberg, Minsk, and even the exotic climes of King of Prussia, Pennsylvania. So the resort offered, as one of its worker-friendly perks, a roommate-matching service. Kerry had signed up, filling out the requisite forms and answering a slew of questions about things she wouldn't even have talked about with the aunt and uncle she lived with. She was slotted into a house in nearby Bird Rock with five people with whom she had in common only the fact that they all worked for Seaside.

After a few weeks of initial discomfort, though, everyone fell into a kind of casual routine. Kerry, Josh, and Mace shared the house with Scott Banner and Brandy Pearson, who had come out from Harvard as a couple, and Rebecca Levine. The couple didn't get to share a room since there were only two bedrooms in the small cottage, and nobody was willing to cram four into one room so that two could have the other. But Brandy and Scott still managed plenty of alone time in the house, and they'd both had tonight off. They had said they were going to a movie, and as Mace pulled his massive baby blue Lincoln Continental onto the narrow driveway, Kerry noticed that Scott's RAV4 was still gone.

"Guess the lovebirds are still out on the town," Josh pointed out, echoing Kerry's observation.

"Too bad for them," Mace said, without a hint of sympathy. The driveway ran alongside the house, crowded on one side by the neighboring house's oleander bushes and on the other by the cottage itself. There was room for both cars if the RAV4 got tucked in first, but when Mace's monstrosity had pulled in as far as it could, the RAV4's rear end wouldn't clear the sidewalk. Which meant he had to park on the street. Mace had urged him just to block the sidewalk a little, but Scott was full of Harvard-induced social activism and refused to in case someone came by in a wheelchair. Kerry admired the stand he took, but couldn't have said for sure if she would be as noble if she had to be the one looking for street parking late at night.

The cottage was dark, as if Brandy and Scott had left during the day and had forgotten that no one would be home until after eleven. Rebecca had been working early shifts, and was no doubt already sound asleep—the girl could sleep anywhere, through anything, Kerry had decided.

The nearest streetlight was half a block away, largely obstructed by a big willow tree that overhung most of the minuscule front yard. A low hedge ringed the front of the house, bisected by a flagstone walkway that led from the sidewalk to the front steps. Their landlord paid for landscaping. If it'd been left up to the six of them, Kerry was sure everything would have died by July.

"Somebody could've left a light on," Josh complained, fumbling in his pocket for keys. "I can't even see the front door."

"Like they're gonna think of that," Mace replied quickly. "Probably too heavy into lip-lock mode when they walked out. And Sleeping Beauty was most likely out before the sun went down."

Having no flashlight handy, Kerry, who was not yet out of the Lincoln, hung back to hold the door open in case its dome light could cast a little illumination to help Josh. With considerable and fluent cursing, Josh managed to jam his key into the lock and got the door open. Inside, he flipped switches, and light blasted out from the coach lamp by the door, the windows, and the gaping doorway.

Light that etched, among other things, a pair of legs sticking out of the hedge. Male legs, it looked like, clad in dark pants, feet in what Kerry guessed were expensive leather ankle-high boots. She realized that a far more appropriate response to noticing the legs would have been to scream rather than, well, *noticing* them.

But the scream, practiced so often recently in dreams, wouldn't come. It caught in her throat like a chicken bone. Instead she barely rasped out Mace's name, since his back was still visible in the doorway.

"*Mace . . .*"

He turned, gave her a questioning look.

"Mace," she said again, a little more forcefully.

"What's up, Kerry?"

She pointed toward the hedge. Taking a step closer, she could see that the man, whoever he was, had crashed through the brush and was lying mostly covered by its greenery. "Umm . . . he doesn't belong there."

Finally Mace noticed him. "Oh, Jesus, Kerry. Get inside, I'll call the cops."

"I don't know if he needs cops," Kerry said, inching closer. "An ambulance, maybe."

"He's just some drunk, Kerry," Mace argued. "Fell down there and couldn't wake up."

But Kerry didn't think so. She'd been around enough drunks—held the hair away from friends' faces when they got sick, dodged clumsily groping hands at parties, even tucked her own uncle Marsh into bed a time or two or ten—to know the stink that wafted around them like a foul cloud. The closer she got to this man, though, the more she knew the smell was all wrong. Instead of the miasma of alcohol, there was a familiar metallic tang. The man in the hedge was very still and silent, and she moved closer still, as Mace watched, frozen, from the doorway.

The smell was blood, and it was thick in the air around the man.

Crap, she thought. *He's been stabbed. Or shot.*

She knew there was no way he hurt himself that much falling through the hedge. He'd have been scratched up—*could even have put out an eye on a branch*—but he wouldn't have opened enough veins to kick up a stench like a blood bank on two-for-one day. Kerry had nursemaided her mom for years while cancer had spread throughout her body, finally taking the older woman. Kerry was no trained doctor, but she'd learned a little something about emergency medical care during the ordeal, and she had a feeling that this guy was going to need everything she could offer and then some.

Another smell, underlying the one of blood, nagged at her, and Kerry suddenly realized that it was a faint electrical stink of ozone, as if lightning had struck close by.

"I don't think he needs the police," she repeated, leaning forward to find the man's wrist in hopes of checking his pulse. By now, she noticed, Josh's lean form had appeared in the doorway, silhouetted behind Mace. "At least not first thing. He needs a paramedic."

The hand she had been groping for clamped around her forearm with surprising strength. "No," the man said, his voice an anxious rasp almost indistinguishable from the rustling sound his motion made in the hedge. "No doctors."

Her heart jumped to her throat, and she tried to yank her arm free. But the man held fast to it, even raising his head a little to look at her. A stray beam from the streetlight shone through the leaves onto his right eye, making it gleam like something from a Poe story. "Promise me, no doctors," he insisted. "Take me in and give me shelter or leave me here, but let me live or die on my own terms."

Mace and Josh had both come down from the doorway and hovered over Kerry and the wounded man like anxious seagulls at the beach, looking for handouts. "Dude, let her go," Mace ordered, snarling. "Or I'll really put a hurtin' on you."

She heard Mace shift as if he really did intend to attack the wounded man, and then she did something that surprised even her. She spread her one free arm—the man on the ground continued to clutch her right arm with a grip so powerful she didn't think she could have shaken it—over the man, as if to protect him from whatever Mace might have in mind. "No!" she shouted. "He's hurt bad enough. Leave him alone or help me bring him inside, but don't be stupid."

"I've got to wonder about your definition of stupid," Mace said, sounding petulant.

"He's right, Kerr," Josh added. "You want to bring some bloody stranger into our house?"

"You guys both missed Sunday school the day they talked about the good Samaritan?" Kerry shot back over her shoulder. "If you don't want to help me, just get out of the way. He's losing blood and he can't stay out here overnight." She pushed her way deeper into the thick hedge, feeling the branches scratch and tear at her skin like a hundred cats' claws, snagging her long, fine black hair and the fabric of the white cotton dress shirt that, with snug black pants, was her restaurant uniform.

She reached around the stranger's head with her left hand, hoping she could ease him up out of the hedge. Holding back the worst of the branches with her own body so he wouldn't suffer any further injury, she found the back of his head and slipped her hand down to support his neck. His hair was long in back, and matted with sticky blood. Never mind the tears, the bloodstains would make her uniform shirt unwearable.

"That's crazy talk," Mace complained behind her. She ignored him and drew the man slowly forward.

Josh unleashed another string of colorful profanities, but he knelt beside Kerry and shoved branches out of the way, helping to bring the wounded man out of the hedge. "I guess we need to get the mug out of our bushes anyway."

"You're both crazy, then," Mace opined. Kerry couldn't see Mace, but from the sound of it, she gathered that he had given up on them both and was on his way back inside. She found herself hoping that it wasn't to get a baseball bat or to call 911.

What do I care? she wondered. The good Samaritan thing had been a flip response to Mace and Josh's moaning, but it wasn't any kind of lifestyle choice she had made. She guessed that, as Josh might say, it meant the reaction she was having in this case was situational. Something about this battered, broken man in their bushes played on her sympathy, and she was unwilling to leave him there or to go against his stated wishes by calling the authorities.

With Josh's assistance she was able to disentangle the man from the hedge. In the light, the blood on his face was shocking—dark and glistening and obviously fresh. He might have been handsome once, but age and the damage caused by whatever had done this to him had taken care of that. She felt, more than ever, an urgency about getting him inside, getting his bleeding stopped, and trying to prevent shock.

"Can you stand up?" she asked him, not sure if he was even still conscious. But he forced his eyes open again, raised his head, and looked at her with something like kindness. His mouth curled into an agonized smile.

"Not a chance," he whispered. Then his head drooped, his eyes closed, his muscles went limp. For the first time, his grip on her forearm eased. She touched his neck, felt the pulse there.

"He's still alive," she declared.

"But he's deadweight," Josh said. Josh was, well . . . "lean" was a polite way to put it. "Scrawny" was more the truth. And the stranger was a big man, probably a little more than six feet tall, weighing a couple hundred pounds. "You think we can carry him?"

Kerry spoke without hesitation, without doubt. "We can carry him. You take his feet."

"Oh, I almost forgot," Josh said. He used the name that the housemates had applied to Kerry ever since they'd become familiar with her stubborn streak, "Bulldog."

Hoisting the stranger's shoulders, she grinned at Josh way down at the other end. "Woof."

Kerry Profitt's diary, August 11–12

Just for fun I looked back to see my first impressions of my housemates. Thinking to compare them, I guess, to current impressions.

Just goes to show how wrong you can be sometimes.

"Can you say insufferable?" I had typed about Josh Quinn. "Gay, Goth, vegan, and adamant about all three. If he keeps it up, I'll be surprised if he survives the summer. Not that he could be 'voted out' or whatever. Not that, to push the metaphor to the breaking point and beyond, this is a reality TV show or anything. *The Real World*, *Big Brother*, *Survivor*—they have nothing on the trials and tribs of six genuine strangers trying to get along in a house without cameras, supercool furniture, and a cash prize on the other end."

There was more, but why cut-and-paste all night when I can simply scan the folder menu and look it up? Suffice to say, his first impression was the kind that almost makes you hope it'll also be a last impression.

Mace Winston, on the other hand. Then, I wrote: "Hmm . . . he's got a body like Michelangelo's *David*—not that I've seen under the fig leaf, figuratively speaking. But handsome, buff, and he tooled up in this sky blue Lincoln Continental—except for the left rear, I think he said quarter-panel, which is kind of rust colored and clearly taken from a different car. He said he found the whole thing in a desert canyon somewhere in New Mexico, full of bullet holes and snakes, but he cleaned it up and fixed it up and here he is. He really does wear the boots and one of those straw hats and he has squinty, twinkly eyes like some movie cowboy and somehow it all works for him. I don't know if there's a brain in his head. Ask me later if I care."

But tonight, when the chips, as they say, were down, Mace turned away and Josh came through. Although the heaving and ho-ing would have gone better had it been the other way around, I'm sure.

Okay.

Ms. Harrington, in eleventh-grade speech, used to give us holy hell when we started with "okay" or "umm." She said it was just a verbal time waster, a way of saying that our thoughts obviously weren't well enough organized to begin with because if they were, we'd start out by saying what we really wanted to say.

Boy, was she right.

So . . . okay. Umm . . .

There's a man in our living room, passed out on that butt-sprung lump of fabric and wood that passes for a sofa. We managed to stop most of the bleeding, put bandages on the worst cuts, got a couple of blankets (mine, since no one else would volunteer theirs) over him, elevated his feet higher than his head. Near his head there's a glass of water, in case he wakes up and is thirsty, and he seems to be breathing okay.

He looks like he lost an argument with a wood chipper. I can't even imagine what happened to him. Hit by a truck that hurled him all the way across our lawn? Picked up by a stray tornado and dropped there?

But he said no doctors, and that's exactly how many he's getting. Why? And why did I argue against calling the police? Rebecca woke up just before Scott and Brandy finally came home. I had the same argument with them that I'd had with Mace, although Scott came over to my side pretty quickly and Rebecca, bless her huge hippie heart, lit a candle and dug right in to help with the bandaging. With Josh already allied, that made four against two—Mace and Brandy. Brandy did a lot of huffing noises and is now either sound asleep, or pretending to be, as I laptop this. Is that a verb yet? If not, how soon?

Other good verbs: To delay. To procrastinate. To put off.

Okay.

Of course, what I wanted to do with my summer was to lead a life that might, by some reasonable definition, be normal. As opposed to the life I've led for the past, well, lifetime. Summer job, summer friends, maybe a summer boyfriend, even. Just, y'know, normal stuff.

I don't think this qualifies.

And to be fair, they're entirely correct (and "they" know who they are). We don't know who he is—he could be dangerous, a felon, a crazy person. Or even, you know, someone from Katy Perry's band, although maybe a little senior for that. But, to continue being fair, he's not the one who said "no cops." That was, not to put too fine a point on it, me. He just said "no doctors," and maybe he's a Christian Scientist or whatever. I was the one who said "no cops," and I'm still not sure why I did that. But it was the right thing to do.

I hope.

Journaling is supposed to help one figure out one's own emotions, right? Tap into the unconscious, puzzle out the mysteries therein? Not tonight, Dr. Freud. I don't know why I trust the old road-kill guy snoozing on the couch. But I do.

Go figure. Go to sleep. Go to hell. Just go. See you tomorrow, if we're not all murdered in our sleep. Or lack thereof.

More later, I hope.

K.

2

Scott Banner was one of those guys who did lots of things well. Kerry hadn't known him all that long, but then it didn't take long to figure that out about him. He got good grades in school, hence the Harvard bit. He worked hard, he could cook and clean quickly and efficiently, which were pluses where Kerry was concerned because that meant fewer household chores that she had to do around the summer house. He played soccer, and he looked fit and trim in the polo shirts, khakis, and Topsiders that he favored, and while Kerry thought he was dressing about twenty years ahead of his age, he somehow managed to pull it off.

His girlfriend Brandy, black, athletic, and as graceful as Kerry was not, appreciated those things about him too, confiding to Kerry that he would make someone a great husband one day, hoping that someone would be her. Kerry thought they made a wonderful couple, occasionally wishing she had someone who matched her as well as Scott and Brandy did each other.

One of the most important things to know about Scott was that he made really excellent coffee. And for those occasions when he wasn't available, there was a spot called Java Coast in downtown La Jolla, next to an English as a foreign language school that attracted vast numbers of young, available men—all foreign, of course, but Kerry had picked up a few words of Spanish, French, German, and Russian over the summer. The mornings that she worked early or that Scott was otherwise unavailable for barista duties, she allowed herself to splurge on the pricey brews there. All of which went to the fact that, on this particular morning, having slept almost not at all, Kerry had the distinct feeling that there just wasn't going to be enough coffee in the world to get her through the day. She had developed a serious caffeine habit over the summer. But some days it was more crucial than others.

Today she sniffed the air hopefully, even before she rolled out of the sack. No fragrant aroma of the glorious bean. So Scott was sleeping in, or Brandy had been ticked enough about the way last night's argument had gone that she had kicked him out of the house or dragged him away for an early breakfast (and accompanied by a stern talking-to).

Or, of course, it meant that the stranger in their living room had in fact been an axe murderer, and all of her housemates were dead.

With that image in her mind, she kicked off the sheets and glanced at herself. Green cotton pajama pants and a tank top provided enough coverage. She padded barefoot across the hardwood floor, pulled the door open. A short hallway led to the living room, and she could smell the man before she saw him. He was still there, and he needed a shower more than ever. But if he had, in fact, murdered the rest of the household, she'd have expected him to smell more like fresh blood—as he had last night—and less like stale sweat.

So all in all, an improvement over where things *could* have been.

And there had been no nightmares during the night, she realized, which was a bonus. She'd had recurrent nightmares before, but not since the days when she was young enough to comfort herself by hugging the rag-doll clown she'd named BoBo. He was long since put away, though, stored in a trunk in her uncle Marsh's attic. Approaching the stranger, she found herself wishing for a moment that she had BoBo here with her, giving her courage as he had done when she was a child.

The living room was dimly lit—curtains still drawn, but they were moth-eaten and sunshine leaked through—and nobody was around. Kerry approached the stranger, whose breath was ragged but steady, and looked at his pale, drawn face. He looked different, somehow, than he had the night before. Still gaunt, but his cheeks seemed less sunken, the hollows of his eyes shallower than they had been. It was almost as if, she thought, the night's sleep had not only allowed him to heal but had made him younger at the same time.

Even so, Rolling Stones young, not Radiohead young. Big difference.

A sound from behind her. Kerry turned. Rebecca, her short-cropped orange hair reaching in every direction at once, stood there in blue fuzzy slippers and a cotton nightgown. Rebecca took a bath every day, never a shower, and she spent a minimum of forty minutes—more often an hour—in the bathroom. Lit candles, put in a bath bomb or bubble bath, something floral. Pampered herself. Kerry admired her dedication even if—in a house with six people and only one bathroom and a half—she often resented the time it took. But a cloud of flowery fragrance usually surrounded Rebecca, as it did now, wafting to Kerry's nose across the room, providing relief from the stranger's stench.

Rebecca blinked away sleep. "I stayed up last night," she said in a quiet voice. "Watching him."

Kerry felt an unexpected surge of jealousy, as if the strange man sleeping on their couch was her find, not anyone else's. She knew it made no sense. *Just tired*, she decided. She hadn't stayed up watching him. Thinking about him, though. "Did he do anything?"

A shrug. "Just slept. Maybe dreamed some—he moaned a little, and kind of scrunched his face up, you know."

"How long did you watch him?" Kerry asked, hoping the answer wasn't long enough to be creepy.

"Just awhile," Rebecca said, shrugging some more. Kerry had learned that was one of her signature moves. Maybe a sign of low self-esteem, as if to accompany her statements with a shrug meant that they shouldn't be taken too seriously. "I think he's getting better."

Kerry had to agree, though it was absurd to think that just a few hours of sleep would make much difference to a man as wounded as he'd been. *Well,* she mentally corrected, *a few hours of sleep and some basic first aid.*

But she had thought the same thing when she first glanced at him. Now, as if disturbed by their soft conversation, the man on the couch groaned and rolled away from them. She waited another few moments, thinking that he might wake up. When he didn't, she looked at Rebecca and stifled a yawn against the back of her hand. "Let's make some java, Beck," she said.

Rebecca happily agreed.

A few hours passed. The day, as they had a tendency to do in San Diego in August, heated up. Kerry put on a green V-neck T-shirt with soft, faded jeans and the red-and-white zigzag sneakers that were even more comfortable than being barefoot, and brought a book into the living room. She sat in the big easy chair that had come with the furnished house, silently turning pages while she watched over her patient. The last thing she wanted was for him to wake up alone, in a strange room, not knowing where he was or who had brought him there. She plugged in a freestanding fan over by the doorway, hoping its whir wouldn't be too loud. The breeze wasn't exactly cool but at least it moved the air around.

Occasionally one of her housemates—none of whom, as it happened, had been murdered in their sleep—would wander by. When Mace came in he stood with his hands on his hips and cocked his chin toward the sleeping man. "Dude still alive?"

"Seems to be," Kerry told him. "Disappointed?"

"Surprised, I guess," Mace answered. "Didn't think he'd make it to dawn."

"I guess he's tougher than he looks," Kerry observed.

"Seems like." He shook his head and moseyed on.

When it was time for Kerry to leave for work, she called in sick. It was the first time she had done so all summer, and a pang of guilt caught in her stomach when she hung up the phone. But her boss, Mr. Hofstadter, wouldn't have understood or accepted the real reason.

Through it all, the man slept. And Kerry wondered about him.

What was his story? How had he wound up in their yard? What had injured him? Was anyone looking for him? These questions, and many more, kept her from concentrating on her book, a paperback chick-lit novel she'd borrowed from Brandy. Her own tastes tended more toward suspense and thrillers, and if there were some exotic locations and romance mixed in, so much the better. But she would read anything she got her hands on, and this one was available.

Every time the man shifted in his sleep, she tensed, thinking he was waking up. The rest of the household went to work. She paced, or sipped a soda, or tried to read, and waited.

Eventually she dozed off in the chair. The book slid to the floor, but that didn't wake her.

Neither did having a blanket draped over her.

Later, she did open her eyes, startled that they had been closed at all. More startled to see that the man was sitting up on the couch, watching her. On her lap she clutched the blanket that had once covered him.

"You didn't have to do all this," he said. His voice was soft and smooth, not the ragged husk of the night before. His eyebrows raised as if to encompass the "all this" to which he referred.

He was definitely younger than he had looked, even that morning. Sleep and recuperation had erased wrinkles, filled furrows. Still years older than her, but not decades. His eyes were steel gray and clear, dancing with a light all their own in the poorly lit room.

She patted at the blanket. "It looks kind of like you're the one who's been taking care of me."

"I owed you," he said, as if that explained everything.

Or, really, anything.

"All I did was—"

He cut her off. His smile was, she realized, quite enchanting. "All you did was take me in, against the wishes of most of your friends. Clean and dress my wounds. Allow me to sleep, undisturbed, for as long as I needed. Accept without question my desire not to be taken to a doctor. Refuse to call the police. That, I have to say, was more than I could have asked, even if I'd been capable of asking, and I appreciate it."

Kerry blinked a couple of times. "Weren't you, like, unconscious for most of that?"

"Yes," he said, flashing her that grin again. She felt it down to her toes. She hadn't noticed what a handsome man he was—or, more accurately, how it had been obscured by the apparent years with which his pain and exhaustion had saddled him. "But not unaware. Thank you for everything."

As he spoke he made to rise from the couch, pushing off with his right hand. But he hadn't even reached his full height when his legs buckled, and he flopped back down. He tossed her a sheepish smile that dimpled his cheeks. "I guess I'm not as strong as I thought."

Kerry rushed to his side to help him, dropping the blanket to the floor. "You shouldn't even be awake, much less trying to stand," she insisted. He was already sitting by the time she reached him, so she wasn't sure what to do with herself. She stood there a few moments, feeling embarrassed, then simply sat down beside him as if that had been her plan all along.

Graciously he ignored her awkwardness and extended a hand. "My name is Daniel Blessing," he said.

She took his hand in her own. His was large, engulfing hers, and as warm as if he'd been holding a cup of hot tea. Holding it felt comfortable, like being hugged by an old friend. After a few moments she realized he was waiting for her to let go, to say her own name, or both. She couldn't understand why she was so flustered around this man.

Except maybe because he should be dead, she thought. *Or at the very least, still comatose. And years older.*

There was something very strange going on here. Part of her wanted to know what it was, but a bigger part—the dominant part, she realized—wondered why she wasn't more concerned about why she trusted him, almost instinctively. Why she had brought him into the house and dismissed the concerns of housemates who didn't want to leave her alone with him.

"Kerry," she managed at last. "I'm Kerry Profitt."

"Yes," he said, as if that name meant something to him. Though, obviously, it couldn't have. His voice and his manner were both, Kerry thought, oddly formal. "Yes, of course. It's a pleasure to meet you, Kerry."

"You too . . . Daniel," she replied. She had almost called him "Mr. Blessing," something about his age and that strange formality making her feel like she ought to treat him as she would a friend of her aunt Betty and uncle Marsh. She regarded his handsome face again: high forehead; intense, heavy-lidded gray eyes; a straight nose that she might have considered large on a different face but that here seemed somehow fitting. His lips were thin but quick to smile. When he did smile, his whole face took part, cheeks creasing, eyes crinkling, dimples at the edges of his mouth carving themselves into his skin. His jawline was pronounced but firm, his chin square. Thick brown hair, which could've used an encounter with water and shampoo, swept away from his brow, covering his ears, flowing over the collar of the Deftones T-shirt they'd borrowed from Mace when his own torn and blood-soaked shirt had to be cut from his damaged body. Impossibly he looked even closer to her age than he had when she'd suddenly awoken—within a decade of her, she guessed now.

"You have questions," he said. He tried to stand again, stopped mid-rise to wince and grasp at his ribs where his worst injury had been, an open gash that looked like he'd been attacked with a meat cleaver. His skin blanched, eyes compressing against the evident pain. But he composed himself and pushed through it.

"Well, yeah, Sherlock."

"I wish I could answer them for you, Kerry. Really, I do. But if I did—well, you saw what I looked like when you brought me in, right?"

She had hardly stopped remembering. His body was lean, with the stringy musculature of someone who worked hard rather than worked out, and yardstick-wide shoulders and a deep chest—but after last night, bruised and shredded, as if he'd made a dozen laps in a demolition derby, only without a car. "Yeah, I saw."

He nodded gravely. "If I answered your questions, then you'd be at risk for the same. And, I suspect, you'd have a harder time surviving it than I did."

"So this is, what, a regular thing for you?" she asked, surprised at his use of the present tense.

He showed that grin again. "Not to this extent, no. And I don't know if I'd use the word 'regular.' But it has happened before and likely will again. I'd rather you didn't get mixed up in it, so that's all I'll say about that." He walked away from the couch, away from her—stiff-legged, clearly sore, but still, considering the shape he had been in, miraculous. "If you don't mind," he called over his shoulder, "I'm starving. Okay if I raid the kitchen?"

Kerry Profitt's diary, August 13

He's gone.

I can't quite sort out how I feel about it. Night before last I risked the wrath of my homies—and maybe our lives—playing Florence Nightingale to a stranger who could have been just what Mace and Brandy were sure he was—a random drunk who'd been bounced off somebody's fender. But once he woke up, once the years fell away from him and he started to speak, it didn't take long to see that he was not that. Still, mega-mystery man.

But we talked and eventually the others came home from work—where, they lied, I had been sorely missed—and Daniel Blessing seemed to draw energy from them. He became enchanting: witty, interesting, the kind of conversationalist to whom you could apply the term "sparkling" without being too off base. Even those who had distrusted him the most had been charmed.

Did he tell us anything about himself other than his name? He did not. And that name is probably as fake as the phone number Rebecca gives out to the tourists who hit on her at work (aside, in case I didn't mention it: While Rebecca considers herself a few pounds overweight, what she is is zaftig. She hides it with the hunching and the baggies, but the powers at Seaside picked her—being the only one of us over twenty-one—to be a cocktail waitress in their oh-so-cleverly named bar, the Schooner. Part of the cocktail waitressing involves wearing a uniform that, while not as desperately provocative as they probably were ten or twenty years ago, is still, let's just say . . . snug. And short-ish. So the aforementioned hitting on? Happens a lot).

So no personal details from (possibly) Mr. Blessing. But he was informed and erudite, able to discuss books and movies and modern music, as well as the state of the world (about which he's not much impressed), environmental and social issues, and even, much to Josh's amazement, film noir of the thirties and forties. By the time people dragged themselves away from the kitchen table to go to bed, he had won them all over. I'm only guessing, but I think Josh may have fallen a little bit in love.

He may not even have been alone in that.

But then, this morning. Not just early-ish, but genuinely early. The kind of early where your eyelids are sort of glued together and the clock's face swims just out of focus. He taps on my door a couple of times, then lets himself in before I can mumble incoherently. He kneels—*kneels!*—beside the bed, takes my hand, kisses it once, says, "Thank you, Kerry Profitt. Thank you so much, for all you've done," and then he stands up and walks out.

I fumbled out of bed, but I heard the front door close before I reached the entrance to my room, and when I hit the street, he was gone. Out of sight. Maybe there was a car waiting for him, though I didn't see or hear one. Maybe one of those big mythological birds picked him up. Or a UFO.

Gone.

I only knew him for a day. And *knew* may be too strong a word, since I know so little about him even now.

So why does it feel like there's a vast emptiness in the house?

Anyone?

3

"I'm worried about Kerry," Brandy confided. She and Scott were both at work—she as a front-desk clerk at the resort, and Scott as a groundskeeper. A couple of times a shift, they made a point of crossing paths, usually when she was on a short break from the desk. With the run of the property, his schedule was less restrictive than hers. And as a groundskeeper whose clothing could frequently be grass-stained or otherwise soiled, him visiting her at the desk was frowned upon. Now they wandered the paved pathways that led from the room complexes down to the tennis courts and pool and the wide sandy beach beyond.

"Why?" Scott wondered. He carried a broom and a long-handled dustpan in his left fist; the fingers of his right hand were twined with Brandy's darker ones.

"It's been, what, four days since that guy left. Daniel?"

"Yeah, I guess so," Scott agreed, not quite getting what she was leading to. But that was the thing about Brandy—directness was not her strong point. She would walk all the way around an issue before she'd step right up to it. "What about it?"

"She's been kind of, I don't know, mopey. Ever since."

"Brandy, she hardly knew the guy. She wanted to play nursemaid, she did, he got better. End of story."

Her grasp tightened on his fingers, and he saw the fire flash in her eyes that always told him when he'd said the wrong thing. It was not an unfamiliar event, but it was never a pleasant one either.

"It *should* be," she insisted. "But it's not, and that's the problem. Haven't you seen her? I don't know if she's laughed once since he left. This is Kerry we're talking about. Girl loves to laugh. But instead she's been acting like her dog died."

Scott knew he was treading dangerous ground. Brandy, a psych major, was perfectly content to psychoanalyze anyone who fell onto her radar screen. Scott preferred life a little closer to the surface of things, where motives and rationales were not examined so closely. And he admired Kerry's surface a great deal. She was absolutely gorgeous—he'd thought that the moment he'd met her, and hadn't stopped since. Long, silken hair of purest jet, big emerald eyes, a lean body that was not as athletic as Brandy's or as curvaceous as Rebecca's, but still feminine and attractive. He'd been with Brandy for three years, and loved her completely. But that didn't mean he didn't think once in a while about what it would be like to be with Kerry.

"You're right, I guess," he ventured, shaking off the mental image of Kerry to focus on Brandy "Maybe seeing him on the couch like that, taking care of him, reminded her of her mom. When she had to take care of her for so long."

Brandy nodded. He'd scored one. "There you go, Scotty," she said, her tone congratulatory. She stopped, released his hand and faced him, moving into lecture mode. Behind her, the Pacific surged up onto the beach, then slipped back into itself in an unending, slightly irregular rhythm. "What defined Kerry for years? Being her mom's nurse and caretaker. Then what happened to her? Her mom died anyway, and she had to move in with an aunt and uncle she can barely stand. Now she's got a nice insurance settlement, but she's working anyway, trying to supplement the money with income from a summer job. She's looking to redefine herself in some other role, but when that guy fell into her lap, almost literally, it took her back to the same place she had been, emotionally, with her mom. And when he left too . . . well, that brought back a lot of feelings, most of them the bad kind."

"Do you have a suggestion?" Scott asked. He readily admitted that he was nuts about Brandy. She was smart and beautiful and very caring, so what was not to like? But when she got like this, sometimes he felt antsy, eggshell-walking.

The first time he'd introduced her to his brother Steve—six years older, married with a kid of his own—Steve had taken him aside and said in a conspiratorial tone, "She's great, Scott. Doesn't seem like someone who puts up with idiots."

"She doesn't," Scott had confirmed.

"Then I have one piece of advice, bro. Don't be an idiot."

Brandy's little brother DJ had been less subtle. "You ever hurt my sister," he said with a sinister smile, "I won't have to do jack. That girl'll have you for breakfast and pick her teeth with your bones."

All things considered, eggshells didn't seem so bad.

"She's got to work through it her own way," Brandy prescribed, drawing Scott back to the current situation. "All we can do is be as supportive as we can, let her talk it out if she wants. Show her we care about her, but not that we want to meddle."

If amateur psychiatry wasn't meddling, Scott wasn't sure what was. But he kept that opinion to himself. Anyway, there was a stretch of lawn that needed mowing, and Brandy's break was over, as was his own. He agreed with her, kissed her good-bye, and went back to work.

With so many new faces to look at every day, Kerry found herself looking forward to getting acquainted with the resort's regulars—those who stayed for a week or so and ate in the restaurant several times instead of availing themselves of La Jolla's many other fine dining opportunities. Some she got to know, on the most superficial of levels, as people on vacation who sometimes had a tendency to talk about their lives—family members, pets they left behind, the old neighborhood back in Lincoln or Tempe or Fort Wayne. Others kept their own confidences, and sometimes Kerry entertained herself by making up her own stories about them, giving them colorful, mysterious histories and reasons for visiting southern California.

Some of these fictions she had e-mailed to her best friend Jessica Tait, who had moved to Florida the year before. Lately Jessica had seemed more and more distant, as if her new life and friends were drawing her away from the bond they'd shared. Kerry mourned the change; losing her mother had been bad enough, losing her best friend on top of it was heart-wrenching. The way she'd grown up had left her with precious few friends anyway, and she valued the ones she had.

Tonight one of the diners in her section was a woman she'd seen several times recently—not for days in a row, as was typical with vacationers who came to the resort, but spread out over many weeks. This was unusual, but not unheard of. Sometimes local residents decided they liked the kitchen's offerings. Carolyn Massey, the chef, had, after all, trained at Le Cordon Bleu in France, and then had a stint under Alice Waters in her Berkeley restaurant, Chez Panisse, before taking over the resort's kitchen. Her meals were always delicious and frequently adventurous.

This guest, though, Kerry noticed partly because the woman always dined alone, and partly because, while she was unfailingly pleasant and polite, there was an air about her that made Kerry believe that she was terribly sad. She was a beautiful woman, with skin so soft and smooth it could have been freshly poured from a bottle, and hair that reminded Kerry of a ray of golden afternoon sunlight shining down on fresh straw. Upon closer inspection, the color of her shoulder-blade-length hair spanned a spectrum, from platinum white to a dark auburn, and the overall effect was lovely. Her features could have belonged to fairy tale royalty, or to the Hollywood kind: wide-set, sparkling blue eyes, a refined yet expressive brow, a nose that was petite but was not so small it was an afterthought. Her lips were full and finely sculpted, and the determined set of her jaw implied that she was no pushover.

In Kerry's mind, the woman was a widow whose wealthy husband had died tragically young. She had tried to put his death behind her, to carry on with her life, but everywhere she went, simple things reminded her of the joy they had felt in their few years together. A song on the radio, a particular vintage of wine, even the cries of gulls on the beach, could bring an unexpected tear to her eye. Nonetheless, she made herself go out, eat in restaurants, drink that wine, listen to the radio, walk on the beach at sunset, intent on enjoying her heartbreaking memories as if he were still there beside her.

Sometimes Kerry added an extra twist to the woman's tale. She was a spy, and her husband had been killed in the line of duty. Or she was an international jewel thief, and he wasn't dead at all but simply doing a long stretch in a prison in Monaco or Majorca. She came to La Jolla because she wasn't wanted for anything in California—yet.

The woman's beauty was ageless, which inspired Kerry to even greater flights of fancy. She could have been in her midtwenties, her late forties, or any place in between. Her outfit was just as timeless—a loose-fitting white silk top that suggested rather than revealed her figure, a tan jacket, also silk, and matching pants with heels, no doubt some Italian brand that Kerry could pronounce no better than she could afford. There were hints of lines at the edges of her eyes and mouth that would, with the years, deepen and most likely make her even more lovely. She would carry her years and experiences well, Kerry believed.

After dinner the woman lingered over a cup of coffee. She exchanged pleasantries from time to time, but whenever Kerry tried to engage her in conversation, she expertly steered away from any personal topics. *Just adds to her mystery,* Kerry thought with some satisfaction.

When she went into the kitchen to pick up an order for the next table over, a party of five who had come in late after what looked like a scorching day on the beach—lobster-red foreheads, shoulders, and arms that would be painful and peeling before long—the last person she expected to see was Daniel Blessing.

But there he was, hovering near the open back door like an unwanted houseguest who wouldn't quite leave. When he saw Kerry, his lips parted in a sudden smile. This time, she noted, it didn't engage his eyes. She smiled back and arched a quizzical eyebrow his way.

"Daniel?" she said, surprised. "What are you doing here?" The cooks, bus staff, and dishwashers all ignored him, as if by prior arrangement. But Kerry had been out in the dining room for several minutes, and he could have had time to slip each one a twenty for all she knew.

He came toward her, unmistakable urgency in his step, and took her by the arm. His grip was so firm it hurt. She tried to pull away, but he held on. "Kerry," he whispered. "I hoped that you'd be safe, that helping me wouldn't put you in danger. I was wrong. You've got to leave here, right now."

Kerry laughed, but it sounded forced even to her. "In case you hadn't noticed, I'm kind of working here, Daniel."

"You're in terrible danger, Kerry. I'm not joking. Or exaggerating. You have to trust me."

That, in spite of herself, she had always done, even that very first night. And she certainly couldn't imagine any reason he might have had for trying to play a trick on her now. Unless this whole thing was one of those ridiculous TV stunts, set up to ridicule her in front of millions, he seemed absolutely serious.

"What's going on, Daniel? I can't just walk out of here."

"You have to," he insisted. He blew out a frustrated breath. "There's a woman out there, sitting by herself at a table."

"The blond one?"

"That's her."

"She's a regular. She's perfectly harmless."

"You're wrong," he said with finality. "Remember how I was the night you found me?"

How could I forget? she wondered. *Three quarters dead, like an animal by the side of a busy highway.* "Of course."

"She's the one who did that to me. She's still after me. And now she's connected me to you." His voice had gotten louder as he tried to convince her, and Kerry noticed that some of the kitchen staff was now paying attention to them. She had to calm this guy down, fast, or she'd be out of a job.

"Look, Daniel," she whispered, "I don't really know you or anything, you know. I'm glad you're better and all, but I kind of need this job, and—"

He squeezed her arm even harder than he had before. "Kerry," he said. She found her gaze drawn to his eyes, such a strange color of gray, but steady and profoundly persuasive. "There's no time for this. She'll be—"

The kitchen door swung open and the woman was there. Now the staff did react. Carolyn Massey, the head chef, came forward with a knife in her hand. She'd been using it to chop fresh vegetables, and she didn't hold it threateningly, but it was still a big, sharp object. "I'm sorry," Carolyn said, "but this kitchen is off limits to everyone except staff." She glanced meaningfully at Kerry and Daniel. "Everyone."

The blond woman barely spared her a glance, but focused her attention on Daniel and on Kerry, who stood between them. "I thought you were nearby," she said. Her voice was ice.

Then, she spoke another word, or maybe two. Kerry couldn't make them out, couldn't even tell what language they were in. As she spoke, she gestured toward Daniel with her right hand, a kind of swooping curlicue of a motion that seemed to encompass much of the kitchen before settling on him.

Daniel was already in motion when the big gas oven's door flipped open, seemingly of its own accord. He shoved Kerry to the side and spoke some equally strange words of his own, making a different sort of two-handed gesture. Kerry couldn't quite process what happened—it was all too fast, and way, way too weird—but it seemed that, in response to the woman's combined words and movement, the oven door had opened itself and a huge gout of flame jetted out toward Daniel, dragon's-breath-like. She felt the blast of heat suck the air from her lungs. But then it seemed that in response to whatever Daniel had done, the flame stopped in midair, as if striking an invisible shield, and turned back toward the woman.

The questions this raised were, of course, innumerable. But she didn't have a chance to ask so much as "What the hell?" before Daniel tugged her out the back door. He kept a tight grip on her arm as he ran for the parking lot, and she had to sprint to keep from falling down and being dragged along behind.

He was silent as he ran, and she had the impression that he was concentrating, intent on something she couldn't even sense. She guessed the woman was probably following them, but if she'd turned to look she'd have fallen for sure. So she let herself be led to a dark, low-slung sports car parked close to the restaurant. The doors sprung open before they reached it, and Daniel pushed her into the leather passenger seat. He ran around to the driver's side, and she could have sworn—though by this point, the evidence of her own senses was clearly not to be trusted—that the engine turned over before he was even sitting down. Slamming his door, he threw the car into reverse and backed from the parking space, then he shifted gears and the little car darted toward the exit.

Finally risking a glance behind them, Kerry saw that the blond woman had indeed followed. She had just gotten into a car of her own, and before Daniel's vehicle had even cleared the first block, she was racing after them.

4

Daniel hung a sharp left turn on Avenida de la Playa, the car's rear end fishtailing through the intersection as they entered the main drag of the La Jolla Shores neighborhood. From outdoor cafés and restaurants, patrons stared as the screech of skidding tires battled the growl of the engine for supremacy. This time of night, there wasn't much vehicular traffic on the street, so Daniel floored the accelerator and the car burst forward like an animal released from a cage.

At La Jolla Shores Drive, he made a screaming right. This street, which connected with Torrey Pines and the "village" section of the resort town, was busier. Kerry gripped the edges of her bucket seat as Daniel swerved around cars and a city bus, then pulled back into a proper lane and rocketed through the major intersection at Torrey Pines. Kerry barely had time to notice that he had gone through a red light—the blare of horns from cars and trucks was lost behind them.

On the other side of Torrey Pines, the road was narrow and wound up the side of Mount Soledad, the hill that loomed over the town, providing a scenic backdrop and multimillion dollar views from its many estates. As they started the climb, Kerry heard another blurting of horns, which she figured was probably caused by the blond woman pulling the same stunt Daniel had.

Daniel cursed under his breath.

"She's still behind us, isn't she?" Kerry asked. The run had shaken her fine hair free from the ponytail she wore for work, and she tried to regather it, but her hands were shaking as much as her voice.

"Sounds like it. I'd be surprised if she wasn't."

"So when are you going to tell me what this is all about?" Kerry demanded, trying to sound more forceful than she felt. "And what that little display in the kitchen was?"

"Another time," Daniel said. His teeth were clenched in concentration. "Hard enough getting to know this car so I can squeeze every last drop of juice out of her."

Getting to know? Kerry thought. A horrible notion struck her. "Isn't this your car?"

"I don't actually *own* a car," Daniel admitted.

"And this isn't a rental?"

He didn't answer. But then, he didn't need to. It was clear now that he'd stolen the car. *And,* she realized, *effectively kidnapped me.*

"I think you should let me out here," she suggested. "I'll walk back to work."

"You really don't want me to do that."

"I really do."

Daniel risked a glance at her even as he muscled the car around a hairpin turn. The floodlit walls and thickly hedged iron fences that separated La Jolla's wealthy from the rest of the world rushed past in a blur. "Kerry, I'll explain everything, I promise. But right now I'm trying to not get us killed, and I'm trying to leave Season behind. Which is another form, need I add, of not getting us killed. If I dropped you off, not only would she slaughter you, but it would slow me down enough to let her catch me. And I have to tell you, I'm not ready to go through that again."

He sounded convincing, or at least convinc*ed*, and Kerry discovered that once again, she trusted him without knowing why. She stopped arguing and let him drive. A moment later they spotted an electric gate sliding shut behind a Mercedes that had just pulled into a driveway "Hold on," Daniel muttered. He stomped on the brake and cranked the steering wheel at the same time. The little car shuddered and turned in an almost ninety-degree angle, and then he shot through the gate just before it closed. On the other side of the gate, he pulled off the driveway so that a high wall hid the car from the street. As he came to a stop and killed the engine, he said another word in whatever unfamiliar tongue he had used at the restaurant, and waggled his hand.

The air around the car seemed to shimmer, as if enveloped by the most severe heat waves this side of the Sahara. Through the weird haze, Kerry saw a silver-haired man and woman emerge from the Mercedes and stare in their direction. "Keep quiet," Daniel warned her in a whisper. "They can't see us, but they can hear us."

"What do you mean, they can't see us?" Kerry wanted to know, echoing his hushed tones.

"Invisibility spell," Daniel replied, tight-lipped. She could see beads of sweat forming at his brow and dripping down his temples as if from intense effort. Outside, the man and woman looked at each other in confusion, and the man shrugged. They turned away and went up to the door of the house, then disappeared inside. A moment later the exterior lights went dark.

Daniel faced Kerry, a finger across his lips in the universal sign for "keep quiet." She did. There would be plenty to say later. For now, though, she would let him call the shots. He was clearly playing with forces way beyond her understanding or control. That fact stirred her to unexpected anger— she'd been swept into a game to which she didn't know the rules; hadn't known, a half hour ago, even existed. She hadn't asked to be included. And yet here she was. She fumed, but silently.

But when he says I can talk again . . .

From the other side of the wall, they heard the growl of a powerful engine, and headlights swept past, shining through the iron gates. Kerry and Daniel sat in silence until the engine noise faded away, moving higher up the hill. A few moments later Daniel started the stolen car again. With a word and a wave at the gate, it slid open and Daniel drove back out onto the street.

Instead of turning right to continue toward the top of Mount Soledad, he made a left, back down the hill toward where they'd started.

"Are you taking me back to work?" Kerry asked.

"I can't do that," he said. "You're not safe there anymore. She knows she can find you there."

There was so much that Kerry didn't understand. "But she wasn't after me," she insisted. "She was after you."

"She'll consider you an ally of mine now. She's ruthless, Kerry. If I took you back there, the rest of your life would be measured in hours, maybe days at the most. I'm sorry, but you can't go back to work, and you can't go back home—she has probably located the house by now. I'm almost sure of it, in fact. How else could she have traced you to the restaurant? I never visited you there, so she must have followed you from home."

"I told you, she eats there all the time," Kerry said. She was still upset, still ticked that this guy had come along and upended her life, yanked her into his own personal drama.

If it hadn't been for what she had seen the woman do in the kitchen, she'd think Daniel suffered from paranoid hallucinations. But she *had* seen it. That overruled her rage and earned him the benefit of the doubt, at least for a while.

Daniel seemed to puzzle over what Kerry had pointed out for a few moments as he drove to the bottom of the hill and hung a right on La Jolla Parkway, heading away from town. "I didn't think that precognition was one of her gifts," he said. "But I suppose it's possible. Maybe she was staking you out, knowing that you and I would somehow come into contact."

The talk of precognition and gifts made Kerry's blood run cold. It sounded like something out of one of those movies full of pounding death metal, where everyone in the audience dresses in black and none of them could pass through an airport scanner without setting off sirens. She shivered and hugged herself, but at the same time felt a sudden weariness, as if all her strength had left her at once. Since the woman had walked into the kitchen, Kerry had been frightened and furious in more or less equal measures. Then the chase, the invisibility, the escape . . . she realized that adrenaline had been charging through her system, and now that the immediate threat had passed, it drained from her. She remained scared—probably more so than before, a combination of fear that she was in the company of a crazy man, and worse, what it might mean if he were not crazy at all—and angry that she had somehow been punished for what she had believed was a simple good deed. *See if I ever help a half-dead man in my bushes again. It's just not worth it.*

"You're going to have to do some explaining, Daniel," she declared. "And it better be good."

"It will be," he assured her with a hint of a smile. That smile, on another occasion, might have won him points, but not now. Now it implied that things were less awful than they were, and Kerry wasn't sure that was possible. "Let's just get someplace safe and comfortable. I'll tell you everything. I owe you that much."

"Got that right." Another horrible thought crossed her mind. "If the house isn't safe, what about the others? My friends?"

"They've got to get out too," Daniel replied. "As quickly as possible. Are they at the house now?"

"Some of them, maybe." Kerry knew Rebecca and Josh were at Seaside. Mace had the day off, though, and Scott and Brandy had worked earlier in the day. She almost reached for her cell phone, but then remembered that her purse was still in her locker at the resort. Cell phone, ID, money, keys . . . everything she needed with her on a daily basis was gone, unless she could somehow get back to work.

And of course, by leaving the way she had, she was pretty sure there would be no job left, even if she could get back. Which meant no further income. She had put aside a little bit over the summer, depositing it via ATM to her account back in Illinois. But her ATM card, naturally, was in her purse.

All in all, this pretty much sucked.

"You've got to warn them," he said. "Get them away from there."

"What am I supposed to tell them? I'm in the dark here, remember?"

"We'll find a safe place," he promised. "When we do, just tell them to meet us there—without telling anyone else where they're going. I know it sounds melodramatic, but their lives really are in danger now."

He took one hand off the steering wheel and squeezed her left shoulder. "Kerry, I truly am sorry you got involved in this. If I could undo it, I would."

Kerry shrugged, and he took his hand away. "Yeah, well, that makes two of us."

5

The apartment Daniel rented—one he found when cruising, stopping after sighting a sign in the window of a building, going inside, paying with enough cash that the landlord was willing to dispense with the paperwork—was on the second floor of a two-story, fake-stucco monstrosity with a red tile roof and an empty pool except for a few inches of scum-filmed rainwater. It had three bedrooms, a long, narrow living room with high ceilings and a skylight, one bathroom, and a kitchen in which two people couldn't pass each other without turning sideways and inhaling. The carpet was microthin, bunched up in spots and separating at the seams in others. Josh, when he saw it, said something about it gloriously representing southern California's "seamy underbelly," but to Kerry it was just a dump.

It was two blocks off Palm Avenue, the main drag of Imperial Beach, a community ten miles south of downtown San Diego, which was about that far south of La Jolla. At the corners on Palm were a fast-food restaurant and a gas station with a minimart, but down the side streets there were only small cottages and low-rent apartment buildings. TVs and music—salsa, hip-hop, classic rock, and Top 40 pop—could be heard from open windows most hours of the day, and night, as it turned out, competing with the constant drone of air conditioners.

It was, Kerry knew, a place she'd be very unlikely to find for herself, which made it perfect for their purposes. The electricity hadn't been turned off yet, and the landlord had agreed to let it stay on under his name for a while in exchange for yet another handful of cash. There was no phone, but Daniel had a cell so she used it to call the summer house, then Seaside. After a couple of tries, she reached everyone and convinced them to leave work or the house and to join her in Imperial Beach. She pleaded, cajoled, and threatened, but they all came. Scott and Brandy brought her laptop and some clothes from the house, in addition to their own things and everyone else's. She gave Rebecca her combination so her friend could get her purse and personal items from work. Within four hours of her escape, as she had come to think of it, from the resort's kitchen, they were all seated together on the floor of the apartment's living room, backs against the walls, legs crossed. Daniel cleared his throat. He was on stage, and, Kerry believed, he knew it. *Looks like you got some 'splainin' to do, Lucy,* she thought, à la Ricky Ricardo.

He started by flashing his friendly grin, but Kerry was having none of that. "I know what I'm about to tell you will sound ridiculous to you," he began. "Unbelievable, even. But I swear to you, it's true. I could make you believe it—that's not a terribly difficult stunt for me—but I won't do that. Instead I want you to believe it on its own merits. Such as they are."

Kerry, having already experienced some of his "stunts," was thrown by his passing remark about being able to make them believe. She interrupted before he could continue. "Daniel, when we first met you," she said, "and I found myself trusting you, for no particular reason . . . was that just because I really trusted you? Or did I have . . . I don't know, *help*?"

"And by 'help,' you mean . . . ?"

"You tell me."

"Was I enchanting you?" he asked. "Even through my pain and semi-consciousness?" He smiled again, looking at the others instead of Kerry. "Yes, I was. I apologize now, but I couldn't take a chance that you'd send me to a hospital, or call the police. I had barely escaped from Season with my life, and she knew that. She'd have been watching for me to show up at a hospital. I needed a place to hide out, to recuperate, and you guys gave me that. I don't know if I thanked you enough for that, for giving me a chance to live."

Rebecca cleared her throat. "Season? Who's that?"

"Is that who we saw at the restaurant?" Kerry asked. "The one who chased us, and—"

"They're still talking about that all over the resort," Rebecca broke in. "You guys are, like, famous. Or infamous, I guess."

Daniel was nodding. "That was her. Season Howe is her name. She's a witch."

Josh made a snorting noise. "Do we get the Ouija board out now?" he asked. "Commune with the spirits of the dead? I think Rebecca has a Stephen King novel we could use for reference."

"It's not as easy as all that," Daniel said matter-of-factly. "It can be done, but according to their rules, not ours."

"Come *on*!" Scott said angrily. His features were long and narrow, their length accentuated by the large lenses on his wire-rimmed glasses and his gaunt cheeks reddened with emotion. "What kind of game are you playing here, Daniel? Why don't you get to the point and tell us what this nonsense is all about?"

"I understand your feelings," Daniel replied, staying calm. "I *am* telling you what it's about. It's about Season Howe. It always has been."

"Maybe you need to give us a little more detail," Brandy suggested. "And the kind we can believe would be good."

"But if he can enchant us," Rebecca tossed out, "how do we know *what* we can believe? We might believe him only to find out that he *made* us believe him!"

"Which, if he could do that," Mace observed quietly, "would mean that he really is able to do this magic stuff he's claimin' to do."

"If I could go on," Daniel said, "without enchanting you or somehow causing you to believe a word that I say, except perhaps by convincing you—"

"That'd be good," Kerry said. "Because our lives? Pretty much uprooted now, thanks to you. It'd be nice if there's a good reason for it all."

"There is," he assured her. He met her gaze for a moment, solidly, and she felt once again the trust she had before. Of course, now it was tempered by the knowledge that he had helped that trust along a good bit, or at least he claimed he had.

"You have seen, Kerry, things tonight that you would never have believed a few days ago, true?"

She blinked a couple of times. "I . . . I *think* I have."

"Trust yourself, if not me," he suggested. "Trust your own senses."

"Well, then . . . yes. I saw what looked like some kind of . . . mystical battle between you and that woman—"

"Season."

"Yeah, her. Season. In the kitchen. Then we ran, and you stole a car—only without a key, or taking any time to hotwire it, or whatever. Then later on you turned it . . . invisible. So yeah, I guess it's safe to say I've seen some strange things tonight."

"The merest glimpse into my life," Daniel said, his voice grave. "Our lives. Season's . . . and mine."

"What is she, some kind of psycho ex-girlfriend?" Mace asked.

Daniel chuckled. "Hardly. An enemy. Always an enemy."

"So you've known her for a long time?" Josh wondered.

"Too long," Daniel said. His gaze had gone distant, as if he were searching his memory for something he couldn't find. "You'll find this hard to believe, I'm sure. In *spite* of the evidence you've seen tonight, Kerry. It all happened so long ago."

"How long?" Kerry asked.

Daniel cleared his throat and met her gaze again, as if only by looking into her eyes could he persuade her of the most outlandish things. "During the spring of 1704, in a town called Slocumb, Virginia—you can still find it on the map, a good map, anyway—Season was accused of witchcraft. There was plenty of evidence against her. She was, after all, a very powerful witch, and she remains one today."

Mace let out a snickering sound, and Daniel fixed him with a heated stare. "I said you'd have a hard time believing me," he reminded them. "But let me finish, please, then question me all you like."

Mace shrugged, and Daniel continued. "Season was guilty, there was no doubt of that. The town's fathers weren't hasty about this accusation. Nonetheless, Season objected to it. She objected with fire and wind and destruction. Her powers were greater than anyone in Slocumb suspected, and when her assault was over, so was the town. There was only one survivor."

"You're kidding," Kerry said, as surprised by the unexpected brutality of the story as by its outlandishness.

Daniel shook his head. "Not at all," he said. "Some of this you can find corroborated in history books. Except they don't know, or don't tell, the real reason the town was destroyed."

"Who was the survivor?" Brandy asked.

"I suppose if you look at it another way, there were three survivors," Daniel said quietly. "Since my mother was pregnant at the time with twins."

"Your mother?" Brandy was the one who spoke up, but it was obvious from the general response that they all had a hard time with this sudden twist in the tale.

"That's right," Daniel said. "Everyone called her Mother Blessing. She was also a witch, but she used her abilities to help the people of Slocumb, and she was not only accepted there, but loved. When Season's rage came, though, Mother Blessing was only able to protect herself . . . and her unborn sons—myself and my twin brother, Abraham. We were born seven months later."

"So you're sayin' you're, like, three hundred years old," Mace stated.

"Close to it," Daniel confirmed.

"No offense, bud, but the femme fatale plot is way old hat," Josh said, looking disgruntled. "And no way I buy the old man bit."

Brandy stood up, shaking her head, face clouded with anger. "Okay, now I know you're yanking our chains. I don't know why or what your scam is, but I don't appreciate you trying to play me and my friends!"

Daniel was silent while she remonstrated him, and when she was finished he spread his hands placatingly. "I told you that you'd have a hard time believing me," he reminded her. "I also said that it might be easier for Kerry, who had already seen things tonight that she would never have believed possible."

Brandy turned to Kerry. "Okay, then, Kerry," she said. "Take a look. Do you believe he's a day over a hundred? Or forty, for that matter?"

Kerry swallowed hard. She wasn't sure what she believed anymore. She wouldn't have believed he could make a car invisible, but he seemed to have done just that. And she had seen how old he had looked when they'd first brought him inside—maybe not three hundred, but certainly far older than he had even a day later.

"I . . . don't know," she admitted. "Given what I have seen, though, I'm willing to give Daniel the benefit of the doubt. At least for now."

"Until what?" Brandy pressed. "Until he makes some even more ridiculous claim? How far out there do you want him to go?"

"What will it take to convince you, Brandy?" he asked, remaining utterly calm in the face of her barrage.

"I don't know," she said. "You keep talking about Kerry, what she's seen. What about the rest of us? Why don't you show us something?"

"I don't use my abilities casually," Daniel explained. "They're not for show-and-tell—"

"Lame excuse," Brandy snapped, pointing at him.

"—but if it will help to convince you," Daniel continued, "then I'll try. Nothing fancy—I'm still getting my strength back after Season's sneak attack the other day."

"Is that how you ended up at our place?" Rebecca asked. "A sneak attack?"

"She took me by surprise, yes. I was unprepared, and she very nearly finished me right then." He closed his eyes, as if to end the conversation, and it worked. The room was almost silent. Kerry heard the breathing of her friends, her pulse pounding in her own head, and that was all.

Then Daniel's eyes snapped open and he turned to glare at Brandy, gesturing toward her with both hands and speaking a soft phrase Kerry couldn't make out. Brandy's pose remained the same—arms clenched tightly across her chest, chin jutting defiantly, legs spread a little—but her location changed. Now, instead of a couple of feet of empty space above her head, the space was beneath her feet. Her head brushed the ceiling. When she realized this, fury danced in her eyes. "Put me down!"

Daniel obliged, and a moment later Brandy was standing once again on the floor, and the others gaped at her, openmouthed. "What the hell was that?" she demanded.

"A demonstration."

"Mass hypnosis, more like," she insisted.

"Touch your hair, Brandy," Kerry urged. Brandy glared at her for a moment, but then put a hand to her head. It came away dusted with the debris her head had scraped off the popcorn-style ceiling. "That's not hypnosis."

Brandy rolled some of the plaster dust between her fingers, examining it as if the truth lay inside. In a way, Kerry figured, it did. Daniel's demonstration didn't make the rest of his absurd story true, but it at least showed that there was more to him than was readily apparent.

More to the world, for that matter.

Kerry Profitt's diary, August 18

So after that my friends, being who they are, couldn't shut up long enough for Daniel to finish telling his story. Which, I don't know about them, but I'd have liked to have heard more of.

I mean, sure, he told bits of it. His mother dedicated her life to hunting down Season Howe, bringing her to some kind of witchy justice for what she did to their town. And when her sons were grown, she dedicated them to the task too. Season, he explained, has been in hiding ever since. She goes where people are—resort towns in season, like La Jolla, are a favorite because the population temporarily swells and it's easy to stay anonymous. She'll go to one for a few years, then move so people don't get to know her too well. Once everyone she's encountered has moved on or died off, then she can start going there again.

Having figured out her pattern, Daniel said, he has been able to get close a few times. But as powerful as he is, she is more so, and she's always managed to avoid or defeat him—or, like this time, turn the tables so that the hunter is the hunted.

But the others were all over him with questions. Stupid ones too—did he know Humphrey Bogart, Josh wanted to know. Answer, no, in case anybody cares. Not that anybody's reading this except me. No way I'm posting it to Facebook. Brandy got completely corny and wanted to know if he'd ever lived on Elm Street, in reference to nightmares, I guess. Which is my department, after all, although not so much lately, blessed be (as they say, or do they, in witchy circles?). Did he fight in the Revolutionary War (Civil War, World Wars I and II)? I think Mace asked him about every war except the Spanish-American. Answers, no, no, no, and no. His war is private, and all-consuming.

War sucks, and his seems to be no exception. To look at him you wouldn't think he had paid too high a price. I mean, he's an older man—way older, if you believe him (do I? "Ask again later," to quote the Magic 8-ball), but for his age, especially the more advanced one he claims, he looks good, or even fantastic. No visible battle damage anymore.

If you look at the whole story, though . . . his mother lost everyone she knew, everyone she cared about, including her husband, to Season Howe's little temper tantrum. She then spent the next several hundred years trying to get revenge. Or justice. Her sons carried on the same fight for her, giving up anything that might resemble a normal life. Every human Daniel has known, until the very recent past, has aged and died on him.

And his brother, Abraham? Oh, yeah, Season killed him. Late 1880s, I think he said.

So it's no wonder he's just a little pissed, right?

More later.
K.

6

The next couple of days reminded Kerry of an extended *Survivor* episode as her roommates shared whispered conversations with one another, formed and broke alliances, and generally acted as if their world had been turned upside down. She was willing to concede that maybe it had. Daniel spent most of his time away from the apartment, not wanting to attract "undue attention," which Kerry took to be synonymous with "Season Howe."

Maybe because it had become clear that Kerry shared a bond with Daniel that the others didn't, she felt as if she were being excluded from most of the discussions. Every now and then someone would come to her, trying to sway her over to their side, but she hadn't been involved at all in the initial choosing of sides. Still, her opinion seemed to be valued, and she had a hard time being left alone at all. When she wanted an ice-cream sandwich one evening and was about to walk to the corner to buy one, Mace insisted on joining her. She found Brandy far more solicitous than usual, offering her tea, cookies, and a sympathetic ear whenever she wanted one. It was, she thought, as if she was the key to something but she didn't even know where the door was, much less what was behind it.

The basic positions were, it was true, pretty clear. Brandy and her camp thought that Daniel was some kind of charlatan, and that they should call the police on him, at the very least. Rebecca's side believed he was practically a messiah, and that they should all team up with him and do anything he asked. Kerry came down somewhere in the middle—she believed most of what Daniel had told them, but she wanted to maintain a healthy skepticism about him until she had a better idea of what he was after.

Besides Brandy and Rebecca, who had staked out positions early, the sides were vague and shifted as often as the wind. Scott kept his opinions mostly to himself, but sided with Brandy more out of default than reason. Josh flew back and forth, depending on who made the last argument, which was not even necessarily the best. Mace felt a powerful loyalty to Rebecca, with whom, against all odds, he had formed a fast friendship over the summer, but he didn't mind telling her from time to time that she was acting stupid.

Daniel hadn't, as yet, made any particular requests of the group. He had moved them from the La Jolla house, he explained, because he felt responsible for exposing them to Season's wrath, and he wanted to protect them. He hung around for the same reason, spending his days out in search of the witch, and his nights close to the apartment in case she sought them out.

The rest of the apartment was quiet one night when Daniel and Kerry sat around the second-hand kitchen table he'd scrounged from somewhere. She traced designs in the cheap linoleum tabletop with the tip of her finger while he sipped from a can of Barq's root beer. He'd been talking about some of the changes he'd seen during his long life. "In those days," he was saying, "you could walk from the Atlantic coast to the Mississippi River without ever coming out from under trees. If you were a monkey, you could make the whole trip without ever touching the ground, limb to limb. It wasn't until you reached the Great Plains and the southwestern deserts that the trees gave way to other sorts of landscapes."

"Could anyone have predicted what would happen?" Kerry asked him.

"That the population would swell and all those people would need places to live, and that those forests would be cleared to provide lumber and paper, until the land was a sea of houses instead of trees? No, I don't think so." His mouth was a grim line, and there was a sadness in his eyes that Kerry could barely fathom.

He's seen so much, she thought. She had come to believe that he was as old as he claimed and that he had abilities far beyond any she had ever conceived of.

"No," he said again. "Some people speculated, of course, that the United States—once we'd given it that name—would grow quickly. But the land, the trees, the animals, the water—we thought those things were abundant enough to last forever." He took another sip from the aluminum can. "Obviously we miscalculated." He smiled. "We should have thought to recycle our aluminum back then, I guess."

She laughed with him, which she was finding easy to do. "Yeah, why were you guys so backward?"

He finished the root beer and set the empty can down on the table. But before he could speak again, one of the bedroom doors opened and the rest of the roommates filed out, grave expressions on their faces.

When Brandy stepped forward as their spokesperson, Kerry was pretty sure she knew what was coming.

"Daniel, we've taken a vote," she began.

"I didn't vote," Kerry interrupted. "Don't I get a say in whatever this is?"

"You can vote, but your vote won't be enough to change the balance," Brandy told her. "If it had been, we'd have included you."

"Thanks for the consideration," Kerry snapped, feeling betrayed by the very people she'd thought were her friends.

"Anyway, Daniel, here's what it comes down to. We've all upset our lives over this mess, some of us have lost our jobs, worried our parents. It's got to end. Summer's almost over anyway, and we'll all be going our separate ways. But for the rest of the summer, for as much of it as we can salvage, we'd like you gone."

There was a moment of silence. Nobody met Kerry's eyes.

"Gone?" he echoed.

"That's right. Don't come around, don't call."

"But Season—"

"None of us has ever seen Season, except Kerry. She's left us alone so far. We'll take our chances."

"You don't know what you're getting into," he warned.

"Whatever it is, you're the one got us into it," Brandy countered. "Now, we're telling you we're done with it."

Daniel glanced at Kerry, but she couldn't bring herself to hold his gaze. She looked away from him, at his pop can sitting on the table, forgotten now. "What . . . what was the vote?" she asked hesitantly.

"Four to one," Brandy answered.

Four to one. That meant . . . Kerry looked at Rebecca. The girl's huge, soft brown eyes brimmed with tears. Brandy and Mace were the only ones who appeared certain. Scott shifted his weight from foot to foot, while Josh looked at his Converse sneakers, his eyes lined with black, the studded stainless steel collar he liked to wear, when not on duty, as tight around his neck as a strangler's hands.

"Four to two," Kerry corrected. But the world tilted sharply up around her in a vertiginous spin—the overhead lights seemed to reverse on themselves, giving out black rays that fought against a pale white background, and blood roared in her ears like an express subway past an abandoned station.

Daniel shoved his chair back on the bunching carpet and stood up. "Thank you, Kerry," he said. "But majority rules, right?"

Does it have to? Kerry wondered. They'd been talking about American history, and she knew there had been times when majority hadn't ruled at all, times when the powerful forced their will upon others. And Kerry had as strong a will as anyone—"stubborn," that's what most people called it, except her mother who had always preferred "determined." Or "Bulldog," as her housemates had named her. She wasn't sure how she could force the others to change their minds, but that didn't mean she couldn't try.

Except she was unable to form a sentence with the floor spinning beneath her feet. "I'll get my things," Daniel said, apparently interpreting her confused silence as acquiescence.

He didn't, as far as she had been able to tell, have many things to get. When they'd found him in their bushes, he had only the clothes on his back. He had been living someplace, though, and he had a knapsack's worth of possessions that he'd gathered from there after installing them all in this apartment. Kerry supposed that it was possible he had a house full of stuff somewhere—obviously, there was still far more that she didn't know about him than that she did. Since the apartment, shabby as it was, actually had more bedrooms than their house had, Brandy and Scott shared one, while Josh and Mace bunked together in another, Rebecca and Kerry in the third. Daniel, when he slept, did so in the living room on a worn, thrift-shop sofa, next to which he stored his leather pack. He crossed the room and picked it up now, moving with graceful economy, surely knowing that all eyes were on him.

Kerry felt her own eyes growing misty. She wasn't sure how much of that was because Rebecca was sniffling, huge round tears rolling down her pudgy cheeks, and how much was because, as briefly as Daniel had been part of her life, she would miss him. She sniffed once, determined not to cry.

"Daniel . . . ," she began, but she wasn't at all sure where she was going with it, and she let it hang there.

He looked at her, as if reading her meaning anyway. "Don't, Kerry," he said. "If you need me, I'll be there."

"But not here," Brandy chimed in.

"Not here."

"And no stalking, dude," Mace added.

"Not a chance," Daniel assured him. He hoisted the backpack onto his shoulder, took a last look around at everyone, gave a smile and a friendly wave, and walked out the door.

Kerry Profitt's diary, August 20

How many times can you lose a person that you never really got a chance to know?

7

For Mace, the whole crazy thing was just too much to cope with.

He'd lost his job the night Kerry had run out of the restaurant with Daniel. He'd been back at his station in a corner of the kitchen, washing dishes, iPod screaming The Strokes into his ear, completely unaware of what was happening until a burst of light caught his attention. His first thought was that someone was taking flash pictures, though why anyone would want to do such a thing in a busy restaurant kitchen was beyond him. But looking up, he caught a glimpse of Kerry and Daniel diving out the door, pursued by a blonde with a reasonably high hotness quotient.

The whole thing was more than a little freaky. Kerry was a friend of his, though, so he dropped a stack of plates, which caught the edge of the big sink and shattered onto the floor, and ran past the stunned kitchen staff and into the parking lot. Two cars roared away. His own car was parked in an employee lot a quarter mile away. He ran for it and lit it up, but way too late—the car Kerry had jetted in was history.

When he made his way back to the kitchen, the restaurant manager, Emil Hofstadter—who Mace was pretty sure had been born John Smith, or something like it, and whose name was as phony as his Swiss accent—had been furious, though he denied having seen anything out of the ordinary. But with no Kerry to take out his anger on, he'd directed it at Mace. Knowing it was completely without justification, Mace sucked it up anyway, figuring it might help protect Kerry from any fallout. But then, a couple of hours later, when Rebecca came in and told him that Kerry had texted her and said they all needed to get out of there, now—even though his shift would have been over in twenty-five minutes—Mace had gone along with her, walking out right in front of a raging Emil. He knew then that the job was history. Emil's arms were crossed over his chest and his face was the color of an eggplant, with veins standing out on his forehead like they were about to burst.

So he'd given up the job, and willingly. Not happily, mind you—he didn't have money in the family like Scott and Brandy, or an insurance settlement like Kerry, and had to work for what he got. But friends came first, even when they had only become friends over the course of the summer. Besides, when Rebecca directed those puppy-dog browns at him, he didn't know how to say no.

But the whole crazy deal with Daniel was just too much to put up with. Even though Brandy had won the battle, and the man had been exiled from the apartment—which he had paid for, which meant, Mace supposed, that he could show up again at any time—Mace still wasn't comfortable hanging around anymore. Occult stuff really gave him the chills. He didn't even like horror movies, unless they were so ridiculously slasherific that there was no way to believe in them. But he thought that messing around with magic was just asking for trouble, the kind that he didn't want to have to cope with.

He didn't *believe* in magic—who would, in their right mind? He figured the stuff Daniel had shown them was nothing but trickery of some kind. And even though Kerry swore some kind of magical battle had gone on in the kitchen that night, there had been no damage left behind and he hadn't seen it, had only observed some bright lights. That didn't mean he was comfortable with it, though.

So the morning after the final confrontation with Daniel, he got up early and packed up Susie, his baby blue Lincoln Continental. He said adios to his summer friends, after coffee and churros from the taco stand on the corner of Palm, with lots of hugs and handshakes. Rebecca cried, as she would, and pulled him close to her, and the curves and valleys of her lush figure beneath her loose clothes made him think twice about what he was doing. But then he saw Kerry, ivory pale, green eyes looking bruised and bloodshot from worrying about Daniel, he guessed, and knew that of all of them, she'd have the hardest time giving up the strange old man—and he her—and if the guy was going to come back into their lives, Mace just didn't want to be there for it.

Susie started right up, as she always did. Rebecca stood on the sidewalk and waved until he was out of sight. He connected his iPod to the cassette deck—damn thing was built before CD players; that and the gas mileage were Susie's main drawbacks—and headed for Interstate 5, which would connect with the I-8, which would merge with the I-10 and take him all the way to Las Cruces. From there the I-70 would lead home to Clovis. In minutes he was on the freeway, and he lowered the window a few inches so the wind would blow on his face as he drove. To Mace, that was one of the joys of a road trip—wind in your face, tunes blaring, blacktop spooling out behind you like film running through a projector.

He'd only gone a few miles, though—hadn't even reached the I-8, which ran east-west across the bottom edge of the southwest—when Susie started to act up. Susie, for whom he cared as if she were a precious thing, started to bump and knock and rattle like she'd been inhabited by a family of poltergeists. There was no reason she should have any problems, given how carefully and meticulously he maintained her, but he couldn't ignore the noises and the shuddering that got worse with each passing mile.

With a curse and an angry slap on the steering wheel, he gave up and pulled off at the next exit. Downtown San Diego loomed ahead of him, the I-8 a few miles beyond that. But here, off to the side of the freeway, there was only a vacant industrial area—warehouses and a railroad track and then a stretch of sloughs and shipyards close to the shore. Mace pulled Susie over in the shade of one of the warehouses and killed the engine.

He sat behind the wheel listening to her tick for a few minutes, letting the engine cool a little. Inside, he fumed, but he tried to keep that from her. A car was a sentient being, or close to it, he believed, and you didn't want to let one know when you were genuinely mad at it. Talking nice was almost always preferable. He apologized for having struck the steering wheel, and then popped the hood.

He couldn't have said where the woman came from. The neighborhood had been deserted, the only sound the steady rush of the nearby freeway, the only smell the sour, fecund stink of the standing water between here and the ocean. But between the time he opened the hood and glanced inside—to see an engine that looked just as cherry as it ever did—and the time that it took for him to go back into the car to get a rag to wipe his hands on, she had come up behind him. He stood up, rubbing at a spot of oil on his left index finger, and she was just standing there, a dozen feet away, looking at him. Tall, blond, wearing faded jeans and a black tank top and an expression like a stern librarian giving her last warning.

"Where is he?" she demanded. As soon as she spoke, Mace realized who she had to be. "Season," Daniel had called her. Mace had seen her before, in the kitchen that night, though only from behind. He recognized the honeyed hair, however, her statuesque carriage, her muscular form.

And anyway, who else could it be? This is just too perfect.

"I don't know what you're talking about," he replied.

"Just tell me where to find Daniel," she said, "and you'll be fine."

He started to speak again, to deny that he knew who she meant, but she narrowed her eyes and parted her lips just a little and he knew that it was pointless. He didn't know *how* she knew—didn't want to know, for that matter. But she did.

"I have no idea," he said. "He was hanging around, but we kicked him out last night. I don't know where he went."

She started toward him then, walking slowly, with pretend casualness, but he didn't trust her intentions for a second. "Let's just see about that," she said. Visions of aliens with mind probes leapt into his head, and he knew that the last thing he wanted was this woman, whatever she was, rooting around in his thoughts.

He ran for Susie's open door and hurled himself inside, grabbing and twisting the key that still hung in her ignition. The engine grumbled but caught, and he yanked the door shut as he stomped on the gas. The blonde stood in the roadway before him, coming toward the car as if she intended to stop it with her own body and tug him out. Mace wasn't thinking clearly, wasn't processing. *Get out of here,* that's what went through his mind, over and over. *Get out of here. Get out—*

But she was in the way and she didn't look like she was moving, and anyway she was trouble, anyone could see that . . .

—of here.

. . . and instead of swerving around her, he turned the wheel ever so slightly, and pointed Susie's enormous bulk right *at* her.

The big car ate up the feet between them. He braced himself for the inevitable impact.

Which didn't come.

He reached the spot where she should have been, but she didn't seem to be there anymore. It took him a moment before he realized it wasn't that she had moved, but that *he* had—his direction of travel had changed. Instead of pushing through her toward the open road, he was hurtling *toward* the cement block wall of the nearest warehouse.

Mace pawed at the wheel and started to correct his course, but even as he did, he knew it was too late. He was moving too fast, had come too close. The wall loomed huge in his windshield, and then—

8

"Mace is dead."

Daniel stood in the doorway, his face drawn, looking worse than at any time Kerry had seen him since that first night. This time it wasn't physical pain he felt, she believed, but emotional. He had come to deliver bad news. And he experienced the hurt of that news himself, maybe even some complicity.

"I'm so sorry," he went on, filling the silence when she didn't say anything. "I feel just terrible."

Confirming her theory. "Did you have anything to do with it?" *Cold,* she thought, *but necessary.*

"No. Yes." He looked at the ground, then back at her, eyes wide and solemn. "Just that . . . while he was allied with the rest of you, he was under my protection. Once he made the decision to leave, he slipped from my sphere of influence. She must have been waiting for something like that, for the scent of any of you. She must have caught up to him. It's the only thing that could have happened."

Somehow the explanation, perfunctory as it was, made it all more real to her, and she herself turned numb. "How . . . ," she began, but couldn't finish. She swallowed hard and stepped aside, wordlessly inviting him in.

"He had pulled off the freeway in an industrial area, for no reason that I can discern, and drove straight into a warehouse wall. The speed and force must have been incredible. Do you want to know more?"

"I . . . want to know everything," she said. Josh, Brandy, and Scott were at work. Rebecca had lost her job at Seaside when she and Mace bailed from the kitchen, and she had gone down to the nearby branch library for some books. Kerry knew that they'd all have questions, lots of them, and she wanted to be able to answer whatever came up.

"The force of impact drove the engine block through the passenger compartment," Daniel elaborated. "He would have been killed instantly. I'm sure he didn't suffer."

"But . . . if it was her . . . why? Would she have . . . tortured him?"

Daniel shrugged, but his face remained grim as he considered the possibility. "Maybe. I doubt it, though. The way they found him . . . if she had had any time with him, I don't think he would have been in the car."

Kerry flopped down on the couch, suddenly feeling unsteady on her feet. A darkness seemed to close in around her, but she didn't know if it was actual or spiritual. Or if it really mattered, in the long run. People died—in the thrillers she liked to read, and her own parents had died—but she had never known of a violent death before, and the thought of it staggered her, made her feel sick. "What, is she just evil? Why would she do that?"

Daniel sat beside her and put a hand on her knee. "I'm sure she's still trying to find me, to use my association with you all to track me and finish me off. I've regained most of my strength since our last serious encounter, but if she still expects that I'm weakened, she'll want to press her advantage." He looked away from her, at the plastered ceiling. "Which makes his death my fault," he said, sounding very somber. "One more in a long line."

Kerry felt that she should argue with him, should claim somehow that Mace took his own chances by leaving. But that wasn't right, she realized, since he had no way of knowing what might have been in store for him if he left. None of them had known that they were still under Daniel's protection, so how could they be aware of what might happen if they left it? No, he was right—Mace's death was on him.

On him . . . and Season Howe.

"As to whether she's evil," Daniel continued, "the answer is very definitely yes. I thought I'd made that clear."

"I guess I don't understand what her game is," Kerry said. Daniel's hand still rested on her knee, and it was getting to the point where she'd have to acknowledge it with a squeeze of her own or shift away from it with whatever message that would send, or it would become like the elephant in the room, impossible to pretend wasn't there. But then probably she was only dwelling on it to distract herself from the fact of Mace's death—the real elephant in the room. "What is she after?"

Apparently he caught on to the knee situation too. He gave a final pat and took his hand away, raising it and his other one chest high in a gesture of uncertainty. "Who knows? I like to think that by keeping the pressure on her, keeping her on the run, I've prevented her from putting any grand plans into motion. But bad things happen every day, everywhere on Earth. Might she be responsible for some of those? Of course."

Kerry rubbed her eyes, as if that would help her discern Season's motives. "But you don't have any proof that she's still up to bad things?" she asked. "Nothing you can pin on her recently?"

"Murdering Mace," he reminded her.

"Yeah," Kerry agreed, feeling the numbness overtake her again. There had just been too much going on emotionally this last week or so. She hadn't been sleeping well, hadn't been eating right. It wore on her, and she was afraid that she was simply shutting down, one part at a time. "Yeah, there's that."

Josh had just parked a Lexus at the north lot and was starting to hoof it back to the valet station when one of his coworkers, Kevin, pulled up to the curb nearby in a gigantic black Escalade. Kevin rolled down the driver's window and leaned his head out. He was big and shaggy, with the sunstreaked blond locks of the surfer he was. He mostly worked nights because he preferred the morning waves. "Dude!" he called. Josh jogged over to him.

"What's up?"

"Hey, you knew that guy Mace, right? Dishwasher?"

"Yeah, he's my—". Kevin's use of the past tense suddenly struck him, and Josh felt his insides turn to hot liquid. "What do you mean?"

"Dude, he got killed," Kevin said casually. "There's some cops askin' for anyone who knew him. Detectives, I guess, in suits. They started with valets because we're right out in front, but it looks like they're gonna work their way around."

"Killed how?" Josh demanded. His legs felt like pipe cleaners, like they were about to buckle under his weight.

"I don't know," Kevin answered. "They were into asking questions, not answerin' 'em."

The specifics of it, Josh knew, weren't really the important thing. The fact was, Mace was dead—unless this whole deal was some colossal misunderstanding, which seemed unlikely. Mace was not the kind of guy to whom Josh would normally be drawn, but over the summer they had become friends anyway, and to think his life had been suddenly snuffed . . .

Then another thought burst into his consciousness, and he believed—no, he *knew*—that this was somehow related to those freaking witches, Season and Daniel. Somehow Mace had been caught in their crossfire and had paid the price for it.

Which meant that any of them could be next.

Scott and Brandy, he thought suddenly. They were working today too, and they had to be found and warned. If the cops could find them, so could the witch.

Without a parting word to Kevin, he broke into a panicked run. Scott could be anywhere, but Brandy would only be one place—the hotel's front desk. It would be the second place the cops would go, after the valet stand.

He needed to call her, get her out of there. As he ran, he tore off his red valet's vest, not wanting to be easily recognizable to the police. He hurled it to the ground, followed it with his bow tie. Now he was just a guy in a white shirt and black pants, running full tilt across the resort grounds, digging a cell phone from his pocket as he did.

Kerry Profitt's diary, August 21

Much to my astonishment, Rebecca didn't cry when we told her about Mace.

I'd have put money on it. The girl is such a soft touch she wants to take in every stray dog, cat, or homeless person we see on the streets, of which, especially that last one, there are plenty. But then, San Diego in summer? Relatively mild, no humidity, not too bad in the bug department (I haven't suffered a mosquito bite since I got here, which is more than I could say for Illinois in the summer). If I was homeless, which so far is only a borderline possibility, there aren't many places I'd rather live.

She said, changing the subject.

Then again, I didn't cry either. Mace Winston, not my favorite person (can you say that about the dead?) was gone, and I felt—and feel—just horrible. I'm sure Rebecca feels the same way. I've never seen her look so sad as when she came in the door, a bunch of library books under her arm, and we told her. But no tears fell. They will tonight, later, I expect. She's still out in the living room as I write this, and I have a feeling that when we're both in here tonight, with the lights out, there are going to be tears on both our pillows.

Mostly what I feel is empty. And angry. As if Mace, who as I pointed out was not my best friend in life, has left a giant hole inside me through his absence. And even though I never expected to see him again anyway after he drove into the sunrise, the idea that he's not out there anymore, the idea that I couldn't call him or see him even if I wanted to, is somehow too horrible to really process.

I'm sure the police notified his parents. Mace had ID on him, they knew who he was. Fortunately not where he was living most recently,

because a whole lot of questions could come up that we have no interest in answering. I was a little surprised to find that, on that question,
at least, Brandy and I were in agreement.

More later.
K.

Later, Kerry heard a clatter on the outside stairs, which meant that Scott,
Brandy, and Josh were home, earlier than anticipated, and the heavy footfalls
indicated that they were upset too. She tossed a wan smile Daniel's way—he
was still on the couch, but she had paced for a while and then settled in a
chair—and waited for the inevitable. Rebecca heard the noise too, and drifted
in from the bedroom she and Kerry shared, exchanging glances with both
Kerry and Daniel.

When the door flew open, Brandy was the first one inside. She took in
the scene quickly. "So you've heard," she said.

"We've heard," Kerry confirmed.

Brandy dropped her purse unceremoniously to the floor; she seemed to
carry the approximate weight of a small city with her at any given time, Kerry
thought. "This is your fault," she said, boring in on Daniel with her glare.

"You're right, Brandy," Daniel agreed. "I am so terribly sorry. It was
because of my association with you that Season Howe killed Mace."

Scott and Josh crowded in behind Brandy, who had stopped just a
couple of feet in front of the door, and had her arms folded, legs wide.
An aggressive stance, Kerry thought, *like she's spoiling for a fight.* Sunlight
splashed in through a part in the curtain, giving her caramel-colored skin
a soft glow.

"Do you know for sure it was her?" Scott asked.

Daniel gave a little shrug. "I didn't witness it, if that's what you mean.
But in my heart, yes, I'm certain. Unless you think Mace would have intentionally driven into a wall."

Scott pulled his glasses off and wiped them on the tail of his tan uniform shirt. "That doesn't sound like him."

"Not at all," Josh agreed. He squeezed behind Scott and planted himself on the floor, legs crossed, back against the wall. Kerry wouldn't have believed he could be any paler than his usual paper-white, but he seemed almost gray now. "Mace was, like, the least suicidal guy I've ever known. And a good driver besides. And even if he would kill himself, which he wouldn't, he'd never do anything to hurt that car."

"No," Brandy echoed. "He wouldn't do that."

"It was Season, then," Scott said, replacing his glasses and blinking behind them. He sounded like he was trying to convince himself, and was slowly coming around to that position. "She killed him."

"That's right," Kerry found herself saying. "That's what Daniel's been telling us."

"But if it wasn't for you he'd still be alive," Brandy declared.

Daniel looked at her calmly. "Most likely, yes."

"And we'd all still have our jobs," Josh said.

Kerry had already noticed that they were home early, but now she realized that Josh wasn't wearing his vest or tie, nor had he carried them in. Brandy still had on the conservative gray skirt and tight short-sleeved top she'd worn that morning, and Scott was in his groundskeeper uniform, but neither of them had work accessories that could as easily be abandoned as Josh's. "You didn't all quit, did you?" she asked.

"Effectively, since we just walked away from them," Brandy said, her dark eyes smoldering. "It was either that or talk to the cops. As it is, I'm sure they'll be calling our families pretty soon, trying to track us down. We're in a serious situation here."

"The police were already there?" Kerry asked, surprised.

"Looking for us, apparently," Brandy replied. "There's an investigation into Mace's death."

"That makes sense," Daniel said. "It just doesn't look like an accident."

"So you saw where it happened?" Scott asked him. He still stood, a half step behind Brandy.

"I did," Daniel answered. "After the fact. I had a sense that something had happened, something involving one of you—"

"Then why weren't you able to stop it?" Brandy demanded.

"It was *after* the fact," Daniel repeated. "As I explained to Kerry and Rebecca, by leaving the rest of you behind, Mace took himself outside my protection."

Brandy shook her head. "There shouldn't even *be* protection," she fumed. "We told you to leave us alone! What part of that don't you get?"

"I couldn't, not completely," Daniel said by way of defense. "I had involved you in something dangerous. Without my protection, what happened to Mace would have happened to all of you by now. Unless—"

"There's an unless?" Rebecca asked, her voice so high it squeaked.

"Unless you give me up," he finished. "If you tell Season where to find me, then she might let you live."

"But Mace didn't . . . ," Kerry began.

"You had sent me away. Mace had no idea where to find me. Even if he'd wanted to save his own life, he wouldn't have been able to."

Brandy slumped as if she'd been deflated. "So really, I . . ."

Scott grabbed her shoulders from behind, like he was trying to keep her from sinking into the floor. "Brandy, no!"

"But it's true," she said quietly. "If I hadn't insisted we make Daniel leave, Mace would still be alive."

"Possibly," Scott countered.

"No," she snapped, turning on him. "I was the one who pushed and pushed to get Daniel out of here. If I hadn't—"

"Scott's right, Brandy," Daniel said, trying to console her. "There's no way to know what might have happened. Mace might have gone anyway, and then he still would have been outside my protection. He could have given me up, told her to find me here. But that doesn't guarantee that she wouldn't have killed him anyway."

"I guess." She sat down on the floor, with Scott helping her down. He remained beside her, like a bodyguard. "But still . . ."

"You can never know what might have happened, Brandy," Daniel assured her. "Or what's going to happen. The best you can do is try to make the right decisions when they present themselves."

"So what's the best decision now?" Josh asked. "I mean, we're basically screwed, right? The cops are looking for us, we've lost our jobs, and this Season witch is going to try to run us down one by one."

"Unless . . . ," Daniel began.

"Unless what?" Kerry asked.

"Unless," he continued, "we take the fight back to her."

9

Daniel didn't have much in the way of a plan, Kerry learned. *But then, if he had, he might not have spent the last three centuries chasing her from place to place.* He admitted as much over fast-food burgers and milk shakes in the apartment that he had moved back into, taking the now-vacant bed that had been used by Mace.

"Season's survival skills are well-honed," he told them. "She's hard to get the drop on, virtually impossible to ambush. Every now and then I get a lead on where she is, but even then, she's so much more powerful than me that I have to plan my strategy carefully, and that's just to give me a fighting chance. I can't say that I've ever had the advantage."

"Can you beat her?" Scott asked. His neatly trimmed collegiate hair, Kerry noticed, was starting to grow a bit long and unruly. "Or is it just not even worth trying?"

"Am I spinning my wheels?" Daniel rephrased Scott's question. "I like to think I'm not. But then I suppose the same is true of anyone on a long, fruitless hunt. Was Ahab wasting his time chasing the white whale all over creation? A lot of people would say yes." He took a deep breath and blew it out slowly. There was, Kerry thought, a sadness in his eyes while he considered the question. "Certainly there are other things I could have done with my life. I could have helped more people, I suppose. Saved more lives in some other capacity. But I believed—I continue to believe—that Season is a threat, a real danger, to everyone whose path she crosses. She's not going away on her own, so someone has to step in and deal with her."

"That's not exactly what I meant," Scott said, his elbows on the cheap table as he wrested a fry from its paper bag. "I meant more, like, can you take her on, or is it pointless to try? But since you bring it up—not to be too nosy or anything—but just how long can you guys live?"

Daniel smiled briefly. "Got it," he answered with a chuckle. "I didn't mean to be evasive. Short answer, this time—yes, I believe I can take her. Not easily, as I've mentioned, and probably not one-on-one in a fair fight. But I've long since given up the idea of fighting her fairly. Question two— I'm not entirely sure. I knew a witch once who claimed to be well over a thousand. He said that he'd narrowly escaped death at the Battle of Hastings, and when I knew him he looked every single one of those thousand and some years. He died shortly after that, of natural causes. Or at least that's what I was told."

"So the fact that Season was an adult when she wrecked your town doesn't necessarily mean that she's likely to die of old age any time soon," Brandy suggested.

"You've seen her, Kerry," Daniel pointed out. "She look like she's on her deathbed to you?"

"I wish," Kerry replied. "But, no. I could only hope to look that good when I'm thirty-five."

Josh had been staring blankly at a corner of the room, and Kerry wasn't sure he had even been tracking the conversation. But now he swiveled his head, neck stiff as if it needed oiling, and fixed his gaze on Daniel. Outside, the sun had gone away, and the glow from the overhead light in the kitchen left the table half dark. "How do we off her, man?" Josh asked. "That's what this is all about, right? How do we freaking kill her?"

Kerry shuddered to hear the question phrased so bluntly. Josh was right, of course. And he had been closest to Mace—well, he and Rebecca. But Rebecca wasn't the kind of person who would think along those lines, under any circumstance. Josh, though—the set of his chin and the hardness of his eyes reminded Kerry of a character from the hard-boiled movies he loved so much. *He could be turned into a killer,* she realized. *Maybe he already has been, and now he just needs the opportunity.*

Daniel shrugged. "First we find her," he said, as if it was that easy. "Then I kill her. Not you. Not any of you. You wouldn't stand a chance against Season Howe."

"Try me," Josh said.

"I'm serious, Josh," Daniel assured him. "Not a chance. She wouldn't even break a sweat against you. But . . ." He paused before he went on, as if choosing his words carefully. Perhaps debating whether to say them at all. ". . . you can help. You can track her down."

"How?" Rebecca asked. "Wouldn't that, like, make us even bigger targets? Like Mace was?"

"Mace was outside my protection, so he was no longer shielded from her," Daniel explained. "It's not a physical thing, not a matter of distance or anything like that. Mace left the rest of you behind, and by doing so he opted out of my protection spell. But the rest of you—you could walk right up to Season, and she'd never know you were the ones who helped me. As long as you all work together." He looked at Kerry. "Except you, Kerry. She's seen you. She can't sense where you are, but if she sees you again, she'll know you."

"I understand," Kerry said.

"But if we find her, then what?" Scott asked. "Aren't we back to square one? We have to let you know where she is, and then you have to get there and somehow do battle against a superior opponent."

"Sounds so easy when you put it that way." Daniel was smiling when he said it, but his grin didn't look particularly mirthful.

Under Daniel's direction—and more significantly, he promised, his protection—they split up the next morning to go look for Season Howe.

Kerry was impressed by his visual aid: he generated, or rather, projected, an almost-photographic image of Season in the inch of black coffee left at the bottom of Scott's cup, clear enough that even those who had never seen the witch in person would recognize her. Daniel didn't want to let the image last for long for fear, he said, that she would somehow be able to lock onto it. So he told everyone to take a good look, and then he stirred the coffee and the image went away.

Season liked crowds, Daniel had said, and transient populations, where strangers weren't unusual. So to cover the most ground possible, they paired off—Scott and Brandy, of course, Rebecca and Josh, Daniel and Kerry. Rebecca and Josh decided they'd scope out downtown San Diego, look into the coffee shops and boutiques of the Gaslamp Quarter and the stores of Horton Plaza. Scott and Brandy—who, since Mace died, was willing to go along even though she still hadn't come around to believing in Daniel—went to scout the beaches. Daniel and Kerry knew that it was impossible for six people to cover the entire city—plus there was always the chance, though Daniel insisted it was remote, that Season had already moved on—but they also knew they had to make the best possible effort. So Kerry and Daniel went to a place where they knew there would be crowds: the San Diego Zoo.

At Daniel's suggestion, everyone had contacted their parents or other adult caretakers—in Kerry's case, it had been a simple e-mail to Uncle Marsh's work account, which Kerry knew would suffice—to let them know that there had been a change of address and phone number, but that they were okay. Since most of their folks used their cell phones anyway, the change wouldn't be a big deal to them. Kerry had rarely spoken to her aunt and uncle since she'd been in California, but then again, she rarely talked to them even when they lived in the same house. Rebecca was close to her parents and three brothers, as were Scott and Brandy to their families, but Josh almost never mentioned his, and Kerry was pretty sure only his mother was still alive.

The zoo was nearly always busy, but on a warm summer afternoon it was almost overwhelmingly so. The line from the ticket booths extended most of the way to the parking lot. Kerry thought she'd die of sunstroke by the time they got inside, the sun not being a friend to her fair skin. But Daniel told her to wait in the shade while he stood in line, and in a few minutes they had passed through the turnstiles. Inside, the air had a differ- ent quality—the exhaust of cars and tour buses was left behind on the other side of the walls, and they moved into a world of exotic scents—scores of plants mixing with the rich, pungent odors of the birds and animals that surrounded them. The scenery was a riot of colors—the Hawaiian shirts and casual clothes of zoo-goers battling for supremacy with the bright plumage of the flamingoes near the front entrance. Daniel didn't add much to the display in his jeans and dark blue T-shirt, but Kerry had opted for a crimson-and-white striped rugby shirt, with the long sleeves pushed up, and white hip huggers.

"Flamingoes were used as the hieroglyphic symbol for the color red, in ancient Egypt," Daniel told her as they threaded their way through the crowd. "And to represent the reincarnation of Ra, the sun god."

Kerry studied his face, looking for signs of age that weren't there. "You're not *that* old, though," she said.

Daniel laughed. "No, not that old. Just old enough to have picked up lots of totally useless information along the way."

"Not totally useless," Kerry argued. "There's the sheer entertainment value. Not to mention the possibility of scoring big on TV game shows."

He smiled, but he was standing up on the balls of his feet, scanning the crowd for any sign of Season. "Yeah, I guess that's true," he admitted.

"Speaking of cash," she pressed. "How do you survive, anyway? You don't seem to be gainfully employed, not that I can tell."

Daniel looked away from the crowd long enough to meet her gaze for a moment. Just under his right jaw line, where she usually didn't notice it, was a scar like a half-curled worm against his skin. She had meant to ask about it before, but never had. "Turns out if you take the long-term view— and I mean, really long term—the stock market isn't a bad place to keep some money. And even a bank account will do pretty well after a hundred years or so of collecting interest."

"What about government records? Social Security, the IRS, stuff like that?" She'd been too absorbed in the craziness of the hunt to give much thought to such mundane questions before, but now that they'd occurred to her, she couldn't stop the flow.

"Nothing that can't be doctored with a simple spell," Daniel explained.

"And doctors? Doesn't your family doctor wonder if you never age?"

"We tend to take care of our own. Don't have much need of doctors." He touched her arm. "And sometimes an angel of mercy appears from nowhere when you need her most."

She felt herself blushing, and turned away. But then she reached up, almost as if she couldn't stop herself, and touched the curled scar. "What's this one? Seems like that might have needed some medical attention."

His face changed slightly, as if a shadow had passed over it, and he rubbed the spot she had just touched. "I could have removed it," he said. His voice had turned to steel. "But that one I got the day she killed Abraham."

"Your brother," Kerry remembered. Twins, he'd said, born shortly after Season had destroyed their town.

"That's right." They had stopped walking, and the flow of humanity coursed around them like a river around boulders. A woman pushing twins in a stroller shot them a dirty look, as if they had intentionally blocked her path, but then picked a side and moved on. "Season did that, with an enchanted blade she carried in those days. Nearly killed me. Took me out of action long enough for her to finish Abe. He was trying to help me, and she cut him too. Left us both for dead. Unlucky for her. She should have finished me off then."

He touched the spot again and then shook his hand, like he could shake off the memory as easily as a few drops of water. Kerry felt bad for bringing up something so obviously painful, and thought she should change the subject. "Why here?" she asked, starting to walk again. Signs ahead of them pointed toward the children's zoo and the Absolutely Apes exhibit. "Why would she be at the zoo?"

"She would be here, or at the beach or the mall or some other place, because her whole goal is not to stand out. She is probably living in a hotel, although it's possible she found a summer rental. Either way, there would be someone—neighbors, hotel staff, a cleaning service—who would notice if she spent these warm summer days holed up in the room. She wants to look like every other out-of-towner here for the season, so she goes to places like this, even if she has no special interest in them."

"And you can't just magically track her down?"

"No more than she can track me, or you while you're under my protection. I've got counterspells, and so does she. If we see each other, then it's war. But if I can't find her before she leaves town, then I've got to start all over."

They made the turn toward the apes exhibit area, for no particular reason that she could determine. There was a part of Kerry that enjoyed just walking through the zoo with a handsome, interesting man. She wished there didn't have to be some kind of epic death hunt going on to darken the day. But at the same time, she knew it was the death hunt that had brought them together, and it remained the main thing they had in common.

"Do you ever get tired of it?" she asked. "Just want to give it up and let her go?"

Again, he stopped in his tracks. Kerry was starting to feel like the queen of hurtful questions. "You don't have to answer that," she said quickly. "It was over the line. I'm sorry."

"It's okay." He took her upper arms in his hands and held on tightly until she thought he might leave bruise marks. "I don't feel like I have to hide anything from you, Kerry. I don't quite know why that is, yet. But I kind of like it. I hope that doesn't scare you."

The only answer that came to her was the honest one. "Yeah, it does, a little. But I'll try to cope."

"The truth is, I get tired of it every day, and every day there are times when I want to give up. But I never do."

"Why not?" *You just have to push,* she thought, even as the words left her mouth. *You big dope.*

"Honestly?" Daniel looked toward the sun, and blinked a couple of times. "I don't know what I'd do with myself. Daytime TV gets pretty dull after a few decades."

Kerry Profitt's diary, August 23

The zoo was a big strikeout, Season-wise. Brandy and Scott washed out too. As did, need I say, Rebecca and Josh. No Season, no Season, and no Season. Not that, in a city the size of San Diego, with more millions than I can remember, but several of them, it's an easy task to find a single person who doesn't especially want to be found. And as Daniel put it, better twelve eyes looking for her than two—especially since she's no doubt looking for us, too, and whoever spots the other first has the advantage.

Can't argue with the reasoning. Of course, to take it a step or two further, twelve hundred eyes would be better yet. Twelve thousand, and maybe there'd be a chance of finding her. This needle-in-the-haystack routine seems so, I don't know, eighteenth century somehow. Like we ought to be able to Google her instead of just looking.

Which, by the way, I just did. There's a hockey player named Howe who's had several good seasons, and likewise some squash news. No witchy stuff, though. So I guess, as Daniel told me while we walked past the big cats (side note—the snow leopards are spectacular!), she has done a good job of maintaining a low profile.

What is most amazing to me is that this works, he says. The low-tech thing, I mean. He has found her before, several times. Done her some damage, too, he says. Of course, she's done the same to him. Many clinches, no knockouts. Sports page girl today, that's me.

Actually, not, so don't ask why the various jock references. I might recognize Tiger Woods or A-Rod on the street, and not many guys can carry off bicycle shorts like Lance Armstrong, but that is, I confess, about the extent of my sports smarts.

I'm frustrated, of course, by the lack of forward momentum of our day—the first real day of what I presume to be many (at least until school beckons and we have to go our separate ways) of hunting Season Howe. But the truth is, it wasn't a bad day at all. I got to roam the zoo, and then the open spaces of Balboa Park as well as its museums and walkways, with Daniel. Who, as it turns out, is full of stories. Living three hundred years would give one plenty of material, I guess. But I sometimes have a hard time remembering what I did last week, and he's coming up with bits like the time, a hundred years ago, when he sat in a dark nickelodeon in New York and watched *The Great Train Robbery*, one of the first movies ever made.

Well, I guess I might remember something like that too. Having spent my "formative years" not exactly going to a ton of movies, I think I remember all the ones I've seen in theaters. Cried at *The Notebook*, but at the wrong parts. Laughed at *The Hangover*, ditto. Guess I'm just culturally illiterate.

But the point is, walking around with Daniel, being entertained by his stories, even as we kept our eyes open for any sign of the big bad witch of the west, was nice. Balboa Park is as beautiful a spot as one could hope for. It all helped drive horrible thoughts of Mace from my mind, and I hope that somehow, wherever he is, he's found some peace. Being with Daniel felt easy, comfortable, even though I haven't known him for long and he is as different from me—being essentially immortal, many-powered and all—as it's possible to be.

All the crazy witch stuff? Turns out when you're faced with it, right in front of you, it's not so hard to believe. A month ago—two weeks ago—I would've sworn that it was all bogus. Today I'll swear till I'm blue in the face (and just what does that old cliché mean, anyway?) that it's true, that there are people—witches—among us with abilities far beyond our imagining.

I asked Daniel, while we walked and searched, about Wiccans. I think the way I phrased it was less than charitable, something like, "so those people who sit around in circles and worship trees and stuff—are they just wannabes? Do they even know that witches like you and Season really exist, and is that what they aspire to?"

But Daniel is, apparently, kinder than I. "A few of them are," he told me. "Aware of us, I mean. Very few. To others, we're nothing more than whispers, rumors, maybe legends, if that. They aren't necessarily trying to become like us, or even thinking that's a possibility. It isn't quite as if they're acolytes. But their activities can help to power us, like we're batteries, recharged by the forces they release into the ether. So they do us a major service. And much of what they do is effective, as far as it goes. Spells to find love or employment, or to help friends through difficult situations: These can all work quite well if carried out correctly."

Okay, the colon I put in there? I made it up. Don't know if that's what he intended, or even if I'm quoting verbatim. He could probably quote something Abraham Lincoln told him in 1862 (kidding, he never met Lincoln, he says), but I don't have that particular skill.

Point is, something about Daniel—maybe because of his special abilities—has made him remarkable in other ways too. He has an astonishing memory, and my guess is that he's just developed his mental faculties in ways most people can't even comprehend. So living for centuries just enhances his recall instead of—as I suspect would happen to me—jumbling experiences together.

Hey, I've been to Disneyland and seen the animatronic Lincoln. If I'd been alive in the 1860s, I probably would think I'd seen the real one.

I pummeled him with questions, over the course of the day. Who he had met, what he had seen. Finally, he told me he kept journals, and he'd let me read them if I was interested. I think it was a ploy to shut me up.

Didn't work.

But I'm still going to read them. How cool is that?

More later.

K.

10

The day after that, they rotated partners and continued the hunt. Kerry found herself paired with Rebecca. She felt an unexpected pang of sorrow at not getting another day with Daniel, who teamed up with Scott, while Brandy and Josh went out together. But she understood the reasoning. If the same two people searched together every time, Daniel suggested, they'd fall into patterns of looking, and maybe become complacent. If they were changed up frequently, they'd be more likely to remain alert and aware. Anyway, she liked Rebecca so she had no real problem with it, just a sense of longing to be with Daniel.

They spent a long day mall-crawling, figuring a woman who looked as good and dressed as nicely as Season Howe would probably be a serious shopper. They started south, at Plaza Bonita, and worked their way north, through Horton Plaza, Mission Valley, and its more upscale neighbor, Fashion Valley; east as far as Grossmont and Parkway Plaza; then up to La Jolla's University Town Center. Each mall seemed to have its own personality, its own core group of shoppers, in spite of the fact that most had the same national chain stores. They saw, throughout their day, a lot of attractive blondes.

Rebecca also saw at Mission Valley a pair of turquoise drop earrings she just had to have. She was wearing a blue chambray work shirt open over a white-blue tank, the tails tied across her belly, with a sky blue and green-and-yellow batik skirt. The turquoise looked like it had been plucked from the ground especially for her.

What they didn't see was Season.

Kerry had seen Rebecca sad, but she'd never seen her anything resembling grumpy before. Driving home from UTC in the Honda Civic Daniel had acquired for them was the closest the girl had come, in Kerry's memory. "This sucks more than anything," Rebecca groused, thumping the steering wheel for emphasis. "I've been trying to think of something that sucks worse than this, and I just can't. I mean, how many stores are there in San Diego county? Thousands? A hundred thousand? How are we supposed to find Season in the middle of all that? Why do we live in such a materialistic society, anyway? If this was a simple village of hunter-gatherers, we'd have come across her long before now."

"If we see her, we see her," Kerry countered. "If we don't, we don't. But if we don't see her and she sees us, we're going to regret it."

"Yeah, but . . ." Rebecca didn't finish the thought.

"I know," Kerry sympathized. "I feel the same way, Beck. We just have to keep trying."

"For how long, Kerry? Are we in this for the rest of our lives?"

"I don't think so," Kerry said. She wasn't entirely sure herself, though. She couldn't see the hunt lasting forever, even though it had already gone on for many lifetimes. "From what Daniel says, I think it's just a summer thing. Season will move on after that, and we'll be able to split up, go back to our own lives."

"And she won't keep looking for us?"

Let's hope, Kerry thought. "I figure she's got other things on her mind. She'll keep an eye out for Daniel. But I expect we'll be okay."

"But you can't be sure," Rebecca challenged.

"No, of course not. Not a hundred percent."

They were just about to pass by the off-ramp that led into La Jolla when an idea flashed into Kerry's head. "Rebecca!" she shouted. "Turn off here."

Rebecca cranked the wheel to the right and shot off the exit, cutting off another car that blared its horn at her. The look on her face was one of near-panic. "Why?"

"Just a thought," Kerry said. "I didn't mean to startle you. I just figured we should swing by the old house, while we're out this way. If Season's looking for us, she might be staking it out."

"So if she is, should we go there?"

"She's never seen you," Kerry reminded her. "I'll keep a low profile. Just one pass."

"Okay. . . ." Rebecca didn't sound convinced, but she drove toward the house they had once shared, in the part of town known as Bird Rock. Kerry wasn't sure what to expect when they got there. The place was full of memories, most happy, some frightening, as when they'd first discovered Daniel. And, of course, memories of poor, lost Mace that weighed on her like a lead blanket.

When they reached their old block, Kerry scrunched down low in the passenger seat, so that only her eyes and the top of her head showed over the window. "Drive slow," she instructed. Rebecca's knuckles were white on the wheel, and there was a bit of a shake to her arms. "We'll be fine." She probably didn't sound all that reassuring, but then, she found that she was more nervous than she had expected to be.

The street, at first glance, looked the same as ever. It was a little after seven thirty, the sun lowering toward the distant horizon, and the trees that lined the street cast long shadows across the blacktop. Houses had lights on in kitchens and living rooms and over front doors, but there was no one visible on the sidewalks, no one out in their yards. On a Saturday morning at least three or four people on the block would be mowing or weeding, trimming hedges, clipping trees. Now, though, the street might as well have been in a ghost town, or a movie set after filming had wrapped for the night.

Rebecca glanced anxiously at Kerry as she slowed the car, bringing them to a crawl as they neared the house. It was dark and didn't look as if anyone new had moved in since they'd left. Kerry tried to scan the cars parked along the sides of the road, in case Season was sitting in one of them watching the place. They all looked empty, and she began to think the detour was yet one more waste of time in a long day full of time wasted. As they passed the house, though, she rose up in her seat a little, staring hard at the building that had, for a brief time, contained her life on this coast. *Funny how a building can be so small, so limited, and yet hold so much inside its walls,* she thought.

And then all other thoughts vanished from her mind. Through a window, she saw something move.

"Stop!" she said, clutching hard at Rebecca's knee.

Rebecca gave a frightened squeal and jammed on the brake, lurching the car. "What?"

"In there," Kerry said, her voice quaking. She pointed toward the house's living-room window. "Look."

The window had four panes. There were curtains over it, the same moth-eaten ones she remembered, still tied back as she'd left them her last day here. In the faint light that filtered in from the street and the setting sun, she could see figures—not just one, as she'd thought initially, but at least two or three—moving about inside. They moved in an odd, graceless fashion that somehow didn't feel right.

"Is it her?" Rebecca asked.

"No. I don't know who it is, but that's definitely not Season."

Rebecca started to lift her foot from the brake, but Kerry stopped her. "Wait a second. I want to get out."

Rebecca's eyes widened in fear. "But, Kerry," she argued, "you don't know who's in there, and you don't know if Season's around."

Kerry agreed, but she didn't want to admit it, even to herself. She had to know what was going on inside that house. Maybe it was something completely innocent—maybe those guys were exterminators or painters, preparing the house to be rented again.

But she didn't think so.

"If Season was hanging around," she pointed out, "she'd have seen us while we sat out here in front of the house."

Rebecca slowly pulled the car to the curb, swiveling her head in every direction to watch for sudden attack. "I'm not too sure about this. . . ."

Neither am I, Kerry thought. She knew better than to give voice to her hesitation, though. She didn't want to freak herself out, much less Rebecca, and she wanted a closer look while she had her courage worked up for it. She couldn't help wishing it were Daniel at the wheel instead of Rebecca, convinced that he'd know what to do. Or at least make her feel safer.

As soon as Rebecca killed the engine, Kerry lunged from the car. Rebecca had coasted a little past the house, so Kerry darted back toward it, hunching over in hopes that she'd be less noticeable. She knew that if whoever was inside looked out, she'd be spotted. But the way they were moving around, it looked like they were searching for something, and she hoped all their attention was inside.

The light was fading fast. Already shadows covered the lawn, and the bushes in which Kerry had first found Daniel took on a dark, menacing appearance. Through the streaked window, she could barely see the forms she had seen just moments before, when the light was slightly better. Trying to get closer, she shoved her way through the thick bushes and pressed her face to the glass. The evening hadn't cooled off, and a film of perspiration coated her forehead, threatening to blind her, but she blinked it away.

From this spot, one could see the whole living room and into the kitchen. The kitchen had a window over the sink facing onto the tiny backyard, which meant it faced west, toward the sunset. She had loved to look through it when it was her turn to do dishes, watching birds and butterflies, and the occasional stray cat, raccoon, or opossum. Now, though, as Kerry focused on the shadowy interior, a shape crossed in front of the kitchen window, and she felt her stomach lurch.

Its form was distinctly human. It wore what seemed to be a long, dark coat, and some kind of shapeless slouch hat. But its features—unless the bad light and her own nervous system conspired to play really unpleasant tricks on her—were barely human, kind of doughy and indistinct. Her first thought was that maybe she was looking at a man who had been scarred in a horrible fire. As she watched him, though, trying to wrap her mind around what she was seeing, another came into view briefly, and he had a similar aspect. Two fire victims seemed unlikely.

Then a third appeared at the window right in front of her. Kerry screamed and ran for the car. She'd left her door open a crack, but had barely touched the seat with her butt when Rebecca peeled out like a race car driver. "What? What'd you see?" Rebecca demanded.

"It was . . . they saw me," Kerry rejoined. "They were horrible, and they saw us!"

11

Josh enjoyed hanging out with Brandy. She was lovely, for one thing, which made her easy to be around. He liked her athletic body and her ready smile. She was tight with Scott, of course, but that was okay—kind of relieved him of any pressure to pretend he might be interested in her as a boyfriend, since, being a girl, she definitely was not his type. But that didn't mean he didn't like to look upon beauty of whatever gender.

The day was a scorching one—each day seemed more so than the last, until Josh had to admit that a heat wave was upon them and even he, accustomed to Vegas summers, was uncomfortably warm—and she wore a knit halter top, a denim mini, and strappy sandals. Josh thought the halter was a bit much—or a bit not enough, maybe—but either way, a fashion faux pas as far as he was concerned. He'd have chosen a nice tank top, maybe, with spaghetti straps and a little more substance. The whole knit thing just smacked of eighties to him. In his baggy black jeans, *Maltese Falcon* movie-poster T-shirt, and spiked collar, he knew he was nobody's idea of a fashion god, but he knew what he liked.

They went into the village section of La Jolla, walking the streets of the shopping district, which centered around Prospect Street and Girard Avenue. The village retained its small resort-town air, with buildings and natural scenery reminiscent of some Mediterranean port of call. The name La Jolla, according to some, meant "the jewel," though others disputed that Chamber of Commerce–sounding translation and claimed that it was really a version of *la joya*, or "the hole," so-called because of an enormous cave that opened to the sea. Small specialty stores lined the streets, intermixed with a few nationwide chains like The Gap and Ralph Lauren. Because restaurants and bars abounded, stores stayed open late, so even though they'd taken time to watch the sun sink into the Pacific from across the grassy expanse of Ellen Browning Scripps Park, most of the shops were still occupied when they went back to browsing.

Season had never seen Brandy or Josh, so they didn't feel too exposed walking in the same general neighborhood where she had last been observed. Kerry had said Season had eaten in the restaurant at Seaside a few times, so chances were good that she was staying in or near La Jolla.

"You think we'll recognize her if we see her?" he asked as they meandered out of what seemed like the fiftieth shoe store they'd visited. "That coffee-cup picture seems to be staying with me pretty well."

"I think he magically implanted it or something," Brandy agreed. "I don't like the idea of him messing with our heads like that."

"There isn't much about him you do like," Josh pointed out. They had agreed not to use names when they talked, because it was possible—remote, but possible—that she or some associate of hers would overhear them. Not that they thought Season had any idea who they were, but caution was the order of the day. "Smoke break," he called.

Brandy scowled at him. "Didn't you just have a smoke break?"

"That was hours ago," he argued, snaking a cigarette from the pack he kept in his hip pocket. "Or at least five shoe stores ago."

"It's like every person in La Jolla needs a new pair of shoes every day." Brandy looked at her own sandals and grimaced. "No wonder they all look so hopeful when we walk in. I really *could* use some."

Josh lit his cigarette and sucked in a lungful of smoke. He knew that Brandy was far too thrifty to buy shoes at one of these trendy shops, though. Her family had some money, according to Scott, but they had climbed to an upper-middle-class lifestyle during Brandy's lifetime, and she still knew what it was like to go without. For his part, Josh would have been happy to try life with money, having never experienced that particular sensation. Since he wouldn't wear leather, his own shoes were canvas and rubber, but the rubber was wearing awfully thin on the bottom. Soon a new semester would start up at UNLV and with it, the cost of textbooks, board, and so on. Even with financial aid, going to college was an expensive proposition.

Of course, if he'd quit smoking, he could save a few hundred bucks a month. But some sacrifices were too terrible to consider.

"I'm serious," he said, trying to draw the conversation back to where he had interrupted it. "You hate him, right? You don't even buy his whole line. So why are you putting yourself through this?"

Brandy squinted at him. "You want to end up like Mace?"

"You really think that's what happened to him?"

"I don't know what else to think. If we'd heard about his death on the news, or if cops had knocked on the door and told us, maybe I'd think it was some freak accident or something. But since Da—since he came and told us about it, I figure it had to be her."

Josh blew a series of smoke rings into the still air. "Or him."

"You think he . . . ?"

"As an entrée back into our good graces? I'm just saying it's possible."

Brandy shook her head. "Anything's possible, Josh. But is it likely? Or have you just watched too many conspiracy movies?"

"He's just one guy, so it's not exactly a conspiracy," Josh observed. "And yeah, maybe I've read a lot of noir crime stories with some pretty convoluted plots. But hey, if those writers could think those stories up, then regular people can come up with some twisted ideas too. And to hear him talk, it sounds like he's loaded with twisted ideas."

"What, now you're saying you don't believe any of this?" Brandy asked.

Josh dropped his cigarette butt to the sidewalk and ground it under his shoe. "I didn't say that," he countered. As much as he liked being with Brandy, sometimes talking to her was exhausting. She had a tendency to question and analyze and interpret even the most casual comments. "At first I thought somebody scared his momma with a Twilight novel when he was in utero, but there's obviously more to him than there is to us. We've all seen that. I'm only saying it doesn't hurt to keep an open mind, you know? Cooperate with him, but keep an eye on him at the same time. Just in case."

Now Brandy nodded her agreement. "You know I've never liked him or trusted him. I'm trying to because if he's right, then our lives might depend on him. Probably they do. But if he's pulling some kind of fast one, I want to be ready to put some major distance between me and him in a heartbeat. And I don't want anybody getting in my way. You know what they say about what you have to do when you're hiking with a friend and a bear charges you?"

Josh spread his arms, indicating his slight frame and his utter lack of a tan. "Not exactly Mr. Outdoors here."

"You don't have to be able to outrun the bear," Brandy elaborated. "As long as you can outrun your friend."

Josh laughed, surprised to hear a sentiment like that coming from Brandy. He guessed he shouldn't have been. *Girl has a pragmatic streak as wide as the Grand Canyon,* he thought. It seemed to put her at odds, sometimes, with her hopelessly idealistic boyfriend Scott, to whom every newspaper or news broadcast held fresh outrage.

"What's the matter with this state?" Scott had exploded at breakfast that morning. "California drinks half the bottled water consumed in the country. But less than thirty percent of the bottles are recycled! Billions of bottles a year go into landfill."

Brandy had calmed him down, as somehow she seemed supremely able to do, but Josh had felt a little sorry for Daniel, having to go out hunting with

Scott today. He was sure to return to the water-bottle crisis several times during the search.

"So you're of the 'keep your friends close and your enemies closer'
school?" Josh asked.

"Pretty much," Brandy replied. "I'm not saying he's our enemy. So far
he hasn't done anything to hurt us, unless he really is responsible for Mace
somehow. And this Sea—the other one," she caught herself, "sounds like a
real piece of work. So I'm willing to give him the benefit of the doubt, at
least until he proves otherwise."

Josh shrugged. "Works for me," he said. "Let's check out the next shoe store."

The next store, in fact, was a children's clothing store—children's clothing
for millionaires, Brandy pointed out when she saw the price tags—and they
only stayed a moment, long enough to ascertain that Season was not picking
up a new bib or a thousand-dollar velvet toddler's dress. After that came an
art gallery specializing, it seemed, in pieces that made no sense at all to Josh's
untrained eye, and then an Oriental rug shop. *Then* a shoe store.

But it wasn't until they had reached a woman's boutique with a cutesy
name that Josh forgot as soon as they had passed beneath the sign, that they
saw her. Josh was eyeing the salesman, who wore bleached-out jeans and a
tight, striped shirt, its sleeves rolled back over muscular forearms, when he
felt Brandy's fingers dig into the flesh of his upper arm.

He looked at her, and she ticked her eyes toward the other side of the
store. An attractive blond woman held up a purple silk shirt in front of
herself and examined the look in a mirror.

"Is that her?" Josh whispered. He couldn't be sure he had actually made
any sound at all. His heart was suddenly pounding as if a marching-band
drummer straddled his back.

But when Brandy said, "It's her," he could hear that. Brandy still hadn't
let go of his arm, and it hurt when she forcibly turned him around and
marched him from the shop.

"What are you doing?" he asked as soon as they hit the sidewalk. "She's inside."

"Right. You see a back door? I didn't. She's not sneaking out. But we need to get *him* down here—nothing we can do by ourselves."

"Gotcha," Josh agreed. He fumbled his cell phone from his pocket.

"Not here," Brandy hissed. She grabbed him again and tugged him down a couple of storefronts. "We don't want her to see us and know something's up. You heard what he said—she's too strong unless he has surprise on his side. If he can take her when she's walking out of a store, unsuspecting, he might have a chance. If she sees some freaked-out Goth boy screaming into his cell phone, she'll be on her guard."

"He'll have to be close by," Josh pointed out. He gestured with the phone, which was still undialed, to where Season was walking out of the store, empty-handed, a small purse dangling on a long strap from her shoulder. *Leather, too,* he thought. *I hate her.*

"We'll just follow her," Brandy said. "Keep tabs on her."

But even that simple plan wouldn't work quite so easily since, apparently done with her shopping, Season approached a BMW Z4 convertible parked at one of the angled spaces by the curb, underneath a streetlight. "Oh, no," Josh moaned. "She's driving."

Street parking being a precious commodity in La Jolla, especially in summer, their own wheels were in a parking garage beneath an office building, more than a block away. "I'll go for the car," Brandy said urgently. "You call him, and keep her in sight."

She took off running without waiting for an answer. As he watched her disappearing form, Josh had no doubt she was, in fact, faster than the bear. Or at least faster than him.

He punched up Daniel's number and hit send. A moment later, the now-familiar voice came on the line. "Yes."

"Sh-she's here," Josh stammered. "In La Jolla. The village. On Girard.

She just came out of a store and got into a car, a silver BMW."

"I'm on my way," Daniel said. "Keep watching her. Let me know where she goes."

"One problem. I'm on foot. Brandy's gone to get the car."

The silver BMW waited for a couple of cars to pass and then began to back carefully from its parking space. Josh started walking quickly toward it, torn between not wanting to attract attention and not wanting to let Season escape his sight.

"Do you know how to hotwire a car?" Daniel asked him. The witch sounded breathless, and Josh figured he was already running to his own wheels.

"Only in theory," Josh said. "I've seen it done in movies. Not in real life."

"Never mind, then. Just keep an eye on her, any way you can."

"I'm trying." Josh broke into a run then, because Season had cleared the parking space and begun driving up Girard, away from Prospect Street and the ocean. There was traffic, though, and she wasn't going very fast. When he reached an intersection, he hurtled into it without looking, and a car trying to cross the wide expanse of Girard squealed its tires, stopping for him. "She's driving," he panted into the phone. "I don't know how long I can keep up."

"Don't lose her!" Daniel ordered. Josh could hear the roar of his engine over the phone. "Can you get the license number?"

Then he heard Scott's voice. "Is Brandy there? Is she all right?"

"Tell him she's fine," Josh replied, huffing. "And I can see B523 . . . can't make out the rest. . . ." Ahead of him the BMW started to accelerate up a long, traffic-free stretch of road. He broke into a sprint, awkwardly trying to hold the phone to his ear as he ran. Every few paces he craned his neck to see if—*please, please!*—Brandy was drawing up behind him.

"Do you still see her?" Daniel demanded urgently.

Josh ran with everything he had, but the BMW reached the intersection.

Her brake lights flashed once, and she made a right turn, immediately vanishing behind the building on the corner. "Nooo!" Josh yelled.

"What?" Daniel wanted to know.

Josh kept up his pace, swallowing sidewalk with every step. But the corner was still too far away—more than a city block, on the other side of a supermarket parking lot. He'd never make it. She would be long out of sight before he could reach it.

"She turned a corner," he breathed into the phone. Finally he stopped running. "I lost her."

"Are you sure?" Daniel asked.

Josh did a quick scan. He could cut through the supermarket's lot. If she'd been stuck at the next light, where Fay Street crossed Pearl Street, he might still get a glimpse of her at that intersection. "There's one more thing I can try," he said, though he wasn't sure how he was going to get his legs to take another step.

"Do it!"

Josh was about to obey when a horn honked on the street beside him. Brandy was finally there in Scott's RAV4. She popped open the passenger door and he forced himself to hurry the four steps to the car. "Up to the corner," he managed, folding in on himself from the ache in his chest and lungs, trying to ignore the sweat that ran in rivers down his sides and soaked his back. "Turn right."

Brandy floored it, racing up the street, braking just enough not to lose control as the car screamed around the corner. The car's rear end fishtailed a little, but the tires bit and held on to the road. Josh put his left hand on the dash in front of him and searched Pearl Street.

No BMW in sight. Brandy drove the length of the street, and he watched every parking lot, every side street. In a few moments they were dipping down toward the ocean. "Which way?" she asked.

Josh could only shake his head.

"We're almost there," Daniel's voice said. Josh had forgotten the phone, still clutched in his right fist. "Do you have her?"

"She's gone," Josh admitted. "We can't see her at all."

"Keep cruising," Daniel said. "Maybe you'll pick her up again. Did she know you were onto her?"

Only if she looked in her mirror and saw a maniac running up the sidewalk, Josh thought. He felt defeated, broken. "I don't know."

Brandy took the road down toward the water. It wound between luxury apartments and condominiums, then, on the ocean side, a few sprawling homes and then nothing but cliffs and coast.

"Where are you?" Daniel asked after another few minutes. "We're at Girard and Pearl."

"She went right there," Josh told him. "We went toward the water."

"We'll turn up La Jolla Boulevard, then," Daniel reported. "Maybe she's heading toward Pacific Beach."

"I'm sorry, Daniel. I really did try."

There was a long moment of silence from the other end, and Josh wasn't sure if Daniel had even heard him. But then he answered. "It's okay, Josh. You guys found her. We can do it again."

12

Scott Banner was pretty sure he was going to die.

Daniel had magical powers or whatever, so he could probably survive the collision of the rented (or stolen, he wasn't entirely sure which) Ford Taurus with any of the half-dozen vehicles it had almost smashed into, not to mention lane dividers and walls, as Daniel piloted it at breakneck speeds from Del Mar to La Jolla. But any of those near misses could have spelled instant extinction for Scott, who held on to his seat belt's shoulder strap for dear life on each occasion.

Fortunately Daniel seemed to have an inordinately sure hand with the wheel, and his touch with the brake—though used sparingly—was also confident and precise. Of course, he drove one-handed, with his cell phone glued to his ear by the other, which made the whole experience that much more nerve-racking. They raced down the coast road (ocean to their right, lagoons to their left), then up the hill past Torrey Pines State Reserve, along the cliffs between the Scripps Institute and the University of California at San Diego, of which the campus looked lovely, if a bit blurry, finally speeding down the hill into La Jolla proper. Fortunately they had already been headed in that general direction, having stopped at one of the beaches to see if Season was there. If they'd been far from the car, or going the other way, Scott wouldn't have wanted to see what shortcuts Daniel might have made to save time.

A few minutes after reaching La Jolla, they rendezvoused with Brandy and Josh in the parking lot of a chain drugstore. Josh still looked out of breath, his pale, sunken cheeks rosy with the effort he'd put into the chase. Scott climbed gratefully from the car and enveloped Brandy in a hug, pulling her close and sniffing the vaguely vanilla-like scent of whatever she used on her thick, luxuriant hair.

"Are you okay?" he asked. "Did she see you?"

Brandy disengaged, shaking her head. When she answered him, her usual antagonism toward Daniel had vanished. "She might have seen Josh. I'm sure she didn't see me—if we'd been close enough for that, we'd still be on her tail. Woman can move."

"How did you find her?"

"We just walked into a dress store and there she was, looking just like she did in that coffee cup," Brandy announced.

"Did you . . . like, cement that image in our heads somehow?" Josh inquired of Daniel. "Because when we saw her, both of us were, like, pow, that's her."

"When I conjured it there was a retention spell involved," Daniel admitted. He didn't sound reluctant or embarrassed about it, Scott noted. Just as if it had been something so mundane he'd forgotten to mention it. *A retention spell. When I conjured it. Like I'd say, "I flipped on the light switch."*

Of course, Scott realized, *to me it is basically magic how the electricity gets from the river, or the coal plant, or whatever, to the light socket. So I guess to him it's just another kind of science. Maybe something anyone can do with the right kind of calculator and test tubes. To the liberal-arts undergrad, all science is magic.*

Daniel turned to Josh. "Can you show me where she was standing?"

Josh pointed in the general direction. "Over there," he replied. "On Girard."

"No," Daniel corrected. "I mean, precisely. Can you show me a spot where you know, with absolute certainty, her feet touched the ground?"

"I can," Brandy volunteered. "In the store. Her bag was bumping into a top I thought looked really cute. Unless they've rearranged the display in the last thirty minutes, I can show it to you."

"Let's go," Daniel said.

Parking being the losing proposition that it was, they left the cars in the drugstore lot—risking tickets or towing, Scott noted, because the lot had FOR CUSTOMERS ONLY signs posted in huge red letters—and walked back to the boutique. On the way Daniel called Kerry's phone and told her to meet them back at the drugstore's parking lot.

In the store the salesman looked at them expectantly when they walked in, but Josh waved and said, "We're only looking," and the guy went behind the counter and sat on a stool with a glum sigh.

Brandy pointed out to Daniel exactly where the witch had been standing when they'd seen her. "Right here," she said. Turning to Scott, she fingered a shimmery green blouse and added, "And if you want to pick up an early birthday present, check this out."

But Scott couldn't even get close enough to see the price tag. Daniel squatted down on the ground and touched his fingers to the floor. Scott was reminded of trackers in Western movies, feeling for the oncoming thunder of a buffalo herd. Then Daniel stood and sniffed the air. After a few moments of that, he froze, standing utterly still, eyes closed, lips parted slightly. It was, Scott believed, exceedingly strange behavior. But he presumed that it meant something. Either that or Daniel was a gifted con man, pulling a fast one on them by acting out the oddest routine he could come up with.

While Daniel performed his awkward gyrations, Brandy took Scott's hand and squeezed. "I guess we did okay," she said softly. "I mean, I wish we hadn't lost her. But at least we spotted her once, right?"

"You sound like a convert," he responded. Secretly he was glad. He'd believed in Daniel almost from the beginning—or, more precisely, he'd believed in Kerry's judgment, and if she wanted Daniel around, that was good enough for him. Brandy had doubted him with such rabid certainty that it had put Scott in an uncomfortable position. If she was coming around, that would make his life easier.

"I wouldn't go that far," she hedged. "But maybe I'm mellowing about it. A little. Now that I know Season Howe is real, I guess."

"Nothing wrong with that," Scott said, hoping he sounded neutral but encouraging.

Without a word to the rest of them, Daniel stalked outside, nose in the air as if he were following a scent. The sales clerk watched them go, confusion written all over his face. Josh tossed him a shrug and a smile, and then trailed after Daniel.

On the sidewalk, Brandy squeezed Scott's hand again and nodded toward Daniel, who came to a stop underneath a streetlight. "He's following her path exactly," she reported. "Walking exactly where she did."

"Weird," Scott uttered. He'd been with Daniel the whole time, so he knew the man couldn't possibly have seen Season's moves. Which meant that somehow, even after this long, he was able to sense where she'd been.

"Uh-huh," Brandy agreed. "Like I said, the realer this gets, the more I'm into it."

"You never said that," Scott reminded her. "At least, not to me."

"Maybe not. But I meant it."

Kerry and Rebecca hadn't been far from La Jolla, still working south through Pacific Beach, when Kerry's phone trilled like an agitated bird. She answered it and heard Daniel's voice, sounding strained and urgent. "Are you all right?"

"Fine. What's up?"

He didn't answer the question, but instead gave her instructions to meet the rest of the group at a drugstore's parking lot. Kerry relayed the message to Rebecca, who turned the car around—avoiding the street they'd raced away from, not so long before—and drove back up to La Jolla. When they got there, they found the RAV4 and the Taurus parked side by side, but saw no sign of the gang. Kerry and Rebecca stood by Rebecca's car, waiting, making uncomfortable small talk. Both of them were still freaked by what Kerry had seen in their old house—Kerry by the sight itself, and Rebecca by Kerry's reaction to it. Kerry thought about the conversation they'd had when she'd jumped back into the car.

"You look like you're being chased by ghosts," Rebecca had said to her.

"I don't know what they were," Kerry had admitted, trying to bring her voice under control. "'Ghosts' is probably as good a word as any."

"You're kidding," Rebecca had said. She had stared at Kerry for so long, Kerry worried they'd run off the road.

"Watch where you're going," Kerry had ordered. "I'd like to live long enough to ask Daniel what those guys were."

"You think they were, like, Season's familiars or something?"

"I thought a familiar was like a black cat. Anyway, he hasn't said anything about her having any. But maybe."

Rebecca had offered a couple more suggestions, but Kerry found she wasn't interested in hearing the theories of someone who—while truly wanting to help—could not possibly have any idea what they were up against. Her monosyllabic answers discouraged Rebecca, who eventually stopped trying to talk to Kerry. Then the phone had gone off. And here they were; Kerry still lost in questions she couldn't answer, Rebecca keeping her distance.

As they waited in the parking lot, though, Kerry understood what had happened, and how she'd shut out Rebecca, who was just about the most well-intentioned person she'd ever known. "Hey," she said apologetically, "I didn't mean to be a shrew or anything. I was just, you know, kind of preoccupied."

Rebecca smiled, her whole face seeming to brighten, though in the harsh light it was a little hard to tell. "That's okay," she said. "Perfectly understandable, considering . . . you know. Whatever you saw."

"That's the big question, isn't it?"

Rebecca reached for Kerry as if to give her a hug, but Kerry didn't feel quite that sisterly yet. Rebecca caught the vibe, though, and just rubbed Kerry's shoulder instead. "One thing I do want to say, though, is how impressed I was."

"Impressed?" *Color me confused,* Kerry thought. *Maybe I set some sort of Olympic sprinting record when I ran away from the house.*

"The way you walked right up to the window, even though you'd seen someone inside," Rebecca explained. "I couldn't have done that. I just about left a puddle in my car seat, waiting for you. I don't think I've ever seen something so brave."

Kerry was complimented to hear her say that, but puzzled by the sentiment. "All I did was check it out," she said. "Nothing special about that."

"You don't think so," Rebecca countered, "because you're a brave person. So it doesn't seem like much."

Kerry felt herself blushing now, heat rising from her chest, engulfing her neck and face. In spite of her pale complexion, she didn't blush often, but once she did, her body committed to it. She turned away from Rebecca, just in time to see Daniel and the others walking from the corner of Girard Avenue and Pearl Street. Daniel led the way, his gait purposeful. Kerry was surprised to feel a small thrill at the sight of him, more or less encompassing the same region as the blush she'd experienced moments before.

When he reached the parking lot, he looked around, and she thought—or hoped—that meant he was seeking her out. His face gave a spark of recognition when he saw her, she believed—a lift of the jaw, a twitch of a smile, a brightening of the eyes. It might have been a trick of the light.

But maybe not. "You're okay?" he asked when he reached her, holding out his hand for hers.

"Why wouldn't I be?" She liked the pressure of his hand grasping hers, engulfing it with warmth and concern.

But after a moment Daniel released her hand and glanced up and down the street. The others caught up to them as he was doing so. "She was here," he said. "You lost her here, on Pearl, right?" This was directed to Josh, who nodded morosely.

"Right."

"She was here?" Kerry asked. "Season?"

"That's right," Brandy said. "Josh and I saw her, but we lost her."

Daniel's gaze darted about again, and Kerry realized he was as alert as a cat in an aviary, ready for Season to return to try something, or just to pass this way again. "I can almost sense her," he explained. "It's like an aftertaste, kind of metallic somehow. It happens when I get close to her."

"Even when you're running from her?" Josh asked. "Like the other night, with Kerry?"

Daniel nodded. "It's how I knew she was in the restaurant."

The admission startled Kerry, though it didn't seem like anyone else realized its import. If he hadn't known Season would be at the restaurant, then he'd have had no reason to go there.

Unless he'd gone to see Kerry.

She couldn't say, at that moment, exactly how she felt about that possibility.

But she thought she liked it.

13

Somehow the seating arrangements for the cars going back to Imperial Beach were shuffled, and Kerry wound up riding with Daniel. Not that she was complaining. In fact, all other considerations aside, she still wanted to ask him about what she had seen in the house. Her initial fear was that he might want to drive by and check it out for himself, but he put that to rest immediately.

"They're simulacra," he said quite matter-of-factly, when she described them.

"They're what?"

"Simulacra. Not really human, but human in structure. They can pass for human, if no one looks too closely."

"Are they . . . do they work for her?" Kerry asked nervously. "For Season?"

Daniel laughed softly as he tooled down the freeway in the dark. "No. No, they work for us."

Shocked, Kerry wasn't sure what to say to that. *Seems like something you should have mentioned,* she thought. But the words wouldn't come out of her mouth.

"Well, for my mother, to be more exact," he went on. "It's a little stunt of hers."

"Your mother?" Kerry realized she sounded stupid parroting what she had just heard, and she had a vague memory of Brandy saying the same words, with very nearly the same surprised tone, many nights before. But the words slipped out of her mouth before she could rein them in.

"Mother Blessing," he confirmed. "That's what everyone calls her. Myself included."

"Seems a little formal," Kerry suggested. "For someone you've known for three hundred years."

"Maybe," Daniel agreed. "But then, she's not much like other mothers. Or at least that's the impression I get, having only had the one."

Kerry felt herself reddening for the second time tonight. "I'm sorry," she said. "I guess I . . . when you told the story about Slocumb, you said your mother had survived. I didn't realize you meant she was still alive."

"Still alive," he confirmed, glancing out the rear window and changing lanes to the right. "Not as well as she used to be, I'm afraid. Witches do age, just more slowly than most."

"And she's still hunting for Season?" Kerry pressed.

"She does what she can."

Daniel moved farther right, exiting the freeway. A couple of minutes to the apartment, and their brief time alone would be over. She found the prospect sad. But then she mentally chastised herself, knowing she shouldn't even be thinking like that. There was nothing between her and Daniel, and there couldn't ever be. He was not just an older man than her, he was older than her great-grandparents would have been if they were still alive. Which, of course, they weren't, because, hey, *old*. She didn't see that when she looked at him. He looked like a man in his mid-twenties, perhaps, now that he was fully healed.

And in addition to being easy to look at, he was charming and fascinating. From time to time she thought him humorless, but then his dry wit would show through, and she'd realize that it was simply that he was preoccupied and that his quest was more important to him than the ability to crack jokes. She could honestly say that she had never known anyone quite like him.

"These simulacra you saw," Daniel said, after they'd reached the surface street. "Mother Blessing didn't tell me she was sending them, but from your description I'm positive that's what they were. They were doubtlessly searching the house for signs of Season."

"But that was our house, not hers."

"Right," Daniel agreed. "And by now she has surely found it and gone inside looking for similar signs of me. In doing so, she might have left behind an energy signature the simulacra could pick up on."

"But you're just speculating, right?"

"Informed speculation, let's say. If Season had developed the ability to manifest and control simulacra, I think I'd know about it."

"Can she just come up with new powers like that?"

Daniel laughed again. "You can, in fact, teach an old dog new tricks," he said. "Or an old witch, at any rate. But creating simulacra really is one of Mother Blessing's trademarks. So chances are good they were hers. Even so, they can be dangerous, so its good you kept your distance."

"I thought they were on our side," Kerry said.

"They are. But they're not truly human, and their powers of reasoning are essentially nonexistent. They take orders, that's all. If you should see any again, I'd recommend you keep well away from them."

"I'll do my best," Kerry promised. Their apartment building loomed before them in the night. "I'd like to know more about her. Your mother, I mean," Kerry heard herself saying, though the thought had never before crossed her mind.

"I told you I'd let you read some of my notebooks," Daniel reminded her. "Why not start tonight?"

I knew the weather was changing as soon as I walked outside and felt the north wind on my face, cold and crisp as a winter's day. The trapper's cabin was in a clearing with a creek running behind it, and ponderosa pines as far as I could see in front. Through the trees I could just see a snowcapped mountain peak. I shouldered my rifle and began the day's hunt.

She had been here, this much I knew. Not so long ago. The cabin I had slept in the night before had been inhabited by her within the past week. I could still smell her on the walls, the floors, the scant furnishings. Not long ago she had slept in that place, though not for the last few nights. The night before I had rested with eyes half open and no fire, just in case she returned. But she did not.

Kerry put the dense leather book down on her bed. Daniel had handed her two of them, both wrapped with leather thongs to hold them closed, both heavier than modern books by almost double. The journals were about six by nine inches, she figured, and held a hundred or so leaves of thick paper on which Daniel had written in an ink that had turned the color of rust. His handwriting was meticulous, and even on the yellowed, flaking pages she found it easy to read. "I don't know what years these cover," he said. "I never have bothered to date the outsides. But I'm sure you'll find one just as impenetrable as the next." She took the volumes, surprised by their unexpected weight, and her fingers had brushed his as she did. He smiled and left her alone in the room. Rebecca was out with Brandy and Scott, talking over the day's events, but Kerry had retired early, anxious to start on Daniel's journals.

During the few minutes that I slept soundly during the night, horrifying nightmares had been my reward. This only confirmed my belief that Season Howe had found refuge under this same roof—even the air inside had been twisted and distorted by contact with her, by the evil miasma she leaves behind everywhere she passes. My dreams had been full of death: carcasses missing their heads, blood flowing freely from their necks; disemboweled men with innards yanked out as if by butcher's hooks, streaming from their bellies; worms and vermin crawling about in the midst of all this carnage. These were not, need I say, normal dreams for me, but were surely caused by her proximity.

I knew, therefore, that she was not far away. But the wind from the north meant two things to me. One, by the time the sun set, the day would be far colder than it was now, and two, a stiff wind would scour her tracks, making it even harder to find her. I had come close, but missed her by days. Now I had to follow a trail that was already growing cold, and I had to do so before weather made the task impossible.

At first I had an easy enough go of it. The same tracks that had led me to the cabin were still visible to me, though most of them would not be to a normal, human tracker. Season had been traveling fast, heedless of such things as broken twigs on the forest floor, or bits of fabric, or long blond hair caught on limbs. And less visible to others were what I have taken to calling her miasmic tracks, the traces of evil that glow in her wake with a foul green tinge. The color of sickness.

I was right where the weather was concerned. By midmorning the air had turned frigid, and the wind bit at my cheeks and hands like a whip. Shortly after noon, a time I marked only by removing a lump of hardtack from my sack and chewing it as I walked, the first snow flurried around me.

My other fear was borne out as well. The ever more powerful winds scattered leaves where her feet might have made impressions, picked up and hurled away those stray hairs and threads, and generally slowed my progress. I began to hope some other trapper's cabin would present itself by dark, or the night would be unpleasant indeed.

To my surprise, though, when I crested a low hill I saw before me a valley containing a small settlement. A mining community; even from the hillside I could see headframes on the opposite slope. A score of buildings, mostly of wood, huddled around one *sad-looking, rutted wagon road. The sun had become a cold, flat disk that looked impossibly distant, and even if Season's tracks had not led me this way I would have sought refuge in the town for the night. As it was, dark had fallen by the time I reached it.*

But when I approached the buildings on the road, I noticed something I had not from above while the sun yet shone. Though it was past dusk, there were no lights in any of them, no flicker of candle or lantern or fireplace glowing through windows. The same wind I had battled all day whistled between the cold, stark buildings. Somewhere a shutter banged; that and the wind were the only sounds besides that of my own feet, trudging on hard-packed earth.

Seeing no one, hearing no other noise, I felt a chill to my core. I should call out, I knew, to see if anyone was about. But what if she was here? Would making my own presence known put me at her mercy? I feared that it might, and decided to investigate at a more cautious pace. I started with the nearest house, and rapped upon the door.

Hearing nothing from within, I opened it. Instantly the reek of death assailed me. Bracing myself I went farther into the house's cold bowels, only to find, in the kitchen, the remains of three people. I could not be certain, but it looked like a man, a woman, and their daughter, a girl of perhaps twelve or thirteen. Fat, lazy flies sated themselves on pools of blood. Gagging, I hurried away from the grisly scene.

But similar sights greeted me in the next house and the next. The town had been massacred—one house, one family, at a time. I was put in mind of Slocumb, although in that instance, of course, the town's death had come all at once in a horrible swirl of destruction, according to the stories Mother Blessing tells. I felt sure that the cause was the same; that the tragedy that had struck this town, whatever it was called, wore the name of Season Howe.

Finally I went into a house and heard, or thought I heard, the scuttling sounds of inhabitants from somewhere in the back. Rats, I told myself, or some other vermin, no doubt feasting on the dead. I readied my rifle and kicked open the door behind which I had heard the noises.

It was no rat, though, or other creature of field and fen. It was a man, wild-eyed and unshaven, staring at me from behind a flintlock pistol of his own, and from behind a mask of madness. His clothes were tattered and covered in blood, but it took me a moment to see the source of the blood. In the corner behind him were the ravaged remains of three other people. My first instinct was that I had caught him in the act of despoiling the remains, possibly even cannibalizing them. But upon regarding him further, his stance appeared defensive, as if he were simply trying to protect them. The antique firearm trained on me enhanced this impression.

"Rest easy, friend," I said. "I am here to help if I can."

When he replied, the madness that flitted across his face came through in his voice as well, high-pitched and anxious. "Nothing to be done. Nothing anyone can do. Go 'way."

"How did this happen?" I asked. "Who did all this?"

He twitched the gun at me. "Go 'way, while you can. Sickness here, sickness spreads."

"I might be able to do something," I said. I knew not what I could truly do to help, but my abilities were beyond those of others, so I prayed that perhaps there was still hope for someone in this forsaken place.

"Too late, way too late," the man said. He giggled when he said it, a sound so girlish it seemed unnatural coming from such a grizzled old man.

"Was there a witch here?" I demanded. "A woman with blond hair and smooth features hiding the evil beneath?"

"She was here, she was here," the man answered. "Too late,

though. Everyone's too late. Months too late. Years. Too, too, too."

"She did this?" I was sure I knew the answer. This looked like Season's handiwork to me. "She killed everyone?"

"Too late, too late," the man said again. His face twitched, and I worried that if his finger tightened on the trigger of that weapon, I would be in sorry shape as well.

Sensing that I would get no useful answers from this tragic soul, I shouldered my own weapon again. "I am sorry to have disturbed you, sir," I told him. "I shall find myself someplace in town to sleep tonight, and then tomorrow I will be on my way. If there is anything I can do to help you, just ask."

The man let out a plaintive mewl then, like a kitten begging for milk. He spoke not, though, made no intelligible request of me, which I would gladly have done my best to fulfill. So I took my leave, shaking my head sadly at the wretched state to which he had fallen, which had, indeed, beset this entire town. If he was the sole survivor, as seemed to be the case, then the town was tragic indeed.

I had barely reached the front door of his house when I heard his ancient weapon discharge. I turned and rushed back into the room in which I had left him. He was still there, but there was no life in him. A new hole had appeared in his forehead, and a spray of blood and bone decorated the horrific scene behind him. The gun was still clutched in his right hand, a thin plume of smoke issuing from its barrel.

I write this in a room of the town's boardinghouse, denoted by a sign beside the door. Downstairs are more dead, but this room I found empty and clean. If there is sickness here, it will affect me not at all. Tomorrow I will perform a cleansing spell to make doubly sure of that and to ease the way for whatever visitor comes here next. But I am not certain that it will do any good. Despite what the man told me—and his madness, I feel sure, makes all of his words suspect—this looks to me like yet another town that has fallen prey to Season's hatred.

I mourn for this nameless town and its people. And I renew my vow to find her, to destroy her, in the name of the people of Slocumb, and now of this place and of any others who have crossed her path.

My candle gutters, my eyes grow heavy. Even in the face of terrible tragedy, sleep makes its demands.

I remain,
Daniel Blessing, Fifteenth of September, 1854.

Kerry closed the book. She hadn't expected to have read this long— Rebecca had come in, wished her good night, and gone to sleep, while Kerry sat turning pages by the light of a bedside lamp. But then, she hadn't expected the story to take on such a horrific aspect. She had thought it would be a record of days, like most she had spent with Daniel—looking for Season, not finding her, getting up and doing it again.

Having read it, though, she felt like she had a more visceral understanding of Daniel's quest, of the urgency of it. *If "urgency" can be applied to an effort that's been ongoing for hundreds of years,* Kerry thought. But who knew what terrors Season had cooked up in that time, if this sort of thing was a habit with her?

Kerry remembered the nightmares she'd been having, in the weeks before Daniel had appeared in their yard—nightmares that had ended at that time, and about which she'd forgotten until reading about the ones that Daniel had in Season's proximity. Could there be some connection to hers? She didn't know how that could be, though. Anyway, they hadn't recurred, even though there was more in her life that might lead to bad dreams now. She felt tired, but she wasn't sure how she'd sleep that night. Determined to try, though, she switched off her light, put her head down on the pillow, and closed her eyes.

14

"I'm going to try to pick up Season's trail where we lost it last night," Daniel announced the next morning. Scott and Brandy hadn't shown themselves yet, but the rest of them were up, eating breakfast, and sipping tea or the coffee that Daniel had brewed.

Having read the part of his journal that she had, Kerry understood that the effort wouldn't necessarily be as hopeless as it sounded. "I'll go with."

Daniel shook his head. "It's not safe."

"Safe?" Kerry echoed, incredulous. "With Season out there somewhere, what does safe even mean? Is there such a concept?"

"I wouldn't argue with the Bulldog if I were you," Rebecca warned Daniel. "She's a tough one."

"I know that," Daniel agreed with a hint of a smile. "Believe me, one doesn't have to know Kerry long to figure that out."

"So?" Kerry pressed, oddly pleased to hear Daniel acknowledge a personality trait she wasn't always so fond of. "There's some forward momentum here, and I want to be along in case anything happens."

"When I find her, I don't want you close by," Daniel protested. "Any of you. The next time we meet it's going to be bad, and I don't want to have to worry about you getting hurt."

"Is that why you didn't take her at the restaurant that night?" Josh wondered. "Because you didn't want Kerry or Mace to get hurt?"

"That, and I wasn't fully recovered from our previous encounter," Daniel admitted. "I am now. And there's Mace to hold her accountable for, on top of everything else she's done."

"I didn't know Mace meant that much to you," Brandy put in sleepily. She shuffled in from her room, rubbing her eyes, a bathrobe tied with a sash over her silk pj's. "You sure didn't show it when he was alive."

"Brandy—" Kerry began, but Daniel cut her off.

"You're right, Brandy," he said. "Mace was no fan of mine, and I probably didn't do enough to win him over. I misread him or I would never have let him try to drive off alone. But he was one of you, and I consider myself responsible for the lot of you, in some ways."

"We can take care of ourselves," Josh countered, sounding defiant.

"You could, before I came along. Now, not so much."

"We've been over this before," Kerry said, casting a sharp look Brandy's way. "Rehashing it now doesn't do us any good."

Brandy stifled a yawn. "Yeah, I know. Sorry." She didn't sound much like she meant it, but Kerry figured that was as good as it would get.

"So when do we leave?" she asked Daniel.

He put his cup into the sink with a clatter and ran hot water over it for a moment. "No time like the present," he said. "Let's go."

Back to La Jolla again. Again Daniel parked near the intersection of Girard and Pearl, which was the last place Josh had definitely seen Season. The morning sun was bright, the skies blue and cloudless, and she could smell the slightest trace of sea air on the gentle breeze, reminding her how much she missed her daily communion with the ocean. Daniel got out of the Taurus and walked to the corner, waited a moment for traffic to clear, and then went out into the street. Glancing both ways to make sure it was safe, he squatted down and touched the pavement with his right hand. He shook his head, moved to a spot farther toward the edge of the lane, and repeated the same process. This time Kerry saw a smile curl the edges of his mouth. He jogged back to the safety of the sidewalk as the next wave of cars came toward the corner.

"She was here," he confirmed. "She came this way."

"That's what Josh said, right?"

"And I didn't doubt him," Daniel explained. "But Season can be trickier than most people think. I needed to know for myself."

"Okay," Kerry said. "So now what?"

"Now we follow." He began walking down Pearl, eyeing the street as if he could see her trail. Maybe he could—maybe that green-tinted track Daniel had followed in the journal still existed.

"On foot?" she asked, surprised. Season had been driving a BMW, according to Josh and Brandy. Following on foot seemed pointless.

"It's much harder to track from a moving vehicle," Daniel told her. "But once we have an idea of what direction she's heading, I may ask you to drive ahead, just so the car is never too far from us."

Kerry shrugged and watched him move on, his face turned toward the street, ignoring the curious looks of people in passing vehicles. That image summed him up, she believed, the intrepid seeker, carrying on his quest no matter what the obstacles, or the opinions, of others might be. She couldn't decide if it made him a humorous figure or a tragic one . . . or simply heroic. *Probably a combination of all three. But considering what Season's done, weighted toward heroic.* She hurried to catch up with him, mindful that she might be sent back for the car at any moment.

Kerry Profitt's diary, August 25

This is when the world stopped making sense:

Daniel and I had spent the morning tracking Season, and making good progress. At least according to Daniel. As far as I could tell, he was just following one random street after another, but he insisted that her car had driven on all these streets. Through Bird Rock and into Pacific Beach we went, me running for the car from time to time, and him even getting into it once in a while, when it looked like she was going in a straight line for a long stretch.

But the day wore on and even he gets hungry sometimes, so we stopped for a pizza at a place on Turquoise Street. We're waiting for the food, sipping our drinks, tired and hungry. And his hand is resting on the table. It's just a hand, tan and muscular, I guess, if a hand can be muscular, with long, lean fingers. Well-shaped, I suppose you'd call it, if you called it anything at all. Little scars here and there, and I know from experience that it's a working man's hand, not an indoors hand. Callused and rough sometimes.

So out of nowhere—and I mean that literally, because as surprised as he was, I think I was even more so—I took his hand in mine. Both of mine, actually. Picked it up off the table and held it, kind of caressing it. He closed his fingers around my hand, but there was shock in his eyes, and a kind of hesitant half smile on his lips.

"I know I have a long way to go in the journals," I said. "But are there many women in there? Besides Season, I mean. You've lived so long, and you're so wonderful and handsome, there must have been some in your past. You never talk about them, though."

Daniel sighed and nodded. "There have been some," he said. "Not so many. And fewer who really meant anything."

"Why?" I felt like someone peeking through her fingers at the scariest part of a horror movie, not wanting to see but wanting to at the same time. Was I sure I needed to hear this?

"Ask again later," quoth the Magic 8-ball.

But he answered me anyway. "It's hard. I'm always on the move, always on the hunt. If I did fall in love with someone, would that slow me down? Probably. Would it give Season an edge she could use against me? Certainly. And then there's the other problem. . . ."

"What problem?"

"If she was a mortal woman, she would age at a normal rate," he said. "I would not. She would grow old and die, and I would still look like I look. That would be so hard, for both of us."

About this time it occurred to me that we were still holding hands, and that his thumb was moving softly over mine in a kind of circular pattern. What are you doing? I asked myself. How awkward was this whole thing going to be?

At the same time, though, I liked it . . .

. . . a lot.

"So you've been playing the field for three centuries," I said, trying to make something vaguely resembling a joke out of it all. "Sounds rough."

"Believe me, there have been times when I've wished it were otherwise," he said. "Times when I wished I could just give up the hunt and settle down with someone. I can't bring myself to do that, though. Not until Season is gone."

The waiter brought the pizza then, and we separated our hands. But even afterward I could feel his hand on mine as if we had never let each other go. I changed the subject, aware that I'd probably been too personal, gone too far.

And anyway, what is my deal? Here I will psychoanalyze myself in hopes of figuring out why I practically threw myself at this guy who is (a) older than me and (b) not quite human.

I haven't, to understate the point, had a lot of experience with boys. Or men, which Daniel clearly is. These last few years—the dating years, according to my friends—have mostly been spent taking care of a sick, and then dying, mother. Friday night, Saturday night? Just as dateless as the rest of the week. Sure, I saw guys at school, during the day. But when school was over I had to rush home, leaving little to nonexistent social time. The occasional party, the occasional groping post-adolescent. Not exactly "seventeen and never been kissed," but close enough.

That being the case, is it surprising that I seem to be hurling myself toward the first male who gives me the time of day? Hormones are hormones, after all, and mine are just as demanding as the next female's. There have, of course, been other males who have looked at me for more than twenty seconds. Mace, I think, I could have had in a heartbeat, if I'd wanted him. But, in spite of the physique, sooo not my type. And Scott has made it clear—not out loud, but through glances and signs and the occasional too-long hug—that he might toss Brandy aside for me, but I couldn't do that to her even if I wanted that. Which I so don't.

But Daniel—unattached, mature, attractive . . . I mean, what's not to like?

Did I mention mature? It keeps coming back to that, doesn't it? And yet my inner Freud says, didn't your father die when you were very young? And didn't that make you feel abandoned as a girl, even before your mother became ill? Is it not possible that you are merely trying to fill the hole left in your heart by a father who was gone from your life all too early?

How do I answer the old Austrian? Or even Brandy, who has her own theories about things psychoanalytic but would surely be in agreement here. Yes, it's possible, Doc. Maybe even likely. But there's something to be said for the way my heart quickens when I'm around him, the way he can make me smile just by being there, the way his touch curls my toes. His scent sends those hormones racing, even when it's only a lingering aroma on the pages of his journal. This is definitely something I'd tell my one-time best bud Jessica about, if I thought she'd be at all interested anymore.

But really, what could I tell her? There's this guy, and he's got magical powers, and he's three hundred years old . . . I guess this is something I just need to work out solo.

On the other hand maybe what I need is to stop thinking about this so much and just feel for a while. Feeling would be nice. . . .

Pacific Beach was loaded with apartment complexes, large and small. In some neighborhoods almost every block had at least one, and in other parts, especially closer to the ocean, apartments greatly outnumbered single-family homes. If Season was living in this area, she had picked a high-density locale with lots of places to hide.

"She's here," Daniel said with what sounded like absolute certainty. It was midafternoon, and though they'd taken a break for lunch, he had essentially been on his feet all day, tracking, tracking.

Kerry looked at the literally dozens of dwellings she could see from this spot. "Which here?"

"I don't know," Daniel answered, and the anger was evident in his voice. "Around here the tracks go every direction. I know this is close to home for her, because she has been over just about every inch of these streets—these, and the ones nearby. Tracks are everywhere. Too many of them—I can't possibly narrow it down any further."

"So you've got, what, six square blocks? What now, door to door?"

"More like a dozen," he said. "Door to door, solo, would take weeks. And I'd be exposed the whole time."

The moment they'd shared while waiting for pizza had seemingly passed as they'd eaten and then returned to the hunt—*I'll have plenty to write in the old diary tonight, though,* Kerry thought—and they were back to business as usual. Except she couldn't quite shake the feeling that something had changed between them, possibly forever.

"Fortunately for you," she said cheerfully, "you aren't solo. Door to door probably isn't absolutely necessary, but if we've got it narrowed down to a dozen blocks, and five people she has never seen—well, four, anyway, and me, who she's only seen briefly—we can cover the neighborhood pretty well. We'll find her, Daniel. We've got her boxed in."

He thought about it for a moment. "The closer we get to her, the more I worry about you," he said. She was pretty sure that, in that instance, the "you" was specific to her and not referring to the whole group. But that might have been wishful thinking.

"It's what we're here for," she reminded him. "I mean, there's nothing else keeping us in San Diego now, right? No jobs, no other friends. We've been stalling our families, especially Brandy, whose parents got a call about Mace and threatened to fly out here. We're in this deep, Daniel. We are here to do this thing. So let us do it."

Daniel considered a few seconds longer, but Kerry didn't see how he could possibly reach any other conclusion. "Okay," he finally said. "Let's round up the others and set a game plan."

15

The next day the stakeout was in place.

Such as it is, Kerry thought. Three cars, six people, and one of the cars, with herself and Daniel in it, had to stay out of the immediate vicinity because they would be too easily recognized. Of course, Season usually kept to herself, Daniel reasoned, so chances were slim that she'd see them. But then, he usually worked alone too, and now he had recruited help. There was nothing to say that Season couldn't do the same, and if she had, Kerry and Daniel would be the ones they'd be watching for.

So Scott and Brandy took one car and parked it on the route that Season would most likely pass by on her way back to La Jolla, since it seemed she still frequented that community. Josh and Rebecca were roamers, cruising the streets of the dozen blocks Daniel had identified as the ones Season used most often. Daniel and Kerry had moved around outside the perimeter, spending most of the day cramped up in the car. Now that it was night, they had parked in a busy neighborhood, near the beach on Garnet Avenue, where restaurants, nightclubs, and bars kept things hopping all day and most of the night.

Everyone was connected by cell phones, though they were instructed only to use those in emergencies. Everyone knew that "emergency" was defined as a Season sighting.

Daniel parked in front of a store that had already closed for the evening. Most of the people on the sidewalks were young and fashionable, drifting from one trendoid watering hole to another. Men were dressed in jeans and untucked shirts, high-heeled women in short skirts with low-cut tops. The crowd was college age, or just a little older. Kerry felt a momentary pang that she was missing out on the fun, instead sitting here on a life-and-death mission that she barely understood. Sure, she was here with Daniel, not alone. But they had been together all day, studiously ignoring the issue of what had happened between them at lunch the day before, while those people were out laughing, eating and drinking, enjoying the San Diego summer night. She didn't have that luxury and couldn't help being a little sorry she was on this side of the windshield instead of that one. *What must a "normal" life be?* she wondered. She'd never had one, and it didn't look like she would any time soon.

"Tell me why we're here again, Daniel," she said, after the silence between them had grown uncomfortable.

"That's a complicated question," he replied with a chuckle. "Do you mean in the cosmic sense? Or the strategic one?"

"I mean, why we're doing all this. Why you don't just accept that Season is always going to be there—if not her, then someone like her—and move on with your life? Try for some happiness while you can, instead of spending all your days on the hunt?"

In the glow from neon signs and streetlights, his face, when he turned to regard her, was serious, even stern. She thought she'd pushed him too far—between the flirting at lunch the day before, and now this, she was losing her grounding, forgetting to switch on the filter that would keep her from saying and doing stupid things. "That is a tough question," he answered. "You know the facile answers. Because Season is evil. Because she destroyed my town, killed my family."

"Before you were born," Kerry reminded him.

"That's true. Have you read my journals yet?"

"Just started," Kerry said. The night was warmer than was typical for San Diego, as if the heat wave that had started up ruled the dark as well as the light, and the windows were open to let air circulate. From outside she heard a burst of laughter, causing her to look out at a group of men seemingly sharing a joke. "But I haven't had much time."

"When you make more progress you'll see that there are other reasons as well," he assured her. "As for what makes me think that I have to be the instrument of justice? That's more complicated, and I'd have to be a smarter man than I am to figure it out."

"But how do you even define justice in a case like this? Does she have to die for justice to be served? Does she have to die by your hand? Where are the boundaries?"

"My preference," Daniel said, after considering for a few moments, "would be to kill her myself. I know that's going to be difficult—if it was easy, I'd have done it long ago. But that's the ideal."

"Is there a second best?" she asked him. "Something you can settle for?"

"In fact, there is." He shifted in his seat, bumping his knees against the steering wheel. "Next year there's an event we call the Convocation, or the Witches' Convocation, more correctly. It comes around twice every millennium, or every five hundred years."

"Like a Woodstock for witches?" Kerry asked.

"More or less. Maybe more like a trade show. But with elements of Woodstock, for sure. It's a gathering. Virtually all the world's serious witches come together—a few hundred of us, all in one place. We share stories, complain about problems, offer one another help and advice. Witches go to learn new spells, to see friends and family, and so on."

Kerry did the mental math. "But you've never been," she observed. "The last one would have been before you were born."

"That's right. I haven't. We all hear stories, though, and I've heard a lot of them. I can't wait for it."

"It does sound kind of fun," Kerry admitted. "But I don't see what it has to do with Season Howe."

"Because I haven't told you yet," Daniel teased. "One of the things that happens is that tribunals are gathered, crimes between witches dealt with. There's also a lot of politicking that goes on—this is the witch world's main chance to form alliances or partnerships, and to push various agendas."

"Now it sounds like a political convention."

Daniel nodded. Outside, a partyer with a few too many drinks under his belt bumped into the car as he made for the curb. Daniel shot him a sharp glance, then turned back to Kerry. "There is an element of that to it," he agreed. "Where Season comes into it is this: If necessary, we can convene a tribunal, effectively putting her on trial for her crimes."

"That sounds like a good thing."

"It is, to a point," Daniel said. "But there's also the chance that she could be acquitted, just like with any trial in your world. There's also the chance that she could form a powerful enough alliance to block any tribunal. She could even use it as a platform to sway more witches over to her side—the Dark Side, to use *Star Wars* terminology. The side of chaos and destruction. If that happened, and the Convocation ended with that alliance intact, the whole world could be looking at a new Dark Age. The last Dark Age, according to all reports, was bad enough. With new technology, new weapons, and current global stresses, the world might never survive another one."

This was a lot to take in, maybe too much. "So . . . you're saying the Dark Age—as in, *the* Dark Ages, medieval times, whatever—was the result of a bunch of bad witches teaming up to make trouble?"

"That's about the size of it," Daniel said. "Look, it's getting a little raucous around here. What do you say we find another place to wait for a while?"

Kerry agreed, and he started the engine and drove around the neighborhood for a few minutes. The phone had been silent all night, and Kerry was pretty sure Season was either staying inside, or she had managed the not-so-difficult task of evading the other two searching vehicles. After circling a particular block a few times, a parking space opened up, and Daniel nosed the car into it.

"We're a block from the beach," he said. "Take a walk?"

She had hardly had a moment to go to the beach since meeting Daniel, and she realized that she missed it fiercely. "Absolutely," she said quickly. "Do we dare leave the car?"

"We'll keep the phone with us, and stay close by," Daniel promised as he opened his door. "I don't really think she's going out tonight."

"I was just thinking the same thing."

"Great minds . . ." Daniel came around to her side of the car and opened her door. Then, like a perfect gentleman, he reached for her hand and helped her out. She could have easily done it herself, but there was something unexpectedly charming about this, a hint of old-fashioned chivalry absent in the males she had known before.

"Why, thank you, sir," she said, beaming at him.

"It's my pleasure, madam," he replied.

Here on the beach, the noise on Garnet was behind them by a couple of blocks, drowned out by the gentle thunder of the surf rolling forward, collapsing on itself, and pulling back, over and over. Wind off the water carried the scents of aquatic flora and fauna and snapped away the sounds from the couple of bonfire parties spread about the beach. Water and sky were equally black, with white stars glittering overhead and glimmering in the sea of foam and moonlight.

When their feet hit the sand, they still hadn't released each other's hands. Without letting go, Kerry kicked her sandals off and picked them up with her free hand. Daniel held on, helping her maintain her balance.

But that, she knew, was only her physical balance. It was her emotional equilibrium that was dizzy now. The cool sand between her toes felt comfortable, and so did his hand in hers, and she decided that it was time for one more push. Either it would go well . . .

. . . or it wouldn't.

"So, this is all a little confusing," she said after a short while.

"What is?" Daniel asked. "The Convocation? Season?"

She gave a little laugh. "I'm past all that," she said. "No, I mean this." She gave his hand a squeeze. "Us. If there is an us. Just what exactly are we doing here?"

"Ahh," he responded. "I think I see what you're getting at. You mean what makes me think that I, an over-the-hill, overly serious geezer with a mission, would have a chance with a beautiful, lively, spirited young woman such as yourself?"

Laughing again, she kicked sand at his feet. "That wasn't exactly what I meant. But I guess it was close enough."

"Then the answer is . . . I have no idea." He stopped walking and turned to face her, releasing her hand but putting both of his own on the sides of her waist. She dropped her sandals to the ground and pressed her hands loosely against the backs of his arms, not trusting her own emotions at this moment, not confident in her own impulses. "I don't know what we're doing," he elaborated. "But I know what I want, and I hope you want the same thing. I think you do." He stopped, took a deep breath, blew it out. "I've been wrong before, though."

"I don't think you are. Not this time," Kerry assured him. "That is, if you want what I suspect you do."

He pressed his hands more firmly against her waist, then took a step forward, sliding his hands around her back and pulling her toward him. She went willingly, happily, letting him guide her to him, loving the feel of his big hands spreading across her back. At the same time, she moved her own hands up his arms and around him, across his wide shoulders, and pulled him down toward her. As if choreographed, she tilted her head back and rose up on the balls of her feet, and he leaned forward. She felt her chest press against his, broad and muscular beneath his light cotton shirt, and then his lips were on hers and his hands moved hungrily across her back. Kerry returned that hunger, and then some, and they hardly noticed as the sea surged toward them, soaking their legs, then pulled back and left them standing in the wet sand, deeper than they'd been just a moment before.

Kerry Profitt's diary, August 26

Dear Diary,

Oh, never mind.

More later.

K.

16

My first impression of New York City, for this trip, anyway, is that they haven't finished building it yet. But it's definitely changed a lot since the last time I was here, which was, I think, 1899 or maybe spring of 1900.

I flew into LaGuardia and caught a cab into the city. I loaded my gear into the cab, and when I told the driver I was going to the Carlyle, his mouth dropped open. "I've been saving up," I told him.

"No foolin'," he said. Apparently I don't look much like your average Carlyle sort. But it's comfortable and centrally located, right next to Central Park. A good location is important when you're trying to find a single woman somewhere in America's biggest city, and you don't know where to begin.

Back to the first impression, though—it was just about dusk when I got my first good look at modern Manhattan. Tall buildings, of course, but all over the skyline are these giant cranes. It's like the Empire State Building and the Chrysler Building and those others I don't know the names of aren't enough—every building in the city has to be a skyscraper.

After the cranes, what I notice next are the lights. Millions of them, twinkling everywhere I look. Lighted windows, lighted signs, lighted billboards. The cabbie drives me through Times Square, at my request, and it's just a crazy riot of light and color. There are signs and posters plastered everywhere for Look Homeward, Angel at the Ethel Barrymore Theatre, which I guess opens this week. Tony Perkins is in it, and it seems to be the talk of the *town at the moment. That and, of course, Thanksgiving, which means turkey dinners and the Macy's parade and Christmas lights, adding to the sparkle in the streets. There are people everywhere—on the sidewalks and spilling onto the streets, dressed to the nines, laughing and having a grand time, it seems. It would be nice to join them, I think, but business before pleasure.*

After giving me the nickel tour and running up the fare at the same time, of course, the cabbie drives me to the Carlyle, which surprises me by being every bit as fancy as he had warned me. Thirty-five stories tall, all beautiful art-deco design, a big fire roaring in the fireplace and formal-dressed staff all over the place—pretty tony for an old witch. But I can afford it, so why not?

In fact, I'm sitting in one of its deluxe beds right now and ready to try it out for real. So I'll set this aside for the night and get back to it when there's something new to report.

I remain,

Daniel Blessing, November 26, 1957

Kerry put the leather book down and jabbed the power button on her laptop. Kerry and Daniel had stayed on the beach, exploring each other with lips and tongues and hands and eyes, until midnight, when Scott had texted Daniel's cell. They had all headed home then, recognizing a major flaw in their plan—that Season could easily slip through their already loose net while they slept—but also accepting the obvious truth that people parked overnight in a residential neighborhood might attract the unwanted attention of the police.

Who still, presumably, wanted to talk to them about Mace's murder.

Kerry Profitt's diary, August . . . oh, who cares.

I'm writing this in bed while Daniel is in bed in the next room, probably trying to ignore Josh's snores.

I'm only guessing that Josh snores, but it seems like he would.

But the important fact of my life is not Josh snoring. Rather, it is that he—should that be HE?—is sleeping just twenty feet from where I am sleeping. Or, not sleeping. In my case.

If I were a different person I'd be scribbling the name "Daniel" across the inside cover of my notebook now, a hundred times, in different colored pens. Some with hearts around them, or flowers.

I'm not that girl, though. I'm laptop chick, ever so much more sophisticated.

Besides, I can just cut-and-paste.

Daniel

Daniel

Daniel

Daniel

See? Maybe loses some of the visceral impact. But I'm still all squooshy with visceral, anyway, from earlier, on the beach. I think my toes are permanently pruned, and did I mention that Pacific Ocean water is cold? I mean, at the moment I was sort of disregarding the part of my body called feet in favor of other parts. But when we stopped, I realized that I was, like, frostbitten or something.

Okay, not. But damn cold just the same. Teeth chattering, even.

Which is when Daniel did the coolest thing. Or one of them, anyway.

He got down on one knee, giving me momentary proposal jitters, I must say, and then he took my feet—crusty and sandy from beach and saltwater, and yuck!—in his hands, one at a time, and held them. But the thing is, when he held them, his hands generated some kind of warming field, like they were mini-toasters and my cold, aching feet were the bread. After a few seconds in his hands, the cold and the pain went away, and my feet felt completely rejuvenated.

He's a one-man spa, that Daniel Blessing.

So we got home and talked for a while about the fruitlessness of the day's long, long stakeout. But we don't have enough people to pull different shifts, so we pretty much have to be out there as many hours as we can, and just tough it out. Meanwhile, Daniel and I were trying hard not to make googly eyes at each other, and we managed not to tell the others what had happened, even though I want to, but on the way home we agreed that it might make them feel awkward, and maybe we should hold off telling anyone for a while.

So then we went to bed. We were able to clasp hands, just for a moment, as we passed in the hall. That was it.

Fortunately I can still feel his lips on mine, still taste him, still remember the crush of his hands on me.

Giddy? Me?

Forcing myself not to write in here until after R had gone to sleep because I was afraid I might just start giggling, or crying, or both, and she'd want to know what was going on and I'd have to tell her. So I got out the journals and skipped around for a bit, finally finding what looked like another story instead of just the "woke up, didn't find her, went to bed" reportage of so many days, read that for a while. Until R's breathing was regular. I'm sure she's out now.

So here I am. Instead of being crushing schoolgirl with my friends, I'm being crushing schoolgirl with a box full of wires and . . . well, whatever is inside computers. Chips? Whatever they look like.

It's all magic to me. I touch keys and words appear on the screen. Magic. Daniel touches my feet, and they warm and stop hurting. Magic. Daniel's mouth presses against mine and every worry I ever had flies out of my head. Magic.

Daniel? You're not just playing a game, are you?

silence

silence

silence

Didn't think so.

More later.

K.

New York is a funny town.

So many people. I'm certain that Season is here somewhere, but I roamed the city all day and didn't pick up a trace of her.

Just about wore through my shoes, though—I'll likely need a new pair before I leave.

The good thing about New York is that you can buy anything here. No problem finding a new pair of shoes. The only hard part might be deciding: loafers, wing tips, what? I guess it'll depend on my mood when I'm in the store.

After having spent all day wandering around in the cold, though—and I'm talking COLD—I decided to check out the balloon preparation for the big parade tomorrow. I braved wind and weather (and skies that promise rain, I fear, for tomorrow) to hike the Upper West Side, watching colorful stretches of rubber slowly take shape. Mighty Mouse, clowns, Popeye the Sailor, a tremendous dachshund, toy soldiers, and other fanciful forms began to billow and shake as gigantic helium tanks filled them. The streets were crowded with revelers and volunteers, the latter working to control their balloons, the former hindering that effort, as often as not.

One old geezer buttonholed me as I watched, anxious for any target for his stories. "I was at the end of the route in '30," he told me. "Right in front of Macy's. In those days, they let the balloons go at parade's end, you know. Just let 'em float away. Most of 'em popped before they cleared the store—noise was terrible, and the bits of rubber raining down stank something awful too. But some of them got away, and Macy's had a reward out for their safe return—one year, two tugboats each caught an end of one of them wiener dogs, and pulled it in two."

"That's fascinating," I told the codger. But I tried to work my way clear of him because I was getting a strange feeling. One I didn't like a bit. Was it Season? I thought it over for a couple of moments, but no, it wasn't that. I was still trying to figure it when I heard a woman scream, not too far away—around the corner, I thought, and about half a block down.

A couple of us took off running toward the sound, but I was the fastest. When I reached her—forty, perhaps, nicely dressed, in a fur-lined coat, with boots and gloves to protect against the chill—she shouted something about her purse and a guy with a knife. She pointed down the block, and I just kept running.

I don't know what happened behind me, if the other men who ran toward her stopped to comfort her, or to call the cops, or what. All I knew is that a few minutes later I was on a block that seemed hundreds of miles removed from the swank Upper West Side blocks where the parade balloons were. Here the brownstones were run-down, with broken windows covered by boards, and trash in the streets. There seemed to be no one out. I could see the blue glow of television sets in a couple of windows, and hear radios blaring from others, but there wasn't a soul to be seen.

Part of me wanted to give up, to turn around. The lady had a fur, she could probably afford the loss of the purse and whatever dough was inside it. And if the guy who hiked her purse lived in this neighborhood, chances were that he'd just gotten away with more than he usually saw in a month. But there was a matter of principle, too. A thief is a thief, whether he steals from rich or poor.

I had touched the lady as I ran past her, though, so it wasn't a terribly difficult thing to track the progress of her purse. Eventually that trail led me to an alley, and in the alley were a half dozen hoodlums, counting out their take. Leonard Bernstein's West Side Story *opened on Broadway this year, and these guys could have been extras from the rumble scene, Sharks or Jets in their leather jackets and pomaded hair.*

And, I was to learn momentarily, switchblades.

One of them looked up and saw me. "You lost or something, Pops?" he asked.

"Pops," I said. "That's funnier than you know."

"I didn't mean it funny," he said back. "You guys think it sounded funny?"

They all agreed that I was the only one who found it funny in the least. Which only made sense, considering I was the only one who knew that I was old enough to be this punk's great-great-grandfather, at the very least.

"Anyhoo," the spokesman said after they had discussed it for a while, "this here is our alley, and unless you have some business with us, I think you oughta scram."

"I do have business with you," I said. "That purse you've got. I've come to take it back to its owner."

They looked at one another then, as if surprised by what I said. I guess they were. They couldn't have known I'd be able to track it this far. They thought they were home safe.

I guess they still did think that. "He's a funny man," the spokesman said. "A truly funny man, is old Pops."

"I'm not being funny," I said. "I'd like the purse, please. And all the money that was in it."

This is when the switchblades came out. Snap, crackle, pop, like the cereal, and suddenly all eight guys had steel in their hands.

I just looked at them, still hoping they'd do it the easy way. "The purse, please," I repeated.

The spokesman grabbed the purse from the one holding it, and waved it toward me. "Whynchoo come get it?" he asked. I'm just putting it down the way it sounded. Whynchoo.

"If that's the way you want it," I said. "I was hoping to spare you some trouble."

They looked at one another again. This time a couple of them looked nervous. I think they were getting the idea that I wasn't someone who was going to back down easily. Since they were used to people who did back down easily, that meant I had some kind of gimmick. Maybe a gun, maybe some friends, they didn't know what. But some secret weapon, because no one would be foolish enough to face down eight switchblade hoods without one.

In fact I did have one. Not any of the ones they might have thought. But a good one, just the same.

There were any number of ways it could have gone. I wanted them to remember it, though. I wanted them to learn something from it. I didn't want them to write it off later as some kind of hallucination, bad liquor or dope, or whatever else they might have imbibed that night. I wanted it to seem as natural as possible. So instead of just knocking them all out, or lifting them off their feet and slamming them magically into the walls of the alley, I decided to go hand-to-hand.

Of course, my hand was a little stronger than their hand. Even with the knives, which would never touch me. But they didn't have to know that. All they'd know was that a seemingly unarmed civilian could stand up to the bunch of them, and win.

I advanced on them at a regular walking pace. Some of the switchblade-wielding fists shook now, as they realized that this was turning ugly. Maybe they were afraid they'd have to kill me, and while they were hoodlums and punks, I thought they probably weren't killers by nature. Maybe they were just plain afraid.

I started with the spokesman, because he annoyed me the most. Easily dodging his knife, I caught his jaw with a right hook, followed with a jab to the gut and then an uppercut to the chin. He went down hard. Now the others were all stabbing at me, but I took them one by one, letting their blades slip past me. A few punches here, a couple of karate chops there, some judo throws for variety. Finally the last two broke out running, down the alley away from me. But that was okay. I wasn't going to chase. I gathered up all the money the ones left behind had on them, on the theory that even if it hadn't come from the purse, they'd stolen it from someone, and tucked it inside the lady's wallet. Then I left them in the alley. They'd wake up in a few hours, never again quite so confident, I hoped, in their own invulnerability.

I found the lady about where I'd left her, answering questions from a uniformed cop who wrote slowly, and with obvious difficulty, in a little notebook. Gave her the purse. Explained that it had been dropped, several blocks away, and I hoped she wasn't too inconvenienced. Ignored the look the cop shot me, like if I wasn't the snatcher, I was probably in league with him. Back on 90th I caught a cab back to the Carlyle, and here I am. It's starting to rain outside.

Interesting day. Interesting city. No Season.

I remain,
Daniel Blessing, November 27, 1957

17

"You get any sleep?"

Scott looked at Kerry like she was some kind of lab specimen. Then again, she felt like some kind of lab specimen, so maybe that was how she did look. When she'd been in the bathroom, she hadn't quite been able to focus on the mirror, which, judging from Scott's greeting, was probably a bonus.

"Not much," she admitted. "I was reading."

"You were?" Rebecca asked. "I didn't even know."

Because you could sleep through nuclear war, Kerry thought. *Or Ozzfest, at least.* She just shrugged and tried to smile, though.

She felt strange this morning. As if she was the same person she had been yesterday, but everything around her had changed. Like she had gone to bed at home, but had woken up in a foreign country. She didn't know the language, the customs, the lay of the land. But she'd made the trip willingly—buying her own ticket, bringing her passport. A strange feeling, that was the only way to describe it.

"Must have been a good book," Scott said. "Keeping you awake and all."

"One of Daniel's journals. It's pretty interesting reading."

"Does it have any advice in it about how to survive a stakeout?" Brandy asked, coming into the kitchen from the bedroom she shared with Scott. "Because all day in a car . . . I thought my legs were permanently frozen in a sitting position."

"You took enough bathroom breaks," Scott teased. "You could have walked around a little more then."

"I'll have to today," Brandy shot back. "I go back into that mini-mart, they're going to start charging me rent."

"Josh suggested using a bottle or a can," Rebecca offered. "I told him if I even saw him bring a bottle or can into the car, I was throwing him out."

Brandy cracked up. "Good for you."

"That's how they do it in real life, I guess," Scott said. "Not that this isn't, you know . . ."

Rebecca flapped her hands at him. "I think that's how it's done in those crime books and movies Josh likes," she replied. "I don't know about real life. I just know I'm not sitting there while Josh whips out a soda bottle."

Daniel wandered in then, hair still mussed from sleeping and a crease from his pillow on his face. Kerry liked it. As she learned more about him, sometimes it was hard to remember that he was human—not quite like her, obviously, but still, at his core. A pillow mark on his face, though—that was as human as it got. He was a long-lived, incredibly powerful man, but he was still a man.

She'd have to remember to kiss that cheek later, where she saw the crease. Maybe some other spots, too.

"I don't blame you a bit, Rebecca," he said as he rummaged in the cabinet for a clean cup. "This is serious business, I'm afraid. But just as I don't want any of you to try to engage Season on your own, I don't want you to injure yourselves, or to be any more put out than is absolutely necessary. We'll stake her out, but we won't kill ourselves doing it, okay?"

"We're already about as put out as we can be," Brandy observed. "Unless you don't count our lives being turned upside down and put in danger."

"Oh, I do," Daniel said. He poured coffee from the pot into his cup, took a sip, grimaced. Kerry had noticed that he nearly always tasted it, even though he invariably put in sugar afterward. *Old habits,* she figured. "Believe me, I know how seriously I've inconvenienced all of you."

"But if we get Season," Kerry put in, "then it's all worth it. Everything. Even . . . even Mace."

She felt Brandy's gaze burning into her. "You sure you want to go there?"

"I feel terrible about Mace, Brandy, you know I do. But Season is responsible for so many deaths, so much sorrow and loss. If we could stop her, think of everyone we'd be helping. All of her future victims."

"We're on board," Scott assured her. "Doesn't mean we have to be thrilled about it. But you don't see any of us turning away, do you?"

"Josh tries to bring a bottle into my car," Rebecca said, trying to sound hard-boiled, "I'll turn him away."

"Yeah, you talk like a tough cookie!" Josh called from behind the closed bathroom door. "We'll just see how tough you really are when the chips are down."

Rebecca laughed and blushed, lifting her breakfast dishes from the table and carrying them to the sink. So far, Kerry decided, she was impressed with all of her friends, for even sticking it out this long, and for being willing to go to all this trouble.

The chips, she was pretty sure, had been down for a long time.

The shopping center was wood-sided, painted brown, reasonably busy. It wasn't much more than a glorified strip mall containing a coffee shop and a bagel shop, a drugstore, office and pet supplies stores, a couple of restaurants, and at one end, a supermarket. But there was enough traffic in and out so no one really noticed that one nondescript Ford Taurus had parked in the slender shade offered by a tree and hadn't moved for a long time.

Anyone looking into the car, though, might notice that the couple in the front seat was locked in passionate embrace, as often as not.

"Should we really be doing this?" Kerry asked when they broke once. It was midafternoon; they'd been on the stakeout since eight that morning. The windows were half open so the occasional breeze could help cool the car's interior. They'd taken one break for ice-cream cones, and a couple of others to replenish their supply of cold bottled water. "The others . . ."

"We don't kiss so loudly that we wouldn't hear the phone," Daniel assured her. "But if you want to stop . . ."

"That's not what I said." At the moment, she could hardly imagine a more pleasant way to pass the time than sitting and talking with Daniel Blessing, interrupted from time to time by a bout of feverish kissing.

"Tonight," Daniel announced, somewhat abruptly, "we'll tell them."

For a moment Kerry was confused. "Tell them . . . oh. *Tell* them. About us."

"There's no reason we should have to keep it a secret," Daniel said. "We're both adults. You're young, yes, but you're as mature a woman as I've ever known."

Kerry felt herself crimsoning. "Thanks. I guess . . . I guess I had to grow up fast, with my mom and dad in the conditions they were in."

"You've done an admirable job." He traced a pattern on her knee with his finger. She wore khaki shorts and a red cotton T-shirt, almost the color she figured her face had turned, because in spite of the August heat, they couldn't run the air-conditioning the whole time they were parked, and his touch was cool, comforting. Somehow Daniel stayed crisp in a white linen shirt with the long sleeves rolled up and faded jeans. "I told you before, I've been with a few women over the years."

She didn't necessarily like to think about that. "Yeah."

"But none of them . . . ever . . . have meant what you have come to mean to me, Kerry. You . . ."

He paused, and she waited for him to finish his sentence. He worked his jaw, she could see the little worm of a scar under it twitch, but nothing came out.

Finally she decided to take him off the hook, finally allowing herself to say what she'd been holding inside, not even certain of her own feelings until just this moment. "I can't say I've been with a lot of guys," she said. "And obviously never with an age difference like we have. But I think I feel the same way. Like there's something about you that I just respond to, that I'm at ease with. It's hard to remember when you weren't in my life, and hard to imagine a future without you in it." She laughed, suddenly even more nervous than she'd expected. Whenever she'd had this kind of conversation in her head, growing up, it had all flowed so easily. "God, isn't this the kind of talk we should be having six months from now, maybe? I'm so bad at this I don't even know what the timing is supposed to be like."

"It's supposed to be whatever feels right," Daniel said, squeezing her leg. "And this does."

"So tonight?" Kerry asked, aware that maybe she was, once again, about to push too hard. "When we tell them? Do you think maybe we can get Rebecca and Josh to share a room?"

Daniel smiled at her, obviously pleased by the suggestion. "It's worth a try," he said.

He leaned toward her, drawing her closer with subtle pressure on her leg, and their lips were almost in contact when his phone chirped at them. He raised an eyebrow in annoyance. "Great timing."

"It's not like we haven't had a chance to kiss today," Kerry reminded him, biting back her own disappointment. "Or like we won't have plenty of time later."

Fishing the phone from his pocket, Daniel pouted. "But I wanted one now."

Kerry stretched toward him and planted one on his cheek, right where the pillow-crease had been. "There you go," she said. "Now answer your phone."

"Pick up, pick up, pick up," Rebecca pleaded, listening to Daniel's phone ring.

"Trying to drive here," Josh said with a growl. He had the wheel of the Civic, and he wore an unpleasant scowl as he tried to maneuver around a

Buick that had lurched from an apartment complex's lot into their way. "You want to put the kibosh on the whining?"

Pick up, pick up, pick up, Rebecca thought anxiously. Josh's mood was foul enough that she didn't want to aggravate it any more. But—

"Hello," Daniel's voice spoke in her ear.

"We found her!" Rebecca realized she'd shouted it, but didn't care. She could almost feel Josh's glare.

"Where are you?"

She glanced at their surroundings. "Heading toward the water, so west, I guess, on Emerald."

"She's driving?" Daniel asked.

"Yes. Driving."

"In what?"

"A car," Rebecca said, flustered. She'd known a minute ago, but the tension and excitement of the chase were getting to her.

"Forest green Nissan Maxima," Josh informed her.

She relayed the message, and added, "We were driving down Emerald, and she passed us, going the other way. Josh pulled over, then turned around. She's a couple of blocks ahead of us."

"Okay, good job, Rebecca," Daniel said sharply. "I'm going to alert Brandy and Scott now. I'll check back in a minute."

He ended the call, and Rebecca put the phone in her lap. Two- and three-story apartment buildings flashed past her window; the fronds of tall palms strobed the sunlight that raked across the windshield. Ahead she could see a van and a big black SUV. "Where is she?" she asked Josh. "I don't see her."

"Don't sweat it, I have her," Josh assured her. "I'm hanging back so she doesn't make us." He tossed her a sideways grin. "You act like I don't know what I'm doing."

"You watch a lot of movies, read some books," Rebecca countered. She was fully aware that her anxiety was making her edgier than usual, more argumentative. But she had every right to be edgy. They were chasing a killer—and worse, a killer with unknown magical powers. "I'm not sure that makes you a genuine expert on surveillance techniques."

Josh's grin turned into an unpleasant sneer. She had always liked Josh, even when the rest of their housemates found him a bit obnoxious. But now that he was in his element—or what he believed was his element, even though he had no particular experience with, or real-life knowledge of, the seamier side of life—he got all bent out of shape when she dared to question his abilities. As if to prove her wrong, he mashed down hard on the accelerator and the car lunged ahead. At the same time he twisted the wheel to the left, swerving into the oncoming traffic lane, which was blessedly empty. He stayed on the gas, pulling ahead of the van, then cutting back into the correct lane. The van's horn bleated, the SUV in the other lane ticked to the side as if worried about being hit. But three blocks ahead of them, just making a right turn, she spotted the green Nissan.

Josh glanced at her, wordlessly triumphant.

18

Brandy flipped the phone open as soon as it rang. "Hey," she said.

"She's on the move." Daniel's voice, brittle with anxiety. "On Emerald, headed west. Toward you."

"Okay," Brandy answered, not sure what other response was needed. If any. She and Scott were parked on Mission, near Beryl, on the route one would take from Pacific Beach to La Jolla.

"Dark green Nissan Maxima," Daniel added.

"We'll watch for her," Brandy promised.

"Don't get right behind her," Daniel warned. "Let her get a few car lengths ahead. Josh and Rebecca will be following too, so you should both take turns pulling up and slipping back. Make sure she doesn't see the same car in her rearview the whole time."

"I got it," Brandy said.

"We're on the way over. I'll check back in a few." Daniel signed off, and she folded the phone. Scott looked at her, curiosity on his face.

"What's up?"

"Get ready for action, Scott. She's coming this way." Brandy repeated the details Daniel had given her. "Let's not lose her this time," she said. "I'd sure love to get all this over with."

Scott nodded as he turned the key in the ignition and gunned the engine. The air inside the car was charged now; the urgency of imminent contact, the anticipation of some kind of conclusion to the summer's madness striking them both. "That makes two of us."

A couple of minutes later the phone rang again. "It's Rebecca," their housemate's voice said when Brandy answered. "She's not coming your way after all. She turned south on Mission, not north."

"We're on it," Brandy acknowledged. She hung up and filled Scott in. So Season wasn't heading for La Jolla this time—or to the freeway, at least, not right away. South on Mission would take her through Pacific Beach, and into Mission Beach. But that would become a dead end; eventually she'd have to turn inland, crossing Mission Bay. Then she could go out Point Loma, which would trap her on a long peninsula, or toward downtown and the freeways.

Scott pulled out of the parking place, waited for a break in traffic, and performed an illegal U-turn in the middle of the block. Now he was headed south on Mission, as well. He stomped on the gas and the car shot forward. Traffic was light, but there were cars on the road, and he wove between lanes to get around them. Brandy found herself clutching her seat, trying not to show fear. They'd have to live through the chase if they would ever get a chance to die at Season's hands, she knew.

Of course, there was the other option, too—the one where they defeated Season and ended the summer in triumph. She hadn't been willing to give much consideration to that scenario, unwilling to get her hopes up. Life, she had found, was somewhat less disappointing if she didn't expect too much out of it to begin with. Allowing herself to imagine that she'd be some kind of hero, would help save the world—*okay, not the world*, she thought, *but at least lives, someone's world*—had been too ambitious for her to even consider.

Now, though, she couldn't help it. She had the sense that some kind of conclusion was coming, some ultimate confrontation. Either they'd walk away from it or Season would, but no way would the status quo be unchanged at the end.

So she hung on and let Scott drive, silently watching the road ahead, his hands tight on the wheel. A trickle of sweat ran down the side of his face, dripping from beneath the temple-piece of his glasses. Brandy worried a little about him, about how he'd deal with this whole thing. He was a smart guy, and she loved him, really loved him like no other boyfriend she'd had. But confrontation wasn't his forte. He was smart but not strong, not in the physical sense, although he was no weakling, either—no Mace, but no Josh, either, and soccer had given him great legs—but in the emotional sense. When life battered him around, he didn't bounce back easily. Even something as seemingly minor as a disagreement in traffic—someone cutting him off or flipping him off—unsettled him for at least a day.

She'd been pleasantly surprised, so far, about how well he'd handled all this, with Daniel and Mace and everything. When things turned really bad, he seemed able to rise to meet the challenges. But she couldn't help wondering when he'd reach his breaking point, when it would all just be too much for him. Judging from the expression on his face now—lips clamped together, eyes wide, jaw as tight as a violin string—that time just might be close. She'd have to keep an eye on him.

"There's Josh and Beck," he said a few minutes later. Brandy saw them too, in the rented Civic they drove.

"We should pass them," she said. "So when she looks in her mirror—"

"I know," Scott interrupted. Brandy had already explained the theory, when reporting what Daniel had told her. She guessed the stress was getting to her too.

"I know, sorry."

"Yeah," he said. "Anyway, that's what I'm doing." He pulled even with the other car, and Brandy waved at Josh and Rebecca. Josh made an ushering gesture with his hand, indicating that they should pull ahead. He had an unlit cigarette clamped between his teeth. Rebecca wouldn't let him smoke while she was in the car, but it looked like he'd been chewing on it. Brandy thought she could see flecks of tobacco on his chin.

Brandy and Scott pulled ahead, though, and all her attention was on the dark green sedan a block or so ahead of them, with only a driver inside.

"That's got to be her," Scott said.

"Yeah," Brandy agreed softly, more nervous than ever now that Season was in view again. This time there would be no losing her, she determined. This time it would all play out to the end. One way or another.

Suddenly every vehicle in San Diego was in Pacific Beach, either stuck in traffic on Garnet or trying to cross it. That was how it seemed to Kerry, anyway. She drove Daniel's car. He had his hands full with his cell, trying to coordinate the movements of three different vehicles, all in pursuit of a fourth, and he'd spread a city map on his lap. He tried to anticipate where Season might be headed, based on where she was. Kerry knew that was a fool's game— Season had proven her unpredictability plenty of times in the past, and could as easily turn around and head right back where she'd come from as continue on any given path. But she didn't bother to share her opinion with Daniel, who, after all, knew his enemy far better than she did.

Ahead, the traffic light turned green, and she started inching forward even before the car in front of her had moved. But three cars in front of that, a pick-up truck with surfboards spiking from the bed was trying to turn left, and sat at the light waiting for a break in the oncoming traffic. By the time the truck had passed through the light, it was turning yellow again, then red. She had moved up all of one space.

"She's not doing this, is she?" Kerry asked, only half-joking.

"What, manipulating the traffic? No, I think that's beyond even her abilities," Daniel replied. "That's the problem with traffic, it can't be controlled. Too much human element. It's barely contained chaos. Almost makes one long for the days of traffic cops, standing in the streets directing the flow."

"Or horses and buggies?" Kerry teased.

"Say what you will," Daniel said. "There were definite advantages.

Quieter, safer, less polluting. The world has given up a lot in the name of progress."

"But we don't have to worry about stepping in horse manure when we cross the street," Kerry pointed out.

"That's true. Then, though, you didn't have to worry about global climate change or growing holes in the ozone layer. You didn't have to worry that you were breathing in carcinogens every day. And that's without even bringing nuclear arms or biological weapons into the equation. Life is easier now, in many ways, and safer in some. But in others, the world has gone completely, screamingly insane."

The light changed again, and Daniel fell silent as Kerry silently urged the cars in front of her to just go straight already. And it worked. This time, she made it through the light. Ahead, Garnet had the undisputed right of way for several blocks, so it was relatively clear sailing.

"Do you really think that?" she asked after a while. "That the world is insane?"

Daniel considered the question for a long moment. "In some ways, I said. And the answer is, yes, I do. Certainly, there have been remarkable improvements, amazing technological advances. We've essentially beaten the worst diseases of history—plague, polio, whooping cough, and so on. We can vaccinate against measles and chicken pox. These things used to cripple and kill, and now they're merely inconvenient, if that. But we've also changed the world in ways we don't even understand, so that we have to deal with new cancers, STDs, various pandemics. We've poisoned the air and water. We build nuclear power plants that have the potential to kill tens of thousands if something goes wrong. In many ways, large and small, from the individual to the corporation to government, we keep inventing new ways to kill, new ways to tyrannize, new ways to destroy people's lives." He chuckled dryly. "I'm sorry, Kerry, I don't mean to pontificate."

"That's okay," she said. Listening to him talk helped her cope with the frustrations of the traffic.

"No, it's not. We have other things on our plate right now." He punched some buttons on the cell phone, listened for a second. Then, "Brandy, where are you? Good, good. We'll be there in a few minutes; just trying to get through traffic."

After he hung up, he pointed at a stop light ahead, at Mission Boulevard. "Left on Mission," he told her.

"Okay," she said. She really did find his diatribe intriguing. When most people talked about the differences between older days and the present, she knew they were only basing their opinions on what they'd read or heard. He had actually lived through the whole thing, though—the settling of America, the westward expansion, the rise and fall of global powers. He was history made flesh.

But thinking about his flesh made her mind veer in other directions, and she shook her head, not wanting to let herself get distracted with thoughts of that. Plenty of time later. Right now she had to drive a car. Daniel was on the phone again, with Rebecca this time, when Kerry made the left onto Mission.

Daniel continued to direct her, and she went where he told her to—left, left, right. Through Crown Point and across the bay on a narrow bridge, then they were on wide avenues and moving fast. Past Sea World, and eventually onto I-5, heading south, but then an abrupt turn onto I-8, going east. That way was the desert and the rest of the country, eventually. Kerry found herself wondering how far they'd go today. Was the witch finally leaving San Diego behind? Part of her gloried at that idea—it would be over then, for her.

But Daniel would go too, wouldn't he? Continuing the hunt.

At Daniel's urging, she sped up, and soon she had the other two cars in sight. They slowed a little, letting her pass, acknowledging her and Daniel as they did so.

And then she could see Season, up ahead, cruising along in her dark green car. Daniel put a hand on Kerry's leg and squeezed. "No closer," he said quietly. That made sense—if she could see Season, then Season could see them. She hung back.

In the city of El Cajon, a few miles east of San Diego, the green car exited the freeway. Josh was back in front by this time. He flipped on his turn signal and followed her, and the other two cars did the same. "It's good we have three cars to work her," Daniel said. "She obviously left Pacific Beach the hard way to try to spot, or avoid, pursuit. I don't think she's seen us yet, but she still might. We'll need to be very careful on these roads."

El Cajon was a small city, and traffic there was nowhere near as heavy as it had been back in San Diego. All three vehicles stayed well behind Season's. Daniel was silent now, grimly focused on the Nissan ahead of them. The three chase cars did a dance, each taking the lead for a while, then falling back to let a different one move closer—never sticking to a pattern, but changing things up each time. Now and again one would pull into a parking lot, and then out again, or stop by the side of the road, only to pull back out after the other two had passed. The last thing anyone wanted was for Season to get stuck at a light long enough for them to catch up to her, to risk stopping right next to her or being obvious about holding back.

The streets Season chose became increasingly empty. She led them away from El Cajon's small downtown area, through residential neighborhoods where the streets were lined with small cottages or faded apartment complexes in shades of salmon or aquamarine. Overgrown yards, sometimes with cars parked in them, were not uncommon here. Fences tended to be chain-link, in various states of repair. Behind some of them, dogs stood guard or lazed in the sun. Being inland and therefore farther from the coast, El Cajon was even more brutally hot than San Diego, and there weren't many people on the streets, but Kerry spotted a few, sitting on shaded porches or walking on the sidewalks under sun hats or, in one instance, an umbrella.

"You have any idea where she's going?" she asked Daniel.

She could see his shrug from the corner of her eye. "No clue," he said. "Up to no good, I'm sure."

"Doesn't that go without saying?"

The question was answered in another couple of minutes, though. Daniel's cell rang, and when he answered, Kerry could make out Brandy's voice, which sounded agitated. Daniel listened for a moment, thanked her, and disconnected. "She's stopping," he told Kerry. "Brandy and Scott are driving past, Rebecca and Josh are stopping behind her."

"What do we do?"

The other cars had already turned a corner that Kerry had not yet reached. Daniel pointed to the parking lot of a strip mall, before the corner, on the left-hand side of the street. "Pull in there," he said. "We'll get closer on foot."

She did as she was directed, parking in front of a taco stand, and they both got out. Daniel kept his phone in his hand. He punched a button. "Rebecca," he said. "Where is she?"

He frowned as he listened to her response, then he put away the phone and looked at Kerry. "There's an herbalist around the corner," he explained. "She's gone in there. Picking up supplies for some kind of spell, most likely."

Anxiety gnawed at Kerry's stomach, as if she'd swallowed a mouse. They were close now, as close as they'd been since that night in the kitchen when Daniel was too weak to give his all. A battle might be only moments away. She wanted it, ached for an end to Daniel's long quest. But was he strong enough now? And if he wasn't, what then? She hardly dared to imagine. "What now? Do we just go in there after her?"

"Three reasons why we don't do that," Daniel said. "One, we don't know who's in there. An herbalist may well be a cover for a witch, maybe an ally of hers. Two, we don't know if she spotted us and is trying to lead us into a trap. She may be watching the street right now from inside, waiting for us to make our move. Three, we don't know the territory. We've had no time to plan, to scout out escape routes, to know what cover there might be. Going in there now could be suicide."

Kerry was confused. "Then why have we followed her all this way?"

"Because we found her," he said simply. "We're not losing her again. That just isn't happening."

19

But they did.

Season stayed in the shop less than five minutes. Kerry and Daniel made their way around the corner and had taken up positions in the recessed doorway of an empty, boarded-up storefront. They could see the Civic up ahead, and Season's Nissan, parked right in front of a shop with a green painted sign that read HERBS 'R' US: REMEDIES AND ROMANCE, and farther ahead, Scott's RAV4. But Season's abrupt reappearance took them by surprise. Daniel and Kerry both had to turn away from the shop, facing into the doorway of the vacant store. They stayed there until they heard engines starting, and then the squeal of tires as Season pulled hurriedly away from the curb.

As soon as she was gone, Daniel grabbed Kerry's hand. "Come on!" he urged. His phone rang, and he answered it as they ran for the car. "I know!" he shouted. "Stay on her!"

By the time they were back in Daniel's Taurus, though, Kerry once again driving, Brandy had called to tell them that Season was gone.

She had made a quick right at the first corner, then a sudden left into an alley. Scott hadn't wanted to be so obvious as to follow her down the alley while she was still in it, so Brandy called Rebecca, intending for that car to go straight instead of making the right. She and Scott would go past the alley and then left, and whichever way Season turned when she reached the alley's end, one of the cars would be nearby.

Except what Season did, apparently, was to go partway down the alley, then back out and go back down the original street, in the opposite direction. Both cars were more than a block away by this time, and Kerry and Daniel, who had started at a disadvantage, weren't close enough yet to catch her.

"Do you think she saw us?" Kerry asked after Daniel explained what had happened.

"Maybe," he said. "Or maybe she's just being careful. She would know that if anyone had been following, her few minutes in the store would have given them time to catch up, maybe even lay a trap."

"I guess it wasn't her trap, though," Kerry observed.

"I called it wrong," he admitted. "Couldn't be sure, though."

"Better safe?"

"Exactly."

"So what now?" she wondered.

"Back to I-8," he said. "As fast as you can. Let's assume she's heading back home, and not away from the city." He began punching buttons on the phone. "I'll text the others."

Ten minutes later, they had her again. She had taken a roundabout way back to the freeway, apparently hoping to shake anyone tailing her. Rebecca and Josh were the farthest back, and when they saw her coming up fast behind them they called the others. Daniel and Kerry pulled off the freeway altogether, so she wouldn't recognize them when she passed. The other two cars stayed on her, and Kerry just re-entered at the same place, so within a very few minutes they were all behind her again. Kerry felt a powerful sense of relief, as if it was all over.

Which, of course, it isn't, she thought. *It hasn't even really begun.*

Forty minutes later, having gone back into Pacific Beach through La Jolla—prompting Daniel to point out that she hadn't taken a direct route anywhere—Season was back on Emerald, with Josh and Rebecca not far behind. She made a right on Everts, and pulled into the driveway of a small clapboard bungalow, at the corner of the alley that ran up the block between

Emerald and Felspar—Pacific Beach's east-west streets being named after minerals. This time, Rebecca and Josh drove past, and the other two cars stopped a block away.

"Isn't that more or less where you picked her up in the first place?" Daniel asked when they called in the report. He listened, nodding, then said, "Okay, sit tight. We're on the way." He made another quick call, telling Brandy and Scott to stay where they were, motor running, just in case. Then he turned to Kerry.

"Okay, drive past the house. Not too fast, not too slow. Just like you're out for a drive with no special destination in mind."

"But won't she see us?" Kerry wondered.

"She might," Daniel said. "If she's looking. Chance we have to take. I need to check out her place."

He sounded a bit too casual about it for her tastes, but Kerry did as she was told. She pulled away from the curb and drove at a slow, steady speed past the bungalow. Its exterior walls were painted white, with brown trim. A front porch seemed to sag under the weight of an old overstuffed chair that had suffered the elements for too long. A screen door was closed, but the heavier door behind that stood open. It looked like the kind of place a college student might live in, Kerry thought, or a young professional still a long way from her potential earning plateau. Not one of the world's most powerful witches. She wasn't sure where the Season of her imagination might live—a gingerbread house or a crumbling castle surrounded by thorn trees, maybe. The yard of this cottage was dried out, mostly dirt with a few hardy weeds, but no thorn trees. The only thing she saw that suggested Season at all was over the door, where a small bundle of greenery had been tacked.

"Is that a charm of some kind?" Kerry asked. "Above the door?"

"Keeps us out," Daniel explained. "It's a ward."

"Really?" Kerry couldn't keep the surprise out of her voice. "That little bunch of leaves can keep you out of a place?"

"It's not just the leaves," he said. They had passed the house now, but he kept looking at it until he couldn't see it anymore. "It's what they represent, how she prepared them, and the way she put them up. Those leaves, properly prepared and blessed, have the power of the trees behind them. Strong enough to stand through the ages, limber enough to survive wind, structured to use rain instead of being worn away by it. With her help, the power of the trees is transferred to the bundle, and then applied to the whole house. I could no more walk in there right now than I could step through a redwood tree."

"Somehow I didn't think a little thing like that would be beyond your abilities," Kerry said, mostly joking.

But Daniel took it seriously. "I didn't say it was," he rejoined. "It just takes some preparation."

Rebecca, Josh, Brandy, and Scott were assigned to keep an eye on the bungalow while that preparation took place. Kerry drove Daniel back to their apartment, way down in Imperial Beach, phone on his lap the whole way in case they called to say she was on the move again. But the phone remained quiet.

Kerry was uneasy about leaving the others behind. The fact that they didn't call was no consolation—what if Season had somehow caught them unaware and done the same to them that she'd done to Mace? She could have called them, but that could be the same as demonstrating a lack of trust in them. She would have felt much better if Daniel had been able to stay close. But that wasn't an option, he assured her. He had work to do, work that couldn't be done until he knew just what they were up against.

The first thing he did when they got into the apartment was to borrow her laptop and go online. There he went to Google Earth and typed in the location of Season's apartment.

When he had zoomed in as far as he was able to online, he gazed at the image for a while. It lost clarity as it got closer, Kerry noted. And they didn't have a printer, so all he could do, she figured, was to look at it on the screen. But he asked her to find a piece of blank paper, and she rummaged through her belongings until she did, a brief letter from her aunt Betty, written on only one side of the page. Daniel spread the paper out flat on the tabletop and then put his hands on the computer screen. He spoke a couple of words in a language that Kerry didn't know, and then touched the paper.

As if it had run through a color laser printer—*or as if by magic, more accurately,* Kerry thought—the image that had appeared on screen transferred to the paper. But looking at it more closely, she realized that it was much more distinct now, that somehow in transferring it, Daniel sharpened it. Now it could have been a photo taken from a few hundred feet up, if that, showing the bungalow, its yard, and the houses and streets around it in crisp detail.

She was astonished. "If you could patent that, you could give Microsoft a run for its money."

Daniel shook his head. "Witches have gone up against Bill Gates before. He still wins. We're not all-powerful, you know."

He turned back to the image he'd made, and studied it. A couple of times he pointed out features to Kerry—the way the fence at the back of her place was leaning in one spot, suggesting weak support posts there; the fact that a neighbor's house behind hers was unfenced so that there was access to Emerald through that property. He traced his finger across the picture like a general planning a military campaign, which Kerry figured wasn't too far from the truth. For the most part, though, he was silent, working through details in his head without sharing them. Kerry knew that if he wanted to share, he would, and that quiet contemplation was probably more important right now.

When he finished with the picture, he excused himself and went into the room he shared with Josh. "I'll be in here for about twenty minutes," he said. "Don't come in, no matter what you might see or hear. I'll be fine.

What I'm going to do isn't dangerous, but it's necessary, and it might sound unpleasant from the outside."

He gave Kerry a last kiss and closed the door. She crossed her arms in front of her chest and stood by the open front window, grateful for whatever breeze slipped through. The apartment was just small enough to be stuffy on these hot days, and though they got a decent cross breeze at night, during the day the air outside wasn't much of a relief. *I always heard San Diego was supposed to have perfect weather,* she thought. She had found out, though, that while it was mostly pleasant, it was far from perfect. She'd learned about June gloom, during which the beaches stayed socked in by overcast skies most of the day, so travelers who had come from far away for the fabled southern California coastline were disappointed by gray, cool days. July had been about as good as it gets, with warm, sunny weather all the time. Even August had started nice, but these last few days had reminded her that San Diego is essentially a desert, albeit one close to the ocean. She hadn't seen a drop of precipitation all summer, which cemented that impression.

Musing on the climate was just one way she tried to ignore the sounds that issued from Daniel's room. The first noises she heard were just strange—deep-sounding bells, like cowbells or heavy wind chimes, with a low moaning sound twining through them. But the sounds quickly became more disturbing—the moan less like wind, more like human voices, then turning to a keening wail, a mourning sound. When Daniel's voice entered the chorus, in evident agony, Kerry started to rush for the door. Remembering his warning, she kept herself from throwing it open, but it took every ounce of willpower. She went back to the window.

When he screamed again, she turned away and crossed to the bathroom, running water full force in the sink, wetting a washcloth and laying it over her face. She pressed the corners against her ears, trying to keep all noise out, to amplify the blood she could hear in her own head, drowning out everything else.

Finally he emerged. He looked like he'd been through hell. His cheeks were drawn and pale, with red splotches on them. His eyes were glassy and unfocused. It looked like he might have blow-dried his hair in a wind tunnel. Kerry went to him and grabbed his hands, which were clammy. "Are you okay, Daniel? What happened in there?"

"I'm fine," he replied. His voice was a dry rasp that sounded like it reached her from some faraway place.

"But . . . what . . . ?" She didn't even know how to finish the question. It was obvious to her that she needed to know more about this whole business before she would know what to ask. He tugged absently at his hands, and Kerry released them.

"Another time," Daniel said. Already he seemed to be improving: color flooding back into his face, eyes clearing. He ran a hand over his head, smoothing the flyaway hair. Now he looked at her, really seeing her for the first time, she thought, since he'd come out of the room, and he smiled. "I'll tell you all about it later," he said. "It's just . . . preparations that have to be made. A little easier if I could have made them over the span of several days, as they should be. But since we didn't know precisely when battle might be joined, I had to hold off." He leaned forward, kissed her forehead. "You okay?"

"I'm . . . I'm not the one who was screaming in pain."

"Is that what you heard?" he asked. Kerry nodded her head, but Daniel didn't elaborate. "Let's go," he said. "We have a wicked witch to kill."

20

"Have you ever been in love, Kerry?" Daniel asked as he drove north on I-5, back toward Pacific Beach and the confrontation they both knew was imminent. "I mean, totally and completely head over heels?" Her heart leapt at the question. *Where is this going?* she wondered. She knew where she hoped he was taking the conversation. She had decided that—lack of personal experience with the emotion aside—she believed she was in love with Daniel. She couldn't stop thinking about him, worrying about him when he was away from her. She wanted to be with him every moment, wanted to feel his hands on her, his lips, the comfortable way they fit together when they walked or stood together, her weight on him and vice versa. There had been a hole in her life, and that hole had been Daniel-sized and Daniel-shaped, and now there was a Daniel in it.

She recognized that she was letting her silence last an awkwardly long time. "No. Never before." She hadn't wanted to come right out and say it, but figured that her reply was ambiguous enough to leave plenty of room for his own interpretation.

"Season was, once," he said simply. Kerry was stunned by the comment, which was so totally opposite from where she had hoped he was leading. "I killed him."

"You did?" was all she could manage.

He sat in silence for a moment, guiding the car up the busy freeway. "That's right. He was a witch—not a terribly powerful or influential one, not in her league or mine, definitely. But probably a nice enough guy, with a few talents of his own. He fell into her sphere of influence somehow, and . . . well, you've seen her. She is a very beautiful woman."

"Yes," Kerry had to agree. "She is that."

Daniel laughed. "Not in your league, of course. But beautiful just the same." Kerry felt her cheeks warming. The thing was, she got the impression he really did feel that way. He wasn't just saying it. When he looked at her and that smile illuminated his features, he seemed to be looking at something glorious, radiant. He could have been admiring one of the world's great pieces of art. But it was Kerry he was looking at. Just Kerry.

"Anyway, he fell in love with her almost at first glance, I guess. I only pieced it all together later, from things I heard. She came to return the feeling, and after a while—this is about two hundred years ago, I guess, in the early nineteenth century—she was as hopelessly in love with him as he was with her. They were together for a decade or so, completely wrapped up in each other. It was kind of sweet to see, but it made her weak. Distracted. Almost like she forgot we were out there, Abraham and I, looking for her."

There was really nothing Kerry could say to this, so she just tried to pay attention while her thoughts thundered along at a thousand miles an hour. *Is this a brush-off?* she wondered. *Is he telling me that he can't afford a relationship, that it's too dangerous, too distracting?*

"We found her in Philadelphia, in summer. It was hot, like this, but humid, too, I remember. Thunderstorms in the afternoons that sounded like the world was falling apart around us. She and her lover—his name was Caleb—had taken a suite of rooms in a fine hotel. But they went out at night, became part of the social scene, and of course stories spread and people talked about the beautiful stranger, and we heard about it. When we got to Philadelphia we watched the hotel for a few days, saw them coming and going, learned their routine. That was what did them in: the routine they had developed."

The freeway exit loomed, but Daniel was so involved in his story, so lost in the past, that he almost missed it. When he noticed the exit, he ticked down the turn signal and darted across three lanes of roadway, just making it.

"Sorry," he said, sounding sheepish. "What was I saying about distraction? It's a dangerous thing."

"I guess it is," Kerry agreed, a little glum.

"We're almost there so I'll make this short," he continued. "Shorter, at least. Abraham and I came to know when they would be in and when they wouldn't. One night we waited until after they had left and then we went in, enchanted the hotel staff, let ourselves into their suite. We waited. We were ready for battle, but Season . . . Season had been making love, not war, for ten years. We knew we could defeat her.

"When they came back to the room, we were ready and they were utterly surprised. Shocked. I still smile when I think about the look on her face, that beautiful face with the blue eyes so wide, the brows raised, the mouth gaping open, lip quivering. Then rage set in. And Abraham and I attacked, both at once, as we'd planned. Season and Caleb both raised defensive shields, but Caleb's wasn't strong enough. Like Season, he was out of fighting fettle, soft and complacent." Daniel's tone changed, became quieter, with an edge that sounded almost bitter, Kerry thought. "I tore him in half without even thinking about it. Literally. Cut him apart at the waist. When his torso slid off his legs and fell to the floor, I could see Season changing in front of me. She hardened, right there, as if the last decade had never happened. She turned ferocious, throwing everything she had at us. We had believed it'd be a rout, but she turned out to be far more formidable than we'd expected, especially with the fury of a love lost powering her."

"Can't really blame her for that," Kerry opined. "I'd be really ticked if . . ." She let the sentence hang, unfinished.

He didn't seem to notice, though. He let go of one hand and fingered the scar on his jaw. "From someplace she drew an enchanted blade, and she pushed—physically pushed, like someone walking through water—her way past the spells I was casting at her, and she cut me with the knife. That put me out of the fight. I was in agony, losing blood, weak—any mortal would have been dead. I went down, passed out, I guess. Meanwhile she finished up with Abraham.

"When I came to"—His voice was tight now, his eyes narrowed to slits—"Abraham was dead. In pieces, like Caleb, only more of them. It looked like she had done it fast—a few slashing blows, one that cut off his right arm at the elbow, one across the left thigh, one at his throat. I must have appeared dead to her already—not surprising, really, since I was covered in blood, and my neck was cut wide open. I woke up in a hotel suite that was drenched in blood, with the remains of my brother and Caleb scattered around me, a knife on the ground, no Season in sight, and hotel personnel staring at me. One of the men vomited on the spot, and another ran to call the police. I was wanted for decades in Philadelphia after that— probably still am, since there's no statute of limitations on murder, but it's not like anyone is still expecting to find me.

"Things got more personal between us after that," he went on. "Season and me, I mean. I had killed someone she loved; she had done the same to me, and nearly finished me as well. However inadvertently, she had framed me for the brutal murder of my own brother. I had always hated her, thanks to my mother's stories, but now the depth of my emotion changed. I didn't just want her dead; I wanted to tear her apart with my bare hands, piece by piece, glorying in the expression of sheer agony on her face while I did it. You've heard the cliché about wanting to dance on someone's grave. I want more than that—I want to dance on her body while it's still steaming, still bloody and warm."

Daniel made the turn onto Emerald. Season's house was less than a block away. The conversational thread was worrying Kerry—instead of leading up to Daniel confessing some kind of deep feelings for her, he was, frankly,

freaking her out with his talk of bloody revenge. She supposed he was steeling himself for the battle at hand, preparing himself by remembering the
reasons for it. But she didn't like it at all.

He braked the car around the corner from Season's bungalow, behind
Scott's RAV4, in the shade of a jacaranda tree. "Sorry, I didn't mean this
to be so grim," he said as he shut off the engine. "What I really meant to
say, Kerry, is that I don't want to see anything happen to you today. I don't
want to repeat what happened to Season and Caleb. Now that I've found
you . . . I don't want to lose you, Kerry. Ever."

Well, that's better, Kerry thought. *Not quite a declaration of undying love, but
close enough for now.* She leaned over and kissed him on the cheek before she
opened her door. The doors of the RAV4 opened at the same time, and Scott
and Brandy stepped out. Even from the sidewalk, Kerry could feel the heat
radiating from the blacktop. She blinked against the sun and scorching air.

"She's still in there," Scott reported. "Unless she's got teleportation technology or something. We've been on this end, and Josh and Rebecca are
parked on the other. She hasn't budged."

"Season has a lot of talents," Daniel said seriously "Teleportation is not,
to my knowledge, one of them."

"Then she's in there," Scott reiterated. "How do we get her out?"

Daniel shook his head. "*We* don't," he said forcefully. "I take it from
here."

Brandy wagged a finger at him. "You got us into this, mister," she
declared. "You can't just shut us out of it now."

Daniel's gaze flitted from one to the other, and even down the block
where Kerry knew Rebecca and Josh were waiting for the word. "This is
where it gets well and truly dangerous," Daniel said. "Deadly. I don't want
you guys anywhere near here. You've done your part, and then some. Today
Season Howe dies, and you can all go about the rest of your lives knowing
that you've done a good thing, you've saved people you'll never meet."

Except we couldn't even save Mace, Kerry thought. "I think we want more than that, Daniel," she told him. "I know I do. After what we've been through, we want to be there for the end. We want to see Season finished, with our own eyes. We want to help if we can."

Brandy nodded, smiling. "Bulldog's got that right."

Scott didn't look as convinced, but as usual he was willing to go along with Brandy. "It's unanimous," he announced.

"What about Josh and Rebecca?" Daniel asked. "They can still get out of here if they want to."

"You'd have to ask them," Scott replied. He handed his cell phone to Daniel. "But I have a feeling I know what they'll say."

Daniel declined the phone, but used his own and called the other two. They walked down the street and around the corner, joining the rest of the group. Kerry felt pleased that they were all together for this—all except Mace, of course, but he wouldn't have wanted anything to do with it anyway. She thought it was important, though, for reasons she couldn't even really enumerate, that they be absolutely unanimous on this one.

As it turned out, they were.

Once the vote had been made clear, Daniel relented and outlined his plan. As soon as he started describing it, Kerry realized that he had expected them to want to take part from the very beginning—that the finger-tracing he'd done on his self-printed aerial photo had taken all of them into account, not just himself. She should have known he couldn't be in all of those places at once. As he'd said of Season, he had many talents, but some things were beyond even his abilities.

Five minutes later, everyone was on the move.

21

Kerry didn't have as far to go as most of the rest. Daniel had pointed out a big red SUV halfway down the short block, almost directly in front of Season's house but across the street, and instructed her to go sit on the ground behind it—right at the rear wheels, so Season wouldn't see her feet beneath the vehicle. Scott and Brandy hopped back in the RAV4 and drove past Season's place, then around the block. An alley bisected the block, lengthwise. Because Season's place was on the short connecting block between the main streets of Emerald and Felspar, the alley ran beside the fence enclosing her yard. They parked the car and got out, positioning themselves so they could see the whole line of Season's back fence. If she tried to run, they'd see her.

Not that they could stop her, at least not for long. But, as Daniel pointed out, all they had to do was slow her down.

It was, they all knew, potentially the most dangerous thing they'd ever attempted. Kerry found herself swallowing, again and again, as if her terror was something stuck in her throat. But it wouldn't go away. She felt cold and raw, like she'd been through a punishing hailstorm.

When Brandy and Scott were in place, a quick text alerted the others. Daniel started Rebecca and Josh on their way—what Josh called the Long Walk—down the block to take up positions at the front corners of Season's yard. While they walked, Daniel tossed Kerry a grin, blew her a kiss, and went to take his own position on the far side of a gray sedan parked on the street in front of the house next to Season's, on the corner of Emerald and Everts. Like Kerry, he ducked down behind the car, hidden from Season's view by the wheels. The dark sky of gloaming made hiding all the easier.

When they were all in position, Daniel gave Rebecca and Josh the high sign. Standing at the corners of her yard, they began to call her name. "Season," they chanted. "Season Howe."

Hearing the chant begin, Brandy and Scott picked it up at the rear of the house. Within moments, all four were calling in unison. "Season. Season Howe."

"When she hears her name, she'll scan you from inside the house," Daniel had warned them. "She'll know that you don't have any magical abilities, though. I'm counting on her being too curious to resist checking you out further, to see what's going on, how you know who she is. She'll come outside."

Apparently Daniel knew her well. Kerry couldn't see what was going on—she was under strict orders not to make any part of herself visible to Season—but at one point, shortly after the four-part harmony kicked in, she thought Josh's voice caught, and then a moment later Rebecca's did the same. *She's scanning them,* Kerry realized with dismay, *and they can feel it. Feel her digging around inside them.*

Ick.

The chanting continued for another thirty seconds or so. Kerry had been worried that other neighbors would freak out at this undeniably odd behavior and call the police or interfere themselves. Daniel had assured her that it wouldn't be a problem, and she hadn't been anxious for him to elaborate on that.

So when she heard a door open and then close, she was pretty sure that it was Season. Doubly so when she heard the woman's voice.

"Who are you? What do you want?"

She would, Daniel had warned, be on full alert when she came outside. She would obviously know that something was going on, that her cover had been blown, but at first she wouldn't know why and by whom. The key to taking her was to keep her off guard, keep her wondering just what was happening, and not to let her raise the proper defense in time.

Now she was outside, though, and that was Kerry's cue. She could barely get her legs to cooperate, and her hands were shaking like crazy, flopping around like two fish on a line. But finally she got her appendages in order and emerged from behind the SUV. When she spoke, her voice even surprised her with the authority she managed to put into it.

"We're here for you, Season Howe," she said. "We know who you are. We know what you are. And we're here to make sure this is your last day on Earth."

The witch was standing on her front porch. Now, she turned to face Kerry. A storm of emotion washed across Season's beautiful face. A moment of shock when she recognized Kerry, or at least a realization that she had seen her before. That was followed by amusement, when, Kerry believed, she understood that she was being called out by five powerless mortals who hadn't even come bearing traditional weapons much less mystical ones. Kerry was gratified by what looked like a moment of doubt, as if she was second-guessing herself, wondering if these five were as powerless as they looked, because if they were, how would they have dared to confront her?

But her face settled into anger, clouded and red, as she regarded Kerry across the street. "I know you," she said, her voice quaking with rage. "You . . . you were with him. With Daniel Blessing."

"That's right," Kerry answered. This part hadn't been scripted, and she was winging it. But she felt emboldened by Season's anger—the witch wouldn't be so mad if she wasn't concerned, she figured.

And she has every reason to be concerned.

Season stepped down from her porch, beckoning Kerry with one crooked finger. "Come here," she commanded. "I want to talk to you."

Kerry maintained her position next to the SUV, so she could duck behind it for cover at any moment. She didn't have to wait long, though. As soon as Season's shoe clicked on the sidewalk in front of her house, Daniel made his move.

He rose up from behind the gray car like a jack-in-the-box. Spoke one of the words that Kerry still couldn't understand, but which Daniel had told her were in an incredibly ancient tongue, long since forgotten by most humans. Made a hurling motion with both hands toward Season, who only now noticed his presence. Again, her expression changed rapidly, rotating through a variety of emotions—surprise, fear, fury—in the space of a quarter second.

That was all the time she had.

Formed from empty air, picking up apparent mass and force as it went, Daniel's spell had created, manifested, or otherwise brought into being a roiling ball of pure energy. At least that's what it looked like to Kerry's admittedly untutored eye. Transparent, it seemed to warp the view behind it, the way heat shimmers the scenery on a summer day. She could only see its outline by watching where the background was clear and where it wavered and shifted.

Season barely had time to register it before the energy ball struck her with a sound like a thunderclap.

The force of the impact drove her to her knees, blasting her hair like a hurricane wind, shredding her blouse. When it was past she glared up at Daniel with fire in her eyes, a thin trickle of blood running from the corner of her mouth.

And another one hit her, laying her out on her back.

Season swore, scrabbled to turn over, to regain her footing. The next one slammed into her before she could stand steadily, but when she went down this time, it was on her stomach.

Daniel kept up the attack. Kerry watched in dumfounded horror. The destructive potential contained inside Daniel had always been theoretical to her—potential, not actual. Seeing it at work was terrifying. She knew it was for the best possible reasons, knew it had to be done.

But that didn't make it easy to watch.

Daniel changed weapons now. Instead of the roiling energy balls, he spoke different words of the ancient language, and bolts of violet lightning seemed to issue from his fingertips, blasting at Season like the weapons of Zeus. Where they struck her, her clothing tore, her skin smoldered.

Still, she lived.

Still, she fixed Daniel Blessing with a murderous glare.

She hadn't had a chance since he had launched his attack to counterattack. He had never let up, not for a moment. His plan, simple as it was, had worked to the letter.

Season Howe was finished, Kerry thought. Daniel had fulfilled his lifelong goal.

Finally, after what seemed an unbearably long and torturous assault, Season was still.

She lay on the walkway leading up to her front steps. Blood streaked the pale cement. Her body looked, in the pale remnants of daylight, as if it had lost an endurance contest with a threshing machine: cuts and tears everywhere, clothing ribboned.

Kerry started toward her, but Daniel waved her away. She glanced around, saw that Brandy and Scott had come up from the back and joined Rebecca and Josh in the street. Brandy's eyes were wide and glittering with fear—at last, Kerry understood, even she believed what the rest already accepted. Kerry would go stand with them, she decided, and wait for Daniel's all clear.

It never came.

Season was dead, anyone could see that. She'd stopped moving long before, except for involuntary motions, her body buffeted about by the force of Daniel's attack. Even then, he had not let up. Finally she was as limp as BoBo, the rag-doll clown Kerry had slept with from the time she was three until after her mother got sick, when Kerry had decided it was time to grow up, to stop playing with toys, because she was the only functional person left in the house.

Still, Daniel approached her with caution. Stood a dozen feet from her and watched the body, looking for any sign of breath, of life. Satisfied, he moved closer. Stopped, watched again. Closer.

Finally crouched over her. Touched her shoulder, rocking her over, onto her back, and releasing.

Limp. Lifeless.

Kerry knew Daniel by now, knew him well enough to recognize the look of relief that washed across his face. Relief, and something else.

Accomplishment. He had done it. *They* had done it—distracted her, made her forget to look for the real threat.

Daniel locked eyes with Kerry, smiling. Kerry tried to look into those eyes, from this distance, tried to tell him with her own gaze that she loved him. That she always had, somehow, from that first night. That she always would.

So neither one of them noticed that the witch moved her hand—just a simple move, really, a flick of the wrist, almost casual. An observer might have thought it was a postmortem reflex.

But it wasn't. There was purpose behind it. Season's lips moved at the same time, uttering an ancient phrase of her own.

And Season's attack, at such close range—even through her own pain, her own seeming defeat—was devastating.

One second Kerry was looking into Daniel's gray eyes and the next, those eyes were scrunched shut, his face twisted in agony, his knees buckling. *Oh, no,* Kerry thought, but the rest of her thought was wordless, just fear piled upon horror upon the misery of seeing the man she loved brought down by a sudden, treacherous blow.

Season moved again, not much more than a twitch—this time, Kerry watched her, a soundless scream on her lips—and again, Daniel was wracked with pain. He fell to his hands and knees in Season's yard, still facing away from her, toward Kerry. His head hung down toward the lawn but he raised it, his gaze meeting Kerry's once again, holding it, and he was trying to mouth something to her when Season struck a third time.

The last time.

Season managed to push herself to her own knees now, and clearly she wasn't dead, after all—should have been, anyone else would have been, but not her. Her face contorted in rage and she moved both hands this time, mouth speaking words Kerry couldn't even hear over the thunderous roar that accompanied her motion, and Daniel—

Kerry tried to focus on his eyes, those warm, loving eyes, not on the rest of it.

—and Daniel let out a last cry, a wail of loss and longing, as Season's blast crushed him like a squirrel under the wheel of a semitruck. His body collapsed, his spine splintered, his limbs suddenly giving out, blood jetting in every direction, landing with a wet splatter like a lawn sprinkler. His eyes shone for a brief moment and then closed, and with a final shudder he fell onto the grass.

And Season stood, rose up to her full height, fists clenched, face still showing traces of anger but also something else, something that looked like sorrow, and she ignored the others huddled in the street, looking only at Kerry.

Kerry swallowed. Season had defeated Daniel—*killed Daniel,* she corrected herself, she never wanted to let go of that knowledge. She would never forgive Season for that. But at the same time, she didn't exactly want Season to unleash that power against her.

Season didn't. Instead she spoke words Kerry could comprehend, though it took her a few moments to track them, to realize what the witch was saying to her.

"This is done now," Season said without preamble. "This was between me and Daniel Blessing. At long last, it's over. He lost. I won. That's all there is to it. Go now, and don't concern yourselves any longer with issues far beyond your ken. Know that I could easily do to you as I did to him, but I'm not. I won't. Just go."

"But . . . ," Kerry began. "You . . . you killed him."

"As he very nearly did me." Season crossed her arms defiantly across her chest. "Go. Before I lose patience."

"He . . ." Kerry felt hands on her arm. Rebecca's voice whispered to her. "Kerry, for God's sake let's get out of here. You saw—"

"I saw."

"—what she did to Daniel. We can't fight her. Come on."

"But . . ."

"She's right," Josh said. "This is lose-lose. Cut your losses and let's go."

Now there were other hands on her, tugging on her. In her yard, standing over Daniel's lifeless form, Season nodded her head. She looked almost sympathetic now, as if she understood what Kerry was feeling.

Maybe she did. Kerry remembered the story Daniel had told, just a few minutes ago, really, about Caleb. The one man Season had loved.

Maybe she'd just had her long-delayed revenge for that.

Well, Kerry thought, *revenge can go two ways.* She let the hands tug her away, toward the waiting car.

Away from Daniel, and Season.

Her eyes filled with tears, her heart with sorrow.

Daniel . . .

Kerry Profitt's diary, September 1

I'm writing this at 33,000 feet, scrunched into the window seat of a 737, nonstop from San Diego to Chicago. The guy next to me is snoring, his bulk slopping over the armrest into my space. It's a red-eye, of course— only appropriate, given my bloodshot, puffy peepers. The plan is to meet Aunt Betty and Uncle Marsh in Chicago, then spend a couple of days there together before I go on to Northwestern. I'm hoping that we'll be able to fill the days—Field Museum, shopping on the Miracle Mile, pizza at Gino's East, coffee in Wicker Park, etc.—enough so that B & M won't fight with each other, or me, too much.

I called Aunt Betty and asked her to bring a few things from the house with her, most especially BoBo the clown. I'm feeling the need for some comforting, some retreat, some healing. Hoping he can help with that.

It took us a couple of days to get past what had happened enough to clear out of the apartment and separate. Josh off to UNLV, Rebecca to UC Santa Cruz, Scott and Brandy beginning the long cross-country drive back to Harvard. And me, on a plane to O'Hare, and a life that suddenly feels like someone else's, not at all like the me I expected a month ago to see sitting on that plane in the dark. In my suitcase, along with my clothes and a couple of personal things, are Daniel's journals, all of them that I could find, anyway. And the letter.

Oh yeah, the letter.

It was on my pillow when I got home that night. It had not been there when I left the apartment—I was in the bedroom last, and Daniel didn't go in at all after coming out from his "preparations" in his room. So, no letter then.

But letter after. Go figure. Daniel has his ways.

It's not long, and of course I've read it so many times it's committed to memory. But considering the way it came into being, who knows when it might vanish again? So I'll put it down here, and if I have a word or two wrong I'll correct it later.

Dearest Kerry,

I liked the way that looked, and read it several times, right off the bat. Even spoke the words out loud, much to Rebecca's surprise. Plus, I was not looking forward to the rest of it, since I was pretty convinced it wasn't good news.

Dearest Kerry,

If you see this letter, it means I did not beat Season after all, and that she destroyed me. If you had to watch that—and, knowing you, I'm guessing you did; certain I couldn't dissuade you if you had put your mind to it—I am sorrier than you will ever know.

It was, of course, never my intent to involve you in this whole business. My fight, not yours, and all of that. Still, since we were thrown together, by fate or whatever you might choose to name it, I am proud and honored that you chose to throw in your lot with me.

But now it's over for you. I know you'll be angry at Season, and sad to have lost me, but please, please don't get it into your head that you can somehow avenge my death. I think I told you once that Season is quite possibly the most powerful of us. I had a chance, though a slim one, and apparently not a good enough one. You wouldn't. You are a remarkable woman, wise and mature and breathtakingly lovely, but you wouldn't last ten seconds against Season Howe.

So put this summer's experiences into your box of memories. Treasure the brief time we had together. Mourn me for a short while, and then get on with the rest of your life. It will be an incredible adventure, and I only wish I could be there to share it with you.

Death, Kerry, is not the end. It's a passage, a process. In some fashion I will be forever with you, and you will always be a part of me.

In life, though I never said it—I didn't want you to feel any obligation to me, and I knew that our time together might be short and end brutally—I loved you. In death, I love you still.

So, forward! Aspire! Achieve!

I remain,

Daniel Blessing

Yeah . . . so what do you do with that?

Captain just announced that he's beginning our descent. In another few minutes, laptops will have to be put away, tray tables stowed, and all that stuff. Then Aunt Betty and Uncle Marsh will be there, and then college. Endings, beginnings. Passages.

More later.

K.

FALL

So, okay, college? Not exactly what I figured it'd be.

I mean, the campus is nice, the classes moderately interesting. My favorite is an American history lecture from one Dr. Page Manning, who is not only a terrific and often funny speaker, but can really make the subject come alive.

Not in the way that Daniel Blessing could, of course. But then, Daniel lived a lot more of it. I think it is his influence, though, that inspired me to take the class in the first place, letting me see history in a way that I never had, as something more than just dates and battles and the names of dead white men. I'm thinking about it as a major.

Minoring in depression, I guess.

I miss him SO much. Like I said, college is okay, but it's full of skimpy-outfitted Rihannas and baggy-pantsed, backward-hat boys trying to grow goatees and personalities at the same time, and after what I went through this summer, what WE went through, Scott and Brandy and Rebecca and Josh and poor Mace, and me—and Daniel, who, like Mace, paid the ultimate price—sitting in lecture halls, taking notes, doing homework in the dorm . . . it all just seems so tame. So removed from the rest of the world.

Not that I'd know what the rest of the world was really like, having spent most of my life removed from it by one thing or another. But still, you know.

It's like the summer was in Technicolor and campus life is in sepia tones. Washed out sepia, at that. I keep finding my mind flashing back to San Diego, to the hunt for Season Howe that consumed us all. And to the final battle that Daniel didn't survive.

I don't know where Season is now, obviously. I couldn't fight her if I did. But I feel like if I saw her today, I'd rip her apart with my bare hands, so pumped up with righteous wrath that she couldn't begin to hold me back.

The nightmares haven't come back, so that's one small blessing (a word I have to remember not to capitalize, or to precede with "Daniel" on certain occasions). But my waking thoughts are so dark, so violent, sometimes so hopeless, that it's hard to see the difference.

No, I take that back. I never really knew where the nightmares came from. I know perfectly well where this darkness originates, though. It comes from having watched the man I love get killed. Murdered, right in front of me, by an evil witch named Season Howe.

And some day, somehow, she's going to pay.

More later.
K.

1

"Kerry?"

Kerry Profitt tore her gaze away from the screen of her laptop. She had lost focus anyway, the words she'd been typing blurred behind a film of tears. "Yeah?"

Sonya, her roommate in Northwestern University's Elder Hall, looked at her from her own desk with motherly concern. Sonya's eyes were big and brown, accentuated all the more by small-lensed but thick glasses and an expression of perpetual curiosity, as if she were a visitor to this world, trying to take in everything at a single glance. Sonya tugged a lock of her short, dark hair away from her cheek and positioned it behind her ear. "You okay?" she asked.

"Yeah, I'm . . . you know. Fine."

"Because you don't look so okay," Sonya went on. "What with the tears kind of splashing on your keyboard, I thought maybe there was something bothering you."

"Well, I guess maybe a little," Kerry admitted. She hadn't given Sonya the What-I-Did-On-My-Summer-Vacation talk, not expecting that her roommate, or, when it came right down to it, anyone else, would believe a word of it. And maybe it'd be worse if they did believe it, because she knew how hard it was to deal with the fact that the world was so much different than she had thought it was. Things she had always believed to be unreal, to be fantasy, had turned out to be absolutely true. It made "real" life seem like a cartoon, like someone else's version of reality. Why force that knowledge onto others?

She had, to cover her sometimes abrupt moments of grieving, told Sonya about the deaths of her parents, and said that they had been topped off by the death of a boyfriend over the summer. She just avoided the minor details, such as precisely how the boyfriend had died, and the fact that he had been a very powerful witch who was almost three hundred years old.

"Daniel?" Sonya asked.

Kerry nodded. "I miss him. A whole lot."

Sonya turned in her chair, and Kerry thought she was about to give her the You've-Got-To-Move-On-With-Your-Life lecture again. But Sonya was wise enough to catch the way that Kerry tensed—a pose that said, *If you start that again I* will *pummel you*—and she restrained herself. "I'm going out with Dougie and Ben," she said instead, naming the two guys she was juggling, though it seemed that Dougie was winning out. "Maybe get some falafel, have a beer. You want to come?"

Kerry appreciated the invitation, and said so. "But I'll stay in," she added. "I still have a bunch of homework to get done before tomorrow."

Sonya shrugged. "As long as you're really doing homework," she said, "and not sitting here by yourself moping."

"No," Kerry tried to assure her. "I'm okay, really."

The truth was she didn't want to have falafel and beer with Dougie and Ben and Sonya. Their interests were not hers, their lives seemed flat and boring somehow. They would talk about professors and classmates, or the latest band that had captured their fancy, or they'd dis some style they hadn't taken up yet but would soon. She'd been part of such conversations in the past, and probably would be again—she remembered, with some fondness, how all she'd wanted at the beginning of the summer was to have a "normal" life, like everyone else's. Now she had an opportunity to have just that, and it couldn't have held less interest for her.

"You say so." Sonya gave her short hair a little flip, pulled a jacket off a hook by the door, and left.

The room, with Sonya out of it, suddenly felt twice its real size. She was a perfectly nice girl, but her presence in the room seemed to suck the air out of it. Kerry knew it was her own fault, not Sonya's—anyone else would be glad to have Sonya for a roommate. *I'm spoiled,* she thought, *that's what it is. I want Daniel, or nothing at all.*

She wondered if it was stupid to spend her life wishing for things she couldn't have. It probably was, she decided—a huge waste of time and energy. Trouble was, she didn't know quite what she could do about it. She was who she was, and if there was a way to change that she didn't know it.

She went to the window and looked at the campus spread out below her third-floor window. Trees flamed yellow and red in the glow cast by streetlights and spilling from the dorm. The Illinois air was crisp but not yet cold—jackets were required at night, but the days were still warm enough for shirts and the occasional sweater. She had always liked this time of year, before—the cool evenings, the back-to-school excitement, then the Halloween season that led to football games and Thanksgiving and Christmas. Even now she could feel herself wanting to be caught up in it.

But if you have to want it, she thought sadly, *it's not really happening, is it? More wishing, that's all.*

I wish I didn't wish so much.

Rebecca Levine soaked in the big clawfooted bathtub of the house she and her friend Erin had rented near downtown Santa Cruz before summer break started. It wasn't much of a house—a run-down Victorian with faded green paint, floorboards that creaked like something from a horror movie, and wiring she was convinced would someday burn the whole thing to the ground. But they had a cat, and the plumbing worked fine and the water in the tub was steaming hot, and she had placed scented candles around the room before she got in. At some point Erin would yell at her to get out because they only had the one bathroom, but until that happened she'd make the most of it.

She had always loved baths, but during the last month of summer she hadn't had much opportunity to indulge. Too much had been going on—and it had been so sad. Now that it was all over, at least for her, she was trying to make up for August's privation. It had taken her a couple of weeks just to relax enough to do it, not to jump every time there was an unexpected noise or a shadow fell across her path. She still wasn't back to what she considered routine, and didn't know if she ever would be. But she was determined not to let that prevent her from indulging herself whenever she could.

Sleep? That was hard to come by, at least sleep uninterrupted by horrible visions and memories of Mace and Daniel and Season Howe. But in here, wet and steamy and alone, she could relax, let her mind float to happy places. Private sandy beaches, mountains thrusting up from canopied jungles, sidewalk cafés on wide Parisian boulevards . . . these were comforting images for Rebecca, and comfort was what she needed most. Holding Reynolds, their mutt of an alley cat, and feeling the motor of his purr while she read helped too. She'd gained almost ten pounds in the last couple of weeks, thanks to the comfort foods she had allowed herself. While she had never been skinny or cared that she wasn't, she recognized that eating her way to sanity was never going to work. So, the baths, the pampering, the self-indulgence.

Her classes this semester were pretty cool, though she was having a hard time getting into them. She was taking a poli sci class focusing on twentieth-century American political history, an introductory psych class, and an entomology class, figuring that the only way to get over a lifelong fear of bugs was to learn more about them. No luck on that, so far. Actually, knowing what insects could do to people only beefed up that particular phobia. At the same time, though, being afraid of creepy-crawlies at least took some of the edge off being afraid that Season Howe might come around at any time.

Rebecca breathed deeply, inhaling the aroma of the lilac-scented bath water and the vanilla candle nearest the tub. She luxuriated in the tactile sensation of the hot water against her skin and tried to push aside all other thoughts and cares.

If only she didn't ever have to come out . . .

"Pop-Tart?"

"Eeew," Brandy said, just as Scott had known she would. "How can you put that stuff in your body?"

He took a bite and spoke with his mouth full, letting crumbs spill out over his lips. "Kind of like this," he said, facing her and enjoying the way her pretty face twisted in revulsion. This one was strawberry, and fresh from the toaster so the filling was especially soft and gooey. She waved him away from her with an urgent motion.

"Yuck! Go away!"

Instead, he lowered his head toward hers, crumbs dropping onto the chemistry text spread in front of her on their dining room table. "Kiss me, baby," he demanded around the mouthful. "Gimme some sugar."

Now Brandy physically pushed him away, her hand against his shoulder. "All the sugar you're getting is already in your mouth," she told him.

Scott decided the joke had gone far enough and he turned away, finishing the bite in a more mannerly fashion. He loved to gross her out because she was such an easy target, but he knew that her tolerance for it was very limited, and on those occasions when he'd pushed too much her reaction had changed from good-humored to genuinely furious without notice. And a furious Brandy Pearson was a sight that Scott Banner didn't want to see too many times in his life.

"Sorry, babe," he said after he'd swallowed and chased the mouthful with a drink of water.

"Sure you are." Her words were clipped, her tone honestly angry. If he hadn't gone over the edge he'd come close to it, that was for sure.

"I'm just teasing, you know that."

"That kind of teasing I can do without."

Brandy had changed, Scott thought, since the summer. Her sense of humor—never her strongest suit to begin with—had diminished some-how, as if life just wasn't as funny as it had once been. He liked it when she laughed, loved the contrast between her even white teeth and her dark face, but these days it happened less and less. Although she had thrown herself into her studies at Harvard, she didn't seem any more removed from him—they held hands as they walked across campus just as they'd done before, they made love from time to time, they kissed when they parted and when they reunited. But the not-laughing thing bothered him, more than he wanted to admit even to himself.

He touched her shoulder gently. "I know. I'm sorry," he said again. He hoped he sounded sincere. The other thing about Brandy—*okay*, he real-ized, *this has always been true, but more so since the summer*—was that he really hated to be on her bad side. Not just because he loved her and wanted to make her happy, but because she was a little scary when she was angry. He'd seen the power of rage now—Season Howe had demonstrated that—and Brandy was nowhere near that kind of level. But still, Scott guessed, he was a little gun-shy.

"Just . . . try to be an adult," she admonished him. "Pretend, anyway."

The rest of their apartment was dark, the only lights burning the ones in the dining area, where they did most of their studying. The table was almost lost under mounds of books and papers, with precious little space left for actual dining. A living room opened onto the dining area, with a computer, TV, and stereo system, and past that their cramped bedroom waited. Scott knew that he needed to put some space between them right now—space and time. If he turned on the TV or music, though, she'd complain that it was interfering with her studying. Instead, he grabbed a short-story anthology off one of the stacks on the table. "I'm going to read for a while," he said, and headed toward the bedroom, where he could find solitude and solace until she decided to join him.

Space. And time.

UNLV would have usurped all of Josh Quinn's time if he'd let it, but the casinos beckoned, and he couldn't bring himself to ignore their call. Every time he saw them, neon shining so bright that the stars dimmed, he felt like Ulysses tied to the mast, trying to resist the sirens.

But there was no one to bind Josh down, and Ulysses hadn't fared all that well either, come to think of it. So whenever he didn't need to be in class—and sometimes when he did—Josh found himself haunting the Strip or the older casinos downtown. *Ocean's 11* country—the original, not the lame remake. On this night, that's where he was, downtown at the Golden Nugget, enveloped in a soundtrack of bells and buzzers and clanging coins. He was too young to gamble by a few years but he had a fake ID that no one ever checked. He didn't have much money to risk at the best of times, and this was not the best of times, so he resigned himself to video poker. It was hard to win big at that, but it was possible to play for a long time on a ten-dollar roll of quarters.

He'd been sitting at the machine for almost forty minutes, puffing on a succession of smokes, feeding the coins in one or two at a time, playing his hands with as much care as he could, considering the machine was also the dealer. He punched the deal button and was dealt two fives—hearts and clubs—the jack of spades, ten of hearts, and seven of diamonds. A nothing hand, pretty much, and he'd blown two quarters on it. Two hearts . . . he could shoot for a flush but that was almost a guaranteed loser. He had a pair, but that wouldn't net him much. Keep the jack and dump the rest?

Finally he kept the two fives, pathetic as they were, and drew three new cards. Nine of spades and two eights. Now with two pair, the machine paid off. Still small change, but it would keep him going for a while.

If he ran out of money then he'd have to start the long walk back home. And if he did that, walking through the shadowed streets away from the lights and the action, then he'd think about her. About Season, and how she'd ripped the life from Daniel Blessing.

He didn't want to think about that. Instead, he fed two more quarters into the slot.

2

Home again, after far too long. The journey was an arduous one, as I had been in San Francisco when I received Mother Blessing's urgent summons. Urgent or no, one can only cross this great nation at a certain speed, even by railroad. Arriving at Norfolk, I hired a carriage and drove to the old Slocumb site, where she keeps a skiff for precisely such visits.

Great Dismal Swamp greeted me as it always does, and this was my first real indication that I had indeed come home. The smells of the brackish water and the white cedar, the screams and cries of blackbirds, warblers, and robins, the mechanical knocking of woodpeckers, the incessant drone of mosquitoes: All these things brought a rush of memory to my mind, memories of my youth growing up among these marshes and bogs, learning the craft at Mother Blessing's side. No matter where I travel—to the jagged peaks of the Rocky Mountains, the softly sculpted dunes of Arabia, the villages of Europe—Great Dismal's walls of trees and thick cover of ferns, mosses, camellia, and dwarf trillium remain the standard of natural beauty in my heart.

As I poled the skiff through the swamp, I watched for the long-missed but always-remembered landmarks—the lightning-split oak, the stand of bald cypress shaped like the corner of a log fort, the trio of stumps rumored to have been cut by George Washington himself, rising up from the water like swimmers seeking air—that would presently lead me to Mother Blessing's cabin.

Soon enough, I was here, and that is when I learned the reason for her call. Mother Blessing lay atop her bed, flushed and fevered, writhing and thrashing in evident pain. I quickly performed a healing spell, glad that even through her delirium, she had been able to reach out to me in time. My spell calmed her and broke her fever, and before long she was sleeping soundly.

While waiting for her to recover, I cleaned the cabin, which had been clearly suffering from neglect due to her illness. By evening she was awake and alert enough to drink some broth I had prepared for her, and to take a cup of tea. After she had her strength back a bit, she told me that a witch down in South Carolina had cursed her after they'd had a disagreement over some small matter.

I write this now by candlelight, with Mother Blessing asleep again in her room, snoring softly. My spells have helped her, and she is of course powerful enough to help herself now that she's on her guard. But tomorrow I must leave for South Carolina, to find the witch and make her remove the curse.

Or else I shall have to kill her. Either way will work.

I remain,

Daniel Blessing, April 7, 1881

Kerry had just shut the journal and replaced the leather thong that held it closed when Sonya and Dougie entered, arm in arm, laughing at some joke Kerry wasn't privy to. "Hey, Kerry," Dougie said by way of greeting. "That doesn't look like any textbook I've ever seen. What is it?"

"It's an old journal," Kerry replied, not wanting to reveal any more than that. Dougie annoyed her—she considered him a typical frat boy but without the frat, all about using his college years to drink and party and have a good time, knowing that at the end of it his degree and his father's connections would guarantee him a good job even if he never set foot in a classroom. She didn't quite know what Sonya saw in him, but then she didn't know Sonya well enough to speculate.

He disentangled himself from Sonya and reached for it. "Lemme see."

Kerry jerked it away from his grasping hands. "It's very old," she insisted, "and fragile."

Dougie screwed his blunt, good-old-boy features into a mask of hurt. "Jeez, I wasn't gonna damage it," he declared. "I just wanted to look at it."

"Kerry's pretty protective of her stuff," Sonya told him. Kerry noted her tone, as if she were talking about someone who wasn't in the room.

"Just the stuff that needs protecting," she countered. "This journal is more than a hundred years old, and the paper is brittle. I can't let anything happen to it."

"It's okay, Kerry—chill," Sonya chided. "No one's going to mess with it. Dougie's just having fun."

"More than you are, it looks like," Dougie added. "Looks like you need a boyfriend, Kerry. You shouldn't be sitting around here on a Saturday night with some moldy old book."

"You don't have to worry about me," Kerry answered, wishing he'd just go away. She sat on her bed and picked up BoBo, her old childhood rag-doll clown. "I'm fine."

"Tell you the truth, Kerry," Sonya said, dropping her voice to a conspiratorial level, "we were kind of hoping you had gone out for a while, if you know what I mean."

Sonya's meaning couldn't have been more clear. *But do I want to do her that favor?* Kerry asked herself. *Do I want to clear out of my own room so she and her horndog boyfriend can have their fun . . . and maybe paw through my stuff—even Daniel's journals—when they're done?*

Resigned, she gathered up the things she'd need to spend an hour in the common area. For about the millionth time since the semester had started, she wished she had a private room.

By the time she had settled on one of the couches in the third-floor lounge, Kerry was fuming. Two girls she knew vaguely shared another couch and spoke in hushed tones about a project they were working on together, but blessedly the TV was off and the faint smell of microwave popcorn that hung in the air when she entered dissipated quickly. She made it clear that she was there to study, not socialize, and she buried herself in the American history text that she should have been reading instead of Daniel's journal. The words seemed dry and lifeless to her, though, especially compared to the journals, or even more, to Daniel's voice, telling her things about her nation's past that had never made it into the history books.

Kerry was trying, really and truly, to immerse herself in school, to put Daniel and Season and the rest of it behind her. And Kerry was someone who did what she put her mind to—they hadn't called her Bulldog over the summer for nothing. So why couldn't she just focus on the work? Why did images of Daniel pop up, unbidden, every time her mind wandered? Why did she keep seeing Season in every blond woman on campus?

The whole situation was just incredibly frustrating. She turned back to the history text and tried to read about the landing at Plymouth Rock, but the words turned to fuzz before her eyes.

Daniel was there, in her dream, looking just as he had in life. His long-sleeved white shirt was clean and crisp, tucked into faded jeans, the sleeves rolled back a couple of times over muscular forearms. His hair was long and windblown, and he was laughing, head thrown back, mouth open, teeth even and white, gray eyes crinkled at the corners and dimples etched into his cheeks. He stood on a hill, at a slight distance from Kerry; she couldn't reach him or even hear his laughter, which should have been booming.

She moved closer to him, or tried to. But for every step forward she took, the hilltop on which he stood seemed to move back. She tried calling out to him, shouting his name, but even her own voice vanished before it reached her ears.

Then a fog rolled in, as if from offshore—thick and wet, blotting out the view, blocking Daniel, then the entire hillside. Within seconds Kerry was alone, an island in a sea of white mist. Then even she was gone, the mist breaking her body into ever smaller chunks until it had disappeared completely.

Kerry Profitt's diary, October 21

And again with the nightmares, now. All I need, right? Having gotten rid of them once—thanks, I am now convinced, to the appearance of Daniel in my life—they are back, and, it seems, with a vengeance. This one wasn't even all that scary in itself—I mean, the imagery wasn't—but the overall feel of it creeped me out big time. Especially the way that Daniel was there, and then he wasn't, and . . .

Oh, never mind. It's different from the dreams I used to have, which I forgot as soon as they ended. And a year from now I won't remember what the dream was, and this entry will make no sense.

Which distinguishes it from the rest of my life how, exactly?

Now Sonya is sleeping hard and I am wide awake, pretty much giving up on the idea of sleeping tonight. And since it's fresh in my mind, I can't stop thinking about the dream.

Its meaning? Obvious, I think. I miss Daniel. He was taken from me. Duh. Bonehead psych, no-brainer.

The part where I disappear? A little tougher, that. Losing my identity? Maybe.

And maybe I should e-mail Brandy for a more comprehensive analysis. She's the doc, after all. I have her addy—we all have each other's, and have sent a few around since splitting up back in SD after the summer. But not as much as I thought we might, almost as if everyone wants to forget what happened, wants to leave Season and Daniel and the summer of our discontent well behind.

And really, who can blame 'em for that? It pretty much sucked. Find a great guy, and he dies. Find out witchcraft is real and scarier than you ever imagined, and the baddest witch around has it in for your new BF. Find out he's been chasing her for almost 300 years, so you help him catch her, only to watch her kill him.

Yeah, summer means fun.

Okay, here's the thing. School is just not happening for me. Sonya . . . ditto. Aunt Betty and Uncle Marsh check in from time to time, but I could be gone from here for a month before they knew it. So really, what's keeping me here? Lack of someplace better to go?

Only, see, I have an idea about that, too.

I've been reading Daniel's journals. That's just about the only thing that's held my interest, in fact. And Daniel is lost to me.

But that doesn't mean that part of my life has to be lost. Mother Blessing is out there, in the Great Dismal Swamp. Season Howe is out there too, still at large, and now owing for yet another crime.

One that I take just a little bit personally.

So here's my theory. I find Mother Blessing, convince her to teach me witchcraft, and then I hunt down Season Howe and give her what she deserves.

Nothing to it, right?

But did I mention people call me Bulldog?

More later.

K.

3

"McKinley's policies, particularly his unwavering support of the gold standard, helped build confidence among business-people and limited the effects of the depression," Professor Crain declared. "Which, incidentally, cemented Republican domination until the 1930s, at which time they lost it, largely due to the much greater Depression, which had been the ultimate result. Short term, the economy seemed to be doing well. But the truth was, that period was called the Gilded Age for a reason. The rich got richer and the poor became ever more destitute, and the gulf between them had never been greater. Long term, that helped lead to a financial collapse that was the most catastrophic in our nation's history."

Rebecca tried to take careful notes when Professor Crain spoke. She had already learned that he mingled historical fact with personal opinion in his lectures, and while he welcomed analysis that differed from his, one had better be prepared to back up one's differences. In any case, she found herself agreeing with him more often that not. Word was, on almost any other college campus he'd have a reputation as a bit of an ideologue, but this was UC Santa Cruz, where nonconformity was the norm and strong opinions were highly valued.

Anyway, his lectures were always stimulating, and the difficulty of his essay tests, while legendary, helped keep her interested. Lately, she'd been having a harder and harder time even getting out of bed in the morning. Reynolds, their cat, had taken to sleeping on the bed with her in the mornings, and as the year progressed and the weather cooled, the cozy comfort of her quilt with a purring cat pressed against her became more and more difficult to leave. Knowing that to miss even one of Professor Crain's lectures would lead to certain disaster come midterms helped spur her up and out of the house. Three afternoons a week, after class, she worked at a local coffee shop called the Human Bean, and that was the other motivating element—if she couldn't make it to school, she likely wouldn't make work either, and she'd be fired long before she flunked out.

After class she stepped from the lecture hall, blinking in the bright sunshine. Hector Gonzales, a classmate she'd become friendly with, followed her outside. "Party tonight," he said as he sidled up beside her. "You got anything going on?"

She didn't. "I don't know if I'm up for a party," she said vaguely.

"It'll be fun. Two kegs, limited guest list—it's at a private house, some friends of mine. Not a frat kind of thing."

She knew that her hesitation stemmed from the same root as her disinterest in leaving the safety of her own bed. One never knew what might happen, around which corner doom might lurk. She'd never been brave, but she also hadn't thought of herself as a fearful person. She was well on her way to becoming one, though. She didn't want to turn into one of those people who were afraid to leave their own homes, but she felt that she was heading down that road. If she never left the safety of her room, she would be okay. It was other people, other places that were dangerous. She didn't want to become antisocial, but if that was the only way to stay safe . . .

She shook her head violently, and when she looked back at Hector he was staring at her with evident concern. "I'm fine, sorry," she assured him. "Just a little fried today."

"I was worried for a second," he said. "You aren't getting that cold that's going around, are you?"

"I don't think so," she said.

"So, what about later then?"

"Give me the address," she replied. "I'll try to make it if I can."

As it turned out, by nightfall she had talked herself into it. She hadn't been to many parties in the early part of this year, and they were, after all, an important part of the college experience. She found the address Hector had given her—a small, Spanish-style bungalow a few blocks from campus—and knew immediately it was the right place. Students spilled out the door into the yard, loud music chasing them the whole way. Strangers greeted her like old friends as she passed them and worked her way through the crowded doorway, looking for Hector. The air inside was thick with beer, hormones, and dance music.

When she found Hector, he was already beyond buzzed, and into the sloppy and obnoxious category. He sat on a couch with an empty bottle in his fist, staring right past her like he didn't even know her. Rebecca felt a twinge of regret—not that she thought she and Hector might turn into anything other than friends, but part of the reason she had come tonight was that she enjoyed talking to him before and after class and wanted to get better acquainted. Clearly, that wasn't happening.

Disappointed, she almost turned and walked out of the house without even having a drink. But the clot of people between her and the door had become almost impenetrable, and the music hammered her skull, so she spun on her heel and headed the other way, looking for a back way out. She was sorry she had come now, just wanted to get home where she belonged.

She pushed her way through a door that she thought led to the kitchen, but there was a girl coming out of it at the same time—a girl a year or two older than she was, Rebecca thought, tall and thin, with a curly mop of dark hair and bright, friendly eyes. "Hey," the girl said, regarding Rebecca carefully. "You're just what we need."

"We?" Rebecca echoed. "What we?"

The girl put a hand on Rebecca's shoulder and leaned close to her ear, as if sharing state secrets. "In the bedroom," she said, causing all sorts of images to flit into Rebecca's mind. "We're holding a séance."

"A séance?" Rebecca repeated. She could barely hear herself speak. "Don't you need, like, quiet and privacy for that?" The fact was, she didn't care what conditions might be required for a séance. She knew, better than these kids, certainly, what the supernatural was all about, and she wanted no part of it.

But the girl hadn't let go of her shoulder. "We'll have all the privacy we need," she assured Rebecca. "Everybody saw the freaky people go into the back bedroom; they won't dare come in. Anyway, there's a lock on the door. We already have four other people besides me, but we want an even number."

"Does that matter?" Rebecca found herself asking.

"I have no idea," the girl said. "It's Shiai's thing. She just sent me to get a sixth person—and a girl, 'cause it's boy-girl, boy-girl, you know."

Rebecca was torn. Mostly, she wanted to get out of here and go home. But she recognized that for what it was—*something*, she thought, *between fear and outright cowardice*. It was silly to be freaked out. These were just kids at a party, wanting to have a good time scaring themselves. The same impulse sent people to horror movies and Stephen King novels. Rebecca decided it wouldn't hurt to hang for a little while, see what these people were like. She could use some new friends, she knew, and maybe she'd find them here. The girl who had stopped her was certainly amiable.

"Okay," Rebecca said quickly, before she could change her mind again. "Lead on."

"I'm Amy," the girl announced, grabbing Rebecca's hand and tugging her down the hall.

"Rebecca."

"Good to meet you, Rebecca." Amy knocked twice on a door, then opened it. "We have success!" she called into a darkened room.

Cheers greeted her entry, and Rebecca started to feel glad that she'd decided to stick around. The room was lit by six candles, marking the six points of a star drawn on the hardwood floor with chalk. It looked more like a Star of David, Rebecca thought—an image she had grown up with—than any kind of magical pentangle or anything she could remember having seen. But then, Daniel Blessing hadn't really seemed to go in for that kind of thing, and he was her only contact with actual magic. So maybe it was authentic.

A person sat behind each candle. As Amy had described, they were seated boy-girl. Amy pointed and named at the same time, and Rebecca struggled to remember to whom she was being introduced. "Brad, Shiai, Donnie, Mark," she said. "And I'm Amy, like I said. And this is Rebecca."

"Hi, guys," Rebecca said, feeling shy now that she was center stage. At least the room was too dark for anyone to see her blush.

"Welcome, Rebecca," Shiai greeted her. Even though she was sitting down, Rebecca could see that she was short and squat, with chin-length blond hair streaked with green. Her sweater was black and snug, her jeans frayed at the hems. "Come on in. Have you ever been part of a séance?"

"Not really," Rebecca answered. No séances, and the occult activity she had been part of she wouldn't talk about here.

"Then you'll fit right in," Mark tossed out. "Neither have we!"

"But I read a book about it," Shiai added. "So I know basically what we're supposed to do."

Rebecca sat on the floor at the one empty star point, crossing her legs like the others had. She remembered having seen Brad on campus; he was tall, probably six and a half feet, with hair past his shoulders, and so was easy to spot and hard to forget. The others she wasn't sure she'd ever seen. Donnie was handsome, dark-haired and olive-skinned, and Mark was a little on the goofy side, with a short brush of red hair, freckles, and a crooked smile that was friendly and funny at the same time.

The company was comfortable for her, but she still had mixed feelings about the idea of a séance. Though she couldn't tell them why, she knew that messing around with the supernatural was not the safe, casual game they seemed to think. Her only consolation was that she didn't really expect them to be able to accomplish their goal—if indeed they had a goal beyond sitting in candlelight together and telling what would amount to ghost stories.

There were a few more moments of laughing and joking, but then Shiai took the lead, putting a finger to her lips. "We need to be quiet and concentrate," she instructed. "We should all join hands."

Rebecca reached out to Mark on her right and Donnie on her left. Their hands were warm, and she noticed that Mark's trembled a little. Nervous about the séance, or about holding hands with a strange girl, she couldn't tell. *It's not like I've been holding hands with a lot of boys lately,* she thought. *Or doing anything else with them, for that matter.* But she kind of liked the sensation.

Shiai moved a seventh candle to the center of the star. "Focus on the flame," she said in a hushed voice. "Try to clear your minds of any stray thoughts."

She stopped speaking then. Music from the front room rattled the door, but Rebecca, in the spirit of the moment, tried to block it out, to concentrate her entire being on the flickering candle before her. After many minutes, the breathing of everyone around her had settled into a steady rhythm. She felt her own body's breath, her heartbeat, the heat of the hands on hers, and then even those things slipped away She might as well have been floating on a cloud in a night-dark sky, staring into the glow of a faraway star. Sound lost distinction, filling the space around her like soft cotton but without meaning. She became cognizant at some point that Shiai was speaking again.

". . . part the veils between this world and the next, and give us a sign of your presence," she was saying. "Slip the ties that bind you to that world and appear before us . . ."

Rebecca stopped paying attention to the words and let them join the music as just a sound that filled the dark room. Gravity had lost its hold, space and time folded in on themselves, and still Shiai droned on . . .

And then the candle's flame leapt from its quarter-inch height to become more than a foot tall, its bright light blasting her darkness-adjusted eyes like a camera's flash. Amy shrieked and Mark let out a loud curse. Rebecca tightened her grip on him and Donnie, her heart suddenly thundering. *This isn't supposed to happen,* she thought, *or it's a trick of some kind, a fake candle.*

But when Shiai continued, her voice was different, tremulous, and Rebecca knew that it was no fake she was part of. "Now tell us who you are," she commanded. "We know that you are here with us—identify yourself."

The candle had only blossomed for a second, and then its flame had returned to normal. Rebecca stared at it again, its light seemingly diminished even more in contrast to the sudden brightness. As Shiai continued, her voice caught, and Rebecca glanced away from the candle at her.

And she saw—where Shiai should have been—a blond woman, older than Shiai, leaner, taller, with a distinct sense of poise and elegance.

Season Howe.

Rebecca screamed.

She felt hands on her—Mark and Donnie and Amy, crowding around, trying to comfort her. She dared another look, and Shiai sat cross-legged across from her, anxious and frightened. "What is it?" she asked. "What's wrong, Rebecca?"

"Yeah, you scared the holy crap outta me," Mark added.

Rebecca swallowed, trying to regain some composure. It was only Shiai, after all.

But for that moment, it had seemed so real.

"Nothing . . . I'm sorry," Rebecca said haltingly. "I should . . . I should go."

"But we're not fin . . ." Brad began. He let the sentence die. The séance, as far as Rebecca was concerned, was finished. The others could stay here as long as they wanted. Rebecca rose unsteadily to her feet, supporting herself on Mark.

"I'm really sorry," she said again. The others tried to soothe her, to reassure her that her outburst had not been a problem.

But it was a problem for her. She hurried from the party as fast as she could, out into the cool night air for the walk home.

It was not really Season, she thought, trying to convince herself. It had only been her imagination running wild, that and the retinal burn from the candle's flare, making her see Shiai in a different way.

Because if it had been Season, that would mean that the witch was somehow looking for her, tracking them on the astral plane or something like that.

And that would just be too scary for words.

After dozing for a few hours, Kerry got to work.

She skipped her morning class, staying in bed until after Sonya left. Outside, a leaden sky glowered angrily, so Kerry was just as happy to remain in the warm comfort of her own space. She tugged on a Northwestern hoodie and cotton drawstring pants, tied her long black hair back with an elastic, and began.

Her first task was to pull all four of Daniel's journals from the bookshelf and scan them for any references to the Great Dismal Swamp, or to Mother Blessing's cabin. There turned out to be very few of either, but whenever she found one with useful details, she made notes. She had always thought it an interesting coincidence that Daniel, like her, kept a journal, and concluded that it wasn't just coincidence, it was one of the factors that drew them together, one of the points of similarity that made them appreciate each other. Daniel's journals—*just like a man,* she thought—were long on incident and short on emotion, while her own diaries were almost all about her feelings and reactions instead of recounting what exactly happened in her life.

Gradually, though, piece by piece, she drew together a mental picture of the Swamp and the route one would take to find Mother Blessing's cabin deep inside it. Of course, whether that mental picture would prove to be at all helpful was yet to be seen. Interestingly, according to his vague descriptions, the Swamp didn't change much over the years, but Mother Blessing seemed to keep her cabin updated, enlarging it and modernizing it from time to time. It had started as a one-room trapper's shack, but in the most recent entries Kerry could find, from the mid-1970s, it was a four-room cabin that sounded almost luxurious.

Noon had come and gone by the time she finished her paging through, and she hadn't even had breakfast. Putting the journals away, she made a trip to the floor's vending machines and bought a prepackaged sandwich, some chips, and an orange soda. She said hello to the few people she passed in the hall, but avoided conversation. Her body was in Evanston, Illinois, but her mind was far away, and she wanted desperately to stay in that place.

Back in the safety of her room, Kerry went online and searched the Net for information about Great Dismal. It turned out to be a national wildlife refuge, which she hadn't known, straddling the border between Virginia and North Carolina. Beyond some descriptions of its history and a few long, scientifically precise accounts of its wide array of flora and fauna, though, there wasn't much to be found that would help her. It was interesting that George Washington had organized a company that drained and logged portions of the Swamp—that backed up Daniel's claim that George had personally cut down some of the trees—but it wasn't information she could use. She couldn't find any really detailed navigational charts, for instance, and nothing so helpful as a map to Mother Blessing's cabin. Not that she'd expected any such thing, of course, and a quick Google search showed no online references whatsoever to Mother Blessing. That was almost surprising, until she realized that Mother Blessing would probably have the power to maintain her privacy to whatever degree she wanted. Season Howe didn't turn up on Internet searches, and neither had Daniel, for that matter.

Again, though, she made notes. At one point she pushed herself away from her computer screen to rest her eyes, and realized that two more hours had passed. *If I put this kind of effort into my schoolwork, the year would be off to a much more promising start,* she thought. But then there was nothing about her schoolwork that struck her with the same kind of urgency.

Around four, the door opened and Sonya returned, wearing a fluffy yellow turtleneck and dark pants. She dumped some notebooks on her desk, looked at Kerry, and blinked a couple of times behind her big glasses. "Have you even left the room?"

"Once," Kerry replied.

"Obviously didn't bother to put on any makeup when you did," Sonya pointed out. "Are you sick?"

"I'm fine," Kerry said. "Just involved in something."

"What is it? You mean a project for one of your classes?"

"Not exactly." Kerry suddenly felt defensive. Not only would Sonya not understand—she would steadfastly refuse to understand—but Kerry didn't want to share this information anyway. If she was going to leave the campus, go to Virginia and find Mother Blessing, she didn't want anyone to know where she'd gone, or why. Possibly she'd tell her summer friends, Rebecca, Scott and Brandy, and Josh, all of whom would be more likely to get it than Sonya. But no one else—certainly no one who might tell Uncle Marsh and Aunt Betty when they came around looking. "It's more personal," she added.

Sonya shrugged. She had, Kerry thought, become good at that—just about everything Kerry did or said merited a shrug as far as Sonya was concerned. That was okay. She'd started off the year hoping they'd become friends, but it hadn't taken long to realize that that wasn't going to happen.

Now she wanted simply to get along well enough to not have her plans actively interfered with.

"Yeah, whatever," Sonya said at length, crossing to her closet. "I just came to get a coat—Dougie and I are going to the game tonight. You want to come?"

It was Friday, a fact that had completely escaped Kerry's notice. That meant one of two possibilities: for the next couple of days, Sonya would either be away with Dougie a lot, which would be great, or she'd be cooped up in the room with Kerry, studying, which would stink.

There was, unfortunately, no way to know which it would be until Sonya volunteered the information. Kerry didn't want to call attention to her curiosity by asking directly. But she tried one vague query, just in case.

"No, thanks. I'm going to stay in and keep working, probably through the weekend. You got any big plans?"

"I'm going to play it by ear," Sonya answered. No help at all. With another shrug and a wave, Sonya donned her jacket and left again. Kerry turned back to the computer.

If Sonya was going to be in the way, that made getting out of here in a hurry that much more important.

Sonya and Dougie went out for an afternoon movie on Saturday, which gave Kerry the opportunity she needed. She had already identified what she'd need to take, so she crammed it all into a duffel: some changes of clothes, especially heavy sweaters and jeans, essentials like underwear and makeup, her laptop, Daniel's journals. Anything else she needed, she could buy. Her bank had Saturday hours, so she'd stopped there earlier in the day and withdrawn what she thought she'd need. Money wasn't a particular problem—if she wasn't going to be in college, then the insurance settlement that she had set aside for that purpose was up for grabs. And she believed that Mother Blessing's would be an education in itself.

Assuming, of course, she doesn't just throw you out, she thought. *And you can find her in the first place.*

Friday's gloomy skies had turned into a driving rain that snatched brown leaves from trees and glued them to the sidewalks and gutters, blown by an icy wind off Lake Michigan. Kerry made a last pass at the room, making sure she was leaving only clothing and schoolbooks she could stand to lose, but nothing of a deeply personal nature. Then she called a cab. Under a yellow umbrella with green frogs emblazoned on it, she waited, half a block from Elder Hall's front door, until it came, its headlights slicing through the downpour. She hopped in as soon as it stopped, tossing her duffel onto the seat next to her, folding her umbrella, and resting it on its point in the empty footwell.

"O'Hare Airport," she told the driver. He was a thin man wearing a bow tie and a cardigan sweater, and when he smiled at her in his rearview mirror his teeth were full of gold.

"What airline, miss?" he asked politely.

She told him and he pulled away from the curb, his movements smooth and precise. "Have you there in a jiffy," he said. "Do you mind the radio?"

"Not at all." This seemed like an auspicious beginning to her trip—a cabbie who was considerate and also knew his way around town. He turned the power on and heavy metal music blared from speakers in both the front and back seats.

He smiled again, flashing gold. "Too loud?"

"Maybe a little." Kerry dug at her ears with her fingers, trying to see if her eardrums had in fact ruptured.

"Sorry." He turned the music down until it was a dull roar. She'd been expecting a violin concerto, maybe even opera. But it was nice to know that people could still surprise her. She settled back into the seat, guitars clashing and drums banging, and enjoyed the short ride to the airport.

Once at O'Hare, Kerry paid the driver and carried her duffel inside. She made sure people noticed her, buying a copy of *Sports Illustrated* along with her gum, because a young woman picking that magazine would be more memorable than one who chose, say, *People* or *Vogue*, at one of the WH Smith shops. She got dinner at a snack counter, and she greeted maintenance and security workers with big smiles and cheery hellos. After spending a couple of hours there she went back outside to the ground transportation area and caught a CTA bus to downtown Chicago's Greyhound station.

On the bus, surrounded by working people heading to or from jobs, and now and then by students, Kerry felt a sudden rush of sorrow for what she was giving up. Any life resembling these people's, she had decided, was destined never to be hers. But she had spent years looking forward to college, to the things she'd learn there, the friends she'd make, the professors and books that would swell her intellect and experience. Instead, she was leaving all that behind for an uncertain future, and the loss of her once-imagined life tugged at her heart, like a slender shadow of the pain she still felt at the loss of Daniel Blessing.

At the Greyhound station, she was considerably less friendly, keeping her gaze downcast and her face blank. She posted a letter she'd written to Aunt Betty earlier in the day—a brief note, really, saying essentially, "Don't look for me, I'll be fine but out of touch for a while"—and caught a 3:15 bus to Madison, Wisconsin.

She had a seat by herself on the bus, but the two men sitting behind her, nattering on about seemingly every tiny thought that flitted across their minds, made her wish she'd brought an iPod with her. Instead she turned to Daniel's journals and lost herself in his exploits for the four-hour bus journey. Panic attacks threatened to set in every time she thought about what she was doing, but Daniel's voice, as she heard it through his words, managed to calm her every time.

Madison was freezing. The bus station there was on a narrow strip of land between two lakes, and the evening air, dark already at seven thirty, felt arctic to her. She pulled the sweatshirt hood over her head and walked up South Bedford until she spotted a cheap motel, the Flamingo Inn—the kind of place where, she believed, no one would pay much attention to anyone else's business. The desk clerk sat behind a thick, scratched Plexiglas window, and Kerry passed cash through a slot to him. He coughed, grinned at her with yellowed teeth and rheumy eyes, and gave her a room key. After a quick look at the room—bed, dresser, TV, minimalist bathroom—she went back into the cold, searching for a drugstore to find what she needed. Again she paid with cash, and she carried her bag back to her underwhelming temporary abode. The desk clerk eyed her as she returned, leering at her as if she were some kind of runaway. In a sense, she guessed she was, but she didn't think of herself that way. As she climbed the dank, musty staircase to her equally unsavory room, she decided that the difference was that she wasn't focused on running *away* from anything. She was running *toward* something—toward a definite goal, a new future, a destination that she would recognize once she found it.

Inside the room again, she locked and bolted the door, took a long, hot shower, and then toweled off and found *Saturday Night Live* on the battered hotel TV. She wasn't really in the mood for comedy, but she wanted to drown out any noise that might issue from the Flamingo Inn's other guests or staff and get ready for bed. The day had been long and wearying, the emotional impact of leaving her old life behind was hitting her hard in these last few minutes, and she found herself suddenly near exhaustion, tears welling in her eyes for no reason.

And tomorrow, she knew, would be longer still.

4

Morning came all too soon, and with it harsh light spilling through curtains barely worthy of the name. Kerry groaned and forced herself out of bed, rubbing her eyes and biting back yawns. She had too much to do to allow herself to sleep in, even though the idea of opening her eyes to her wretched hotel room filled her with dread.

The night before she had shampooed her hair carefully—long, dark, lustrous hair she had grown out and tended for years. She almost had to choke back tears as she regarded her reflection in the mirror, knowing what had to happen next. From the drugstore bag she removed a pair of new scissors. *I can't believe I'm doing this,* she thought as she took six inches of her tresses into her hand. *But what has to be done . . .*

Before she cut, though, she drew her hand down three more inches. *No use getting carried away,* she decided. A *little* change was better than none at all. Anyway, there would be more to it than the cut. Once she'd snipped away the extra inches—and the split ends that had resulted from a couple of months of virtually ignoring any maintenance beyond simple shampooing in the shower—she took the blue temporary dye she'd purchased at the drugstore and worked it into her raven locks. She knew she couldn't do much about the color without bleaching first, which she wasn't willing to do. But she figured even this little bit would create blue highlights, which people would remember—and which people who knew Kerry Profitt would never associate with her. This was the theory she had developed of disappearing: be as completely unlike yourself as possible, and they'll never find you.

Of course, she didn't expect that a huge effort would be thrown into tracking her down in the first place. Aunt Betty and Uncle Marsh would make some kind of attempt, but when it came to putting money into hiring a private detective or anything like that, Uncle Marsh would draw the line. She was nearly eighteen, and she'd written a letter saying she was going away intentionally and was fine—that would be enough for him. Really, her disappearance would make his life easier. No more trying to keep track of and care for a teenager he'd never asked for in the first place. No more having his wife's loyalties divided when they fought, which they had done with some regularity during the months she'd lived in their house. Uncle Marsh was a drinker, and when he drank he got obnoxious—loud and demanding and unreasonable. Aunt Betty—Kerry couldn't figure out if she admired this, or despised it—had learned to put up with it, to ignore him or cajole him or otherwise accept his behavior. Kerry never could, never even cared to try, and that attitude had caused plenty of tension around the place.

So okay, she thought, *maybe I am running away a little bit. Running from a life I didn't choose, one that was handed to me without any input from me. But it's what I'm heading toward that keeps me going.*

When her blued hair was dried, she put on a nondescript red sweater and jeans. Much as she loved her trademark red checkered tennies, she chose to leave those in her duffel in favor of plain leather hiking boots—better in Madison's weather, and not as memorable. She packed up the rest of her belongings and checked out of the hotel; the desk clerk was a woman this time, not the same guy as last night, which was what she'd counted on. She dropped the key into the tray under the Plexiglas window, and since she'd already paid cash there was no further transaction necessary. Then she took her duffel and waited at a bus stop until a city bus came along. After paying the fare, she sat on the bus for almost an hour, riding through one neighborhood after another until she spotted what she was looking for.

Happy Jack's Wheel World was one of those used car lots that was not associated with a new car dealership but was simply a wide parking lot crammed with various models of vehicles, from a faded pink Jeep to a plum-colored Toyota minivan that looked as if it had never been on the road. Prices were painted on cardboard signs and leaned up against the windshields of the cars. Kerry had never owned a car and didn't really know what used ones should cost, but these prices seemed reasonable to her. After she looked for about fifteen seconds, a man who could only be Happy Jack—his huge bulk resplendent in a sport coat the color of spilled mustard and plaid pants that could have blinded a pro golfer—came out of a small office, smiling as if to prove his identity.

He shook her hand with all the energy of a spastic squirrel. "Looking for some wheels, miss?" he asked, his voice higher than she'd have expected for someone so large. "I'm sure I can put you into something that's just right for you."

Kerry didn't want a long conversation with this guy. She wanted to get in a car and get out of Dodge, or at least Madison. Her inclination was toward something small and economical, not a gas guzzler—although the Jeep would have been okay too, except for the pink part. Too showy. The last thing she wanted was to call attention to herself.

Finally, she pointed at the minivan—absolutely the last thing she could picture Kerry Profitt driving. "I'll take that one," she declared.

Happy Jack chuckled wetly. "You want me to wrap it up, or are you going to eat it here?"

Fifteen minutes later she drove it off the lot. Even paying cash, she'd had to do paperwork, and since she didn't have a fake ID, her name and former address were down on paper. She decided it didn't matter, though. She was still a long way from her destination, and from this point she would become untraceable, just a girl with bluish hair inscribing an arc across a corner of America.

Kerry Profitt's diary, October 23

On the theory that big cities are more anonymous than small towns, I picked St. Louis to stop in tonight. I've been here before, of course—from Cairo, it's the nearest "big city," so it's where I'd go with Mom and Dad for special shopping trips, cultural events, museums, and of course the zoo. That was a long time ago, though—a lifetime. In THIS lifetime, on this journey, I picked one of the dozens of roadside motels outside the city, more or less at random—they all look pretty much the same, and while free HBO and in-room coffee are nice, I'm not inclined to use a pool, spa, or weight room, so one is basically as good as the next.

Outside my window trucks grind through their gears as they climb the ramp back onto the interstate. My route from Madison, in case posterity cares, was Interstate 90 to Highway 20 to Interstate 39 to 55, with a lunch stop in Bloomington and bathroom breaks whenever the urge struck. I don't have a schedule and no one's waiting for me, so I've decided to move as fast as I can without killing myself too much. I'll drive, I'll stop, I'll drive some more. I think I did as much driving today as in the rest of my life combined, but it was all highway and I got pretty comfortable with it. Tomorrow it's Interstate 64 east, which will take me all the way to Norfolk.

Then things get tricky. Daniel had said that the former site of Slocumb can still be found on some maps, but not on most standard road maps or online. Daniel's journals are a little vague on how exactly to get to his mother's hideaway—and anyway, even when he uses specific directions, it's usually not much more helpful than "turn right at the big tree." Which, by now, might be surrounded by bigger trees, or chopped down, or whatever. I guess the important thing is finding the Great Dismal Swamp, which is easy, since it's a national wildlife refuge and all, and it's on every map. Then somehow, once I'm there, finding my way to Mother Blessing. Which I'm sure won't be easy. But I'm equally sure that I'll do it. It's meant to be.

Yawn, stretch. Sitting behind a wheel for hours on end is hard—I don't know how those truckers outside do it all day and sometimes all night. I feel like I need to walk a couple of miles just to unkink, but I'm too tired to try. After this I'm going to send an e-mail to the La Jolla gang, my fellow veterans of the Season hunt, and then take a hot bath.

Then bed. At least this room is cleaner and more comfortable than the one at the Flamingo Inn. Thank the goddess for anonymously institutional chain motels, I guess.

And hey, free HBO. Maybe I can watch while I sleep.

More later.

K., the vanished one.

Brandy went into the bedroom and shook Scott's shoulder. He moaned and turned over, looking up at her, his pale, narrow face puffy with sleep, eyes blinking blindly. "Put on your glasses," she instructed. "E-mail from Kerry. You've got to see."

"You can't read it to me?"

"You've got to get up anyway," she reminded him. Mornings had never been his favorite time. "You have a ten o'clock lecture. It's almost nine."

He stifled a yawn, grabbed his glasses, pushed back the covers, and swung his legs off the bed. His chest was bare, with striped cotton pajama pants covering his legs. Scott was not a particularly impressive physical specimen, but Brandy liked him and the sight warmed her heart a little. Once he was upright she took his hand and led him into the living room, where the computer monitor glowed patiently. Rubbing his eyes, he sat down on the chair in front of the desk, and she read it again over his shoulder.

"Guys," it began, "I'm dropping off the radar for a while. I'll be fine. Please PLEASE don't worry about me. And don't try to find me (not that you would). I'll be in touch when I can. Where I'm going, what I'm doing, is very important—I think to all of us. I'll tell you about it (broken record here) when I can. Summing up: DON'T WORRY. WHEN I CAN. And I love you guys. K."

Scott read the e-mail slowly, or maybe twice, before turning back to Brandy. "What do you think she's up to?"

"Like I'd know? You have the same information I do."

He rose from the chair, folding his arms defensively over his chest. "I wasn't looking for certainty, just speculation, Brandy. You don't have any guesses?"

Brandy shrugged. "It's Kerry. Who knows how that girl thinks? If I understood her, I wouldn't have been so shocked to find out she and Daniel were, you know, a thing." It continued to annoy Brandy that she hadn't guessed that, since she liked to think of herself as a good judge of character and an astute amateur—for now—psychologist. She had known there was a strong connection between them, but she hadn't realized that it had blossomed into anything physical or romantic. By the time Kerry let on, Daniel was already dead.

She suspected that it hadn't been just romance driving Kerry's feelings. Kerry had lost her father, years before, and then nursed her mother through a long and difficult illness. When they'd found Daniel Blessing in their front yard, he had been injured, near death, and Kerry had once again been drawn to nursemaid duty. Brandy thought that some of what she'd felt for Daniel had been projection, layering her feelings about her parents, who were beyond her help, onto him.

"It's something to do with Season," Scott suggested, worry tightening his voice. Rebecca had called on Saturday afternoon, telling them about the Season sighting she had had—which she had later thoroughly discounted— at a party the night before. She had convinced herself that the whole thing was a figment of her imagination, but she'd been a little freaked by it anyway. She said she'd tried to call Kerry but there had been no answer at her dorm room. Now, apparently, they knew why. "She wouldn't do something like this unless it was. She's got a lead on Season."

"You're probably right," Brandy agreed. "I don't see her getting so worked up over anything else."

Scott's lips were pressed together in a tight line, and he looked at Brandy as if she should have some kind of answer. "We've got to help her."

"Did you read the girl's e-mail?" Brandy countered impatiently. "I'm talking about the part where she specifically tells us not to."

"Yeah, but—"

"But nothing, Scott. She says not to worry about her, and not to try to find her. So your response is, let's worry and then go looking?"

"Of course she'd say those things, Brandy," Scott argued. "Kerry isn't the kind of girl to say, 'Please worry about me.'"

"But you don't think she's the kind of girl who'd ask for help if she needed it?"

"I guess she would. Maybe."

"That's right, Scott," Brandy assured him. "Kerry's not stupid. She knows she can't take Season on by herself—hell, she knows all of us together couldn't take Season. She's not going to do anything rash."

"I suppose."

The good thing about Scott was that Brandy knew all the buttons, all the levers. He could be brought around to her point of view on just about any matter Brandy cared to make the effort on. There was, she thought, a certain amount of satisfaction and comfort in that—in knowing that when it counted, she could have her way.

Manipulative? Maybe. But with a purpose.

And as far as I'm concerned, getting what I want is a good purpose.

5

In addition to Roanoke Island, there was another small town on the eastern seaboard that suffered a mysterious fate, albeit more than a hundred years later.

Slocumb, Virginia, less than a dozen miles from the North Carolina state line, was founded in or around 1641 by John Slocumb, one of the earliest settlers to exhibit any interest in the forbidding region that came to be known as the Great Dismal Swamp. Slocumb, a trapper and explorer, led a group of settlers forty-some strong from the Jamestown colony to this new settlement on the edge of the Swamp, where it was believed oysters; beaver, mink, and deer hides; and alligator skins could provide a steady income for those willing to work hard and brave the Swamp's uncharted depths.

In 1665 the tiny village of Slocumb experienced a bit of a population explosion when William Drummond, then governor of North Carolina, discovered the lake which still bears his name, and commercial activity, mostly trapping, really began to take off.

But from a high point of seventy-some residents, in the spring of 1704, Slocumb's population suddenly—apparently in the space of a few days—dropped to zero. No one seems to know quite what happened, and there are no records to explain the mystery. What is known is that there was a great fire, which not only burned down the township but also ignited the eastern edge of the Swamp. No surviving Slocumbites, if there were any, were ever reported after the fire. Volunteers from the nearby towns fruitlessly battled the blaze off and on for a month's time before giving up on it completely, and they claimed that the fire had overrun the town, burning every structure to the ground.

Mysterious, unpleasant rumors began to spread about what may have happened to Slocumb's populace, including stories of massacre by Native Americans or runaway slaves, the infernal workings of witches and devils, and the awful idea that everyone in town had been caught by surprise when the fire broke out at night and thus burned to death in their homes.

Whatever the cause, no attempt was ever made to resettle the town's site.

—Edginton's History of the Coastlands, 1937

Kerry spent her third night on the road in Portsmouth, Virginia, where there was a library in which she was able to find a reproduction of a map of Virginia from three centuries before. Of course, the roads that existed now weren't shown on it. But she got a sense of where Slocumb had been, and by comparing that to current maps and skimming through some histories of the Great Dismal Swamp area, she pinpointed where she thought its site must be.

Not sure what to expect there, she bought an inflatable boat, plenty of insect repellent and sunscreen in a handy combination form, a couple of flashlights and batteries, and some portable food and water. It crossed her mind that a gun might not be a bad idea, given that there were wild animals in there. But she hated guns, and she decided she wouldn't sacrifice her principles for a measure of comfort that might be illusory. Anyway, if the place really was a wildlife refuge, shooting at the critters was no doubt frowned upon. Better to just watch her step and not take stupid chances.

Except, the whole thing's a big fat stupid chance.

Fully outfitted, she drove the minivan down Highway 17, past the tiny town of Deep Creek. The main occupations here seemed to be fishing and selling cold beer. Kerry figured that in hotter weather, the cold beer would be a popular item. Even now, it was quite a bit warmer than it had been in Chicago or Madison; there seemed to be some sort of Indian summer thing going on. The people she saw from her van were mostly men wearing T-shirts or short-sleeved shirts, many open over chests burned brick red from years of exposure to the hot sun.

Not far to the east of here was the Intracoastal Waterway, a series of inland channels upon which one could navigate all the way from Key West to Boston, if one had a boat and the inclination. Kerry had the boat—well, *a* boat, though she doubted that her little rubber dinghy would survive such an ambitious journey. And, she had to admit, she also had a little curiosity about the idea of traversing the country north to south on water without ever sailing open ocean. But that adventure would have to wait its turn. She had another one in mind for now, and who knew how consuming it would turn out to be? Maybe if she and her boat survived it, they'd try the Intracoastal next.

After Season Howe had been dealt with.

This region was notable, too, because it was the part of the country she'd been studying in her history class before she made the decision to leave Northwestern. Roanoke Island, the colony that claimed the first child of Europeans born in North America—and from which the entire settlements population had mysteriously disappeared without trace—was on North Carolina's Outer Banks, just a short distance across the state line. She'd always been fascinated by that story, and by the cryptic word *Croatoan* that was found left behind in their wake. That had all happened before Daniel was born, she realized, but maybe not before his mother was. Yet another reason to find Mother Blessing.

Finally, she found the spot on the roadway that she was searching for, a turnoff unlabeled except by a mile marker a dozen or so feet before it. She took a narrow lane that led off the highway to the right. Tall reeds towered over the van on both sides of the road, creating the impression that she was driving into a tunnel of some kind. Ahead, all she could see past the tops of the reeds was a wall of trees that looked impenetrable from here. Already, just moments after leaving the main road, Kerry felt as if she'd left civilization far behind her and ventured into some primeval world.

The road wound to the right and then left again, but always leading basically west, away from the sea and toward the heart of the Great Dismal Swamp. Kerry didn't know the names of any of the trees or plants she saw, but their effect on her was overwhelming—everything was green and incredibly lush. *This must be the most fertile spot on Earth,* she thought, *or one of them, anyway.* She'd never been very successful at growing houseplants, but from the looks of things around here if she'd had some of the local climate, soil, and water, she'd be queen of the green thumbs.

She drove with her window rolled halfway down, the warm air brushing her left arm and cheek thick with the rich, fecund aromas of the Swamp. The edge of the road was pebbled, and beyond the stones, the reeds stood in murky, stagnant water. The whole experience was like nothing she'd ever seen—or smelled.

After another ten minutes or so, the road came to an abrupt end. For a moment Kerry's heart fell; she thought she'd figured the way incorrectly or made a wrong turn. But then she spotted an old, unpaved track, made impassable to cars by the trees that had fallen across it, but still clearly something that had been considered a road at one time. Now it was little more than a space between trees, choked with weeds and brush, leading into the darkness of what looked like impenetrable jungle.

This was a development she hadn't counted on. But then this whole trip had been made without a real plan, just flying by the seat of her pants. No reason this part of it should suddenly be easy or predictable. Bringing the van to a halt at the edge of the roadway, right tires on the graveled shoulder, she was sure it wouldn't be.

The heat surprised her. When she'd been driving through it, her movement had made it feel comfortable. But now that she stood in it, listening only to the ticking of the Toyota's engine and the cries of unseen birds, it settled around her in a great, damp blanket of humidity. Clouds of gnats swarmed around her like manifestations of the temperature. She flapped her hands at them, then remembered the combination sunscreen/insect repellent in the van and went to retrieve it. A few moments later, suitably slathered, she braved the elements again. Gnats still crowded her, but kept a slightly greater distance; the sun, filtered as it was through the overhanging trees, still hammered mercilessly upon her.

The stretch of old roadway through the trees was relatively short, and after less than fifteen minutes it stopped, opening onto a wide clearing at the other side of which, Kerry supposed, the Great Dismal started up in earnest. On the far side of the clearing, the woods looked dark, benighted in spite of the early hour and the pounding sun.

But it was the clearing itself that struck her the most. This, she surmised, was the lost town of Slocumb. Not a building stood, but the blackened remains of charred timbers still rested where they had fallen back in 1704. Outlines were visible where once houses had been, and among them the paths of the lanes that connected them. The whole thing looked like a carefully preserved archaeological site.

What was most remarkable about it, though—the part that made her body shiver, in spite of the heat—was the fact that there was not a blade of grass, not a single weed—much less the mass of trees and roots and reeds and ferns that covered the rest of the landscape—anywhere within the confines of the Slocumb site.

It was as if a manic gardener had picked the site clean. The pathways between buildings were sandy and rock-strewn, and there was evidence of broken, crumbled oyster shells everywhere. The burned, skeletal remains of the buildings were as free of vegetation as the lunar surface. Even the air smelled different, lacking the musky, dank aroma of the surrounding swampland. Instead, it had a kind of sour stench that made Kerry think of the meat that had spoiled in her mom's freezer when a power outage had kept the electricity off for three days. Kerry hesitated to enter the space, but after a moment's consideration decided that she had to. All of Daniel's directions into the swamp had been from the other side, where the town site bordered the Great Dismal.

She shook off the sense of unease, as well as she could, at any rate, and ventured into the clearing. The air felt thinner here, rarefied, and maybe five or ten degrees cooler than the humid air outside the space. *This,* Kerry suddenly knew, *is the work of Season Howe. She did more than destroy the town; she put some kind of curse on the land so it would never recover.* It was no wonder the history books tended to ignore Slocumb—how could anyone explain this lifeless anomaly in the midst of one of the country's greatest swamps using only the limited vocabulary of science and accepted belief?

When she reached the first dwelling, its boards long since petrified as fire-blackened cinders, Kerry realized something else about this place. There was no noise here, not even the bird cries that had been omnipresent since stopping the van; no frogs croaking or crickets chirping could be heard from this place. And the cloud of gnats that had followed her every step of the way, even after she'd slathered on the insect repellent, had stopped at the edge of the clearing, refusing to enter. Only Kerry was foolish enough to tread this ground, it seemed. The silence was unnerving; the complete absence of life nearly terrifying. The tiny hairs on her neck and arms stood on end, as if Kerry had been subject to a jolt of electricity. She tried to swallow her fear and walk on, but her steps, instead of being courageous and determined, were small, hesitant, and she tried to keep a clear path at her back in case sudden retreat was called for.

Perhaps an archaeologist foolish enough to brave the place might have found something of worth in the ruined buildings, but all Kerry could see were ashes and scorched logs. The ground was solid beneath her feet, less spongy than the trail she had taken here from the van, but even so the people who built this village hadn't used stone foundations. A few piles of rocks that might once have been chimneys lay here and there, but rocks big enough for building seemed impossible to find—probably if they existed at all they had long ago sunk beneath the waters of the swamp. So for the most part, the construction had been wood, which had all burned.

After what seemed like hours, but was probably not more than ten or fifteen minutes even at her cautious pace, Kerry reached the other side of the clearing. Here the forest rose up thick and menacing, with patches of thorny blackberries filling in the space between tree trunks. She saw no way to walk through that morass without a machete, which she didn't have, and even with one the going would be slow.

But between the clearing and the trees was a narrow ditch filled with water that looked like soup, a dark, reddish brown color. Leaves floated on it, and it rippled in spots where there may have been submerged objects. It was maybe a dozen feet across at its widest point, and only half that right where she stood. She couldn't get a sense of how deep it was, even when she tossed in a handful of pebbles from the clearing. They simply plopped against its tranquil surface and disappeared. After rimming the clearing, though, the ditch turned to the west and disappeared into the trees, which meant, Kerry believed, that this was the waterway that Daniel had taken to his mother's house in the Swamp so many years before.

Which also meant, she knew, that it was the path she had to take.

She'd left her supplies in the van while scouting the lay of the land. Now she regretted that decision, for it meant crossing the clearing twice more. But there was no other way to reach the ditch, at least none that she could see—the forest was impenetrable on every other side of the town's site. Biting back terror, she steeled herself and turned back, back onto the most forbidding piece of real estate she had ever imagined, back through the silence and the utter absence of life.

6

There's this theory that the weight of any object is inversely proportionate to how useless it turns out to be—the less one needs it, the more it ends up weighing, and vice versa. So the flashlight I brought with me weighed about an ounce, or maybe a negative ounce, since the inside of the Great Dismal Swamp at night is so ridiculously dark, but the can of beans I brought, because beans on a camp-out just seemed right, weighed about forty pounds. Had I brought a can opener, it might have dropped to just five or ten pounds—even less if I liked beans to begin with.

Okay, the theory is one I just made up. I don't think that invalidates its scientific truth, though.

Here's the thing. I maybe should have bought the Jeep instead of the van, because maybe I could have driven a bit closer to the barren stretch of land that used to be Slocumb. But I didn't, which meant I had to leave the van where it was and carry all my gear, including the inflatable boat, which—the exception that proves the rule—weighed about a thousand pounds more than it had in the store. Eventually I had to put some of the stuff down and make multiple trips to the ditch at the edge of town (or rather, former town), which I had decided was going to be my pathway into the depths of the Dismal.

Eventually, though—and ask me if I mind saying that walking back and forth across that bizarre, haunted piece of land was freaking me out in a gigantamous way, because it was—I had everything where I needed it. The boat, wonder of wonders, inflated when I pulled on the goobie, just like it was supposed to. And it didn't even sink when I loaded all the junk in it, like the forty-pound beans. If I'd had a bottle of champagne I'd have christened it, except for the part about how shards of glass from a broken bottle would probably shred an inflatable boat, and the other part about how I don't drink, but at this point in my admittedly bizarre journey I might have considered taking it up.

So without christening I just launched. No motor or anything, sadly—it was all driven by Kerry-power. Me and my little toy oar, which was really too small to be useful, but fit in the box with the boat. At first it didn't seem too bad, but after a while it started to get old. And then when the overhanging brambles and branches and logs (and other names for spiky wooden things) started hanging down so low over the ditch that I pretty much had to lie down in the boat to keep from having my scalp ripped off, rowing became that much harder.

Plus, did I mention the dark? Scrolling back. Yep, mentioned. But hey, if ever there was something that merited repetition, it's that. Seemed like it would have been kind of late evening, in the real world, but inside the Swamp where the sun just doesn't reach, it was full dark way before I was expecting it. When I realized the light was going I looked around for someplace relatively dry and flat to stop, not wanting to spend the night on the boat. And after a while I found it—found this, in fact, the lean-to under which I am sitting and running down my laptop battery.

And what else is interesting is the way insects are drawn to laptops, which, who knew? I wonder if Mac has a way to clean blood and guts off the screen, because they keep committing suicide by slamming themselves into it.

Before the juice runs out, then, a summary of my position. Somewhere in the middle of the Swamp, except I don't know precisely where. I didn't exactly watch for the landmarks I read about in Daniel's journals because I was too busy watching for someplace to spend the night, which means that even if they still exist, I might have missed some of them, which means that I might be hopelessly lost. And I don't exactly know where I'm supposed to be going anyway. In spite of the insect repellent, I am being eaten alive by bugs. The Swamp makes strange noises—rustlings and hissings and moanings in addition to the more recognizable croaking and chirping, and I think it's really things in the Swamp, not the Swamp itself, which is actually a lot worse.

And all this gab is just a way of not admitting that I am freakin' SCARED TO DEATH out here . . . which, you know, who likes to admit that? But then again, it's the truth, so why not?

The books say people used to get lost and die in the swamp on a fairly regular basis. If I don't find Mother Blessing, will I die out here? If I do find Mother Blessing, will she turn me away, which could still mean dying out here? Or will she take me in like I hope she does? What is she like, anyway? I could write about that for hours, but the battery will never last.

More later.

K.

Mother Blessing was a surprise.

Kerry had begun to think she'd never find Daniel Blessing's mother. The Great Dismal was just too big, too dense, too full of dangers. She saw a black bear her first morning out; fortunately, the bear saw her, too, and turned back the way he had come, vanishing down a trail that seemed too narrow for a human, much less a huge furry beast. She had barely reined in her galloping heart when the creek before her, wider now and flowing faster than when it had merely been a ditch, parted to reveal an alligator drifting to the surface a few feet ahead of her. Kerry had a quick mental picture of it tearing into her inflatable boat with its razor-sharp teeth and sinking her, then finishing her off at its leisure. *This was a bad idea,* she thought, *a stupendously bad idea in a lifetime chock full of bad ideas.*

"I taste bad!" she shouted at the beast. "Really bad! That's what everyone tells me, anyway. Kerry, you taste bad. And you smell funny too."

Apparently she was convincing enough, because the gator drifted past her without biting her boat. For a couple of hours after that, she started to get used to the Swamp, even to enjoy it. Tall trees arced over her head, creating an effect like a green cathedral. The fragrant forest floor was festooned with wide-leafed ferns. Butterflies and birds flitted and flew;

squirrels scampered up the sides of trees; great multihued spiders spun webs like fishnets between tree trunks. There was a quiet charm to the place that she appreciated in a way she would never have expected the night before, when she had been so afraid she had barely managed to sleep at all.

As the day wore on, her nearly sleepless night began to catch up with her, and the beauty of the Swamp combined with the gentle motion of the boat to lull her into a kind of stupor. So when she first noticed the men watching her from the banks, she didn't think anything of it. After a couple of minutes, though, she realized that there was something wrong about it. Men shouldn't watch her here—she was a unique enough sight in a place like this that any other human would hail her, not simply observe from the cover of thick underbrush. She tried to focus on the spot where she thought she'd seen one of them, but he was gone. Maybe a leaf shuddered slightly with his passing, or maybe it was a wisp of a breeze that moved it.

But Kerry was on the alert now, wide awake, senses sharpened. If she saw anything else she'd be ready.

Or so she thought.

The creek forked, and Kerry chose to go to the right. But though she paddled that way, the current had another idea, and it pushed her toward the left. She thought she remembered something in the journals about the right fork, and she tried to fight the pull. She lost the struggle, though, and gave it up after a few minutes, concentrating instead on keeping the boat steady against the sudden surge. It was more important not to capsize than to worry about which fork she should take when, for all practical purposes, she had no idea where she was or where she should be.

Just when she had the little boat settled on the water, Kerry caught another glimpse of movement through the thick trees. For a moment she thought it was a deer, or maybe—her heart pounded in fear—another bear. *What are you supposed to do in the event of a bear attack?* She tried to remember. *Make noise? Play dead? Run like hell?* Making noise seemed like the easiest, especially since trying to run might involve drowning, or a close-up encounter with an alligator or a water moccasin. For a moment she thought maybe she'd be okay if she stayed in the boat and the bear was on land, but then she remembered pictures of bears standing in rushing rivers, fishing for lunch. *So much for that idea.*

She brought the little paddle up out of the water and laid it across the boat's bow, trying to sit very still to minimize any sound. Maybe it hadn't noticed her at all. Through the trees, another flash of motion—something big and dark— caught her eye. This time she heard a noise, too, a rustling of leaves.

So it's not just shifting shadows.

As quietly as she could, she slipped the paddle back into the water and rowed for the opposite bank. The banks on both sides were sheer, with trees right to the edge, roots erupting from the cutaways. She wasn't sure where she'd be able to climb out of the boat, but she wanted to at least have a chance if some creature came at her.

The foliage across the water shifted again, as if something with serious weight were coming through it in her direction. That was all it took to spur Kerry. With two more powerful sweeps of the oar she made the far bank. There was a rope tied to a ring at the boat's bow, and she quickly looped it around the root of a tree. Then, setting her feet widely for best balance, she stood, clutching at a narrow tree trunk for more support. Putting one foot up on the bank, she hoisted herself from the boat and slid between two trees just as the dark figure on the far shore loomed into view.

It was not a bear, but a man.

Everything she'd read about the Great Dismal rushed back into her consciousness: a haven for people dodging the law, runaway slaves before the Civil War and Emancipation, and for criminals in every age, as well as a prime spot for hunters and fishers. If the man across the way had innocent intent he'd have said something by now, surely, not approached her with stealth and silence.

The ground under her feet was soft and spongy, the trees close together, with ferns and trailing vines covering the lower reaches and tangles of thickets tearing at her legs. Placing her feet was difficult, but she didn't intend to just stand there and let someone sneak up on her. As fast as she could manage, she pushed her way through the underbrush and around the trees, putting distance between herself and the creek. Once she had a rhythm going, she was able to get up a reasonable speed.

She was going so quickly, in fact, that she didn't, at first, notice the man who stood in front of her. When she did, it was too late—he swung something heavy at her and she tried to dodge, but a tree trunk blocked her way. A flash of light accompanied the impact, and then everything went dark.

I have to be dreaming, Kerry thought. *This can't be real.*

She seemed to be in an actual bed, with crisp, clean sheets pulled up around her. A dull ache throbbed at her right temple, but it wasn't any worse than an average headache, and there was none of the nausea she might have expected given the fact that she had apparently been clubbed into unconsciousness. The odors around her—she hadn't yet opened her eyes—were clean, almost antiseptic, not the pungent aroma of the swamp. And there were two exceedingly strange sounds: one a kind of electrical hum, and one a labored, artificial-breathing noise, as if Darth Vader were standing beside the bed holding a small appliance.

Or a light saber.

Having gathered as much—seemingly contradictory—information as possible, Kerry opened her eyes.

The first thing she saw was a woman smiling at her from a motorized scooter-style wheelchair. She was an enormous woman in her fifties or sixties, big in every way, from her teased, bleached beehive of a hairdo to her vast bosom and belly, barely confined in a plaid smock the size of a pup tent, to the thighs straining royal blue polyester stretch pants. A clear plastic mask across her nose and mouth was attached by tubes to oxygen tanks mounted on the scooter's rear. The scooter had wide rubber tires and a shallow basket mounted on the handlebars.

"Welcome back, darlin'," the woman said, her Southern accent thick as the trees in the Great Dismal. "I've been wonderin' when you'd be joinin' me. I'm so sorry for the way my boys brought you here."

"Here?" Kerry asked weakly.

"My house, of course," the woman replied. "Y'all were lookin' for me, weren't you?"

Kerry tried to raise herself up on one elbow. "You . . . you're . . ."

The woman breathed loudly into her mask, and then favored Kerry with another broad, slightly grotesque smile. "Folks call me Mother Blessing."

7

"Scott," Brandy said, her tone arch. "What are you doing?"

He turned away from the computer screen. "Checking e-mail."

"Didn't you check it, like, an hour ago? And an hour before that? Since when have you become compulsive?"

Her arms were crossed over her chest and her lips were pressed together so tightly they practically disappeared. Her stance, the tilt of her head, and the tone of her voice put him instantly on edge. "Well, it's just . . . you know. I'm hoping we hear something from Kerry."

Brandy made a *tch* noise and shook her head ever so slightly. "She said she'd be in touch when she could, right? I'm sure she's fine."

"Yeah, but we don't know that. And if we don't check, how are we going to know if she's trying to get in touch?"

"I swear, sometimes it seems like you think about that girl more than you think about me," Brandy said, turning away from him.

Scott came out of the chair and went to her. "You know that's not true, Brandy," he said. He wrapped his arms around her, but there was nothing yielding about her flesh; she didn't lean into him. Her velour top was soft, but that was just surface. It was like trying to hug a velvet bag of saw blades.

The thing was, maybe she wasn't wrong. "You know I love you, babe."

"You keep telling me so," Brandy admitted. But what she left unsaid was whether his words were convincing to her.

"I do," he assured her. He was about to say more, but the computer chimed softly, indicating an incoming e-mail. He felt Brandy's muscles tense even more. He rubbed a shoulder that seemed to resist his touch, and then returned to his seat. "It's from Josh," he said, unable to keep the disappointment from his voice.

When Brandy spoke again, she sounded distinctly uninterested. "What does he have to say?"

Scott scanned the message. It was short; their friend hadn't heard from Kerry either. "I'll read it," he said. "'Hey guys. Just checking in. School is, you know, school. Grades are fine, so no worries there. The rest of life keeps plugging along. No significant other, although there are a couple of guys here who might be potentials. You have any news from Kerry since she went AWOL? I haven't heard a thing, and I'm a little on the nervous side. Love you, Josh.'"

"See, I'm not the only one who's worried about her."

"I guess it's a man thing," Brandy said. "We women know we can take care of ourselves."

"Somehow I doubt that Josh's interest would be the same as mine," Scott pointed out. Realizing how that might be interpreted, though, he quickly tried to cover himself. "Not that I have any interest of that kind. Just, if I did, you know, Josh wouldn't. Kerry being a female and all."

"I understood you the first time," Brandy said. Her tone had gone from arch to glacial. Scott wondered if it was possible to make more wrong moves in one relationship than he did in this one and have any hope of keeping it together. Before he could add anything, though, Brandy walked toward the bedroom. Her body was tight and confined and there was no invitation in the way she walked; instead he got a vibe from her that was somewhere between a shrug and a flipping of the middle finger.

Just as well, he thought. *Anything else I said would only have dug me in deeper.*

Mother Blessing's house, Kerry discovered, was as surprising as the woman herself. It looked like any average ranch house—hardwood floors, plaster walls painted eggshell white, oak cabinets and avocado-green appliances in the modern kitchen. But outside the windows, the gloom of the Swamp pressed up against it, and through the screens Kerry could hear the buzzing of insects and smell the Swamp's fetid aroma clashing with an indoor odor that reminded her of pine-scented cleaning solutions.

After giving Kerry a moment of privacy to pull on a voluminous pink cotton bathrobe, Mother Blessing led her on a tour of the place, seemingly as proud of her house as a new mother might be of her child. With her motorized scooter making agile turns and pirouettes, the woman took Kerry from the guest room, in which Kerry had awakened, down the hall to the bathroom, pointing out her own master bedroom across the way, then further through the single-story house to a kitchen and dining room, and then past the entryway into a living room that opened onto a screened-in porch. Once Kerry had the lay of the land, Mother Blessing led her back into the kitchen, where she took a pitcher of iced tea from the refrigerator.

"Sweet's okay, isn't it?" the woman asked cheerfully. "I hope so, because it's hard to take the sweet out once it's in there, isn't it?"

Kerry thought she was still in shock from the attack, because this whole scene seemed more than a little surreal to her. "Yes, I . . . I suppose it is. Probably."

"Not that it can't be done," Mother Blessing went on, pouring tea into two plastic tumblers with bright, primary-colored polka dots on the sides. "Just about anything can be done, if one's got the determination and know-how, right?"

Kerry simply nodded. She wasn't quite sure how to broach the more urgent topics that were on her mind, such as Daniel's death at the hands of Season Howe or the attack, seemingly at the hands of Mother Blessing's accomplices, that had brought her to this place. *Not that this isn't where I was trying to get to anyway,* she thought, *but I'd rather have done it without the lump on the head.*

Mother Blessing rolled over to the dining table with the two glasses and a bag of Oreos in the basket mounted on her handlebars and parked herself on the one side that didn't have a steel-framed chair. "Have yourself a sit-down," she urged Kerry, sliding one of the drinks across the table for her. "I know y'all have had a rough few days, and my boys didn't help matters none, I'm sorry to say."

Kerry shrugged and took one of the chairs. She knew that both of Mother Blessing's sons were dead. "By your 'boys,' you mean . . ."

"Simulacra," Mother Blessing said matter-of-factly. "Y'all know what that is?"

"Daniel told me." Simulacra, he had explained once, were humanlike figures magically molded from whatever substance was near where they were needed—in this case, Kerry guessed, maybe from swamp muck, leaves, and branches. He had also said that they were kind of a specialty of Mother Blessing's. Now that his name had come up, she felt she had to tell Mother Blessing what had become of her son. "You know, about Daniel? That—"

"That he's moved on to the next plane?" Mother Blessing interrupted. The wide, toothy smile half-hidden behind her breathing mask didn't falter. "Yes, I knew right away. As soon as Season did it."

"So you know it was Season, too," Kerry commented. "I was there."

"You meant a lot to him," Mother Blessing said. "Soon as I saw y'all, I knew you were Kerry. That porcelain skin, the big green eyes, the dark hair—course, Daniel didn't say anythin' about it being blue, but I figure that could be new." Kerry was shocked; she hadn't known that he had been in touch with his mother at all during the time they were together. The impression she had had was that mother and son were not particularly close. But then it was clear there was still a lot about the Blessing family she didn't know. She swallowed, fighting back sudden tears.

"It is," she managed. "The blue. And the feeling is . . . mutual . . . about Daniel. You don't seem . . ."

Mother Blessing blinked at her, breathing heavily. Her oxygen tanks hissed softly. "I'm not as angry as you expected? People die—even *our* people. Even witches. It's a passage, that's all."

"Daniel said something like that too. But he still took it seriously. He never forgave Season for killing Abraham."

"Nor have I, child. Season has much to answer for. I mean to see that she does."

Kerry sipped her tea and watched Mother Blessing pull her oxygen mask aside so she could do the same. The older woman followed it with an Oreo. They might as well have been swapping recipes or hair-care tips, Kerry thought. "That's why I . . . why I came looking for you," she said. "I want revenge. On Season. For Daniel, and for our friend Mace, and for . . . well, everything. I want to see justice done." Kerry steeled herself, knowing her request was probably premature. "I didn't know myself why I wanted so badly to find you, but now I do. What I want is for you to help me . . . to teach me. To make me powerful enough to fight her."

Mother Blessing laughed suddenly, little bits of Oreo spraying the varnished wood tabletop. Her laughter shook her enormous frame and turned to coughing, then choking. Kerry was afraid the woman would die right here in front of her, but she didn't know what to do about it. Through her paroxysms, Mother Blessing snatched up her oxygen mask and held it over her nose and mouth until gradually she was able to control her breathing again. When she looked at Kerry again, mascara-streaked tears ran down both cheeks.

"Child," she said finally. "Y'all are a spirited one, aren't you?"

Now that she had declared her purpose, Kerry saw no reason to back down. "I'm sorry," she said, "but I am completely serious. Daniel said the craft could be learned, that one didn't have to be born a witch."

"Daniel was right," Mother Blessing agreed. "It's not easy, and it's not something that can be taken lightly. It can be done, of course. I'm not sure

I'm the right teacher, though. My days of power are somewhat behind me, I'm afraid."

Kerry touched the side of her head where it was still tender. "Powerful enough to have me brought here unconscious by your simulacra," she pointed out. "And, I'd guess, powerful enough to have patched me up, since this doesn't hurt nearly as much as it seems like it ought to."

Mother Blessing made a dismissive motion with her hand. "Nothing," she declared. "A couple of herbs, an ointment. And I am sorry about the simulacra, child. They didn't rightly know who you were, did they? I knew you were tryin' to find me, of course—soon as you entered the Dismal, I knew that. But not the who or the why. If I'd have known it was you, my invitation would've been much more neighborly, wouldn't it?"

You tell me, Kerry thought. She didn't give voice to it, though. She was asking this woman, this utter stranger, for a huge favor. She didn't want to start on an accusatory note. Even if the woman had bashed her head in, however remotely. "I guess that's true," she said, accepting the semi-apology that Mother Blessing had offered.

"Of course I know a little about y'all," Mother Blessing went on. "Through Daniel. But even so, I don't know you myself. How do I know if I can trust y'all with the kind of power you're talkin' about, the kind that could make y'all a challenge to Season? How do I even know you haven't joined up with her?"

Kerry felt her face flush with anger. "I wouldn't!" she raged. "I couldn't team up with that . . . that . . ." She had been about to say "witch," but realized that in this company that wasn't necessarily a powerful epithet. So she just let the sentence trail off, knowing that her meaning was clear. "She killed the man I love."

Mother Blessing regarded her for a moment, silent. Then she nodded slowly. "So she did."

"You can't possibly believe I'd be . . . in . . . in *cahoots* with her or something."

"I'm just sayin' I don't know what to believe, child. I have years—centuries—of hate built up for Season. Y'all have, what, a couple of months? If I'm supposed to teach you what it takes to defeat her, I have to know you're goin' to stick it out. I have to know y'all are as committed as you say, don't I?"

"Well, I'm here," Kerry pointed out. "I left college, and everyone I know, to come here. I tracked you down—as well as I could, anyway, and if your 'boys' hadn't attacked me I'd still be out there in the Swamp looking for you. I have—oh, crap!" She suddenly remembered her gear, which she'd left in the boat when she ran from the simulacra. "My boat—I have some of Daniel's journals in it, and my laptop!"

"That's all in the closet in the guest room," Mother Blessing assured her with a patting motion of her hand. "Don't you worry about that."

Relieved, Kerry blew out a sigh. "I've been reading his journals, studying them," she said. "Trying to learn as much as I can about Season, her habits, her weaknesses."

"I've got more of those journals here," Mother Blessing told her. "On that bookcase in the living room."

Kerry had known there must be more somewhere, since there were chronological gaps from book to book. "I'd love to read them."

Mother Blessing examined her again. Kerry felt like she was under a microscope, or an X-ray device—as if the woman were somehow looking beneath skin and muscle and bone to what lay deep inside, in the innermost reaches of her heart. "Maybe you will," Mother Blessing said. "Maybe you just will. You know, what you're askin', that's a lot of responsibility. I'm not as young as I once was, and I'm not sure I can keep up with a spirited little chickadee like y'all. Might could be a strain on my heart."

Kerry was heartened by this development. "Does that mean I can stay?" she asked, unable to keep the hope from her voice.

Mother Blessing didn't answer right away. Kerry understood that this was one of her conversational traits: taking a long time to answer, letting the other person feel off guard. Asking questions was another one, even though they weren't meant to be answered. This time, she did both.

"I guess y'all can stay on for a spell. We can get better acquainted before we make any big decisions, can't we?"

8

Josh Quinn's mother was downstairs in her home office, which was where she seemed to live these days. Except, her office, Josh knew, was also the location of her wet bar, and if what she did in there had anything to do with work, then she had given up her real estate license in favor of rehearsing for a role in a remake of *Leaving Las Vegas*. He'd tried to talk to her about it, but nothing doing. He'd even, for what it was worth, left brochures for substance-abuse clinics and a copy of AA's *Little Red Book* where she'd be sure to find them.

But she could ignore a hint just as easily as he could drop it. Maybe easier. All she had to do was pretend not to notice what she was dumping in the trash, whereas Josh had to actually go out and acquire the stuff he brought home for her. Most of it he found on campus without much trouble, but even picking it up and glancing at it meant acknowledging that perhaps he had an addiction problem of his own brewing, and—*like mother, like son*—that wasn't something he wanted to dwell on.

He shut down his computer and headed downstairs. He thought about calling Henry, a friend from school who he had believed might become more than a friend if the circumstances were right. Last time he'd called Henry for a date, though, the conversation had been awkward, and he had ended up not following through. Henry was attractive and articulate, and Josh liked him a lot. But on the phone the other night, there had been a sudden moment when Josh had realized that his friend's experience of the world was so limited that they were like residents of two different planets. They both shared an affinity for noir books and films, for instance. But Henry's entire understanding of violence came from pop culture, and when Josh objected to his hyperbolic comment that he'd like to kill one of his professors, he hadn't understood that Josh viewed killing and violent death through a more realistic lens than he once had. Josh had been unable to overcome that mental hurdle for a few minutes, and Henry had noticed his hesitation. Things had gone downhill from there, and Josh hung up a short while later, thoroughly embarrassed. Rather than put himself through that again, he decided to just go out by himself.

For a moment he considered putting on a light trenchcoat, but decided against it. He had on a long-sleeved black T, tight black artificial leather pants, and high boots with silvery buckles running up the insides, and he was pretty sure he'd be warm enough this evening. Stopping outside his mom's office door just long enough to call "I'm going out!"—and hearing no reply—he went out.

Downtown was a couple of miles from home, the Strip even farther. Tonight, though, he didn't want the slightly seedy, no-frills atmosphere of downtown. He wanted to immerse himself in spectacle, in themed entertainment as carefully thought out as Disneyland, albeit with a slightly different focus. The choices were many: Casinos were disguised as fantasy versions of New York, Rio, Paris, Venice, ancient Rome, medieval Europe, the high seas. He could mingle with acrobats and clowns at the circus or pharaohs in ancient Egypt. This time choosing none of the above, he hiked until he could flag a cab, then asked the driver to take him to the Mandalay Bay. He'd never quite figured out what its theme was—some sort of generic Balinese paradise that didn't quite have the courage to commit to its *Gilligan's Island* roots—and that ambiguity suited his mood tonight. Plus, he enjoyed the fact that sections of it had sunk sixteen inches into the ground after it was built, requiring hundreds of steel pipes bored into its foundation to stabilize it. Somehow that seemed to sum up the Vegas experience for him—just do it, and worry about the consequences later.

If Mother Blessing was a surprise, what Kerry saw when she left the house was even more of a shock.

The day had been exhausting, what with the not having slept much and the various excitements of traveling through the Swamp, including but not limited to being chased and clobbered by simulacra. So, despite her nap and the sweet tea's caffeine, after talking with Mother Blessing for a while, Kerry was ready to sleep again. Mother Blessing took her back to the guest room, showed her where her things had been stowed, and left her to get some rest.

Kerry tugged on a tank top and some pajama pants she'd brought, and climbed into bed, clutching BoBo, the clown doll that had made the journey with her. In spite of her exhaustion, though, the day's events echoed in her mind and sleep was hard to achieve. The double bed was comfortable and roomy, and she had two good pillows—a big improvement over the night before, when her bed was the ground in some hunter's ancient lean-to with the Swamp's wildlife investigating her—but still she tossed and turned for more than an hour before finally drifting off.

Once she finally succumbed, her sleep was deep and without dreams.

She woke early the following morning, when the Swamp was quiet and still and the day's first light was sending yellow streamers across a rosy sky. Curious, Kerry moved through the silent house, still clad only in her nightwear, and slipped out the front door. The Great Dismal seemed a different world from this angle, beyond Mother Blessing's slatted wooden walkway—magical and mysterious, though in a cheerful way, not threatening at all.

But when Kerry turned back toward the house she felt a sense of dislocation that almost made her lose her balance. She faced not a suburban-style ranch house, but a tiny swamp shack, something a trapper might have lived in during the few days it took to set a line of traps. The boards were old and warped, with spaces between some big enough for rats to pass through, the windows covered with what looked like nailed-down tar paper. The waters of the Swamp seeped under the walkway right up to the walls, with trees pressing in against the cabin from three sides.

That's not what I came out of, Kerry thought anxiously. Worried that the whole house might have been a fevered dream, a result of the knock she'd taken to the head—or that it might have been real, but was gone now—she hurried back to the shack's front door, which was at least in the same place as the door through which she had exited. She threw it open quickly, and the scene inside the entryway was just as she remembered: nicely floored with hardwood, walls of eggshell white, a sideboard holding a series of potted herbs, and some framed still lifes hanging on the wall above it.

Confused, Kerry stood in the doorway. Inside was Mother Blessing's house as she remembered it, complete with the artificial pine scent of whatever she cleaned with. But when she stuck her head out of the door and looked at the outside, she saw the ramshackle cabin. The disjunction made her head hurt, so she gave up trying to figure it out. As she walked back to the guest room, Mother Blessing's bedroom door opened. Kerry waited for her to emerge, then described what had happened. She wondered if there was an explanation.

"What do y'all expect, child?" Mother Blessing asked her. "It's magic."

"But . . . which one is real?" Kerry pressed.

"That depends, doesn't it?"

"On what?"

"On if y'all are inside or out, silly," Mother Blessing said. She made it sound like it made sense, and Kerry decided to leave it at that. But she knew that she couldn't take anything about this place at face value.

Kerry Profitt's diary, October 26

After showering in the hall bathroom and dressing in "my" room, I came back out to find that Mother Blessing was up to something in the kitchen that she didn't want me witnessing. Apparently the kitchen is not just where she dishes up the sweet tea, Oreos, and Scooter Pies that seem to be her primary foodstuffs; and by the way, how has she lived to this advanced age (though not necessarily in good health, given the ever-present oxygen mask, etc.) on such a diet? The kitchen is also where she practices her magic, or whips up her potions, or whatever she's doing in there.

Right now, I could go for a Scooter Pie. Or a steak. Yesterday I was too bushed to really care much about food, but today my hunger is catching up to me, and with the kitchen off-limits I only have the stuff I brought in my duffel to sustain me. I've had some trail mix, but the idea that there's a whole kitchen just out of reach is starting to consume me. I'm imagining a pantry stocked with everything I could ever want to chow down on, though in fact it's probably just loaded with more types of cookies, with maybe a few five-gallon jars of mayonnaise and some cases of Velveeta.

Maybe I'm being unfair, or stereotyping the poor woman needlessly. So far, though, I'm getting a really strange vibe from Mother Blessing. She doesn't trust me, that's clear—hence the no-admittance-to-the-kitchen-while-she's-working rule. But it seems like there's more than just that going on—she's trying to be a gracious hostess, I think, because she knows Daniel loved me and maybe because that's what Southern women do. I'd never have pegged her for a witch, though—look at me, Ms. Expert all of a sudden! For one thing, I would expect a witch to maintain herself in a healthier state. Daniel made it clear that he was something of an anomaly, that not all witches spend their whole lives either preparing for battle, battling, or recovering from battle, like he did. But it seems like she would have to be at least a little concerned about Season coming after her, even if she has no other enemies. And except for the simulacra in the Swamp, which seemed to have been dispatched specifically to find me, I haven't seen any defenses at all. Maybe the house's disguise helps with that, though I'm not sure how. If anything, it seems to create the impression of a defenseless place—something a good, stiff wind could knock over.

So the sense of Mother Blessing that I get, obnoxiously prejudiced as it is, is that she's a woman I'd expect to see wheeling her little cart through Piggly Wiggly, stocking up on Ding Dongs and Twinkies, rather than a witch of enormous power and influence.

But Daniel indicated that she was the latter—that when the Witches' Convocation comes around next year, she'll be a participant of considerable importance, though also one that Season might try to railroad in witchy court.

For Daniel's sake, I've got to see if there's anything I can do to help prevent that. But also, and more importantly, from my perspective, I've decided that what I really want is for Mother Blessing to prepare me to take Season on in battle. Daniel asked me not to seek revenge, and I'd love to honor that request. But the truth is, I'm not spiritually advanced enough for that. I guess I'm not as decent a person as he believed I was. Because as small and petty as revenge is supposed to be, it's what I want. The idea of it is one of the only ways I've made it through these last months, since Daniel's death, with any sanity at all.

And of course the other aspect of it is that if Season is allowed to live, she'll keep doing the things she does. I don't have any illusions that now that she's killed Daniel, she'll suddenly reform. On the contrary—without him tracking her constantly, she might feel more free to wreak havoc wherever she goes.

She's got to be stopped. I don't know if Mother Blessing is the right person to help me stop her, but I don't have a whole lot of options at this point. So until she throws me out bodily, this is where I'll stay.

I haven't asked her yet, but my cell can't get a signal and I have my doubts about the place's wireless capabilities. There's not a phone or a computer in sight, so I don't know if I can call or e-mail my buds. I'll just have to hope they're doing okay and not worrying about me.

More later.

K.

* * *

Just when Kerry thought she'd either faint from hunger or be reduced to finishing off her camping supplies—which she had hoped to preserve in case she wound up back in the Swamp—Mother Blessing called her into the kitchen. The smells that greeted her were heavenly, and she saw that Mother Blessing had prepared two plates with pork chops, dirty rice, greens, and mashed potatoes.

"I thought y'all might be hungry," Mother Blessing said with a welcoming smile. The oxygen mask hung from its strap around her neck. She delivered a couple of plastic tumblers of iced tea to the table. "Ready for supper?"

"More than ready," Kerry answered happily. "Starving, in fact."

"Well, sit yourself down, child," the older woman invited. "I didn't mean to leave y'all settin' out there by yourself for so long."

Kerry tried to set aside the anger she'd felt earlier. "I know you didn't plan to have a houseguest," she said. "I can't expect you to rearrange your whole life for me."

Mother Blessing parked her scooter at the table. "It's just a real busy time for me, honey. Just a few more days to All Hallows' Eve, you know."

Kerry didn't follow at first. "You get a lot of trick-or-treaters way back here in the Swamp?"

Mother Blessing laughed so hard that Kerry feared another choking incident. "Goodness no, child," she said when she was able. "It's the most holy day in our calendar."

"Oh." Kerry felt embarrassed by her lapse. "Of course."

"If y'all are serious about learnin' our craft, you've got to know these things."

Kerry could barely contain her excitement. "Do you mean it? You'll teach me?"

Mother Blessing chuckled, but this time without near-asphyxiation.

"Did I say that, child? I didn't hear myself say that. But I haven't ruled it out, either, have I? I'll give it some thought these next few days, and y'all think about whether it's what you really want. Once you start down that path it ain't so easy to turn around, is it? You don't want to get into something that you don't really want to see the finish of."

"I do, though," Kerry insisted. "My friends, during the summer? The ones who helped Daniel find Season? They called me Bulldog, because once I put my mind to something, I don't let it go. And there's never been anything I've been more dedicated to than this. I can guarantee that."

Mother Blessing nodded her huge head, that billow of platinum hair twitching around it as if it had a mind of its own. "I won't be surprised to learn the truth of that," she said. "Not at all, child. Not at all."

9

Mother Blessing has told me the story since I was old enough to pull myself to my feet with my tiny hands on her knees, but I realize now that I've never put it down on paper. Since she's not the type who ever would, I suppose, it falls upon me to do so, in case something should happen to me and it should never be told. Here it is, then, as she has told it—and of all the billions of people on Earth, she is the only one who would know.

Well, she and one other. But that person's version of the story, if she tells it at all, is surely not to be trusted. So the best I can do is to commit to history the facts as I know them.

At the dawn of the eighteenth century, Slocumb was a village of industry and high moral standing. The village claimed seventy-six residents at that time, most taking their living from the Swamp, or farming the fertile land at its edges. John Slocumb had died but his family had stayed on, with two of his sons working his fields and a third hunting and trapping, living the life of a swamp hermit deep inside the Great Dismal. There were other families Mother Blessing knew well too: the Mortons, the Tanners, the Wallmers, and more.

Kerry sat back in Mother Blessing's leather recliner chair—which also, its owner had pointed out, tipped back almost flat, rocked, and had hidden rollers inside which would massage Kerry while she read, if she chose—and held the journal against her chest. Reading it, she heard Daniel's voice in her head, almost as if he were there with her again. Missing him was a physical sensation, an ache in her gut that faded from time to time, but never abandoned her completely. She wondered if everyone's first love was the same way, or if this was something unique to them. She had tried to broach the subject with Mother Blessing, but the woman had seemed uninterested in or uncomfortable discussing her son's relationship with a girl who was his junior by almost three centuries.

This wasn't the only topic Mother Blessing chose to avoid. While she had hinted that she'd be willing to teach Kerry witchcraft, she hadn't yet committed to a plan of action, or even allowed their brief conversations to drift back in that direction. Now she was back in her kitchen with the door closed.

Kerry had staked out her spot in the living room, anxious to read more of Daniel's journals and to learn whatever she could about his life and craft—especially here, in his boyhood home, where she almost thought she could sense his presence. There was a tall bookcase in the living room with a few random best-sellers from years past, as well as a stack of the heavy leather volumes that were obviously Daniel's journals. An ancient TV stood in one corner with a lace doily on top and a potted plastic flower centered on that. Kerry didn't understand why anyone would have a fake plant in the middle of one of the most fertile spots in the country, but the list of things about Mother Blessing that she didn't understand was a long one. *The more I learn, the longer it gets,* she thought. *I didn't necessarily have an idea of what she'd be like before I got here, but whatever I thought, she isn't it.*

Besides the recliner there was a wrought iron couch that looked particularly uninviting, and, in the corner opposite the television, a straight-backed wooden chair that looked like something one might see in a Shaker household. The chair looked about as comfortable as sitting on a rock, but it appeared to Kerry to be very old, maybe dating back to the early days of Slocumb itself.

Which reminded her about the journal. She listened for Mother Blessing for a moment, but all she heard from the kitchen was a tuneless humming. She opened the book again.

The people of Slocumb didn't have a lot of time for fun and games. The Swamp provided for them, but not easily. They had to wrench their living from it, making use of its wood and water, its creatures, its abundant plant life.

But while these were honest and hardworking citizens, God-fearing and sober, near the end of the century a darkness seemed to settle over the village. Crops failed, children died young, and even the Swamp seemed to turn against the townsfolk. A rogue bear came into town on several occasions, attacking, mauling, and killing. Alligators left the Swamp and hid in the creek that ran along the edge of town, preying on swine, young cattle, and even people who strayed too near. Each incident seemed accidental, random, but they added up quickly; within the space of six months a full quarter of the town's residents were either dead or crippled in some way.

Once the extent of the devastation became known, rumors began to spread as to the cause. These were religious people, of course, but also superstitious and ignorant ones. So the explanations didn't revolve around bad luck or unhealthful environmental conditions, but swung to curses and witchcraft.

Living in Slocumb were two suspects: Mother Blessing herself, and Season Howe. Mother Blessing was known as a woman of extraordinary empathy and unusual talents. Season was less beloved, and little trusted by the townspeople. She kept to herself, living in a small house where, it was said, inhuman creatures came to visit her in the dark of night, including the Devil himself on some occasions. Suspicions were voiced in whispers, but no accusations were made, no action taken.

Then, one freakishly cold October morning, as a rare snow dusted the Swamp, a widow woman named Flinders woke to a silent household.

October, Kerry thought. *So this month is an anniversary, of sorts.* Mother Blessing hadn't said anything about that, and Daniel had never pinpointed a date when he told her the story, only mentioning the year. The thought of poor, as yet unborn Daniel and the horrible things that were about to happen to his hometown made her feel sad for him. But she kept reading, wanting to know more.

She had three children under the age of seven, born before her husband was killed in the Swamp by a bear who hadn't been as badly wounded as Mr. Flinders had thought. Most mornings the children were noisy, playing or squabbling in their room, but on this morning not a sound escaped their door, and when Mrs. Flinders went to look inside, a scene of unimaginable carnage greeted her horrified eyes.

Her three young ones were all dead in their beds, throats savagely torn as if by animal claws, blood soaking the bedding and pooling on the wooden floor. The window was wide open and a chill wind blew flurries of snow into the room. A scream caught in Mrs. Flinders's throat, and it wasn't until she crossed to the window and looked outside to see the tracks in the snow—animal tracks such as a wolf might make, she believed—that it finally broke free, shattering the early morning stillness.

Neighbors came running, and then the town's constable and two of its three clergymen. A hunting party was quickly gathered and the tracks followed through the snow that had fallen during the night. But at the Swamp's boundary the tracks suddenly disappeared, as if, the constable said, the beast had suddenly sprouted wings and taken flight.

The clergymen agreed that there could be only one explanation. Witchcraft.

The names of Season Howe and Mother Blessing sprang to everyone's lips. The tracking party split into two, one branch heading for each of the suspected witches' homes. Mother Blessing was sound asleep beside her husband—my father, Winthrop

Blessing—when a determined rapping on the front door roused them. Both grumbled as they opened the door to find Parson Coopersmith—a dour-faced man whose black clothes and ghastly pallor would have made him as suited for undertaker's work as for the pulpit—standing at the front of a pack of a half-dozen men armed with muskets, axes, and, in one case, a pitchfork.

Mother Blessing knew at a single glance that this could not be good news. The men's faces were grim, their eyes hard, and of course there were the weapons they bore. "What brings you here?" Mother Blessing asked without preamble. Winthrop Blessing, never a strong man, according to his wife's stories, stood mute beside her.

"There has been an incident," Parson Coopersmith declared. "The widow Flinders's children have been murdered in their beds. Every indication is that witchcraft is behind it."

"Witchcraft?" Mother Blessing asked him. When she tells the story she says that she was acting like a natural performer, since she had never publicly admitted to witchcraft, though many in town knew her ways and came to her for help from time to time. "Then why come to me?"

"There are tales," Parson Coopersmith said diplomatically. "You and I have never had any troubles, Mother Blessing. But this . . . this has gone on too long, and we can no longer turn our backs on this activity."

"You believe my wife to be a witch?" Winthrop asked angrily, finally rousing himself. "And a murderer?"

"I believe her to be a possible witch," the parson said, "and therefore suspect in this matter."

Mother Blessing felt her confidence shake at this point. She well knew that it was not their responsibility to prove that she was a witch; rather, the accusation having been made, it was now her job to prove that she was not—an impossible task.

A couple of contradictory ideas came to her. She could run,

though that would certainly mean giving up her home in Slocumb forever. She could fight—and win—but that would demonstrate her witchcraft beyond question, and even though these men would never talk, she wouldn't be able to keep their deaths a secret. Or she could go along with them and accept the task of proving her own innocence, which could not be done, since anything she said or did would now be suspect. There were, she knew, no good options. Time and circumstance had gone against her, and all the good she had ever done for the townsfolk couldn't save her now.

"Leave this house at once, Parson," Winthrop demanded, perhaps recognizing himself the impossible choice that confronted his wife.

But she ignored my father's outburst. "Allow me to dress properly," Mother Blessing insisted. "I won't meet my fate in my nightclothes, and you men should be ashamed for facing me in them."

There were murmurs of dissent from the group, but Parson Coopersmith quickly and loudly overruled the others. "As you would, Mother Blessing. Make haste, though."

Mother Blessing closed the door on them. She could hear them arguing, some afraid that she would grow wings and fly out a window so they wouldn't be able to stop her. If she could do that, of course, she could have done so at the door just as easily. But they were frightened and superstitious, and she supposed that she was lucky no one with a musket had fired upon her as soon as she showed herself. She dressed as rapidly as she could, doing her best to ignore their fearful comments, while reassuring her anxious husband that she would be fine.

Of course, she knew that if witchcraft had indeed figured into the murders, like as not Season Howe was behind it. But one witch didn't talk about another, even in such a dire circumstance.

As it turned out, she didn't need to bring up Season's name. Another group of men had gone to Season's home, and her response had not been as calm and reasoned as Mother Blessing's had been. Instead, she had answered their accusation with the proof they sought, a powerful demonstration of witchcraft that killed them all where they stood.

Her assault was witnessed, however, and even before Parson Coopersmith and his group returned to the town center with Mother Blessing, an alarm had been sounded. From every corner of Slocumb men ran toward Season's home, only to find themselves beaten back by her magical blasts. Parson Coopersmith and his men heard the commotion and charged forward, dragging Mother Blessing along with them. Winthrop armed himself with a musket and joined the group.

Mother Blessing tells me that as they neared Season's the very quality of the air changed. There was so much magic in the air the color of the sky was affected, purpling over Slocumb even though it was early morning, and a smell like burning skunks filled the town. Her guess was that Season had lost control of herself—that in her rage or terror she had unleashed so much magic that it was feeding her own extreme emotions, which then spurred her on to greater efforts in an ever escalating cycle of destruction. Those who had first approached her were all dead now, as were any others who had been nearby.

And still it continued. Parson Coopersmith raised a cross toward Season and advanced on her, shouting out a prayer with every step. But Season uttered words in the ancient tongue and gestured toward him, and a moment later his head was ripped from his body and sent flying, rolling to a stop near Mother Blessing's shoes. The body stood a moment longer, and then dropped the cross to the dirt and collapsed.

Panic spread through Slocumb at that point, and those who had given thought to attacking Season changed their minds. Instead of going after the witch, they ran for cover. Season didn't care, though. Mother Blessing saw her standing *in front of her home, her pretty face twisted in unreasoning fury, unleashing wave after wave of incredibly powerful magics. Dust swirled away from Season, choking the streets, and a ferocious hurricane-force wind picked up, bending trees and tearing shingles from houses.*

Mother Blessing tried then to stop her. Except for Winthrop Blessing, who proved to have some backbone after all, the men surrounding her had all run away, leaving her exposed in the road. She had left the house empty-handed, though, not anticipating a challenge like this. She tried a few spells, but they were blown back from Season by the furious power of the other witch's magic.

Mother Blessing realized at that moment that even she was powerless to rein in Season's wrath. Season Howe had lost all sanity, all the rationality that normally kept her in check. There was no stopping her now, not unless she could somehow calm herself down. And that didn't seem to be happening. Finally, even Winthrop was caught in her attack: he picked up a fallen musket and fired a ball at her, but Season simply reversed its course, driving it through his skull with enough force to shatter it, blowing bits of brain almost all the way into the Swamp.

Lashed by wind, stung by flying dust, pummeled by chunks of wood and debris, and agonizing over the death of her husband, Mother Blessing had no choice but to retreat. She escaped into the depths of the Swamp, from which she could still hear the screams and cries of dying villagers, could smell the smoke as one building after another caught fire in an inferno that burned in the Swamp for more than a month.

By the time Season's preternatural tantrum quieted, two days and nights had passed. Mother Blessing dared to venture from her safe haven only to find the town leveled, the swamp ablaze, and every last soul in Slocumb dead. Except her, and the two unborn in her belly: my brother Abraham and myself. Season,

252 - YEAR OF THE WICKED

who had caused the destruction, whose rage had destroyed a town, was gone.

And Mother Blessing dedicated her life, and those of her sons, to hunting her down. That task continues.

I remain,

Daniel Blessing, March 23, 1797

10

Rebecca Levine walked away from campus toward her shared Victorian, her loose, flowing batik skirt fluttering against her legs in the gentle breeze, her soft peasant top open at the neck. She caught glimpses from time to time of the Pacific shimmering in the distance. She had always loved the ocean, loved the natural beauty that surrounded Santa Cruz. But the ocean now reminded her of La Jolla, and that reminded her of Season Howe and Daniel Blessing. Rebecca had never seen anyone killed before—didn't even like violent movies and TV shows—and the sight had been utterly horrifying. She wanted to surround herself with grace and beauty, to forget the vision that would not be forgotten.

She found herself thinking about it at odd moments. When she was sitting in class, listening to even the most stirring lecturer, she would suddenly realize that her mind had drifted, that she was back on that street in San Diego, watching Season cut Daniel Blessing down with her mystical attacks. Or else she would remember the séance at which Shiai had turned, momentarily, into Season—though she had persuaded herself that she had been carried away by the moment, that it had just been an awful hallucination. Sweat would pour down Rebecca's sides, her fingernails digging into her palms, her heart pounding. She knew her grades were suffering because of the stress, knew that she needed to pay better attention in class, but she couldn't force her mind to comply.

When things had been tough during her childhood, Rebecca's mother had had an odd habit of reminding her that her great-grandparents had survived the concentration camp at Buchenwald. "If you think your life is really so hard, think about theirs for a while," she would say. "Then maybe you'll understand that your problems aren't as big as you think."

It had worked, most of the time, when she was a kid. But then she'd been part of a big family—mother, father, and three brothers—and there was always noise and activity going on that she could use to bring herself out of her occasional funks. Now she didn't have that, her problems seemed far worse than they had ever been, and even thinking of the great-grandparents she had never met didn't quite do the trick.

When she reached the house, she was covered with a thin sheen of perspiration; Indian summer had brought a heat wave to northern California and the walk home had been hot and dry. The house was dark, it was cool inside, and she was almost to the refrigerator for an Odwalla when the phone rang. There was an extension mounted on the wall in the kitchen, so Rebecca reached it almost immediately.

"Hello?"

"Rebecca?" The voice sounded familiar, but strange.

"Kerry, is that you?"

"Yeah," Kerry responded. "It's me."

"Where are you?" Rebecca asked anxiously. She hadn't heard from Kerry since that cryptic e-mail—hadn't even had a chance to tell her about the séance. Now that they were actually speaking, though, it seemed unimportant. "You sound so weird."

"It's a little hard to explain," Kerry said. "And I don't know how much time I have. I'm calling via my built-in microphone, since there's no phone here. Or cell service, wi-fi cable, satellite, or anything else."

Rebecca didn't understand. "So then what are you on? Cable? Satellite?"

"I don't really know myself," Kerry said. "But if I had to guess, I'd say magic."

Rebecca felt herself blanch. "Kerry, you're not . . ."

"I'm fine, Beck. Really. Don't worry about me. You know I can take care of myself."

"But why are you messing around with magic?" Rebecca asked.

"Someone's got to stop Season," Kerry said flatly.

"But . . . you?"

"I don't know if I can," Kerry admitted. "But I know that if I don't prepare myself and try to do it, I'll never succeed."

"I guess that's true," Rebecca said. She felt like there had to be something she could say to her friend to change her course, to make her realize what she was doing. Kerry was brave and capable, and she'd seen for herself what Season could do—had felt it more than the rest of them, Rebecca was sure, because she and Daniel had been in love. Even so, she thought, maybe Kerry underestimated what she might be getting herself into.

"Listen, Beck, I'm being way careful. I'm learning witchcraft—Daniel's mother is starting to teach me. I'm not going to do anything rash. I just wanted to let you know how you could get ahold of me—assuming this connection keeps working. Like I said, I'm not really sure how it's working now."

She told Rebecca she couldn't be telephoned. Or if she could, she wasn't sure how, but that she could check e-mail again at her existing e-mail address, and probably could call if necessary. When Kerry disconnected, Rebecca was confused all over again. How could she get e-mail without being connected to the Internet? But they had spoken, somehow, so clearly the physical laws that she had once believed in didn't apply here.

Having promised that she'd let the others know how they could reach Kerry, Rebecca booted up her own computer and sat down to write one of the oddest e-mails she could remember.

Mother Blessing had emerged from the kitchen while Kerry sat in the living room trying to fathom what it must have been like to be the last living person in Slocumb, with the homes smoldering pits of ash and coal, the bodies of her husband and friends and neighbors strewn everywhere, acrid smoke painting the air, and a layer of ash overlaying everything. "Are y'all ready?" Mother Blessing asked before Kerry even knew she was in the room.

Kerry started, closing the journal she still had open on her lap. *Is it time for dinner?* she wondered. She knew time had passed while she'd been reading, but she had no idea how much. "Ready for what?"

"Your first lesson," Mother Blessing said.

"Really? Do you mean it?" Kerry asked excitedly. This was why she'd come, what she'd been waiting for. But instead of teaching her a spell or mixing a potion, Mother Blessing sent her into the Great Dismal Swamp to look for a particular type of plant.

Slogging across the wet, uneven ground, Kerry felt more like a lackey than a student. Mother Blessing had shown her a picture of the plant she was looking for—a white, five-petaled flower with broad green leaves—given her a bag, and instructed her to bring back a sack full of its roots.

"The craft is as much about knowin' the natural world around us as anything else," she informed Kerry. "Our Swamp here is a bounty of blessings, but y'all have to know what to ask of it, and how, and it'll help you when it can. Ain't a better place on Earth for a witch to find what she needs, or if there is I'd like to know about it. And there ain't a better way to get to know it than on your hands and knees."

The task took Kerry the rest of the afternoon, and by the time she returned to the house—still ramshackle ruin from the outside, suburban spotless on the inside—she was soaked, cold, scratched, bug-eaten, and miserable. But she had her bag of roots. And that's when Mother Blessing surprised her with the laptop setup, which she promised would be able to communicate with the Internet, even though she wouldn't explain just how. Kerry tried it out for a few minutes, retrieving e-mails sent to her account over the past many days, then using her built-in microphone to try calling her friends. The first one she was able to reach was Rebecca. She knew Rebecca would contact the others and talk to them, and she felt more comfortable spreading the word that way than sending out e-mails she wasn't sure would get through, or that might be magically intercepted somehow. Kerry didn't know if Season Howe kept track of Mother Blessing, but just in case, she didn't want to do anything that might bring Season's wrath down upon them.

At least, not until she was ready.

After a hot shower and a filling meal, Kerry followed Mother Blessing into the kitchen. Mother Blessing set two cutting boards out on the table with two sharp knives and the bag of roots. When Kerry sat down across from her, Mother Blessing took up one of the knives and one of the roots and, with skillful, precise movements, skinned the outer surface of the root, revealing a moist, white interior, which she tossed into a ceramic bowl. "This is the part we need," she said. "The outside's nothin', might as well be bark. The power's in here, where the root takes in nutrients from the soil, takes in water, and transmits it all up into the body of the plant. A plant's just like a person, has to eat and drink in order to live and grow, doesn't it?"

Kerry almost laughed, thinking of the fried foods and soft drinks and sweetened tea that Mother Blessing seemed to live on, wondering how long a plant would survive on a diet like hers. She was the last person Kerry would expect to give lessons on nutrition—even plant nutrition. But Kerry knew better than to give voice to such a comment. Mother Blessing seemed to be beginning her lessons, and Kerry didn't want to interrupt her, especially with something that might be considered insulting.

"What's the connection?" she asked, picking up her own knife and a section of root. "Between witchcraft and things like plant roots. I just don't quite get it."

"Our power doesn't come from us, child," Mother Blessing explained.

"Or from the Devil, as some would have you believe. It comes from the Earth, through the Earth. It comes from the plants and animals and the rocks and the sky and the water. Some call the source the Goddess, or Mother Nature, or other names. But it's all the same in the end—we don't possess the power, we just channel the power that's around us all the time. That's why I wanted y'all to start getting used to nature—really muckin' around in it, y'know, instead of just moving blindly through it like y'all have been doin' your whole life."

"I haven't been . . ." Kerry started to object. But then she gave it a moment's thought and realized that she probably had been. She had always been drawn to the beauty of nature, the rivers near her home in Cairo, the ocean, the trees and skies and mountains she had seen. But seeing beauty wasn't the same as knowing nature, as being on a first-name basis with it. Kerry thought that that was what Mother Blessing was getting at, and why she had spent the afternoon in the Swamp, digging through mud with her bare hands, uprooting plants. "I guess you're right," she said after reflecting.

"Y'all are gonna find out I often am," Mother Blessing said with a chuckle.

Kerry held her piece of root toward the pot, its outer surface scraped away, its inside liberated. "Can I taste it?" she asked. "Is it poisonous or anything?"

Mother Blessing shrugged. "Find out."

Kerry raised an eyebrow. That seemed like the hard way to learn a lesson. *But hard lessons stick, right?* She brought the root to her lips, opened her mouth, touched it to her tongue. It was bitter, and a little on the hot side. Not especially pleasant, but she didn't think it would kill her. With the knife she cut off a tiny sliver; she put it on her tongue, feeling its heat, then swallowed it. "I hope that wasn't a bad idea."

"Well, we'll just see if you live or die, child," Mother Blessing said casually. "I expect it'll be live."

"Let's hope."

"Unless, of course, you harbor evil thoughts, right?"

Kerry raised both eyebrows at that. "What if I do?"

"Then it could be bad," Mother Blessing said. She was very matter-of-fact about the whole thing, still carving up her roots.

"But . . . doesn't everyone?"

Mother Blessing laughed out loud. "That's right, child," she declared. "Lesson number two. And three. Life, and magic, are about balance, including the balance of good and evil that exists in all of us."

"That's two?" Kerry queried. "So then what's number three?"

"Don't ever let 'em get you down. Even if they're your teachers. Or your enemies. Psychological warfare, Kerry. It's as important to us as spells and magics. If I'd have let y'all think you'd eaten poison it could've actually made y'all sick to your stomach."

"Like people who believe they're cursed, so they exhibit the symptoms of the curse?"

"That's right." Mother Blessing tossed another root into the bowl. "Sometimes they just believe it. Then again, sometimes they don't believe in curses, but they get the symptoms anyway. Because sometimes the curses are real, aren't they?"

"I . . . I suppose sometimes they are."

"Better believe it," Mother Blessing said, her tone suddenly serious. "Sometimes they're as real as can be."

11

So it's Samhain, which Mother Blessing pronounces SOW-waaain, stretching the final syllable out in her Southern way. I've always just called it Halloween, and thought it was all about trick-or-treating and gorging on candy, but apparently there's a lot more to it than that in the Blessing world. This is one of the most important nights of the year in her calendar, up there with the solstices.

She says I get to celebrate with her tonight, but first I had to have another lesson in the Swamp. She gave me a chart and my little skiff and sent me to Lake Drummond, the biggest body of water within the boundaries of Great Dismal Swamp. There was a jug in the boat that I was supposed to fill with water from the lake. The best tasting water on Earth, she said, because of the cypress trees that constantly freshen it.

"Magic is all in how y'all use the energies that surround us, child," she said when she was giving me my instructions. "Energy is everywhere—how else would trees grow, and the grass, not to mention people? It's how rocks form, how wind blows, how water runs. The world is full of energy, and most people walk around in it without even knowing it's there, much less how to use it. That's where our kind are different." She stopped then, and laughed like she does, a high-pitched kind of titter that seems strange coming from someone her size and age. "Well, like I'm different, anyway, and it won't be too long for y'all now, will it?"

"I don't know," I told her. So far we had been talking only about theory—she hadn't yet SHOWN me anything, or told me how to do anything except chop up roots. In a way it was a complete reversal—Daniel had shown me plenty, but told me precious little. He hadn't, of course, shown me much by way of demonstration; it was mostly just him doing what he had to do to keep me safe. "Will it?"

"Let's us get through tonight, Kerry Profitt," she said—the first time she ever used my full name, I believe. "Then we can see what we see."

Which I took to mean that after Samhain is over, she'll start teaching me the good stuff. So I went out into the Swamp—it had cooled considerably over the past few days, and was starting to feel like fall outside—and followed her directions. This time I was less scared than I had been before, and more attuned to the world of the Swamp. It's a green world, every shade imaginable and then some. From the thickets at foot level to the tops of the tall trees blocking out the sun, green is the predominant color. I know that if I study with Mother Blessing long enough I'll learn the names of all these trees, and more than that, I'll know their properties: what they can do, what they can provide. I saw, moving about in the trees, a stunning array of birds—black, gray, brown, white, blue, yet more green. Also squirrels, a flash of fur that might have been a fox, and several alligators floating through the still water like sentient logs.

Instead of traveling through the Swamp worried or frightened, this time I passed through it in a state of wonder, breathing in the rich, fertile aromas, listening to the burble of the creeks, the calls and whistles and shrieks of the birds, the buzz and whisper of insects, really SEEING everything for the first time. Mother Blessing's directions were as clear as if the boat itself knew where we were going—which, hey, maybe so, considering who we're talking about—and Lake Drummond was amazing. I dipped my head down to it and drank some of the water straight from the lake, and she was right—I've never tasted anything so fresh and sweet. Rimmed by trees, like castle walls around a big, calm pool, the area was quiet as death, which is a creepy kind of simile—or at least that's what I would have thought before talking to Mother Blessing so much. She is a little strange about death. She misses her sons, but she says that death is just another part of life, just a passage, which Daniel also told me. She says death returns a person's energy to the world, so ultimately it's a good thing. Hard for me to see it that way, but maybe in time I will.

Going back to Mother Blessing's was almost, in a strange way, disappointing—like having to go back inside was punishment because it meant I couldn't stay outside. The sun was lowering, though, and I didn't want to be out in the swamp alone at night, and I especially didn't want to miss the Samhain celebration. She's in her room now, getting ready, and I've washed the swamp muck off me and am just waiting, and waiting . . .

More later.
K.

Las Vegas on Halloween night was a zoo. *Worse than a zoo,* Josh thought, *because in a zoo the animals are contained. In Vegas, they're everywhere.* The Strip was clogged with traffic, and Josh had to shoulder his way through the homeless people, tourists, and partyers filling the wide sidewalks that served no function except to connect the huge casinos. The lights were always glaringly bright here, the cars in the streets always loud, the people always determinedly cheerful, but with an edge of desperation, as if they knew they were expected to have a good time here and thought if they didn't that it was because of some personal failing on their part.

But on Halloween, it was all magnified a hundred times. Walking into the Mandalay Bay, where he had found a slot machine he particularly enjoyed because it seemed to like him, he saw people in costume—women mostly, though a few men as well—drinking and gaming and carrying on all around him. There were an inordinate number of cops around, but tonight they were all female, and their uniforms consisted mostly of hot pants and low-cut, figure-hugging tops, with high heels and maybe a nightstick or a pair of handcuffs hanging from their belts. But it wasn't all police officers: There were similarly sexed-up firefighters, nurses, and maids, and among the men pirates and pimps seemed to be the themes of the moment. For a change, laughter and loud voices clashed with the familiar electronic chiming, dinging, and clanging of the casino machines.

Recognizing that his usual Goth look—augmented tonight by a belted black trench coat that Humphrey Bogart would have worn proudly—could be construed by some as a costume, Josh hugged the casino wall until he reached the bank of slots where the machine he liked was located. It was called the Whirlwind, and whenever two like objects showed up on the pay line, whichever wheel didn't match went into action again, spinning around like mad to give the player one more chance at three matches across. One could play up to three coins at a time, with jackpots commensurately larger the more a player put into the machine. Josh hadn't had any huge payouts, but he'd left the other night with sixty dollars more in his wallet than he'd started with. Tonight he had twenty bucks in his pocket, no early classes the next day, and the intention of making his money last for a while.

His first five credits were no go—he might as well have tossed them down a storm drain. On his next spin, he won two credits. He anted up another credit and played all three. Zero. Ditto the next four credits. This was turning out to be not nearly as enjoyable nor as lucrative as the other night. Of course, there was still an advantage to not being at home, either listening to his mother get wasted or fighting with her about taking better care of herself. That was a pretty big plus.

By the time he had reached his last credit from his first ten dollars, he was lighting one smoke after another with his Zippo, waving away the cocktail waitresses in their skimpy outfits, and trying to ignore an obnoxiously loud couple—she in skintight black leather, he in a Laughlin T-shirt, baggy shorts, and a Utah Jazz ball cap—who were either flirting or fighting but apparently hadn't decided which they wanted to go with. Barely twenty minutes had passed—at this rate, he'd be through all the money he'd brought with him in no time, and therefore reduced to either going home or finding someplace where he could hang out for free. And most of the free options didn't pass his annoyance threshold test.

He started to dig into the pocket of his black jeans for the second ten but stopped himself as soon as his finger touched it. Obviously, the machine was cold. The Whirlwind had worn itself out for now. It needed a breather, and so did he. He left the machine, giving it some time to get its mojo back.

Instead of going right to another game, he wandered into the big lounge in the center of the playing floor. The live band had taken a break, which was good since he couldn't stand their watered-down version of rock music. He didn't order a drink, but instead drifted at the edge of the drinkers, listening to snatches of conversation and looking at the wild Halloween outfits. Throughout most of the casino the circulation system whisked virtually all odor from the air, but here a cloud of smoke hung thick and heavy.

"Video discs," he heard one man say to his companion, a bitter edge in his voice.

"What about 'em?" the other man asked. This man was in his sixties, gray hair long and curled at his shoulders, wearing a Western-style jacket and a bolo tie. The first man looked to Josh like a businessman on casual Friday—he wore a neat polo shirt, khaki pants, and deck shoes and had both a cell phone and pager clipped to his belt.

"I was all set," he said. "Perfectly positioned. Big, beautiful store. Good credit ratings with all my suppliers. Well trained staff. Plowed all my profits back into the business, growing it, ready to be there when every home had a video-disc player."

"And what happened?"

"DVDs." The man practically spat the word. "Freaky little things. Who'd have thought you could even fit a whole movie on such a little tiny thing? And what makes it better than a full-on laser disc? At least you can see the cover art on a laser disc."

"What'd you do?"

"I adapted. Got heavy into DVDs, built seven stores across the region."

"Sounds great. What happened?"

"As soon as I opened the seventh, movie downloads hit. Killed me all over again."

"What are you selling now?"

"Women's shoes. I hate my life."

"Sorry that—" the second man began. He stopped short and was quiet for a long moment. Josh had paused to listen but didn't want to be caught staring, so he was about to move on when the man finally spoke. "Sorry, it's just . . . I was here, I guess, forty years ago. Forty-two, I think it was. Not at this hotel, it didn't exist then, but downtown at the Lucky Strike. I met a woman at the blackjack tables, and we got on well, and next thing you know I was buying her dinner and, you know. We went out a few times, had a kind of a fling while I was in town. I haven't really thought much about her in the last decade or three, I guess. Just one of those things that happens when you're younger, and it's a pleasant memory but a vague one at best."

"What about her?" the first man asked, sounding confused. Josh was equally befuddled, and if the guy didn't get to the point, he was going to give up and go back to the Whirlwind.

"I could swear she just walked by," the man said. He seemed a little confused himself.

"Maybe she did. Maybe she never left Las Vegas."

"Yeah, maybe, but . . . well, if it's her, she hasn't aged a day since then. I mean, it was a long time ago, but she was a looker, you know, not the kind of girl you forget. I'd say maybe it's her daughter but there's no way a daughter would be an identical duplicate of her mother, is there? No, more likely it was someone who just sort of looks like her, and just being back in Vegas made me think it was her."

"That sounds right," the bitter man said. "Memory plays tricks. It's not a perfect storage device like a handy laser disc or anything, right?"

"Yeah," the guy said again. "Yeah, I guess so. But it's just weird, you know. Kind of creepy."

Josh was shaking his head, ready to get back to his last ten bucks and block out the world's strangeness with the rush of the win and the noise of the machines, when he had a sudden insight that sent a chill down his spine. *A woman who didn't age in forty years? That could describe Season Howe.* Daniel Blessing hadn't aged in hundreds of years, and from everything he'd said about Season, the same went for her. The chances that it was Season were slim, he knew. More likely the man was as nuts as he sounded, or his memory was as bad as he said. Or the woman under discussion was some kind of female Dorian Gray with a really heinous-looking portrait out in her garage.

But on the other hand, he knew from what Daniel had told them that Vegas would be just the kind of place Season might go to hide out. Full of transients, all the anonymity she could want. In Vegas people didn't ask too many questions; they didn't want to know a lot about anyone because they didn't want anyone to know a lot about them. If nothing else, Las Vegas was a good place to keep secrets.

Either way, he had to know. He hadn't seen the woman the old guy had been talking about, but he'd never forget what Season Howe looked like. The idea of trying to track her down by himself—even with thousands of people around—seemed absurdly dangerous. But no more so than letting her roam around his stomping grounds without knowing where she was. And Rebecca thought she had seen her once. Maybe Season was regretting having let them live, back in San Diego. *Besides,* he thought, his mind racing now as he tried to avoid surging panic, *if I find her, I can call the others, and maybe someone will have a good idea.*

He wasn't sure where to look, though. Since he hadn't been watching the man, but simply eavesdropping on what had seemed a fairly mundane conversation, he didn't know in which direction the man had been looking when she passed by. And the casino was not only crowded but, like all the big casinos, laid out in an intentionally chaotic fashion so that one couldn't walk a straight line but had to pass the maximum number of slots and gaming tables to get from one place to another.

The best Josh could do was pick a direction and strike out. If that didn't pay off, he'd work his way around and hope that he saw Season before she saw him. The worst thing would be if he couldn't find her, because then there was always the chance that she would find him. She had spared him once—spared all of them except Daniel, that day outside her San Diego hideout—but if she spotted him here and thought he was looking for her, he doubted that he'd get the same consideration again.

Josh had come to think of the casinos as a kind of refuge, where he could go to get sucked into the thrill of the game and forget his problems. He had forsaken most of his friends for them, with few regrets. But if Season was indeed loose here, his sanctuary was violated, his comfort zone suddenly a potential death trap.

Nearly frantic, he chose to go to the left, and he dashed off in that direction, scanning the way ahead, dodging gamblers even as he cranked his head in every direction to eye those sitting at the machines he passed. He kept going that way until he reached one of the far walls, then peered through the windows as best he could into the restaurant there. Plenty of blondes, some very attractive, but no Season. He turned and went to his right, staying near the wall for a while, passing another restaurant, then struck out to his right again, cutting through another swath of casino.

He was afraid that he was calling attention to himself, darting this way and that, looking hard at every blond head he saw. He half expected security to snatch him up at any moment.

Still no sign of her. He tried to carve the casino into a regular pattern in his mind so he could make sure he covered all of it—notwithstanding the probability that she was not sitting still someplace, but was moving around just as much as he was, so he could miss her anyway—but its walkways were so irregular that that was hard to do.

Finally, Josh gave up. There was a plain-clothes security agent giving him a hard eye—he recognized the guy from other trips here, and the man was always loitering, never playing, which marked him as an undercover man. Josh hadn't seen Season anywhere. Probably his first impression was the right one: Either the old guy had been wrong altogether, or he had seen someone who looked like his old flame, but that someone was not Season Howe.

As he headed for the nearest exit, Josh felt his heart rate start to calm, his breathing become more regular. He had been, he realized now, dangerously close to a full-fledged panic attack. It had all been a false alarm, though. He wouldn't be returning to this particular casino for a while, but at least he didn't have to worry about Season Howe.

He was almost out the door when he saw her.

12

Scott didn't pace. It might almost have been better if he did. Instead, he sat down at the couch, turned on the TV, ran through the channels using the remote. Finding nothing of interest, he turned it off again, drummed his fingers on the couch, then rose and went to the kitchen, where he rummaged through the pantry. Again finding nothing, he went back to the couch, drummed for a while longer, then clicked the TV back on.

Brandy, sitting at the dining room table and trying to cram for a midterm, thought she would scream. Or kill him. Or kill him and then scream. Earlier, occasional trick-or-treaters had interrupted his agonized fidgeting, but their numbers had trickled and then they'd stopped coming altogether.

"Can you *please* try to control yourself?" she asked, impatience evident in her voice. She had given up trying to hide it.

"What? Am I bothering you?" *Clueless.*

"Brilliant deduction, Sherlock." She couldn't put a finger on precisely *when* she had stopped loving Scott. But this was the moment at which she became aware that she had, and it struck her hard, like a physical blow, and made her queasy, almost nauseous. She had, for a long time, loved the guy sitting there on the couch looking at her from behind his glasses like some lost little boy. But she didn't now. He had drifted away from her somehow. They had much in common, still—mutual friends, mutual interests—but that was a friendship, not a love affair or a lifetime commitment.

"It's just that I'm worried about her."

"About Kerry."

Scott nodded affirmation.

And there it is, Brandy thought. *The wedge that's come between us.*

"You think about her more than you do about me," she said simply. "About us."

He looked as surprised as if she'd slapped him. His thin cheeks crimsoned. "That's not true. It's just . . ."

"It *is* true," Brandy said. "You can't get her off your mind. Since we came back from San Diego, you've talked about Kerry more than anything else. Your grades are slipping because you worry so much about her. You check e-mail, what, twenty times a day, just in case she's sent one? Thirty?"

"She's important. To us," Scott argued. He came off the couch now, walking toward her, and Brandy felt threatened by his approach. No, not threatened, that was wrong. Disturbed, though—she wanted distance. If he put his arms around her, held her close, if she breathed in the familiar scent of him, it would weaken her resolve. Somehow, this seemed important to her right now. Earlier, they'd taken turns answering the door to their apartment as trick-or-treaters came in search of candy, but since that had petered off they'd been alone with only the sounds of the TV and his finger-drumming disturbing the silence, grating on her nerves, pushing her toward a decision she had never wanted to make.

"She's important to you," Brandy shot back. "Okay, to both of us. But only one of us is obsessed with her. One of us thinks she can take care of herself."

"Not against Season," Scott rejoined.

"We don't know that she's fighting Season," Brandy said. "In fact, we have every reason to believe that she's not, and that she's perfectly safe with Mother Blessing, like she told Rebecca."

"I wish she'd called here—" Scott began.

"Is that it? You're ticked that she talked to Rebecca instead of you? She said she tried here, didn't get an answer."

"We have voice mail," Scott pointed out defensively.

"Yeah, we do. And Rebecca said she was calling via her laptop, with some sort of magical force connecting it to the Net. So maybe whatever magic made that work doesn't play well with voice mail. Maybe it wasn't even Kerry, maybe it was her audio doppelgänger."

"It's just . . . I worry about her. I think she's up to something dangerous. I think she's the key to Season, somehow, and . . . I don't know." Instead of approaching Brandy, he flopped back down on the couch, as if he sensed the coldness with which she would have greeted his advance. It was almost as if she'd put up an invisible force field around herself, which was, in fact, what she had been trying to project. "Okay, yeah, you're right, I worry about her. She's our friend, is that a bad thing?"

"It is when it's to the exclusion of the rest of your life," Brandy offered. "Do you remember the last time you kissed me? I don't mean kissing back if I kiss you, but the last time you took the initiative? The last time you made love to me? The last time you even took my hand as we walked across campus? You've been so distracted, so—I have to say obsessed, again—with Kerry that you haven't been paying attention to anything or anyone else, including me. I've looked through your notebooks, Scott. Your notes are terrible. I don't think you're going to pass any of your classes. You can't live like this—or, I don't know, maybe you can, but I can't."

She paused, and Scott's gaze bored into her as if he were looking for the Brandy he'd once known behind this new, cruel mask. Finally, he spoke again. "What . . . what are you saying? It's . . . we're over? Is that it, Brandy? Because if it is, if you'd let what we have, what we've meant to each other, end because of . . . because of something like this, of me worrying about a mutual friend who's in trouble—she left her school, she went to some swamp—you know, that really sucks."

"Maybe it does." Brandy had to try hard not to shrug, but that would look too callous, even for her. "But it's her *Deliverance* fantasy; she's where she wants to be. You know, I'm sorry, Scott. This is not what I wanted at all. I wanted us to be together forever. But, see, by definition that requires both of us participating, and you haven't been. I don't see that changing. I think you love Kerry—or if not, your concern for Kerry outweighs every other aspect of your emotional life, which might as well be the same thing."

Finally, Scott seemed to understand what was happening, and anger clouded his face. She saw him looking at her, narrowed eyes twitching as if he were searching her face to see if she meant what she was saying. She was pretty sure that she did. At any rate, she'd said it—it was out there in the room now, like a tiger let out of a cage, and it couldn't be put back in.

She only hoped it didn't draw blood.

"Brandy, I . . ." Scott let the sentence hang, unfinished. He swallowed, and she thought she saw a tear forming at the corner of his eye. *At least that would be something,* she thought, *an emotional response that really was directed at me and not at Kerry.* But he sniffed once and rubbed his eyes with his knuckles, and when he blinked and looked her way again it was gone, if it had ever been there.

He looked like he was about to say something else when the phone rang. *This is a test,* she thought. *If he lunges for the phone, hoping it's Kerry or news of Kerry, then I'm right about this. If he understands that we're fighting for our own survival, as a couple, and lets it ring—*

He lunged. "Hello?"

He was quiet for a minute, his face growing ever more somber. "Okay," he said after a while. "Yeah, thanks. We'll be there."

He hung up the phone, left his place on the couch and came back into the kitchen. She didn't like the look on his face. "That was Josh," he said, and Brandy thought she detected a tremor in his voice. He opened the refrigerator and leaned inside, hunting for something, raising his voice so she could hear him. "He's found Season. We have to go to Las Vegas."

"What, right now?" Brandy asked, surprised. "We're kind of in the middle of something here. And Las Vegas is, like, two thousand miles away."

Scott swung around toward her, a Coke in his hand. "Brandy, you may not like it, but you're in this. You're part of this. Remember when Rebecca thought she saw her? If Season's in Las Vegas she might be hunting Josh—hunting all of us. Or she might just be trying to hide out. Either way, something's got to be done."

"What can we do?" she asked. She felt a sudden panic—she had hoped their Season-fighting days were far behind them, for the rest of their lives. "We can't hurt her. Even Daniel couldn't beat her."

"We can't just leave her alone," Scott insisted. "Josh could be in trouble. And if she's after him, she'll come for us, too. We have to try to do something. Rebecca's going to try to reach Kerry. Maybe with the help of Daniel's mother, she can . . ."

"Kerry's going to save the day?" Brandy asked archly. "You just keep thinking that."

Scott threw his hands into the air. "Okay, whatever," he said. "I'm going to the airport to get the first flight to Vegas. You can come or not. Suit yourself. And anyway, *Deliverance* is hillbillies, not swamp rats." He headed into the bedroom, and a moment later Brandy heard the sounds of drawers being flung open, his closet ransacked, as he packed for the impromptu trip.

She only thought it over for a few minutes, listening to him prepare. She hadn't consciously changed her mind about loving him—almost as if a switch had been thrown, it was just over. He had demonstrated that his concerns were elsewhere, and that was all it took. The process, she was sure, had started a while ago; his obsession with Kerry had simply been the crucial card that brought all the others down.

But notwithstanding that, he was right. She was in this witch hunt as much as he was, or as much as any of them with the possible exception of Kerry. And even if she was no longer in love with Scott, she didn't want him to be injured. Maybe Kerry could take care of herself, but Scott couldn't. Someone had to be there to keep an eye on him.

She went into the bedroom to gather the things she'd need. *I hope this is a short trip,* she thought anxiously. *I'm going to have to make up that midterm.*

"Samhain is a very special night," Mother Blessing explained. She was wearing a green, velvety robe, and while Kerry bathed in a specially scented tub, she had placed a similar robe on Kerry's bed. After Kerry donned the robe, marveling at its soft, luxurious fabric, they met in what had been the kitchen, except that, through some mystical process Kerry couldn't yet fathom, it had become a courtyard, open to the moon and the stars and an aromatic breeze off the Swamp.

The floor, once vinyl tiles, was now earthen. Candles flickered everywhere—short, fat ones on the bare ground; tall, narrow tapers in multitiered candelabra; tea lights in glass dishes or simply arranged in lines upon the stone altar that stood at one end of the impossible arena. When Mother Blessing had pushed the door open and motored into this place, Kerry hadn't believed her eyes. She tried surreptitiously to feel the ground with her hands, rolling dirt between her fingers to convince herself that it was real.

During her childhood, Halloween had been a very special event for Kerry—the one night she could really lose herself in imagination, in fantasy, giving herself permission to be someone else for the evening. She loved the costumes, the witches and jack-o'-lanterns and black cats, parties with bobbing for apples and other games, knocking on the doors of strangers and being rewarded for it with candy. She had never imagined a night like this one, though . . . had never believed that the witches were real.

"We celebrate the Old Ones on this night," Mother Blessing continued. "We thank them for the gifts they've given us this past year, and we ask them to bless the crops which are to be harvested." She allowed herself a chuckle. "Course, I don't do a lot of harvestin' myself, so that part's just kind of traditional. But still, someone's doin' it, and I use the crops plenty. Just don't pick 'em."

The Old Ones, Kerry knew from Mother Blessing's lectures, were the God and the Goddess. Mother Blessing had stressed that they were two facets of deity, and that other religions and cultures might see them differently—as a single deity, or as an entire pantheon full of gods and demigods. But in Mother Blessing's world, they were two: male and female, opposite sides of the coin. The God represented war, power, rationality, and the seed; the Goddess emotion, beauty, art, and the womb. "Sexist, ain't it?" she had said with a laugh. "But not really, because they're both all of those things. Or they contain all those things within them. Or their aspects can be seen in those things. It's a fluid system, child, that's the important part. However you want to think of it is the way it will work for you. It's only crucial that you do think of it, that you commune with them, because they *are* the power. You channel the power, nature provides the power, but they are part and parcel of the power."

"I think I understand," Kerry assured her. She was afraid of sounding simplistic, but it was a lot to take in and she was still processing. "I haven't done a lot of harvesting myself, but I'm sure happy there are fresh fruits and vegetables and grains."

"That's right," Mother Blessing said. She placed several objects on the altar: a cup, a bell, a knife. "Tonight is also a night of great power," she went on, her voice taking on a warning tone. "So our ritual must be cautious. We want to honor those who have passed, and to prepare for their eventual return. But we don't want to call them—on Samhain, that is far too easy to do and far too dangerous to contemplate."

"The dead can come back?" Kerry asked, hope sparking within her for a moment. Maybe there was a way to see Daniel again, to be with him . . .

"The dead always come back," Mother Blessing replied. "But not as those we remember. And not in frogs or rocks or, I expect, lawyers. Just as new people, with some trace fragments of who they were before buried deep inside them. But if they're summoned on Samhain and they're not ready to return . . . well, you don't want to know, do you?"

Actually, Kerry thought, *I kind of do*. But she decided she wouldn't let on about that. This whole thing was so exciting—finally being allowed to take part in a ritual, and such an important one at that. She felt that Mother Blessing was gradually learning to trust her. If she performed well here—which she figured meant keeping out of the way, not accidentally breaking anything, and doing whatever Mother Blessing asked of her— then surely Mother Blessing would ramp up her training, start in with the real goods. She knew it would be a long time before she could do the kinds of things that Daniel had, but baby steps were better than not walking at all.

Mother Blessing turned her cart around and was about to wheel away from the altar when a look of surprise washed over her face. She stopped cold and stared at the ground, as if listening intently to a voice Kerry couldn't hear. When she looked up again it was directly at Kerry. "Someone's trying to reach you."

Kerry said the first thing that popped into her mind. "The dead?"

"The living," Mother Blessing answered. "I hate to see our Samhain rites interrupted, but you had better see what they want. It's urgent."

"How . . . ?"

"Check your computer," Mother Blessing said. "You'll be able to get through. Tonight, magic is easy. The veils between worlds are thin. Go, child, go."

Kerry took a last look around at the unlikely courtyard, the candles, the objects arrayed on the altar, and herself and Mother Blessing in matching green robes. *I'll never learn this*, she thought angrily, *if I can't have some uninterrupted time to do it in*.

But she knew that Mother Blessing wouldn't send her away if there weren't a good reason. She went out through the door—into the rest of the house, just as if she'd been in the normal kitchen all along—and dashed down to her room. The laptop was in the cabinet next to her bed. As she booted up, she wondered what could possibly be so important.

13

Josh had figured he'd live his whole life without ever once saying—at least in any kind of serious way—the words "Follow that cab." But when he finally spotted Season at the Mandalay Bay, she was walking out the front door, and by the time Josh reached the door, a doorman was closing a taxi door behind her. Josh had jumped into the next cab in line and uttered those eternal words, and as the taxi pulled out into the street, he was glad he hadn't gambled away his second ten. And hoped the ride would be a short one.

Both cabs rolled out onto Las Vegas Boulevard—the Strip—and were immediately stuck in gridlock. The Strip was thick with vehicles: huge stretch limos, SUVs, hotel shuttles, and cabs mixing with normal passenger cars and the occasional city bus in a ballet of steel, glass, and rubber performed to a soundtrack of honking horns, screeching brakes, and squealing tires. Josh was half afraid that his cab would accidentally catch up to or pass the one Season rode in, and that either she'd see him or his driver would misunderstand the nature of the request and, thinking he was trying to join her, would flag the other driver down or radio him.

As it turned out, though, that didn't happen. Season's cab stayed ahead of theirs, turning off the Strip at Flamingo and cutting down to the Maryland Parkway, which ran parallel to Las Vegas Boulevard but without as much traffic. Josh watched the dollars mount up on the taxi's meter as the car swallowed up the miles toward downtown. He knew he should call the rest of the summer gang, but he didn't want the cabbie to hear what he had to say; bad enough that by not having a destination, but asking the driver to follow another car, he was creating a memory that would stick with the guy.

Finally, the other cab stopped at a motel near downtown, the Come-On Inn. It was nothing special—not the kind of place Josh would have expected Season to stay. But then again, he thought, if privacy was her primary consideration, the big casinos probably weren't ideal. They had cameras everywhere, they had staff who tried to remember the guests, especially regulars. At this place one could probably get a room without even showing identification, and the staff most likely made a point of not prying into a guest's affairs.

Josh glanced at the meter again. Thirteen bucks, and still climbing. He had just the ten, a few singles, and some loose change on him. "Stop here," he said. He reached into his pocket, pulled out the ten, a couple singles, and some change. When the driver reached around to collect, Josh hurled it all into the front seat. "Sorry!" Josh shouted. He grabbed the door handle, opened it and darted from the cab while the driver fumbled with the money.

The guy shouted at him, but Josh ran into the shadows behind a vacant commercial building. He stayed there for a few minutes, breathing hard, his heart pounding, while the cab circled the block. Josh felt terrible—he hated to rip off an honest cab driver just trying to make a living—but this was an emergency situation. As it was, he'd been left with just a couple of quarters and two singles. *Damn Whirlwind,* he thought.

When the coast was clear, Josh emerged from the shadows, just in time to see an upstairs door close behind Season. He moved a little closer until he could see the number on it: 17. Behind heavy drapes, a light turned on. It looked as if she was alone in the room, and, he hoped, in there for the night.

Now he dug out his cell phone, scrolled through his saved numbers, and dialed Rebecca. "Happy Halloween," she answered cheerfully.

"Beck? It's Josh."

"Hi, Josh, how are you?"

"Listen, Rebecca, this isn't a social call. It's Season. I found her."

There was a long silence from the other end. When Rebecca spoke again, there was a tremor in her voice, and Josh felt sorry for having to put her through this. "If this is a Halloween prank, Josh, it's not a very funny one."

"It's not a joke, Beck. She's here, in Vegas. I just tailed her to her hotel. We have to do something."

"What can we do, Josh? You're better off getting out of there before she sees you."

"But . . . Rebecca, she's not going to stop being a threat. To us and to others. Don't you think we should try to fight her while we have the advantage?"

"What advantage is that? She has all the power."

"We have surprise," Josh countered, hoping he didn't sound as foolishly desperate as he felt.

"We had that before, too. And we also had Daniel. Look at where it got him."

"Yeah, but she was ready for Daniel. She knew he was around, knew she'd be facing him sometime. She doesn't know that we know where she is."

"Because she's not worried about us, because we can't do a thing to her," Rebecca pointed out. "We're powerless against her, Josh. Get out of there while you can."

"Maybe we're not so powerless after all, Beck," he argued. "Didn't you say that Kerry was learning magic from Mother Blessing? Maybe there's something she can do."

Another pause from Rebecca. Her hesitation surprised him. Sure, it was stupid to think they had any chance against Season. But it was suicidal to just leave her roaming freely around his town. "Maybe," she said at last. "Are you sure she hasn't seen you?"

"I'm sure." Josh realized that another advantage of this crummy motel was that in any of the big hotels, security would have thrown him off the premises before too long. Here, though, he should be able to keep an eye on her door at all times. "Can you try to get through to Kerry? I'll call Scott and Brandy. I'm sure if we all get together we can think of something. But it's got to be fast—I don't want to lose her again."

Rebecca sighed loudly enough that he wasn't sure he needed the phone to hear it. "Okay," she said. "I'll reach Kerry, somehow, and then I'll catch the first plane out there. I'll call you when I get there, and you can tell me where you are."

"That's great, Rebecca. Thanks. I really think this is important."

After he disconnected the call he tried to figure out why he thought that. She was right, of course. They had no way to mount a successful offense against Season Howe. Unless, that is, Kerry had learned some really impressive magic in the weeks she'd been gone. Even so, the chance that in such a brief period of training she had picked up any skills that Daniel hadn't acquired after hundreds of years was worse than slim.

But really, he thought, *that doesn't matter. Daniel died. Mace died. Others will die. Now that we have a lead on her, we have to play it out, no matter what. To turn our backs on her would be the only unforgivable thing.*

He scrolled down to Scott and Brandy's number and pushed talk.

With every passing day in the Great Dismal, Kerry felt more comfortable there—so much so that when she had to leave, she was surprised by a pang of regret, as if she were leaving a home she'd known for years. She bade Mother Blessing good-bye before first light, having missed the whole Samhain observance, which the older woman had said had had to go on as scheduled before midnight changed the date. After the ritual was over, Mother Blessing had called her back into the kitchen, which was, once again, just a kitchen, and they had sat down together at the table with glasses of milk and a plate of cookies between them.

"Y'all have to go," Mother Blessing had said.

Kerry had come to the same conclusion, but she had expected to have to convince Mother Blessing. That the witch herself suggested it came as a surprise. "I know," she agreed. "I'm just not sure what I can do."

"You'll do whatever you can. The woman is just evil. You know why she was at a casino instead of celebrating Samhain like she should've been? She thinks she's nontraditional, but it's the tradition that is so important to the craft. She just likes to do things her own way, no matter what." Kerry could tell from Mother Blessing's tone, and the sneer on her lips, that this was an enormous sin in her eyes. "I want y'all to understand why it's so important that Season Howe be stopped," Mother Blessing continued. "And sooner better than later."

"Well, to start with, she's a killer, right?" Kerry offered.

"She is that, true," Mother Blessing said. "More urgently, though, did Daniel ever tell y'all about the Witches' Convocation?"

"Yes, he mentioned it." Every five hundred years all the world's witches gathered for a festival, a sharing of information, and a combination social and business gathering. Kerry remembered, with a pain in her chest like a spike to the heart, that he had been looking forward to his first one.

"Well," Mother Blessing went on, "this one's the first since Season destroyed Slocumb. I'm fixing to bring charges against her for it. But word is she's got a counterattack planned—that she's thinkin' she'll demand sanctions against us for chasin' after her for so long, and she'll use that as a forum to deflect blame for Slocumb onto someone else. Maybe even me."

Kerry was astonished to hear this. "Could she get away with that?"

Mother Blessing tucked a cookie neatly into her mouth and chewed while nodding. "It's all political," she said when she had swallowed it. "If she could sway enough votes to her side, she could pull it off."

"What would the sanctions be?" Kerry wanted to know.

Now Mother Blessing shrugged. "Could be just about anything. I might have to give up magic until the next Convocation. I might have to pay a fine of some kind. Could be I'd even have to pay with my life."

Kerry had been about to sip some milk, but now she put the glass down hard. "You're kidding."

"I wouldn't joke about something like that, would I, child?"

"I guess not. It just seems sort of extreme."

Another shrug. "If her accusations were true, it might be a fair judgment. Since they're not, though, I have to keep her from bringin' 'em if I can. Be better to stop her before she ever makes it to the Convocation so I don't have to worry about tryin' to outmaneuver her once we're there."

After sorting through the logistics of how to get to Vegas from the Swamp, Kerry had turned in for a few hours of restless sleep. As soon as the morning light filtered through the trees into the Swamp, she was in Mother Blessing's skiff, rowing for the old Slocumb site, where her van still waited. By the time she reached it her arms and shoulders were sore from the workout, and she was covered with a film of sweat in spite of the cool of the morning. She hiked across the wasted, barren land with a deeper appreciation for what had occurred there than she'd had before reading Daniel's account of that catastrophic day. When she reached her minivan she thought for a moment that she saw shadows slipping away from it into the reeds. She wasn't entirely sure, but it wouldn't have surprised her to know that Mother Blessing had sent simulacra to guard it until her return.

The van started right up. Sitting behind the wheel felt oddly foreign to her, as if hiking through the Swamp had already become her everyday life, and the world of cars and roads and cities a kind of half-remembered dream. But she hadn't forgotten how to drive, so she put the vehicle into gear, turned it around and headed back toward the highway, back toward Norfolk and an airport from which she could fly to Las Vegas.

Season was there. She wasn't sure what she'd do to Season—Mother Blessing had armed her with some potent spells, though she'd had no time to practice them—but that would come. The important thing was finding her again. Confronting her.

Making sure she paid for what she did to Daniel. And making sure she would never make it to the Witches' Convocation, where she might compound her crimes by blaming them on Mother Blessing.

Kerry's resolve was tempered steel. The Bulldog was back.

14

Josh spent the night huddled in the doorway of the vacant building, drawing his coat around him for whatever warmth it could offer, smoking for the same reason, wishing he had a car he could sit in or a credit card so he could take a room at the Come-On Inn for himself. Las Vegas was a desert city, which meant that on summer days the sun could be merciless, but on October-melting-into-November nights, the same lack of cloud cover that let the sun beat down during the day allowed the city's heat to be quickly dissipated. The result was nights that felt positively arctic, at least by Josh's standards. He figured frostbite was not a genuine concern, but he'd spent more comfortable nights, and he couldn't think of many worse.

Finally, though, the sun did reappear above the eastern horizon, and with its glow the city began to awaken. Parts of it, of course, never slept—the casinos were open 24/7—but most of the city, away from the bright lights and high rollers, operated on a more traditional schedule. As the sun warmed the air, birds began to chirp their morning songs, cars and buses emerged onto the streets, and Josh felt his bones start to thaw.

He also realized another downside to his plan. His stomach woke up too, and it began churning hungrily. He'd hardly slept, he'd had nothing to eat or drink, and he'd been smoking like a chimney. He needed to eat something now, and have some water, or he'd be sick. But there was nothing he could see within immediate range, no handy market or diner, and if he went looking for something he could buy or steal he'd run the risk of missing Season, should she emerge from her hidey-hole. He wondered what Philip Marlowe would do in this situation, or Mike Hammer. Fictional private eyes didn't need to eat as regularly as real people, he decided, so they'd probably just buck it up, maybe knock back a shot of whiskey, and continue the surveillance. Sooner or later someone would knock them out, and then they'd have the opportunity to grab a few winks and maybe a sandwich.

The sound of his cell phone's electronic tune startled him. He fished it from his pocket with a shaking hand. "Yeah?"

"Hi, Josh." Rebecca Levine. She sounded close, but that was meaningless.

"Beck, hey. Where are you?"

"At the airport," she said.

"McCarran?"

"Here in Las Vegas."

He moved the phone from his ear long enough to check the time. Seven-fifteen. "Listen," he said, regretting the words even before he spoke them. "I think our bird's gonna stay in her cage a while longer. Why don't you rent a car, but then stay at the airport a while? Brandy and Scott are supposed to get here at 10:12. You might as well wait and bring them when you come."

"I talked to Kerry last night," Rebecca reported. "She'll be here this morning too."

"That's great," Josh said. "I'm glad you were able to reach her."

"Is everything okay?"

"I could use some grub," Josh admitted. "And I'm sure I need a shower. But I'm fine, I guess. No movement from Season after she went into her room last night."

"It's so amazing that you found her," Rebecca said. Josh thought he caught a hint of disbelief in her voice, as if Rebecca questioned whether it was, in fact, simply coincidence that put Josh and Season in the same building at the same time. Josh didn't know how to answer that, because he'd had the same concern himself.

If it's not coincidence, then we could be playing right into her hands.

That idea chilled him to his core. But in fact, he remembered, Rebecca had seen her first—or had thought she had. Which didn't mean this wasn't a trap of some kind. In fact, the more he dwelled on it, the more it seemed to confirm that idea. "Yeah," he said simply. "I don't know what we're going to do now, but at least we've got her pinned down."

"I think Kerry will have some ideas," Rebecca offered.

"She'd better. I sure don't."

"She will." Rebecca sounded more like someone trying to project confidence than someone who actually felt it, but Josh was willing to take what he could get. "You've got my number, so if anything comes up, give me a call, okay?"

"Absolutely," Josh assured her. The fact was, as much as he liked Rebecca, he could think of no one less useful for surveillance or combat, if it came to that. Her manner of dress tended toward flowing skirts and tie-dye, which would make her stand out in a crowd or in a casino—not that Josh didn't, in his Goth blacks and jet hair. But at least during the night his chosen wardrobe had helped him blend into the shadows. Then there was the fact that Rebecca was just about the most peaceful soul he'd ever known. He was vegan, but even so, he was willing to swat a hungry mosquito. Rebecca would argue for the creature's life, then extend her arm to it. She had needed to be informed of Season's reappearance because she was part of the original group that had faced the witch during the summer, but keeping her at the airport, taking care of logistical things like renting a car, was the best use for her.

Still, he thought as he squirmed in the doorway, *I could have had her pick up some granola or something.*

Two more hours had passed when the door to Room 17 opened. Josh looked around anxiously, hoping to spot a cab. If she was going somewhere by car, or had a ride coming, he was out of luck. This was what he had hoped wouldn't happen until Rebecca showed up with the others in her rental. He watched Season step outside onto the walkway that ran past all the second-floor doors, her honey-blond hair catching the morning sun. She wore what looked like a brown leather suit, snug pants and a jeans-style jacket with a white shirt underneath it. Josh pressed himself back against the door, as deep in shadow as he could get, while she slowly surveyed the neighborhood.

Instead of getting into a car, though, Season descended the staircase and walked across the street to a bus stop. Almost no one used public transportation in Vegas, Josh knew, except those so economically disadvantaged that they just couldn't afford a car. Which was probably precisely why Season was using it—if she were hiding out she'd want to vary her routine, not be predictable. Cab last night, bus this morning. Made perfect sense.

But that didn't solve his predicament. He had an idea that might, though. So far, no bus was in sight. Bus stops weren't too terribly spread out around this neighborhood. He had an opportunity, then, if he hurried, to reach the next bus stop down the line, and to get on the bus before Season did. Of course, that came with a couple of pitfalls, too. If he missed the bus he'd lose Season. If she changed her mind and didn't take the bus, or crossed the street and hopped one going in another direction, he was screwed. And if she recognized him once she got on, she'd . . . well, it didn't help to dwell on such things. It was a gamble, but Josh was a gambler. He ran.

He went around behind the building next to which he'd spent the night, knowing as he did that letting Season out of his sight only decreased the odds in his favor. But if she saw him running, her guard would certainly be raised. This way she'd only have a brief glimpse of him, if at all, when he ran across the distant intersection more than a block away from the one where she waited at the bus stop. Josh put aside his exhaustion, his hunger, and his fear, and sprinted full-out. Two blocks beyond Season's location, he cut back over to the street she was on.

From here, he looked in both directions, spotting a bus stop one more block away. He started for it at the same time that a city bus swung around the corner, coming toward him. He had been running with everything he had—he was not, he'd readily admit, exactly track-star material—but now he reached deep down inside, knowing he had to find a little more speed, a little more endurance, if he hoped to beat the smoke-belching vehicle. Feet pounding pavement, head jarring with every step, aching lungs sucking air, he ran, finally reaching the bus stop just as the bus lurched to the curb.

The driver looked curiously at him as he boarded, but it was all Josh could do to drop his fare into the slot and request a transfer. Trying to catch his breath, he moved toward the back of the bus. He spotted an open window seat next to a wrinkled Latino man with a steel lunchbox on his lap, and ignored several empty seats to take that one, to eliminate the chance that Season might sit next to him. The man frowned, but relented and allowed Josh to squeeze past him.

When the bus rumbled up to the next stop, Josh scrunched down in the seat as far as he could, just looking over the seat back in front of him from the tops of his eyes. For a terrible moment he feared that Season had changed her mind, that she wasn't getting on after all, and that he would be taking a bus ride to nowhere while she slipped away. But then her familiar features showed up in the doorway, another ray of light striking her—as if illuminated by an admiring sun—just before she came into the bus's shadow. She didn't even glance his way, but took an available seat near the front.

The horrible thought struck him, once again, that this was not in fact Season Howe, but simply some innocent young woman who happened to resemble her. *Wouldn't Season sense me sitting here?* he wondered. *Wouldn't she just know?*

But when he saw her run her fingers through her hair or glance toward the back of the bus, he knew again that it was indeed Season. At those moments he quickly looked away, lest the old "I know someone is watching me" radar kick in and alert her to his presence.

Josh's next challenge came when she got off the bus, just outside the New York–New York casino. Should he stay on until the next stop and risk losing her in the crowd? Or get off here and risk being seen? He decided that being seen was the lesser of the two worries, since there were so many people in the casino and so many places she might go. He stayed in his seat until she was off the bus, then he rose, pushed past lunchbox guy, and darted for the back door. By the time he made it off, she was already headed toward the casino's entrance.

He tore his cell from his pocket, breathlessly punched Rebecca's number. When she answered, he said, "Beck, she's at New York. Where are you?"

"Kerry's just shown up," Rebecca answered. "We'll be there in a few minutes."

"Okay," he said. "Take Tropicana to the Strip and turn right."

"I've been memorizing the map," she assured him. "We'll be right there. Don't do anything stupid."

Sprinting for the door, he broke the connection. By any reasonable definition, this whole thing was stupid. The fact that Season Howe was entering a small-scale reproduction of New York City—complete with Statue of Liberty, Times Square, and fireboats in the harbor—was absurd.

But that was Vegas.

Inside, she had already blended in with the rest of the crowd: tourists, gamblers, employees, and sightseers gawking at the replica Big Apple that filled the huge building. Josh tried to slow his pace, not wanting to appear frantic or to chance missing her if she'd simply stepped behind something or someone. She was inside now—it'd be a while before she made it back out. He'd find her.

By the time he did, though, panic had almost overtaken him. He felt like the casino was as crowded as the real New York, like there were nine million people in the place and he was only looking for one. He eventually spotted her, though, sitting at a hundred-dollar-minimum blackjack table, looking as at home as if she owned the place. This, he realized, was probably a great way for a witch to generate cash flow: A few magically altered cards at the right moment could keep her in the green for a long time, and the pit bosses would never be able to figure out how she was cheating. Josh felt a moment's envy—this was the kind of action he craved but could never afford. Maybe if he'd been in league with Season instead of with the good guys, he'd be sitting next to her instead of wearing the same stinking clothes he'd had on all night, ragged and hungry and beyond exhausted.

He had made his choices, though. He hung back and watched her play, the pile of chips before her growing steadily. After a little while, he realized he wasn't the only one watching her. From a bank of slots nearby, two men glared at her with eerie yellow eyes. There was something not right about them, he noticed. When they started to move it became even more apparent. They weren't men at all; he could see bits of casino debris stuck to them—no, stuck *in* them, as if it were part of them—cigarette butts and change cups, plastic and paper coin rolls. These were manufactured men—Josh searched his memory for the term Daniel Blessing had used. *Simulacra.* It came to him just as they headed for her. She hadn't seen them yet, and he knew that if she did, it would spook her—no way would she still be around when Kerry and the others showed up. He was sure the simulacra couldn't defeat her alone; if they'd been able to, Daniel's quest would have ended ages before.

He was also pretty sure that Kerry and the gang wouldn't be able to beat her either. But if she was hunting them down, then they had to at least try. And he didn't know what tricks Mother Blessing might have outfitted Kerry with. No matter what, he had to keep the simulacra from scaring off Season before Kerry arrived.

He did the only thing he could think of. He moved in front of them, putting his hands out to stop them. "Wait," he said urgently, trying to keep his voice low so as not to attract casino security. "I know what you are. You work for Mother Blessing, right?"

The two barely spared him a glance. He could see that he was right, though; there was nothing natural about these creatures. *Men* was the wrong word for them. They ignored his entreaties, as if deaf to him. One of them swept an arm sideways, catching Josh in the chest and hurling him into the slot machines. Pain shot through his back and flashes of light filled his vision. But he forced himself to his feet again, and dashed toward the creatures, knowing even as he did so that it was too late now to prevent a scene. His gambler's instincts, though, told him that if the simulacra got to Season first, he'd never get another shot at her, and he wasn't willing to let that happen. "Stop!" he called. "You'll blow everything."

This time one of the simulacra turned toward him. Its face was feature-less but its body language spoke volumes, and Josh got the sense that it would not interrupt its mission for anything. The thing snatched up a stool from in front of a video poker machine, tearing it loose from its moorings, and drove its jagged base into Josh's chest. Fire lanced into him, obscuring the comparatively minor pain he'd felt before. This was like nothing he'd ever experienced: The whole world was turning dark, except for the white-hot bolt of agony at his chest.

Josh felt himself slumping backward, falling to the floor. The world moved before him in slow motion. The simulacra, having forgotten him, advanced on Season. She came up from her seat, her pretty face set with a determined scowl, sparing only a glance for Josh before she faced the two not-men. All around, people went into slo-mo action, like something from a Peckinpah battle sequence: civilians ducking for cover, security forces converging on the scene. Josh heard screams, but distantly, as if through some kind of filter.

One of the simulacra overturned a craps table as it rushed toward her.

Chips spun everywhere, arcing through the air like rainbows. Again, voices were raised, but they sounded to Josh like deep bellows, like foghorns on faraway shores, and when the table hit the ground, the crash came to him slowly, as if he were underwater.

But then Season went into action, and it was a beautiful thing to behold: practiced, efficient, without a wasted motion. She spoke words Josh couldn't hear, inscribed gestures in the air that his eyes couldn't track. Bursts of glowing energy pulsed from her upraised hands. The simulacra halted in their tracks, caught in beams of light that pummeled them like hurricane winds. They tried to push forward against her magical field, but it tore at them, tattering their makeshift clothing, keeping them at bay. Now they both howled their anguish, and this Josh could hear even over the dull rush that filled his ears: long, drawn-out screams as they began to disassemble. Pieces of trash, a mannequin's arm, a hunk of partially shredded black tire, strips of wire—Josh saw them all come into focus as they tore away from the simulacra's bodies under Season's steady assault. The image was fascinating and terrible at the same time—nonliving beings dismantling bit by bit—and Josh couldn't help being impressed by Season's bold stance as she stood there, unshaken by their attack, unmoved by the commotion around her, until her task was done.

Finally it was.

The simulacra gone, Season shook off the meaty hands of the security officers who tried to grab her and headed straight for Josh. She swam in and out of focus as she neared. Josh was cold, so cold, but at least his chest had stopped hurting, and that was something. He started to think that maybe he'd survive this after all, until he saw Season bearing down on him. His eyes fluttered closed; he fought them open again, and she was nearer.

The expression on her face as she knelt before him was the scariest thing he'd seen yet. It was concerned, almost tender—her clear blue eyes wide, moist lips parted—but at the same time utterly without hope. Her words confirmed this impression. "It's too late for me to help you," she said soft

"But thank you for what you did. Maybe this will help."

She touched his cheek, fingers as gentle as a whisper, and spoke a
word. Instantly, all the pain faded away. The cold vanished. Josh felt as con
fortable as he ever had in his life. He was dying. He had known that, but
where moments before he had been in utter agony, now he felt at peace with
it. That was Season's gift to him, and it was not one he could take lightly.

He touched his chest, feeling the tacky blood that flowed there, soaking
his clothing and skin. In the dim distance he saw Season running, twirl-
ing like a quarterback to elude the security forces trying to tackle her. He
couldn't help thinking that they had all misjudged her, and he knew they
were coming, Kerry and the rest, and had to be told. He just had to hang
on long enough to let them know. Or he had to send them a message some
other way.

He tried to free his cell phone from his pocket but it slipped from his
wet hands and clattered away. He didn't have the strength to lift it anyway,
he was sure. Dipping his finger in his own blood, Josh Quinn began to
write on the side of a slot machine.

15

When Kerry came down the escalator into the central baggage-claim area of Las Vegas's McCarran Airport, Rebecca, Scott, and Brandy were waiting for her, Rebecca holding a big, hastily lettered sign that said "Bulldog Profitt." Kerry began to laugh immediately, the first good, long belly laugh she'd had in a long time. The others surrounded her and enmeshed her into a textbook-quality group hug that lasted until the laughter faded and the import of the trip began to settle among them again.

As Rebecca directed them to the parking structure where the rental car waited, Scott inclined his head toward a young woman dressed in a skimpy showgirl's outfit, complete with feathered headgear, holding a sign welcoming visitors to the resort she represented. Then he pointed at the double rank of slot machines filling the center of the baggage-claim area. "No wonder Season likes this place," he said lightly. "It's like a surrealist's bad dream. No one would even notice her here."

Rebecca, resplendent in a long broomstick skirt and an embroidered denim top, nodded her head. "I read someplace that more fugitives from justice pick Las Vegas to hide out in than any other city."

"I believe that," Brandy chimed in. She looked stylish as ever in a peach-colored, long-sleeve thermal top with low-rise twill pants and black Paul Frank sneakers, and she tossed Kerry a smile like they were long-lost sisters. "After all, Josh lives here."

"He likes crime stories," Scott countered. "I don't think he's so big on actual crime."

"I'm just saying," Brandy shot back. "The spoon doesn't fall far from the kettle, or something like that."

Rebecca cracked up again. "That doesn't even make any sense," she said, her face turning red.

"It's Josh we're talking about," Brandy reminded her. "Who said making sense entered into it?"

The banter continued until they were in the car and Rebecca, after giving them a brief update on her last text from Josh, focused on driving. Scott and Brandy sat in back, hushed, while Kerry watched out the windows.

Emergency vehicles overtook them on the short trip from the airport—police cars, fire trucks, ambulances, lights flashing, sirens blaring. Traffic already jammed Las Vegas Boulevard, but somehow the cars on the street managed to pull to the sides, and the official vehicles wove through. Kerry wrinkled her forehead. "I've got a bad feeling about this," she said. "Hurry up, Beck."

Rebecca nodded grimly and pulled out, beating most of the other cars back into the lane after the emergency vehicles had passed through. "I'm on it," she said, flooring the accelerator. The rented Maxima lunged forward. Kerry was impressed by the way Rebecca handled the car. Ignoring the complaining horns, she muscled it from one lane to the next, pushing her way through before traffic had a chance to jam up again.

Within minutes, New York's skyline, or an approximation of it wrapped by a roller coaster, loomed on the left. Rebecca turned into the self-parking structure and the four of them ran from the car into the casino, Rebecca trying furiously to reach Josh on his cell phone. It rang and rang, she reported, but he did not answer. Kerry swallowed hard, expecting the worst.

Inside, the worst was what they found. Uniformed police officers were shooing away gamblers and onlookers, trying to spread yellow crime-scene tape across a wide swath of the casino floor. People stood around with stunned looks on their faces, some in tears, some strangely excited, as if they'd just seen a show put on by the establishment and felt they'd gotten their money's worth. Kerry shoved her way through the clot of people, craning her head to see around the cops, EMTs, and firefighters. The first thing she noticed was a strange assortment of trash strewn around the floor—the wheel of a shopping cart, a paper cup from an overpriced coffee shop, some general casino litter. Anyone else looking at the random junk would have wondered why it was all there, but to Kerry there was only one possible answer: simulacra had been here. She'd told Mother Blessing she was going to Las Vegas to investigate a Season sighting; the old witch must have sent her own scouts ahead.

But then her eyes rested on another sight, one that chilled her to the core, as if she'd just taken a cold shower inside a deep freeze.

Josh—or rather, a crumpled shape that had once been Josh, had once contained the essence of him—was splayed against a bank of slot machines. In the center of his chest a hole gaped, red and meaty, and blood from it had poured down his torn shirt, pooling on the ground between his legs.

Next to him, on the side of one of the slots, were four letters, scrawled in blood by a shaky hand.

SEAS

As if there were any doubt, Kerry thought. "Leave it to Josh," she said quietly to Scott, who had come up beside her. She pointed to the writing. "He fingered his own killer."

"Just like something out of one of those hard-boiled movies he loves," Scott answered. His voice broke when he said it, and Kerry knew he was close to tears. That was okay.

So was she.

Kerry Profitt's diary, November 1

We couldn't stay at NY-NY—couldn't bring ourselves to—so we're across the street at the MGM Grand. It's my first time here, and I'd like to think there's something grand about it, but the fact is that we are all just staying the night because we're too drained to actually make any moves toward going home.

Three down:

Mace Winston.

Daniel Blessing.

Josh Quinn.

Pausing to look at my friends . . .

Scott Banner sits in a chair, staring out the window. Brandy Pearson's reading a textbook she brought with her, sitting on the bed with her legs folded beneath her, making herself as small as possible. Something's wrong there—trouble between those two, though neither one has said a word about it. Neither has said much of anything, come to think of it, since we saw Josh. They asked me a couple of questions about Mother Blessing and the Swamp, I asked them a few about school and their lives. I don't think any of us heard the answers. But I don't think Scott and Brandy have touched each other once since I got here, if you don't count that group hug. Rebecca Levine, beautiful flower child, has barely stopped weeping since we saw Josh's body. Now she stares vacantly at the TV, watching a moronic reality show with the sound turned so low I can barely hear it. Which is fine with me.

Rebecca also told me something apparently everyone else has known for some time now—that she thought she saw Season at some bogus séance. Which maybe wasn't as bogus as she thought. Maybe Season has been hunting us down, one by one.

So I can't help wondering: Which one is next? Season has taken three friends from me so far. Not just from me, from the world. Three flames snuffed, three lights extinguished. Three people who could have changed the world. Would Mace have discovered a cure for cancer? Not likely, I guess. But he might have coached a baseball team and befriended a sad, fatherless boy, and isn't that just as valuable an accomplishment? Josh might never have composed a stirring symphony but he might have skipped through a park on a sunny spring day, bringing smiles to the faces of every-one who saw him. Daniel . . .

Daniel saved lives, dedicated himself to bringing Season Howe to jus-tice, and still found time to love me. To change my life, to pull me out of my own self-obsessed rut and give me some kind of direction, a goal, a desire to affect something larger than just myself.

We can never measure the impact we have on others, never know when a friendly word to a cashier at the market or a smile bestowed on a stranger or a few bucks to a charity might strike at just the right time to make someone's day, or give someone hope, or lend the tools someone needs to rebuild something that's broken. And so we can never know which life, cut short, might be one that the world needed. Since it's unlikely that Josh, Mace, or Daniel would have eventually become supervillains or anything, the loss of these lives, the tragedy of their early endings, is that their gifts, whatever they were to be, will never be realized. Okay, I guess it's hard to apply that to three-hundred-year-old Daniel, but still, he seemed young to me, and he had an important task that was left unfinished.

Not that their lives were wasted. They gave to me, to the others in this room, to their families, and to strangers. Rebecca wanted us to go see Josh's mother, but the rest of us talked her out of that—considering what we've found ourselves mixed up in, we've all agreed to keep parents, family, and friends out of the loop. Safer for them, safer for us. I'm sure Josh never told his mom anything about us, and if we had shown up with our crazy stories, it would have just made a hard day even worse.

We don't know if Season is still in Vegas. Rebecca was the last one to talk to Josh, but he never told her where he staked Season out last night, so we don't even know where she was staying. Chances are, though, given that she battled simulacra, she knows her cover here is blown and she's already on the move. By plane, car, train, bus? Don't know.

I leave in the morning, back to Virginia, back to the Great Dismal. So do the others, Brandy and Scott for Harvard, Rebecca for UC Santa Cruz. My college pals, and me, witchy apprentice girl.

I don't know what they're all learning. But I know what my major is, what my course of study has to be. Intense, comprehensive, accelerated.

How to kill Season Howe.

More later.
K.

16

The sky over the Great Dismal Swamp was heavy and gray, lowering overhead like a leaden shroud, which suited Kerry's mood just fine. She had parked the minivan in its usual spot and rowed back through the ever-more-familiar Swamp to Mother Blessing's ramshackle cabin/comfortable suburban home (depending on whether one was outside or in). Kerry thought she felt eyes tracking her the whole way, but whether it was simulacra or snakes, birds, and other swamp wildlife, she couldn't have said.

Mother Blessing met her with a bottle of Coke and a tray of ham sandwiches on Wonder bread, and they sat together in the kitchen while Kerry filled her in on what had happened. The older woman was sympathetic, listening attentively until Kerry declared that she was exhausted and needed to get some sleep. Mother Blessing patted Kerry's arm. "Y'all get a good night's sleep, child. Tomorrow'll be a busy day."

"Busy with what?" Kerry asked, stifling a yawn. She had hardly slept at all the night before; images of Josh and Daniel filled her head. Though she'd dozed a little on the flight home, she really was weary to the bone.

"Well, it's time you learned some serious magic, isn't it?" Mother Blessing said. "Someone's got to stand up to Season, and I guess it might just as well be you."

"Are you sure I can do that?" Kerry asked excitedly. She wanted it more than anything, but she'd thought she'd have to persuade Mother Blessing. Now she was almost afraid that the witch had made the promise in hopes that Kerry would realize she was asking too much and back off. She almost wished Mother

Blessing had waited until the morning to make this announcement—now, tired as she was, she feared she'd have a hard time sleeping. Everything she'd been shown so far was basic stuff, beginner's tricks and a bunch of theory. But she'd seen Daniel and Season at work, knew there was far more to be learned.

Mother Blessing nodded gravely. "I reckon we'll find out, Kerry," she said. "Tomorrow. Y'all get to bed now."

Kerry did as she was told, and to her surprise, as soon as she put her head on the pillow, she felt consciousness fading away. Tragedy and possibility whirled around in her mind, each feeding on the other, but soon enough they both emptied into nothingness and she slept.

"Most magical systems won't let one practitioner do harm to another," Mother Blessing explained the next day. They were back in the kitchen, which seemed to be where the woman spent most of her time, day and night. Kerry sat at the table in a heavy cable-knit sweater and soft, forest-green fleece pants, her long dark hair tugged into a tight ponytail. Dressed in her usual stretch polyesters under a shapeless housecoat, Mother Blessing rode her scooter, rolling it this way and that like a lecturer pacing while she spoke. "Violence is limited, in those systems, to the evil, the outlaws or renegades. Black magicians who call up destructive demons, for instance, are hated by white magicians. If Wiccans knew half of what they could do by simply taking their studies a few steps further, applying their powers in different ways, their little flowered headpieces would most likely melt off them." She had a small smile on her face when she said that, and a twinkle in her eye, but Kerry knew that didn't mean she didn't believe what she was saying.

"The difference here is that we use violent magic only in self-defense, or in the defense of others. Y'all know Season well enough now to understand that there's no stoppin' her, short of killin' her. Now, there's plenty of witches out there who'd think we were evil to contemplate such a thing, but when it comes to evil, I have to think that letting Season continue her reign of terror is just about the worst thing a person could do."

"From what I've seen," Kerry said, "I'd have to agree."

"Of course." Mother Blessing spoke as if no other opinion was even worth considering. "Y'all have been touched by her foul deeds. She's impacted your life. Those others, the ones who'd defend her, they don't know her like we do. They haven't lost two sons and a husband to her, or a lover, or a whole town full of neighbors and friends."

"That's probably true."

"Bet your sweet patootie it is," Mother Blessing said with a chuckle. "So the question is, what do we do about her? What steps are y'all willin' to take to make sure she can't keep doin' what she's been doin'?"

Kerry had thought long and hard about just that question. "Whatever it takes," she said decisively. "I'd do anything."

"I'm delighted to hear it, child." She wheeled in close to Kerry, leaning forward, her bulk almost spilling out of her scooter. "What's really required to go the extra step is depth of commitment. If you're willin' to go where the magic takes you, it'll carry the weight."

"I'm willing," Kerry affirmed. If she had any doubts along the way she could simply call up the pictures of Daniel and Josh emblazoned into her memory.

"That's fine, just fine." Mother Blessing wrapped her big, fleshy hands around Kerry's. They felt warmer than human hands could rightfully be, as if they burned with the inner fire of her dark magics. Kerry would embrace that darkness, if it would lead to revenge. This was why she'd come here.

Then Mother Blessing released her hands and backed away from her, rolling toward a kitchen cupboard. She opened the door and withdrew a book—a slim volume, but covered in soft leather like Daniel's journals. It looked incredibly old, the leather creased and cracked, the pages yellow with age. Mother Blessing put it in her scooter's basket and drove close enough for Kerry to reach it. "Take the book, child," she said. "First thing you've got to do is learn the Old Tongue."

"What's that?" Kerry asked.

"The words of power. They come from a language forgotten by humans, a language that predates the written word. There was a time when magic was commonplace, swirling through the air like smog does today. People understood it better'n we do electricity today—course, there wasn't as many people about, and not all of 'em knew how to use magic. But they all knew someone who did, and they respected their shamans, instead of burnin' 'em at the stake or forcin' 'em into hiding."

Kerry figured that there was some personal bias tinting Mother Blessing's commentary—if living a hermit's life in a disguised home deep in the Swamp wasn't being forced into hiding, she didn't know what was. Daniel, too, had been good at disguising his nature. And Season was nothing if not expert at running and hiding. If these three—the most powerful witches Kerry had ever imagined—were all forced into seclusion by the world's distrust of magic, then it was not surprising that Mother Blessing had strong feelings about the matter.

Taking the book from the basket, Kerry flipped through its brittle pages. At first glance, it was completely illegible. There were no words in it, not in any kind of writing she could decipher—just scribbles, seemingly random markings that might have been the scratchings of an animal's claws. She looked up, confused. "How am I supposed to . . . ?"

"Give it some time," Mother Blessing assured her. "Look it over at night, before you go to sleep."

Kerry closed the book and put it on the table, still confused but willing to give her the benefit of the doubt.

"When y'all speak the Old Tongue," Mother Blessing continued, "it draws the power of the Old Ones into you. Since y'all will be taught how to use that power, the right combination of words and gestures focuses the power and directs it where you want it. Gesture is as important as words, Kerry, and don't forget that. It's the combination that makes y'all's magic effective."

She pointed across the kitchen to where a copper-bottomed pot hung on the wall. "As a for instance," she said, "see that pot?"

"I see it."

"Okay, now watch me." Mother Blessing raised her hands and curled her fingers. She took her right hand and, with the thumb sticking up, tucked the two lower fingers flat against her palm, and crooked the middle two as if holding onto a pole. She splayed the fingers of her left hand as far apart as she could while bringing the thumb down crosswise across her palm. "Looks awkward, but it ain't bad," she explained. "You'll get used to it."

Pointing both hands toward the pot, she said a single word that sounded to Kerry like "bibblehead." As soon as the word had escaped her lips, the pot vibrated against the wall, shaking free of the hook that held it there, and floated across the room, as if carried by spectral hands, to land safely in the basket of Mother Blessing's scooter.

"What was that word?" Kerry asked her. Before she spoke it she made sure her own hands were neatly crossed on her lap, just in case. "'Bibblehead'?"

"B-I-B-E-L-H-E-T, I think," Mother Blessing spelled out. "Actual spellin' ain't all that important—it's the speakin' of it that counts. I couldn't define it, either, just know that it'll do what I want it to do. That's what y'all have got to achieve—the knowledge that the words and gestures'll be there when you need 'em, without having to think about 'em too much. Thinkin' things through'll get you killed. It's got to be automatic."

"But . . . that could take years!" Kerry complained. "You've been at it for what, centuries."

"That's right, child," Mother Blessing agreed. "But once y'all start in to learning, you'll be surprised how fast it goes. Power feeds power, Kerry. It's like it's all floatin' out there lookin' for a home, like liquid searchin' for the lowest point, and when it finds one, it flows in fast and strong."

She took the pot from the basket and put it on the table in front of Kerry. "Put it back," she instructed.

Kerry started to rise, lifting the pot from the table. "No," Mother Blessing said sharply. "Not that way."

Kerry understood what she meant, but not how to accomplish the task. "But . . ."

"Do like this," Mother Blessing said. She folded the fingers of both hands toward her palms, making hooks of them, then raised the thumbs and pointed them toward the wall where the pot had been. She held her right hand about a hand's breadth higher than the left. Kerry duplicated the pose as best she could, until Mother Blessing nodded her satisfaction. "That's good," she said. "Now hold the pose."

Kerry did so, and Mother Blessing unfolded her own hands, lowering them to her handlebars. "Now, say the word *'beshitoon.'*"

"Beshi . . . ?"

"Beshitoon," Mother Blessing repeated.

Kerry held the position with her hands and attempted the word. "Bes—*beshitoon*," she said hesitantly.

Nothing happened.

"Say it like you mean it, child," Mother Blessing chided her.

Kerry hesitated a moment, her hands starting to quake from the effort of holding them still. She visualized the pot floating back across the room and hanging itself up on the hook again. *I can do this,* she thought. *Mother Blessing wouldn't be pushing me if she didn't know I could.*

"Beshitoon."

The pot rattled on the tabletop, as if trying to make up its mind, then ascended into the air. Slowly, taking its time, but moving in almost precisely the line Kerry had visualized, it drifted across the room. Reaching the far wall, it lowered itself until the hook had slipped inside the hole in its handle. Then it was still, and the room silent.

"There you go," Mother Blessing said softly. "Nothin' to it, is there?"

I wouldn't say that, Kerry thought. But excitement coursed through her. She had *done* that! She had taken power from the air around her and directed it toward a specific goal, and that goal, however minor, had been achieved!

"I did magic," Kerry said finally. "I really did."

"You really did, child," Mother Blessing confirmed. "Congratulations."

Kerry Profitt's diary, November 4

I did magic.

Yeah, I know, big whoop. I moved a pot. Could have used some scrubbing—the copper bottom was a bit on the tarnished side—but I didn't take it that far. One step at a time, right? Today I move, tomorrow I may scrub.

Or not.

The thing is, this is why I came to the Swamp. This is why I sought out Mother Blessing. She trained Daniel, right? So she can train me, too. Can, and more importantly, is willing to. Even anxious. She knows that Season is out of control. And the closer it gets to next year's Witches' Convocation, the more important it is to take Season out of commission. Which means that I don't have much time to perfect my skills. I don't have centuries, or even years. I have weeks, months.

I was going to write in here last night, after my day's training, but instead I did as Mother Blessing suggested, and I looked through the book she gave me, the one with the Old Tongue in it. Look at it before you go to sleep, she had said, in that delightful accent of hers that makes everything sound like music. So I did. Still looked like chicken scratches to me.

But then I went to sleep, and in my dreams the writing became clear. It was so realistic that when I woke up, I grabbed the book and looked again. And guess what?

I could read it!

Well, not READ it, precisely. The words still don't make any sense, words like bibblehead and beshitoon. But it was as if they were all written down using our alphabet. No more scribbles and scratches. Don't ask me how—magic, I guess—but now at least I can sound out the words, know how I'm supposed to say them. I still need Mother Blessing to tell me which ones should be used for what, and what gestures to combine with them—seems like I'm particularly dangerous right now, because if I accidentally spoke one of them while unconsciously making some gesture or other, I could blow something up or hurt someone.

But yesterday I knew squat about this stuff, and today I've not only done magic, but I'm able to read the words in the book. Power flows to power, she says. The more I achieve, the more will come to me.

I wouldn't want to be Season Howe a couple of months from now. Because I intend to flow a lot of power this way, in a hurry.

Impatient, me? Perish the thought.

More later.
K.

17

Erin pounded on her door.

"You're going to miss class again, Beck!" she shouted. Rebecca tunneled deeper into her blankets, wedged a pillow over her head.

She didn't want to go to class. She didn't want to get out of bed. She hadn't wanted to since Halloween, since . . . since Josh had died at the hands of Season Howe.

She couldn't stop dwelling on the sight of Josh, murdered, body cooling up against a bank of slot machines. Every time she closed her eyes, it seemed, he was there—either that or the image of Season herself. She had become convinced now that she'd been right after all, at that séance—that Season was looking for them, hunting them down. If that was true, there was hardly any purpose in getting out of bed. When Season came for her, it wouldn't matter where she was.

Kerry, at least, was trying to learn how to defend herself against the witch. Rebecca didn't have that option. She was defenseless, and every day that she listened to Erin—every day that she got out of bed—she was only one day closer to the inevitable confrontation.

She knew that she was slipping into clinical depression. Erin had said as much, had even offered to take her down to the student health center and help her sign up for counseling. But Rebecca knew that no counseling could help her with her problem.

Every now and then she talked with Scott or Brandy—Kerry was out of reach again, and their little summer group was getting smaller and smaller—and that helped a little, mostly because she could speak freely with them, didn't have to hide what was really on her mind. But they were far away, and she was here in Santa Cruz, alone.

Erin knocked again and Rebecca shoved her pillow aside. "Okay!" she called. "I'm getting up, okay?"

"Fine," she heard Erin answer.

This would, she had decided, be the last year she and Erin shared a place. She didn't know what would happen next year.

But then, she didn't know if she'd be alive by next year. Certainly not if Season Howe had anything to say about it.

There was, it turned out, a lot more to the whole witchcraft thing than simply reciting strange-sounding words and making funny hand motions. Mother Blessing made Kerry spend hours in the Swamp becoming intimately famil-iar with dwarf trillium, silky camellia, fiddlehead, and log fern, discerning Tupelo bald cypress from Atlantic white cedar from maple-blackgum, tasting the bark of red maple, crushing pine needles in her hands and inhaling the bitter scent, picking bunches of paw paw, blackgum, devil's walking stick, and wild grapes for the table. Not all magic could simply be scooped from the ether, she explained. Some had to be distilled from plants and trees, teased from animals, dug from the very earth.

Kerry learned how to tell apart the tracks and scat of the swamp's big mam-mals: the paw of the bobcat and the black bear, the hoof of the white-tailed deer, the smaller track of gray fox and red, of raccoon and mink and gray squirrel. She came to recognize the calls of different warblers, the Swainson's and the Wayne's and the Myrtle, the chirps of the ovenbird and the hermit thrush, the sounds of the robins and blackbirds that swarmed in as the month progressed as if drawn by the fiery leaves on autumn trees. She took pleasure in the staccato rapping of the pileated woodpecker; she went to sleep at night wondering what the barred owl was talking about, or cringing at the plaintive cry of the bobcat; she woke to the *yakkety-yak* of the wood duck. With great care, Mother Blessing taught her to extract venom from the cottonmouth, the canebrake rattler, and the copperhead, and how to tell them apart from the dozen or so nonpoisonous varieties of snake that lived nearby.

Every night, Kerry went to bed with aching muscles and a head swimming with new information and vivid images, her tongue tripping over the foreign words and phrases she had learned that day. And each day she woke early and leapt from her bed, ready to repeat the process, to absorb more knowledge, to glean more wisdom from the Swamp and its inhabitants—and, of course, from Mother Blessing herself. The days grew ever shorter—darkness came early now—but Kerry packed them full. Makeup was a thing of the past—a quick shower, a brush through her hair and a band to hold it back, some jeans and a sweater or maybe sweat pants and a long-sleeved T-shirt, and she was ready for the day. She barely took time to notice that her physical efforts were making her ever stronger, her arms and shoulders firm and supple, her waist tight, her thighs and calves bunched with strength.

When she was inside, she worked with Mother Blessing on learning the correct pronunciation of the Old Tongue, on practicing magical gestures until her hands screamed with aching. And she read, still working her way through Daniel's journals, front to back, beginning to end. She couldn't remember a time in her life that had been so filled with activity, days so long and with never a moment to be bored—hardly even any time, but for the few seconds between undressing and falling asleep, to reflect on anything.

During one of the rare moments of downtime, she had turned on the TV for the first time, and had not been at all surprised to find that it received more than a hundred channels, none of which seemed worth watching. This house was like that, though—she could take long, steaming showers without worrying that the hot water tank (if there was one; she had never seen it) would run out. The lights and the heat always worked, though there seemed to be no electrical or gas lines to the place. Mother Blessing could, she figured, solve the world's energy problems in seconds if she wanted to. But then the energy companies wouldn't be able to make any money, and they'd probably prove a far more nefarious adversary than even Season Howe.

Kerry knew that this was a time of preparation, a schooling time, but it didn't feel like a step on the way to somewhere; it felt like a destination achieved. As if she had already made it to where she was going.

It was, she decided one night in the moments before sound sleep overtook her, a happy time. In spite of everything that had led her to this point. She had rarely been quite so content.

She found that strange.

Now that I am older and have seen more of the wide world, I realize that there were great advantages to growing up where I did, to reaching maturity—and spending many months after that—in the Great Dismal. It was, and probably remains, a magical place to be a child, full of mystery and, yes, some danger. The sheer variety of plants and animals made every day an adventure: How many children my age went to school with alligators and came home with black bears? How many knew that every time they left the house there was the distinct possibility that, before suppertime, they could become hopelessly lost, never again to see their mother and brother? How many could see millions upon millions of blackbirds erupt from the Swamp, filling the sky in a steady stream that blacked out the sun for most of a day before they had all flown away?

Precious few, I'd wager. And though, in the way of small children everywhere, I didn't always appreciate it while it was happening, I certainly do now. I'm glad Mother Blessing didn't let Season drive her away from the Swamp, but only deep into it, that horrible day when she ruined Slocumb, house by house, burning each one with her magical fires until the screams of those inside faded away, keeping the flames hot until every trace of habitation was gone. Mother Blessing did the right thing by hiding out, by refusing to return to Slocumb until a safe period had passed, for in her fury Season Howe was certainly more than herself, channeling evil unknown and unknowable, not to be stopped by any earthly intercession.

But the Swamp: I was writing of the Swamp. Each day a new lesson, a new joy, sometimes a new fear, but always with Mother Blessing, and usually Abraham, to help me through it all. And so many surprises, for anyone willing to open his eyes and look for them. I met George Washington there, in 1763. I didn't know yet, of course, what a courageous leader of soldiers he would turn out to be, but he was already known as an intelligent man, and a decent one, with a sharp eye for business.

And one day in November of 1894 when I was back visiting Mother Blessing—depressed at my inability to find Season, who had been successfully avoiding me for months, and feeling like a complete disaster, a worthless fool who would never amount to anything—I met a sad-eyed young man roaming the Swamp on foot, looking, he said, for the best way to kill himself.

"Best," I asked, "in the sense of most assured? Or most dramatic?"

"I should like it to make a statement," he said after considering my question. "I believe I should like people to talk about it."

"Is there, perhaps, some certain individual who you would especially desire to hear the news?" I inquired, believing I was beginning to understand the nature of his predicament. He sat down on the log of a fallen gum tree and looked at me as if deciding whether or not I was trustworthy enough to reveal his story to.

"I was late in Canton, Massachusetts," said he at length, "where I surprised my lady love by arriving unannounced at her door bearing a most special gift. I thought that this lady would welcome me. Certainly I hoped so, having ridden all night by train."

"What was the gift?" I asked the young man.

"Two books of poetry, written especially with her in mind," he said. "One for her and the other for me. There existed only the one copy of each book. But upon being given hers, she simply held it at arm's length, as though I had given her a toad or a snake, and closed the door on me.

"In my grief, I wandered back to the railroad yard and tore my own volume to shreds. On the journey home, I determined that without Miss White, I had no reason to live. So I am here, in the most aptly named Great Dismal, where I should like to find an appropriately dramatic way to close the door on my existence."

I scratched my chin again and considered his predicament. "Hmmm," I said. "A number of options present themselves. Have you considered trying to make the acquaintance of a brown bear, or an alligator, or perhaps a poisonous snake? Although any of those might leave you merely crippled or ill, not dead. Perhaps you could find a tree in the process of being felled and stand on the wrong side of it; the woodcutters, though, might see you and insist you move away."

"You seem quite well versed in the ways the Swamp can put finish to a fellow."

"Swamp born and bred, sir, though I have traveled more than a little in my day."

He regarded me for a long time, nodding his head. Finally he said, "I suppose the most certain way would be to walk into the Swamp with no provisions. One way or another I should not survive the journey."

"That seems to work, yes," I agreed.

"But if my body was never found, then the news of my passing might never reach Miss White."

"It is true," I said, "that she would likely never know with certainty."

The young man raised his arms in evident frustration. "What is the point of it?" he thundered. "To come all this way, to the most dismal spot in Creation, and still not find a suitable end?"

314 - YEAR OF THE WICKED

"Very little point that I can see," I agreed again.

The young man spared me a smile then, the first that I had seen, and it was like a flicker of sunshine breaking through storm clouds. "Then perhaps it is my plan that is faulty, and the better course would be to go on living after all."

I pointed my index finger at him. "And to live such a life that Miss White would learn to regret having spurned you," I added.

He smiled again, this time as if the sun had warmed the sky and burned the clouds away. "Yes," he said happily. "I think that might be the better course of action after all."

"I am happy to hear it," I told the man.

He took my hand then, and shook it with great effusiveness. "I thank you, sir. Be well, and remember the name of Robert Frost, in the event that some day it should come to mean something to anyone. Especially to Miss Elinor White."

I gave him my own name, and he smiled again and walked away. I felt better about myself immediately: Having saved a life, I felt the depression that had gripped me lift at once, and I knew that I would, in fact, find Season again and destroy her.

And that young man? He did become something special after all.

I remember the story today because I heard on the radio that Robert Frost died yesterday. While I don't believe he was a witch or prolonged his life through any special magical powers, there was certainly magic within that man. He won four Pulitzer prizes for his magnificent poetry, and just over two years ago he became the first poet to read a poem at the inauguration of an American president.

I, for one, salute his passing—much delayed, and we are all the better for that. And his moving on serves to remind me of the special joys and pleasures of life in the Great Dismal, so thank you, Mr. Frost, for all your gifts.

I remain,

Daniel Blessing, January 30, 1963

18

Just when Kerry was starting to think that her life was destined to be devoted to studying and nothing else, Mother Blessing surprised her.

"How long's it been since you got yourself a new outfit, honey?" she asked one morning, startling Kerry from her reading. She was constantly amazed by the things Daniel had seen and done, by the sweep of history he had lived. But the idea that he had effectively saved the life of Robert Frost, whose poetry she had loved in high school, had blown her away. She had been reflecting on that when Mother Blessing mentioned her wardrobe, and the disconnect seemed almost surreal. "I swear, the clothes you're wearin' look like they're fixin' to come apart at the seams."

Honestly, Kerry hadn't even been thinking about clothes, or hair or makeup or anything else. There didn't seem to be time in the day for such things, and there was no one to get dressed up for except Mother Blessing. Since the older woman's idea of dolling herself up usually involved wearing stretch pants with slightly fewer stains than usual, Kerry felt that the bar of presentability had been lowered, and that was fine with her. Now that Mother Blessing mentioned it, though, Kerry remembered that there was a certain therapeutic value to shopping that she appreciated.

"I guess it's been a while," she answered. She didn't want to sound too anxious, though, in case this was some kind of test. "If you think we have time . . ."

Mother Blessing's smile looked genuine, though. She was not an attractive woman, but when she really smiled, a sense of true joy showed through.

"Child, we don't answer to nobody but ourselves. We want to make the time, then that's just what we'll do."

A simulacrum rowed Kerry and Mother Blessing out of the Swamp in the old witch's boat, to where the creek went right up, behind Edgar Brandvold's property in Wallaceton, Virginia. Edgar was a man who looked as old as Mother Blessing was, though he couldn't have been more than eighty or so, whereas Mother Blessing, while she looked like someone in her fifties, was obviously several hundred years old. When they arrived, the simulacrum lifted Mother Blessing's scooter up onto old Edgar's driveway, then lifted her up onto it. She cruised up to the front door of Edgar's sagging frame house, which looked as much like a shack as the magical facade of Mother Blessing's place, and rapped on his door. A few minutes later a stoop-shouldered mass of wrinkles with thick glasses and a knob-headed cane came out, waved, smiled at Kerry and the simulacrum as if he'd known them both for decades, and unlocked his garage, a former carriage house that looked to be in even worse shape than the main house.

"Howdy, Mother Blessin'!" he called loudly. His voice was deep and sonorous, unexpected in such an apparently ancient fellow. He wore baggy brown pants and a plaid shirt under a ratty blue cardigan sweater, like some kind of Mr. Rogers gone to seed. "Lovely day. You gon' take a ride?"

"That's right, Edgar," Mother Blessing answered brightly. "Miss Kerry here's got some shoppin' she needs to get done."

Edgar opened the carriage house doors widely and Kerry saw her van in its shadowed interior. "What's that doing here?" she asked. Last time she had seen it, it was still parked in its spot near the old Slocumb site, on the other side of the Great Dismal.

"I had it brought around," Mother Blessing explained. "Thought it'd be best if Edgar kept an eye on it."

The simulacrum stepped toward Edgar, who seemed well accustomed to such temporary creatures, and took the key from the old man's hand. "Y'all drive safe now, hear?" Edgar said.

"Always do," Mother Blessing answered for the voiceless being, which opened the driver's door and climbed up behind the wheel.

"I could drive," Kerry offered, a little fearful about the reactions other motorists might have to the plainly nonhuman thing.

"Wouldn't hear of it," Mother Blessing replied, shaking her hands at the very idea. "Ain't nothing like havin' a chauffeur take you where you need to go."

"But he's . . . not exactly convincing," Kerry argued.

"Folks see what they expect to see," Mother Blessing insisted. "Or if I'm around, what I want 'em to see."

The simulacrum at least seemed to know what it was doing. It backed the van smoothly out of the long, narrow garage, then stopped and climbed out, leaving the engine idling. Opening the big side door, it easily lifted Mother Blessing off her scooter, as if she were weightless, and deposited her in the front passenger seat. Then it put the scooter up into the cargo area of the van. There was a single back seat with a seat belt, and at Mother Blessing's suggestion Kerry got into that. The van had a distinctly earthy aroma to it, but she didn't know if that was from sitting cooped up in a small garage by a creek, or from the presence of the simulacrum, who was composed of leaves, vines, mud, and other swamp debris, in the enclosed space. The simulacrum got back behind the wheel and put the van in gear. With a cheery farewell to old Edgar, they headed up the road toward Norfolk.

"One thing I've been wondering about," Kerry began, after they'd been driving a few minutes. Seeing Edgar Brandvold looking so much older than Mother Blessing had reminded her of her curiosity. "If it's not too personal to ask."

"Well, y'all just ask it, and if it's too personal I won't be shy about sayin' so," Mother Blessing replied.

"It's just . . . Daniel looked like he was in his mid-twenties. Season looks like mid-thirties at the oldest. You look like someone in her fifties, maybe. But I know you're all much older than that—so how exactly does the aging process work for witches? Now that I'm learning, will I stop aging and always look like this?"

Mother Blessing regarded her for a few moments, as if she were weighing the relative merits of appearing to be a teenager for hundreds of years. "It's mostly a function of peak power," she said then. "It takes different witches different lengths of time to achieve their strongest capabilities. At that time, the aging process more or less freezes up. I guess I was a slow learner, and it wasn't until I was in my fifties that I reached my peak. My overall health was better—that's gone downhill in recent years, I'm afraid, though I'm still not aging much."

Kerry nodded. "That makes sense, I guess."

"Don't much matter if it does or not," Mother Blessing answered. "It's how it is."

Twenty minutes later, they turned into the parking lot of a bland-looking discount clothing store. "They'll have everything y'all might need here," Mother Blessing announced.

Kerry couldn't prevent the crestfallen expression from washing over her face. She still had plenty of money left over from her college account; since reaching the Swamp, the only thing she'd had to spend it on was the brief trip to Las Vegas. "Isn't there a mall someplace?"

Mother Blessing eyed her with surprise for a moment, then smiled. "Turn around," she told the driver, who obeyed instantly—had, in fact, been starting to obey before the witch gave the verbal command. "Course there's a mall. Teenage girl needs more than a place like this, don't she? Let's us find you somewhere with real shops."

Kerry Profitt's diary, November 17

In the dream, I'm driving in a car. This one I can remember, so I don't think it's the same dream I used to have in the weeks before I met Daniel. Nothing special about the car—it's not the van I bought or any particular car at all that I can tell. But I'm stuck in traffic.

And as I'm sitting there, looking at all the other cars around me, wishing I could just floor it and move already, water starts to bubble up through the floorboards. (Were they ever actual boards, at one time? Just a digression. They sure aren't now.)

Rapidly, the water rises. I try to open a door or a window to let it out, but nothing doing. I can't get anything open. Now I'm in water up to my waist—it's not cold, I notice, but pleasantly body temperature, and I'm not nearly as panicked as I probably should be. Still, it rises.

And rises. And then it's over my head, and I'm still there, seatbelted in, unable to go anywhere or do anything about it. Noises sound funny, like, you know, when you're underwater. Finally, I notice, traffic eases up a little and I can move again. I press the accelerator down and start to edge forward, unable to breathe now, my lungs constricting, really and truly beginning to drown.

But as I do, I'm looking out the car windows at the other cars around and I see that the drivers of those are all underwater inside their cars too. Only the thing is, they don't seem to mind. They're breathing normally—well, normally if humans could breathe underwater. Bubbles float up from their mouths and noses, but they look just like people do in traffic, some smiling, some talking, some angry or impatient. Just people in cars. And we're all underwater.

But I'm the only one who's drowning.

Once again, I need Doc Brandy to tell me just what this all means, and she's not around. Brandy ain't handy.

My guess? Maybe it's telling me that I'm becoming different from all the normal people out there, the people who are not witches—or even halfway to becoming one. Alienation from my peers. Evidence of my journey and how it diverts from that of everyone else I've ever known.

Or not. Who knows?

More later.
K.

* * *

"Strike!"

Kerry heard Mother Blessing's voice in her head, even though the woman was miles away, back in her cabin. She had drilled Kerry on this so many times, though, it seemed as if she were right here with her. Kerry did as she'd been taught: She hurled herself to the peat, tucking her head, rolling on one shoulder, and coming up on her feet, hands splayed out in the proper ritualistic position. *"Hastamel!"* she shouted as she rose, and a burst of energy shot from her hands, tearing a chunk of vegetation off the simulacrum with which she sparred. The thing grunted with pain—part of Mother Blessing's commitment to realism, Kerry figured—and dropped to its knees. Kerry knew she'd missed any vital organs, so she repositioned her hands and spoke a defensive spell. If the thing had been a witch, it could have gotten off a blast.

Since it wasn't, she only defended herself against an imaginary spell, and then she shot an impulse wave at it. The creature's head separated from its shoulders and it went down hard in the dirt. Kerry allowed herself a congratulatory moment, but she cut it short when a noise behind her alerted her to the fact that this one hadn't been alone.

She spun around, throwing up a blocking spell and then following that with another sharp, directed burst that punched a hole the size of a soccer ball through this one's chest. These sparring matches were wearying, and she became frustrated when there was one opponent after another after another, even sometimes half a dozen all at once. But they were also necessary, she knew. Daniel had found himself in all kinds of dangerous situations over the course of his long life, and—until that last battle—had survived them all. If Kerry was going to survive, she needed to train until she dropped, and then pick herself up and train some more.

She may have resented Mother Blessing while she was putting her through the mental and physical agony of the exercise, but when it saved her life some day, she'd thank her mentor. She tried to keep sight of that knowledge, to let it help her through these difficult days.

The second simulacrum fell, and Kerry found that there were only two, for now. She was allowed a moment's respite, a chance to catch her breath and let her racing heart calm a bit. After a few minutes the Swamp's normal sounds resumed: birds cried, insects buzzed, a faraway frog croaked its basso profundo solo.

Kerry stood for a few moments, just enjoying the day. It was cold enough in the Swamp that she had the hood of her new lime-green fleece snugged around her head, and fake fur-lined boots with a fake suede finish—bought out of consideration for Josh's feelings about wearing real leather—on her feet, but the sky was crisp and cloudless. Between the flame-red tops of two maples she watched a great blue heron skate across the sky and out of sight. Her appreciation for the natural world was far greater than it had ever been now that she had a better sense of how inextricably humanity was tied to it.

I wish Rebecca were here, she thought, *and Brandy and Scott, too. I wish they could all go through what I have, learn what I have.* She'd had other friends, of course. But with the loss of her parents, and then her ordeal over the summer, most of those people had drifted away from her. She didn't miss anyone from Northwestern, not really. She barely thought of them at all, except a couple of times when she found herself imagining how much Dr. Manning, her history professor, would love to talk to Mother Blessing and hear some early American history from someone who'd been there. But Rebecca, Scott, and Brandy—they held important positions in her heart, and she couldn't help believing each would find valuable lessons here in the Swamp, even if they didn't care to learn magic.

It's not magic to understand that what happens to nature affects all of us, she thought. *To know that the wholesale extinction of species can only be bad for everyone, that humans won't be the last species to become extinct, or that no species except humans has ever been single-handedly responsible for the extinction of any other. And it doesn't take magic to comprehend that power flows from nature through us, or that we have to give back to nature some of what we take from it, if we want the interrelationship to continue.*

Kerry laughed. *Listen to me,* she thought, even though she hadn't spoken a word out loud, not wanting to disturb the Swamp's natural choir with a human voice. *I sound like some kind of green. And I thought Rebecca was our resident hippie.* But she wasn't thinking along political lines, or about social policy, just about what Mother Blessing had taught her of the need to respect nature and worship it as a manifestation of the Old Ones from whom all witchy power sprang. Along with that respect, which also applied to her tools—her cauldron, her athame, her wand, and the rest of the things Mother Blessing had helped her make or find—came a new appreciation. No tree, rock, implement, or person lasted forever. While it was in one's life, then, it had to be cared for and held precious.

The faintest rustle of a footfall on dry leaves alerted her, and Kerry spun, dropping to a crouch and raising her hands in a warding gesture. *"Shellitush!"* she shouted, generating a protective field around her. But this wasn't a simulacrum, she saw. Instead, emerging from the cover of a nearby cypress stump, an enormous black bear regarded her, one paw up on the stump, one hanging free, back feet firmly on the ground. Its head bobbed a little, as if listening to some silent tune, but its nose wrinkled slightly and she suspected it was sniffing her, catching the odor that sailed on a barely perceptible breeze. Its eyes were obsidian; its mouth open, tongue lolling over big teeth in an accidental impression of a smile. The big animal looked happy, even friendly. But she knew that it was not. Not that it would intentionally hurt her. If it felt threatened or trapped, it would certainly try. Otherwise, it bore her no ill will, just as surely as it didn't want to be her friend.

Kerry tried to project her thoughts toward the bear. She wasn't a meal, she wasn't a danger. She was simply a mildly interesting side note in the day's activities. After a few moments, as if it understood, the bear dropped down from the trunk, turned around, and loped away into the brush.

Kerry glanced toward the simulacra, both of which had decomposed back into the swamp stuff from which they were made, and then disappeared. She had a long walk back to the cabin, and the day was getting no warmer. Looking for the position of the sun to catch her bearings, Kerry headed for home.

19

"I died once," Scott said. "You didn't know that, huh?"

Brandy looked across the table at him. Mugs of hot chocolate steamed between them, and outside bundled-up students rushed to and fro, slipping on icy sidewalks. It would get colder, but already the weather had turned sour. Thanksgiving was tomorrow, and Scott wanted an invitation to her place for the day—an invitation that would not be offered.

She and Scott had agreed to get together twice a week for lunch, coffee, or sometimes dinner or a movie. Not dating—she wouldn't go that far, and at her insistence it was strictly hands off. When they'd returned from Las Vegas, she had declared that it was over between them. He had packed up his things and moved out, leaving her in an apartment that she had to struggle to pay for. She had considered getting a roommate, but there was only one bedroom, and she valued her privacy. So far, her parents were helping out, but she knew she would have to move after the first of the year.

"No," she answered. She took a sip of the hot chocolate. It had been topped with whipped cream and just a hint of cinnamon. "No, I don't think I did. You never told me, did you?"

"No, it's . . . it's weird," he said. "I don't talk about it, really. I thought about it, after . . . you know, after Mace died. And then in Vegas, with Josh and everything. But it didn't seem appropriate, somehow. Because I came back, and they didn't."

"You came back? I mean, obviously, you're here. But what happened?" It seemed like the kind of thing a guy would tell someone he was in love with, living with. But hearing it this way just helped cement her conclusion that Scott wasn't ready for a real commitment.

He looked away from her when he told the story. These meetings were hard on him, Brandy knew, but still he insisted he wanted them. She was convinced that he thought she would reconsider, take him back.

He was wrong.

"I was eight," he said. "My dad was driving, mom in the front seat, me in back. I was wearing my seat belt, of course, but I was kind of lying down in the seat, you know, flopping around like kids do. We were going through an intersection when some maniac in a big pickup truck ran a red light and slammed right into us. Dad says the car spun around a dozen times, but he's always been kind of prone to exaggeration. Anyway, we bounced off a couple of other cars, slammed into a light pole. The car was almost cut in half, and I was banged up pretty bad. The paramedics on the scene thought I was gone—they actually wrote me off and went to work on my mom, who was the one with the most minor injuries. There happened to be a doctor there, and he didn't have any trauma equipment or anything, but he checked my pulse, my breathing. He declared me dead.

"I don't remember any of this—I only remember being told about it later on, when I was older. But after they had all turned their backs on me, I revived somehow. I started to scream, and they were really freaked out that I was even alive."

"I can see how that might be surprising," Brandy admitted.

"Yeah. I was out for a couple minutes, I guess. My mom said if it had been any longer they would have worried about long-term brain damage. She said she'd never been so glad to hear me holler bloody murder."

"I bet." Scott's mom was a little stiff, a little too old–New England for her tastes, but still a nice enough lady.

Scott drank some cocoa, went quiet for a minute. Finally, he put his mug down, ran a finger across his lips to wipe away any chocolate remnants. "So anyway," he said, "I guess the moral of the story is that you don't always know for sure if something is really dead. Sometimes it'll surprise you."

And there it is, Brandy thought. *He doesn't give up easily. You almost have to admire that.*

Almost.

She wasn't about to get sucked into it, though. She made up an excuse and left him in the coffee shop. Ten minutes later she was sliding down the sidewalks herself. It *was* over. It was because she said it was, and one person didn't make a couple all by himself, no matter how much he wanted it.

Anyway, she thought, *he only wants it because Kerry's not here.*

They hadn't heard from her since leaving Vegas. She had gone back to the Swamp, back to finish her training, she had said. After Josh's death, none of them had had much to say to one another. Kerry, Rebecca, and Scott had all retreated into their own minds, into their own worlds. She had done the same, Brandy knew. They had promised to stay in touch, and Rebecca had called a couple of times since then, and of course she still saw Scott.

But everything had changed. Brandy had realized it was changing even before Josh's death, but that had hurried it along, made it all somehow more definitive.

Life might be short. *Too short to waste in a relationship in which you're only a stand-in for someone else,* she decided. She didn't know if Season was really hunting them, although it certainly seemed as if that might be the case.

If she was, then Brandy had a lot of living to squeeze into a finite amount of time. Being with Scott wasn't really how she wanted to spend it.

So she had moved on. She just hoped he would be able to do the same.

Thanksgiving brought a perfect fall day, with a clear sky, a snap to the air, and leaves like brittle flame. Kerry rowed herself to the Slocumb site and tugged the skiff up onto the bank at the edge of that blasted, forsaken landscape.

She had listened to some of Mother Blessing's stories about that fateful day, and had read various accounts of it in Daniel's journals. It had made such an impression on his mother, and through her on his own life, that he came back to it again and again.

Kerry found herself drawn to the place too, trying to picture what it had been like on that day so long ago. She walked across the scorched earth, noting the location of each building. Season had burned each one individually to the ground. The places where the roads had been laid out were still clearly distinguishable, now that she knew what to look for, and where structures had been, fire-blackened earth made precise geometric shapes. Wind had blown across this land, softening the edges, but as she'd noticed before, not a blade of grass had grown here since that time, not a dandelion or one of the ferns that were everywhere just a few feet away.

She had never quite understood how Mother Blessing had such precise knowledge of Season's actions on that day, since by her own account she had taken refuge in the Swamp as soon as it became clear that Season's rage had made her too powerful to fight. Kerry had asked, a time or two, but Mother Blessing had glossed over the issue as skillfully as a math teacher dodging the question of just when in life someone might have a need for advanced trigonometry. Probably, she had just relived the incident so many times in her own mind that she thought she remembered things she couldn't possibly have seen. At any rate, the damage had been done, that long-ago day. The Swamp had grown back, even after the fire that burned for months afterward—everyplace but here, of course. Mother Blessing had lived, had borne her sons and raised them. The world kept turning.

But for the people of Slocumb, the people Mother Blessing had known, had lived among, the world had ended that day. Kerry didn't know if Season's murderous ways had begun that day—if, having snapped, she'd never fully regained her sanity—or if she'd already embraced evil, and in fact had been responsible for the initial killings that had led up to the day's events.

Really, Kerry thought, *it doesn't matter. Season can't keep killing people I care about. Or strangers, for that matter. She's got to be stopped.*

She still had a lot to learn, a lot of drilling, a lot of practice before magic became as second nature to her as it would need to be to take on Season. But she was already more powerful than she had been three weeks ago when Josh had been killed, and a far more imposing person than she was a few months ago when she was trying to be a student at Northwestern, wanting nothing more than an "ordinary" life.

There is, she decided, *very little value to being ordinary.*

But there were times she wished for life to be a bit more like what she had grown up expecting, and this was one of them. The days and weeks had flown by; Thanksgiving was upon them. As a little girl, she had always loved that day, enjoying the televised parades, the football games, the way the house smelled, the warmth of her mother's kitchen, and the good spirits of the friends and relatives who came over. Mother Blessing's house couldn't be the same, but being there, so close to the region where the first European settlers made their homes, Kerry felt that some celebration was warranted. The older witch had agreed, so Kerry had gone out to shop for the requisite groceries: a turkey that Mother Blessing would fry, Southern style, in a deep pot she owned, and stuffing, cranberry sauce, fresh potatoes, green beans, and whatever else crossed her mind when she got to the market.

After spending a few minutes at the Slocumb site, soaking in the atmosphere and seeing it differently now that she had heard more stories about it, she rowed all the way over to Edgar Brandvold's place. He came out and unlocked the carriage house for her, wishing her a very happy Thanksgiving and revealing that he planned to spend the afternoon watching football. Kerry got in the minivan and drove to Deep Creek, where the nearest grocery store was. She loaded up with the things she needed and a few incidentals—Nehi and Coca-Cola for Mother Blessing, some herbal teas and a couple of bags of chocolate for herself—and took it all back to the van.

She appreciated Edgar Brandvold's willingness to garage the van for her. She had always been worried that someone would happen across it when she left it out in the open near Slocumb, and though it hadn't happened yet, hunting season had started and the Swamp was full of strangers. Now that she had met Edgar and knew he was an ally of Mother Blessing's, she felt comfortable asking him to help out.

When she pulled into his long drive, though, she knew at once that something was wrong. Edgar was nowhere to be seen, even when she honked her horn, and the door to his ramshackle house hung open. She remembered that when he'd come out before, it had been closed, and that he had closed it behind him with the unstudied efficiency of long habit. He didn't seem like the kind of man who'd forget and leave it open.

She killed her engine and climbed out of the van. The house and yard were quiet; only the ticking of her van and the cry of some faraway bird broke the silence. Dust that she had kicked up driving in hung on the still air.

Edgar's house was old, and the boards that composed it looked as if they'd never been painted, though surely they had been once. A gallery edged the front and one side, and the roof bowed low over the door. Missing shingles gave it a gap-toothed look. The house's windows were black, empty. Through the open front door Kerry could see nothing at all.

Steeling herself, fear welling up inside her, she walked across the yard and put her right foot on the first of three steps up to the gallery. The wood beneath her was worn thin, with nails sticking up from it. Old Edgar wasn't big on maintenance, that much was clear. Kerry had already announced her presence by honking, so she climbed the stairs and rapped her knuckles against the open door.

"Mr. Brandvold!" she called. Now she could see an entryway with a small side table for keys or mail and a worn staircase beyond. Her words echoed in the small space but were not answered.

She went in. "Mr. Brandvold, are you here?" The loud creak of a floor-board underfoot startled her, cranking up her anxiety another notch. In spite of the cool day she felt sweat beading on her lip. She went through a doorway into a parlor jammed with enough furniture for a whole house: chairs, sofas, a TV, a table holding a radio and several magazines, other tables in front of the chairs and sofas and lining the walls behind them, and lamps, all turned off, scattered here and there through it all.

Edgar Brandvold sat in one of the chairs, hands at his sides, eyes open. He looked relaxed, like a man peacefully watching television. But his blue cardigan sweater was purpled and moist, and fat, lazy flies were walking around on it.

His knob-headed cane had been driven through his heart.

Kerry caught the coppery smell of blood—and something else at the same time. The second smell was familiar, but it took her a moment to place it. A smell that reminded her of electricity.

Then it came to her.

The stink of ozone. The smell of destructive magic, of murder.

She turned and ran from the house, dashed across the yard, threw herself into the van and slammed her fist down on the door lock. She hadn't taken the key out of the ignition, so she cranked it, and as the engine roared to life she stomped down on the accelerator, cutting a wide arc across the yard as she sped away.

It wasn't until she was back on the road toward Deep Creek that she realized her mistake. This had been no ordinary killing. This could only be the work of Season Howe. She must have tortured Edgar to learn the whereabouts of Mother Blessing—which meant that Kerry needed to get into the Swamp, back to Mother Blessing, as fast as she could. Instead of driving away, she should have thrown the skiff into the creek and rowed for her life. Convincing herself to go back to Edgar's place, though, was almost beyond her capability, even though the only other place she knew her way well enough from was the Slocumb site . . . and if there was one place she didn't want to go while Season was around, that was it.

Choices . . .

The highway was empty, so when she jammed her foot down on the brake there was no one behind her to smash into her van's rear. She performed a shaky three-point turn and headed back the way she had come, back toward Wallaceton.

Back toward Season's last known location.

Chances were, though, that Season had already moved on. Obviously, she had determined that Edgar was connected in some way with Mother Blessing. So if he knew enough to tell her, before his horrible end, how to find Mother Blessing, then Season was already in the Swamp, and there was precious little time for Kerry to warn her mentor. If he did not, though, then Season would be looking for some other clue, and chances were, Slocumb would be on her list of destinations.

Kerry raced back into Edgar's yard, pulled as close to the creek as she dared, and dragged her skiff out of the van. She spared a moment's thought for the groceries and then abandoned them. There would be no Thanksgiving anyway, if Season got to Mother Blessing before she did. Climbing into the boat, she sat down and dipped her paddle in the water, glad that the autumn's activities had built her muscles. She would need to row as she never had before.

20

By the time Kerry reached Mother Blessing's home—*my home,* she thought defiantly, *as much as anyplace else is*—the once-blue sky had turned dark gray and begun to weep. She grounded the skiff at the edge of the small property and ran inside.

"Mother Blessing!" she called anxiously. "Are you—"

The door to Mother Blessing's bedroom banged open and the old witch rolled out into the hallway on her familiar scooter. Her brow was furrowed, her lips tightly compressed. "I know, child," she said. "Season is in the Swamp."

"Edgar . . ." Kerry began, barely able to formulate a sentence. "She killed him!"

"I thought as much," Mother Blessing acknowledged. "I have eyes in the Swamp, Kerry. I know she's lookin' for us. Lookin' for me. It's not too late for y'all to get yourself gone, though. Things are like to turn ugly round here."

Kerry hadn't considered running for a moment, couldn't quite believe Mother Blessing was making the offer. "It's my fight too."

Mother Blessing spared her a smile at that. "I was hopin' you'd feel that way. Let's get to work."

"How do you get ready for something like this?" Kerry asked anxiously. She could hear the first heavy drops of a hard rain hammering against the roof. "When Daniel was preparing to battle Season, he locked himself in a room and I heard the strangest noises—bells, wind, screams."

Mother Blessing rolled toward the kitchen as she answered. "He took himself out of the world for a few minutes, sounds like," she said. "Purifyin' is important before a fight, if there's time. If he was pressed for time, then he'd have done it by goin' someplace where time has a different meaning, where a short spell for you was a day or more for him."

"You mean . . . when I was standing outside the room waiting for him, he wasn't even in there?"

The old witch opened the refrigerator and rummaged around inside. "Yes and no," she said. "There's no easy answer to a question like that, and no right one either."

Kerry was almost afraid to ask the next one. "Are we . . . going someplace like that?"

"We don't even have that much time," Mother Blessing answered quickly. "We just got to be as pure as we are."

Kerry thought about making a crack to the effect that the only man she'd spoken with in a month was in his eighties and dead, but it didn't seem funny, even to her. She let it go and watched Mother Blessing's preparations. As a sudden fierce wind began howling outside, her mentor took out potions made long ago and stored in glass bottles in the icebox, then wheeled around and retrieved various implements from her cupboards. These were, for the most part, things Kerry hadn't seen before: a long sword she was sure she'd need both hands to lift, an old thorned stick that could be used as a wand, and, most frighteningly, a rifle or shotgun, Kerry wasn't sure which.

"What's that for?" Kerry asked, surprised. "Daniel didn't use anything like that."

"And he lost, didn't he?" Mother Blessing answered, her words clipped, her voice glacial. "I don't intend to."

Kerry couldn't argue with that, so she held her tongue. Mother Blessing moved rapidly, mixing the contents of some of the bottles, lighting candles, chanting softly to herself in words that Kerry recognized as the Old Tongue, even though she couldn't make out the meaning. Once Mother Blessing had combined some of the various fluids, she rubbed the mixture on the blade of the sword. She poured another concoction into a bowl, where it steamed like something from a mad-scientist movie, and into that she emptied a box of bullets. Her efficiency was wondrous to behold, even as her actions filled Kerry's heart with terror.

Mother Blessing pointed at the bowl of ammunition and tossed Kerry a dishtowel. "Dry those," she instructed. Kerry held her hand over the rim of the bowl and poured the liquid out into the sink, cringing inwardly as the cold steel of the bullets bumped against her flesh. She spread the towel on the counter and scooped them out onto it, then folded it over them and rubbed them dry. She had always hated guns; the thought that she might be asked to use one repulsed her. After a moment she checked the bullets.

"They're dry."

"Load it," Mother Blessing said.

Kerry looked at the forbidding weapon. "I . . . I don't know how."

Mother Blessing huffed at her and took the gun in her own hands, drawing the towel toward herself over the counter. Kerry felt like she ought to apologize, but then thought better of it. The woman had no reason to assume that Kerry would know how to use a rifle; she shouldn't get upset when it turned out she didn't.

Still, it was true that while Mother Blessing did almost all of the preparatory work, Season—if the weather outside was any indicator, and Kerry couldn't help feeling like it must be—was drawing ever closer. The rain beat at the roof and walls like fists, causing her to wonder if it had turned to hail. The wind buffeted the walls, seeping in through whatever cracks it could. In fifteen minutes the temperature had dropped at least thirty degrees.

Before Kerry could even process the drastic meteorological changes, though, there was a noise like a clap of thunder right outside. The whole house shook as if a sixteen-wheeler had run into it. Mother Blessing looked up at Kerry with a wry grin. "She's here."

"Do we have any simulacra?" Kerry asked.

"If she's outside, she's already gone through them."

"But . . . are we ready?" Kerry asked.

The witch was already in motion, wheeling her scooter around and heading out of the kitchen, toward the front door. "As we're gonna be. Got no time to be readier." Over her shoulder, she added, "Bring that stuff, willya?"

Kerry gathered up the sword, the stick, and the loaded gun and followed her. She caught up to Mother Blessing just inside the front door, where, to her astonishment, the older woman was climbing off the scooter. She had never seen Mother Blessing stand or walk, and had just assumed that both were impossible for her. But she was doing both now, and though her bulk made it difficult, she was able to maneuver herself to some degree. She tugged open the door, which blew inward with a great gust of wind, and stepped out into the lashing rain.

"This is still the South," Mother Blessing declared loudly. Kerry couldn't see who the witch was talking to, but she knew just the same. "We're hospitable folks here—y'all don't need to raise such a ruckus just to visit."

As Mother Blessing took a couple more steps away from the door, Kerry came closer to it and was able to see Season Howe standing on the firm ground outside the house. She couldn't spot any indication of how Season had arrived—there was no boat visible, nor any other form of transportation. But then again, Kerry couldn't see much; the curtain of rain reduced visibility to just a few yards.

Season looked like she had the last time Kerry had seen her: stern, severe, but undeniably beautiful. Her honey-blond hair was plastered to her head by the rain; wet black leathers, like a motorcyclist's, hugged her slim figure. Arms folded over her chest, she stared up at Mother Blessing on the wooden walkway outside the house, spared a casual glance for Kerry, whose arms were still laden with Mother Blessing's weapons, then looked back at the real threat.

"I decided I'm tired of you sending intermediaries after me," Season said, her voice calm and even. "Especially after I saw in Las Vegas that you are using these children again." Here her gaze ticked toward Kerry for a moment. "And not even children versed in the craft, but simply cannon fodder. You should be ashamed."

"Not that y'all will believe me," Mother Blessing argued, "but those 'children' weren't workin' on my behalf. They got their own issues with you."

"Is that right? I thought *you* were the one who wanted my hide—you and the sons you sacrificed."

Kerry was close enough to Mother Blessing to feel her go tense at that—*surprising,* she thought, *because I've been tense for a couple of hours now*—the woman's spine straightening, her fists clenching. "You leave them out of this."

"If you had left them out of it, they'd still be alive," Season observed. There was no cruelty in her tone, though there obviously was in the words she spoke. Mother Blessing took another step toward her.

"This house is under protection," she warned.

"And how far does that extend?" Season asked, almost cheerfully. "Since you're outside the house."

"Far enough."

The two witches faced each other, neither speaking for a moment. Kerry couldn't see Mother Blessing's eyes, but she was sure they were locked on Season's. The very air between them seemed charged somehow, as if to step into their path would be inviting electrocution.

"This has gone on too long," Season said after a few moments. Her voice sounded tighter now, as if she were starting to feel the tension. "Let's end it."

"Sounds good to me," Mother Blessing agreed. She raised her hands in a gesture with which Kerry had grown very familiar. *Lahatsi,* she thought, even before her mentor spoke the word.

"*Lahatsi!*" Mother Blessing shouted. She raised her hands as high as her bulk would allow and Kerry saw the energy ball that formed between them. Then Mother Blessing drew back and hurled it at Season.

Season didn't even speak, just flicked her wrist, almost casually, and the energy ball was diverted from its course. It hit a stand of cypress trees nearby and burst into flames, which sizzled and were extinguished in moments by the powerful rain. Watching the ease with which Season turned away what Kerry had believed to be a devastating attack, she realized with a shiver of fear that Season was the more skilled, the more potent, of the two combatants.

Which is bad, because Season has to die.

Not to mention that Kerry didn't want to be on the losing side of another fight to the death.

Season brought her hands together in a gesture that Kerry didn't know and then spread them quickly. A wave of power rippled the air, coming right toward them. Mother Blessing raised her hands in a warding gesture, and Kerry reflexively did the same. It worked; the energy wave dissipated harmlessly around them.

Mother Blessing turned partially, glancing behind her to make sure Kerry was there. She took the stick and the gun from Kerry's hands, leaving her only the sword. "We'll need weapons," she said simply. "Use that, Kerry. Kill her."

"Me?" Kerry felt her stomach clench, her insides turn to liquid. She had never fought with a sword in her life. *But then,* she told herself, *there are a lot of things you've never done before. Doesn't mean you can't do them.* Half convinced by her own pep talk, she gripped the sword by its handle, holding it in both of her fists. To her astonishment, flames licked up and down the blade, as if gasoline had been spread on the steel and then ignited. Raindrops hissed on its fire as they struck it, evaporating instantly.

With the fire came new confidence—confidence she thought might have been magically instilled, but was good enough just the same. She pressed past Mother Blessing and went down the steps toward Season, fiery blade held out in front of her.

Season took a step back as Kerry approached, her eyes widening slightly, which added to Kerry's sensation of well-being. *This can work,* she realized. *She's genuinely worried that I can beat her.*

As she moved toward Season, she felt more sure of what to do, how to wield the flaming sword, as if the weapon itself were teaching her its technique. She advanced, blade flicking this way and that, weaving a web of light and flame. Season raised her right hand and manifested a similar weapon, a sword made from pure magical energy. She waved it around for a moment, as if gauging its heft, and it made a whistling noise as it cut through the air. Then she lunged suddenly toward Kerry, right leg thrown forward, left hand back, like a fencer. Kerry didn't even have to think—the fiery sword drew her hand across her body to parry the lunge, and Season's mystical blade slid harmlessly to Kerry's side.

Kerry moved easily from the parry to an attack, her own sword thrusting itself forward at Season, drawing her body into a straight line as it did. Season, her face all intense concentration now, blocked the thrust with a grunt of effort. The move threw her off balance, her feet slipping on the wet ground, and Kerry pressed her attack, twisting her blade around Season's and driving forward again. This time, the tip of it touched Season's leathers before the witch managed to bat it aside.

Season retreated two quick steps and raised her sword again. "This can only end badly for you," she warned through clenched teeth. "You don't know what you're in the middle of."

"The plan is for it to end badly for *you,*" Kerry corrected. She stood her ground, feet planted, legs spread for stability. Every muscle that she had built up over the fall was functioning at peak performance. Mother Blessing had been right—she may not have been ready, but she was as ready as she'd ever be, and far more prepared than she had expected.

"Plans don't always work out the way they're supposed to," Season pointed out. "I would have thought you'd have learned that by now."

"You killed Daniel," Kerry reminded her, fury tightening her voice. "That's all I need to know."

"Like I said, you have no idea what you're mixed up in, girl. If you back off now I'll try not to hurt you."

There was something in the witch's blue eyes that looked plaintive, even sympathetic. But Kerry was in no mood for it. She feinted to Season's left and then drove her sword, hard, toward Season's right. The witch parried, then drew her energy blade back and brought it forward again, slamming it into Kerry's with enough force to rip the flaming sword from her grasp. It spun twice in the air and splashed into swamp water, its flames dousing as it did.

All trace of sympathy gone from her face now, as if Kerry's resolve had steeled her own, Season charged in for the kill.

She lunged, the tip of her mystic blade slicing the air toward Kerry. Before it reached her, though, Kerry heard a sharp report from behind her, then another, and a third. Season's advance halted and she staggered back, blue eyes widening, mouth dropping open. Kerry whirled to see Mother Blessing sighting down the barrel of the rifle, which had a trail of smoke rising up from its opening. The woman fired again, the muzzle flash impossibly bright against the dark sky. Four spots appeared on Season's black leathers, dark against dark, wet on wet.

Then Season bent forward at the waist, hands going up to her mouth. Kerry felt an unexpected sadness. She couldn't decide if it was because she hadn't been the one to finish Season off, or if it was something more than that, a kind of sorrow that the whole affair was ended. But ended it seemed to be.

Season had another surprise in store, though. She moved her hands a few inches away from her lips and spat four bullets into them, each one slick with her own blood. Holding them out before her, she smiled and dropped them to the ground. "You've got to do better than that," she said with a chuckle.

Mother Blessing hurled the weapon away, and raised the stick. "Not the gun and not the sword," she said, "but the rod will vanquish you."

Now Season's dry chuckle turned into a full-throated laugh. "That thing?" she asked. "Do you forget who gave you that, daughter?"

"Y'all are on my ground," Mother Blessing said sharply. "And Kerry is strong, stronger than she has any right to be. There'll be no walkin' away, not from this fight. Not this time." But Kerry noticed that in spite of the certainty of the words, the hand holding the old stick was shaking a little, and there was a quiver in the voice. She couldn't have imagined Mother Blessing being scared by anything, but there it was.

"I didn't come here to walk away," Season reminded her. "I came to make sure you don't. To make sure you aren't going to continue to haunt me for the rest of my days."

"I don't need to haunt what's dead," Mother Blessing said, her voice cracking even more. She held out the stick like it was a weapon and said, *"Manistera!"*

The stick crackled with energy, traces of blue lightning running up and down its length. After a moment, the energy lanced toward Season. But the witch deflected it with a quiet word and hastily upraised hands. Her magical sword was gone now, back to whatever place she had conjured it from.

Season clapped her hands together hard, creating a sound like a sonic boom. Kerry threw her hands over her ears too late. The boom echoed in them, and she had a feeling they'd ring for hours, if not days. But the blast of power that began at Season's clap and rippled out toward Mother Blessing like a stone in a pond was sliced by the older woman's rod. Where it passed, leaves and bark were torn from trees, mud upturned, water churned in the creek. Mother Blessing, Kerry, and the house seemed unaffected.

Season didn't release her hands, though. She kept them clasped together, and as long as she did, the wave continued. Kerry felt it pressing against her like a surging tide. Mother Blessing felt it too, she saw, and though she tried hard to hold onto her stick—*her rod,* Kerry mentally corrected—the force of Season's attack whittled away at it, bit by bit, until all that was left was the tiniest twig. As that happened, tears came to Mother Blessing's eyes—tears of rage or tears of sorrow, Kerry wasn't sure—and the older woman, who she had come to think of as all but invulnerable, was driven to her knees. The sight filled Kerry with terror more than anything else that had happened so far.

Finally, Mother Blessing threw the twig aside and brought her hands up in a *"Lashifoth!"* defense. Kerry joined in, shouting the word simultaneously with her and making the appropriate motions.

A golden glow engulfed them—the punishing rain actually bounced off its blurred edges—and Season's attack ceased. Still, Season didn't look particularly frightened or upset. "You didn't really think that stick would stop me, did you, daughter?" she asked. "A gift from me to you? Your first rod."

"I remember," Mother Blessing said, almost spitting the words. She crooked her finger at Kerry. "Help me up," she commanded.

Kerry wasn't sure she'd be able to budge the woman, but she hurried to comply. She didn't want Season to try anything more while Mother Blessing was on her knees.

"You're right," Season admitted then. "I am demonstrably more powerful than you, but on your home ground, and with your little helper, neither of us can get the upper hand. I had hoped to bring this little conflict to a close today, but apparently that's not to be."

Mother Blessing looked at Kerry, her eyes narrow, her mouth twisted into a scowl of utter hatred. "Don't let her go!"

Kerry already had her hands on Mother Blessing's arms, trying to hoist the enormous woman to her feet. "What can I—?" she began.

Season interrupted her question. "Nothing. There's nothing you can do, child. Except perhaps ask the woman you call Mother Blessing to explain what happened here today. Make her tell you the *whole* story. The real story."

Kerry looked from one to the other—Mother Blessing, struggling to regain her footing, her face a mask of fury, and Season Howe, beautiful and calm even though her leather jacket still showed four bullet holes. As she watched, Season grew less distinct. Kerry thought at first that she was walking backward, getting lost in the still-pounding rain. But her legs weren't moving, and she wasn't getting smaller. She was just . . . *vanishing* was the only word that came to mind. Becoming less substantial. Kerry could see the trees behind her, through her, and the rain and the Swamp, and then she was gone altogether.

Mother Blessing got a grip on Kerry's shoulders and forced herself to her feet. She looked at where Season had been a moment before, spat in that general direction, and stormed inside, slamming the door behind her. Kerry opened it again and walked in, wanting to talk to the woman, but Mother Blessing was already back on her scooter, wheeling toward her bedroom. When she reached it, she slammed that door, too.

And Kerry was alone with a million questions.

Kerry Profitt's diary, November 24

There's something very wrong here. I can't ask Mother Blessing about it because (a) she hasn't come out of her room since the battle to end all battles that wasn't, and (b) because if what I think is true IS true, then she's been lying to me all along.

To me, and maybe to others.

See, the thing is, Season Howe addressed her as "daughter." Not once, but twice. I know, it could be some sort of traditional witchy form of address, indicating love and respect, but . . .

No, really. That was what I tried to convince myself she meant. Figure of speech, right? Problem there is that the rest of Season's speech seemed pretty precise—not one for flowery speeches, that witch.

And there's more. If Season gave Mother Blessing her first rod, that implies, at the very least, some sort of teacher-pupil relationship. Which could also be a mother-daughter relationship.

If Season is Mother Blessing's mother, then what else hasn't Mother Blessing told me? Or Daniel—because I'm sure if he knew Season was his grandmother, he'd have said something. Apparent age, among witches, doesn't mean much, as Mother Blessing herself told me. Mother Blessing looks older than Daniel and Season, but none of them look anywhere near their actual ages. So Season could easily be older than Mother Blessing.

I had a lot of questions before, but now I have . . . well, A LOT a lot. Like why was she so willing to send me to Las Vegas after Season, knowing that I had just barely begun my magical training? Was she testing me somehow? Testing my willingness to fight, my courage, my hatred of Season? Or maybe testing Season's strength? And having my van moved—sure, she let me find out about it, introduced me to Edgar. But why didn't she tell me when she did it, or even ask permission? My van, after all. And the biggie that's been haunting me is this—I've wondered how Mother Blessing could have described the destruction of Slocumb so well, when supposedly she was already on her way into hiding, trying to protect her unborn children. But what if the answer is that it wasn't Season who destroyed Slocumb, but Mother Blessing? That's a big stretch, I know. But it's one answer to something that's been gnawing at me. And it goes back to the fact that Mother Blessing has been hiding things, lying to me.

I hate that. Hate lies, hate liars. I had grown to respect Mother Blessing—she's a real character, and a bit of a handful, but she was teaching me a lot, and I was willing to use what she taught to help her further her goal. Since it was the same as my own goal—revenge for Daniel's murder.

If she's been dishonest with me this whole time, though, that changes things. It doesn't change the fact that Season killed Daniel (although it adds, like, this whole layer of almost Shakespearean irony to it, doesn't it? Mother persuades son to kill his grandmother, but grandmother turns the tables . . .). What it changes are all the whys, and some of the whos, if not the whats.

It also changes my plans. I wanted to stay here, to learn as much as I could from Mother Blessing, to try to get close to her since she is my only link now to Daniel—not that she's the easiest person to get to know, since she will almost never actually talk about herself. But now . . .

. . . now, I think I need to get away from here. Fast.

To paraphrase old Willie S., there's something rotten, but it ain't in Denmark. It's right here in the Great Dismal. And I have this feeling that the longer I sit in "my" room, typing on this laptop, the rottener it's getting. I think it'd be best to get myself gone before MB comes out of her room looking for me.

Is it because I've been thinking about Josh and his noir movies that the phrase "you know too much" comes to mind? Because whenever there's someone in those movies who knows too much, the person who says it is always trying to kill them.

I think maybe I know too much.

Guess it's time to go.

More later.

K.

WINTER

I am ready to run.

Not that I brought much with me to Mother Blessing's that I need to take away, but there are a few things—my old red-checked tennies, a couple of sweatshirts and some jeans I've grown attached to, my stash of cash, this laptop, BoBo the clown doll, and some of Daniel's journals—that I don't want to leave behind.

By now I know my way through the Swamp, so I'm not that concerned about provisions for the trip—no need to weigh myself down with energy bars or anything. But when I leave here this time, I'm never coming back. I don't want to forget anything that I might want later.

And, truth? I don't want to leave anything that Mother Blessing might be able to use to track me down.

But by the time I threw the few things I want to take into a duffel bag, Mother Blessing came out of her room and started wheeling around the house, slamming doors and cursing and shouting out—certainly for my benefit—things like "I can't believe what a liar that Season Howe is!"

I was hoping to get out of the house before she emerged from seclusion, so I'd be gone well before she knew I was missing. Because, let's face it, Thanksgiving hadn't exactly turned out like I'd planned. The groceries I had bought were still in my van—the turkey no doubt well thawed by now—at Edgar Brandvold's place, but Edgar had been murdered. I thought by Season Howe, since she seems to make a habit of killing people I know, including Daniel Blessing, Mother Blessing's son and the man I loved. But now everything I thought I knew about Mother Blessing and Season has been turned upside down, with the new information that Season is apparently Mother's mother. And, according to Season, there are other things Mother Blessing hasn't told me as well, which feed into certain questions I have run up against. Such as, which one was really the mega-destructo queen who trashed Slocumb, Virginia, three hundred years ago?

Confusion reigns. All I know for sure is that nothing is for sure. Maybe Mother Blessing killed Edgar to make me think Season had done it. Maybe Mother Blessing destroyed Slocumb and then sent her sons—Abraham and Daniel, both now deceased at Season's hands—after Season, to hide her own guilt.

Almost certainly Mother Blessing has been less than honest with me. And also almost certainly, she knows that since our confrontation with Season I am suspicious of her. The combination, it seems to me, is a dangerous one, which is why I really want to get gone.

But now she's banging around the house, and if I leave my room she'll see me. I'm trying to wait her out, hoping she'll give up and go to bed, and then I can scram.

The Great Dismal Swamp at night isn't exactly my favorite place. Dark, full of bugs and gators and snakes and the occasional bear. But right now, it beats the heck out of staying in this house an instant longer than I absolutely have to.

More later.
K.

1

Mother Blessing's door slammed again.

She'd been doing this for an hour—coming out of her room, rolling around the halls, the rubber wheels of her scooter squeaking on hardwood floors, then going back in. Slamming doors like an eight-year-old throwing a tantrum.

Except most eight-year-olds weren't potentially lethal.

Is she in for the night this time? Kerry wondered. *Or just for a couple of minutes?*

The answer could, literally, be that proverbial matter of life and death.

Gotta get out of here gotta get out of here gotta get out . . .

The door opened. Wheels squeaked. Barely breathing, Kerry closed her laptop and listened. Mother Blessing had stopped shouting so much, but she was muttering something under her breath that Kerry couldn't make out. Panic gripped Kerry for a moment—the scooter was coming all the way down the hall to the guest room, the room in which Kerry had spent much of the autumn, learning magic at Mother Blessing's side. Given what had transpired earlier—Season Howe informing Kerry, in front of Mother Blessing, that most of what she had been told about the mutual history of the two witches was wrong—Kerry couldn't help feeling that Mother Blessing would not be in a jovial mood when next they met.

Kerry had power. She knew that now. She had learned well, and magic seemed to come naturally to her.

But she was nowhere near Mother Blessing's level. If the old witch decided that it would be advantageous now to just take Kerry out, there would be little Kerry could do to dissuade her.

She held her breath for several seconds, but then the scooter's wheels squeaked again as Mother Blessing turned away from her door. Kerry heard the door to Mother Blessing's room open, and then slam shut again.

Is she working up her courage? Kerry thought. *Why? What kind of threat could I be to her?*

Sounds from Mother Blessing's room filtered down the hallway to her. They could have been the sounds of Mother Blessing preparing for bed—it was past ten now, her typical bedtime—but rain still hammered the roof, and it was hard to be sure.

Kerry waited another half hour. The minutes dragged by like days, weeks. Finally the noises from Mother Blessing's room died out.

Kerry was convinced that if she stayed, tomorrow would bring a confrontation with the old witch that she would probably not survive. She had successfully dodged it for tonight, probably because Mother Blessing herself was so weakened from the afternoon's magical battle with Season that she hadn't wanted to force the issue.

By morning Mother Blessing would have regained her strength. She would want to discuss the things Season had said—a discussion that would lead inexorably to Kerry's concerns that she had been lied to since arriving at the cabin in the Swamp earlier in the fall. If Kerry lived long enough, she would most likely accuse Mother Blessing of having lied to her own sons as well—of sending them off to kill a witch they didn't even know was their grandmother.

If Kerry was to get another day older, she had to leave tonight.

She had been ready for hours now, but she waited still longer. She wanted Mother Blessing to be deeply asleep. The old house's floors could creak when she walked across them, and the last thing she wanted was for Mother Blessing to wake up and find her on her way out. That would precipitate the very confrontation Kerry was trying to avoid.

Every minute was torture, every tick of the guest room wall clock ago-nizing. She almost took out her laptop to write some more in her journal, but then stopped herself. She wanted to be alert, aware, in case Mother Blessing woke up. Losing herself in her diaries was a distraction she couldn't afford. She couldn't even pace, for fear that her steps would wake the witch whose house she shared.

Midnight passed. *The witching hour,* she thought. Except for Mother Blessing, who, witch or no, almost always slept right through it.

But then, I guess I'm a witch too, now. Not as skilled and practiced as Mother Blessing or Season Howe. But if being a witch is defined by doing witchcraft, then I am one. So I can observe the witching hour all by my lonesome.

She waited, and let Mother Blessing sleep.

When the clock ticked over to twelve thirty, Kerry decided she had waited long enough. Her bag was already packed. She tied her long black hair back with a leather thong, pulled a coat from the closet, wrapped it around herself against the cold and rain she knew were waiting outside in the dark, and opened her door. Her room was at the end of a hallway, and she had to go past Mother Blessing's room to get out of the house. She stepped as lightly as she could manage, holding the duffel away from her body so it didn't rub against her jeans. In her other hand she carried boots, which she would only pull on when she was at the door.

She had almost made it when Mother Blessing's bedroom door opened, spilling light, and her scooter nosed out into the hall. Kerry's heart leapt into her throat as she spun around to see Mother Blessing glaring at her over her oxygen mask. The woman's breathing was labored, her voice muffled when she spoke.

"Where are y'all goin'?"

This was precisely what Kerry had hoped to avoid. She hadn't wanted a confrontation or a scene. She simply wanted to vanish, as she had from Northwestern University when she had decided that she wanted to come here, to the Swamp, to have Mother Blessing teach her magic so she could take revenge on Season Howe.

That worked out great, huh? she thought.

Now, facing Mother Blessing's glare, Kerry delivered the line she'd been practicing. "I'm . . . uh . . . going after Season," she said. "She can't be too far away yet."

Mother Blessing just stared, her breathing Darth Vader–esque through the mask.

"You've taught me a lot," Kerry went on. Her mind screamed at her to *shut up, already!* but her mouth didn't comply. "I think it's time to move on, though. Got to stay on Season's trail until I can kill her."

Mother Blessing stared. Finally she spoke again. "I don't think that's a good idea."

"Yeah, well, I kind of do," Kerry returned, defiance starting to rise in her. "So, thanks a lot and all, but I've got to get going."

"No."

Obviously conversation wasn't a good idea. Kerry dropped the duffel, tugged on her boots, picked it up again. Another glance at Mother Blessing, who was rolling in her direction now, her mouth scowling behind the oxygen mask, and Kerry stepped out the door.

"No!" she heard Mother Blessing cry behind her.

Kerry slammed the door and ran through driving rain to the shallow-bottomed skiff Mother Blessing kept for traveling out of the Swamp. She hurled the duffel in, pushed it off the bank, climbed in, and shoved the oars into the oarlocks. As she started to row, she glanced back toward the house—which always looked like a tumbledown old trapper's cabin from the outside—and saw Mother Blessing silhouetted in the doorway, her arms raised in the air.

That, she thought, terrified, *is not good.*

But with strength that came from working hard around the Swamp for weeks, she dipped the oars into the murky water and pulled.

It was impossible to tell where the water ended and the trees began, and just as hard to know where the tops of the trees merged with the sky. Moonlight filtered through only in rare spots. Trees were a wall of black against black. The toads, crickets, night birds, the rare and piercing howl of a bobcat, were all but drowned out by the pounding rain and the occasional crack of thunder, adding to Kerry's confusion and disorientation.

At this moment, however, she was more concerned with steering the shallow boat between the trees and not grounding it than with direction. She needed to find her way through the honeycomb of canals and creeks to someplace where she could catch a ride far away from here, but it wouldn't do her any good to get away from Mother Blessing if she killed herself trying. Since she wasn't sure who had killed Edgar Brandvold, or why—and since she had told Mother Blessing that she'd left the minivan at his place when she arrived and found Edgar murdered—she didn't want to risk going back there. Mother Blessing had not been happy about her leaving, and if she were going to try to stop Kerry—or to send her simulacra to do that— the van would be the obvious place to start.

A flash of lightning momentarily illuminated a barricade of tree trunks right before her. Kerry put her oars to water and pulled backward, trying to brake herself, to lessen the impact of imminent collision. At what she figured was the last moment, she raised an oar and thrust it out before her to stave off the bank. She felt the oar hit the bank, felt the boat stop in the water just before it rammed.

But when she tried to lower the oar to the water again, something held it fast. She yanked at it, but to no avail. Whatever had her oar wasn't letting go—and, she realized, it was drawing her in toward the bank.

Simulacra? Kerry wondered. If she'd just snagged it on something, she would be able to free it, she was certain. She had a flashlight with her but hadn't bothered to use it, since it would have meant taking a hand off the oars. Now, though, she released the stuck oar and grabbed for the flashlight at the top of her duffel bag. She drew it out and flicked it on.

Something had her oar, all right, but it wasn't one of Mother Blessing's manufactured men. It was a bald cypress root sticking out from the bank. It had wound itself three times around the end of the oar and was waving it like a magician with a wand.

Kerry knew the root could not have grabbed the oar like that without help. Mother Blessing was trying to stop her—and using the Swamp to do it!

While she watched, another root snaked toward her. She ducked away from its grasp. It came again, and she bashed it with the flashlight.

That wouldn't hold it for long. She clicked off the light and jammed it back into the duffel, zipping the bag closed to keep out the rain. With her remaining oar—no way would she be able to fight the tree for the other one, not while it had dozens of roots that might attack her—she pulled hard against the water, alternating sides of the skiff to keep on an even course.

She was only a few yards away from where she'd lost her oar when she felt something damp brush her face. *A spiderweb,* she thought, *or some low-hanging Spanish moss.* Either was possible here. She swiped at it with one hand—and it snaked around her wrist, pulling tighter as she tried to tug away.

Kerry screamed and yanked her arm. Whatever it was—she thought she felt leaves on it, like a vine of some kind—wouldn't let go. She swung at it with the oar but couldn't break its grip. It started to lift her up out of the boat.

Panic threatened to overtake her as she struggled against the vine. Another one wrapped around her waist and tightened there, like a belt cinching up. Her free right hand dropped to her own belt, but the knife she wore sometimes in the Swamp wasn't there, and she remembered tossing it into the duffel when she'd packed.

When the next vine looped around her throat, she thought it was all over. It closed tightly on her, cutting off her airway. By now she was mostly out of the skiff, could feel with her feet that it was drifting away from her.

Which was when she remembered that she was a witch too.

A kind of calm settled over Kerry's racing mind. Mother Blessing was turning the Swamp against her through magic. But she wasn't the only magic-user around. She had taught Kerry quite a few tricks—but more important, she had taught her philosophies and systems. She may not have known a specific spell to free herself from living vines, but that didn't mean she was defenseless.

With her throat closed off and one hand out of commission, speaking the Old Tongue and making the correct gestures was tricky. But she managed to croak out the word *"Kalaksit!"* and curl the fingers of her free hand toward her palm while splaying the thumb out. White flame crackled at her fingertips. She felt herself relaxing even more, letting the now-familiar sensation wash over her—the thrill of power, the rush of magic. Raindrops sizzled against her fire. Aiming by the light the flickering flames provided, she pointed at the vine that encircled her throat and willed the fire into a narrow, straight blast. It cut the vine as keenly as a laser.

Next came the one around her waist, and then her arm. Kerry dropped back down to the skiff, but unbalanced, she went over backward, landing faceup in the shallow water. She allowed herself a bitter smile. It hardly mattered; she was already drenched from the rain. The flames at her fingertips died in the creek, but that was okay. She could always make more.

She climbed back into the skiff, found the remaining oar, and started to row.

Okay, then, she thought as she churned the water, driving the boat quickly up the creek.

Mother Blessing is definitely opposed to me leaving. Don't know yet if she's homicidal about it, but she's obviously serious.

Kerry rowed and rowed. Her arms started to ache, her shoulders and back protesting from the effort. The rain gave up, and by the time light started to show itself, patches of silver and pink visible through the leafy ceiling to the east, she knew something was wrong. She had been making for the old Slocumb site—the blasted, cursed township Season and Mother Blessing had once shared—and she should have reached it within a few hours. Navigation had been difficult in the dark, but even so. . . .

More light filtered in through the trees and Kerry saw a bank that she recognized, with roots reaching through the bluff of clay and diving into the water, a big, pale mushroom sticking out of one like a dinner plate wedged halfway in. She had seen that bank at least an hour or two before, on one of the occasions when she'd taken out her flashlight to gauge her path. She was positive she hadn't been rowing in circles—the Swamp wasn't so well organized that one could even do that intentionally. Which could only mean that the Swamp itself was shifting, changing itself around in an effort to keep her here.

What if it isn't Mother Blessing? Kerry wondered as the icy hands of fear gripped her again. *What if it's Season—or the Swamp itself? What if it doesn't want me to leave? Will I ever get out then?*

But Kerry Profitt was the Bulldog, she reminded herself. It didn't matter who—or what—was trying to keep her here. The only thing that mattered was that she was determined to get out, and so she would. She drifted past the familiar bank. Now that the sun had come up, she knew which direction east was. Slocumb was to the east, and a highway ran alongside the Great Dismal in that direction. She would find an exit, at one spot or another.

Kerry had traveled maybe another half mile when the water started moving faster under her boat. It took her in the direction she wanted to go, so she let the current carry her, using the oar only to keep herself away from the banks. A family of feral pigs watched her race by from a bluff; crows and three snowy egrets took flight at her rapid approach.

Then the creek widened, and ahead she could see where it joined with a broader canal. By now she was completely lost—she was nowhere she had ever been before, or, more likely, the Swamp had never been configured in just this way before. She put the oar to water to help ease herself into the canal, but when her smaller tributary hit the larger one, the water there rushed faster than she had ever seen water move here. It was like a river's rapids, not like the near-stagnant swamp water she was used to. Her heart raced as she tried to steady the shallow skiff, but the little boat was no match for the sudden flow.

Water roared in her ears and splashed ahead of the skiff, and Kerry found herself spinning around and around, the oar useless to stop her. Then the tiny craft was hurled against a jagged bank, where it splintered. Kerry snatched up her duffel bag as the water rushed in, and hurled it up onto the bank. The water in the Swamp was rarely deep, but things lived in it that she didn't want to encounter if she could help it—water moccasins and alligators foremost among them. Grabbing exposed roots, she pulled herself onto dry land, where she sat down hard and watched the boards that had once been the skiff separate and float away.

The waterways were the highways of the Swamp, Kerry knew. There were trails on land, but they were mostly animal paths, unsuited for anything as big and ungainly as a human being. Kerry was slender enough for most trails, but when they wound underneath spreading ferns and fallen trunks, they could be impassable even for her.

Still, it didn't look like she had much choice now. She headed vaguely east until she found a faint track and then followed it.

And still Mother Blessing wasn't done with her, she discovered. After maybe a mile or so, Kerry discovered that she was being followed. She heard the chuffing sound of a big cat first and froze in place. Slowly, carefully, she turned and looked back down her trail, and after a few minutes a bobcat showed itself, its strange golden eyes fixed on her. But the bobcat wasn't alone—a black bear parted the brush and stood beside the feline. Kerry knew that would never happen in nature—only Mother Blessing's intercession could have made those two creatures into allies.

Knowing that didn't make Kerry feel any better about it. Either one, bear or bobcat, could do a lot of damage if it attacked her. Both acting together, impossible as it was to imagine, could easily tear her to shreds.

She could defend herself, of course. But the idea of hurting either of those animals, forced against their own natures to cooperate in her destruction, was repellent to Kerry.

Fighting the tremor in her knees, the urge to run, she turned away slowly, showing them her back. She then continued down the trail she had found, heading into the morning sun, moving at a steady clip—not running, but not slow.

Behind her, she heard the animals keeping pace.

To panic, to run, would certainly bring them both charging down on her. This way they remained at bay, tracking without charging, while she tried to think of a way to reverse the spell that had enchanted them.

No such reversal came to mind. Kerry was exhausted. She hadn't slept since yesterday morning, Thanksgiving, which seemed a lifetime ago, and then the battle with Season, the effort of rowing all night—it was no wonder answers weren't coming to her as quickly as they might have.

Finally an idea occurred to her. The animals had been set on her trail by Mother Blessing, no doubt with malicious intent. They hadn't attacked her yet, but Kerry was convinced that they would when their instincts told them she was a threat or when she tried to run. She didn't know how she could alter the programming, but she was pretty sure she could change their target. She stopped, then spun around, facing them again. Speaking a couple of the magic words she had learned, gesturing with both hands, she pointed toward a nearby puddle and raised the water from it. With the water that now hovered in the air between herself and the animals, she sculpted the image of Mother Blessing—all three hundred pounds or more of her, complete with scooter, oxygen tanks, and beehive hairdo. She tried to look into the eyes of each animal, and she drove into their minds the concept that this person was their enemy, their mutual target. Finally she hurled the water sculpture at them. Bear and cat both flinched away, but it splashed against them, harmless but soaking.

When it was over, both creatures regarded Kerry almost casually, and then looked this way and that, up and down the path. They were no longer fixed on her, she believed. She waved her arms at them, and they backed away, turning and going back the way they had come.

Kerry didn't know how long Mother Blessing's spell would last—or how long her own would, for that matter. But if it held, and if these two unlikely companions found their way to Mother Blessing's cabin, the old witch was in for an unpleasant surprise.

The path twisted and turned, widening here, narrowing to almost nothingness there. Always it led east, which was where Kerry had decided salvation lay anyway. So she stayed with it as best she could.

In another hour or so, she could hear the rush of cars on the highway. She struggled to place her weary feet. The duffel was so heavy she was regretting having brought it. The world no longer seemed to conspire against her—when vines snatched at her ankles or thorns tore at her sleeves, they were simply doing what vines and thorns naturally did. But she was almost ready to admit defeat anyway, not sure how long she could continue the hike. The sound of cars perked her up a little. But they were still at some distance, with plenty of thick swamp between her and them.

She drove herself on. When her mind started to wander, when she began to lose her focus, to fall asleep on her feet, she reminded herself of Mace Winston, whom Season had killed back in San Diego during the summer. That summer had changed everything for her—had taken a life that was moving in one direction, as surely as the creek that had carried her skiff, and spun it around just like the canal had done the little boat. Summer had introduced her to Daniel Blessing, three hundred years old and, as it turned out, the love of her life. She allowed the memory of his smile, kind and genuine, to fill her for a moment. It brought her a few seconds of peace, reminded her why she was doing all this. He was the handsomest man she'd ever seen—centuries old, sure, but witchcraft, she had learned, was the original Botox and didn't even involve needles or deadly germs.

But the summer had also brought Season Howe into her life, and Season had killed Mace, and later Daniel. Then, during the fall, when Kerry was in the Swamp learning from Daniel's mother, Season had apparently tracked down Rebecca in Santa Cruz, and Josh in Las Vegas. Josh hadn't survived the encounter. The only ones remaining from the summer house in La Jolla were herself, Rebecca, Brandy, and Scott.

Finally Season had shown up here, in the Great Dismal. Where it had all started, so many years before. Here she hadn't been able to defeat Mother Blessing and Kerry, but neither had they been able to triumph over her. It almost didn't matter—the things Season had said were enough to make Kerry rethink everything that had happened since August. She had been motivated by thoughts of revenge against Season ever since Daniel had died.

Now it wasn't so much revenge that spurred her on, although that was still a factor. Now—just since yesterday afternoon—what Kerry discovered she wanted most in the world was the truth. She wanted to know who had destroyed Slocumb. She wanted to understand the relationship between Season and Mother Blessing, wanted to know what Daniel and his brother Abraham had known about it.

That quest, instead of just simple revenge, kept her putting one foot before the other, ducking branches, dodging thorns. She tried to remain alert, worried that Mother Blessing would have turned the Swamp against her in ways she hadn't encountered yet. But her eyes grew bleary and her concentration flagged.

Until finally she topped a low rise and saw, at the bottom of a weed-choked slope, the highway she sought. Highway 17 ran north-south here, along the edge of the Great Dismal Swamp. It would take her away—away from Mother Blessing, away from Season Howe.

It was so beautiful, that strip of lined asphalt, that Kerry thought she would cry.

2

Kerry didn't know exactly what she looked like, but she was pretty sure she was a horrific mess. A full night and all morning in the Swamp, in the rain, falling out of the boat—all after an epic battle—would do it to anyone, she decided. She hadn't spent time on her appearance since yesterday morning, when she'd cleaned up and brushed her hair and even put on a little makeup because she was going into Deep Creek to do the holiday feast shopping.

If she were driving and spotted herself hitchhiking, she would lock her doors and speed up.

She couldn't do much about her physical appearance—not without a shower and a hairbrush and maybe a new wardrobe. But that didn't mean she had to let passing motorists know what she really looked like. Casting a glamour was one of the first tricks Mother Blessing had taught her. It was basic, and while it didn't necessarily have anything to do with the more common definition of "glamour," there was no reason it couldn't apply. She decided she would look like a clean-cut, friendly student, in the Swamp to study its biology or something. She visualized what she wanted people to see, changing as little of herself as possible. The muddy, torn coat became a clean sweatshirt with a UVA logo on it, the shredded jeans were crisp and new, the fouled, mud-caked boots were shiny green duck boots. She imagined her hair as she liked it best, loose and flowing in the breeze, raven-dark and fine. She visualized herself only lightly made up, her natural porcelain complexion undisguised, her green eyes almost luminous. As a finishing touch she imagined a faint scent of lilac, instead of the swamp mud and sweat she really smelled like.

Once that was accomplished, she ventured out to the edge of the roadway and stuck out her thumb when the next batch of vehicles raced up the highway. She wanted to go north, toward Portsmouth and Norfolk, and points beyond. But either of those nearby cities would do for a start.

Six months before, Kerry would have been petrified to even consider hitchhiking anywhere. She still understood that it was not the safest mode of transport, particularly for a young woman. But compared with what she had survived in the past twenty-four hours alone, it was a piece of cake.

The third car that came along stopped for her. A man in his early thirties drove, a pretty woman by his side. In the back was an array of photography equipment—camera bags, tripods, backpacks, and the like. The woman rolled down her window as Kerry jogged up to the car.

"Where are you heading?" she asked.

"Portsmouth, I guess," Kerry told her.

"We're going to Newport News," the woman said, "so that's on the way. If you can find a place to sit with all that junk in the back, you're welcome to ride."

"I don't take up much space," Kerry promised. She climbed into the back. The driver pulled back out into the lane, and the woman started to say something else. But the motion of the car on the highway lulled Kerry, and though she tried to listen, within minutes she had slipped into a deep sleep.

The Friday after Thanksgiving is, retail legend has it, the busiest shopping day of the year. Brandy Pearson saw no reason to doubt the conventional wisdom. Her parents lived in Needham, a Boston suburb, and she had foolishly tried to go to one of the town's independent bookstores to find something to read during the Thanksgiving break that wasn't required for one class or other. She didn't have anything particular in mind—she enjoyed chick-lit, legal thrillers, suspense, and the occasional romance, as well as popular biographies, and she figured she could easily find something in one of those categories that caught her eye.

So she fought the bundled-up throngs, trying to peer past anxious shoppers at the covers and spines of the books on the store's shelves. She browsed new hardcover fiction first, picking up and putting back at least a dozen books. She had experienced a lot in the past several months, since San Diego and the discovery that witches were real—and deadly. She had mourned Mace and Josh and even Daniel, who had drawn them all into it. She had broken up with Scott, who had been, for a time, the guy she thought was forever. Now she found that fiction that took some matters too lightly—the existence of the supernatural, life and death, love and hate—didn't appeal to her anymore. She picked up a book with a knife on the cover—she had heard somewhere that knives on book covers were guaranteed sellers—flipped it open, read the cover flap. Then she put it back where she'd found it.

"Do you taste them too?" a voice asked from behind her. "Or just squeeze them to see if they're ripe?"

Half-expecting to see someone she knew, Brandy turned around. But the young man who had spoken was a stranger—*a handsome stranger,* she corrected herself, but a stranger just the same. He was about her age or a little older, early twenties, maybe. His friendly smile revealed even, white teeth. His hair was short, neatly cropped, his eyes were wide and cheerful. His skin was several shades darker than her own, set off nicely by a cream-colored dress shirt underneath his heavy winter coat. Clean blue jeans and expensive leather shoes made up the rest of the ensemble. Brandy had to approve.

"If you take them home too early they just spoil," she replied. "Vine-ripened is always best, at least for hardcovers. Paperbacks you can keep in a bag for a few days if you need to, and they'll usually turn out just fine."

"I see you know a lot about the care and feeding," the man said. "Maybe you can give me a lesson sometime."

Is he asking me out? Brandy wondered. *We just met, like, seconds ago. We haven't met, really. Well, one way to fix that.*

She extended her hand. "I'm Brandy Pearson," she said with a smile. "World-famous expert on book botany."

"Adam Castle," he said, taking her hand in his. His hand was large and warm, and he shook hers with a firm grip and then released it. "Not world famous at all."

"Give it time," she said. "I'm sure you'll find your niche."

"I'm afraid my specialty is a little more mundane. Urban planning."

A browser reaching for a new Dean Koontz novel jostled Brandy. "Nothing wrong with that," she said, sidestepping so as not to take another elbow to the ribs, and glad she wore a heavy woolen pea coat over her lavender turtleneck and black yoga pants. "Especially if you can urbanly plan a shopping experience where there's some kind of consideration for personal space."

The shopper put the Koontz book down, shot Brandy a glare, and said, "Excuse me," as he moved down to the next shelf unit.

Adam laughed. "Ouch. You don't pull any punches, do you, Brandy?"

"Only when there's a good reason to," Brandy replied. "Which, it seems, is pretty rare."

"Yeah, you're right about that, I think," he said. "And to answer your question, yes, I think I do have some interesting ideas about retail spaces. Of course, this is an example of what I like—smaller independent stores, as opposed to big-box chains. But there are ways to situate them, and to organize the insides, that create a more efficient and user-friendly shopping experience, and . . . you were just saying that, right? You didn't really want to hear my theories."

"Not that they're not fascinating," Brandy assured him. "Because I'm sure they are, in the right setting. I just don't think this is it."

Adam laughed again. Brandy found herself responding to his laughter— it was honest, with a lack of self-consciousness that she found refreshing.

She knew virtually nothing about this man except that he was strangely appealing. She wasn't in the market for a relationship, especially so soon after breaking up with Scott. But there was some kind of instant connection going on here, it seemed. This guy was cute, he made her laugh, and he seemed to have a few brains in his head, all of which were qualities that Brandy appreciated.

She wasn't the kind of person who could just fall into a romance, anyway, even if she had been looking for one. She was too analytical for that. She tried to look at every aspect of a person or situation and make up her mind based on the facts as she found them. The fact that she was even thinking in romantic terms, just minutes after seeing Adam's face for the first time in her life, was unusual for her, and she figured that when she took the time to analyze her own reaction she might find that it was meaningful in that context. Her immediate response to him indicated to her that there might be something there worth responding to.

But on a friendship basis only, she decided. *I am not looking for a new boyfriend already.*

Adam seemed to be thinking along similar lines. He ticked his head toward the bookshop's coffee bar, where a few empty tables stood among people reading through magazines, chatting, or working on laptop computers. "Would you like to get something to drink?" he asked her. "And then we can talk about what the right setting might be."

Brandy had to think about the invitation for almost three whole seconds before she accepted.

The Charles River separated Cambridge, home of Harvard University, from Boston. The river wasn't visible from Scott Banner's family home on Marlborough Street in the Back Bay, but one knew it was nearby just the same—its edges choked with ice at this time of year, hardy runners blowing out clouds of steam as they jogged its footpaths.

The house was ridiculously large, Scott had always thought, five stories of red brick on the outside, its roof turreted and dotted with four chimneys. Snow webbed the trees in front of it. Old New England money had paid for the house, and Scott Banner's father—now known as Judge Banner, though he'd spent most of his professional life as a partner at a downtown law firm—was perfectly happy to take full advantage of the privileges life had cast his way.

Scott knew that his gut response might be written off as typical teen rebellion. But even as he relaxed on a leather couch in the media room, watching old movies on the plasma TV, he couldn't help thinking about the millions of hungry people who could be fed for the cost of this one house. His father was a philanthropist who gave heavily to dozens of worthy causes, but Scott had decided that someday when he inherited all of this, he'd sell the house, live a more reasonable lifestyle, and share with the needy the wealth that had been passed down to him.

For now it was a nice place to relax after the Thanksgiving feast of the day before. The grand dining room had been full, with family friends and relatives spilling off the main table, which seated twenty-four, and using two additional tables that had been set up for the overflow. The meal had been huge—again, bringing Scott a rush of guilt over those who got their only Thanksgiving turkey from a shelter, if they even had that option. After dinner the party had split into different rooms: Scott and his older brother Steve had gone into the game room and taken all comers on at the pool table, while others had gone to the media room for football, or onto the patio in back, heated with standing propane warmers, for cigars and brandy.

Last year, he kept remembering, he and Brandy had been together on Thanksgiving, spending part of the day here and part at her family's home in Needham. The contrast had been marked—her parents were well-off, but they had earned it themselves, and their lifestyle was comfortable but not ostentatious. Her family seemed to like him, and his family definitely enjoyed her company. He must have explained thirty times yesterday why she wasn't with him for the meal.

The truth was, he had a hard time figuring it out for himself.

She accused him of secretly longing for Kerry Profitt. And when he was honest with himself, he couldn't really deny that charge. Kerry was a remarkable young woman—beautiful, brave, and resourceful. Of the group of them who had been thrown together in a house during the summer, she had been through the worst of it. Scott's heart had gone out to her, and that, plus the undeniable physical attraction he felt, created the situation that bugged Brandy so.

His brother Steve came into the room, glancing at the movie playing on the big screen. "Can't go wrong with Indy," he said. "Well, maybe except for that middle one."

"That's why I'm on number three," Scott agreed.

Steve sat in a club chair next to Scott's couch. Like Scott, his eyesight was terrible, but unlike Scott he'd been willing to have lasers beamed into his eyes to correct it. He was a little taller than Scott, sandy-haired and tennis-fit. "You've been pretty down last couple of days, little bro," Steve said. "What's up?"

Scott shrugged. There was so much he couldn't tell Steve—about Season Howe, and the friends who had died. "I guess a little class consciousness," he said. "Feeling bad that we're the haves in a world of have-nots."

"Feel free to join the Peace Corps, dude," Steve suggested. They'd had this discussion before.

"Maybe I will," Scott said. With a grin, he added, "You tell Mom."

Steve was six years older than Scott, and they had been close since childhood. In the last couple of years they'd grown apart, largely because they hardly ever saw each other—Scott was busy with Harvard, while Steve was busy climbing the tenure track at Amherst. Even so, it wasn't hard for one brother to tell when the other was hedging something. "Is it Brandy?" Steve asked. "Must've hurt yesterday when people kept asking where she was."

Scott nodded. "Yeah, that's part of it. A big part, I guess. I just miss her a lot, you know?"

"Understood," Steve said. He was married to a girl he'd known since his senior year of high school, so Scott was pretty sure he had no recent experience with break-ups. "Life goes on, right?" Steve added.

"That's what they say."

"She was a good lady," Steve said. "I know you'll miss her a lot. But you know what? There are plenty of good ladies out there. You'll find another before you know it."

The problem was, Scott had already found another. Kerry. Only he'd found her too soon, when neither of them had been ready for each other. Now that maybe they were—now that he was ready, at least—she was MIA, somewhere down in the swamps with Mother Blessing. Out of touch, but not out of mind.

He hoped she would contact him over the holidays, because he was turning over an idea in his mind, persuading himself to commit to it, and it would involve her. At least, after the fact.

He couldn't say anything about that to Steve, however, or tell his brother how much he hoped she was okay. He hated the fact that he was unable to reach her—he could send e-mails to her address, which she could sometimes log on and receive through some magical Internet access Mother Blessing had arranged. But there were no guarantees that she'd get them, and he couldn't call her, and he had no way of knowing for certain that she was safe down there.

"You're right," he said after a while. "Brandy's great, but there'll be others. Like Linda, right?"

"Exactly," Steve agreed. "Just like that. Give it some time, that's all I'm saying."

"I hear you." Scott nodded and glanced toward the screen, where Indiana Jones was in mortal danger yet again. Somehow he always pulled out of it.

Like Kerry, he was gutsy and resourceful. Like Indy, Kerry had always managed to survive.

So far.

Scott only hoped that if there ever came a time when she needed him to help her do so, he would be there for her.

New York at Thanksgiving was a magical city. The usual bustle went on, but people's moods seemed improved somehow—strangers smiled at one another on the sidewalks instead of growling. Horns still honked, but the blasts were shorter, not as angry. Rebecca Levine was willing to admit that it might simply have been her imagination, that because she loved the holiday season she projected that feeling on those she saw.

But she had grown accustomed to the Santa Cruz lifestyle; the small California beach town felt like home to her now. She had grown up in the city, in her family's Upper West Side apartment. Her room was still there, and it was still home in a way, but the city felt alien now, crowded and impersonal. It was only at this time of year, between Thanksgiving and New Year's Eve, that she really enjoyed being back.

She had stayed in yesterday, watching the Macy's parade on TV but unwilling to brave the crowds to see it in person. Today she ventured out into the wind and cold, partly just to see the city in her favorite dressing, and partly to get away from her family. Her father had taken a few days off from his insurance company job to spend time with her, since she was out from California. Her mother only worked part-time, and little sister Miriam was off from high school for a week. So privacy was hard to come by in the apartment, and after sharing a comparatively large house with just Erin, Rebecca had become accustomed to plenty of privacy.

Plus, people kept trying to cheer her up.

That was probably okay, probably what families were supposed to do. Miriam, especially, was relentless, regaling Rebecca nonstop with stories about who was going out with whom, and who had said what, and what did people think about this, until Rebecca thought she was about to explode.

Because the world wasn't about which girl liked what boy who didn't like her back. At least Rebecca's wasn't.

In Rebecca's world, Season Howe existed. Witchcraft was real—and terrifyingly deadly. Friends died. Witches could use stupid college kid séances to hunt people down.

There was a lot in life to be thankful for, but having the blinders ripped off, being exposed to the truth about the supernatural world that paralleled the one most people thought of as real, wasn't part of that.

Rebecca would rather have lived in blissful ignorance of the whole thing. But that ignorance had been torn away from her, and there was no going back. It meant building walls between herself and her family, because there were so many things she couldn't talk to them about. Every conversation had to be parsed to make sure she didn't accidentally say something about Mother Blessing, or Josh's brutal murder, or Season.

So getting away from the apartment, losing herself in the happy holiday crowds, was her answer. At least short-term.

Rebecca had a few more weeks of school before the long winter break, which meant she'd have to go back to Santa Cruz. She found that the prospect pleased her.

In Santa Cruz she'd be alone. But at least she wouldn't be alone in the midst of her whole family.

She thought maybe that was better.

Kerry Profitt's diary, November 26

Never let it be said that a night's sleep can't do a world of good.

Okay, to be completely accurate, more than a night. I crashed almost as soon as I got into the Hendersons' car—and a good thing for me they were basically honest folks, right?—and didn't wake up until we were in Portsmouth. Then once they shook me into consciousness, they drove around until they found a hotel that they were comfortable letting me stay in. Never mind that they still didn't know the first thing about me, except maybe that I snored and drooled a little (okay, maybe not, but who knows? It's not like I was awake and watching). Never mind, too, that I'd have been satisfied at that point with a cot and a soft rock for a pillow.

But the place they found was clean and tidy, with locks on the doors and starched sheets and everything. I checked in, paid in advance with cash, went up to my ninth-floor room. Once I got there, I realized that I was ravenous.

So guess what: room service!

No greens or pork chops or Scooter Pies or any of that stuff that Mother Blessing lives on, either. I ordered a steak, medium-rare, with fries, a salad, and a slice of cheesecake. Ate every bite. Then I took a bath that lasted more than an hour, running more hot water every time it turned too cool. When I started to get so sleepy I worried about drowning, I got out, toweled off, and climbed in between the crisp white sheets.

That must have been about six. In the p.m.

When I woke up again it was past noon. Princess Aurora, much?

Now I'm sitting on the queen-size bed, the big TV with cable channels and everything running to give me some company, typing this on the trusty laptop that, miraculously, survived my escape from the Swamp. Outside the floor-to-ceiling windows, the sun is setting, the sky over the Atlantic is purple and indigo with a few streaks of salmon. There's a sandwich on the way up, courtesy of room service again—well, I guess it's not courtesy if you pay for it, right? But still . . .

Still, the point is that now I'm awake and fed and there's a laundry room in the building, so soon I'll have clean clothes, and downstairs there's one of those little overpriced hotel shops, so I have makeup—real makeup, for the first time in months! So . . .

. . . it's time to figure out what's next.

And that, dear diary, is the hard part.

I got away from Mother Blessing. For now, at least, which is not to say that she won't send someone—or something—after me still. She's kind of run out of sons, but she still can manufacture simulacra to hunt for her.

Not that I'm as big a problem for her as Season is. But I get the feeling she was a little ticked off that I ran out on her like that. And I get the additional—and related—feeling that she is a sore loser. So I've got to watch my step, Mother Blessing-wise.

And the other thing is that Season is still out there in the great wide world someplace. She is still, whatever the real story between her and Mother Blessing, the person who killed Daniel. And Mace and Josh. She's got a lot to answer for.

I've got a few new tricks up my metaphorical sleeve that I didn't have before, thanks to Mother Blessing (I keep wanting to write Mama B., but somehow, even though I know she'll never read this diary, I can't quite bring myself to do it). I know enough to get myself out of a swamp that wants to keep me there. What I don't know, I'm pretty certain, is enough to be much more than a momentary headache for Season Howe. I definitely am not skilled enough to defeat her in one-on-one combat, unless maybe she was comatose. And tied up.

Even then it wouldn't be a given.

So my quandary—and isn't that a great word, quandary?—is, how do I hone my skills now? How do I learn more, so that I can go after Season with some hope of winning? Who is there to teach me all the things I don't know?

I can't beat Season. But I can't really rest until Season is beaten. I can't beat Mother Blessing, but I can't give up until I know what really happened in Slocumb, and whether Mother Blessing, as I'm coming to believe, bears a lot more responsibility for what happened to Daniel than I originally thought.

Hence, quandary. Dilemma. Perplexity, even.

Hark—a knock at the door. Room service.

More later.

K.

3

Kerry stayed in the Portsmouth hotel for two more nights, watching the world from the ninth floor, behind the protection of a dead bolt. The TV stayed on most of that time as Kerry caught up on the various news items, reality shows, sitcoms, and personal hygiene commercials she had missed during her time in the Swamp. All in all, she decided, she really hadn't missed much of any importance at all.

But on the last night she started to feel uneasy. This was far too close to Mother Blessing for any kind of real comfort. And she didn't have any fake ID, so she had checked in under her own name. It wouldn't take much effort to find her here.

If anyone was looking. That was the big question mark, the great unknown. She had every reason to suspect that Season might be—she had, after all, shown up at Rebecca's séance and then found Josh in Las Vegas.

Or was it Josh who found her? That part was never completely clear. If that was the case, then maybe the séance sighting was the optical illusion Rebecca had first thought it was. Maybe Season wasn't hunting them after all.

Which would be good, because it would take some of the heat off Kerry while she figured out how to go about hunting Season herself.

Her first priority had to be getting out of this neighborhood. Where to go, she hadn't yet determined. She didn't think she had to cover her tracks as much as she had when she had run away from Northwestern to come down here. Then, she had worried that her aunt Betty and uncle Marsh would call the cops when they learned she was missing, and she needed to make sure she couldn't be easily found. She knew Mother Blessing would have her own methods of searching for her, but she highly doubted that involving the authorities would be one of them.

When she woke up the next morning, she had the answer.

Hide in plain sight, she thought. She would go home—back to Illinois, back to Aunt Betty and Uncle Marsh. Then even if there was any kind of search effort going on, it would be called off. Mother Blessing would never think she would go back there, so it would be the last place she'd look. The other alternative was going back to Northwestern, but she was pretty sure she'd have been expelled by now, what with the not going to class or making her tuition payments.

She called for room service one last time, showered, ate breakfast. When she was done with that, she packed her duffel again and caught a hotel shuttle to the airport. There was a flight to Chicago that afternoon that she could get on, and then a commuter plane down to Cairo. Still weary, she dozed on the longer flight, but on the commuter she stayed awake, drinking bottled water and paging through a magazine.

From the airport she took a taxi. At nine thirty, she knocked on the door of her aunt and uncle's home, a single-story ranch house with snow on the front lawn and the blue glow of a TV showing in a window.

Uncle Marsh opened the door with a half-empty highball glass in his hand and a questioning look in his eyes. He stood unsteadily in the doorway for a moment, as if unsure of what he was seeing.

"Hi, Uncle Marsh," Kerry said meekly.

He put an arm around her shoulders and drew her into the house. His breath reeked of alcohol. "Call off the Coast Guard, Betty!" he called. "Look what the cat dragged in!"

Aunt Betty emerged from the kitchen carrying a dishtowel and a china plate, which dropped from her hand the instant she saw Kerry standing in the entryway. It hit the ground and smashed into a hundred pieces. "Kerry!" she cried, and ran toward her niece.

Standing there, enveloped by her closest living relatives, Kerry had a moment of wondering why she had ever left this house. But that only lasted for a few moments. Aunt Betty was weeping openly and clinging to her, repeating, "We were so worried about you," over and over. Uncle Marsh knuckled Kerry lightly on the chin and said, "I was just joking about the Coast Guard. We figured if you'd wanted us to know where you were, you'd have told us."

And then it all came flooding back. Uncle Marsh was a drunk, a harsh man who had taken every tenderness ever offered him and turned it away, using a crude sense of humor like a shield against the blades of kindness. Aunt Betty gave new meaning to the term codependent, and the worse Uncle Marsh behaved toward her—or anyone else, for that matter, within earshot of her—the more she decided he needed to be protected. From what, Kerry was never really sure. But she became his one-woman security squad, running interference, keeping him safe from his own worst instincts. She wept openly and often, which drove him mad. The madder he got, the more she decided that he was being persecuted, and the more she wept.

Kerry hadn't been inside for ten minutes before she realized that coming back here was one of the biggest mistakes she had ever made. She would have been better off letting them think she was dead. At least then they could have continued driving each other crazy without dragging her back into it.

The next morning she sat at the table having breakfast with Aunt Betty. Uncle Marsh was still asleep—sleeping off the effects of the previous night's alcohol intake, Kerry guessed, although Aunt Betty insisted that he had been "working awfully hard lately." Kerry had managed to forestall the inquisition last night by claiming exhaustion, but she knew it couldn't be dodged forever.

"I called the police last night and told them to stop looking for you, Kerry," Aunt Betty said over the rim of a bone china teacup. She was a bird-like woman, thin and frail, with bad eyes for which she wore glasses whose lenses were nearly as big as her entire head, a pointed beak of a nose protruding from between them. Her hair was brown, but from a bottle, because it should have been gray years before. She held her cup in two bony hands. "We really were terribly worried about you when you just disappeared. The college called, and that girl you shared a room with, Sophia—"

"Sonya," Kerry corrected. She pushed runny scrambled eggs around on her plate with her fork. There were many ways to describe Aunt Betty, but "skilled chef" would never be one of them.

"Right, Sonya. She was no help at all. She said you were antisocial—which Marsh and I, of course, knew wasn't true—and that you had probably gone to live in a cave somewhere. Well, I said that was just the most ridiculous thing I had ever heard, that my niece wasn't the kind of girl who would live in a cave, and that you were perfectly nice and very reliable, and if you were gone, then obviously something had happened to you. You were kidnapped, or murdered, or something like that."

"Well, I'm fine," Kerry said. She bit into some rubbery bacon.

"I can see that, and I'm so glad to hear it. I told the police that, of course, after I saw you. The detective who's had your case, a young man, Pembroke or something like that, he called back first thing this morning while you were sleeping, and said that he'll be by this afternoon to talk to you. He'd like to know where you've been, of course, and he'd like to know whatever happened to you.

"We all would like to know that, of course. I'm sure it was something just dreadful."

She continued yammering on, speaking words that Kerry was no longer listening to, without seeming to notice that Kerry hadn't replied. What could she tell the police? "Sorry, detective, but I was off learning magic so I can kill the witch who killed my boyfriend. Next time, I'll call more often."

Yeah, that'll fly.

She had managed to convince herself that Uncle Marsh and Aunt Betty would be glad she had disappeared. They no longer bore any financial burden on her behalf, if they ever had—an insurance settlement, after her mother's death, had paid for Kerry's college, and even though there wasn't much of an estate left after all her mom's medical bills, the sale of the house they had lived in had netted some money for her aunt and uncle.

And Uncle Marsh had wasted no time—as soon as she left for school, not even waiting for her to vanish completely—in turning "her" room back into the den it had been before she had come to live in their house. She had spent the night on a foldaway couch in there, with Marsh's big-screen TV and wet bar. She always thought their house looked like something decorated from a thrift store, except that the reverse was true: Their furnishings were the kind that ended up at thrift stores, but they were the original owners. There were lots of items that looked like carefully tooled wood, except that they were really molded wood-grain plastic, lots of veneers, lots of composition board. Everything except real wood, it seemed.

Given her uncle's speed at eliminating every trace of Kerry from the house, the fact that they'd called the police at all was a little staggering. The idea that she would have to explain her whereabouts to the authorities was terrifying. How thoroughly would they check her story out, if at all? If she claimed to have run away to San Francisco, or Sweden, would they ask for addresses? Known associates? Would they expect some kind of verification of her statement? If she turned out to simply be a runaway, instead of a kidnap victim, would they want to be repaid for the expense of their investigation?

She doubted that, but on the rest of it she was completely in the dark. She hadn't anticipated anything like this when she came back here.

"Aunt Betty," she said, interrupting whatever her aunt was going on about now. "I'm not sure I'm really . . . you know, up to talking to the police today. Can't we just tell them that I'm fine, and let it go at that? I mean, don't they have better things to do than investigate people who aren't missing anymore?"

"Well, but they'll want to try to find whoever took you," Aunt Betty said.

"No one took me, Aunt Betty. I . . . had something I needed to do. I went to where I could do it. I . . . well, I didn't do it all, not really. Not yet. But I did some of it, and then I came back."

Aunt Betty regarded her, the teacup cradled in both hands again like something rare and precious. "You just . . . left?"

"I'm almost eighteen, Aunt Betty. I'm capable of making my own decisions. It was something very important."

"It must have been," the older woman said. "Aren't you going to tell me what it was?"

Kerry looked at her plate. "I can't."

"I see." A long pause, and then the teacup clattered in its saucer. Aunt Betty's hands were trembling, and when Kerry looked up, she saw tears welling in her aunt's eyes. "Noreen trusted us," she said. She almost never used her sister's name, it was always "your mother." "I'm sorry you can't."

"It isn't that, Aunt Betty," Kerry said, already knowing the conversation had veered from difficult to hopeless. "It's just . . . it's hard to explain. I can't explain. Not without telling you . . . telling you everything. And I can't do that. I guess I'm asking you to trust me, this time."

"I see." Again with that. She always said that when, of course, she didn't see—when she couldn't see at all. Soon the tears would be flowing, and the sacrifices they had made would be drawn into the discussion—sacrifices which were real, Kerry had no doubt about that. She appreciated completely the fact that they had opened their house to a child who was not their daughter, whom they had never asked for.

"I'm so sorry, Aunt Betty," Kerry said, hoping to head all that off at the pass. "I really . . . I wish it hadn't happened the way it did. I wish I could tell you the whole story. I honestly do. But . . . it's something you're better off not knowing, you've got to believe that."

"Yes, well . . ." Tears ran down Aunt Betty's cheeks now, and she dabbed at them with a paper napkin. At least she hadn't started sobbing. That was the worst.

"Haven't you ever known something you wish you didn't, Aunt Betty?" Kerry pressed. She blinked, feeling tears of her own coming on now. "Something that you couldn't tell another soul about, something that was just too huge and too terrible to share? That's what I have, what I know. I can't tell you what it is, and you wouldn't believe me, probably, if I did. And if by some miracle I could convince you, it still wouldn't do you any good to know it. It would only make you miserable, in fact. So why share it? Why work so hard to persuade you of something that you can't do anything about and that will only make you hurt? I can't do it to you and Uncle Marsh. I'm sorry that it's this way, but it is. There's nothing I can do about that now. No way I can undo it. The best I can do is try to make it right, and even if I do that, you'll never know about it. . . . But I will.

"So that's what I have to try to do. And you—you'll just have to try to understand that I love you, and you'll have to either trust me, or—or not trust me, I guess. I hope it's trust, but it really doesn't make much difference, either way, in the long run."

Kerry snatched her napkin from her lap and blew her nose. Aunt Betty was sobbing now, long looping sobs that Kerry had always thought must have been a real hit at funerals. And Kerry was crying too, tears falling from her cheeks and splashing into the watery eggs and rubbery bacon she hadn't eaten. Tears that came from knowing that she had somehow stepped off the path her life was supposed to have taken onto a different one, a road that was dark and frightening, for which there was no map and no guide. Tears for her mother, who couldn't be around to try to deal with this new and sinister aspect of her life, and tears for her aunt, who was but could never understand it. Tears, too, for Daniel, whom she had known for so short a span and loved so hard, who had both set her on this path and tried to protect her from it.

Both women cried now, sitting at the breakfast table, each consumed by her own private grief that Kerry suspected had little, if anything, to do with the other's.

Which was when Uncle Marsh wandered in, unshaven, his white hair askew, in a sleeveless white T-shirt and flannel pajama bottoms, scratching his belly under the shirt.

"Who died?" he asked.

And Kerry started to laugh through her tears.

4

Kerry hadn't unpacked her bag yet, so it didn't take her long to get ready to move on again. Aunt Betty called the police detective she had been talking to and told him that the whole affair had been a misunderstanding, that Kerry had left school of her own free will and now was back. The detective peppered her with questions for a few minutes, but agreed to close the books on the case. Kerry was still a little surprised that there had been a case with open books in the first place.

She found herself oddly touched by it, and by Aunt Betty's willingness to help. Uncle Marsh remained his typical grumpy self, and Kerry tried to limit her interaction with him to just the right amount so that she might actually miss him when she left.

Even though she had barely arrived, there was still a lot to get done. Aunt Betty drove her downtown to a branch of her bank, where she withdrew a few thousand more dollars from her insurance money to cover expenses wherever her new course took her. When they got back home, Aunt Betty suggested that Kerry take a look inside some boxes she had stored in the attic—things that had belonged to Kerry's parents, as well as some of Kerry's childhood items—while she made lunch.

The attic was close and musty, and even though the air outside was near freezing, Kerry found it uncomfortably warm up there. Aunt Betty had separated out the boxes that had come from Kerry's parents' house, so Kerry knew just which ones to look at. Each box was taped across the top.

Kerry took a knife up with her and sliced through the tape carefully so she wouldn't damage any of the contents.

She had no memory of this stuff being packed up, even though she must have been around. Her mother's death had been hard on her, but in a way—after nursing her through illness for more than a year, alone because her father had died a couple of years before that—it had been both a heartbreak and a relief. Her mother's long suffering had finally come to an end, and Kerry, having been pressed into service at too young an age, could have what was left of her teen years.

Well, we know how that worked out, Kerry thought grimly. Her first summer out of high school had been spent in San Diego for a summer resort job. That had ended when Daniel Blessing had stumbled, injured, into her life, and she and her housemates had been swept up into his world—a world of dangerous witchcraft and intrigue.

Not so much the teenage dream, she knew. It was okay, though. She had learned long ago that adaptability was one of her strong points—a key to survival, really. *Go where the river takes you.*

But during that period, right after her mother's death, she had been an emotional basket case, she remembered. Aunt Betty and Uncle Marsh had packed up the house and sold most of the furnishings and the property. They had been named Kerry's guardians and the executors of her mom's will. Which made it not especially shocking that she would have been unaware of precisely what had been saved and stored up here.

Some of the things she found were expected, but they still brought a lump to her throat. Her parents' wedding album and a couple of additional albums of family photos, including shots of Kerry as a little girl, dark haired, wide eyed, and skinny. Her dad had called her string bean until she was twelve, when she declared that he was never to use that term around her again. Old documents: tax information, birth and death certificates, medical records. A few objects that probably could have been sold or that

Aunt Betty herself could have used—some jewelry, an antique music box with intricate gold filigree, a set of fine silverware that had been a wedding present from Kerry's grandmother and that had always remained inside its cherry-wood box, "for company."

Then there were the boxes that had come from Kerry's room, where less stuff had been disposed of. Kerry found old school papers, mostly forgotten, including some that made her smile with fond memories of certain teachers and friends. Books she'd liked over the years, going back to *Where the Wild Things Are* and Dr. Seuss, all the way up through her poetry phase in high school, including such diverse poets as Sylvia Plath, Robert Frost, Walt Whitman, and Pablo Neruda. A small selection of mysteries, including Nancy Drews and Agatha Christies. Mostly, after about the sixth grade, she had read books from school libraries or Cairo's public library system and from her parents' library, so her own collection was limited. But she found herself glad that Aunt Betty had saved these, and she hoped that one of these days she'd be able to settle in one place so that she could have them again.

She found old toys, locked diaries, drawings she had made, yearbooks friends had signed for her. Nothing earth-shattering, but looking through the boxes somehow crystallized things for her. Her life had been one thing, now it was another. The past was part of her; there was no denying its influence. But it didn't define her by itself, and it didn't control her direction from here. She found that she could remember it with a sense of pleasant nostalgia without feeling that she had to be dragged back into the life she had left behind.

Her life, Kerry decided, was like these boxes. The part of it that was her childhood, that included her parents, could be wrapped up in paper and sealed inside one box. It would never change; it was what it was. The precious part spent with Daniel could go into a second box. The third box had to remain open—it included everything since Daniel's death, and it was an unfinished project. There would come a time, she believed, when it could be wrapped and stored as well, but she didn't know what the shape of it would be at that time.

Whether she'd be alive to do the wrapping was anybody's guess.

Kerry spent one more night under Aunt Betty and Uncle Marsh's roof. The next day they drove her to the airport. Aunt Betty welled up again; Uncle Marsh was gruff and offhand about the whole thing. Kerry figured he was just glad to get his house back, while Aunt Betty had seen her as a kind of reinforcement in her ongoing struggle with his drinking, his temper, and his generally unpleasant attitude. But she would never leave him, Kerry knew, never even force the issue of him changing his ways, because the worse he got the more she protected him from himself and others.

As she walked through the terminal, past the point where only ticketed passengers could go, she found herself glad for the short time she had spent with them—happy she had been able to spend it, but also happy that it had been so brief. She had an hour to wait for her flight, so she sat in the waiting area and studied every blond head she saw, just in case one might be Season. Not seeing her, she took one of Daniel's journals from her duffel and started to flip through it, looking for a section she hadn't read yet.

> *There comes a time in the life of every young man when he must leave the home of his parents and make his own way in the world, for good or ill. In my case, this time was doubly complicated. First, I have a twin, Abraham, so there are two of us, not one, striking out to find our fortunes. And second, our father has been gone for our entire life, so when we left, that meant Mother Blessing would truly be alone for the first time in a very long while.*
>
> *Perhaps triply complicated would be more apt, for there was yet another matter to consider. We were not leaving simply to start*

families and households of our own. We were leaving with a very particular purpose in mind—one that has been instilled in us from our earliest days.

Mother Blessing had trained us and instructed us. We were ready, we were equipped, and we were anxious to go forth into the world to find and destroy Season Howe. As we have learned since infancy, she killed our father, demolished our town, and drove our mother into hiding in the Swamp. Mother Blessing alone knows the truth of that day, so long ago in Slocumb, and Season will likely not rest until she has murdered the last surviving witness of her crime. Abe and I are to locate her and make sure she can never accomplish that sordid goal.

Though Season has had years to hide herself away, we are not without clues. There is, in the community of witchcraft, some small amount of communication. Season has been seen, and spoken to, here and there. Reports of her whereabouts occasionally reach Mother Blessing. A pattern has been observed.

Season Howe, unlike Mother Blessing, does not confine herself to a specific location. She moves from place to place, occupying new homes like a hermit crab inhabiting the shell of some other creature. She seems to make few alliances, and those temporary and short-lived. She wants for little, and seems always to have means at her disposal. Though it is unusual for a woman to travel alone, she does so often, and not just within the colonies but also to foreign lands.

Our most recent report, although it was several months old by the time word reached Mother Blessing in the Swamp, had her in the city of Providence, in Rhode Island. Abe and I packed a trunk, loaded it into a wagon, and set off, striving for manly composure in the face of Mother Blessing's weeping. She had known that we must depart, of course, for it was she who set us on our path, she who taught us from childhood what our task in life must be. Even so, the actual doing of it, setting out on that journey, was a sorrowful event for us all, as it must always be.

And yet our circumstance is not like that of others, as Abe and I discussed on the road today. Other men of our age are indeed setting out to build their own lives. But we are different, we know. We have every expectation of living far longer than they. In a very few years they will be twenty, their lives likely half over already. When we reach twenty our lives will still be in the beginning stages, still in relative infancy. We will likely still not have achieved the full measure of our powers, but at some point thereafter our aging will cease, or at least slow considerably. Time, which has passed for us at much the same pace as it has for other boys, will, from this point forward, mean something very different. The days will pass, but each one will be the merest moment in time for us, each year as an hour or less.

Abraham and I know this to be true, and yet we struggle with the idea. We are not immortal, but we are witch born and witch bred, and so as close to that exalted state as mortal man can be.

Our journey is just begun. We may find Season at its end, and we may not. But if she eludes us now, we will have time enough to seek her out again.

We will, in fact, have all the time in the world.

I remain,

Daniel Blessing, Ninth of August, 1720

Her flight called, Kerry wrapped the leather thong around the book and tied it. He had been just sixteen when he wrote that, she realized. Younger than she was now—a boy, by contemporary standards. But that was a different world—she would have been considered an old maid, unmarried a week before her eighteenth birthday. If all this had been revealed to her at sixteen, she was sure she would have fallen apart, completely unable to handle it. She supposed she had been relatively mature for her age, since she was effectively running a household and helping to care for a mother who could barely get out of bed. But there was a big difference between that and being willing to accept evidence of witchcraft, of magical feuds that had been raging for longer than there had been a United States.

All in all she thought she had handled it pretty well. And continued to do so. Like Daniel in his journal entry, she was leaving home—or the place that had once been her home, if only briefly—with no certainty of when, or if, she would return. The last time she had gone away she had done it in secret, but this time her aunt and uncle knew where she was going, if not why. Last time she had been consumed with a specific desire: to find Mother Blessing and learn magic. This time her goal was more vague. She wanted to find Season, but didn't know where to look. She did know, however, that she didn't want to make Cairo her base of operations—she couldn't bring herself to live in Aunt Betty and Uncle Marsh's home again and didn't want to expose them to possible danger even if she could.

A few minutes later, Kerry was buckled into her seat and a flight attendant was demonstrating how oxygen masks would fall from above in the event of a sudden loss of cabin pressure. As the plane headed down the runway, a sense of ease fell over her. With no specific urgency before her, no crisis under way, she was more relaxed and comfortable than she had been in a long time.

She hoped the feeling would last a while.

5

Kerry flew into San Jose, and Rebecca Levine met her at the airport. She hadn't seen Rebecca since Las Vegas, when Josh had died. They had talked a couple of times since then, most recently when she had called from Aunt Betty's to tell Rebecca she was headed for California. But they hadn't spent any real time together since summer, in San Diego, before the group had split up to go their separate ways.

When she came out of the gate, Rebecca ran to her with a squeal, embracing her like a long-lost sister. "Kerry!" she shrieked. "Oh my God, it's so good to see you!"

"Hey, Beck," Kerry replied, a little more subdued. "It's great to see you too."

"We have so much to talk about," Rebecca gushed. Kerry thought her enthusiasm sounded a little forced, and when she pulled away from the hug she realized that Rebecca had lost weight, probably twenty pounds or so. Her typically loose clothing—in blues and golds today, a pleated long skirt with striped tights under it and a voluminous fuzzy sweater—hung on her, and there were dark circles under her eyes. A red paisley bandanna covered copper hair that looked like it could use some attention. Rebecca hadn't complained of any problems on the phone, but it was obvious at a glance that something was very wrong.

"I guess we do," Kerry agreed. She had carried on her one bag, so they walked straight outside to Rebecca's parked car. It was dark out, and cool, but not nearly as cold as Illinois had been. As they walked, Rebecca babbled casually about classes, her roommate Erin, and life in Santa Cruz.

It wasn't until they were on the freeway, heading south over the coastal hills, that she stopped her constant, upbeat chatter. She glanced over at Kerry. "I'm . . . uh . . . I'm not doing so well," she admitted.

"I kinda guessed that," Kerry said.

"Yeah, I know. I'm a mess."

"That's overstating it," Kerry answered. "But I've seen you looking better."

"Yeah," Rebecca said again. She returned her attention to the freeway, driving with both hands firmly on the wheel. "I don't know exactly what it is. I went home for Thanksgiving, but I just couldn't wait to get back here, you know? I wanted to be here. Dad said I was becoming a hermit and I needed to snap out of it. He's probably right, but he let me come anyway."

"You said you had only been back for a day when I called," Kerry remembered. "How was New York?"

"I don't know. I love New York at this time of year. I thought it would snap me out of this . . . this funk that I've been in. But instead it just got worse. It's like, when there are that many people on the streets, and a significant percentage of them have their heads covered, you can't even tell which ones are blond. Any of them could be Season. I thought I saw her a few days ago when I went down to Ground Zero, and I screamed. People looked at me like I was freaking insane. I guess maybe I am."

Kerry had known it wouldn't be long until Season's name came up. She was the great uniter, the common bond that held their summer group together long after they would ordinarily have lost touch. "I don't think you're crazy, Beck," she said, stroking Rebecca's arm. "Season is a scary person. You saw her, or thought you did, and then she killed Josh. And then—you don't know this yet, so don't let it freak you out more, because I'm here and okay—she came to the Swamp. Mother Blessing and I fought her."

Rebecca almost lost control of the car, swerving into another lane, and a horn blasted behind them. "Oh, jeez, I'm sorry!" she said after she had corrected her course. "Kerry, are you okay? What happened?"

Kerry told her about the assault on Mother Blessing's cabin, and about the things Season had said—and implied. She explained her suspicions—that Mother Blessing seemed to know an awful lot about the destruction of Slocumb for someone who claimed to have run away to hide in the Swamp; that she had apparently kept from her sons, and from everyone else, the fact that Season was her own mother; that she had tried to keep Kerry in the Swamp by force when she'd started to run away.

"I don't know anything for certain, really," she admitted after she had detailed the whole story. "And I'm sure if we asked her, Mother Blessing would have all kinds of excuses and explanations. But I just get a bad vibe from her—and I've come to trust feelings like that, intuitions, vibrations, a lot more since I started learning witchcraft. There's more to them than we sometimes think."

"Seems like there's more to lots of things," Rebecca agreed. She paid attention to the road as they came down a long slope, with the lights of Santa Cruz spreading before them. "There's home," she announced.

"It looks nice," Kerry said. The town hugged the shore—she could see moonlight sparkling on the water. The city was not big, but a small, comfortable size.

"It's great," Rebecca said. "When it's daylight I'll show you the boardwalk and the beach and all that good stuff. It still feels like an old-time California beach town."

"That's cool." But Kerry couldn't help thinking that an old-time California beach town would be full of blondes. She was worried about Rebecca, concerned that her friend was letting her fear of Season develop into full-blown paranoia. While she was here, she'd have to focus on helping Rebecca get better—sleeping and eating on a regular schedule, going to school, and not worrying too much about things she couldn't control.

She glanced at Rebecca, driving with one hand now while she nibbled on the fingernails of the other.

This might be a lot of work, she thought.

Kerry Profitt's diary, December 16

Beethoven's birthday. At least, according to the old Peanuts cartoons. I haven't run across any specific references in Daniel's journals, but Beethoven lived and died during his lifetime, so I suppose it's possible they crossed paths at some point. It always strikes me as weird that someone I knew was alive at the same time as people who I think of as practically prehistoric.

Santa Cruz is a pretty awesome little town. It doesn't have the natural beauty that La Jolla did, but it's more laid-back, less glitzily commercial than La Jolla. Rebecca was right, now that I have spent some time here—it does have a kind of old-fashioned charm to it. The boardwalk has carnival games and a roller coaster (that you'll never catch me on), and the beach is full of surfers in wet suits. Of course, it's winter—probably in summer it's also full of sun worshippers and families.

Near the beach is a railroad trestle that looks sort of like the one in *Stand By Me*, except for the lack of adolescents about to get run over by a train. Plenty of adolescents hanging around it, though, and jumping from it for kicks.

Not me. I'm sitting on the rocks nearby, watching them as I write in my too-long-neglected journal. The day is cold, with a brisk wind coming in off the water, making me glad I'm not trying to write the old-fashioned way. The laptop screen doesn't blow around like notebook paper would. I'm bundled up in a watch cap and coat and jeans and my red-checked tennies with thick white socks, and anyway, as a Midwestern girl, I'm still used to real winters, not this kind, so I am not overly concerned.

Except, of course, about Rebecca.

I don't think she sleeps for more than three hours at a stretch, ever. I've been staying at her house for a while now, crashing on the living room sofa, and I hear her at all hours. She says she's going to sleep, but then I wake up and she's reading, or she's online, or she's sipping hot chocolate by her window, looking out at an empty street.

As if she's afraid someone will be out there.

Which, duh. She is.

I have tried to tell her she's safe with me here. I've done a couple of little demonstrations, some handy tricks I picked up back in the Swamp. But she knows I still am not nearly powerful enough to beat Season, if she decided to come around.

And maybe it's worse with me here. Maybe, since I've seen Season more recently than she has—and since Mother Blessing is a little miffed at me too—she's afraid that my presence here makes this place even more likely to be visited sometime. She could be right. That's the thing. None of us know Season's mind, or Mother Blessing's for that matter.

For the first week or so I thought she was doing better. I got her eating regular meals, even though it meant getting up early enough to cook her some breakfast before her first class. I woke her up, walked her to campus, hung out there or went downtown while she was in class. Met her in the afternoon and came back here with her. She had a job earlier in the fall, but apparently she just stopped going. Usually a good way to become "formerly employed."

Then it was my eighteenth birthday, and she wanted to have a big celebration. Planned it out. She would invite a bunch of people, have snacks, drinks, music. She talked about it for days. December 9 came, and hey, I'm legally an adult for most purposes. I can vote, I can join the army, I can do lots of things.

What I couldn't do was get Rebecca out of bed.

Missed her first class. Halfway through what would have been her second, she finally emerged. Puffy-eyed, teary. "I'm canceling the party," she said. "I can't do it. I haven't been able to go to a party since that night."

Now, the party? Not really that big a deal to me. Turning 18 is cool and I'm glad I made it this far—and, as an aside, I totally loved the pen she bought me, silver and chunky, with purple trim and a clip so I can hang it on my backpack or whatever, so happy birthday to me—but I don't need a bunch of strangers to validate that. What bothered me was, she wanted to cancel it because months ago she went to a party at which there was a séance, and at that séance she thought maybe this blond chick turned into Season Howe for a second.

And okay, it freaked her out. Can't blame her for that.

But is she going to let that one incident rule her life? I mean, we all watched Season kill Daniel in front of a house, but that hasn't kept her out of houses. We know Mace was killed by his car, or in it, and ditto for cars.

Me? Never so much the party girl to begin with. But I wouldn't let one Season sighting keep me away from them forever, especially if they were something I liked in the first place.

I've spent the week since then trying to keep her steady, but it seems like she's getting worse, not better. Sleeping less. Eating when I sit down with her and watch her, but I don't think she eats a bite if I'm not right there. I hear her at night sometimes, crying, when she thinks I'm asleep.

Paging Doc Brandy. Rebecca has a serious problem here, and it's something I am not equipped to deal with, I guess. I mean, shaking her a lot and shouting, "Snap out of it, girl!" probably won't help, right?

Beyond that, I'm fresh out of ideas. And she's not going to have a very happy Hanukkah if I can't figure something out fast.

More later.

K.

In the run-up to the holidays, the ski resorts were full of people. New England was loaded with resorts, of course—winter sports were practically a religion here. But Scott guessed that New Hampshire's were the most prized, particularly those centered in the White Mountains. He seemed to spend most of his day in traffic, jammed between SUVs with skis and snowboards on their roof racks, loaded with folks in bright-colored outfits and dark tans.

These were his people, but they were not. He was of their social class and background, and had he chosen to be a ski bum or a 'boarder, he could have. But the whole thing just seemed too elite for his tastes—he couldn't enjoy an expensive hobby knowing that there were millions of people who couldn't afford a square meal, much less lift tickets and Rossignols. He knew it was a foolish attitude that marked him as a buzzkill to many people. He certainly wasn't opposed to fun, but there it was.

Still, he could afford the clothes and he had the car—okay, his SUV was just a RAV4, not a Hummer or anything, but it would pass. If only he could get through the traffic and find a parking space.

And the other problem was that there were so many resorts to choose from. His theory was that if, as Daniel had said, Season Howe liked to hide by moving from resort area to resort area, staying where populations were transient and most people didn't delve into the affairs of strangers, then in winter she'd be most likely to hang out at winter sports resorts. There was, of course, another alternative—that she might go to Florida or someplace warm for the winter, but he was just one guy and he couldn't be everywhere. The other alternative, worse yet, was that she would leave the country altogether.

That would just stink. Because Scott was determined to find her. School was out for a while, he had no girlfriend, no job, nothing to tie him to Cambridge or Boston. Sure, it'd be great if he could be home in time to spend Christmas with the family. But they'd just load him down with pricey gifts he couldn't really use and didn't want.

What he wanted was Season.

He thought he had developed something that resembled a plan. Nothing concrete, more of a feeling that might be worked into a real plan if he toyed with it. His idea was that Season's guard was probably up when there were other witches around, other magic users. Even in Las Vegas, when Josh was killed, Kerry had said she saw evidence of some of Mother Blessing's simulacra around.

So Scott reasoned that if there were no witches, no simulacra, no magic, maybe she would be more relaxed. If he could catch her with her defenses down, maybe a simple human-style killing would suffice.

So here he was, cruising the ski resorts of New Hampshire, with murder on his mind.

In Boston's combat zone, a guy with the money to spend could put his hands on just about anything he wanted to acquire. In this case what he had acquired, during one truly terrifying evening at some of the seediest bars he had ever imagined, was a Kel-Tec P11. It was a few years old, the guy said, a nine-mil with a ten-shot magazine and polymer grips. He barely knew what all that meant, just knew that the gun and a box of ammunition set him back a thousand bucks—and maybe ten years of his life, which he was pretty sure had run out of him in horrific sweat while he was making the buy. He was not a gun guy, and the idea of buying one and using it went against everything he had thought he stood for.

But he had seen Season. She might be a witch, but she was still a human being. A bullet could kill her.

All he had to do was find her.

He started at the aptly named Gunstock and worked his way north, through King Pine and Cranmore and then east into the White Mountains. Black Mountain, Attitash Bear Peak, the Waterville Valley. Which was where he was now, in the parking lot at the beautiful Golden Eagle Lodge, trying to angle into a parking spot that a full-size Ford Expedition had just given up on. Scott was pretty sure he could slide the RAV4 into the space, though, if he could just get the right approach.

He waited for a couple of other vehicles to go past, and then he backed and filled until he made it in. He killed the ignition with a little flush of triumph and stepped outside into the blinding sun and snow.

Walking toward the lodge, he was once again reminded that ski areas were crawling with blondes. He had to hope he could recognize Season if he saw her, and that she didn't recognize him. He didn't want to get into a confrontation with her—Brandy had always said he was an all-time champion at conflict avoidance, and she was usually right about that sort of thing. He just wanted to sneak up on her and drop her.

Surviving was another big part of his almost-plan, because the deal was, once Season was down, he would call Kerry at Rebecca's place, where, according to her latest e-mails, she had gone to stay. Part of the whole conflict-avoidance thing also meant that he was not exactly the big heroic type. But that didn't mean he never wanted to be, and if he could single-handedly off the big bad witch, that would be about as heroic as it got. Kerry could not fail to be impressed by that.

Even Brandy would take notice. But at this point Kerry's attention was more important to him. Brandy had hurt him, while Kerry had never really noticed him, romantically speaking—she was so hung up on Daniel she hadn't had eyes for anyone else. Now he could change that.

6

It was funny how one could see familiar places through fresh eyes, just by spending time with a new person. Adam Castle was a relative newcomer to Boston, having moved to the area just over a year before from Washington, D.C., to work on his master's degree at Harvard. But cities were his element, his passion, and he had delved into this one, quickly digging past its tourist facade and learning it like a native. He had taken Brandy to lunch at the Locke-Ober Café, an old-time, formal dining establishment where the waiters wore tuxedoes, even for lunch, and male guests were expected to wear jackets, and to one of the best dinners she'd ever had at Rialto, in the Charles Hotel in Harvard Square—a building she had seen a thousand times but had never thought to eat in.

Now he and Brandy walked hand in hand through the Quincy Market. In summer she liked to sit at the outdoor cafés and watch all the people, but this time of year, the indoors was much more comfortable. It was still crowded with tourists and locals alike, buying food at the market stalls or eating and drinking at the cafés. Musicians roamed the cobblestone promenade aisles and a juggler commanded a small crowd in one spot. A mime worked the masses too, but Brandy and Adam managed to dodge him.

People-watching had always been one of Brandy's favorite leisure-time pursuits. It fed her interest in psychology, her curiosity about the factors that make people act the way they do. Now everything had changed slightly. There was a new awareness that not everyone she saw was what they appeared to be from the outside—that some of them might, in fact, be more conversant with the supernatural than she'd have guessed. One couldn't go through experiences like she had, she theorized, without having those experiences color one's perceptions. People were still people, but her impressions of them had changed, as if she were eyeing them through a window glazed with ice, so reality shifted a fraction of an inch to the side.

"How did you like San Diego?" Adam asked her, once he had filled her with more information about Quincy Market than she had ever known.

"It was beautiful," she answered without even thinking about it. "The weather was just gorgeous. You know what they say, America's Finest City."

"That's what they say," Adam agreed. "But that's in terms of climate only. There are plenty of cities that beat it on almost every other score. For charm and natural beauty, San Francisco has it all over San Diego. For architectural beauty, Chicago. For sheer scale, of course, New York is the champ. San Diego has no history, especially if you compare it with Philadelphia or right here in Boston. In terms of being livable, its infrastructure is nothing compared to D.C., or New York, or Boston—there's no worthwhile public transportation there, and it's hard to get from one spot to another."

"Sounds like you've spent some time there," Brandy observed.

"Just a weekend," Adam admitted. "But I pack a lot into a weekend, and I've studied it."

"Maybe you should give it another try, and just spend a few days relaxing on the beach."

Adam shrugged. They stopped to look at a market stall selling oysters and every kind of lobster imaginable, from live ones to magnets, postcards, stuffed animals, and ceramic figures. "I will one of these days, I'm sure," he said. "But there are plenty of other places I'd like to see first."

"I hope you get to them all," she said. She was starting to hope she'd see some of them with him. This was their ninth date in two weeks, and she had already started thinking of him as her boyfriend. He made her laugh, he taught her things, and he had an easy self-confidence that made her comfortable right from the beginning.

Perhaps most important, she realized, was that when she was with him she didn't think about Season all the time. She began to see a possibility of life beyond Season, a life in which she didn't startle every time she saw a blond head on a slender female body. She would never forget the horror of that summer and fall, but someday it might just be a distant memory— something that had happened, instead of something that might happen again. She pressed herself up against Adam's arm.

That would be something worth fighting for.

Rebecca wasn't a very strict observer of the Jewish faith, but Kerry had bought her a Hanukkah present anyway: a digital camera. Kerry figured it was something that would take Rebecca outside herself, would force her to interact with the rest of the world, even if from behind a barrier of metal and glass. Of course, she didn't detail her reasoning for Rebecca, who loved the gift.

They had taken it to the boardwalk on a bright, sunny early morning at the end of the semester, the day before Rebecca was to leave for New York to be with her family. Rebecca was framing a shot of the roller coaster when her cell phone broke into song. She handed the camera to Kerry and tugged the phone from her coat pocket. "Hello?"

Kerry watched Rebecca's face change. Her mood had been good today, cheerful, and she'd answered the phone with a smile. But as she listened to the voice on the other end, her smile crumpled into something else. Her lower lip started to quiver, her eyes widened, her forehead creased like a freshly plowed field. After listening for a minute, she handed the phone to Kerry and walked away.

"Hello?" Kerry asked, inadvertently echoing Rebecca's response.

"Hey, Kerry." It was Scott Banner's voice, but he sounded anxious, upset.

"What's wrong, Scott?"

"I—I found her, Kerry. I found Season. She's in New Hampshire. But—well, can you come out here? Fast? She hasn't seen me yet, but I'm afraid she will."

"Sure, of course," Kerry said. "Soon as I can get a flight. Be sure you stay safe, okay?"

"I'm trying," Scott promised. "But I don't want to lose her either."

"I know, but staying out of her way is the most important thing. How did you find her?"

"A wild guess," Scott said. "I figured, you know, winter, ski resorts. I've been making the rounds up here and finally spotted her."

"That's amazing," Kerry said. The familiar and terrifying notion that maybe Season wanted to be found came to her—the idea that Season wanted to pick them off, one by one. "But listen, you keep a low profile. She's dangerous." *To say the least.*

"I know, Kerry."

Yeah, he knows, she thought. *But he went there anyway, by himself, looking for her. What was he thinking?*

It wouldn't help to harangue him. She just needed to keep him safe somehow. "Have you told Brandy?"

"I was going to call her next," he said. "I figure we need all hands on deck."

"No," Kerry said sharply. "If you haven't told her, don't." She looked at Rebecca, who stood fifty yards away on the beach, her red coat and yellow cargos standing out in sharp contrast to the blue-gray sea and blue sky. A stiff wind whipped her hair, and she looked very small against the wide background. "I'm not going to bring Rebecca, either. I don't want to put them in any danger if I don't have to."

"But . . . Kerry . . . ," he began.

"I know what I'm doing, Scott." *Which is a lie, of course, but maybe he'll buy it.* "You're just going to have to trust me."

"Okay," he said. "The nearest airport is a tiny one in Laconia, so get a flight into there and then call me. I'll keep tabs on her until then."

"I'll let you know when to expect me. Good job tracking her down."

"Thanks, Kerr." He sounded a little more relaxed than when she had first taken the phone.

"And you be careful!"

"You don't have to worry about that," he assured her.

I already am, she thought.

Kerry said good-bye and ended the call. Rebecca was still down on the beach, looking out at the sea with her arms wrapped around herself. Kerry walked down toward her, but the thunder of the surf and rush of the wind covered the sound of her approach. When she touched Rebecca's shoulder, the girl almost screamed.

"Jeez, Kerry, you scared the crap out of me!" When she turned around, Kerry saw that she had been crying. Mascara streaked her face.

"I'm sorry," Kerry said, spreading her arms. Rebecca moved into them and they shared a hug. Kerry's long black hair flew around them, mixing with Rebecca's, shorter and red. Kerry couldn't help remembering her first kiss with Daniel, also on a beach, several hundred miles to the south. "I didn't mean to startle you, Beck."

"It's okay," Rebecca said into Kerry's shoulder. She pulled away and looked into Kerry's eyes, her own brown ones still moist. "So, should I pack for New Hampshire?"

"No."

Rebecca's face brightened immediately, like the sun breaking through clouds. "You mean it? We're not going after her this time?"

"You're not," Kerry explained. "You've got to go to New York. I'm going alone."

The clouds returned. "Kerry, no!"

"I have to, Rebecca. Scott can't handle her by himself, and the longer he stays there the more danger he's in."

"Then why doesn't he just clear out of there?" Rebecca insisted, tears beginning to flow again. "Who says she has to be our problem?"

Kerry dug her sneaker in the sand. "She's our problem because we inherited her. She's our problem because she killed Mace and Daniel and Josh. And because it looks like maybe she's tracking us down, one at a time. Which means that Scott could be in a lot of trouble if I don't get there soon."

Rebecca's mouth hardened. "And what can you do about her, Kerry? You said you and Mother Blessing together couldn't take her."

"Yeah, well, that's just something I'll have to figure out when I get there," Kerry said.

"There's no way I can talk you out of this?"

"No, Rebecca. I don't really know how to explain—it's like, my destiny is linked with Season's now. As long as she's out there, my life isn't completely my own. I have to go."

Rebecca sniffled and wiped her eyes with her hand. "Doesn't mean I'm not going to try," she vowed.

"All the way to the airport if you want," Kerry agreed.

They stopped by Rebecca's house on the way out. Kerry said good-bye to Erin, Rebecca's housemate, whom she had only seen a handful of times since arriving, and packed up her few belongings. Once again she would get on an airplane that would take her toward Season Howe. She knew Rebecca's arguments made sense—if she just told Scott to get out of there, if they never went after Season again, she might just forget about them, right? Let them live out their lives in peace?

Maybe. And then again, maybe she really was hunting them. Maybe it wasn't happenstance that Scott found her, and Josh before that. If that was the case, then leaving her alone didn't help any of them.

Besides, Kerry wanted answers almost as much as she wanted revenge. She had been killing time in Santa Cruz, cooling her heels and getting stale, without even realizing it. Now she had a direction again, a purpose.

Scott had spent days cruising ski resorts before he spotted her. Countless blondes, many with stocking caps covering their hair, had passed before his eyes. He was growing frustrated, starting to think the whole plan was just crazy. *There's an entire world to choose from,* he thought. *Why would she pick New England just because it's convenient for me?*

At the same time, the longer his hunt stretched out, the more relaxed he became. He forgot, for brief periods of time, about the gun in his jacket pocket, though the memory of it always crashed back over him like a tidal wave of anxiety. He enjoyed the fit, attractive bodies around him, in more colors of spandex and nylon than he had known existed. The sun, the clean mountain air, the pure white snow, and the physical beauty, both of the natural region and the resort buildings themselves, all lulled him into a kind of contented languor. He was sipping a Coke in a huge, soft chair near a roaring fire in a lodge, its walls log and stone, when he saw an attractive blonde walking past the window with a pair of skis balanced on her shoulder, clad in a snug black ski outfit.

For a quarter of a second Scott forgot why he was even here. He appreciated her beauty and had a moment's sense of familiarity. Abruptly, though, he realized *why* she was familiar, and more urgently, why it mattered. He slammed the Coke down on the closest table, left a few bucks for the waitress, and wove around skiers until he found a door.

Outside, of course, the air was frigid and the walkway jammed with people, many, like the blonde he'd seen, carrying their skis. Scott looked around frantically. He had only caught a glimpse of her, and it had been months since that day in San Diego. He could easily have been wrong.

But at the moment that he had thought that the woman was Season, his whole body went cold. It was, in the words of the old cliché, as if someone had walked over his grave. Which always seemed a little strange, since why would that be a problem to someone who wasn't dead yet?

Still, it seemed suddenly, disturbingly appropriate. Scott put his hand inside his jacket pocket, closed it on the little nine-mil he carried there. Its cold steel brought him scant comfort.

He dodged and ducked, and finally he spotted the familiar form. Her clothes were skintight spandex, but she had taken off her cap and tucked it into a pocket. She stood at a coffee cart with her back to him. Scott slowed his pace and walked past the cart, then, trying to appear far more casual than he felt, he stopped and turned, looking past the cart at the blonde.

There could be no mistaking that face—the cheekbones, the vivid, almost cobalt blue eyes, like infinite sky, framed by short golden hair that curled toward a strong jaw.

It was the face of Season Howe.

He spun away quickly, before she could spot him. She was a dozen feet away. The gun was suddenly hot in his hand. He could walk up to her before she left the cart, or with her hands full of hot coffee and skis. A couple of shots in the head, close range. Sure, he'd go to prison, and it would kind of mess up the whole plan of ending up with Kerry.

But he would also be putting an end to a monster. Preventing a killer from killing again. There was something to be said for that.

Even if Kerry had to visit him in jail.

The gun was loaded, the safety off—he double-checked that with his thumb, inside his pocket. He'd never actually fired the thing, but he had practiced inside his Plymouth motel room for the last few nights. He understood it in theory, if not in practice.

Besides, how hard can it be?

In spite of the cold air, Scott felt sweat pouring from him. His hand slipped on the gun's grip. The world seemed like it was spinning too fast, colors whirling around him. He was light-headed and nothing sounded right, his ears rang as if he was deep underwater. He took a few steps toward Season but his knees felt like jelly, his feet wouldn't connect firmly with the ground.

It wasn't going to work. Before he reached Season—before, he hoped, Season saw him—Scott turned away, walked in the other direction until he found a vacant seat on a bench. *Who am I trying to kid?* he wondered. *I'm no gunman.* With shaking hands he drew his cell phone from its inside pocket, glad he had Rebecca's number programmed in. No way he'd be able to dial right now.

He punched send and waited.

Kerry would know what to do.

7

Kerry Profitt's diary, December 23

I'm almost getting used to writing in this journal on airplanes going to or from an encounter with Season Howe. I say almost because it's always an adventure seeing how far the person sitting in front of me is going to push his seat back, and whether I can actually see the screen as I type. This particular one is really pushing his luck—just about asking for someone to flick the bald spot on his head with her finger. I guess that someone would be me. Lucky for him I'm not the violent sort.

Or am I? It occurs to me (a little late, maybe? Am I not examining my life enough or something?) that I have spent most of the last five months, going on half a year, on an effort—unsuccessful so far—to commit a violent act against a person. A person I have plenty of reason to be mad at, but whom I really don't know.

That's not like me—at least, not like the me I used to be. I don't know if "meek" would be the word I'd have used to describe me. "Mild"? Maybe. I have always had a stubborn streak, and if something got in the way of getting what I thought was important, I was willing to do whatever it took, steamroller anyone. (Poor Ms. Tomkins, back in eighth grade, who really didn't understand how important my friends and I thought it was to have an anime club in school. A short-lived fad, at least where I was concerned. But man, did we hound her.) But actual violence? One of the reasons I lost interest in anime was the amount of violence in it.

So I guess there's a new me in town. I'll try to decide if I like her or not.

Glancing at the business type sitting in the seat next to me, also laptopping. Only on his there are, like, spreadsheets and numbers and stuff that looks suspiciously like work. I haven't done any of that since

the Seaside Resort, and I can hardly remember what it feels like to cash
a paycheck.

That's okay—I bet Mr. Business Type doesn't know what it feels like
to cast a spell. He probably doesn't even believe in magic, which is so
ingrained in me now I can hardly remember NOT believing in magic. Seems
so . . . naïve, now. People don't believe because they don't want to believe.
Because the world is simpler, they think, without it.

Well, tell you what, people. The world is a freaking complicated place.
Magic doesn't make that more or less true. But with magic, if I need to,
I can make you think I've had a shower and changed my clothes in the
last twenty-four, even if I haven't. Let's see you top that with technology.

Ha!

More later.

K.

It turned out to be not so easy to fly from San Jose to Laconia, as Scott
had recommended. Instead Kerry flew into Chicago's O'Hare, from
which she phoned Aunt Betty to tell her she was fine. From Chicago she
flew into Manchester, New Hampshire, and then hung around for several
hours until she could catch a puddle jumper into Laconia.

There were only ten seats on the plane, of which four were occupied. The
single flight attendant made Kerry and her three fellow passengers spread
out on the little plane to make sure it was balanced, an idea that filled Kerry
with dread, and then it took off, lurching and bouncing all the way into
Laconia. The town turned out to be relatively flat, though surrounded by
lakes, including Lake Winnipesaukee, which was large but maybe, Kerry
thought, not quite as big as its name.

It was almost midnight when she arrived, and she was both exhausted
and anxious. The closer they came to landing in Laconia, the more frightened she became. She remembered Las Vegas, when everyone but Josh
had hung around the airport waiting for her. She would probably never

know just how late they had been, but she guessed it was only minutes—minutes that had cost Josh Quinn his life.

Now, with Scott's life potentially in the balance, Kerry couldn't dial his phone number fast enough. He answered on the second ring.

"Kerry?"

"Hi, Scott. I'm here. Where are you?"

"You're in Laconia?"

"Right. At the airport here."

"Okay, you're going to have to get a car," he said. "You're still almost an hour away."

An hour? Anything can happen in an hour, Kerry thought. "Are you safe?" she asked. "Do you know where she is?"

"I think so," Scott said. "She's in a hotel room here at Loon Mountain. I couldn't get a room in the same place, but I've been hanging around as much as I can. Haven't been kicked out yet."

"And she doesn't know you're there?"

"I'm pretty sure not. She seems to be enjoying herself and not paying any attention to me."

Kerry felt a flash of anger at that idea. *Enjoying herself. While we run around like mad, just trying to stay sane and alive, she's up in the mountains having fun.*

"Okay," she said. "Tell me how to get there."

She wasn't sure how she would get a car—no one was likely to rent to her, even if there had been any rental places open at this hour. She looked frantically around the terminal building, and finally a dour-looking man—central casting New England, she thought—ambled toward her with a broom in his hands. He wore a janitor's uniform with a name patch that said MITCH. "You look like you're lost, miss," he said. "Somethin' I can do?"

"I'm trying to get to a place called Loon Mountain," she said.

He spoke slowly, and there was something on his face that might have been a smile. *Or maybe gas,* she thought. "Well, you could wait till mornin'. Be a bus then."

"That's great," she replied sarcastically. "But I really have to get there tonight. As fast as possible."

Moving just as slowly as he spoke, Mitch glanced at a clock. "Well, I get off at twelve," he said. "I could give you a ride up there, you want."

"It's after twelve," Kerry pointed out. The clock read 12:06.

"Ayup, that it is. Just workin' late," Mitch said. "I don't sleep too good these nights."

He apparently doesn't tell time too good, either, Kerry noted, but she didn't want to mention that if he was going to do her a favor. She recognized the danger inherent in accepting a ride from a stranger, on a dark night, into unfamiliar mountains. But then, the hitchhiking thing had gone okay. And she figured she could handle Mitch if he got out of hand. If he drove like he did everything else, she could probably get out and run at any point and still make better time than he could.

"Okay, I guess," she said. "Are you going that way?"

"Nobody's goin' that way. That's your whole problem, isn't it?"

"Well, yes, I suppose it is."

He carried the broom over to a janitor's closet. "Wait right there, miss," he said. "I'll be back directly."

Kerry spent the few moments that he was gone running through self-defense spells in her head. She felt comfortable with them. Unless old Mitch turned out to be a witch, there was nothing he could do to hurt her. And if he tried anything, then she'd wind up driving after all, and he'd have a long walk home.

A minute later he came back from the closet wearing an anorak and tugging on furry gloves. He made that expression again, like someone trying on a new smile to see if it fit. "You ready to go?"

"I've been ready," she said.

"Kind of impatient, aren't you?" he asked.

"You could say that."

"I just did."

Kerry tried to walk fast, but Mitch just kind of shuffled along at his own pace, and she knew she couldn't get too far ahead since she didn't know where they were going. Once they were in the parking lot, it became clear—there were only a scattered handful of vehicles there, and Mitch plodded toward the oldest one, a truck that might have been state-of-the-art in the 1950s, but not since. He opened the passenger door for Kerry and then climbed in behind the wheel.

"You say you're in a hurry?" he asked her, although he knew full well, she was sure, what the answer would be.

"You know, that old life and death thing," she answered.

He put the ancient truck into gear and stomped on the accelerator. The truck left rubber behind in the parking lot and roared onto the street. "Well, then I reckon we ought to get a move on," he said. He kept both hands on the wheel in a death grip, as if afraid it would get away from him if he relaxed. But dark, sleepy Laconia zipped past outside the windows much faster than Kerry would have believed possible. Within fifteen minutes they were climbing up into the White Mountains. Snow gleamed silver, reflecting the moon overhead, trees strobed past, and Mitch drove silently, his eyes forward, his lips pressed together. Kerry figured that his picture would be in the dictionary under "taciturn," maybe cross-referenced with "crusty."

But she wasn't going to complain. The guy was going more than an hour out of his way just to get her where she needed to go. He hadn't mentioned money, or any other reward, and he hadn't asked her any questions. She was grateful for his help and delighted that a human being would make the effort to assist another in this cynical age.

About forty minutes after they had left the airport, Mitch pointed out the windshield at an array of buildings glowing in the darkness. "Loon Mountain Lodge," he said.

"Wow, that was fast."

"What you wanted, right?"

"That's right," Kerry agreed. She dug her phone out. "I've got to find out where my friend is."

"Asleep, if he knows what's good for him," Mitch commented.

"Well, if he knew that he wouldn't be here at all," Kerry said. "That's never been his strong point."

"People don't know how important sleep is," Mitch said. "Take it from me."

"I've had plenty the last couple of weeks," Kerry told him. "But I don't always. I know what you mean." She dialed Scott and he picked up immediately.

"Where are you?" he asked.

"We're here, basically," she said. "Where are you?"

"Come to the parking lot closest to the lodge," Scott replied. "I'm in the RAV4. Look in the second row."

Kerry relayed the directions to Mitch. "Okay, we're just about there." She disconnected and scanned the snow-laden cars, trucks, and SUVs. Near the end of the row, she saw his black Toyota. "There it is!" she shouted. As they pulled up, Scott got out of the vehicle. He wore a dark blue down coat with the hood pulled up, a knit cap on his head beneath the hood, jeans, and snow boots. His breath steamed as he stood by the SUV, waiting.

"That's him?" Mitch asked. "Looks cold."

"That's him," Kerry agreed happily. "Thank you so much for the ride. Can I pay for gas or something?"

"Nope," Mitch answered. "I'd stayed at the airport I'd've been makin' messes just to have somethin' to clean up. You just have sense enough to get in out of the cold, that's all I ask."

"It's a deal." She shook Mitch's big hand—slowly—and then climbed down from the truck. As soon as her feet hit icy pavement, Scott enveloped her in a hug.

"Kerry," he breathed. "I'm so glad you're here."

Kerry couldn't help laughing. "You must be freezing," she declared. "Haven't you been running the heat?"

"Off and on," Scott admitted. "But I haven't wanted to sit there with the engine running because I figured that would attract attention."

"Can we go inside?" Kerry asked. She was an Illinois girl, used to harsh plains winters, but time in California and southern Virginia seemed to have thinned her blood. She rubbed her arms vigorously through her heavy coat. "It is really cold out here."

"We could," Scott said. "But there are various doors out of the building. Unless Season's planning to leave on skis, she'll have to take the road. We can see it from here, but if we're inside we could miss her."

"Maybe. But if we turn into a couple of corpsesicles out here, she could waltz right past us anyway."

Scott nodded. "Good point."

"Do you have any reason to think she's going to skip out tonight?" Kerry wondered.

He contemplated a moment before answering. "She put in a pretty full day on the slopes," he said. "Ate a big dinner, couple glasses of wine."

"Sounds like you kept a close eye on her," Kerry commented.

"I did what I could without being too obvious. Anyway, I figure once she hits the sack, she's there to stay. At least, that's what a human would do."

"She's a witch, but she's still human. Just . . . differently abled, as they say."

"Well, whatever she is, I bet she's sound asleep. Like we should be."

"Will we be too obvious if we go in now?"

"It's, what, a little after one? The bars are still open in there. We'll fit in."

He locked up the RAV4 and they started the trudge up to the lodge. "By the way," he said as they walked. "Merry Christmas Eve."

"Oh, yeah." She had forgotten, in her weariness and worry, that when midnight hit it had become Christmas Eve. "Heck of a way to spend a holiday, huh?"

Scott put a gloved hand on her shoulder. "I'm not complaining."

8

The Loon Mountain Lodge was all peaked roofs and large windows. Some faced onto the parking lot, but the best looked out toward the slopes. When they got inside, Kerry saw that Scott had been correct—in spite of the late hour, there were still plenty of merrymakers inside wishing one another happy holidays. It wouldn't last; they wouldn't be able to stay inside all night, she knew, without getting a room. And Scott had said the hotel was full. So they'd be heading back to the RAV4 in a while. But at least until then they could warm their bones a little.

Neither one was old enough to get into the bar, but there was enough spillover into the lobby that they felt comfortable just taking a seat there. A fire crackled in a big stone fireplace with a wooden mantel, scenting the air with the tang of wood smoke. On the mantel, pine branches decorated with glass Christmas balls crowded a couple of antique duck decoys. In a corner away from the fire stood a Christmas tree, at least ten feet tall, fully decorated, with giant boxes strewn underneath it as if waiting for the next morning.

Scott sat close to Kerry, his knees touching hers. His cheeks were flushed with the cold, his eyes glittering. Something about him seemed different than when she had last seen him, in Las Vegas after Josh's death. He seemed more . . . alive, maybe. Like his internal batteries had been running low, but were now recharged.

Kerry had only had a few short conversations with him since then, too involved in her own life, she guessed, to delve into his. She felt uncomfortable bringing up Brandy, but didn't see any way around it. "I'm sorry," she began. "About, you know, Brandy."

Scott nodded, then shrugged. "Life happens," he said. "She was ready to try something different, I guess. I'm doing okay, though. I think maybe I was ready for it too, but just didn't know it yet."

"Are you . . . seeing anyone?" she asked.

"No." His answer was immediate and emphatic. "No, not at all. She is, I guess. I don't know him, but she's mentioned a guy named Adam a couple of times."

"Are you okay with that?"

"Like I have a choice? Sure, I'm okay. Just time to move on, right? I guess you haven't had time for any . . ." He let the question trail off, but she knew what he meant.

The truth was, since Daniel had died she had hardly thought about romance at all. He was the man she had wanted to be with, the only one she had ever met with whom she could imagine a future. "Nope. No time at all."

"You'll . . . you'll find the right guy," Scott assured her. "You'll probably find out he was right there the whole time, and you just didn't know it. You've just had a lot on your plate."

"That's for sure," she agreed.

"Listen, I should tell you," he said, changing the subject abruptly. "When I came here, I brought a gun. I was going to kill her."

"Season?" She couldn't keep the surprise from her voice.

"Of course, Season. What, you don't think a gun could kill her?"

"I know it can't," Kerry stated firmly. "Mother Blessing shot her four times with a rifle, close-up. She just spat the bullets out into her hand."

It was Scott's turn to be surprised. His color had already started to pale from being inside, out of the cold, but now he blanched. "You're kidding me."

"Not at all." She sat back in the seat—he moved to stay close to her, she noticed—and told him the whole story of the battle outside Mother Blessing's cabin in the Swamp.

When she was finished, his hand was on her knee, squeezing it. "I don't see how you could have done all that, Kerry," he said. "I'd have been absolutely terrified."

"What makes you think I wasn't?"

Late-night had turned to middle-of-the night while they talked, and the bar crowd had started to thin. "We should get out of here," Kerry observed. "They're going to charge us for a room pretty soon. Can we stay warm enough in your car?"

"I've got a blanket," he answered. "I think if we huddle we'll be all right."

"Okay, then. Huddle it is." She rose and led him out of the building. It bothered her that Season was inside sleeping—she wanted to go back in and bring things to a head right now, but she knew that wasn't the way to go. Instead, they went to Scott's RAV4, put the seats back as far as they'd go, and snuggled close to one another underneath his blanket. He ran the heater for a few minutes until the car warmed up a bit, and soon they were toasty.

Scott had never been Kerry's idea of gorgeous. But it had been a long time since she'd had a man's body pressed against her. Feeling his warmth and solid bulk, she found the idea of kissing him swimming to the forefront of her thoughts. By the time it occurred to her, though, his breathing was regular and deep. He was out. Kerry tried to stay awake, to keep watch, but the day had been long and she was worn out. Within minutes, they were both sound asleep.

Kerry assumed that the skiers getting the earliest starts were not the ones who had been up drinking all night, but there were plenty of them. She woke up feeling pretty well rested despite the difficult conditions and late night, but famished and needing some grooming time. She was dying to take a shower and wash her hair, which had been tied back into a ponytail since she'd left California the day before. *Shampoo would be great,* she thought. *And conditioner. And an exfoliating scrub . . .*

Thinking like that wouldn't help. She shook Scott awake.

"Hey," she said brightly. "It's Christmas Eve. I'm starving, and if I don't brush my teeth my breath is going to kill somebody. Let's go inside."

Scott blinked a few times and found his glasses on the dash. "Okay," he said. "I could go for food. And dental hygiene."

They went back inside and found a restaurant where they could eat and watch the lobby, just in case Season woke early too. They still hadn't seen her when they were done. Over the last of their coffee, Kerry brought up what she knew would be a difficult subject.

"It's time for you to head out, Scott."

"What do you mean, head out?"

"I mean . . . when I confront Season this time, it's got to be alone. I need to do this by myself."

He looked at her like he couldn't believe what he had heard. "By yourself? You can't!"

"I have to. There's no other way for it to work." She didn't describe exactly what her plan was, but he'd never go along with it anyway. That was why she needed him gone.

"Kerry, no."

"Scott. It's not a request. I'm sorry, but you've got to go."

He was still shaking his head, still not going along with it. She was going to have to be harsh, she feared. It was for his own good. There was no telling what fireworks might happen when she confronted Season.

"I can—whatever you need me to do, Kerry, I'll do it," he insisted. "Just let me stay with you."

"You can't, Scott. It won't work. I'm glad you found her, that was great.

And I appreciate you keeping me warm all night and everything. But your part is done now, and it's my turn."

"Your turn? Kerry, it's always you. Why not let me help?"

"You've done the part you can do." Kerry was firm. "Now the best thing you can do to help is to go away, before she comes out."

Scott frowned angrily. "Okay," he said, getting up in a huff. "If that's how you want it, that's what you get. I thought we were partners here, but I guess not."

"That's right," Kerry said. "No partners this time out. It's a solo deal."

"Whatever," he said. He grabbed his backpack off the restaurant floor. "I hope you're not making a big mistake," he said as he stormed away.

Oh, you and me both, Kerry thought. She hated to make him angry, but he'd never have left otherwise. And as much as it hurt her to see him so upset, he really was better off.

Now, of course, came the really hard part. It had been one thing to make a big show of courage and resolve in order to drive Scott away. But she had to follow through—she had to confront Season, all by herself, and not let the resolve she had faked so convincingly turn into outright terror.

Hands trembling, she left the restaurant and went back into the lobby to wait for Season.

Fortunately the wait wasn't too long—otherwise, Kerry believed, she might have lost her nerve altogether. But less than twenty minutes after paying the breakfast bill and finding a chair in the lobby, she saw Season's sleek form, clad in tight royal blue ski attire, heading for the back door.

Swallowing hard, steeling herself for anything, Kerry followed Season outside. She wanted to catch the witch before she got too far, and definitely before she realized Kerry was here. Catching her off-guard seemed like the only way this had even a chance of working.

"Season!" she said sharply once they were both outside. She thought Season tensed for a moment—a sudden lifting of shoulder blades, straightening of spine—but then she kept walking. *Not going by that name here,* *then,* Kerry reasoned. *But she'll answer to it anyway.* She moved closer to Season, who had increased her pace.

"Season Howe," she said again. This time her voice was lower. She knew Season would be listening for it.

And this time Season turned—casually, as if just looking around to admire the beautiful morning—and faced her. Her expression didn't reveal any surprise or consternation—she had a pleasant smile fixed on her pretty face, and it stayed there while she regarded Kerry. Still casual, she moved some of her neatly trimmed honey-blond hair off her face. "I'm surprised to see you," she said. Her voice was soft, almost friendly.

She's good, Kerry thought. *Anyone watching us would think we were old pals.*

"I want to talk," Kerry assured her. "That's all, just talk."

"I don't think we really have anything to say to each other."

"Oh, you're wrong, Season. We have plenty of things to discuss, trust me."

Season laughed. "Have you ever given me a reason to trust you?"

"I've never given you any reason not to."

"You've tried to kill me."

Kerry's turn to laugh. "Point taken. And vice versa, I have to say."

"Maybe I should do it again now," Season said. "I could, you know."

"I know that," Kerry said. "I know you could try, at least. But I know a few tricks now too." Which was almost a lie—she knew nothing now that she hadn't that last day in the Swamp. She hadn't quite exhausted her repertoire that time, because Mother Blessing had been calling the shots. But she hadn't picked up anything new since then.

Season smiled again. "Enough to stop me? Show me."

They were talking on a busy walkway, with skiers bustling past them on their way to the lifts. So far no one had paid them any attention, because their poses and attitudes were nonchalant. Kerry wanted to keep it that way, but it was looking like Season would need some convincing if she were not to blast Kerry on the spot.

She needed to demonstrate her skills, but in a way that would not draw any notice. Beside her was a wooden railing, with a snowy expanse beyond that led to the base of the slopes. Not far away, cable lifts ferried skiers up to the runs, which were already strewn with colorful specks, like sprinkles on a frosted doughnut, except that these sprinkles were moving swiftly downhill. Close to the lodge, the snow was dotted with trees and rocks. She ticked her head toward it, and Season's gaze followed. Kerry concentrated, gesturing toward the ground, and said, *"Ashashalika,"* one of the old words of magic.

Rocks shifted, shaking off their dusting of snow. Big ones rolled quickly to the points Kerry had visualized, and smaller ones filled in the spaces between. When they had settled, they spelled out SH in the snow.

Season laughed again, a sound that Kerry realized was a pleasant one. Season was pretty, she was cultured, she had good manners. It was just too bad she was an evil killer.

"Cute," she said. "But how does it keep me from killing you?"

"It doesn't," Kerry admitted. "But I can't show you that kind of thing without drawing a lot of eyeballs this way. I don't think either of us wants that."

"You're probably right," Season said. "But I could cloak us, and kill you just the same."

"Oh, cloaking," Kerry said, feigning surprise. She had pulled it off, drawn Season right where she wanted her. "If you want cloaking, look." She brought her hands together, touched her thumbs, and then spread them wide, which dissipated one of the cloaking spells that had kept her real stunt from Season's eyes. As far as any other onlookers were concerned, she and Season were just standing and talking—Mother Blessing had taught her that the real test of a witch's cloaking skills was the ability to reveal something to one person or group while keeping it hidden from others.

But what Season saw was a cartoon-style weight labeled 16 TONS hanging in the air, inches above her head.

"Oh, bravo," Season said, clapping her hands. "Misdirection *and* a genuine threat, cloaked. You're better than I thought."

Coming from Season Howe, that was real praise, and Kerry felt a flush of pride. "Thanks," she said. Another word of the Old Tongue, another gesture, and the weight had vanished, the rocks returned to their original positions.

Season regarded her closely for a moment, her head shaking slowly from side to side. "You really have a lot of guts to do this," she said. "Or you're stupider than you look. And I don't think that's the case."

"No, it would be a bad idea to count on that."

"We should get out of here, then," Season suggested. "If we're going to talk, I mean."

"I kind of like it public," Kerry countered, still trying to sound bolder than she felt. "How do I know you wouldn't take me someplace just to kill me?"

"I guess you don't," Season replied, turning the tables. "You'll just have to trust me."

9

Scott couldn't believe what Kerry had said to him. Everything he had done was for her. Hunting Season, finding her, keeping her in sight all day—even risking his life by buying that stupid gun. All for Kerry . . . and then she just dumped him from the whole thing. *Get lost, basically. Go away, little boy, you've done your chore for the day. Merry Christmas Eve, but I'm done with you.*

As if that wasn't bad enough, she had completely ignored the subtext of his remarks, blown it off as if she hadn't understood. He was offering himself to her, and she either didn't notice or wasn't interested. She had a lot on her mind, so it was possible, even probable that she might have missed some cues. And it probably came out of left field—he didn't know if she had ever been aware of his attraction to her.

Still, he didn't think he'd been overly subtle. Especially with the whole snuggling through the night thing. He thought it was one of the best nights of his life—fraught with the terror of possible discovery by Season, and on the cold side, but still . . . amazing just to be near to Kerry.

And then she just turned it all away. Sent him packing.

Well, she might not think he had anything to contribute, but he knew better.

He walked all the way out to the RAV4, furious at her. He tossed his backpack into the cargo area and was about to get in behind the driver's seat when he thought better of it. *Who says she gets to make the rules?* Scott wondered. He stuffed his keys back into his pocket and returned to the hotel. Much as he had done with Season, he stayed out of Kerry's view but kept an eye on her. It was only a few minutes until Season showed up and Kerry chased her outside.

He hadn't been able to get close enough to hear, but he could see just fine. They feigned a perfectly friendly conversation, but from Kerry's body language and some of her movements, he knew there was more to it than met the eye. Then Season led Kerry away—straight toward the parking lot. Scott had to spin away and insert himself between a couple of skiers to make sure they didn't spot him, but after their backs were turned he followed.

Outside, Season led Kerry to a black Jeep 4X4. Scott ran to the RAV4, jumped in, and cranked the engine. By the time Season was leaving the parking lot, he was three cars behind. He opened his cell phone and dialed.

"Hello?" she answered a moment later. "Scott?"

"Brandy, listen, I know you don't want me calling you, but this is important. Season Howe just kidnapped Kerry."

"Kidnapped? What are you talking about, Scott? Where are you?"

"I'm at Loon Mountain, in New Hampshire," he said, the words spilling out of him in a torrent. "I came up here looking for Season, and I found her. So I called Kerry. She came out, and then she wanted to confront Season by herself. But I watched. I think they did some magic stuff, and then Season took her away in a Jeep. I'm following them."

"Scott," Brandy said, and her concern sounded genuine. "You be really careful. I know you like Kerry, but she's different than we are now. She has powers that we don't. She can take care of herself."

"She can't take Season by herself."

"You don't know that."

"Yes, I do," Scott protested. He had to make a hard left turn, so he held the phone between his cheek and shoulder while he did. "She told me this story—she and Mother Blessing together couldn't beat Season, and that was only a few weeks ago. Before she went to stay with Rebecca."

Brandy was quiet for a second, taking that in. "Okay. So where are you, exactly?"

"I'm driving. I'm following them. North on I-93."

"But they don't know you're behind them?"

"I sure hope not."

"Make sure you keep it that way. If Kerry sees you back there, Season will figure it out."

Scott eyed the horizon ahead. Storm clouds glowered; the sky was a ferocious leaden gray. "It looks like the weather is turning, too," he reported.

"Scott, I'm coming up there. It'll take me a while from here, but I'll leave as soon as I can."

"If you're going to come up, Brandy," Scott replied, "maybe you should call Rebecca. Kerry said she's in New York visiting her folks. Maybe she can come too. The more the better."

"Okay, I'll try her," Brandy promised. "And I'll have my phone, so keep me posted. And be careful!"

He ended the call. People kept telling him to be careful, like he was some kind of simpleton. Kerry had warned him to be careful, and look where it got her. Snatched by Season and driven up into the mountains.

It occurred to him to try Kerry's phone. He punched her number, and it rang three times before she answered it.

"Kerry, is everything okay?" he asked.

"Yes, Scott. Everything is fine."

"Can you talk freely?"

"Sure, why not?" She sounded normal, relaxed. Not like Season was holding a mystical gun to her head.

"I was just wondering. If you need me for anything, you can call me. You know that, right?"

"I know, Scott. Thanks."

"Okay. Talk to you later." He ended the call, feeling like an idiot. Either she was being kidnapped or she wasn't. Would a kidnapper let her keep her cell phone? Maybe, if she knew it couldn't help her.

He hung back, at least a half mile behind—just far enough to keep them in sight from time to time, but not so close that they'd realize they were being followed. The radio brought in a mixture of reggae, ska, and punk from a college station in Manchester, keeping him alert. After an hour or so, the station began to fade, and snowflakes started to slap against his windshield. They didn't stick, but before long he had to turn on his headlights and wipers. He started to feel hungry. He could use a bathroom. And his shoulders were getting sore from the driving. But they kept going, so he did. Season had left the interstate but continued on what seemed to be a fairly major two-lane highway.

His mind whirled with conflicting thoughts of Kerry. He was sick with worry about her. Had Season hypnotized her, or enchanted her somehow? Why else would she get in a car with a known killer—one she had battled just weeks before?

And then those thoughts mixed with his memories of earlier—of the joy he had felt when he'd seen her step down from that old truck. Even in the dim light of the parking lot, her big green eyes had seemed to glow, her smile radiating like a small sun. His heart had swelled at the sight of her and at the sensation of holding her in his arms—and of her returning the hug—when they'd embraced. Her scent filled him with a happiness he could barely believe.

He wasn't sure if other people felt things with the intensity he did, but he had often suspected not. For others, emotion sometimes seemed secondary to the regular grind of life. Brandy, for instance, prioritized feelings after intellect, after psychology, or her interpretation of it. And his own parents loved each other, or said they did, and had been married for more than a quarter of a century. But while they tried to have dinner together a couple of nights a week, one or the other always seemed to be off at a meeting or function that the other wasn't part of. Work or obligations got the best of people, he believed, forcing them to put off their emotional lives and well-being for later, which couldn't be healthy.

But not Scott. He found himself trying sometimes—making an effort to, as Brandy said, sublimate his feelings. But they wouldn't be put in a box. They *were* him—surface, inside, everything. The rest of him was just the clothes they were dressed in.

And right now his emotions were a stew of love and terror—but they were rapidly being mixed with anxiety about driving in the worsening storm.

When Season and Kerry pulled off the highway he almost missed them. He had spaced out, the snow creating a field of pure white ahead of him, and his focus was all on not losing the road. So when he realized that he couldn't see their taillights anymore, it was almost too late. At the last moment he spotted the small side road leading off to the right, higher up into the White Mountains. He yanked the wheel hard, and the SUV's rear wheels started to fishtail out from under him. He corrected by turning into the skid, and brought the vehicle under control in time to avoid going off the road or flipping over. If anyone had been coming up fast behind him, it would have been trouble. And there was precious little traffic—if he'd gone off the road, it could have been a long time before someone found him. He let go of the wheel long enough to wipe the sweat from his eyes, then nosed the RAV4 toward the side road.

The wind was really blowing now, coating everything with snow. Tracks showed on this little road, but there was already snow sticking to the black-top, beginning to cover them up. Trees and bushes and hillsides were frosted as thickly as a wedding cake.

At least there was just one way they could have gone. The road only led up.

Scott pressed down on the accelerator. His wheels slid on the snow and ice, but then they caught and carried him forward. He realized, too late, that he hadn't even noticed if this road had a name, or a sign—if he had to tell Brandy how to find him up here, he'd be out of luck.

Wipers flailing, he drove on through a nearly impenetrable curtain of snow. He was getting genuinely worried now—this was starting to look like a blizzard, or a whiteout. If he was stranded up here, without food or water or shelter, he could be in some serious trouble.

But Kerry already was, he was convinced. He couldn't back off.

The road wound up a mountain, becoming narrower. Trees hemmed it in on both sides, looming dark and menacing in the dim light. The roadway was completely covered by snow now, and his tracks seemed to fill as soon as he passed.

So when he reached a fork in the road, he had no idea which way to go.

Both directions looked equally unappealing. Both seemed to lead deeper into thickly forested mountains. Neither had so much as a signpost or marker. He realized that he couldn't remember when he'd seen the last human, the last car other than Season's Jeep. He might as well have been in a primeval wilderness. He picked the right fork, because that seemed more of a continuation of the road he was already on, while the left would require actually turning off that road. But after driving that way for about ten minutes, he still hadn't caught sight of the Jeep, and the snow was, if anything, falling faster than before. The road was practically obliterated by it. Even with four-wheel drive, it was treacherously slippery. And if he had picked wrong, then with every passing minute they were getting farther and farther away on the other road, their tracks wiped away by the blizzard.

At a loss for any other options, Scott stopped his vehicle and killed the engine. He stepped out into the snow, listening. The air smelled like pine; falling snowflakes kissed his cheeks and eyelids. He had hoped to hear the roar of Season's Jeep, but there was only utter silence—not a bird, not a distant airplane, not the chirp of a cricket.

He tried Kerry's phone again. No service.

He ducked back inside, got the gun from his backpack. He hated the thing. Aiming for a faraway tree, he threw it as far as he could. It hit some branches and fell through them, crashing to the ground beneath. Snow shaken loose by its passage dropped over it. Then the silence returned, made somehow more absolute than before.

He could have been the last person on Earth.

This was just *perfect.*

Christmas Eve. Taking the new honey to meet the folks for Christmas dinner. And the ex calls and says drop everything, never mind your life, the girl I have the hots for now is in danger.

Ninety percent of the world's females, Brandy figured, would have offered a two-word response. But then, ninety percent of the world's population—more like ninety-nine point nine, probably, with a few more nines thrown in for good measure—were blissfully unaware that beings like Season Howe existed. That knowledge, combined with the belief that Season had targeted their little summer group for extinction, meant that Brandy's reaction would have to be somewhat different than the vast majority's.

Instead of telling him to get lost—or any of the other combinations of two words that came to mind—her answer had to be "I'm coming." It wasn't fair. But then, no one had ordained that life had to be fair. In fact, it often seemed that the better it was going in one area or another, balance decreed that it had to get worse somewhere else.

So: Adam good, Season bad. And as good as Adam was, on the scale Season's badness was far, far worse.

Which meant her response wasn't in doubt. The only question remaining was, how did she tell her parents and Adam that she was going to New Hampshire for Christmas, instead of their house?

Her mom would want her head. Her dad would sulk unpleasantly. DJ, her little brother, would probably threaten bodily harm. The various relatives—aunts, uncles, cousins—who were expected would be overly concerned and offer bits of helpful advice to the family. Of course, she wouldn't be around so she wouldn't have to listen to that part, but she'd get plenty of complaints about it when she got back.

Bright side, she thought, *maybe I'll get killed and won't have to face them at all.*

Not funny, she amended. *Ask Josh and Mace if it's funny.*

Still, there were times when one needed black humor to fend off the real horrors of life, and this was looking like one of those times. If she couldn't make unpleasant jokes about it, she probably couldn't face it at all.

Brandy realized that sitting in her apartment stewing wasn't going to do any good—this was one of those occasions where the sooner she acted, the better. She picked the phone out of her lap and dialed Rebecca's cell.

While she drove through the gathering storm, Season chatted casually about a wide variety of subjects, from clothes to cars, environmental issues to restaurants and resorts all around the world. She was well informed and erudite, and Kerry couldn't help enjoying the conversation.

The only thing Season refused to discuss was what Kerry had wanted to talk about in the first place. "We can talk about all of that, but not here, not in the car," Season had said when Kerry pressed the issue. "When we get where we're going." But she wouldn't tell Kerry where it was they were going, only that it was someplace safe, someplace they wouldn't be disturbed.

Kerry was terrified by the whole idea of going anywhere with Season.

But curiosity outweighed her terror. Season had made some explosive charges at Mother Blessing's place, and Kerry was determined to get to the truth about them. Was Season Mother Blessing's mother and Daniel's grandmother? Who was really responsible for the tragedy at Slocumb, Virginia, in

1704, which had kicked off this whole multicentury war of witches? These were the issues that Kerry was really concerned with, not which European chef made the best chocolate desserts—although chocolate still ranked pretty high on the priority scale.

She rode along beside Season, commenting or asking a question on occasion and answering some about her own earlier life—before San Diego—and found herself surprised at the witch's geniality. The radio played holiday music that made a strange counterpoint to the ride. She didn't relax—that was a leap of faith she wasn't ready to take, not when the woman behind the wheel had the power to end her life with a word or two. But she became somewhat less tense as the drive wore on, at least until the storm blew in and erased visibility down to a few yards. Season expressed full confidence in her Jeep's ability to handle the snowy roads, and Kerry could see that she was a capable driver. *But then,* she thought, *she's had a century of practice, so why not? Probably started out driving a Model T.*

They drove deeper into the wilderness, and Season became less chatty as she had to struggle more with just keeping her wheels on the road—or seeing the road at all. It was still only early afternoon, but the sky was twilight-dark, the world reduced to nothing but snowflakes flickering in the headlights. Looming over everything were the mountains, rounded and stolid, like hunched-over elders quietly disapproving of everything they observed. Kerry knew these mountains were older than the Rockies she had flown over twice, earlier in the year. Those had knife-edged peaks that looked like they could slice open the airplane. But these, while less imposing, were still higher than anything back home in Illinois, or down in the flat mid-Atlantic region.

Finally, when Kerry was starting to worry that they really would become trapped by the ever-thicker downfall, Season pulled off the road onto a barely-there driveway and stopped with her headlights shining on a small wooden cabin nestled in a stand of tall pines. Snow had drifted in front of the cabin's door and piled on its rooftop, but the structure seemed sound enough.

"Here we are," Season announced.

"*Where* we are?"

"Where we're going. Kind of a little hideaway I have."

"I thought you liked being where there were lots of people around," Kerry mentioned. "The whole safety in numbers thing, like with the resorts?"

"I do," Season confirmed. "But I also know that, strategically, sometimes it's important to be able to change the way I do things. Can't be predictable all the time. So I have a few of these kinds of places scattered around the country, for emergency use."

"Are we still in New Hampshire?"

"Yes," Season replied. "I like to keep my hideaways within an hour or so of the resorts I frequent. Weather permitting, of course."

Kerry looked at the weather. "Think we'll be snowed in?"

"Almost definitely," Season said. "We'll be fine, though. There are plenty of supplies and firewood inside."

"Okay, then. Might as well get to it." She opened the Jeep door and grabbed her duffel from the backseat. "Guess it's going to be a white Christmas for us."

10

The cabin was, in fact, much more impressive inside than out. That seemed to be a habit with witches, Kerry thought, remembering the way Mother Blessing's place in the Swamp had looked like a falling-down old trapper's cabin from the outside, but a modern suburban home on the inside.

Witches had other advantages, too. Starting a fire was no problem for Season, who simply laid some logs into a gigantic stone fireplace and ignited them magically. Within minutes the place had already started to warm up, and Kerry was able to shed her coat and look around a little.

The interior reflected the cabin theme from outside, but in a much more luxurious way than Kerry would have guessed from the primitive facade. The walls were knotty pine, but highly polished, warm, and rich-looking. The hardwood floor was dotted with beautiful rugs. Season's furniture was rustic but comfortable, all wood, well crafted and padded. A counter or breakfast bar separated the huge main room from a kitchen area with cabinets in the same golden pine as the floors. The place had two bedrooms, and Season showed Kerry which one would be hers—a cozy space with a big wooden bed covered by a lush comforter. The room was tucked under the eaves at the back of the house, timbered ceiling slanting away toward what looked, through the one small window, like unlimited, infinite pine forest.

We really are alone up here, Kerry thought, with a sensation of dread. *Anything could happen. They'd never find my body.*

But if Season had intended to kill her, she could have done so at any time. Why bother bringing her up here, showing her a bedroom, getting towels from a linen closet for her?

No reason that Kerry could determine. Which could only mean that Season hadn't brought her here to kill her, but to talk, as she had insisted.

Well, that was fine. That's what Kerry wanted too. She had hoped to do it nearer civilization, where she could get away if she needed to. But she wasn't the one calling the shots. Since they'd climbed into the Jeep, Season had been, literally as well as figuratively, in the driver's seat.

Season had suggested that Kerry take a shower, and given how nasty she felt, Kerry had happily agreed. She took her towels into the hall bathroom— her own master suite, Season said, had another—and was delighted to find that it was just as deluxe as the rest of the place. The fixtures were gleaming brass, the tub enclosed in sparkling glass. When Kerry undressed and turned on the shower, the water rushed forth steaming hot. Bottles of shampoo, conditioner, and cleanser were lined up on a shelf inside the tub enclosure. Twenty minutes later, showered, having found a brand-new toothbrush and a tube of toothpaste lying next to the sink, she felt like a new person. She wrapped her long black hair up in one of the towels, wrapped the other one around herself, and went back across the hall to the bedroom. When she opened the bathroom door, she realized that Season had been busy too— cooking aromas competed with the wood burning in the fireplace, and the smell instantly reminded Kerry of how long it had been since breakfast.

Back in her room she dug a clean pair of sweatpants, a thick green cable-knit sweater, and fuzzy white socks from her duffel. After rubbing lotion into her hands, arms, and legs, she dressed quickly. She carried the towels back into the bathroom to hang, tied her hair back, applied a little eyeliner. She could have done more, but she felt more presentable than she had in days, and the smells from the kitchen were making her crazy.

"I hope pasta's okay," Season said when Kerry found her. She had a big pot boiling on the stove. She'd changed into a soft tan turtleneck and faded jeans and wore her hair loose. "It was fast and easy. There's garlic bread, too, and some salad."

"Pasta's fine," Kerry said. She was afraid that she might actually start to drool. "Smells wonderful."

"Thanks," Season said with a smile. "I like to cook, but I don't really get much chance to."

"How did you get fresh salad vegetables here if you haven't been here lately?" Kerry wondered.

Season just laughed.

"Oh," Kerry said, realizing the foolishness of her question. There wasn't much Season couldn't do, apparently—conjuring some fresh lettuce, tomatoes, and cucumbers wouldn't be much of a trick for her.

There was a rough-hewn pine dining table beside the breakfast bar, on which Season had put out thick white linen place mats and heavy pewter tableware. "Can I do anything?" Kerry asked.

"It's just about ready," Season said by way of reply. She picked up the pot with two massive potholders and carried it to the sink, where she dumped it into a colander. "Meat sauce all right with you?"

"Yeah, that's fine," Kerry said. "Thanks for this, by the way. I am just starving."

"Me too." She put the pasta back into the pot and put it back on its burner. On another burner a pot of red sauce simmered noisily. Season poured the red sauce over the pasta, stirring the two together, and let it cook for a couple of minutes. "This makes it so the sauce doesn't just slide off the pasta," she explained. "Holds the heat in, too, so it stays warm longer."

"Works for me," Kerry said. She appreciated the effort, although right at this moment she was less concerned with technique and more with actually eating.

"Can you grab the bread?" Season asked. She was busy stirring the pasta and sauce, so Kerry picked up the potholders and went to the oven. Inside, the crusty garlic bread was just the right shade of golden brown. She drew it out and put it on the cutting board that Season indicated, carrying that to the table and setting it down.

"I think we're ready," Season announced. "What do you want to drink?"

"What is there?" Kerry asked. But at Season's smile, she answered for herself. "Oh, right—everything. I'll have a peach Snapple, I guess."

"It's in the fridge," Season said, putting the pasta into a serving dish. "Help yourself."

Kerry opened the refrigerator. There was indeed a peach Snapple there, on the top shelf.

And nothing else. Kerry took the bottle, leaving the refrigerator empty. She suspected it had not been empty a minute earlier, and probably wasn't now.

So Season had a sense of humor, on top of everything else. That was unexpected, but the kind of surprise—like this lunch—that Kerry could use more of.

After they had eaten—both largely silent, more interested in consuming than conversing—Kerry cleared the dishes and they retired to the living room to sit by the fire. Outside, night had fallen, but snowflakes continued to drop past the light from the cabin's windows. Season took a glass of red wine in and sat on the rug in front of the fireplace, setting her glass down on the hearth. She carried in a bowl of mixed nuts and a plate of cookies and put them on a coffee table. Kerry brewed some orange pekoe tea and joined her, taking a seat on a cushy couch. Season watched her get comfortable, a serious expression on her lovely face. She chewed a little on her lower lip, which Kerry found surprisingly girlish for someone as old as Season was.

Then again, if you get right down to it, walking and breathing are pretty girlish for someone as old as her. Especially if she's really Daniel's grandmother.

After a minute Season broke the silence. "You've got some questions,

Kerry," she said. "Not all at once, please. And I reserve the right not to answer everything right away. I'm tired, and I don't want to talk all evening."

This presented Kerry with a quandary. How would she know which questions to ask and which to avoid? There was so much she wanted to know— not just about the areas in which Season and Mother Blessing contradicted each other, but about Season's long war with Daniel, and about her powers and abilities. She was still furious at Season, but the long day with her had exposed a human side that she had never expected to find, and that tempered her rage somewhat. Season may have been a monster, but she wasn't all monster, all the time.

"Start at the beginning, then," she said finally. "What happened that day in Slocumb?"

Season shook her head. "Not tonight," she replied. "That story's too long for now. Next?"

Most of Kerry's questions were going to involve long, complex answers, she figured. She hoped Season wouldn't try to dodge them all. "Okay," she said after coming up with a different approach. "The way I see it, you killed three of my friends: Daniel Blessing, Mace Winston, and Josh Quinn. And poor old Edgar Brandvold. How can you justify murder?"

Season took a sip of wine and studied Kerry with her deep blue eyes. "Murder has been justified in human society since the first caveman clobbered another one over the head with a stick," she said. "But you're not here for a civics lesson, so I'll take them one at a time.

"Yes, I killed Daniel. From your reaction at the time, and some things you've said and done since then, I take it he meant something to you."

"We were in love," Kerry said quietly. She didn't want to start talking about that, didn't want to shed any tears for him in front of his murderer.

"I thought it was something like that. For your sake, I'm sorry. For my own, though—he had been chasing me for centuries, Kerry. We've battled many times, done some damage, but there was never anything final. Never a conclusion. I was tired of running, tired of having to look over my shoulder, of never sitting still or trusting anyone. And he was never going to let up."

"That's true."

"And I shouldn't need to remind you, Kerry, that when it happened, he attacked me. You were there. You saw it all. He hit me with everything he had, thought he had killed me. And I was hurt, bad. Just not as hurt as he believed."

Kerry remembered the day vividly, especially in her nightmares. It had happened just as Season described. They had trapped Season in her rented house—Daniel, Kerry, Brandy, Scott, Rebecca, and Josh—and lured her outside, where Daniel had unleashed a barrage of magical attacks against her. As Season said, she had gone down. Even Kerry thought she was finished. But from somewhere, she had summoned an unexpected reserve of strength. With Daniel's guard down she had been able to claim the advantage, and she had bested him, while Kerry and her friends looked on in horror.

"Okay, yeah," Kerry admitted. "That's true. But—"

"There are no buts, Kerry," Season said. "He would not have just given up. There was no talking to him, no rational discussion. He wanted me dead, and he wanted it to happen before the next Witches' Convocation. You know what that is?"

Mother Blessing had told Kerry about the Convocation, a gathering of witches held every five hundred years to discuss problems and techniques and to try witches accused of crimes. "Yes."

"If I thought he would let up, if he would have let me live until the Convocation, where I could have taken some legal action, that would have been fine. Obviously, I've spent the last few hundred years running and hiding, trying to avoid violence, instead of seeking him out and just finishing it off. But the closer we got to the Convocation, the more he came after me. Finally, I'd had enough. At that moment, with all of you there, he almost got me, and I did what I had to do."

Kerry didn't want to admit there was any truth at all in what Season was saying. She wanted to hold on to her anger, to wave it like a flag. Whatever the circumstances, Season had been the one who struck a fatal blow, not Daniel.

She knew, however, that Daniel would have if he'd been able. His intention had been to kill Season or die trying. She had simply held the better hand, or played her cards more skillfully. Either way, Season's version of things rang true.

"It happened more or less like that with Abraham, too—Daniel's brother. Have you heard about him?"

"Daniel said they ambushed you in your room," Kerry told her.

"That's right. And killed my lover. I fought back hard. I killed Abraham, and thought I had killed Daniel then too." She took another sip of wine and looked away from Kerry. "My life would have been a lot simpler if I'd made sure."

"What about Mace?" Kerry asked. "What threat was he to you?"

Season glanced up again. "I don't know the name. He was the one with the big blue car?"

"That was Suzie," Kerry replied. She was still stuffed from the meal, but she took a couple of nuts and nibbled on them. "The car, I mean. Yes, Mace had a big blue Lincoln."

"Yes. That one might have been avoidable," Season admitted. "I knew I had injured Daniel, but he'd escaped before I could finish him. I thought if I could track him down quickly enough, before he had healed . . . I could end things that much sooner. But he had come into contact with you and your friends, somehow, and he was screening you all from me. When that one—Mace, you said?"

"Right, Mace Winston. Kind of a hick, but sweet, you know?"

Season nodded, biting a cookie. "When he left your group, he suddenly came onto my radar. That's a metaphor, by the way—not real radar. So I interrupted his escape to question him about where Daniel might be found. He tried to resist. I admit that I overreacted. I didn't mean to kill him, but I did. I'm terribly sorry for that."

"Not so sorry that you didn't kill Josh, too."

Season looked confused. "I'm sorry? You mentioned that name before, too. I don't know who you mean."

"Oh, come on," Kerry said, anger simmering to the surface again. "Josh. Pale-faced Goth boy, Las Vegas. Do you kill so many people you can't remember them all?"

Season put her wineglass down and pointed a finger at Kerry. "Oh, now I know who you're talking about. I was there when he died, but I didn't kill him."

"He wrote your name in his own blood on the side of a slot machine," Kerry said.

"I didn't know that," Season admitted. "But it doesn't change anything. Maybe he wrote it because he recognized me, or because I was the last person to speak to him."

"Because you killed him."

"I didn't, Kerry," Season insisted. "I've admitted to the ones I did, even Mace, which was accidental. Why would I lie about this one?"

"Why did you talk to him, then?" Kerry pressed.

"He helped me, or tried to. A couple of Mother Blessing's simulacra were attacking me in the casino. He stepped in front of them, slowed them down. It was like—like he was trying to reason with them. You know simulacra?"

"I've met a few."

"Reasoning isn't their forte," Season understated. "If he was one of your friends, I would have thought he'd have been egging them on."

"He knew we were coming. We were in the parking structure, I think, when it happened. Or almost there. Maybe he wanted them to hold off until we arrived so we could all attack you together."

Season shrugged. "Perhaps. All I know is that the simulacra didn't react well to being thwarted. They removed your friend from their path the only way they knew how. After I dispatched them, I checked on him—on Josh—but it was too late. He was already fading. And casino security was on the way. I made him comfortable in his last moments, so at least he wouldn't be in pain, and I left."

Kerry found herself wanting to believe that, even though she didn't know if she should. But she liked the idea that Josh's death had been without pain.

"You said one other name, earlier," Season reminded her.

Daniel, Mace, Josh, Kerry thought. Those were the deaths she had carried around inside her for so long, the reasons she had wanted Season Howe dead. Then it came back to her. "Oh, yeah. Edgar Brandvold. Down in Wallaceton, Virginia. Outside the Swamp."

"Oh, right," Season said. "A longtime ally of Mother Blessing's."

"He did her favors from time to time," Kerry countered. "Brought her groceries, that kind of thing."

"More than that," Season said. "He was a kind of early warning system for her. She'd taught him a few tricks, and he patrolled the eastern border of the Swamp to make sure her privacy wasn't compromised. When I found him, he cast a spell, tried to tear my head off. But I've got pretty good reflexes. I dodged and counterattacked. His reflexes weren't so good."

"His walking stick was driven through his heart."

"A girl's gotta do what a girl's gotta do. It was a walking stick when you saw it. It was a serpent before that, with a mouth the size of a car door, trying to chomp on me."

The story sounded just ridiculous enough to be true. And Kerry had seen equally bizarre things. She had wondered why Season had killed Edgar—the man seemed ancient and frail, like he couldn't possibly have been a threat. It seemed clearer now.

"Okay, I guess I can buy that. So then, what—"

Season held up a hand to stop her. "That's enough for one night," she said. "I'm beat. Driving through that snow really took a lot out of me. And it's early enough that I can shower and get a good night's sleep. Let's turn in now, and we can talk more tomorrow."

"But—"

"If we don't go to sleep," Season cautioned, "then Santa Claus won't come."

"There isn't even a tree," Kerry pointed out. "Somehow, I doubt that Santa is going to visit this place. There aren't any good little girls here anyway."

"You might be surprised," Season said. "Never count the old guy out." She stood up and took the dirty dishes to the kitchen. "Tomorrow!" she called back over her shoulder.

"Okay," Kerry said. "But tomorrow everything's fair game."

"I promise."

And I'm going to hold you to that, Season, Kerry thought. *That's a promise you won't get out of.*

11

Kerry Profitt's diary, December 24

All righty, then.

It wouldn't be fair, I guess, to say that twenty-four hours ago I had been ready to kill Season Howe on sight. I had already decided at that point that I wanted to talk to her first, to try to get some things straight in my own mind. I wanted a clearer picture of what it was I had become involved in.

Then I would kill her.

And now . . .

Is it called the Stockholm Syndrome? Something like that. Wherein kidnap victims begin to identify with their captors, sometimes even helping protect them from the police. Although it's not fair, probably, to say that someone going, "Hey, let's take a ride so we can talk," and the other someone going, "Okay," is the same as being kidnapped.

She's not exactly holding me here against my will. Except it's not like I could leave, at least not easily, given that we are a million miles from civilization and I have no actual idea of where.

But I came willingly, and I don't feel like I'm in real danger from her. That could change. I'm not sure I'll sleep all that soundly tonight, and it has nothing to do with listening for reindeer hooves on the roof. But I don't think she'd have fed me and talked to me about having killed Daniel, and Mace, and Edgar, but not Josh, if she was just going to turn around and kill me.

I'm not sure, in fact, why she brought me here, why she agreed to tell me all this. Maybe that's something she'll reveal tomorrow.

That would be good, because I could sure use a clue here. Once again I'm feeling kind of out in the wilderness without a map, which is not only literally true but metaphorically as well. I still don't know what happened in Slocumb, but if Season is to be believed, then Mother Blessing, not Season, is really responsible for Josh's death. And Mother Blessing knew, when I got back to her place from Las Vegas, that I was devastated by what had happened there.

So why would she continue to let me think Season was responsible, if she knew full well that she wasn't? That would be . . .

Hello! Clue much? If she wanted some proxy stand-in to take over the hunt for Season when Daniel was gone, what better way to keep that person interested than throwing the body of a friend or two down and letting her think Season had done it?

And, once again, Kerry the slow-witted comes to realize there's much more to Mother Blessing than meets the eye. And none of it good.

So tonight. Kind of strange, sitting around with the killer of the man I loved, sharing cookies and nuts, drinking and talking. And underneath it all—also kind of strange—feeling like, hey, I'm glad I haven't killed her, because she's kind of neat.

"Kind of neat." Too old-fashioned? Kind of rad, maybe. Kind of phat. Whatever, it's Christmas Eve, and if there is ever a time when old-fashioned is apropos, this is it. "Apropos," also old-fashioned, methinks.

And "methinks," again also.

Methinks I'm dodging the central issue here, which has to do with not killing Season after all. But she makes a kind of sense that I am having a hard time disregarding. Yes, she killed Daniel, and I hate her for that. But she's right: He was trying to kill her. I really thought he had killed her. She was so brutalized, so still—I thought she was dead, and so did he. But she wasn't, and then he was, and it was just about that fast.

And tonight, when she was talking about the necessity of killing him and Abraham, she was looking right at me, flat and level, letting me see that she was telling me the truth. But then she turned away. Not like someone who was lying might, but . . . when she turned back, it looked like there might have been a tear in her eye.

A trick? Too much wine? Anything's possible, right? But the fact is, it looked like talking about their deaths choked her up.

Like, maybe, a grandmother would cry when talking about the deaths of her grandsons.

Sleep on that, Kerry Profitt.

It's almost midnight. Merry Christmas.

K.

"Merry Christmas!"

After coming down off the mountain, Scott had paid higher-than-premium fare for a short-term condo rental near Berlin, New Hampshire, offering enough to make the people who had really rented it happy to go bunk with friends, knowing that their ski holiday had netted them a significant profit. But he had figured they'd need a base of operations if they were going to have any hope of finding Kerry.

"They" came at seven o'clock on Christmas morning. Scott woke to their insistent ringing. Bleary-eyed, he pawed for his glasses. He had slept poorly, worrying about Kerry, but a couple of hours ago had finally drifted off. Then the doorbell started in. On the way out of the bedroom he caught a glimpse of himself in the mirror—bed-head sent his brown hair shooting off in every direction at once. He had slept in a T-shirt and boxers, so he tugged on yesterday's jeans, then opened the door for Brandy and Rebecca, who, in spite of having been on the road for hours and hours, both looked at least ten times more awake than he felt. They entered with holiday greetings at least twenty times more cheerful than he could return, given the circumstances.

"Hey, you guys," he said. Brandy accepted a quick hug, even returning it with a couple of friendly pats on the back. Her familiar, slightly fruity scent brought a rush of emotion flooding into him, even more than the sight and feel of her did.

"Did we wake you?"

"Well, it's either that or I always look this bad," Scott said. "I'll hope for the former."

Brandy shook off her vintage fake-fur-lined coat and handed it to Scott. Fortunately, the place had come with a standing coatrack, so he didn't have to try to figure out someplace to put it. "You don't look—well, okay, yes you do. You look awful. You want to get some more sleep?"

He turned to Rebecca, who squeezed him tighter than Brandy had. "Don't listen to her," Rebecca said. "Anyone has a right to look like they spent the night under a bus if they want to."

"Gee, thanks, Beck," Scott said, stifling a yawn. "I'll make coffee. You want some?"

Brandy shook her head. Underneath her coat she wore a red wool turtleneck and brown denim pants. Her hair was tightly braided and lay close to her scalp. "Caffeine is what got us here. I think we sampled every energy drink on the market. If I have any more, I'll start bouncing off your walls. Which, by the way, nice place. How'd you score it?"

"Found someone willing to accept a wheelbarrow full of cash. Don't tell the landlord, because he doesn't know."

Brandy smiled. "You're becoming very resourceful, Scott," she said. "Good job."

"Definitely," Rebecca added. She doffed her puffy blue ski coat, revealing a gray UC Santa Cruz sweatshirt with pink corduroy pants and black lace-up pleather boots.

"You don't know the half of it." He was thinking of the gun he'd acquired. That had been resourceful. *And stupid,* he added.

"I'm sure not." Brandy went into the living room, furnished in Modern Rental oaks and earth tones, and took a seat on a sofa.

"Have a seat," he said, after the fact.

"Thanks," Rebecca replied. *Other people are always more polite than exes,* Scott observed. He crossed through the living room into the condo's kitchenette to start the coffee. He needed a jolt, even if no one else did.

"What do we do now?" Brandy asked. "Is there a plan?"

Scott was suddenly, unreasonably infuriated by her. "I don't know, Brandy! I don't have a plan. All I know is that Kerry is out there somewhere, that Season's got her, and we have to find them!"

Brandy got up off the sofa, putting her hands out. "Whoa, Scott. I know you're frantic over this. I am too, believe me. But let's keep our eye on the real problem, okay? Don't take your frustrations out on me."

"Yeah, I'm sorry, Brandy," he said, deflated just as quickly as he had blown up. She was right, he wasn't mad at her. He was just mad.

"I was looking at a New Hampshire map on the way here," Brandy pointed out. "And there must be, like, thousands of square miles of wilderness up here."

"Probably," he agreed glumly. He stared at the coffee, willing it to brew faster. He was either going to have to go back to bed or down the whole pot, and Brandy seemed intent on talking.

"So how are we going to—"

"Brandy!" he interrupted, unable to keep his emotions in check. "I just said I don't have a plan, okay? I don't know how we're going to find her! I just know that we have to—that if we don't, Season's going to kill her! That's what she does."

"Okay, you guys," Rebecca said, obviously uneasy with their arguing. "We'll figure something out. Or she'll get in touch with us. Have you tried her phone lately?"

"I tried it all day and night yesterday. She's out of range, or else she has it turned off."

"That'll make things tougher," Brandy pointed out. "But there's got to be a way. You know where you lost them, right?"

"Yeah, basically," Scott replied. "But it was snowing like crazy. I'm pretty sure I can find it again, but there are no tracks or anything."

"But maybe we can come up with some kind of organized search pattern," Rebecca suggested. "Mark off a grid and take it section by section."

"We'd have to have snowmobiles for that," Scott countered. "It's really wilderness up there—not many roads, lots of open country and forest."

"But they were in a car of some kind," Brandy said. "So there must be a way to get to where they are on roads."

"They were in a Jeep," Scott answered. "They were sticking to roads as far as I saw, but it's possible that they didn't have to. They could have taken some little dirt road, or even left the roads altogether."

"You still have the RAV4, right?" Rebecca asked him.

"Yeah," he said. "It's got four-wheel drive, but it's not the off-roader the Jeep is. They could definitely get to places I can't."

"Okay," Brandy said. "But at least it gives us a place to start. And if we get going soon, we'll have a full day of light. The longer we sit around here the less time we'll have to search."

That was true, Scott knew. But the coffeemaker was just beginning to fill the pot. He had not had enough sleep to function at his best all day. While he knew that caffeine was no substitute for sleep, it looked like it was the best he was going to get.

Rebecca had gone almost immediately to Grand Central Station upon receiving the anxious call from Brandy. She had been expecting it ever since Kerry had taken off for New Hampshire. Kerry was brave and smart, but she wouldn't be able to cope with Season all by herself. It had been stupid of Rebecca to let her go off and try. She had hoped that Kerry could keep Scott out of trouble, but now it seemed she was in danger herself. That knowledge was the only reason Rebecca had been willing to come, to risk facing Season again. Kerry should have gathered them all from the beginning—not that there was much the rest of them could have done that Kerry couldn't, but at least they'd have been together. Taking them one by one seemed to be Season's standard procedure, and they couldn't let her continue to do that.

Her parents had been upset, but not outrageously so. Their holiday was over anyway. She had been on a train within an hour. Four hours after that—four hours of increasing anxiety, mingled with some outright terror—she was in Boston.

Brandy met her at the train station looking terrible—her eyes bloodshot and puffy, the skin under her nose raw. She had obviously been crying.

Once they were settled in the car, heading out of town, she had asked Brandy what was wrong.

"It's just . . . this whole thing stinks," Brandy answered. "I'm seeing this great new guy—his name is Adam, you'd love him, Rebecca. Really, you would. Anyway, things have been moving kind of fast, and it seems like we're pretty serious about each other. He was going to go with me to my folks' house for Christmas dinner. We were both super nervous about it, but I was looking forward to it too, because Adam is really mature and charming and everything. He would have blown Mom away."

"But then, you know, Scott had to go all *America's Most Wanted* on us."

Rebecca was shocked. "Brandy! It's not like he made Season take her."

"No, I know," Brandy admitted. "I don't mean to make light of it. Kerry's in trouble and we've got to be there for her, just like she would be for us. It's just—the timing was incredibly sucky. I told Adam I had to cancel, and he was all pouty and sad. I think it would have been better if he'd been mad, but he wasn't. He was just, 'Okay, if that's what you really want to do.' Which, of course, it's not. But it's what I have to do, and he didn't seem to get that."

"What did your parents say?" Rebecca asked.

Brandy concentrated on her driving for a minute. Rebecca figured she was probably trying to compose a response. "Let's just say they weren't happy," she said finally. "Mom just about blew a gasket. 'I've been cooking for three days! Everyone's expecting to see you, and to meet Adam! What do you mean, you have to go?' That kind of thing. DJ thought it was Adam's fault somehow and offered to break his legs."

"You tell him to break Season's instead?"

"If I dared to tell him about Season, he'd try it. And of course she'd fry him."

"Like she'll do to us if she gets a chance."

"Well, yeah," Brandy agreed. "Anyway, there was a scene. Mom shrieking, Dad kind of humphing, DJ storming around hitting things. It wasn't pretty."

"Doesn't sound like it."

Rebecca was glad to be with Brandy, happy to see her friend in spite of the unpleasant reason for the reunion. Conversation drifted to less emotionally charged topics as the miles melted away behind them. The farther north they went, the worse the weather grew, until what should have been a four-hour drive turned into eight. Christmas carols and caffeine helped them stay alert and on the road, but even those things couldn't help stave off the very real horror Rebecca felt as they got closer to where Season had last been seen. Rebecca worried about Kerry, but she worried about herself and the others, too.

And now they were here, in Scott's emergency rental. And Kerry, the reason for their hurried trip, was somewhere out there.

12

Kerry slept better than she'd expected—*better than I had a right to, under the circumstances,* she thought—and when she got up in the morning, donning the fuzzy terry cloth robe that hung on the back of her bedroom door, Season was already busy in the kitchen. The cabin smelled like bacon and garlic, which were both happy aromas as far as she was concerned.

"Merry Christmas," Season said when she saw her. She wore a white sweater with a red reindeer shape on it and black pants.

"Merry Christmas," Kerry echoed. "That smells great."

"I hope you're hungry," Season said. "There are omelets, garlic home fries, bacon, and juice. And I made a pot of Earl Grey."

"Mmm," Kerry said. "Sounds wonderful."

"Well, you were right. Santa didn't find us. So I figured we could eat our sorrows away."

"I'm in favor of that idea." Kerry still felt strange, socializing like this with Season. But she had slept all night under the witch's roof, and she had not been attacked. She was still here, still in one piece. The more she got to know Season, the more she believed that they had all been wrong about her. Not completely wrong, since she had admitted to killing Mace and Daniel. But wrong in some very significant ways nonetheless.

A few minutes later Season had dished up breakfast, and Kerry sat across from her at the table. The food tasted delicious—Season could become a chef, if she ever decided to give up the witch gig.

They ate in relative silence, Kerry realizing with the first few mouthfuls how truly ravenous she was. After they were done and Kerry was washing dishes, Season made her an offer.

"For your Christmas present," she said, "I'll answer ten questions for you."

"Just ten?" Kerry replied.

"Choose carefully," Season admonished with a smile. "Now you're down to nine."

"Oh, jeez," Kerry said. "It's going to be like that? That wasn't a question, so don't count it."

"Whenever you're ready," Season said. "Have you looked outside? We're not going anywhere today, so I'm not in any hurry."

Kerry hadn't, but she wasn't surprised. The way the snow had still been coming down when she'd gone to bed, she would have been amazed if any of the roads they took here had still been passable.

Nine questions, though. And she had to be careful how she phrased them, obviously. It wouldn't do to waste another one.

She finished washing out the last pan and pulled a towel from its hook to begin drying. "Okay," she said. "Here goes. Is Mother Blessing your real daughter?"

Season looked directly at her. "Yes," she said simply.

"I hope that's not all the elaboration I get," Kerry said, careful to phrase it as a statement.

"I'm not trying to be difficult, Kerry," Season said. "But there are rules about this kind of thing. And before you spend a question asking what kind of thing I mean, I'll just tell you: Witches aren't supposed to give non-witches unnecessary information about our kind."

"But I am—I mean, I'm becoming a witch. Mother Blessing was teaching me. She said you didn't have to be born a witch, but you could be trained."

"And she was right. That's the only reason I'm giving you this chance now. If you were completely non-witch, you wouldn't even get this much.

Daniel broke more rules than you'll ever know when he told you everything he did. Had he survived until the Convocation, he'd have been severely disciplined."

"Well, I think that sucks," Kerry said. "He loved me, and he wanted to protect me."

"I didn't say that I thought he did anything wrong," Season said. "Only that he broke the rules. I'm trying to be more careful. But I won't leave you with just yes or no answers. Yes, she is my daughter. She wasn't always, as you might guess, called Mother Blessing. When she was born, her father and I called her Myrtle. It was traditional in those days for the children of witches to have names from nature."

She stopped, and Kerry guessed that meant the answer was complete. She was going to have to be very careful, with just eight questions remaining. She could jump around, asking the first things that came to mind. But that would probably be a good way of ensuring that when they were done, big holes in her understanding remained. She had to play it smarter to make sure she got the whole story.

With the last of the dishes dried, she came out from behind the kitchen counter. She still hadn't dressed, but it was a lazy Christmas Day and she didn't care. The fuzzy robe kept her warm and comfortable. "Let's sit down," she suggested.

Season followed her to the living room. As on the night before, a fire crackled in the fireplace, giving the room a homey, pleasant feel. Kerry sat in a soft chair while Season stretched out on the couch.

"Who was Mother Blessing's father, then?" she asked.

"His name was Forest. We married young—but then, everyone did in those days. That was in 1649, in England. Charles I was beheaded, Charles II crowned, and I was married, all in the same year. It was an eventful time."

"Sounds like it."

"Anyway, Forest and I had many good years together. We moved to the colonies, where it seemed there was more freedom, and we were less likely to be hanged for witchcraft. I was pregnant before I learned that Forest was, in fact, evil—he had been hiding it well, but not well enough, as it turned out. I left him and moved to Slocumb with young Myrtle, my only child. We were happy there, for a while, and the people came to accept my skills, seeking my help when they needed something I could provide.

"But Myrtle, as it happened, inherited her father's nature, not mine. Evil can only be repressed for so long; eventually it reveals itself. The same happened, sadly, with Myrtle. I think having a child herself set it off."

A child? Kerry wondered. She had only ever heard about Daniel and Abraham—twins, and born after Slocumb's demise. She had to ask.

"What happened to that child?"

"I think I want more tea," Season said instead of answering. "How about you?"

"No, I'm fine," Kerry replied.

Season went into the kitchen, and came back a moment later with a steaming mug. "Sorry," she said. "All this talking makes my throat dry."

"That's okay," Kerry assured her.

"You wanted to know what became of my first grandson. That's part of a longer story. The easy answer is, he died, but you want more than that. I won't count that one, but find another way to ask."

Kerry thought that over. That question had almost been wasted, because she had been suckered into rushing it. She didn't want to do that again. After a minute, she had figured out how to phrase it. "What was the progression of events that led to the destruction of Slocumb?"

Season smiled, and Kerry felt like a student who has come up with the correct answer to a tough problem. "Are you comfortable, Kerry?" she asked. "Don't have to go to the bathroom or anything? Because this one might need a long answer."

Kerry performed a quick mental diagnosis. "I'm fine," she said. "Go ahead."

"All right." Season sipped her tea and smiled again. "Well done, by the way."

"Thanks."

"As I said, Myrtle and I lived in Slocumb. She grew to adulthood there, married a man named Winthrop Blessing—a useless man, I'm afraid, of small mind and scant courage—and had a child of her own. Again, I think it was that event that somehow brought out her dark side. I had been well liked in Slocumb, and Myrtle had been too, until then.

"But she was her father's daughter, after all. Things began to happen in Slocumb, sinister things. Children disappearing, or dying young. Crops failing. Lights appearing in the Swamp, leading hunters to their deaths. Animals going rogue, terrorizing the townsfolk.

"I should have known it was her, should have been able to stop it. But I was blinded, I guess. She was my daughter, and even though we had been estranged by that time, I still couldn't bring myself to suspect anything like that. Besides, it had been a long time since I had known Forest, so I guess I had forgotten just how horrible some witches could be.

"What I didn't know was that Forest had come to town. Somehow he heard that he had a grandson—Darius, she had called him, having already abandoned the tradition of naming children from nature and begun to express her perverse irony by choosing biblical names—and he wanted to see the boy. So he sought Myrtle out—or Mother Blessing, as she called herself by then. He didn't tell me he was there, gave me no indication that he had come to visit. But when he and Myrtle got together, they fed one another's madness."

Season paused for a minute. She was staring into space as she talked, with a complete lack of self-consciousness. Kerry thought Season was remembering too deeply, the pain of long-ago events drawing itself clearly on her face.

"If you want to finish this later . . . ," Kerry offered.

But Season shook her head. "No, I'm sorry. I'll keep going. There was an—an incident. A widow with three young children woke one morning to find all three children dead, horribly, brutally slaughtered in their beds. Wolf tracks were seen outside in a light snow that had fallen, although no one believed that a wolf had climbed in through a window and silently murdered three children.

"The whole town was up in arms. Some blamed me, some blamed Mother Blessing. I knew it must have been her, of course. But by that point, nobody wanted to listen to reason. They wanted all witches gone, or better yet, dead, and they set out to make that happen.

"Cornered, Mother Blessing and Forest fought back, hard. I did too—fighting for my own life. The town, not that big to begin with, became a magical battleground where no one was safe. Before it was all over, the townspeople had killed Forest and Darius. Mother Blessing's response to that—to two deaths she had prompted in the first place—was to go mad, to level the whole town.

"I tried to stop her, but she was beyond control at that point, her fury having made her a wild woman. And then, to top it off, when the town was a smoking ruin and people from other towns nearby came to offer help, she blamed me. I had been injured in the battle, could barely defend myself, and suddenly they were raising a virtual army against me, going town to town to recruit able-bodied men willing to chase me into the Swamp.

"So I did the only thing I could do. I ran. My grandson, my former husband, my daughter's husband, had all died, and I was made to run like a coward. I found out later that not only did my daughter tell the locals that I was responsible for the devastation in Slocumb, but she went to every witch she could find and spread the same story. Her version of things has become the accepted wisdom, while I've never had a chance to tell mine. Not in any official way, at least."

Kerry sat silently when Season was done, taking it all in. It was much like the story that Mother Blessing had told Daniel, which Kerry had read in his journal. But it was unlike it in other ways, important ways. Ways that rang true to her. In Daniel's version, Mother Blessing had escaped the town before the worst of the destruction began, but still somehow managed to know what had happened, point by point. Season admitted to having stayed through the worst of it, only to leave after the fact when she was blamed for her daughter's crimes.

"I guess I'll have some of that tea now," Kerry said after a little while.

"Do you believe me?" Season asked her.

"I still don't know what to believe," Kerry admitted. She went into the kitchen for some of Season's Earl Grey. In a small microwave oven, she heated a cup. "But what you say makes sense, I think. I'm surprised Daniel never said anything about there being another brother."

"I doubt if she ever told him," Season said. "By the time he was born, she had cemented her story. I was responsible. If she brought Forest and Darius into it, that might have muddied the waters."

"I guess that's true," Kerry said, sitting back down with her tea. "We can take a break if you want."

"I'm okay," Season said. "Thanks for offering, but let's just keep going."

"All right," Kerry said. *Glutton for punishment,* she thought. If this had been her playing true confessions—not that she had much to confess—she'd have been ready for a time-out. But she had thought of her next question, one to which she already had Mother Blessing's answer. "What happens next, in terms of Slocumb? I understand the Witches' Convocation is coming up."

"That's correct," Season said. "Next spring. There I'll finally get a chance to tell my side of the story, and Mother Blessing will tell hers. It'll be a fair hearing, the first one there's been. One of us will be acquitted and the other will have to pay some penalty.

"But there are more important things at stake here. I doubt that Mother Blessing talks about this much, because she's on the wrong side of it. There is a balance of power in the world, an eternal struggle between order and chaos. Mostly these are natural forces at play. Nature has a tendency toward entropy, but at the same time, its designs are magnificently detailed and precise. Think of a forest left completely on its own—trees grow, trees fall, the underbrush goes wild, until the whole place is completely chaotic—you could never find your way through it. But at the same time, think about the complicated interrelationship between species that allows the forest to grow. Think about the precision with which you can measure the age of the tree by counting its rings. The struggle never ends.

"But witches can help push it toward their preferred way. I try to battle for order. Even my garden, when I had the time and opportunity to grow one, was structured, arranged formally, weeded and tended on a daily basis. No overgrown forest for me.

"Mother Blessing and her sons have kept me on the run so much, though, that I haven't had much time to pull my weight. The scales are tipping—slowly at first, but now faster and faster—toward chaos. If she keeps me from making my contribution—or worse, if she can go to the Convocation and have my powers stripped—then it'll be very hard to stop her from getting her way. Every witch must play his or her part in the balance, and without me in the mix, our side is losing.

"So the Convocation is terribly important, for a number of reasons. But just as important, Mother Blessing can't be allowed to keep me out of action. Things have become too unstable, too desperate."

Kerry wasn't quite sure how to respond to that. It was a whole new and unexpected level. Season was right—Mother Blessing had never given the slightest indication that the stakes were so high. Kerry had been led to believe that, while there might be lives at stake, they were primarily those of witches and of people who had accidentally been drawn into their battles. But now Season's talk of order and chaos made it seem like those few lives were just the tip of the proverbial iceberg, and many, many more might hang in the balance.

"Now I need a break," Kerry said. "That's a lot to take in."

"I know," Season agreed. "I would have broken it to you in an easier way if I could have, but you have to have all the data if you're going to understand it."

"Well, I'm feeling pretty data-rich at this point. I'd like to knock off for a while. Maybe a soak in the tub would help me absorb some of this."

"Sure, no problem," Season said. "You've still got five questions to go."

13

Scott drove Rebecca and Brandy back up to the point where he'd lost Season and Kerry. Snow had covered the little side road, as he had thought, but it had stopped falling, at least for a while, and a heavy gray sky sat atop the peaks as if tethered to them. In four-wheel drive he was able to get up the road to where it forked. From there both roads were buried under drifts—a formless expanse of white spreading in every direction, with trees and snow-topped mountains as background.

"This is where I don't know which way they went," he explained. "I tried one direction for a while, but the snow was falling so heavily I was afraid I'd get stuck. I worked my way back down the hill, and that's when I went into town."

"But that was late yesterday," Brandy observed. "So we don't know if they're still in this area. Or if this was just a back road they took up into Canada or something."

"That's true," Scott admitted.

"Which means we could drive around up here for days, looking for all kinds of side tracks off into the mountains," Rebecca said, "and still never get close to them."

"That's what I'm thinking," Brandy said. "Maybe if we had a helicopter or, I don't know, a spy satellite or something, then this would be a reasonable way to search for them. But without that, this is really a wild goose chase."

Scott stopped the SUV and gripped the wheel, looking glumly at Brandy in the passenger seat. "I told you I didn't have a plan."

"I know," Brandy said mockingly. "And I fully expected that from you."

He made a face at her. "Don't start, Brandy . . ."

"Don't either of you start," Rebecca wailed. "I hate it that you're not together, and if you guys argue I'm just going to cry."

"Crying's not going to help," Scott said. "I should know. I thought I was going to bawl like an infant yesterday when I lost them."

"Because that would have been so manly?"

"Brandy!" Rebecca poked her in the shoulder. Scott caught the motion, and Brandy's wince, out of the corner of his eye and felt secretly glad. Rebecca may not have been on his side, but she wasn't going to sit idly by and let Brandy torment him either.

"So, Mrs. Einstein, do you have any better ideas?" he asked.

If Brandy felt insulted by the nickname, she didn't show it. "We're here now," she replied. "We might as well make the effort. If you couldn't travel much farther, maybe they couldn't either—or maybe they didn't have to. They might be just around the corner."

Scott looked at the snow, the trees. "If there were any corners."

"It's a figurative corner," Brandy shot back. "Like the figurative corners on your blockhead."

"If you guys don't quit it, I'm going to get out and walk," Rebecca threatened.

"That'd probably be a better way to find them," Brandy opined. "More likely to see their tracks than from a car."

"But also cold," Scott added.

"There is that," Rebecca agreed. "And with my delicate constitution, not to mention thin blood from all that time in California, maybe I'd better not. So you guys just chill out."

"I'm sorry, Rebecca," Brandy said, turning in her seat to regard their friend. "I guess there's a little leftover tension here, and we're trying to defuse it in a, sort of, you know, good-natured way."

Scott couldn't restrain a bitter laugh. "A *little* tension?"

Brandy turned back to him. "We're riding in a car together and we haven't pulled out any sharp objects," she said. "I'd call that pretty minor."

"Could we, maybe, start looking for Kerry?" Rebecca pleaded. "This is worse than being with you both when all you wanted to do was make out."

Scott remembered those days fondly. He still cared about Brandy—probably still loved her, if he let himself accept the truth. But he knew now that he loved Kerry more. If anything happened to her—if, by his reluctance to interfere yesterday when he'd seen Season leading her away, she was injured or killed—he didn't know how he would live with himself. He guessed that he would be like Kerry had been when Season killed Daniel—driven by lust for revenge. And next time, when he had Season in his sights, he wouldn't back down, wouldn't allow himself to be afraid. He was already regretting having thrown that gun away. No way to find it, not before the spring thaw, and by then, he guessed, the moisture would have ruined it.

But he couldn't let himself think like that for more than a couple of moments, or he'd be drawn into a spiral of despondency. Kerry was safe, she was alive, and he would find her before anything bad happened. He *had* to.

He put the RAV4 into low gear and felt its tires slip a little before they bit through the snow to grip the road. This time he took the left fork that he had ignored before. "We're going this way," he announced, hoping to change the subject away from the uncomfortable topic of him and Brandy. "Keep your eyes peeled for any sign of them."

"I always wondered about that phrase," Rebecca said. "Is that peeling your eyes like they were grapes? Peeling grapes is hard, and I'm not sure it would actually help you see better."

"I think the implication is that your eyelids are the peel," Brandy told her. "So by peeling your eyes, you're opening them."

"Why not just say 'Keep your eyes open,' then? Makes a lot more sense than peeled."

"If old sayings made sense," Scott ventured, "they probably wouldn't be so memorable. 'A stitch in time saves nine'? It'd be just as easy to say something like, 'Hey, better fix that before it gets worse.' I mean, why nine? Because it sort of rhymes with time, only not really?"

"Yeah," Brandy put in. "Or 'One bad apple ruins the whole bunch.' Does it really? And if it does, how long do you have to leave it in there before they're all ruined? If you leave it long enough, is it really that apple ruining it, or just the fact that you've ignored your apples too long?"

"I thought it was 'One bad apple doesn't ruin the whole bunch,'" Rebecca said.

"Well, then," Brandy said, suitably chastened. "I guess that's different."

The road was hard to follow, and Scott let the conversation continue on without him while he gave all his focus to crawling forward, cutting through the drifted snow without losing the packed earth underneath. This direction led into a meadow scooped from the mountains as if with a shallow spoon. In spring it would probably be a riot of color as wildflower blooms filled its grassy expanse, but now it was just more white in a landscape of it. At the other side of the meadow, Scott could see where the roadway carved a notch through a stand of pines. The SUV growled as he pushed on and up, and a few minutes later they passed into the shade of the trees. There hadn't been much sun to begin with, and now that it was gone, a chill enveloped the vehicle. Scott shivered and cranked the heater up another notch.

He hoped his sudden chill was just from the temperature outside and not from anything else—not from any sense of foreboding that came from heading into the deep woods.

But he wouldn't have put money on it.

Somehow Christmas Day often seemed like the longest day of the year, although Kerry knew it wasn't. She supposed it must be the lack of pressing commitments. People didn't expect much of others on Christmas, most businesses were closed so there wasn't much reason to leave home, and relaxing was the order of the day.

In Season's New Hampshire refuge, the same rule applied. The witch had indicated that leaving would be almost impossible, so deep was the snow outside. After their morning talk, Kerry had taken a long bath, letting the hot water soak her completely. Then she had dressed, checked in on Season, and gone back to her room for a nap.

But sleep wasn't in the cards for her. She sprawled on the bed for a while, tossed and turned, tried to get comfy. But her mind was racing, everything Season had told her roiling around in it trying to find purchase. It seemed every time she believed she had a handle on how the world was really laid out, she discovered new information that completely redrew the map. *Christopher Columbus must have felt this way,* she thought. *Only, sometimes I think I really am sailing right off the edge.*

When she needed grounding, needed to reconnect to those things in her crazy life that seemed to truly make sense, she turned to Daniel Blessing. All she had left of him now were memories and his journals, so she took one of those heavy leather volumes from her duffel bag and slipped off the thong that held it closed. Turning a few pages, she found a passage she had never read.

> *The town wasn't much more than a flat spot where someone had scraped away the desert and built a couple of saloons, a church or three, a stable, a jail, and a random scattering of houses. I hadn't come for the scenery, however, or for the fine cuisine. I had come in search of a man named Stearns, who, I was told, had a score to settle with Season Howe and maybe reason to know where she was. Seeing as I had a score or two of my own, I reckoned maybe we could be friends.*

When I rode in this afternoon, it was through brutal, punishing sun and heat. My horse was stumbling for the last half mile or so, even though I imagined he could smell the water waiting at the stable. I imagined that I could smell it too, and gave some thought to leaving the horse there if he fell and finishing the trip on foot.

Luckily, the horse held out. We covered that last stretch and made it to the relatively cool shade of the livery stable, where he dunked his muzzle into the trough and drank deep. It was all I could do not to join him, but I left him there and headed to the nearest saloon. A sign painted on the wall above the door said it was the Lucky Sack, but there wasn't much about it that looked lucky to me.

I had never let that stop me in the past, and wasn't about to now. I walked in out of the dusty late afternoon sunlight. A barkeep stood behind a plank balanced across two barrels, with a row of bottles and some glasses on a shelf behind him. Eight other men, mostly crowded around two tables but for a couple of lone drinkers, looked up when I entered. I suppose I must have looked like a threat—a stranger, rare in these parts to begin with, and one who carried a Colt strapped to his side. I almost never used the gun, of course. I had other, more effective weapons at my disposal. But I carried it to forestall any questions about why I wasn't armed, which had come up with depressing regularity until I'd bought this one.

I ordered a whiskey and a water from the barkeep, a portly fellow in a stained shirt and fraying suspenders holding up his britches. He put two glasses down in front of me without a smile. I did smile as I put my coins on his plank, overpaying by a wide margin.

"That's too much," he said.

"Not necessarily," I said. "You have rooms to let here?"

"Couple, upstairs. You might have to share."

"That's okay," I told him. I drank the water down, asked for another one. He brought it. This time he smiled a little, or at least his bushy mustache twitched.

"Anything else?" he asked.

Parched, I drained the second water. "Yeah," I said when I was done. "I'm looking for a man named Stearns. Know him?"

The barkeep blanched visibly. "Never heard of him."

"You always turn white when you hear a name for the first time?" I asked him.

"I didn't," he said. He turned away and started to wipe out glasses with a filthy rag.

"You did," I said. "And I hope you didn't dry these glasses with that thing."

"Look, mister, you don't like the way I do business, you can just move along."

"I got nothing against your business practices," I said, which wasn't entirely true. "I just don't like being lied to."

When he came back over to me his voice was low and the look on his face was surly. "I don't need the trouble, okay?" he said with a snarl. "Sayin' that name out loud around here is like askin' for a fight to start."

"One starts, I'll finish it," I said softly. "Just tell me where I can find this Stearns."

He looked around like he was afraid someone would jump him if he talked to me, and then he leaned closer, still wiping out a glass with that rag. "I couldn't tell you if I wanted to," he whispered. "People don't find Stearns. He finds them."

"What does that mean?" I asked. "Either he lives somewhere around here or he doesn't."

"That's what you'd think," the barkeep said. "But it ain't always the truth."

I couldn't figure out what he was talking about, but I knew

better than to push too hard. Surely few knew better than I that things weren't always what they seemed, and that sometimes asking questions only revealed answers that you didn't really want to know.

"So just by asking you about him, he'll come to me?"

"If he wants to," the barkeep answered. "He don't do things he don't want to do, way I hear it."

"A man of mystery."

"Don't laugh about him," the barkeep warned me. "Way I hear it, he don't like that."

"Well, give me a room, then," I said. "I'll have some dinner and then see if old Mr. Stearns pays me a visit."

And I did just what I said I would. I wandered around the town, what there was of it, for a little while. Ate some stringy steak and biscuits for dinner, and then went up to the room, which in fact I didn't have to share. And I waited. Eventually, I slept.

I didn't even hear him come into the room, which is rare for me. I woke up when I heard the click of his revolver. When I opened my eyes he was pointing it at me.

"You must be Stearns."

"What makes you think so?"

"I was told if I looked for you, you'd find me."

He smiled. The room was dark but there was some moonlight leaking in through a window, and I could see that he was lean and rangy, with a droopy mustache and some gold in his teeth. His eyes were narrow and dark, and I had the feeling they didn't miss much. The pistol in his hand looked like it had seen plenty of use. There was no shake there, either, like there usually would have been when someone snuck into another man's room and pointed a gun at him. Mr. Stearns was just as calm as he could be.

"Why were you looking?" he asked.

"We have a mutual acquaintance," I said. I sat up a little

in the bed now, my hands spread on the blanket in front of me so he could see I wasn't making a play for the Colt. "Name of Season Howe."

"Not sure I know that name," he said.

"No one around here seems to know anyone else," I said. "You don't have to worry that I'm a friend of hers or anything. I aim to kill her."

Stearns smiled at that, uncocked his gun, and slid it into his holster. "Well, why didn't you say so?" he asked. "What do you call yourself?"

I told him my name. He nodded slowly, as if he had to think on it for a while. "What's your gripe with Season Howe?" he asked after a bit.

"Let's just say she owes a price that's bigger than she can pay in this lifetime," I said. Not knowing Stearns, I didn't want to go into detail.

"That's true," he said. "You don't know the half of it."

"I know enough."

"Sounds like you've really got it in for her," Stearns said. "I like the sound of that. And I can see you're a man who can handle her."

This man Stearns was full of surprises. "What makes you say that?"

"Well, being a witch and all, I mean. Same as her, that's all."

Which was what I thought he was getting at, but I didn't expect he'd come right out and say. He said it without hesitation, like he just knew it was true. So I didn't see any reason to deny it. I just sat there on that uncomfortable slab of a bed staring at him.

"You're wondering how I know," Stearns said. "Can't blame you." He moved closer to me, tilting his head up toward the ceiling. Beneath the edge of his whiskers I could clearly see the raw, choppy line where his throat had been cut. "I got a score to settle too, but I can't do it by myself," he said. To demonstrate further, he reached toward my bed, but his hand passed right through it with no resistance.

"I can see how that might be a problem for you," I admitted.

"Reckon you'll have to set things right for both of us," he said. "I can tell you where to find her—information is easy to come by on this side of the divide. She's in Durango. I don't know for how long, so I'd be on my way in the morning if I was you."

I was going to say something else, but didn't. Next thing I knew, I was waking up at first light. The whole thing might have been a dream—there's no sign that Stearns was ever here at all. So I'm putting this down just as it happened, in case I forget any of the details later.

After I get some breakfast in me, I'm lighting out for Durango. I have a feeling it wasn't a dream.

And I have a feeling that if I pass the town cemetery on the way out and look at the markers there, I'll see one with the name "Stearns" on it.

I remain,

Daniel Blessing, Twentieth of July, 1871

Kerry closed up the book and put it back in her bag. She knew there was a long tradition of ghost stories at Christmas—even the old chestnut "A Christmas Carol" was a ghost story, after all. This one she would once have read as a ghost story and felt a little shiver at, but knowing that Daniel had put it down—and that, at least when he wrote it, he believed every word he wrote—gave her a serious case of the creeps. Sure she had seen plenty of strange and spooky things over these past few months, but this little tale struck her as especially frightening.

Still, somehow she couldn't help feeling a little encouraged by what she had read too. There were times when she felt like she was the only person who was constantly surprised by others—like she just didn't have a handle on who people were and how they acted. She was glad to know that Daniel could be fooled too.

Maybe she hadn't been wrong to trust Mother Blessing. At least until she showed her true colors. Lacking evidence that someone presented themselves as something other than what they were, a person could go crazy not trusting anyone. *And where,* she wondered, *would that get you? That's probably why people become hermits—living in caves because they just don't know who they can believe and who they can't.*

Kerry preferred to trust first, and doubt, if there was a reason to, later. She had doubted Season—with perfectly good reason—but now that seemed to be turning around. Would it turn into trust? No telling yet. But that possibility was open now, where it wouldn't have been even a few days before.

She thought that, in some way, Daniel might approve.

14

Scott kept cranking the heat higher and higher, but the air outside grew colder as the afternoon dragged on. Brandy zipped up her coat and shoved her hands into her fleece gloves. But she didn't get really nervous until Scott said, "You know what would really stink? Running out of gas up here."

"Yeah, that would stink, all right," Rebecca agreed. "Does running your heat use extra gas?"

"I know running the air-conditioning does," Scott said. "I guess heat probably does too."

"Turn it off, then, if you're getting low," Brandy urged.

"But we'll freeze," Scott protested.

"We'll freeze if we run out of gas," Brandy countered. "Or have you seen a service station that I missed somewhere in the last hundred miles or so?"

"We haven't gone anywhere near that far," Scott said.

"I'm talking square miles."

"Okay," Scott said, beginning the complicated process of turning around on a narrow, snowbound road. "It's getting late anyway, and we don't want to be caught up here after dark."

"I sure don't," Rebecca said.

Brandy didn't answer. She was trying not to give Scott a hard time, but she felt like the day had been mostly wasted. They had cruised through the woods, up and down whatever little dirt roads they could find beneath the snow. But there was no rhyme or reason to it, no actual plan beyond just looking and keeping their fingers crossed. They hadn't seen any buildings or stray Jeeps, but New Hampshire was a big place, and not far from here was the Canadian border.

She had gone along with the day's agenda—or lack thereof—so she couldn't blame anyone but herself. Now it would be night soon, and their search would be ended until tomorrow. Who knew what could happen in that time?

Merry Christmas, Kerry, she thought bitterly. *Sorry we failed you.*

But tomorrow, she swore, would be different. Tomorrow they would use their heads, would approach the problem logically. "No more of this driving aimlessly," she said. "Soon as it's light, we've got to get smart about finding Kerry."

"You have any ideas, Brandy?" Scott asked. "Because you didn't when I was looking for some earlier."

"Maybe I do," Brandy replied. "I was thinking: If we were the police, we wouldn't look for a missing person by driving around the neighborhood, would we?"

"I guess not," Scott said.

"Of course not. We'd ask questions. We'd investigate. That's what we'll do tomorrow—we'll hit the little towns around here and see if anyone knows Season, or if anyone's seen her. If she's hiding out in this area, then she must buy food from someone. If she has a place to live, she must have bought or rented it from an agency or somebody like that. So we ask around."

"I like it, Brandy," Rebecca said. "It makes sense to me."

"Can I just remind you both that she's a witch?" Scott shot back. "We don't know if she needs a grocery store, or if she can just conjure up a meal from thin air."

"Well, she'd have to buy gas, then. Something. At least it's a chance," Brandy insisted. "It's better than trying to cover a million square miles of wilderness."

"Do you think we should call in the real authorities?" Rebecca suggested. "I mean, if Kerry's been kidnapped for real, maybe we should be getting the FBI or the National Guard or something after her."

Brandy snorted. "You want to try to explain Season to the New Hampshire state police? You're gutsier than me."

"Yeah, okay, maybe that wouldn't work," Rebecca admitted. "But it just seems like we need some, I don't know, reinforcements or something."

"Reinforcements would be great, but I wouldn't hold my breath," Scott said. "I think we're it."

"What about Mother Blessing?" Brandy asked. "Could we ask her for help somehow?"

"I don't think we'd want to do that," Rebecca cautioned. "It sounded like she and Kerry had kind of a falling-out."

"But she still hates Season, right?" Brandy pressed. "We were talking about stupid old sayings earlier, and 'The enemy of my enemy is my friend' fits into that."

"You were wrong about the apple one," Scott reminded her. "What if you're wrong about this one too? What if it's something like, 'The friend of my enemy is my enemy'?"

Brandy shrugged. They were on their way back down the hill, coming out of the trees, but still a long way from civilization. The sun was a pale copper ball perched at the crest of the mountains. "Same idea," she said. "Mother Blessing and Season are enemies. Season has Kerry. Anyone who could help, I think we ought to consider."

"Yeah, but Beck and I have had more time than you have with Kerry recently," Scott argued. "She didn't give me the whole scoop—you know how she's been, always holding stuff back—but I got the same sense that Rebecca did. Kerry and Mother Blessing didn't part on the greatest terms."

"Whatever," Brandy said, throwing up her hands. Here she was intentionally trying not to ignite some kind of great debate, but she was in the middle of one anyway. All she wanted was to make sure Kerry was safe. Then she would make the argument that what they really needed was to leave Season alone, to stop this crazy hunt for her. Sure, there was a chance that Season was after them. They continued to get mixed up with her because they were worried about that possibility. But realistically, if they just went about their own business, ignored Season, wouldn't she do the same to them? They weren't really a threat—that had been proven time and again.

She didn't know how the others would feel about it. She wasn't even really sure if she cared anymore. She missed Adam, she missed her family. It was Christmas! And instead of celebrating her favorite holiday of the year with loved ones, she was traipsing all over the White Mountains with her ex-boyfriend and someone she had known for one summer.

That was messed up.

"Okay," Scott said as he urged the SUV onto yet another ribbon of trail. "Tomorrow we do it your way, Brandy. We'll hit the towns, question the local yokels. Anybody have a picture of Kerry? It'd be easier if we had one of Season, but anything is better than nothing, right?"

"No picture here," Brandy said.

"I have one on my website," Rebecca offered.

"You have a website?"

"I've just been working on it the last couple of weeks," she said. "Kerry bought me a digital camera, and I've been putting up some pictures."

"That's just peachy," Brandy said. "So all we have to do is go into the grocery stores and gas stations and ask people to browse the Net for a while."

"No, silly," Rebecca answered. "We just need to find a computer that we can print from. Maybe one of the hotels around here has a business center, or there's an Internet café or something around."

"At the risk of starting another bizarre digression," Scott said, "we'll be going through a few towns on the way back to the condo. Everybody keep your eyes peeled."

Kerry and Season bundled up and went for a walk in the woods. The bitingly cold air smelled freshly scrubbed, the snow crunched loudly underfoot, and a few of the hardier birds whistled and fluttered from branch to branch overhead. The sun hung in the sky like a decoration, with no discernible purpose, since Kerry couldn't tell any difference in temperature between shade and bright sunlight.

"This is what winter should be like, to me," Season said. "I've spent plenty of them in warmer climes, but I can never get used to listening to Christmas music while the palm trees sway, or going out in January in shorts and sleeveless tops. It just seems wrong to me."

"I wouldn't mind the chance to find out," Kerry said. "I kind of liked the couple of weeks I spent in Santa Cruz. And Rebecca said it's relatively cool there because it's right on the water and everything—back down in San Diego, she said, it'd be a lot warmer."

"That's true. And down in Baja, or the Florida Keys, it's warmer still. But it's just not winter to me. I guess I'm old-fashioned or something. I think winter should be the time you put on a lot of clothes, drink hot chocolate or eggnog, and complain about the cold."

"And go sledding," Kerry added. "Sledding's good. I haven't done it since I was a kid, but . . ." She waved a hand toward a slope that faced them through the trees. "That'd be a great spot for it."

"You're right," Season agreed, a broad smile on her face. "Shall we?"

Kerry looked at her for a moment, confused. "But . . . with what sleds?"

"Kerry," Season said, shaking her head sadly. "Witches, remember?" She spoke one of the old words and gestured toward the slope. Kerry saw a faraway flash of light, and then two colorful objects appeared against the white snow.

"Sleds?"

"Flexible Flyers," Season confirmed.

"I am so there." Kerry broke into a run, and Season started in right behind her. When she was a kid, back in Cairo, there had been a street near her house that was steep and straight. On winter weekends the residents there closed the street off and ran hoses down it, icing it up, making a sled run out of it. There was always the unhelpful neighbor who left a car or truck parked at the curb, but most pulled into driveways or garages to clear the path. Someone would build a bonfire at the top of the hill at night, and the adults would gather around it for drinks and conversation while the kids sledded. Kerry had spent many happy winter hours streaking down that hill, and the few frightening moments, when her sled was caught on the ice and seemed determined to plow her into one of the parked cars or a fellow sledder, just made the whole experience that much more memorable.

A few minutes later Kerry huffed her way up to the top of the slope, leaving a trail of deep bootprints in her wake. The sled she found looked brand-new, but at the same time it looked like one that had hung high up in her parents' garage when she'd been little—supposedly it had been her dad's when he was a kid. It was made of blond wood slats with red metal rails, and it had the familiar arrow logo in the middle.

"This is great!" she shouted when Season caught up.

"Take her out for a spin," Season suggested.

Kerry hesitated for just a second, part of her still looking for the trap, the angle. She had been at war with Season. Could this be for real? But then she felt the combination of sun warm on her face and snow cold at her feet. That was real. The sled felt real, too. She grabbed its edges, ran a few steps, and then hurled herself on top of it as it rocketed down the slope. The sled gained speed as the hill grew steeper. Wind pummeled Kerry's face, snow flew as she sliced through it. A shriek behind her told her that Season was on her way down too.

At the bottom of the slope, she had to turn away from a couple of large rocks jutting up through the snow, and then from a creek that carved through the valley. She ended her ride in a spray of snow and a fit of laughter.

Season rolled her sled at the hill's end, and she came up laughing hysterically. "That was so fun!" she shouted. "This was such a good idea, Kerry!"

"I know!" Kerry called back. She was already using the attached length of rope to drag her sled back up the hill for another ride, her earlier moment of paranoia almost—but not completely—shoved away. Season caught up to her on the climb.

"I'm so glad you thought of this, Kerry. It's been a long time since I've done something just for fun."

"If I was a witch I'd do fun stuff all the time," Kerry replied.

Season grabbed her arm. "If?"

Kerry realized what she meant. She did not yet always think of herself as a witch, even though she'd been trained by Mother Blessing and could do things far beyond the abilities of most other people. To hear Season confirm her status somehow carried a lot of weight with her. "Yeah, okay," she said. "I guess I am a witch. But I've been kind of, you know, preoccupied." *With killing you,* she thought but didn't say. She was sure Season understood that anyway.

"Me too," Season said. "Having to be on edge all the time, literally for centuries . . . it interferes with my enjoyment of things."

Kerry nodded. "Even before—before I met Daniel and got all mixed up in this, I had kind of given up on fun," she admitted. "I was too busy taking care of Mom, and then going to school, working . . . I kind of let fun go by the wayside."

They had just reached the top of the slope. Season threw her sled down to the snow. "So let's go again!" she cried, pushing off and starting her trip.

Kerry spun and started hers as well, shooting down the hill behind Season.

* * *

Later they sat in Season's living room, nursing cups of hot chocolate. Kerry's cheeks were chapped, and they hurt from smiling so much and laughing so hard, but the fire and the warm beverage helped. They had sledded until the sun started to slide behind the hills, staining the snow as surely as if someone had spilled a bucket of red ink on it, and the air turned so cold that both were shivering almost uncontrollably. Kerry noticed near the end that her sled was literally breaking down—its hard edges softening, becoming less distinct, bits of it just disappearing from view. Season explained that most magically created items couldn't last very long—they were made by repurposing other materials, which needed to return to their original state before too long. Food was an exception to that rule—it was composed of tiny bits of organic material from so many different sources that they weren't missed.

At a quiet moment in the conversation, Season offered Kerry a gentle reminder. "You have five questions left. Do you still want to use them?"

Kerry had been turning things over in her mind, trying to narrow down what she wanted to ask about. But her major questions had already been answered, and the rest of it seemed small-time compared with the things she'd asked earlier.

"Okay," Kerry said after contemplating awhile. "We were talking about having fun earlier, and I know you have tended to hide out in resort-type areas. Daniel said it's because the population in those places changes a lot, swelling during their main seasons, so you can come and go without really being noticed. And I know you were in Las Vegas in the fall, because that's where Josh saw you. I also know you were in a casino on Samhain, which, I've got to tell you, really ticked off Mother Blessing. So what I want to know is, what is a witch doing in a casino on the holiest night of the year?"

Season considered her answer only briefly. "I'm not surprised that

Mother Blessing was perturbed by that," she said. "She likes to make a big issue of being all traditional. When, of course, if she was truly that traditional she would never have done the things she did, back in Slocumb or since."

"Like what?" Kerry asked, before realizing what she was saying. *Another one down.*

"Witches aren't evil by nature," Season replied. She had changed into a soft cream-colored sweater and brown pants, but in honor of Christmas her socks were red and green striped. Once again she sat on a rug on the floor, leaning on the hearth, where her mug rested. "Or at least we're not supposed to be. Most of us are not, but there is a minority that are—that's why the natural slide toward entropy, or chaos, is so hard to resist. It was not traditional of her to allow the deaths of children that she could have prevented. It was not traditional of her to put me in the awful position of having to kill my own grandsons. But let me go out for an evening's entertainment, and she's offended?"

"Samhain is, in fact, a holy night to most witches," Season went on. "And it's perfectly appropriate to celebrate it with ritual and solemn observance. But it's also fine to celebrate it with a party, or by having a good time in some other way. There is no single way that Samhain must be observed, regardless of what Mother Blessing might say. I paid attention to Samhain in my own way, and part of that was going to a casino—the closest thing there is to a truly holy place in money-worshipping Las Vegas—to enjoy myself. And was attacked by her simulacra. Surely she knew I was there because your friend called you."

Which means, Kerry extrapolated, *that I got Josh killed. If it hadn't been for me, Mother Blessing would never have known where to send the artificial men who killed him.* The realization hit her like a truck. *Good thing she doesn't know where Season is now, or I'd be in real trouble.*

"Can I—I mean, I'd like to save the rest of my questions for another time," Kerry said. Her sudden insight depressed her, and she felt very tired. "If that's okay. I think I'm ready to call it a night."

"If that's what you want, Kerry."

"Yeah, I think so. But thanks for a great Christmas, Season."

Season appeared to be unexpectedly touched by Kerry's sentiment. She swallowed, and her hand went to her chest. "Thank you," she said. "I hope I've cleared some things up for you."

"A lot," Kerry assured her. "Doesn't mean I don't still have a long way to go. But you've helped."

"Good night, then, Kerry. I'll see you in the morning."

Kerry wished Season a good night, and then retired to her room.

Kerry Profitt's diary, December 25

Well, that was certainly one of the strangest Christmases ever.

A fantastic one, for the most part. If you don't count the lack of a tree with presents underneath it. Which I kind of do, but I'm trying to look beyond that.

Anyway, there's more to life than presents and material things. Back when I was mall-happy I'd never have believed I would ever think that. And the truth is, even though I'm snowed into this cabin with no one around but Season, I still put on clean underwear today, and socks, and did my makeup, and brushed my hair. Not that good grooming is necessarily the same as being materialistic, but I guess what I'm saying is that I'm not going all Flintstones or anything. More like Gilligan's Island, I guess, where the women had plenty of clothing and makeup even though they were only going on a three-hour tour.

And what would life be without old TV references to keep us sane? Thank the Goddess for TV Land, I say.

Well, enough of that. And enough digressing, keeping me from the main point of this little diatribe, which is . . .

. . . is . . .

First of all, I really can't remember the last time I just let loose and laughed like that. I guess some of those nights at home with the La Jolla gang, when Mace would start complaining about modern life and our strange back-east ways, and then Scott would go off on him—all in fun, of course, but fun with an edge to it.

So the walk in the snow, and the sledding, and the fact that we didn't have to drag our sleds home because they never really existed somehow . . . I don't quite get that, but at least no trees had to die for our enjoyment—that was all great.

So was the other part, in a different way. Just relaxing with Season, getting some questions answered. I am horrified—just wrenched apart—by the idea that I got Josh killed. I couldn't have known, of course. I trusted Daniel's mother. My mistake.

And now, it seems, I am starting to trust Season. Another mistake? I already know she's a murderer, so the answer should be a resounding "Duh!" But maybe it's my own naïveté. . . . I can't bring myself to doubt her when she speaks so frankly. She could be telling me one lie after another. Without evidence to the contrary, I just don't know. I'm reminded of those first days with Daniel, when I trusted him instinctively, or so I thought, but I found out later that, in fact, he had enchanted us.

We always say we are "enchanted" by people to whom we feel an instant, inexplicable attraction. Maybe we are, but that kind of enchantment is different from this kind—less manipulative, I guess. A matter of chemistry and pheromones and personal taste.

I don't know that Season has intentionally enchanted me. But I don't know that she hasn't.

Is trusting her some kind of betrayal of Daniel? Or of my vow to avenge his death? Should I go in there right now and just kill Season? I'm sure she trusts me enough now to let me get close. One of those carving knives, from the kitchen. It would be over in a second, except for cleaning up.

But would it be the right thing to do? Not just because she killed Daniel, but in the greater scheme. And listen to me (well, okay, read me), thinking about the greater scheme. Like my actions can affect the whole world.

Except, to hear her tell it, maybe they can. Which means I have to think before I act.

I hate that.

I also hate not knowing who to trust.

I guess I've got to stay on my guard. If I catch Season in a lie, or turn up something that proves she isn't telling the truth, then I call her on it. Or I make like a tree and "leaf." Except around here, most of the trees are pines and so the bad pun doesn't even work. Unless needles are leaves, in which case . . . oh, never mind.

It would be so much easier if . . . if it was easier. Same could be said for the rest of life, right? Think it ever is?

Me neither.

More later.

K.

15

Berlin had a copy shop with Internet connections, but it didn't open until ten, so they got a late start on their day. Rebecca brought up her website and saved the photo of Kerry—really of the two of them together, taken by Erin on one of the few occasions she had been around while Kerry had been visiting. Erin had a new boyfriend, and she'd been spending most of her time at his place, leaving Rebecca in the house alone. She had loved having Kerry visit, because she didn't like being home by herself—didn't like being anywhere by herself, she had realized. Being by herself just gave her too much time to think.

Once the photo was downloaded, it was an easy matter to crop herself out. She wanted the picture to show just Kerry, to keep any confusion to a minimum when they started spreading it around. It was a small file, fine for online viewing, but it printed blurry and grainy. Still, Kerry's pale skin, long dark hair, and huge green eyes were visible. They had been in Rebecca's kitchen, and there was a yellow wall behind Kerry that set her off nicely.

The first person they showed it to was named Frank, according to the tag on his shirt. He worked in the copy shop, and Rebecca slid it across the counter while Scott paid for the computer time. "Have you seen this girl?" she asked. "She might be with an older woman, a very pretty blonde."

Frank looked at the picture for a long time—maybe taking some time to admire as well as checking to see if he recognized her. "Nope," he said after a while. "Think I'd remember her."

"Okay, thanks," Brandy said, snatching the picture away.

They went outside onto Berlin's main drag—mostly brick buildings, very traditionally New England-styled. Here and there a cupola or clock tower broke the rooflines. Many businesses were closed, their storefronts boarded over or shuttered up. Signs for commercial real estate agencies hung on most of them, but they looked like they'd been there a long time. Rebecca remembered a mill they had seen on the river the day before— empty and abandoned, like a ghost town. For a minute she had thought it looked that way because of Christmas; no one would be working the mill on Christmas. But a closer look proved that to be false: The parking lots were blanketed in untouched snow, the buildings had broken-out windows and caved-in walls.

They tried a restaurant, a coffee shop, a drugstore, a gas station, but in each place they had the same response. No one remembered having seen Kerry or recognized the description of Season.

Finally, after searching for more than an hour, they reached the office of Bald Cap Realty and pushed through the heavy glass door. An old heater made the air smell stale. There were two people inside sitting at desks behind a long wooden counter. The woman looked up first—fiftyish, lean and bespectacled, with brown curls framing her pinched face. "Can I help you?" she asked, her tone suspicious. *No way do we look like we're shopping for a house,* Rebecca realized.

"We're wondering if you've seen someone," Brandy began.

Rebecca put the photo down on the counter. "This person," she said. "Or another one. They might be together."

Scott took over. "The other one is a pretty blonde, older than the girl in the picture. Mid-thirties, maybe. Striking blue eyes, the kind you don't forget. They're not from around here, so you'd have noticed their accents, maybe."

"That sounds familiar," the man said, rising from his own desk. He was younger than the woman, but not by much. Round and balding, but with a gray beard hugging his chin. He buttoned his red blazer as he approached the counter, seemingly out of long habit. "An attractive blonde, you say?"

"What is this about?" the suspicious woman asked.

"We're afraid they might be in trouble," Brandy said, repeating the line they had agreed on in case anyone asked. "We haven't heard from them in several days, but we know they had a place around here."

The man looked at Kerry's picture. "Haven't seen her," he said.

"The older one was here first," Scott interjected. "This one just came a couple of days ago."

"You remember, Margaret," the man said. "Couple years ago, that property up by Mount Cabot?"

"Hush, Steven," the woman called Margaret said sharply. "Why don't you young people go to the police if you think there's something wrong?"

"We don't really know if it's as bad as all that, ma'am," Rebecca said. "We'd hate to get everybody stirred up if it turns out to be nothing."

"But if you know where on Mount Cabot," Brandy added, "we'd sure appreciate a tip."

"We have nothing more to tell you," Margaret said.

"Okay, then, thanks for all your help," Scott said sarcastically.

As they left the office, Rebecca tried to remember where Mount Cabot was on their map. It wasn't much to go on, but it was better than they'd had before.

"Are you crazy?" Margaret fumed after they had left. "Don't you remember what she said?"

"Not exactly," Steven admitted. "What was it?"

"She paid us both an extra ten percent if we'd promise to keep quiet about her buying that place."

Steven sighed. "That was two years ago," he said. "I'm sure she just meant for a while, not forever."

"It was three," Margaret said. "And she didn't put any time limitations on it. Maybe you don't take your commitments seriously, but I do."

"Look, I'm sorry, Margaret. I didn't think it was a big deal, and I forgot." Of course it *was* a big deal to Margaret—it was always a big deal when anyone let her down in any way, or revealed that they were merely human. Margaret liked to think of herself as godlike, while everyone around her failed in their attempts to achieve her exalted level. Steven thought it was probably difficult to go through life surrounded by abject failures and the willfully unkempt, but Margaret seemed to thrive on her demonstrated superiority over all beings.

"Well, I just think you would keep the desires of our customers in mind," Margaret huffed.

Before Steven could answer, the door opened again. *Probably those same kids coming back for something they forgot,* he figured. He hadn't expected much business the morning after Christmas. He was surprised they were willing to brave Margaret again, but if they were he had to give them credit.

But when he turned back toward the door, it wasn't the kids at all, or anyone else that he had ever seen. It was two men—*well, things that are like men, anyway,* he corrected. They were mostly brown, the brown of the mud by the banks of the Androscoggin River, and slick like that mud, but there were other components as well. He thought he recognized the spokes of a bicycle wheel, a crushed aluminum soft drink can, and a plastic bag from a supermarket mixed in with the river mud. They wore no clothing, just mud from head to foot.

Then he blinked, because he couldn't really be recognizing those things, that made no sense at all. It was just because the men were coming in from outside and the light was behind them, that was it. He was about to rub his eyes and say something when Margaret screamed.

"It's—it's all right, Margaret," Steven said. When he addressed the . . . the *things*, he tried to sound forceful, but his voice caught and it came out squeaky and uncertain. "Look here, what do you want?"

One of them came forward and leaned its fists down on the wooden counter. Steven was sure he could see mud squish out from between its fingers, but then suck back in somehow. He felt a chill that went to the core of his being.

The thing spoke then, and its voice was surprising. Not in its inhumanity, he expected that. But this was at once inhuman and yet feminine, in some way, like this creature was only a speaker box for a female talking through it remotely. "Season Howe," the strange voice said. "Where is she?"

"I don't—I don't know who you mean," Steven said. He knew full well, but how could these bizarre man-shaped concoctions know that?

"Season Howe," the thing said again.

Margaret had begun to sob as soon as her initial scream died, and she was still sobbing now, sitting in her desk chair with her face buried in her hands. Through the sobs, she said, "She's the one those kids were looking for, you fool. On Mount Cabot. Just tell them what they want to know, get them out of here."

The thing leaning on the counter, the mud-man, looked into Steven's eyes with an eye that was nothing more than a thumb-size space in his crudely sculpted head. There seemed to be some kind of intelligence there just the same, Steven thought. He would go to his grave believing that the thing read him like a book. "I—I didn't recognize the name," he sputtered. "But she—she's right. Mount Cabot. That's where she is. Where her cabin is, anyway."

"Mount Cabot," it repeated, in that same semi-feminine voice.

"That's right," Steven said. He was terrified, afraid that he would lose control of himself at any moment, that these horrible creatures would drive him completely mad. He was a hairsbreadth away from becoming a gibbering idiot, rolling into a ball and hiding in the footwell of his desk. "Mount Cabot. Now please, just go—"

Before he could finish the thought, the thing came across the counter at him, moving fast and . . . and fluidly, not like a man but like a liquid, splashing itself at him. Margaret screamed again, and Steven saw that the other one was on her, arms swinging, fists pumping. Then Margaret was silent, and Steven felt a wet, slick hand contract on his own throat, felt muddy fingers clamp over his mouth and nose. He couldn't breathe, and when he tried he sucked mud in, inhaled it; it filled him up, and then it was over his eyes too, or the world had gone mercifully dark.

Six dead people. That was more than the town had seen in—well, ever, as far as Will Blossom knew.

Ordinarily there wasn't much a constable had to do to keep order in Berlin, New Hampshire. Not much crime. Most people didn't have much to steal, anyway, except the tourists and skiers who came during the season. They found themselves victimized from time to time, but Will didn't feel too bad about that. They left their car doors unlocked and their fancy stereos disappeared, that was too bad. He would rather it didn't happen, but the end result was that they usually bought new car stereos, sometimes before they even left town, and that was good for the local economy.

The town's only gang was a pack of punk kids who couldn't make the high school football team, smoked cigarettes, and pushed around smaller kids for their lunch money sometimes. At least that's what Chief Blossom liked to think. The truth, which he seldom allowed himself to contemplate, was that there were other things going on under the surface of the town that he didn't like or understand. Sometimes there were kids who wound up in the river, or on a hospital slab. Someone was responsible for that. He didn't know if it was a gang or simply random circumstance.

But as long as it didn't affect most of the townspeople, he didn't push too hard on it.

He was understaffed, of course. Every law enforcement agency was these days. And there had been a little more crime since the last big mill on the river had closed. Someone stealing a few cans of food, a loaf of bread, those things he could overlook. Life was hard all around, and he didn't leave himself out of that equation. The less he had to do to claim his bimonthly paycheck, the better he liked it.

So this morning he was a very unhappy man. The phone in his office was ringing off the hook, and every time it did it brought more bad news. He had already been out of the office more than he'd been in it today. Carla, his dispatcher, had a stack of pink message slips in her hand when he came in this time, and she shoved them into Will's fist.

"More calls," she said. "I'd have called you on your wireless but I knew you were just about here. You're going out again, though."

He had been dreaming about the chocolate bar in his desk drawer and a Coke to wash it down with. "I don't want to go out," he protested, knowing it was pointless. This was going to be one of those days that didn't let up, and then it would lead into a week or more of the same—funerals and distraught family members and demands for answers. He would find those answers, one way or another.

"You got a big staff of investigators going to do it for you?"

"I'm going out again," he relented. "Where am I going?"

"Depends," Carla said. "You want to work them in order of when they called in? Or maybe alphabetically?"

"In order," Will said.

"Then you're going to the Tas-T-Scoop, Virgil's Café, Notions 'n' Things, and Bald Cap Realty."

"I know that's the name of the mountain," Will said. "But doesn't it sound like something an actor would wear if he needed to be bald?"

"You're wasting time, Will."

"I'm delaying the inevitable, Carla," he protested. "That's different."

"In what way?"

He couldn't think of any. "Okay, maybe not. Anyone else needs me, call me."

He left the office to go back into his town. The town he was supposed to keep safe, and in which half a dozen people had already died today. Maybe starting last night, he amended, since he didn't know precisely what time the murders had started to occur.

The scary thing was, nobody had put it all together yet. Some people knew a victim or two, but no one outside of his department knew how many there were. When they did, it would be trouble. Panic. He didn't want that.

He just wasn't sure how to avoid it.

He drove down to the Tas-T-Scoop. Kitty Russell was there in her colorful uniform, with the little striped cap and everything. But her eyes were red and her nose was running, and she was shaking like a leaf in a nor'easter. Will got out of his car and walked over to where she sat on a bench in the dining area, pointedly not looking toward the counter.

"What's wrong, Kitty?" he asked, afraid he already knew the answer. "What happened?"

She tried to point to the Formica counter, but her muscles failed her and her arm fell limply to her side. "It's—it's Mr. Penrose," she said through her tears. "He—he—he's back there."

Will massaged her back for a moment. "I'll just take a look, Kitty. You stay right here. Everything's going to be okay. You're safe, I promise you that. Okay?"

"O—okay . . . ," she said, without apparent conviction.

He left her and let himself through the opening into the kitchen area of the ice-cream parlor. *Who'd buy ice cream on a day like today, anyway?* he wondered. *Penrose should have just stayed home, and let Kitty stay home too. They'd both have been better off.*

On the floor behind the counter he saw just what he expected to see— what he'd seen at every other stop this morning. Same as Hoot Buffington, and Sandra Cliff, and Nat Landers. Penrose was dead. His clothes were foul, muddy, and they stank like the Androscoggin on a hot day. Mud caked his chin and neck, dribbled from his slack mouth. His eyes were open.

He looked terrified, even in death.

Will Blossom shuddered. He was a little terrified himself.

16

Writing about TV shows in her journal the night before had made Kerry realize how much she missed television. That, and the fact that TV had been part of her family's Christmas tradition: Charlie Brown, the Grinch, Rudolph, *Miracle on 34th Street* and *Holiday Inn* and *A Christmas Story*. It had been just ages since she had sat down and watched TV. A couple of days at the hotel in Portsmouth, and not for months before that. Maybe she'd been too busy living her life to simply observe, but on some level she felt removed from the rest of the country because they had gone on watching while she had been doing other things. TV might be overrated, but it helped define America in a very real way, and she missed that attachment to her fellow citizens.

Besides, being stuck up on this mountain with Season was starting to wear on her. She liked the sledding and the fireplace and the conversation, but she craved communication, connection. She wondered if there was some sort of plan. When would the roads open—or had they already? When would they come down from the mountain? And, maybe most important, how did her new perception of Season fit into her life? What came next?

In the morning, while Season slept in, Kerry tugged on sweats, tied her hair back, and scouted around the cabin. No telephone—and her own cell, she had determined long ago, had no signal up here—no radio, no TV. Even Mother Blessing had owned a TV.

But, Kerry remembered, *witch.*

She racked her brain for a long while, but couldn't come up with a spell that would make a TV appear where there was none.

While she dwelled on it, sitting on the living room couch with her ankles crossed, knees up, hands resting on knees and chin on hands, Season came in.

"Good morning, Kerry," she said. She looked warm and comfy in a man's loose-fitting corduroy shirt and soft, flared gray pants.

"Do you have a TV? Wait—does that count—no, strike that. I'm hoping that doesn't count as one of my remaining questions. I'm still not sure how these stupid rules are supposed to work."

"Rules can be stupid," Season agreed. "But often you'll find that the stupidest ones aren't so bad once you realize why they're there."

"That doesn't answer my . . . my not a question."

"I won't count it, okay? And the other answer is no, no TV. But if you'd like to watch some today, you can."

"I was just feeling a little, you know, cut off from the world. This hermit deal isn't so much me, I guess. I'd kind of like to talk to my friends, too."

"I think we can arrange both," Season said. "Let's have some breakfast first, and then we'll get on that." She went into the kitchen and Kerry got off the couch to follow her. She had come to like watching Season cook, although not as much as she liked the eating part.

Season cracked a few brown eggs into a bowl. "I think an omelet would be good today. Sound all right to you? Maybe with biscuits and some fresh fruit."

"Sounds yummy," Kerry said. "Why—and I guess this one can count— why do witches like to cook so much? Mother Blessing did too, and even Daniel was a good cook. I mean, you could just kind of *poof!* and there's an entire meal, right?"

"I could, yes," Season agreed. "I think part of it may be that we enjoy the process, though. Most witches I've met are good cooks. It's not unlike witchcraft, when you get down to it. We take natural ingredients, combine them in a specified manner, and the end result is something that isn't what it was, something that's new and different and functional. A lot of spells work the same way."

"That makes sense, I guess."

Season's hands flew with practiced assuredness. Kerry was a pretty fair cook herself—she had taken over the culinary duties at home once her mom got too sick—but her repertoire was basic. Breakfast was far more likely to be cereal and toast than Belgian waffles, sausages, and strawberries cut into the shape of roses. Anyway, there were lots of choices of breakfast cereal. She hadn't counted them all, of course, but in her local supermarket if you stood at one end of the cereal aisle you could almost see the curvature of the Earth in the shelves. She figured you could easily eat cereal every day for the rest of your life, a different box at a time, and never have to repeat yourself because they'd just keep coming up with new ones. Soon the cabin was filled with wonderful aromas that pushed any thoughts of such basic foods from her head.

"So . . . what comes next?" Kerry asked as they ate Season's delicious food. She felt awkward about it, but knew the subject had to be broached sometime. "I mean . . . you know. With . . . all this? I guess I don't want to kill you as much as I used to."

"Well, that's a relief," Season said with a warm smile. "I don't want to kill you either. I really am not a killer by nature."

"I think I've figured that out," Kerry admitted. "It was hard, though. Took me a long time to accept."

"Understandable. You've been through a lot, and you've seen a lot of awful things. And we've been on the opposite sides of most of it. I guess the only way to answer your question is to ask you one. What do you want? There's probably no reason you have to stay involved in any of this.

You can go back to school, go on with your own life, and leave our little intrigues behind. At least that's what I'd do if it was my choice."

Kerry dwelled on that for a moment. Back to Northwestern? Back to live with Aunt Betty and Uncle Marsh? Neither of those choices had very much appeal. She was eighteen—not a little girl, barely an adult by society's standards—but without the hunt for Season, without Daniel, she was completely adrift.

"I've been thinking about it a lot," she said. "But I haven't come to any firm decisions. Part of me would like to keep studying witchcraft, I think. That's the only thing that has really interested me lately."

Season looked a little surprised by Kerry's comment. "I would think you'd want to leave it as far behind you as possible, as fast as you could. I don't want you to jump into anything without giving it a lot of thought. It's not so easy to do, and there are a lot of sacrifices that have to be made, especially if you're not born into the community."

"I get what you're saying," Kerry said. "But I don't know. It seems like something I'm good at. Maybe I could make some kind of contribution."

"You probably could," Season agreed. "More omelet?"

After Kerry had done the dishes, she came into the living room to see Season looking at a TV set that stood on the hearth. It wasn't plugged into anything, Kerry noted, but there was a picture on its screen just the same.

"Cable or satellite?" she joked.

"Astral plane," Season answered with a grin. "Much clearer reception."

She held a remote control that looked perfectly authentic to Kerry. Pointing it at the TV, she started clicking through the channels. "Anything in particular you want to watch?"

"I've been so out of touch I don't even know what's on anymore," Kerry moaned. "And a million new songs are probably out, by a thousand new bands I've never even heard of. And movies? Is Josh Hartnett even a star anymore?"

Before Season could answer, something on the TV screen caught her eye. ". . . gruesome murders in Berlin this morning have authorities baffled. The early morning killing spree has left seven dead. Berlin police chief William Blossom has asked all residents to stay inside with their doors locked as much as possible, until more is known about who has committed these savage crimes . . ."

"Look," Season said in a hushed voice. The screen showed a reporter standing outside a café in what must have been Berlin. There were muddy handprints on the doorjamb behind him, and more tracks of mud on the ground. Season pushed a button on the remote and the screen froze, as if they were watching a DVD or TiVo, and not a broadcast with the word "Live" in the corner. She pushed another button—*That's some remote,* Kerry couldn't help thinking—and the picture zoomed in on the muddy foot-prints.

Mixed in with the mud, Kerry could see cigarette butts, stray leaves, bits of paper, and other detritus. "Is that—?" she began.

"Simulacra," Season said anxiously.

"But they're—they're killing people! Why would they do that?"

Season's voice was solemn, her brow furrowed with concern. "That's what they're best at." She eyed Kerry for a moment, then shook her head. "Sorry," she added. "That was flip. This is serious, and you deserve a real answer. Here's what I think: Mother Blessing is using them to look for me. She has tracked me to this area somehow. Instead of coming herself, she's sent the simulacra to find me. But she doesn't want anyone who sees them to be able to tell anyone else about them."

"Usually when she's with one," Kerry remembered, "she uses a glamour to make sure no one really sees them."

"That's right," Season agreed. "From this distance, though, it would be all she could do to keep them animated. So she would command them to kill any witnesses after they got whatever information they could."

Kerry shuddered. Sometimes she forgot just how brutal Mother Blessing could be. "Can we stop them?"

"We have to try," Season said. "But we have to get down there, fast."

Scott, Rebecca, and Brandy had just reached the RAV4, parked at a curb a few blocks from the real estate office, when they saw the police car race down the street past them, siren blaring, roof lights flashing. Scott realized that they'd been hearing sirens around town for the last twenty or thirty minutes, but they had been so busy trying to track down any information about Season that they had barely paid any attention.

"I wonder what's going on," he said. He wasn't curious enough to want to backtrack and find out—he was more concerned with getting on to Mount Cabot and finding Kerry. So much time had gone by since she had disappeared; he had a horrible feeling, sitting in his gut like a lead weight, that they would be too late to help her. It had taken only seconds for Season to kill Daniel, and Daniel had been a much more formidable opponent than Kerry would be. The only saving grace was that Season had taken Kerry away, instead of just finishing her off on the spot—to Scott, that suggested that the witch had some use for Kerry. If so, Kerry might still be alive.

But every minute might count.

"Looks serious," Rebecca added. She nodded toward a nearby intersection, which an ambulance screamed through at top speed.

"None of our business," Scott said. He fished his keys from his pocket to open the SUV. But before he reached the door, a dark shape separated from the nearby building and lumbered toward them. It took Scott a moment to realize that the figure was dark not because of shadows—as soon as it peeled away from the building's face, it moved into bright sunlight—but because it was, top to bottom, rich brown mud, not flesh or clothes.

"Umm . . . Scott . . . ?" Rebecca's voice quavered with fear, and he knew she had seen it too. His own voice seemed to fail him, as if it were out of his reach somehow.

But Brandy stepped up, the only indication of her own emotions a barely noticeable shaking of her legs, like her knees wouldn't quite lock under her. "It must be a . . . what do you call them? Simulacra? One of Daniel's mother's . . . things."

The man-shaped creature continued toward them with its odd gait, and Scott found his voice. "What do you want?" he asked. The thing's arms were at its sides, and there was nothing sinister or threatening in its demeanor. But when it stopped a few feet from them, its head cocked as if listening for something, it didn't speak, didn't answer in any way. "Tell us what you want," Scott insisted.

Finally, the simulacrum uttered one word, in a raspy, high-pitched voice that didn't seem to match up with its large, bulky body. "Season."

The three of them stood in place, stunned by the being's statement. Scott realized they shouldn't be—Brandy was almost certainly right, this thing was a simulacrum, and they were Mother Blessing's creations. It was only natural that the creature would be looking for Season.

"Mother Blessing must have . . . I don't know, tapped our phones or something," he speculated. "Or she's keeping tabs on us somehow, anyway. So when we found out where Season is, she sent her simulacrum. I don't think he wants to hurt us, or he already would have."

"Are you—do you want to go with us? To find Season?" Brandy asked the thing.

"But remember," Rebecca put in, "Kerry said Mother Blessing was kind of crazy or something when she left. I'm not sure she's actually on Kerry's side."

"She's against Season," Scott reminded them. "That means she's okay with me right now. If we find them—when we find them—we're going to need whatever help we can get to fight Season."

"Season," the simulacrum repeated in the same strange voice.

"How did you find us?" Brandy asked.

"Season."

"Kind of a one-track mind."

"If Mother Blessing can 'see' through its eyes, then she might have recognized us," Rebecca guessed. "She probably knows what we look like."

"We're going to find Season," Scott told the creature. "Do you want to go with us?"

The simulacrum shambled toward the SUV, which Scott took as an affirmative. "I guess we have company."

"It—he can ride in back with me," Rebecca offered. Turning to it, she added, "You don't mind if I open the window a little, do you?"

Scott understood—the closer it came, the more odiferous he realized it was, with a smell like rancid fish. He wondered if he'd ever be able to clean his vehicle sufficiently after this. It left mud tracks on the ground with every step, and he was afraid that after sitting on his backseat for the hour or so it would take to get up to Mount Cabot and find Season, there would be a permanent stain.

But cars were replaceable. Kerry wasn't. They all piled in, the simulacrum scrunching itself in next to Rebecca. As soon as it was seated its head drooped to its chest, as if it had gone to sleep. *That's fine*, Scott thought as he started the vehicle and pulled away from the curb. *It won't be needed again until we find Season. And then we're going to want it to have all the strength it can manage.*

As they drove out of town, more sirens split the morning air.

17

Season's Jeep roared easily through the half-melted snow of Christmas Eve's storm. Season had warned Kerry that if the simulacra were so close they might not be able to return to the cabin, so they had taken a few minutes to pack up necessary belongings and thrown their bags into the back of the vehicle.

"How do you think she could have found us?" Kerry asked as they bounced down the snow-packed road away from the cabin.

"I don't know," Season said. Her knuckles were white on the steering wheel. "You didn't tell those friends of yours where we've been, did you?"

"I hate to shatter any illusions," Kerry replied, "but I don't even know where we've been. With the snow and everything, I was lost as soon as you left I-93. Anyway, at the cabin my phone didn't have any signal, so I couldn't have told them even if I wanted to."

"Well, somehow she figured it out," Season stated.

The "she," Kerry knew, was Mother Blessing. And Season was right—she might well have been looking for either of them, or both. The news report on the TV had been brief, but terrifying—if Mother Blessing was willing to let her simulacra kill half a dozen innocent people in one morning, she had stepped things up considerably. Maybe she knew that Season and Kerry were together, and she believed they might be forming an alliance. That would be something, Kerry was sure, that Mother Blessing would go to almost any lengths to stop.

And it intensified her sense that teaming up with Season was the right thing to do—that Mother Blessing, not Season, was the real enemy. The long struggle between them had taken too many lives, but it was Mother Blessing who pressed the issue, who wouldn't let up. Season's responses, Kerry had come to accept, had been mostly defensive. Running and hiding weren't the actions of an aggressor.

Season would be aggressive now, Kerry was sure. The set of her jaw, the determined way she muscled the Jeep around turns and over the unpaved road—everything Kerry saw pointed to a Season who was outraged and ready for anything. Finally, their wheels hit pavement, and Season stomped on the gas, hurtling the Jeep toward Berlin and the ultimate confrontation.

The beast in the backseat made Brandy nervous, but she knew that it would be an important ally in the confrontation to come. She, Scott, and Rebecca had no magic, no special powers. They could find Season and Kerry, and then . . . they could yell and scream at the witch, maybe throw rocks at her. That was about the extent of their ability to cause her harm.

With the simulacrum in tow, maybe they could succeed in freeing Kerry from Season's grasp. She knew Season had beat simulacra before, but at least it was *something*. *Which,* she reasoned, *is better than nothing.*

Scott raced toward Mount Cabot with a seriousness of expression that Brandy at once admired and despised. Clearly the danger to Kerry was foremost in his mind, and it may not even have occurred to him that by trying to rescue her, all he was doing was putting the rest of them into equal jeopardy. She hadn't tried to dissuade him—besides understanding that the effort would have been pointless, she wanted to force a showdown too. She hated the idea that Season was taking them one by one, like a fox picking off sheep who wandered too far from the flock. They needed to present a united front, to let Season know once and for all that she had to face them together or leave them alone.

Stinky mud-man would help make their case. They didn't have much power, but they had powerful friends. Maybe that would be enough.

As they sped up the road, she noticed a vehicle coming toward them. Scott spotted it too, and, glancing at him, Brandy saw his eyes widen in surprise. "It's the Jeep!" he said, almost breathless.

"Season's Jeep?" Rebecca asked from the back.

"Looks like it," Scott said.

Brandy narrowed her eyes, trying to sharpen her focus. There were at least two people in the oncoming Jeep, but that was all she could make out at this distance. Scott didn't wait for confirmation. He pulled the RAV4 over to the side of the road, off the pavement, and jumped out. Standing at the edge of the roadway, he flapped his arms like a crazed penguin trying to fly.

Twenty yards away, the Jeep pulled over. Its doors opened and Season and Kerry got out.

Kerry didn't look like a prisoner.

The two women started toward them. Kerry, Brandy saw, had a wide smile on her face. *She's all right, then,* Brandy thought happily. She realized how tense she'd been only when her tension started to dissipate at the sight.

But a dozen yards away, Season put a hand against Kerry's chest, holding her back, and pointed toward them. Both women's faces changed, expressions of joy becoming looks of concern. They stopped their advance and took what could only be defensive positions.

"Scott . . . ," Brandy warned. He had already started toward them, but he read the body language and halted in his tracks.

"What—," he started to say, but he let the rest of it die in his throat.

Season's posture—and Kerry's—were unmistakable. They were ready for war.

The sight of Scott's RAV4 pulling off the road had made Kerry's heart leap. "There they are!" she shouted gleefully. "We have to stop!"

"Okay," Season said. "For a minute. Just long enough to bring them up to speed. Then we have to get into Berlin to find those simulacra before they hurt anyone else."

"Deal," Kerry agreed. Season halted the Jeep and they both tumbled out, heading down the slope toward Scott, Brandy, and Rebecca. *They all came,* Kerry thought, her heart swelling. *Those guys are the best.*

Then Season's hand was on her, and they both came to a dead stop. "Look," Season cautioned. "Simulacra."

At first glance, Kerry saw only one, unfolding itself from the backseat of Scott's ride. But it was alone only for a moment. As Kerry watched, more shaped themselves from the packed snow and dirt beside the road, from pine needles and stray leaves, from litter and the tread of a shredded tire and a hubcap someone had lost. They formed from the ground up, a head first, then, as more matter clung together, growing taller and broader until they each stood on two strong legs. There were two, then four, then ten, and finally an even dozen, standing around Kerry's friends.

No, she corrected herself, *standing* with *my friends. Allied with them.*

"They—," she began.

Season confirmed her unfinished statement. "They're with Mother Blessing now."

"But—they can't be."

"No one else uses simulacra like she does."

"But someone could," Kerry suggested.

"Could, maybe. They don't. That's just the way it is."

"That doesn't mean—"

"Kerry, we don't have time to argue. They are there with the simulacra. One came in their car. Don't deny what's right in front of you."

Kerry felt her voice catch in her throat. "What—what are we going to do?"

"We're going to fight," Season answered. Kerry recognized that she had already taken a defensive posture, ready for the simulacra to attack. "The only alternative is to die, and I'm not keen on that one."

"Don't hurt my friends," Kerry pleaded. "We have to talk to them, make them explain what's going on."

"I'll try," Season agreed. But then she didn't speak anymore, because the army of snowmen rushed toward them, a massive wave of human-shaped debris.

Season spoke a few words of the Old Tongue, and a sudden, violet glow formed around her hands, which crackled with power. Kerry caught on and echoed her. She felt the energy tingle as her own hands sparked and the glow surrounded them also. A scent like fresh watermelon in the summer filled the air. Neither witch waited for the simulacra to get any closer, but both blasted at them—Season first, Kerry close behind—with energy pulses that radiated from splayed fingers. Where the pulses hit, simulacra burst apart, snow and earth and other ingredients flying apart, returning to their pre-enchanted states.

But they moved fast, and before Kerry and Season could dispatch all of them, Kerry felt a hard-packed fist slam into her ribs. The simulacrum had charged in so quickly she hadn't even seen it come, focused as she was on a more distant target. She doubled over and it swung again, its heavy hand smashing into her face and driving her down into the snow. She tried to blast it but the distraction had dissipated her energy field. She started to say the old words again. The thing gave her no opportunity, though—it came at her again, this time kicking at her. She dodged the foot, barely, and tried to grab its leg, hoping to pull it off balance. It was too fast, and she too weak from the brutal beating. She missed. It launched another kick that looked like it would take her head off.

Then the simulacrum blew apart, and Kerry, shielding her face from the sudden shower of snow and dirt, saw Season toss her a smile. "You owe me one!" Season shouted. "Now get back into the game!"

Season was surrounded by them, Kerry realized. The dozen that had initially formed had been joined by many more, a virtual army of the pseudomen. Even Season was in danger of being overrun by them, and yet she had taken the time to save Kerry from one.

Kerry forced herself back to her feet, wincing at the pain in her ribs, the throbbing of her face. The determination that had earned her the nickname Bulldog filled her with a sense of purpose. *"Malificant!"* she shouted to the skies, raising her arms as if to grab a cloud. *"Konatifat benilias!"*

This time the glow wasn't confined to her hands, and the electrical sensation rippled through her whole body. Kerry had made herself a living weapon. She didn't hesitate, but unleashed her power on the simulacra, throwing off blast after blast. Each one found its target, blowing another simulacrum back to its component materials. She began with the ones closing in on her, and then turned to the ones surrounding Season. As she destroyed one after another, she felt herself reveling in the power she wielded, taking a kind of joy from the destruction of her unliving enemies.

When it was over, when no more simulacra rose from the ground, she felt almost let down. She relaxed, shook herself, let the power slip back into the universe from which she had called it, and saw Season doing the same. They went to one another and shared a quick embrace, and Season's whispered "You were great" brought Kerry a swell of pride she hadn't felt in a long time.

Then Kerry turned toward her friends, toward Scott, Brandy, and Rebecca, who still stood beside Scott's SUV.

She expected to see happiness written on those familiar faces, pleasure that their foes had been defeated, that she and Season had prevailed. The happiness of a reunion with old comrades. She hadn't seen any of them since she had sent Scott away, and she had known she was hurting him terribly when she did. She wanted to hug him, to let him know she hadn't meant any of it, was only concerned for his safety. She wanted to hug all of them, to enjoy the reunion, to get past the adrenaline rush of the battle in the company of friends.

That was what she expected.

What she saw instead was absolute terror. Rebecca shrank visibly under her gaze, crossing her arms over her chest and taking a step toward the vehicle. Brandy and Scott stood their ground. None of them spoke, but their faces said it all.

They were afraid of Kerry. After all they had been through, all she had done for them . . . now she horrified them. They had seen her power—and her capacity for violence—and instead of being impressed, or pleased, or heartened, all it had done was scare them.

She had been one of them. Now she was something else. Something . . . other.

Kerry had become a witch, and her friends were frightened of witches. Who could blame them, really, considering what they had seen, what they knew?

But reasoning through it, understanding their reactions, didn't make any of it any easier to take.

Kerry thought that her wounded heart, which had so recently begun to heal, would finally break.

SPRING

It's hard to describe exactly what I was feeling, standing there beside the road that led down to Berlin, New Hampshire, looking at the expressions on the faces of my friends and realizing that they were afraid of me.

Because we're talking about *me*. Not only am I the kind of person who wouldn't, as they say, hurt a fly, I'm the kind who the fly could probably beat up. Old stringbean Profitt, that's me. Arms more like Minnie Mouse than Popeye.

Lately, however, I've learned that one doesn't have to be all buff and weight-liftery to be powerful. And it's that kind of power—the kind that comes from understanding one's relationship to the ebb and flow of natural forces—that made Brandy, Rebecca, and Scott so afraid of me. They saw me with Season Howe—whom they had known only as a hated enemy—battling Mother Blessing's simulacra.

And since one of those simulacra had come up from Berlin in the car with my buds, while I was coming down the selfsame mountainside in a car with Season, they unsurprisingly assumed that I had gone over to Season's side.

Which, to be fair, I had.

But also to be fair, Season isn't the monster they thought she was. And Mother Blessing, whom they still believed was trustworthy, is a monster.

All in all, a confusing situation. Which didn't make it any easier to look at their faces and know they feared me.

I did what I had to do at that minute. Mentally and physically drained as I was from the fight, I made like a cross between an auctioneer and Dr. Phil and fast-talked them out of panicking and running away. Then I persuaded them to follow us, in Scott's car, back up the hill to Season's cabin. Once we got there, Season made us some hot spiced apple cider while I laid the whole story out for them—starting at the beginning, which was 1704 and the destruction of Slocumb, Virginia. I told them how Daniel Blessing had always been told by his mother that it was Season who destroyed Slocumb, and how when Daniel and his twin brother Abraham were old enough, Mother Blessing sent them out on their quest for revenge. Or *her* quest, to be more precise. But it turns out that Mother Blessing is a stinking liar, and she's spent all these years blaming Season for something she did herself. In the process, she cost both of her sons their lives, and got our friends Mace and Josh killed too.

Okay, technically, Season is the one who killed Mace. She doesn't get off the hook for that one so easily. But the winds of war, I think somebody once said, can shift in an instant. When she killed Mace, he had been hooked up with us, and we were hooked up with Daniel, and Daniel was trying to kill Season. So self-defense? Kind of hard to argue with.

In the end, I must have been persuasive. Scott and Rebecca were easy, of course—Scott because he majorly crushes on me, and Rebecca because she always wants to believe the best of anybody. Brandy was tougher, as I had known she would be. But finally she came over to my side as well. Season helped—she speaks well for herself, articulate and bright and convincing. By the end of it they had all agreed to spend the night there, in the cabin, with the understanding that we'd move out by first light. It isn't safe here anymore, Season told us. Mother Blessing had been able to track us this far, had even been able to get one of her magically constructed pseudo-men to join up with them. She was getting too close, and we had to abandon this hidey-hole and go somewhere else.

The hugs and kisses and tears that should have accompanied our reunion—the first time we had all been together since Josh's death in Las Vegas—came then, at the end of the evening instead of the beginning. We were all wrung out emotionally by then, all exhausted. With the prospect of a very early morning facing us, we went to our assigned sleeping areas—I'm still in the bed I've been in since Christmas Eve—to get some shut-eye.

Except of course, me being me, a day like this requires some journaling time as well. But sunup is going to feel awfully early, so I should probably fold up the trusty laptop and actually shut that aforementioned eye.

Both of them, even.

More later.

K.

1

In the morning Season pounded on the door to her room, and Kerry started, as surprised as if someone had lit a firecracker under her feet. She sat up in bed, took stock quickly of where she was, rubbed her bleary eyes. Another four hours of unconsciousness would have been good, another six even better. Christmas Day had been relaxing, but it was bookended by days that were anything but, and she was feeling the strain.

She heard the sounds of her friends being similarly roused, though, so she climbed out of bed and dressed hurriedly. She'd showered the night before, knowing from hard experience that any time she could grab a shower she had better avail herself of it, because it might be the last for a while. It meant sleeping with wet hair—and lots of it, given the length of Kerry's dark tresses. But that was a small price to pay for the pleasure of being able to stand her own company all day.

Even moving as quickly as she could, by the time she made it out, Season had put together one of her signature breakfast feasts. Kerry was a little too sleepy to take full advantage, but she managed an English muffin, a couple of cups of strong black tea, and a slice of bacon. Scott Banner filled his plate with a little of everything—scrambled eggs, hash browns, fruit, two kinds of toast, and bacon.

Brandy Pearson looked at his plate and snorted. "You have eaten before, right?" she prodded.

"Let him indulge," Season said. "We're not taking it with us, and I won't be coming back here again for a good long time, if ever. Might as well not waste it."

Scott simply nodded at Season's defense and shoveled another forkful of eggs into his mouth. He'd put on a bulky wool sweater with black jeans and the all-weather hiking boots he had been wearing the day before. Kerry thought he had put on a few pounds since summer, when they had all shared a house together in La Jolla, California. The weight looked good on him, filling out his gaunt cheeks a bit.

Rebecca Levine had taken too many off, and Kerry was still worried about her. She had hoped the redheaded free spirit would stay down in New York—or better yet, back in school at Santa Cruz—and far away from Season and the whole long-unresolved conflict. But here she was, too big-hearted to let her friends face danger without being there too.

Brandy was the one Kerry had gone the longest without seeing. Her thick black hair was tied down with a red scarf, and her off-white sweater beautifully complemented her cocoa skin. Brandy had always been a girl who could put herself together, even when trouble was brewing. She shrugged off Season's defense of Scott and took another bite of the honeydew that, along with a cup of coffee, seemed to comprise her entire breakfast.

"You said before that we have to leave here," Brandy observed. "I get that. But where are we going? If Mother Blessing could track you guys down here, where will we be safe?"

Season set down her own coffee mug and regarded Brandy calmly. "I wish I had an answer for that," she said. "The truth is, I don't know. I can only strategize, but I have no guarantees."

"Okay, what's your strategy?" Rebecca asked.

"Here's what I've been thinking," Season replied. "We need to split up. Together, we'll be far too easy to find now that she has a line on all of us. Without you, Kerry, or her sons, she has no champions left, but she still has power, and even though we can beat her simulacra, there's still the chance that they could catch us by surprise. Or she could join the fight herself. I can beat Mother Blessing in a fair fight on neutral ground, I'm sure. But I don't think a fair fight is what she has in mind."

"So we all have to go different places?" Rebecca asked. The idea obviously caused her concern, and she didn't get her hands into her lap quickly enough to hide their quaking from Kerry.

"For the most part," Season said, "I think you should all go back home. You back to Santa Cruz, Scott and Brandy back to Boston. Resume your normal lives and activities, as much as possible. That way even if she does locate you again, there won't be any advantage to her to harass you, because you'll be out of it."

"Will we?" Scott asked. "Because I'm getting the distinct impression that this whole deal is kind of like the mob, or the CIA. Once you're in you can never really get out."

Season's nod was barely perceptible, but it was there. "There's some truth to that, Scott. I won't lie and say that you'll be completely safe. It depends partly on Mother Blessing. But if she observes you and understands that you're not in contact with me, that you're just going about your lives, then your chances are that much better. If we all stayed together, then you'd always be in jeopardy."

"Who is this 'we,' then?" Brandy wanted to know. "I notice you didn't say anything about Kerry going home."

"Maybe that's because I don't have one anymore," Kerry pointed out.

"Kerry is in this much more deeply than the rest of you," Season said. "She's a witch, Mother Blessing knows her well, and she's a target. She's probably in more danger because, skilled as she is, she still has a long way to go. If Mother Blessing really came at her, Kerry couldn't win. She needs to stay with me, for her own protection and training." Season paused, making eye contact with Kerry. "Does that sound okay to you, Kerry?"

If she had been asked even twelve hours earlier, Kerry would have hesitated. She hadn't decided quite how she felt about Season. The witch had, after all, killed Daniel, who was the only man Kerry had ever loved. And she had no real proof of her contention that it was Mother Blessing, and not herself, who was behind the slaughter in Slocumb. Her story rang truer than Mother Blessing's did, but Kerry was no expert lie detector. It was one witch's word against another's.

So she couldn't have said exactly why, but she agreed almost immediately. "Sure," she said. "I've got nowhere better to go, right?"

"That's one way to look at it."

Kerry knew there were several other ways to look at it too, but they all added up to the same response. She really was running out of other options. She had made a powerful enemy in Mother Blessing. She had left her Aunt Betty and Uncle Marsh behind too many times, and wasn't so sure she'd be welcome back there. Her parents were dead, and her best friends in the world were the people in this room with her—the only people who could ever really know what she had been through since August.

And she figured Season was right in her evaluation of Kerry's abilities. She could do more witchy stuff than she'd been able to a few months before, but that probably meant she was just powerful enough to harm herself and others. She still needed tutelage, a mentor, and if Season wanted to be that, Kerry was happy to avail herself of the opportunity.

"Okay, then," she said cheerily. "I guess you're stuck with me."

Brandy eyed them both suspiciously. "But where are you guys going?" she inquired.

"I think it's best not to tell you," Season replied. "Not because we don't trust you—clearly, Kerry trusts you with her life, and that's good enough for me. But the fewer people who know, the safer everyone is."

"I don't like it at all," Brandy said. "But I guess I see your point."

"I'll be in touch as often as I can," Kerry promised. "So you guys don't have to worry about me."

"I'll still worry," Scott said.

Brandy nodded. "Don't take away Scott's favorite leisure-time activity. He's a gold medalist when it comes to worrying about you."

"I'm fine," Kerry stated flatly. "I've been in a couple of tight spots, but I've always come out okay. You don't need to worry about me, Scott. Especially if I'm with Season."

"I know," Scott said, blinking behind his glasses. "I mean, I understand that, intellectually. But it's not so easy when I don't know where you are or what you're doing. I always find myself thinking about the worst thing that could be happening, and assuming that *is* what's happening."

Rebecca laughed, covering her mouth with one hand. "But the truth is that whatever is really happening is usually even *worse* than Scott's imagination."

"Look, you guys." Kerry really hoped that she could persuade them of her safety, just as she had convinced them last night that she hadn't turned traitor or fallen under some kind of evil mind-control power of Season's. She knew what she was doing—okay, maybe that was a stretch. But she had some sense that she was doing the best thing for herself. These days—since the night she had met Daniel Blessing, really, changing her life forever—that was the most she could ask for. "I know I've said this before, but I really need you all to support me in this. And that means not worrying too much about me. You've all got your own lives to live, and I have mine. Mine is taking me in some directions that I didn't expect—but I think everyone probably finds out that's true, at some point or other. I mean, did your parents grow up thinking that they'd be pharmacists or lawyers or whatever? So I'm not taking the usual path. But I'm taking my own path, and you're taking yours, and we all just have to have some faith in one another's decision making."

Brandy snorted. "She's talking to you, Scott."

Kerry couldn't suppress a grin. "Thanks for not taking me seriously, Brandy," she said. "I could hardly believe that was me talking."

"It was a little drippy," Rebecca agreed. "But still—it made sense."

"Rebecca's right," Scott put in. "I don't mean to freak you out or anything, Kerry. I guess I'm just a worrywart by nature. But I do respect your decisions. If you and Season think you'll be safer, then Brandy and I will just go home and let you guys go wherever."

Season had been silent for a long time, just listening and letting the four friends work out their issues. Now she broke her silence. "I do think that's for the best," she said.

Kerry was glad the conversation had gone her way. "Sounds like it to me, too."

Scott looked at Brandy. "You need a ride, lady?"

"I guess I'm going your way," Brandy said. "If you think you have room for me."

"There's always room for you, Brandy," Scott said. "If you don't mind the stink of that mud-man we had in the backseat."

Brandy looked as if she was thinking it over. "I guess I can put up with it as far as Boston," she admitted. "If we can stop at a car wash on the way. But we should probably be hitting the road—I'll have a lot of explaining to do when we get there."

Kerry was sorry their reunion had been so brief. One of these days, she wanted time to really catch up with her friends, to find out what was going on in their lives instead of just telling them what was up in hers. This wasn't going to be that time, though. Season was right—the sooner they vacated this cabin, the safer they'd all be.

2

"I've been doing some thinking," Rebecca said on the way to the airport in Burlington, Vermont, the nearest city with what passed for a "major" airport. "You guys should fly to California with me."

"That doesn't really help with the splitting up thing," Kerry answered. She guessed that Rebecca just really didn't want to be left alone again—even with her hardly-there roommate Erin. "Anyway, aren't you going back to New York, to spend the rest of the holidays with your folks?"

"I don't want to put them in any danger," Rebecca explained. "And anyway, I don't think I'd ever really feel safe there. California is about as far away from Mother Blessing as I can get, and Manhattan is so crowded that I'd never know who was real and who was one of her simulacra. In Santa Cruz you see the same familiar faces every day, and I'm more comfortable there.

"Anyway," she went on, "I wasn't thinking that you'd go to Santa Cruz with me. California is a huge state. I have these friends who own property up in Bolinas, on the coast up above San Francisco. They get tourists, but mostly it's this really out-of-the-way place where people value their privacy. Half the people up there are old-time hippies, and the rest are artists or hermits of one kind or another. There are a lot of marijuana farmers, too. They tend to be a suspicious bunch and don't like outsiders nosing around much. If you were there, I think you'd be pretty safe from Mother Blessing's minions."

"But we'd be outsiders too," Kerry said. She rode shotgun, and Rebecca sat in the back of Season's Jeep, which they would abandon at the airport.

Kerry wondered momentarily how many vehicles Season had left behind in her life. Enough to fill a stadium parking lot, probably.

"Yeah, but you'd have someplace to be, so it would be okay."

"If we had the permission of your friends to use their place," Season added. "But getting that permission might endanger them."

"I'm sure I could swing that without telling them what it's for," Rebecca said. "That privacy thing cuts both ways. People who don't want others knowing their business are usually happy not to know yours."

"Sounds like it's worth checking out," Kerry suggested. "Unless you already have someplace in mind, Season."

Season glanced over at her and smiled, then faced the road once more. "I like it precisely because it's something I wouldn't have thought of," she said. "It's good to break out of old patterns if you're hiding from someone who knows you well. I'm pretty sure Mother Blessing is aware of most of my tricks by now."

"I'll call them," Rebecca said. "And when we get to the airport we can all fly together to San Francisco. From there I can get a shuttle to Santa Cruz, and you guys can rent a car or something to head up to Bolinas." Kerry heard a rustling as Rebecca dug out her cell phone and then dialed it. Kerry only half paid attention as Rebecca worked on persuading her friends, the Morgans, to let Season and Kerry use their place.

She realized she was happy to be on the move again. Since August she had spent a fair bit of time on the road, running toward or away from one witch or another. Rootless, her only permanent home now had a white line running down its middle—either that or two wings and jet engines that lifted her far above the Earth. Motion was the only constant, staying in one place too long the greatest danger. This had been Season's reality for centuries, and now it was also Kerry's. She wasn't sure if she truly liked it, but she was getting used to it.

If nothing else, she had learned the virtue of flexibility.

* * *

Scott pulled his RAV4 away from the curb after dropping Brandy at her parents' home in Needham, where she had wanted to go instead of back to her own apartment. He had wanted to be invited in. Even though he was a little nervous about seeing her brothers, afraid they blamed him for their breakup and maybe for her missing Christmas, he liked her family and missed spending time with them. She didn't extend that invitation, though. They had chatted amicably enough on the drive down from New Hampshire, with Brandy slipping in the occasional stinging barb, as she had a habit of doing. But she had grown quieter as they closed on the Boston area, her mood almost visibly darkening. He knew she was worried about Adam Castle, her new boyfriend, and about facing her family after skipping out on them at Christmas. At the end of the trip, she quietly thanked him for the ride and gave him a perfunctory hug.

Scott was still not thrilled with the idea that Brandy had a new boyfriend, but he was trying to adjust. He and Brandy had been a good thing for a long time, but that was over. He and Kerry could be a good thing too, he was sure, but it was looking like that would never happen. He glanced in his rearview mirror as he drove away from her block, watching it recede behind him like some kind of suburban metaphor for the longest romantic relationship of his life.

He knew he would still see Brandy from time to time, no matter what. Kerry too—or at least he devoutly hoped so. She would be farther away, however, and he would continue to worry about her, no matter what she wanted. Season would be a better ally for her than he could ever be, but he nonetheless felt better when she was someplace where he could keep an eye on her. Now she was no doubt winging or riding somewhere halfway across the continent, and he was back in the position of having to wait for her to get in touch with him whenever the mood struck her.

As he turned the corner he stole one last glance at Brandy's house. But in his mind's eye he could see Kerry's slow but genuine smile, her green eyes flashing like twin emeralds catching the sun, her long black hair falling over her face and then being swept away, and he knew that such a beautiful vision would never leave him, no matter what else happened in his life.

The San Francisco airport was a terrible place for good-byes. It was crowded and busy, with travelers bustling in every direction, all pulling wheeled suitcases as if they were oversized, blocky dogs, with security people, flight attendants, pilots and staff, and families waiting for or dropping off their loved ones. It meant there was no real privacy, no place for the kind of conversation Rebecca, Season, and Kerry really needed to have.

Instead of trying to talk in detail, they resorted to a kind of code. "So," Rebecca said. "You have my number. If you need anything, just call. Otherwise, my friends are expecting you to be at their place. If it goes more than a couple of months, it wouldn't hurt to call up, but I don't think they're planning on being back up there until early summer. I told you where the key is, right?"

"Yes," Season said. "We know where to look for it."

"And you have my cell, right?" Kerry asked redundantly, knowing full well that Rebecca did. What she didn't know was whether she'd have coverage in Bolinas—it sounded pretty rural, the way Rebecca described it. But she had also said it was a tourist destination, so maybe her phone would work fine. At the very worst, she could always augment it magically, as Mother Blessing had done with her laptop in the Great Dismal Swamp. "If you see or hear any signs of her, you let us know, okay? Don't take any chances with her." Obviously, everyone knew who the "her" referred to.

"Hello," Rebecca said. "Do you know me? Do you remember me being someone who takes chances?"

"You've taken a lot of them, Beck," Kerry said. "I just want you to be safe, okay?"

"That's what I want too," Rebecca assured her. "Well, for both of us—all of us—to be safe."

"The sooner we split up the safer we'll be," Season said. She scanned the crowds like a wary hawk. "I'm sorry, I'm not trying to rush you, Rebecca, but we really need to get going."

"I know," Rebecca said. "It'll be late by the time I get home too. I just . . . I don't want you guys to go."

"I don't either, Beck," Kerry said, suddenly sorry for her friend. Of all her summer friends, Rebecca might have been the least capable of dealing with the kinds of things they had learned—the existence of real witches, the magic, the constant danger. Kerry knew that going back to college in Santa Cruz, living in that big, ramshackle house with Erin, and being so far from the others was going to be tougher on her than on anyone else. She wished there was something she could do to make it easier.

But there wasn't. Inviting Rebecca to stay with them up in Bolinas would just expose her to even more potential danger. Season was right—Rebecca was safest living her own normal life, far away from them. She wouldn't like it, at least at first, but it was for the best.

Kerry wrapped her arms around her friend and gave her a firm squeeze. Rebecca returned it, sniffling a little as she did. *No tears,* Kerry mentally pleaded. *I don't know if I can take it.*

When she pulled away, there was moisture in Rebecca's eyes, but none escaped. Kerry blinked back a little of her own, and then Rebecca turned away and headed for the shuttles. Kerry and Season stood there for a few minutes, until Rebecca was out of sight. Then Kerry turned to the older woman.

"What now? We can't take a cab to Bolinas, right?"

"For tonight?" Season asked, almost incredulous. "We're in San Francisco, girl. Let's get a hotel room and do it right."

Kerry Profitt's diary, December 27

As it happens, Season's idea of doing it right was not precisely the same as mine would have been. Not that I'm club-girl or anything. But a little shopping might have been fun. It was pretty late at night by the time we were checked in at the Mark Hopkins, but still, big city, right? Something must have been open.

Instead, Season got us a cab and went into North Beach, where she took me to a hole-in-the-wall Italian restaurant that I never would have looked twice at. Once I was inside, though, it was like Pavlov's dog all over again—the aroma was heavenly and I was suddenly so famished it was like I had never eaten the cardboard baguette sandwich they served on the plane. Which, in fact, I hadn't, because, you know, cardboard.

I just let her order, because the whole menu was in Italian and I was too hungry to even read English. I won't try to re-create the dinner here—let's just say that everything I ate was so good that my mouth thought it had died and gone to heaven, leaving the rest of me earthbound. The staff treated us both like old friends, although Season swore that's just the way they are, and she had never seen any of them before.

After dinner we walked around North Beach for a while, just watching the people, tourists and locals alike. It's quite a show. We chatted about the people we saw and the weather—cool, but nothing like Chicago or New Hampshire, with a fog that eventually rolled in off the bay like someone pulling a blanket over a bed. Basically, we covered everything except Mother Blessing and what lay ahead of us.

Which was fine. I dwell on that stuff enough as it is. It was good to have my attention distracted by something else for a bit.

I almost typed "for a spell" but decided that would be just too witchy of me. Witchy and old-fashioned, which kind of go together, considering that other than me, the youngest witch I know is, like, three hundred and some years older than I am.

Now we're back in the room—_très luxe!_—and Season's getting ready for bed while I do the dear diary thing. But she'll come out soon and then it's my turn, and then another early start in the morning. I'm a little trepidatious, I admit, about what tomorrow holds, and the day after that, and so on. Me and Season Howe, teamed up? Who'd have ever thought?

More later.

K.

"I'll be Margaret Thurston," Season said. "And you're my niece, Melissa King."

They were in the back of a taxi, bouncing over San Francisco's famous hills on the way to a used car lot Season had found listed in the hotel room's phone book.

"But you'll have to show some identification to buy a car, right?" Kerry asked. "I did, when I bought that van to go down to the Great Dismal."

Season just looked at her, smiling. It took Kerry a few seconds to realize her mistake.

"Oh," she said when she caught on.

To demonstrate, Season opened her wallet and handed it over. Inside it, every identifying item showed the name Margaret Thurston: a valid California driver's license with a Bay Area address, several credit cards, a Social Security card, even a library card. A checkbook had the same name, with a local address imprinted on the checks. "And mine all say Melissa King, right?"

"That's right."

Kerry double-checked the window between the front and back seats. It was mostly closed, but there was a narrow gap through which passengers could speak to the driver. The driver had her radio on, though, playing loud reggae music, so Kerry figured as long as they spoke in low tones they wouldn't be overheard.

"So on top of everything else, you could be a world-class counterfeiter," Kerry said. "Do you manufacture your own money, too?"

"I don't," Season answered. Under a tan leather jacket, she wore a snug blue turtleneck that was almost as vibrant as her piercing blue eyes, with faded brown jeans and black boots, and her blond hair hung loose, framing her face. "I know I wouldn't ever make so much of it that I'd have a real impact on the national economy, but the possibility exists—a witch could manufacture so much cash, and flood the markets with it, that it could devalue our currency. Because I want to make sure that never happens, I only spend money that I earn."

"But you don't have a job," Kerry pointed out.

"Maybe 'earn' isn't the right word," Season admitted. "I have investments, under various names. I gamble sometimes, although I try to resist the temptation to push the odds in my favor. I have a bank account in most cities, collecting interest. Every few years I move them around, because an account in constant use for a hundred years might raise some eyebrows. One of those accounts is here in the Bay Area, under the name Margaret Thurston. I have as much as I need, especially since I make a lot of my own clothing and food."

Kerry thought of her own bank account, established with money from an insurance settlement after her mother's death. She had tapped it a few times since summer, never putting anything back in. There were still several thousand dollars in it, but if she continued on as she had been it wouldn't last a whole lot longer. Would she follow in Season's footsteps, constantly on the move and making witchery her lifelong career? Or was this just another phase in her life that she'd pass through in a little while? She had a hard time picturing herself doing anything more mundane after this experience. Working a food service job or being stuck inside an office seemed like they'd be claustrophobic at best. And her experience with higher education—vanishing from Northwestern a few weeks into her first term—was not promising so far.

She wanted to talk to Season about it, to find out more about her early life and how she had made the decision to be a witch—if there were even any other options open to her—but the cab pulled to the curb beside a sprawling car lot, decorated with multicolored pennants on ropes and sporting dozens of gleaming, polished vehicles. "Here you go, ladies," the driver said through the window. Season pushed a twenty through the window at her, and the two witches stepped out onto the sidewalk.

"Let me do the talking," Season said. "The van you bought was okay for you, but I think we're going to want four-wheel drive up in the country. And you never pay sticker at a place like this."

Another vital life lesson from Season Howe, Kerry thought as a salesman approached. He grinned like a hungry shark, and Kerry realized she was happy to let Season handle the negotiation.

3

An hour later they were crossing the rust-red span of the Golden Gate Bridge, heading north out of the city. Bolinas wasn't far up the coast, but it sat on the end of a little spur of land, separated from the rest of the state by the Point Reyes National Seashore. That isolated it enough that the locals felt they had their much-sought-after privacy.

Through a spattering rain, Season drove the old silver Dodge Raider they'd settled on, up Highway One through affluent Marin County. They made one stop, at a supermarket where they laid in some provisions—"real food," Kerry called it, as opposed to the magically created kind.

As they neared Point Reyes the rain picked up, a solid curtain of it through which visibility was almost nonexistent. Heading into the park, sheets of water filled the narrow roadways. Kerry noticed that Season's knuckles were white on the wheel, and her easy chatter of earlier in the drive had died. All her focus was on the task of negotiating the road. The beauty of Point Reyes was unmistakable, but Kerry could barely see it, and she knew that Season was missing it altogether. She hoped they'd have a chance to come back sometime, to explore the oddly twisted pines and the wind-and-water-sculpted cliffs.

Instead of letting up as they progressed, the storm just dumped ever more rain on them—glimpses of the ocean were redundant, as there seemed to be as much water falling from the sky as in the Pacific. A few cars passed them, their occupants looking like tourists distressed that their trip to Stinson Beach had been ruined by the downpour. But they soon turned off the main road onto an old country lane that led away from Bolinas's minimal "downtown" and through rolling, grassy hills.

The storm let up a little, and Kerry noticed that Season visibly relaxed now that she was off the main road. So she decided to bring up a question that had been on her mind for a long time—one of those that she thought of, then forgot to ask, on a regular basis, usually remembering again at only the most inopportune moments.

"Season, that storm, when you attacked Mother Blessing's place in the Swamp—did you cause that? Or was it one of her defenses? Or just a natural occurrence?"

Season glanced at her. "I guess this is as good a time as any to bring up something I wanted to talk about," she said, apparently ignoring Kerry's question altogether.

"What?"

"I've offered to teach you, to help you develop your obviously significant gifts. And for the last few days, I've pretty much been willing to answer any question you threw my way. But once we get settled into our new place, we'll be going back to a routine like we had at Christmas."

"The no-more-than-ten-questions thing? Why?"

"We might change the number—maybe fifteen per day, or something like that, since we'll be working closely together. But the reason we'll be working together is so you can learn. To do that, you have to be focused. Asking a million questions about any trivial matter that pops into your head is a scattershot way of learning, and it's not that effective. If you have to think your questions through, really narrow down what you need to know and sift out those things you can figure out on your own, then you'll learn much more quickly, and you'll retain more."

"I guess that makes sense," Kerry admitted. She felt a little thwarted by the idea, although Season's reasoning seemed sound. "But you said that starts when we get settled?"

"Right."

"Which means I can ask questions now, right?"

"Uh-huh," Season answered. Most of her attention was still on the road, keeping the vehicle in contact with the wet pavement and trying to follow the directions they'd been given.

"So why are you doing this? Why take me under your wing like this? What's in it for you?"

Season hazarded another, longer glance at Kerry before facing front again. "I thought it was obvious," she said. "Like I told you, you are a gifted witch. A kind of diamond in the rough, I suppose. But anyone who learned as much as you in those few weeks with Mother Blessing is a person to be reckoned with."

Kerry thought her heart would burst with pride at that description. She wasn't sure she could live up to it, but she would definitely try.

"Part of being a witch is giving back to the community of witches," Season went on. "One way to do that is to help teach and develop young witches, so that the traditions are carried on. In this case, of course, there's also a much more practical consideration."

"What's that?"

"Mother Blessing and I have been at each other's throats for centuries," Season explained. "We've each won some battles, but the overall war goes on. One of these days, one of us is going to have to prevail. I would much rather have you on my side in the conflict than hers, because frankly, I could use some allies here."

Kerry started to say that she was honored that Season would consider her aid anything to be desired, but as she was composing her thoughts, Season interrupted. "And that storm in the Great Dismal, by the way, was mine. Mother Blessing knew I was coming, but I was hoping to mask my exact progress to some extent, so she wouldn't know precisely where I was or when I'd reach her home."

"It worked," Kerry said. "She was trying to prepare, but you caught her before she was completely ready."

"And still, I couldn't beat her," Season recalled. "Partly because she is most powerful on her home ground, where she has lived for so long. And partly because she had your help."

"Did I really make that big a difference?" Kerry asked, surprised.

"Do you really have to ask?"

Before Kerry could answer the question, Season pulled off the little country lane onto a rutted dirt track, just the width of two sets of wheels. "Here we are," she said, ticking her head toward a mailbox with a street number painted on it.

The track wound between spreading oaks, down into a little incline where a wood-sided house stood. It was a single story, with a porch across the front. Its blue paint, faded, blistered, and peeling from the sun and weather, was rain-darkened, and water dripped from its eaves. The roof had seen better days, but Kerry figured if it was dry inside, after the storm that had blown through today, then it would hold up fine.

Season parked at the end of the drive, in a little dirt circle right before the front door. "Home again, home again," she said.

They had left New Hampshire with very little. Kerry brought her usual duffel containing a few changes of clothes, some of Daniel's journals, and her laptop computer. Season had a leather backpack that seemed to contain anything she would ever need. Kerry was convinced that if she ever looked inside, it would be empty, and that Season just conjured what she wanted from it. They hauled the groceries inside and dumped the bags on a table made from raw oak planks, sanded but not sealed or painted. The kitchen was small, but clean water ran from the tap, the refrigerator was cold, and the gas oven and stove seemed to work. The owners had an interesting sense of color—the kitchen's walls were fire-engine red and bright blue, while the floor was yellow and the appliances white and gold.

The rest of the house echoed the general color chaos. Wooden walls were painted in seemingly whatever color had struck someone's fancy at a given moment, or maybe just in whatever was on sale at the hardware store. Most of the floors were unpainted, but there were exceptions, including a forest green one with red polka dots.

There seemed to be a great deal of wildlife—spiders, ants, flies, and other less immediately identifiable creepy-crawlies—inside the house that Kerry would just as soon have had living outside instead. She figured that it was a function of the house having been unoccupied for a stretch, and that once she and Season had made the place their own, the bugs would move out. Living in the Swamp had given her a greater tolerance for insect life than she'd ever had before, and learning witchcraft had impressed on her the role that all living things played in the world. Mother Blessing had told her it was scientific fact that if all the insects in the world were to suddenly vanish, all other life on the planet would end within two weeks. Mother Blessing had made a lot of outrageous claims, but Kerry couldn't help suspecting there was some truth to that one.

In spite of the colors and the creatures, the house was cozy and plenty comfortable enough for Kerry's liking. The furniture was old, mismatched, and lived in, as if it had grown up organically within the house. A door led from the kitchen into a small grassy backyard with a few rows of herbs and vegetables, overgrown now but offering the promise of fresh food with only a little work and attention. Beyond that were woods that seemed to go on forever. The room Kerry chose as her bedroom was next to the only bathroom, and though it was a little smaller than the other bedroom, it had a built-in window seat where she could already imagine herself reading and writing at night.

In the middle of the afternoon, after Kerry had hung up her clothes in the room's tiny closet and shoved some furniture around so she'd be able to see trees out the window from her bed, Season called her into the kitchen.

Two cups of hot tea and a plate of cookies were set out on the table. Season sat in one of the four random chairs that surrounded it, looking expectantly at Kerry. It was clear that she'd been summoned for a particular reason, so Kerry took a chair and drew one of the cups to her. She wasn't going to waste one of her questions by asking what was up.

"I wanted to tell you what is really going on here," Season said after a moment. "Why Mother Blessing has stepped up the pace of attacks against me, and why staying with me puts you in considerable danger."

"Okay." Outside, the rain continued to beat down on the roof, creating a kind of staccato background music for their conversation.

"You know about the Witches' Convocation," Season declared plainly. "It starts on the first day of spring. One of the important functions of the Convocation is to rule on disputes between witches, as well as on crimes against witchcraft and crimes by witches against humanity. We firmly believe in policing ourselves, so that the outside world never decides it has to take action against us."

"Which means that the Convocation will finally address what happened in Slocumb," Kerry said, careful in her phrasing. She was determined to save her questions.

"That's right," Season agreed. "We have a very rigid and highly developed system of justice, which is prepared to deal with all of those issues I just described. The Slocumb incident will definitely have a hearing in Witches' Tribunal. Mother Blessing has been spreading her version of things ever since it happened, and even though her version is a lie, there's a little bit of that 'common knowledge' thing operating in her favor."

"People tend to believe something they've heard over and over, even if there's no truth to it," Kerry stated.

"Exactly. I've tried to get my story out there too, but it's been harder for me. For one thing, I didn't know she was spreading her tales for a long time, until they started filtering back to me. And then, she had me on the run for so long that it was hard to get a fair hearing—I looked guilty simply because I wasn't sitting still and waiting for her to finish me off."

"That's not fair."

"That's true. But then, fairness is what the Convocation is for. I'll be at a disadvantage because so many will have heard Mother Blessing's side of it, but the hearing will be as impartial as possible. Which is why Mother Blessing would love to get rid of me before it happens. She could use the Slocumb incident as a defense when the hearing about my death came up, as it certainly would. But that would be an easier sell for her, since she wouldn't have to worry about my testimony contradicting hers."

"So she'd like to kill you before it starts, but even if she doesn't, she stands a good chance of beating you in court?"

"That about sums it up," Season admitted sadly. "She isn't guaranteed to win. I happen to believe that the truth will sway the Tribunal to my side. And I think there's a way to prove that truth. But I'm going to need your help."

"My help?"

"That's right. I need someone I can trust completely, someone familiar with the facts, and someone who is very powerful and skilled."

"But I have a long way to go before I'm those things."

"And it's not quite January," Season replied. "Which is why we need to train so hard between now and the Convocation. I'm going to want you by my side, Kerry. More than that. I'm going to need you. Will you be there for me?"

Stunned that she was being asked, being trusted with so much, at first it was all Kerry could do to nod her head. "Of course," she said finally. "I'll do whatever I can."

"That's good," Season said, a warm smile spreading over her face. "That's the best I can ask for."

4

Mother Blessing wheeled angrily around her home in the Great Dismal Swamp, her motorized scooter's rubber tires squeaking on the hardwood floors. Somehow Season Howe had survived her onslaught. It had taken every ounce of strength Mother Blessing could bring to bear to create nearly a hundred simulacra, and still the witch had defeated them. If only she had been able to manifest them all at once instead of one at a time, however quickly. That might have proven too much even for someone of Season's abilities.

But that great an effort, over such a distance, was beyond her. She had lain for days in her bed after the post-Christmas assault, exhausted by her efforts. It was only now, a couple of days after the passing of the year, that she was able to get around again. The immediate aftereffects of her spell had passed, but the fury hadn't.

Allowing Kerry Profitt to receive communications while she was here in this house had been a stroke of genius. Doing so had enabled Mother Blessing to learn who was close to Kerry, who might be keeping tabs on her whereabouts. So when the urgent call had passed from one to the next—*We've found Season!*—Mother Blessing had known approximately where to begin looking. By watching through the eyes of her simulacrum scouts, she had spotted the young interlopers, and they had led her right to Kerry and Season.

It only added to her rage that Kerry and Season seemed to have teamed up. She had groomed Kerry to be an arrow that she could let fly at Season at any time. For that weapon to be turned so quickly against her was nothing short of infuriating.

But there was no one in the house to shout at, no one to complain to or abuse. So she slammed doors and made sharp turns with her scooter, envisioning the faces of her enemies on the floor and wishing she could roll over them as easily.

A new year had begun. The Convocation would be upon her in a matter of weeks. There was a chance that she would prevail in the Witches' Tribunal, but there was also always a chance that she would not. Far better to finally get Season out of the way before then.

And she could do it, she was convinced. Her mistake had always been in sending others to do the job. Her sons had turned out to be weak—not ruthless enough, or possibly not determined enough. She didn't know what the problem was, but they obviously had some failing that she had not recognized before. Kerry Profitt might have been forged into a useful weapon, given time, but she had been young, inexperienced, and Season had come before Mother Blessing had had a chance to finish with her.

So the task fell to her. Had she recognized this fact years ago, perhaps this war would have been long since over. She had always thought there was time, plenty of time. But suddenly the Convocation loomed. If it had been an annual event, or even a centennial one, perhaps she'd have been better prepared for it. Over the course of five hundred years, though—and this being the first and possibly the only one of her lifetime—it had kind of crept up on her.

It would take her a while to be ready for another battle. Weeks, maybe. Months would be better, but she didn't have months. Any moves against Season this close to the Convocation would automatically be suspect.

On the other hand, Season's presence at the Witches' Tribunal would be more perilous still.

She would just have to make sure that Season didn't show up for the Witches' Convocation. No matter what it took.

Dawn hadn't even cracked, if that's what dawn really did, when Kerry rolled out of bed at Season's summons. For the last several weeks, Season had been running her ragged. Up at first light, warming up, performing calisthenics in the cold morning air. Then a long run, at least five miles, before breakfast. Kerry kept thinking she'd get used to it, but so far she hadn't. Every night she went to bed with muscles sore from the day's workout, and every morning she woke up with aches worse than she'd had the night before.

After the run and a big breakfast, she and Season went out into the fields, forests, and beaches of the area for nature lessons. This area wasn't as rich in biological diversity as the Great Dismal Swamp had been, but it was still abundant in its plant species, and only slightly less so in animal life. And as Season explained, variety wasn't an absolute necessity—more important was the practitioner's connection with the natural forces that flowed through those plants and animals. Kerry, Season noted, had an almost innate ability to make that connection.

She could sit in the middle of a meadow with the wind pushing the tall grasses toward her, and the susurrus of the grass seemed to be a private conversation that only Kerry could understand. She could wait patiently with her arms extended in a forest glade, and birds would drop down to her hands. She had to overcome her distaste for insects, but once she had, they would crawl up her arms and legs without stinging, biting, or otherwise molesting her. Even the enormous elephant seals on the beach at Point Reyes responded to her. She made eye contact with one, which then rolled over onto its back, flippers extended out toward her, and uttered three long, deep-throated squeals in her direction.

After time spent communing with nature, the daily schedule called for a reading period. Kerry knew that Season had not brought an entire library's worth of magical texts with her to the Bolinas house, but the books were there, and Season assigned a heavy study regimen. These books reinforced what Mother Blessing and Season had taught her, but went into considerably greater detail about the origins of witchcraft, the theory behind individual spells, and even some of the great witches of the past.

The reading period was followed by lunch, and then by one-on-one instruction from Season, putting some of the things she had read into practical use. This usually took most of the afternoon, but if there was time, Season put her through more physical training.

"Stamina is just as important as knowing the ancient words of power backward and forward," Season explained on one of the many occasions when Kerry complained about the hard workouts. After dinner they sat around together, making small talk or discussing the events of the day. "It does you absolutely no good to know the words you say if you don't have the strength to put behind the spells. And if the first couple of spells knock you on your tail, you won't be around long enough to become an experienced witch."

"Yeah, but if the workout kills me, what good does all the knowledge do?"

"People almost always survive exercise," Season answered with a smile.

"And if I'd wanted to join the Marines, I would have."

"Are you calling me a drill sergeant, Private Profitt?"

"Hey, if the combat boot fits . . ."

The thing was, Kerry believed it was working. She had been in the best shape of her life when she'd been in the Swamp with Mother Blessing, but now, after just a few weeks with Season, she was even stronger. Her stomach was flat, her thighs and calves hard and sinewy, her arms and shoulders rippling with muscle. The old "no pain, no gain" saying seemed to have a lot of truth to it. Kerry definitely had the pain, but the gain was also unmistakable.

And the changes weren't confined to the physical. Kerry realized that she was sleeping more soundly—and falling asleep earlier, thanks to the way too early wake-up call—and her mood was generally positive and upbeat.

In this way the days sped by quickly—days of wind and weather, of frantic activity, of cramming her head so full of information that she was sure it would explode.

One night in late January, Season sat across from Kerry in the house's living room, crowded with a sofa, several chairs, and an assortment of tables that looked like they'd been purchased at flea markets over the years. Outside, yet another winter storm battered the roof. Season looked cozy in a red polar fleece top and black corduroy jeans. Kerry had layered a couple of T-shirts together, and sitting near the fire she was perfectly comfortable in those and blue jeans.

"I've noticed something interesting these last couple of weeks," Season began. She had poured herself a cup of hot tea, and on the oak coffee table she placed a cardboard box full of herbs she and Kerry had collected early on and hung in the kitchen to dry, and an old stone mortar and pestle. Kerry put down the book she was reading—a thriller from the 1970s that she'd found on a shelf in the house, not one of the magical texts—and looked at Season.

"What is it?" she asked.

Season put some of the herbs into the mortar before she answered. "Teaching you, working with you, has had an unexpected benefit for me as well," she said.

Kerry waited for her to continue. Season had a habit of revealing things at her own pace, no matter what.

"I've been pretty consumed," Season went on finally, grinding away with the pestle, "with either running from, or battling, Mother Blessing and her minions. It's taken so much of my time and energy that there hasn't been much left for anything else. Watching you, trying to see the world—and witchcraft—through your eyes, I've remembered what drew me to witch-craft in the first place."

"You were drawn?" Kerry asked. "You weren't born into it?"

"My father was a witch," Season replied. "Not my mother. She wanted nothing to do with it, and in fact convinced him to renounce his gift. Those were dangerous times for witches in Europe, so it was probably a good deci-sion in terms of prolonging his life. But it meant that I had aunts and one surviving grandmother who could tell me stories about the craft and point me in the right direction when I had made up my mind."

"And when you did, obviously you decided to go the witchy route," Kerry observed.

"Not at first. But there weren't a lot of opportunities for women in those days. I could have worked as a scullery maid, or married, or joined a con-vent. None of those particularly suited me, even then. My father always tried to impress upon me that I was different, special somehow. I guess I believed him. And then I watched women all around me leading miserable lives but saw that my aunts and grandmother were not only healthy and well kept, but commanded respect in their villages. With those role models, I could hardly turn my back."

"So they fulfilled the mentor role for you . . ."

"That I am trying to do for you, Kerry. That's right. And by doing so, I've reconnected to some of that sense of discovery I felt in those days. Learning how the world really works, how everything is connected. Feeling the excite-ment of creating a spell and watching it come about. There's a thrill of creativ-ity that happens, which I've kind of lost track of."

"I know what you mean," Kerry said. "I feel the same thing when one works just right."

"Watching you, seeing the spark in your eyes, that's what reminded me of it all. I'm indebted to you, Kerry. Thanks for showing it to me again."

Kerry was nonplussed—not for the first time since meeting Season.

"I—I'm the one who should be indebted, Season," she stammered. "You could have killed me, or at least sent me back to Mother Blessing. But you agreed to take me on, just like that—I can still hardly believe my luck."

"I think you're failing to see the big picture, Kerry. It's not just you who needs me. We both need each other." She took the pestle out of the mortar, in which she had crushed the dried herbs to a fine powder. "Think about that, okay?"

Kerry Profitt's diary, January 24

So Season owes me? The first impression test tells me that's crazy. So do the second and third. I owe her, huge. But what I've done *for* her could be measured in a teaspoon, I think. If you had a microscope to find it.

I mean, that whole thing she said earlier this evening about having connected somehow with the reasons she became a witch. A little touchy-feely, maybe, but still really sweet. And maybe there's even a modicum of truth to it—"modicum" being a word I was reacquainted with in one of Season's books, and I like it. It's kind of like forgetting how good popsicles taste on a hot day, and then you take a little kid to the store and buy him one, and you get your own, and when you lick it you remember why you liked them in the first place.

Or something like that. Only probably more profound.

But she told me to think about the fact that we both need each other, so that's what I've been doing. I can come up with plenty of reasons I need her: so I don't get killed, so I don't kill myself, so I can continue my training, so I can become the witch I'd like to be, etc. etc.

As for why she needs me . . . ? To help her battle Mother Blessing, I guess. And for whatever is coming at the Convocation, for which she told me she'll need my help. But I still don't know with what. The Convocation is a couple of months away, but getting closer all the time. Every now and then she drops hints about it, things she's heard over the years, and it sounds *amazing*. I can't wait to see it for myself.

I guess I have to, though. Wait, I mean.

What's it going to be like? Has a girl ever looked forward to something with such delirious anticipation?

Well, it so happens that I didn't go to my prom. I guess this is my consolation prize.

Although if you want the truth, this is about a million times cooler.

More later.

K.

5

Rebecca stood on the boardwalk, quiet this time of day. On a weekend, or later in the evening, it would be bustling with people playing for a chance at cheap prizes, lining up for the roller coaster, eating corn dogs and cotton candy. It was like a county fair or a circus all year long, except even more threadbare than most, with a sense of desperation underlying it, as if anyone who couldn't have fun here was just out of luck altogether.

Rebecca wasn't having any fun.

February had already bled into March. The school year was passing by, and she was attending class (well, most of the time—she should have been in class now, instead of at the beach) and trying to pay attention. Her grades had been passable, though not excellent. Nowhere near what she could have done if she had "applied herself"—a phrase Rebecca had heard many times during her school career—but at least she wasn't flunking out.

But although she got up every morning, ate a meal, went to school, did homework, read a little, the whole thing seemed like an exercise, a rehearsal for real life instead of life itself. She spent every day waiting for something that didn't come.

She knew what the problem was, of course, and it had more than one part. She lived on the edge of fear now, never knowing when Mother Blessing, or Season, or some other witch entirely might re-enter her life. Death followed in the wake of witches, that was her experience. And she couldn't quite believe that witches were gone from her life. Kerry Profitt, after all, seemed well on her way to becoming one. And the last time she had talked to Kerry, a month or so before, they were still up in Bolinas at the Morgans' place, and Kerry seemed to be more excited by her new path than ever.

So that was the first part—one of these days, Kerry or one of the witches associated with her would show up, and her life would be spun topsy-turvy again.

The second part was the fear that the first part wouldn't happen after all.

Because now Rebecca knew what most people never did. She understood that there was another aspect to life. And while that aspect was often terrifying, it was also exciting. Even the terror made her feel more *alive* than anything else she had ever encountered. The whole thing—the thrill of the chase, the shiver of horror when she learned that something she had believed was nonsense, or legend at best, was true—she couldn't shake her hunger for it.

Is that why Kerry threw herself into it? Rebecca wondered as she stared off into the blue distance, looking at the line where sky met sea. *Is she addicted too?*

And can addictions ever be good for you?

It was one of those Boston days when people begin to believe that spring will come around again. The gutters ran with melting snow, which for at least a week had been dirty and blackened by exhaust and grime. Joggers ran along the banks of the Charles in shorts and T-shirts instead of all bundled up in sweats. Light green leaves caught the brilliant sunlight, adding grace notes to branches that had been bare and gray for months.

Ordinarily, Brandy would have loved being out on a day like this.

But not today.

Today Adam Castle had decided to pick a fight.

They had gone for a walk to enjoy the springlike weather. Brandy wore a light leather jacket over a cashmere sweater, with black pants and black flats. Adam had on blue jeans, white athletic shoes, and a navy Cambridge sweatshirt. Both had felt relieved at not having to put on a winter coat.

When they got back to his apartment, Adam stopped just inside the door and turned to Brandy. "I've been trying to figure out a way to say this for a long time," he said. "And I just can't think of anything except coming right out with it."

Brandy felt like she'd been sucker punched. She prided herself on being able to read people, but she hadn't known there was anything weighing on Adam beyond the usual work stuff. She closed the door gently behind herself. "With what? What's wrong, Adam?"

"It's . . . I feel like you don't trust me, Brandy. Like there's a whole huge part of your life you don't let me see. It's like you're one of those people who has a second family in a different city."

Now the sucker punch sensation turned into a twisting of her gut, because Adam had proven to be extraordinarily perceptive. He was exactly right. She had been keeping something from him—something huge. She felt like she couldn't explain about Season Howe and Mother Blessing and Kerry. So she had made up stories about her summer job in San Diego, and then others to explain things like her sudden trip to New Hampshire at Christmas. The lies she had fabricated then demanded other lies to support them, and she had found herself constructing a whole network of untruth.

Still, she had thought her psychological insight and studies had allowed her to pull it off. Now, learning that she hadn't, she felt terrible about the whole thing.

Just not terrible enough to confess, she thought. *Some things he really is best off not knowing.*

"I don't know what you mean, Adam," she said, after a hesitation that she recognized had stretched a little too long.

"Are you sure?" he pressed. "Do you really want me to run down the

laundry list of little lies I've caught you in, or times you've evaded questions? Because I can, Brandy. I've dwelled on it long enough."

"That's not what I'm saying, Adam." She searched his face, dark and
scowling, for any sign of the man she had come to care about so deeply. She
couldn't yet bring herself to use the word "love," but the very fact that it
floated at the edge of her consciousness meant something. At any rate, she
enjoyed his company and didn't want to lose him.

"Then what?" he asked. "Either I'm right or I'm wrong."

"You're . . . you're wrong, then."

He flopped down on his couch, his hands folded into tight fists. "You're
sure about that. You haven't been hiding anything from me. That trip out
of town at Christmas, the one you took with your ex and came back from
all exhausted and freaked out—you were visiting a sick friend? Come on,
Brandy, that story's always been lame."

"That's not what I said, and you know it," Brandy objected.

"Sorry," Adam said with an angry sneer. "Not a sick friend. A friend in
trouble. What kind of trouble you never told me, though."

"Because it was none of your business," Brandy fired back. "If she
had wanted strangers to know her personal issues she would have said
so. You don't know her, and you don't need to know what she was going
through—you just need to know that she needed me, and that should be
good enough for you."

"Should be," Adam said. "But it isn't. Not on top of everything else. I'm
sorry, Brandy, but I can't be in a relationship with half of someone. If you
can't open your whole life to me, then it's just not going to work."

"I . . . I've given you as much of myself as I can, Adam," Brandy said, aware
that she was on the verge of sounding like she was pleading. She wouldn't go
that far, though. Not for Adam or any other man. He was smart, funny,
good-looking, and successful. A real prize. But not prize enough to humiliate
herself over.

"That's not all of you, though." His eyes had been burning a hole through her, but now he went to the window and looked away, toward the far side of the river. "It's not enough."

"Adam, hasn't there ever been anything in your life that you just had to keep to yourself? Something that was maybe too private, or too dangerous, for other people to know?"

Adam let out a soft chuckle, but one with no humor in it. "What are you now, Brandy? Some kind of spy?"

"That's not what I'm trying to say, Adam."

"I wish you knew what you were trying to say, then, because it isn't working."

"But . . . Adam," Brandy said, bordering on desperation again. She couldn't tell him the truth, and he would have to live with that. "You've got to just understand on this one. You can't push it."

He spun around to face her again. "I *am* pushing it, Brandy. Consider yourself pushed. You've admitted that you've been lying, hiding things from me. That's what I needed to know. Now you have two options. You can either tell me the truth—all of it, from jump—or you can admit that your secrets are more important to you than I am."

Now anger that had been simmering below the surface pushed itself up. "You know what I'm hearing, Adam?" she asked. "I'm hearing that you don't trust me. I would never ask you questions about parts of your life that are off-limits to me—and I recognize, even if you don't, that everyone has places they don't invite others into. No one's an open book, Adam, so don't pretend that you are."

Adam looked startled by the ferocity of her attack. "Don't turn this around on me, Brandy, I'm warning you . . ."

"You're warning me? Adam, obviously there's a lot you don't know about how human beings work. I don't have time to teach it all to you, though— not if you can't bring yourself to have a little faith in me."

"Brandy . . ." Adam didn't finish the thought. Brandy picked up her purse from the chair where she'd dropped it.

"Think about it. You have my number," she declared. She let herself out and closed the door firmly when she went. Out in the hallway, tears sprang to her eyes. She hadn't meant to storm out—hadn't even meant to spin the whole argument around and make him the bad guy. After all, she *was* keeping secrets.

Secrets of life and death. Secrets she couldn't tell anyone outside the small circle of her summer friends, no matter what.

Dabbing at her eyes with her right hand, she started for the stairs.

Adam sat on his living room sofa, still amazed at what had just transpired. *Did she break up with me?* he wondered. *Because I thought I was breaking up with her.*

Hadn't worked out quite as he expected, though. He had stewed in his suspicions for long enough to work up a good head of moral indignation. Then somehow she had yanked his footing out from under him and made it seem like he was the one with the problem.

Well, I guess I am, he thought. *And my problem is named Brandy Pearson.*

She had been gone less than five minutes when he heard a heavy footfall in the hallway outside his apartment. Brandy? His heart leaped at the thought that she had returned already—confusing, since until he heard the sound he had wanted her out of his life. *Emotions are like that,* he thought. *Can't expect consistency from them.*

He had his hand on the door before she even knocked, and had started to pull it open when a powerful thrust knocked him off his feet.

"Brandy?" he asked, startled. Even furious, she shouldn't be that strong. And when the dark figure swung into the apartment, slamming the door, he knew it wasn't her at all. It was a man—or something like one, anyway. The guy was enormous, the size of a linebacker, and dark, and he looked like he'd fallen into a vat of acid or something. His features were indistinct, as if his face were melting on the spot. And something else—he looked as if he'd been put together from mud and dirty snow, with leaves and branches for skeletal structure. And he stank like the worst locker room Adam had ever been in, multiplied by a thousand.

All this flitted through Adam's mind in less than a second, and he realized that something was terribly wrong. He needed to get out of here, get away from the thing, call for help. Something. But the impossible creature moved quickly, crossing the floor space between the door and where Adam had fallen before Adam could even scramble to his feet. One second he could see the phone, on a side table next to the sofa, not seven feet away. The next, a strong and somehow unclean fist smashed into his face, driving him down again. Intense pain made him screw up his face and shut his eyes. He was pretty sure the thing had broken his nose.

He tried to scramble for the phone again, but he couldn't see through the pain and the tears, and then he felt the creature's hands on him, lifting him into the air and slamming him down again. Miraculously, this time it had chosen to throw him down on the sofa, almost as if it didn't actually want to snap his spine.

Adam forced his eyes to open, just as the thing put its rudimentary face close to his. One of its knees was pressing down on his chest, in real danger, Adam thought, of collapsing his lung. The stench of it was overwhelming, and he nearly gagged. But then the monster spoke in a strangely high and feminine voice, with the most absurd Southern accent.

"Tell me where she is," the voice said. It came from the bizarre man-shaped creature, but Adam could tell it was not *of* him. "Tell me and I won't have to hurt you."

"I—I don't know who you're talking about," Adam managed. "B—Brandy?"

"Season!" the voice answered. Even through the filter of the strange creature, Adam could tell that there was rage behind the response.

"I don't know any Season," he said helplessly.

"Where is she?" the thing demanded again.

"I don't—" The words had barely escaped his lips when the monster swung at him again, its giant fist crashing into his face. It hit him again and again, and he felt blood spray down his shirt, teeth loosen in his mouth, and bones crumble beneath its hammering fists.

6

I've made kind of a point of keeping away from wars, these last many years. Not because I don't love my country, but simply because I have been involved in what amounts to a war of my own, a long, seemingly never-ending campaign against Season Howe. I am both a foot-soldier and an officer in this war, although I grant General status only to Mother Blessing (with whom communication has been sparse of late). And, I suppose, to Season, who is a one-woman army of no small ability.

Kerry held Daniel's journal open on her lap and glanced out the window. Season had said she had an important challenge for her today, and she'd gone to scout conditions. The weather was lovely—clear and crisp, with only a few wispy clouds dotting the blue sky. Kerry didn't know what other conditions might be pertinent, and Season hadn't said.

She liked to read Daniel's diaries, if only as a way to keep his voice in her head and his life connected to hers. For a while they had been an important learning tool, teaching her things about witchcraft—as well as guiding her to Mother Blessing's home in the Swamp—but now she mostly read them for her own emotional well-being rather than for their educational value.

She turned back to the heavy leather volume and kept reading.

But this current conflict, I am sad to say, has become nearly impossible to avoid altogether. It rages across most of the nation, pitting North against South, neighbor against neighbor. As one who takes a somewhat longer view of history than most, I believe there might have been ways to avoid it, but then I am no politician.

Probably it's best that I am not, for I don't have the temperament for it. Endless discussion and compromise are not my strengths, and though there are certainly politicians who are also decisive men of action, I fear they are few and far between. More of them would rather talk about action than act.

These last few days, however, have been hard for me because I find myself in the middle of it, near a place called Chancellorsville, in my home state of Virginia. I had gone home to the Great Dismal to see Mother Blessing, since my leads on Season had more or less run out, and I hoped that Mother Blessing could find some new way of locating her. There was, of course, military troop movement all around me as I journeyed, but I made myself hard to see and was able to travel unmolested.

I spent two days in my mother's house in the Swamp, enjoying her company and her cooking and being back home for a short while. But then she said she thought that Season had been seen in Washington, so I rode out and headed north.

It didn't take long to realize that there was more troop activity than ever. Confederate forces, the troops of Stonewall Jackson, were manning bulwarks, trying to stand against the advance of Union general Hooker. Hooker, I've heard, hoped to crush the armies of Jackson and Robert E. Lee, but he hesitated too long and Jackson's army surrounded his.

I could see the smoke from miles away, like the entire forest was ablaze. And I could hear the thunder of cannon and later, of rifles. But I had chosen my path and had foolishly decided that keeping to my chosen course was more beneficial than delaying my arrival in Washington by picking a new one. I could weave my way unnoticed through the battle, I was convinced.

I was wrong.

By the time I realized my mistake, I was in the middle of it. The fighting was all around me. The forest was, in fact, on fire. Soldiers ran in every direction, from every direction. Minié balls and bullets flew past. I spoke a few words to Augustus, my horse, to calm him, as the fire and the noise and chaos were driving the poor beast to distraction. I shielded him from the worst of it.

But before I thought to extend the shield to myself, I was hit. A fierce blow knocked me from the saddle, and as I fell to the ground I realized my shoulder had been smashed. I tried to regain my feet, then fell again. Augustus, loyal creature that he is, stayed beside me, but I could not use his strength to help me. Moments later I lost consciousness.

I woke up some time later in a field hospital. A nurse, her uniform torn and bloody, smiled so sweetly that for a moment I thought that she must be a heaven-sent angel. But then she wiped a lock of hair off her face and her hands left a trail of blood across her cheek, and I knew that I yet lived. No angel in heaven ever looked quite so ghastly, I am certain. Confirmation came a moment later, in the form of a jagged-toothed saw she held in the other hand.

"I see you're awake," she said to me.

"I seem to be," I replied. I inhaled, and the stench of spoiled meat and sewage filled my nostrils. I tried not to show my displeasure. The nurse, it seemed, had become immune to it, just as she seemed to be able to disregard the moans and cries of the injured and infirm that sounded all around us.

"Sorry to see that," she said. "Doc says you've got to lose that arm. Be easier to cut, you were still out."

I glanced at my shoulder, a mangled, repugnant mess of blood and raw meat. I could hardly blame the doctor, who I had not seen as of yet, for wanting to remove as much of it as possible.

Of course, I could have healed it myself given some time and a *few herbs and unguents. I probably could have found the appropriate items in the forest myself, if the soldiers had not been in the middle of burning it to the ground.*

But now I was in the middle of a field hospital, laid out on a table covered only by a filthy blanket, with, when I turned to look, at least a hundred other wounded soldiers all around me—the source of the shouts of pain, and also of the stink that surrounded me.

If I got up and walked into the woods, surely the nurse would raise some kind of alarm. But if I stayed where I was, she would wield that saw against me. Restoring my shoulder and arm, once they had been butchered, would strain my abilities to the utmost.

If I even survived the surgery. I could see by the pile of bodies stacked up against the wall of a nearby tent that many did not.

"You ready for me to do it?" the nurse asked, indicating with the saw what she meant. "Or do you need a slug of something first?"

I would need several slugs, of some concoction stronger than she might have available, before I would let her near me with that instrument of torture.

"I'm sorry," I told her, "but I have no intention of letting you saw into me with that."

"I don't take it off, gangrene'll set in," she told me. "It'll kill you."

"That's a chance I'll take," I said. I knew that I could mend myself before that happened. But only if I could make my escape from this tool-wielding devil, whom I had once seen as an angel.

"Doctor's orders," she insisted.

I sat up on the rickety table, an action which, to judge from her face, surprised her. She probably hadn't thought I had the strength. "Miss, I do not see a doctor at present. Perhaps if you were to turn your back and attend to some other patient, I would be able to spare you the trouble of either cutting off my limb or further debating with me about it."

She gave me a suspicious glare. "You ain't thinking about killing yourself?"

"*Quite the contrary,*" I assured her. "*I'm talking about saving myself.*"

She looked hurt. "*Most of my patients survive,*" she declared.

Somehow I did not feel comforted. She seemed to be growing more anxious by the minute, and I was worried that she would call out to someone. The more time that went by, the greater the danger that she would be joined by a doctor or another soldier. I decided that it was time to act, if I was going to save myself.

I glanced around quickly, to make sure that we were not yet observed, and then performed a hasty immobilization spell. I was still weak from my wound, and it would not have worked had she been braced against it or expecting it. But for the moment she was stunned into paralysis, simply standing with the wicked saw clutched in her hands and her eyes wide open, watching me.

With her incapacitated, I gingerly climbed off the table, making sure not to upend it. Walking as swiftly as I dared, trying not to attract attention to myself, I made my way through the field of injured, dying, and dead, back toward a corral where I hoped to find Augustus.

I had thought that I was successful in not being seen, but it turned out that I was mistaken. Just as I reached the far edge of the field hospital, a young, hollow-eyed soldier who sat against a tent wall smoking a cigar spoke to me. His left arm was in a bloodied sling, and recent cuts spiderwebbed his cheek and jaw. "*I seen someone else do that,*" he said.

"*Do what?*" I pretended to be utterly innocent.

"*What you done there. Freeze that girl like that.*"

"*I did no such . . . where else did you see that?*" A sudden thought changed my sentence midway through.

"*Not twenty miles up the road,*" the young man said. He coughed, a deep, unhealthy, racking cough. "*She was like a vision, too. Lot prettier'n you, that's for sure.*"

"*A woman, then?*"

"A woman, sure enough." He began to cough again, and this time I wasn't sure he would ever stop. Finally he brought it under control and looked at me with liquid eyes. "She stayed at the camp for three days, helping with the wounded. Fixed up many a man I thought would never see another dawn. Finally said she had to move on. But one time, right before she did, one of the boys got a little too friendly with her. She froze him solid, just like you done."

"Do you know where she might have gone?"

He laughed, which triggered another coughing fit. "Wish I did," he managed to rasp.

I thanked him and went to look for Augustus. Was it Season he had seen? From his vague description, it could have been. But the Season Howe I was seeking—spending three days helping the wounded in a filthy Army field hospital? More like her, I should think, to wipe them all out with no second thoughts.

Still, if Season it was, then she is not far ahead of me. I put pen to paper in a public house not a day's ride from Washington. If she is still there, perhaps I'll find her in the next day or two.

I remain,

Daniel Blessing, Fifth of May, 1863

It didn't take long for Brandy to realize that she had done Adam a terrible disservice. He had been right, after all. She was hiding things from him. He had every reason not to trust her, and the fact that he didn't was only an accurate assessment of the situation, not a reflection on him.

Three blocks from his place, she stopped short. Probably he'd been leading up to breaking it off with her. She could live with it, if that was the case—she had broken up, and been broken up with, and though she preferred the former, neither one would kill her. She was too strong, too independent for that.

So she owed it to him to at least let him have his say, owed him the respect he had earned by being so good to her for so long. If at the end of it he still wanted to call it quits, then fine. She would be okay with it, she was sure.

She turned around and headed back to his apartment. With each step it felt as if a great weight were being lifted off her shoulders. She had felt guilty about walking away, about minimizing his concerns with her own smokescreen. What she was doing now was a better thing, and she felt good about it.

When she reached the front door to his building she felt a moment's concern. The door was ajar, and she distinctly remembered having shut it when she left. That had been a few minutes before, though, so someone else could have gone out—even Adam himself, she supposed—and left it open.

But worse, there was a muddy print on the door, almost head-high for her. A putrid smell wafted from it. The first thought that entered Brandy's mind almost made her run screaming from the building.

Simulacrum!

There was no guarantee that was it, however, and any number of other possible explanations presented themselves. The melting snows had left the whole city wet and muddy. Anyone could have gotten some gunk on his hands and touched the door. . . .

Still, her heart was pounding as she slipped through the door and into the lobby.

The smell in here was worse, and there were wet footprints on the stairs that led up to Adam's place. Big footprints. Brandy eyed them, swallowing back her terror but ready to run at the slightest provocation.

She already had her cell in her hand as she followed the huge footprints up. Scott's number was still programmed in, so she scrolled to it and held her finger over the send button. Walking as quickly as she could while still remaining silent, she hurried down the hall toward Adam's door, stepping beside, instead of on top of, those awful prints.

At Adam's door, the worst was confirmed.

A massive mud print marred its finish. Inside she could hear voices—one of them was Adam's, but it sounded garbled, like he was talking with water in his mouth. She couldn't make out any words, but she knew that it was bad.

She also knew she couldn't handle it alone.

She pressed send.

Scott lived only a few miles from Adam's apartment. He hopped in the RAV4 as soon as he got Brandy's panicked call and drove like a madman the whole way. Ten minutes after his phone had rung, he was screeching to a stop outside the building. Brandy waited outside, terror contorting her face.

He left the car in the street and ran to her, gripping her upper arms anxiously. "Are you okay, Brandy?" he asked.

She nodded and wiped away tears. "I couldn't stay up there and listen," she said, her voice breaking. She was bordering on hysterical, he thought, as bad as he had ever seen her. "He's hurting Adam."

"There was nothing you could have done about it," Scott assured her. He put his arms around her, and she moved into his hug in a way she hadn't done for a very long time.

"I—I tried to call Kerry," Brandy said, "but I couldn't get through to her. But I reached Rebecca. She promised to keep trying Kerry."

"That's the best thing you could have done. If it is a simulacrum, there's nothing we can do against it."

"Scott, we have to try. Maybe we can just hit it with clubs or something. Anything. It'll kill Adam!"

He hated to ask the obvious, but it needed to be asked. "How do you know it hasn't already?"

"I was up there a couple of minutes ago," she said. "I stood out in the hallway again, just to check. I could still hear Adam's voice, crying for help."

"And there's nobody else in the building?" Scott asked.

"Most everybody works during the day," Brandy said. "There's no super or on-site manager or anything."

Scott nodded. It was just a small building, a family home that had been converted to apartments a decade or two ago. Eight apartments, he guessed, at the most, spread over two stories.

"Okay, then," he said, hoping he sounded much braver than he felt. "Let's go do this."

He led the way into Adam's building, with Brandy clutching his arm so tightly he thought he would lose circulation. Inside, the place stank to high heaven. Heading up the stairs, his courage almost left him—his knees wobbled so much he wasn't sure he could actually make it up unassisted.

Somehow, though, he did. Brandy pointed out Adam's door, as if the giant mud splat on it didn't give it away. Scott thought the whole exercise was kind of silly—there was no way the two of them could do any damage to one of Mother Blessing's manufactured men. But Brandy wanted him to try, so he would. He was no hero, but for him the equation was that simple. Brandy wanted him to try.

In her time of need, she had called him.

Adam's door was closed, but not locked. Scott gulped in a deep breath and hurled it open, afraid of what he would see.

The sight that met him couldn't have been much worse.

Blood was everywhere—more than he thought could possibly come from someone who was still alive. Adam's place was cool and modern, with lots of black steel, glass, and chrome. The glass was spattered with red, the chrome was smeared, and only the black didn't show blood. His off-white Berber carpeting looked like a grisly rainstorm had showered it. Windows looked tinted.

But Adam was still alive. He had rolled into a ball on his sofa, broken and battered. The simulacrum towered over him, no longer beating him but instead simply intimidating the poor man with his unnatural presence. Adam whimpered, and his breathing sounded wet and shallow.

"Get away from him!" Scott demanded. His own throat felt very dry, his muscles tense. If the thing attacked him, he'd end up like Adam or worse. Adam was bigger and stronger than he was. The biggest difference between them was that Scott knew precisely what he was facing. *And somehow,* he thought, *I don't think that's necessarily an advantage.*

Slowly the simulacrum turned, as if gradually becoming aware that there was someone else in the room. It straightened as it regarded Scott and Brandy. Then, as if triggered by the realization of their presence, it charged.

"Scott!" Brandy's voice was little more than an exhalation of breath behind him. Scott trembled, keeping his body between the creature and Brandy. He had been allies with one of these beings once, for a short time. It rode in his car with him. But he had been afraid of it even then. Now he was petrified.

The best he could do was to raise his hands defensively as the creature came toward him. His knees locked, seemingly of their own accord.

Then it was upon him, its surface slick and viscous, its stench overwhelming. Scott opened his hands and clamped them down on the simulacrum's arms, trying to break its charge. The creature barreled into him, knocking him backward a few steps, and Scott felt Brandy's hands on his back, bracing him. Still, the thing's momentum shoved them both back against the wall. Its strength was enormous; Scott knew it could easily tear his head off.

Except it didn't.

Instead, where he held it, the monster began to come undone.

Wet glops of mud and snow fell to Adam's carpeted floor. Bits of tree debris and trash followed. The thing seemed to collapse in on itself and then spill down as if melting under Scott's touch.

"Scott," Brandy said from behind him, only this time her tone was much different than the last time she had spoken his name. Something like awe sounded in her voice. "Scott, what's happening to it?"

He held on to the thing, afraid that if he let go the process would reverse and the monster would re-form. "I don't know," he said. "I guess it doesn't like me."

"I guess it doesn't," Brandy echoed.

The disintegration continued until there was nothing left for Scott to grip. Gunk covered his shoes and left a big pile on the floor, but within moments even that started to dissipate, as if it were evaporating.

"I . . . this is just bizarre," Scott said. "I don't get it."

"I don't either," Brandy said. "But I'm not complaining."

Neither am I, Scott thought. *Neither am I.*

His relief was checked by a sudden anxiety, however. "We'd better check on Adam," he pointed out. "He probably needs a doctor."

Brandy shoved past him to do just that. "We'll need some kind of a story," she said. "We can't tell the paramedics what really attacked him. We'd spend the rest of our lives in a mental hospital. Or prison." She knelt beside Adam and started stroking him gently, comfortingly, speaking so softly that Scott couldn't hear what she was saying. Adam just remained curled in his fetal position, crying quietly.

She was right, Scott knew. They had to come up with a story, and fast. He was already on his way to the phone to dial 911. Help would be here soon, and they'd need to be able to tell them *something*.

The simulacrum was almost completely broken down already, with just a few bits of random detritus remaining on the floor amid a big muddy stain.

"Okay," Scott said after considering for a few moments. "Here's what we'll say. . . ." Before he had a chance to finish, the emergency operator came on the line, and Scott gave her Adam's address.

By the time he was done, he had almost started breathing normally again. The immediate danger was past.

But one thing was all too certain. Mother Blessing was on their trail again.

Once again Mother Blessing knew the fury of being thwarted by people for whom she had no respect. Those meddling teenagers should have fallen immediately before the might of her creation. Instead, her simulacrum had been defeated by that boy—the one she thought she had been attacking in the first place. She remembered, from her interception of Kerry's communications, that the boyfriend kept better tabs on her location than the girl did. So now that she was ready to continue the battle—to end it—she had waited until she could catch them apart.

But somehow, it had been the wrong boyfriend. He had looked wrong as soon as she saw him through the eyes of her creation. She was committed by then, so she just kept at it, trying to pry from him information that he no doubt truly didn't have. It wasn't until she saw the girl and the boy enter together that she really understood her mistake. The girl was a tramp, or they had broken up.

And even when she realized what had happened, she hadn't known the power that rested in the boy's hands. He was unnatural. He had died, and yet lived—that was the only thing that could explain the simulacrum's response. A creation like that couldn't cohere in the face of the unnatural. A simulacrum's grip on life, Mother Blessing knew, was too tenuous—meeting anything else whose life was false or wrong would cause its immediate dissipation.

So she was angry with them, these children who had defeated her far too often, considering who and what they were. Insignificant insects who muddled along by accident and who needed to be stamped out. They would pay the price, though—once Season was no longer a problem, these others would taste her revenge too, and they would find it painful indeed.

At the same time, she was heartened. Because the girl had made two other calls—one to Kerry, which had not been answered, so Mother Blessing couldn't discern its destination, but the second to Rebecca Levine. Another of their troublesome pack. Rebecca, though, seemed to know where Kerry was. The implication of their conversation was that Kerry was somewhere not too far away—somewhere Rebecca could drive to in a relatively brief time, if need be.

Rebecca was in California. Which meant that she needed to be in California, too. Mother Blessing would not trust a simulacrum to do the whole job this time. So close to Season, she had to be on the scene in person, just in case.

She would leave immediately. This was a war that needed to be finished, and with the Convocation almost upon them, the end had to come soon.

7

Kerry clambered up the side of the cliff as rapidly as she could. Loose dirt and soft stone gave way beneath her hands, but she pressed herself to the wall and dug in with fingers and feet. Jags of rock scraped her cheek. She allowed herself a couple of quick breaths, a moment to collect her thoughts. *What spell can help me here?* she wondered.

None, she decided. This was one of those moments that required physical strength, agility, and courage, not witchcraft. Short of some kind of antigravity spell—or the traditional flying broomstick, which seemed pretty much in the realm of the absurdly mythical—she was on her own.

She glanced up to see how much farther she had to go, and how far out the overhang extended at the top. Heights had never been a particular problem for her, but she decided that there was no advantage to looking down. Nothing but a narrow ribbon of sand, big sharp rocks, and churning surf, thirty feet below her where the ocean carved away the coastline.

Above, Kerry saw some likely handholds, so she stretched for the closest one, shoved the fingers of her right hand into a narrow crevice, and pulled herself up. She raised her right foot to the little shelf on which her right hand had rested a few moments earlier, found firm footing there, and then felt above with her left hand. It was a slow process, but she was no practiced climber.

Almost thirty minutes—and as many scrapes and bruises—later, the overhang was within reach. This would be the tricky part. She'd have to work her way out hand over hand, digging in with her toes, until her back was almost parallel to that narrow beach way down below. The overhang was only four or five feet out, so she wouldn't be in that precarious pose for long, but even a minute or two was distressing. She'd have greatly preferred to scale a section of cliff that was straight at the top—but then, she'd have preferred a hunky instructor and one of those spiffy fluorescent-colored nylon ropes, too. All of which, no doubt, were reasons why Season had picked this spot, which contained none of the above. Kerry had only sneakers, track pants, and a T-shirt on—if she fell, it was going to hurt.

Nothing to be gained by waiting, she decided. She began the excruciating process of holding herself as close as she could to the wall while she inched up and out, feeling gravity trying to yank her back to earth at every moment. Her terror at this stage was almost palpable, and she worried that her palms would sweat so much that she'd lose her grip on the rock face.

A few minutes later, however, she had hold of the upper edge. Some loose dirt and pebbles slid out from under her fingertips, cascading over the cliff and down past her. The clatter when it landed below sounded very far away. Beneath the loose stuff, though, was good solid rock. She pressed her fingers into it so hard she thought she would wear grooves in it.

The last step was to get her left hand up there and haul herself over the top. But her left hand was wedged tightly into a crack in the overhang, and she felt like that was the only thing holding her in place. Her right hand was gripping the upper edge, but if it started to slip, or the edge gave way, there would be nothing to hang on to there.

Stuck, she knew she couldn't make any more progress unless she did something. Gingerly, trying to adhere herself to the face, to glue her feet in position, she worked her left hand free and finger-crawled it up, inch by slow, perilous inch. Finally, she was able to reach the lip with that hand as well.

Now it was a simple matter of letting go with her feet so she could hoist herself up to the top.

Sure. Simple.

But before she got a chance, she heard a movement at the top. A footfall, she thought.

"Season?"

No response.

"Season, is that you?" Kerry demanded urgently.

Still no verbal response came. But Kerry gradually became aware of a shadow, a dark form coming over the edge. She hung on to the lip with fingers that trembled from the strain and the anxiety and made herself look up at it.

A tall, sinister man grinned down at her, wearing a long coat that fluttered in the wind at the top of the cliff. His smile looked about as genuine as a ninety-dollar bill.

"Going somewhere?" he asked.

"You want to give me a hand?" Kerry replied, pretty sure she wouldn't accept it if he did. He wasn't one of Mother Blessing's simulacra, she could tell, but that didn't mean he wasn't an ally of some other kind. And she was in about as vulnerable a position as it was possible to find.

"How about a push?" he answered.

Which was all she needed to confirm that he was not exactly a friend. It would be hard to make the right hand gestures while clinging to the edge of the cliff, but she needed to do something to protect herself. So she forced the fingers of her left hand into the appropriate position and spoke one of the ancient words. *"Kalaifa!"*

The man flew from her sight as if swatted away by a giant gust of wind. She knew he had been knocked about twenty feet back, but he was most likely uninjured, unless he'd been speared by a tree branch or something. If he had been just a practical joker, then he'd be fine. If he had more homicidal motives, the immediate threat had been removed and she'd be able to deal with him when she reached the top.

If she hurried. He could still come back and they'd have to do the whole dance all over again. Forcing herself to move faster, she dug in with the fingers of both hands and drew them forward on the top shelf of the cliff, getting some rock and earth under her forearms. The man could already be on his feet, and if he returned all he'd have to do would be to break the grip of one of her hands. Kerry made the decision to finish this now, and kicked free with both feet. She used the momentum to release with her right hand and reach farther out, grabbing ground up to her armpit. Now she could pull her head up over the top. The man was still in the dirt where she had thrown him, glaring at her. She tossed him a quick smile and began hoisting herself up.

A moment later she was safely on the top of the cliff, standing up and dusting herself off.

The man turned indistinct, as if she were looking at him through a wall of Jell-O, and then took on solid form again. This time the form was that of Season Howe, who rubbed her bottom as she smiled at Kerry.

"Ow," she said. "Good job, Kerry."

"Thanks." Kerry touched one of the raw spots on her cheek. "Now maybe you can tell me what that was all about."

"A test," Season said simply. "In the time we have left before the Convocation, there's not a whole lot I can still teach you. But I can test what you've learned, and make sure your reactions are appropriate. So far, so good."

Kerry Profitt's diary, March 12

The ways in which this whole business is like school are numerous. I have always loved reading and writing, but the reading program Season has put me on is almost ridiculous—especially since so many of her magic texts were written back in practically prehistoric times, so the language is all stiff and ancient. Thanks to Season's magic translator (just like with the books Mother Blessing showed me, way back when), I can read the books that look like Latin or Greek or German or whatever. At first glance they're in a foreign language, but when I look at them again, I can make out the words just as if they were written in English. Sometimes bad English, but English just the same. Fortunately I have Daniel's journals, and a few books the Morgans have left around the house, to give me a break.

And then the testing part! Like earlier today, when I had to scale this giant freaking cliff while she stood at the top, casting a glamour to make herself look like some kind of scary bad guy. I never had a midterm like that in high school. Would have reduced class size a bit if we had, I guess. Don't let the PTA know.

I get the idea behind it, of course. We don't know exactly what we're going to be facing, either in more possible battles with Mother Blessing or at the Witches' Convocation. Chances are I won't be forced to climb any cliffs. But I might be put into situations where physical strength and/or bravery are required. So better to know now that I can do it, right? If I had fallen today, ouch. Broken leg, whatever. Or maybe Season had some kind of plan to magically break my fall, although of course she wouldn't have told me that. But if I didn't learn my limits, and then wimped out while facing one of MB's bad things, it could be serious trouble for me and for Season.

So, the testing. And in between, the reading. And in between all of that, the purification rites. Also important, Season says. Not that I've been around any guys with whom to be impure, but she says it's not just that. It's the atmosphere, which is chock-full of pollution and nasty microbes and stuff. It's the gunk we pick up from flies and doorknobs and those buttons you press on the hot air hand dryer in the ladies' room, and also that whole breathing thing. In other words, not just purity of spirit but also of body. Helps make the magic work better, somehow. The impurities in a witch's system act like little blocking agents, she says, impeding the flow of the forces that we channel through ourselves. Like shopping carts and old cars tossed into a riverbed. Take out all the crap and everything moves more smoothly down the correct channels.

The purification rituals take many forms. My favorite is the long, hot baths with lilac petals floating in the tub. Not so great is the standing with arms outstretched and a ten-pound weight in each hand for thirty minutes, while counting backward from a thousand. Season swears both kinds are necessary, along with several others. At least she does them with me (although with the bath one, we go one at a time). By the time we go to the Convocation we will be two pure chicks, I gotta say. And looking just fine in our plain white robes, which is what we wear for this drill.

More later.
K.

By the time they left Adam at Mass General, he had been admitted and sedated. He had tried to give the paramedics and the police his version of events, but Brandy and Scott had been there to intercede with their own translation of his garbled tale.

They had agreed to stick as close to the literal truth as possible. The way they told it, Adam and Brandy had had a fight, and Brandy walked out. But she had second thoughts and went back. By the time she got back, someone had broken into the apartment. Brandy could hear a struggle or heated argument through the door but was afraid to go in, so she called Scott. He came over, and by the time they went inside the assailant had fled. They found Adam, beaten and hysterically raving about a monster—no doubt a really big burglar—and called 911. No, neither of them had seen the assailant—he must have run away while Brandy was waiting outside for Scott. No, she couldn't think of any enemies Adam might have, and she couldn't identify anything that was missing. But she had only known him for a few months, and there might, of course, have been something in his past that she didn't know about.

The police and medical personnel seemed to buy the story. She and Scott told it essentially the same way when they were questioned separately and together, and anyway, it all made so much more sense than Adam's ravings. The fact that Adam's were true didn't enter into it—it was the appearance of truth they were after, not the real thing. Anyway, Brandy reasoned, they weren't under oath, so it wasn't like they were committing perjury.

Lying, yes. But with good cause.

When they were allowed to leave, they sat in Scott's car out in the hospital parking lot, giving themselves some decompression time before he took her home. Brandy looked over at Scott, illuminated by light that washed in from one of the hospital's streetlamps. He looked different than he had before, even at Christmas, somehow—strong, capable, decisive. There was a set to his jaw, a sense of determination expressed by a slight stiffening of his lips, a resolve signaled by a narrowing of his eyes, that she had never seen before.

She liked what she saw.

"You were pretty amazing, Scott," she said quietly.

"What? I had no idea that thing would fall apart. I still wish I knew why."

"I don't mean just that," Brandy said. She didn't want him to think it had been an empty compliment, or worse, a backhanded one. Because that kind of thing had never been beyond her. But it wasn't her intention now. "I mean, that was cool too. But the whole thing. Answering when I called, riding to the rescue like that. A lot of guys wouldn't do that if their ex called up and said her new boyfriend was in trouble."

"What, I'm supposed to just shrug and say, 'whatever'?" Scott answered. "He means a lot to you. You mean a lot to me. That's just the way it is."

"That's exactly what I mean," Brandy said. "You don't even think it's special. You just did it, because that's what a person does. In your world, at least."

Scott shrugged, as if he didn't even get what a big deal it was.

Which was when Brandy realized that the warm spot she held for him in her heart had never completely gone away. Sure, it had cooled. Right down to a frosty chill, for a while. But the embers had still been glowing, she just hadn't seen them. Now, though, she felt as if they were being fanned, fresh air being blown in by one of those big old-fashioned bellows. Heat radiated from her core.

She leaned toward him, touching his arm. "Scott, I—"

"Listen, Brandy," he interrupted, completely oblivious. He stared straight out the windshield as he spoke, not even looking at her. "You'll probably kick me or something for saying this, but it's something I have to get off my chest. I was an idiot."

"You were?"

"Absolutely," Scott insisted. "I mean, I was kind of obsessed with Kerry. You knew that—you probably knew it before I did. But that was just stupid, that grass is always greener stuff. Kerry's an amazing person, sure. But so are you. You're beautiful, and you're the most insightful, perceptive person I've ever known, and you were right in front of me the whole time. Right in my own apartment, my own bed. So getting all hung up on Kerry like that, and spoiling what we had . . . well, I was a dope. I'm sorry. If there was any way I could undo it, I would."

Brandy could hardly believe what she was hearing. Especially since it was so close to what she was feeling right now. She recognized that it might simply have been a reaction to their mutual brush with death, which often drew people together in an artificial intimacy.

But she didn't think so. Instead, she thought the experience had knocked blinders away from their eyes that they had consciously placed there, not realizing what a mistake it had been.

She placed a hand on his leg and squeezed gently. "I think maybe we can work on it."

His face brightened instantly, and he finally met her gaze. "Do you mean it?"

"Sure," she said without hesitation. "If people can decide to break up, they can certainly decide to un-break up, right?"

"Isn't that usually called making up?"

"Yes," Brandy admitted. "But that sounded too much like a golden oldie. Then again, there's always making out. Which maybe we could talk about too."

"Talking about it seems so . . . I don't know. Counterproductive."

She snuggled a little closer to him. "Well, I guess we don't have to do that much talking."

He started to lean toward her, then suddenly sat upright. "Oh, crap!"

"What?" she asked, startled. She turned in her seat, to see if he had noticed something out her window. *Another attacker?*

"I just remembered, in all the craziness with Adam and everything, we never called Rebecca to tell her we're okay. We should do that, and make sure she lets Kerry know what's happened."

Brandy realized her heart was racing and adrenaline pumping from his sudden motion. "Okay," she said. "Let's give her a call." Rebecca, being Rebecca, would almost certainly be freaking out by now, Brandy knew. She dug her cell from her purse and flipped it open abruptly—glad that Scott had remembered, but upset because she would rather that his attention had been solely focused on her at that moment.

Just the way he is, I guess, she thought. *If I'm going to be with him—and it looks like maybe I am, strange as that seems—I've just got to be able to live with it.* She knew she would have to visit Adam in the hospital. There would be awkward questions. But then, life refused to be as orderly as she wanted.

She dialed Rebecca, and a moment later their friend, breathless and anxious, came on the line.

8

Exactly what she feared had happened. It was all starting up again, and this time a complete noncombatant, the proverbial innocent bystander, had been injured. And Mother Blessing was still after them—this proved it, without a doubt.

Rebecca couldn't reach Kerry and Season on the phone. She rushed about the house, in a near panic. She had to go up to Bolinas, had to find them and let them know what was happening. It would only be a few hours by car. She wanted to wait for Erin to get home from a late class, but as the minutes ticked by she began to worry that Erin wouldn't be coming home—that she was studying late in the library, or had a date, or something. She paced, she tried to sit and gather her thoughts, but then she squirmed and jumped to her feet again. *Come home, come home, come home,* she silently pleaded. But Erin didn't, and the girl refused to carry a cell phone or pager to class. Something about respecting the lecturer, which Rebecca kind of understood. But then, Erin had never been attacked by a witch.

Since it didn't look like she would show up any time soon, Rebecca settled for leaving her housemate a note. That was probably better anyway, she decided upon reflection, because with a note, Erin couldn't ask any nosy questions. She scrawled, "Erin, I'm out of town for a day or so. I'll call you when I can. Love, Beck," on a sheet of ripped-out notebook paper and pinned it to the kitchen table with a salt shaker.

She didn't, in fact, know if she would even spend a single night away, or if she'd be driving back here much later that night. But if she found Season and Kerry tonight, there was every likelihood that they would insist she stay over. It would be very late by the time she reached the Morgan house. And if she didn't find them at first, she wouldn't be back here until she did, however long that might take.

She tossed some clean underwear, a blouse, and a skirt into her backpack, then put in a toothbrush and toothpaste and a hairbrush. Certain there were things she was forgetting, she decided that nothing else was that important anyway. Outside, a hard, steady rain had been pounding Santa Cruz all evening. Her old VW was parked across the street, and she had almost reached it when she remembered her wallet and cell phone, inside on top of her dresser. She ran back in, fetched those items, stuffed them into the backpack with everything else.

Back in the rain, she dashed toward the car, already wet from her first aborted attempt.

Before she reached it, however, an abrupt movement caught her eye. A dark shape separated from the background, and Rebecca realized it was someone coming toward her. She broke into an all-out sprint, but the shape was much too fast for her. By the time she tried to jam her key into the car's door lock, he was on her.

The man slammed into her, hard, and one of his hands grabbed her wrist, yanking it away from the car door. Only a faint glow filtered from the streetlights through the heavy rain, but that, and the smell, were enough to tell Rebecca that she didn't face a man at all, but one of Mother Blessing's awful simulacra.

She twisted out of its grasp, maybe helped by the rain—its hands seemed slick, and she slid from between them as if she'd been oiled—but she only made it a couple of staggered steps before she tripped over her own feet. The thing came at her again, swatting her as she tried to rise and knocking her sprawling in the wet street. Her face skidded on the pavement, her fingers clutching at it as she tried desperately to right herself. So far the thing had made no sound, and she knew that she should scream but couldn't seem to find her breath.

Instead, she pushed herself to her knees again, and then to her feet, and then it had her, one powerful arm wrapped about her middle. She finally was able to let out a scream, but the creature clamped its other hand over her mouth. Rebecca struggled against it, kicking and squirming, all to no avail. It was far stronger than she was, and she couldn't hurt it. After a moment it moved its hand up to cover her nose as well as her mouth. She gulped for breath but couldn't find it, and seconds after that, the darkness of the night had engulfed her completely.

"A lot of people think witches are inherently evil," Season said. She and Kerry sat in the cramped living room, listening to the wind whistle in the eaves. "That we're in league with the devil. That we're always having unnatural relations with goats. In fact, if there's a devil, I've never met him, and while I enjoy feta cheese on Greek salads, that's the closest I've been to a goat in at least a hundred years."

Kerry laughed at that. It was late and she was in sweats and fuzzy socks, ready for bed. She had been on her way there when Season called her into the living room, apparently in a reflective mood.

"That's why witches have been persecuted so much?" Kerry asked. She had become used to Season's enforcement of the fifteen-questions routine, and it didn't apply after "school hours" were over. "Because of the goats?"

"One of the reasons," Season acknowledged with a nod. "People often tend to fear what they don't understand. Since our abilities are beyond the scope of most people, beyond what they can possibly ever experience for themselves, they decide that there must be something sinister behind us.

"Of course, witches like Mother Blessing don't help matters any. Whenever people have unreasonable fears and prejudices, if they can point to a specific individual who seems to embody that prejudice, then it's that much easier for them to lump all the rest of that group in the same category. Mother Blessing and the few other witches around who are genuinely evil make good poster children for those who hate witches."

"What if witches made themselves known to the world at large?" Kerry wondered. "If you weren't all hiding all the time, if witches were common knowledge, maybe they'd be accepted better?"

Season hesitated for a moment before answering, looking deep into Kerry's eyes as she did. "How often has that proven not to be true?" she said finally. "Think about African Americans, who were enslaved for hundreds of years, and are still having a hard time being admitted into parts of American society, a hundred and some years after emancipation. As a group, they still don't have income equity with whites. Think about gay people—we've known about them forever, and look at their struggles with acceptance. I'm not saying that witches are a persecuted minority, exactly. We are, but in a very different way. There are so few of us we'll never have a big voting bloc or anything like that, even if there were issues on which we would want to vote in lockstep. But we aren't lacking for power. It's not political, necessarily, but we have other forms of power."

"Okay, point taken," Kerry admitted. "Maybe coming out as witches isn't the best idea."

"It's never been anything but trouble in the past," Season agreed. "A lot of us still have bad memories of the Inquisition, and Salem, that kind of thing. We seem to be better off staying in the shadows. The whole low-profile bit."

"I guess it's a good thing I have the voice of experience here to guide me," Kerry said, "so I don't shoot my mouth off at the Convocation and say something stupid."

"You're lucky you're so young for your first Convocation," Season pointed out. "By the time you go to your second, you'll be the one with all the experience."

That'll be five hundred years, Kerry thought, blown over by the hugeness of that concept. *Will I even still be alive then?* "That's a pretty big commitment," she said.

Season cocked her head to the right and showed her a surprised face. "I thought you were ready to make it."

Kerry didn't quite know what to say. "I . . . I thought I was too. I mean, I think I am. But . . . you know, I'm young. What if I decide I'd rather be a firefighter or a dentist or something?"

"You're joking."

"About those two particular career choices, yes. Not that there's anything wrong with them. But you know what I mean. I'm eighteen. How many eighteen-year-olds do you know who figure out what they want to do with the rest of their lives at that age and then stick to it? Most people I've known haven't even stuck to a single college major, much less a career. Much less a career that could last well beyond the usual forty years or so."

Season let out a small sigh. "I know it's asking a lot, Kerry," she said. "Witches live a very long time. It's a serious commitment. Believe me, there have been times that I've regretted the decision too. But not many, and they always pass."

"Well, you're kind of stuck, right? I mean, once you pass a hundred and twenty or so, it must be kind of hard to suddenly decide you didn't mean to be a witch after all."

"It happens," Season admitted. "Just not very often, and the consequences aren't pretty."

"I bet not," Kerry agreed. She tried unsuccessfully to stifle a huge yawn. "I'm totally beat," she said. "I guess I'll see you in the morning."

"Another big day," Season promised. "Almost time to leave for the Convocation."

Another yawn escaped Kerry. "I can't wait."

* * *

When Rebecca woke up, she felt sick and sore all over. It took her a minute to realize that some of the soreness was because she hadn't been able to move her arms or legs for what must have been hours—she was tied to a stiff wooden chair in what looked like a long-abandoned kitchen. Light streamed in through warped sheets of plywood nailed over a window, illuminating a stained and faded linoleum floor and gutted cabinets, the sink and appliances long since taken away. There were two other chairs in the room with her, and a wall calendar from 1996, but nothing else except dust, cobwebs, and a black growth on one wall that must have been mold.

Light, she realized. She had been here all night, then. As she tried to turn in the chair to see what was behind her, a wave of nausea passed through her. Her head throbbed, as if someone had been using it to drive nails through concrete.

She remembered the night before—being grabbed on her way to the car. One of Mother Blessing's artificial goons. She couldn't recall anything at all after that, so he must have knocked her out, then brought her—where? Wherever this was, some old empty house. Hours had passed, though, so she could be just about anywhere. Maybe not even in Santa Cruz anymore. She couldn't smell the ocean, but the house's close, musty air overwhelmed any odors that might have leaked in from outside.

The house had a hollow feel, as if it had been vacant for a long time. She was pretty sure she was completely alone. If the thing that had brought her here—or anyone else—was here now, she couldn't see him. She couldn't see much, though. She could try to jerk the whole chair around, but at the moment such a violent motion would probably only succeed in making her vomit or pass out again. *Anyway,* she thought, *the old witch makes those things out of found materials, right? So he could just be a bunch of spiderwebs and mold right now, but ready to pop up as soon as I make a move.*

The most pressing question was the hardest to answer. Why? What good did it do Mother Blessing to have Rebecca locked away in a house? There had been the attack on Brandy's boyfriend, too—was there some new battle going on that they were all going to be sucked into? Had things heated up to this point?

Well, duh, she thought. *I wouldn't be tied to a chair if* something *wasn't going on.*

Through the nausea, she realized two urgent things. She was very hungry, and she really, really had to pee.

Somehow, it didn't look like either need would be satisfied very soon.

From somewhere behind her—somewhere else in the house—a door opened, groaning on its hinges, then closed with a loud bang. Rebecca started, as if the bang had been immediately behind her head. She suddenly felt terribly vulnerable. She was completely immobilized, unable even to turn around to face whoever had entered the house. She could hear floorboards squeaking as if under a ponderous weight. Slowly, the squeaking came nearer.

Rebecca's eyes were wide with fright. Who was it? The simulacrum that had brought her here? Someone else—even a random stranger? Maybe it was someone who could rescue her. That was a pleasant thought, but probably too good to be true. It was far more likely to be someone with a nefarious motive. A few minutes before she had been wishing that there was someone else with her, but now she realized that alone was far safer than trapped here with the wrong kind of company.

"Who's there?" she demanded, trying to sound belligerent, as if she had any control whatsoever over the situation. "Speak up!"

"Now, don't y'all worry 'bout me," a feminine voice said. The Southern accent was so thick it almost sounded cartoonish to Rebecca's ears, accustomed as she was to the way New Yorkers and Californians spoke. "I'm just here to have a little talk, aren't I?"

"How would I know?" Rebecca replied. "Why don't you untie me so we can have a real conversation?"

A soft chuckle. "Well, now, I don't think that'd be very smart, do you? Not very smart at all, Miss Levine. Or can I call y'all Rebecca?"

"Untie me, and you can call me anything you want," Rebecca shot back. The speaker still hadn't shown herself, but Rebecca knew who it was. Who it had to be. Mother Blessing. Daniel's mother. Kerry had described her way of speaking, even imitated her a couple of times. And, of course, Rebecca herself had heard the voice before, only filtered through the voice box of an inhuman being, one of the witch's simulacra. "Are you going to let me see you, Mother Blessing?"

Another laugh met this question. "Well, ain't you just the cleverest little thing?" More moaning floorboards. Rebecca could hear the huffs of the woman's breath as she walked, seemingly with effort, across the kitchen. A moment later, a vast field of powder blue polyester hove into view. Mother Blessing was enormous, one of the biggest women Rebecca had ever seen. If her thighs, wrapped in that tight polyester, were tree trunks, her waist was one of those redwoods that they cut tunnels through to let cars drive under. She smiled a ghastly grin at Rebecca, the Pan-Cake creasing and cracking on her face, the foothills of blue eye shadow leading toward mountains of platinum hair piled on her head in one of the world's biggest beehives.

"No mirror where you live?" Rebecca asked defiantly.

One of Mother Blessing's meaty hands slapped her across the face. *The woman can move fast when she wants to,* Rebecca realized. She had barely seen the slap coming. Even if she had, she wouldn't have been able to dodge it.

"I'm sure y'all are smarter than that," Mother Blessing said. There was no humor in her voice anymore, nothing but anger and an edge of bitterness. "I'm sure y'all don't want to make this any harder on either of us than it has to be."

"That all depends," Rebecca said, her insolent attitude only heightened by the slap. "Just what is 'this' going to be?"

"Just a short little conversation," Mother Blessing assured her. "Y'all are going to tell me where to find Season and Kerry, and then I'll untie you and leave you alone. Now, that sounds fair, doesn't it?"

"Yeah, fair," Rebecca said. "Only, I don't think so. In fact, I think you ought to take yourself a flying—"

Again, Mother Blessing moved faster than Rebecca could have imagined. This time, the slap spun her head around to one side, and she saw flashes of bright light when it connected.

Note to self, Rebecca thought. *No profanities around this freak.*

9

Scott was almost frantic.

Hours had passed since they had called Rebecca to warn her about the attack on Adam, and what that might portend for the rest of them. Rebecca had promised to get in touch with Kerry and let her know about it. Kerry and Season were the only ones who would know what to do, how to respond.

If at all. If there was any reasonable response possible.

But Rebecca had not called back. He and Brandy had taken turns trying her, at home and on her cell, through the night. Neither had slept much. Rebecca's roommate Erin had finally unplugged her phone, apparently, after answering with less and less good humor, then finally insisting that they stop calling. But they hadn't. And they wouldn't, until they talked to Rebecca, or Kerry.

Now the sun had risen, shining down onto New England. It would still be dark in California, Scott knew, but not for long. Daylight would race across the continent, illuminating forests and villages, cities and plains, mountains and rivers, and finally the far coast.

The coast where Rebecca was in some kind of trouble—where Mother Blessing was closing in on them. Scott was certain of it.

"We need to catch a plane," he announced when Brandy came into the room. Her hair was a mess, her eyes puffy and bloodshot from lack of sleep, and she sipped from a Red Bull. They were at her apartment, where they had spent the night. She had tried to grab a few winks from time to time, unsuccessfully. Scott had alternated between pacing, dialing the phone, and staring out the window at the dark city. Once he had taken a shower, just to try to clear the cobwebs from his mind, but then he'd had to put back on the same clothes, reeking with sweat from the fight and everything since. The mood that had come over them before, the definite rekindling of heat between them, hadn't gone away, but it had been overshadowed by other events.

"Do we have a reservation?" Brandy asked, confused.

"No," he said. "So I guess we're paying full fare. Don't worry, I'll take care of it. But we have to get to California. San Jose is closest, I guess, to Santa Cruz. I wish we knew where Kerry and Season were so we could go straight there, but we need to check in on Rebecca anyway."

"Don't you think that might be a little extreme, Scott?" Brandy wondered. "A cross-country flight because she's been away from her phone for a few hours?"

"Was what that thing did to Adam extreme?"

Brandy nodded, catching on. "I'll get my purse."

Rebecca tried to think about anything except the pain.

Her friends had often called her a retro hippie, and she figured that was why she fit in so well at UC Santa Cruz—even in the twenty-first century, it was the biggest hippie school in the state.

Part of what made her a hippie, she guessed, was her preference for non-violence, for passive resistance to injustice. It had been the most effective technique for those protesting the Vietnam War or fighting for civil rights in the sixties. Don't fight back, show that you are above violence by refusing to sink to that level. Demonstrate that there's a better way.

She tried to cling to that belief, but it was hard. Her flesh had been burned by at least fifty matches. She'd been pinched, pulled, slapped, punched hard in the abdomen. Her hair had been pulled, twisted, and yanked. If Mother Blessing had had a pair of pliers Rebecca was sure her fingernails would be gone by now, and probably only the lack of plumbing in the house had kept the old water torture thing from happening.

But she had refused to tell the witch anything. Friendship was more important than physical discomfort, and violence was an insult that could be dealt with only by absolute rejection. Telling Mother Blessing where Kerry was would be disastrous, and Rebecca would withstand any torture rather than reveal her location.

At least she would try.

Kerry was her friend, someone for whom Rebecca would do anything she could. Anything on Earth.

She had stopped trying to reason with the woman. Mother Blessing wanted what she wanted, and there was no getting past that barrier. She had said she wanted to talk, but that wasn't true. She only wanted to listen, and then just to the specific answer that she sought.

Rebecca had tried, early on, to persuade Mother Blessing of the hopelessness of her effort. "Do you know what my last name is?" she had asked, ignoring the fact that the old witch had used it when she first came into the kitchen. "It's Levine. That's my dad's name. My mother was a Yelinsky. Her grandparents lived in Poland in the 1930s. They were Jewish. You know what that means, right? You were around in those days. Of course, you were probably on the other side."

Mother Blessing hadn't responded—verbally, at least. Instead she had struck another match and held the flame in front of Rebecca's eyes. Rebecca had blown it out, and Mother Blessing had quickly jammed the still-burning head into the soft skin right beneath Rebecca's left eye.

Rebecca screamed, and tears that she thought had dried up started to fall again. "It means they were in a concentration camp," Rebecca said when she could compose herself enough to speak. "They lived through worse torture than you could even imagine with your pitifully small mind. And I'm here, which means they survived it. They survived all that horror, so there is nothing you can do to me—"

Another match struck. "You can make this stop," Mother Blessing whispered, repeating the same chorus she had been singing for a while now. "You can put an end to the whole thing. It's easy. Just tell me what I want to know."

"—nothing you can do to me that is worse than what they went through. There is no way you can make me tell you anything, so just give it up. If you do, I won't tell Season what you've done, and she won't kick your butt for it."

Stories of her family's history had meant nothing to Mother Blessing, so Rebecca stopped speaking them out loud. But they meant a great deal to her. Her great-grandparents were many years gone now, but she had met them as a young girl. She had seen the numbers tattooed on their wrists, had heard the tales they told to adult friends when they thought young Rebecca was sound asleep in her bed. She filled her mind with those tales, the unspeakable things her great-grandparents had seen, had lived through, and with thoughts of Kerry, good, brave Kerry, and she bit the insides of her cheeks until she tasted blood, and she withstood the pain.

She had to.

She *couldn't* give up, *couldn't* turn over Kerry and Season to the old witch. Mother Blessing was a coward who preferred to let others do her dirty work for her. Rebecca didn't know much about her, but she knew that. The fact that she was here, that she was getting her own hands dirty, meant that things were coming to a head. Some kind of endgame was in the works.

Well, Rebecca would be happy to see it all end. But on Kerry's schedule, and Season's. On their terms. Not Mother Blessing's.

She had never thought of herself as a particularly courageous person, though she had been moved and touched when Kerry had told her that she was. She still didn't think so. *Stubborn, yes. Intransigent. Not brave.*

She didn't even think she was brave when she finally lost consciousness.

* * *

The girl would *not* give up.

Mother Blessing had thought she was the softest of the bunch, the weakest link, as it were. A couple of hard tugs on her shiny red hair and the girl would rat out her friends just to make it stop.

She was surprised, and, she had to admit, somewhat impressed, by the girl's fortitude. Annoyed, too. It just made her work harder than she had hoped to. Sweat filmed her forehead and upper lip, and she was dying for some sweet tea and a Hershey bar. There was none of that in this house, however. It was an abandoned place on the edge of town, this awful Santa Cruz place, with plywood over the windows and a CONDEMNED sign tacked to the front door. Mother Blessing couldn't wait to get out of the house, out of Santa Cruz. If she never had to come back to California again it would be too soon. Her son had died in California, after all. And met Kerry in California.

In some ways, this was where it had all started, this recent cycle of violence and war that led toward the Convocation. *Fitting that it should end here,* she thought.

The girl had lapsed into unconsciousness now, though. Mother Blessing hadn't expected to have to expend this kind of effort on her, but since she had, she was angry with the girl, and therefore less inclined than she might otherwise have been to spare her any unnecessary discomfort.

So since the girl wouldn't talk, she would extract the information she wanted in a different way. A little easier for her, a lot harder on the girl. Mother Blessing offered a halfhearted shrug. Didn't really matter to her, one way or the other.

She looked at Rebecca Levine, her head slumped forward onto her chest, mouth slack, body finally relaxed against the cords that held her in the chair. She was a pretty girl who could have grown into a beautiful woman. Not now, though. Pity she had brought this on herself. Mother

Blessing put her right hand on Rebecca's head, feeling the girl's soft hair and the tight, unyielding flesh underneath, close against her skull. She applied more pressure, and at the same time spoke a single word in the ancient language of magic.

Her fingertips dug through the flesh, as if it were no more dense than the thick mud of her home swamp. Pressing harder, they bit into the skull, crumbling bone like stale bread. Beneath the skull there was brain matter, softer still and a little wet beneath her probing hand.

Mother Blessing closed her eyes and concentrated as her fingers rooted around in Rebecca's brain. The girl's thoughts flew into her mind scatter-shot, as if someone were drumming on the remote control of a TV with a thousand channels. Worries about school and work and Mother Blessing herself, fears, joys, loves, and hates. The simple pleasure of sand between her toes at the beach, and the more recent horror of being attacked in the dark and awakening, bound, all alone in a strange place. A recipe for chocolate chip cookies. A memory of a winter morning in Central Park with her father, trying to ice-skate for the first time. An image of a pelican skimming across the waves, its wingtips dipping into the water.

And finally, a name—Morgan—and a town.

Bolinas.

That's where Kerry and Season were.

Mother Blessing pulled her hand out of Rebecca's skull and shook her fingers as if she had just touched raw sewage.

"There, now, that wasn't so bad, was it?" she asked the lifeless girl.

Rebecca, of course, didn't respond.

That was okay. She had what she needed. She would leave Rebecca's body here. Somebody would find it, one of these days, but probably not soon. Not in this abandoned place. And Mother Blessing would never be connected to it, at any rate.

Anyway, she needed to get to Bolinas, wherever that was. She had a map of California that she'd bought at the airport out in her stolen car.

No simulacra this time. They had helped with Rebecca, to a point. But they wouldn't stand up against Season and Kerry. That had been proven. Still, she needed to keep them pinned down until she could get there herself, needed to make sure they didn't run away yet again.

She had an idea, though. One that would do the job just fine.

She could almost taste victory now, and it was sweet.

10

A steady spring rain had tapped against walls and windows all evening. Kerry was amazed that there had been so much rain in northern California over the winter and in the days leading up toward the Convocation. Season assured her that everything she thought she knew about weather was changing, faster than she could probably imagine.

"Call it global warming, global climate change, whatever you want," Season said. "It's happening. Most people don't live long enough to see the progression firsthand, but I have. Up in the Sierra Nevada mountains, not so far from here, glaciers are receding, and winter's snows melt much sooner than they used to. The Antarctic ice shelf is thinning and weakening. Ocean currents are changing. It's getting worse, and it's happening in a hurry. The snap of a finger in geologic time. It's already reaching the point that people who haven't lived as long as me can observe some of the changes, if they're paying attention."

"Can't you—or we, you know, witches, can't we do something about it?" Kerry asked anxiously.

"You think we aren't?" Season responded. "You should see what things would be like if we weren't butting in as much as we're able. We have a group constantly trying to help mitigate the damage that humans do to one another and to their planet, but there's only so much they can accomplish. As a people, we seem able to create war, famine, environmental catastrophe, and crime no matter what. Against that, witches can only try to hold the line. I told you that we're engaged in a continual struggle between chaos and order. The human tendency supports the chaos side, so it's an uphill climb. But we're still trying, all the time."

Kerry was about to respond when a loud crack sounded outside, and virtually simultaneously the living room window shattered, glass crashing to the floor in great shards. A hot buzz swept through the room and thudded into the far wall, between the two women. Kerry jumped, her heart slamming into her throat. "What—?"

"Get down!" Season commanded. She dove across the space separating them and pushed Kerry to the floor. They both landed hard against the threadbare rug. "Someone's shooting at us," Season explained.

Kerry hadn't known what to expect, but somehow that was worse than anything she would have thought of. She was accustomed to magical attacks, or as close to accustomed to them as she figured one could be. But a bullet . . . that was so brutal, so cold. Witchcraft, magic—these things were part of nature, inextricably tied to it. A few ounces of lead formed into a killing instrument was decidedly unnatural and filled Kerry with revulsion.

"Who . . . ?" she began. She didn't bother to finish. *Who else?* Somehow Mother Blessing had found them.

She didn't usually use bullets, though. She had seen for herself how useless they were against Season.

Against Season . . . but not against Kerry. Had that shot been meant just for her? Take out Season's ally, and then go up against Season one-on-one? Kerry shivered, and not just from the cold air that streamed in through the broken window.

"We should find out who," Season suggested. Staying low, she crawled to the wall beneath the large window. She motioned to Kerry to keep down, even as she lifted her own head to the windowsill and peered out.

"Who's out there?" Kerry inquired urgently. Her terror was quickly moving toward rage. She felt violated by the attack and wanted to take some kind of action.

"It's—down!" Season dropped her own head below the edge of the window again, just as another bullet whipped through some of the remaining glass. Shards showered onto her head.

"There are a few of them," Season told her.

"But who are they?"

"I don't know," Season answered. "They just look like regular guys. Like hunters, I guess. A couple in camouflage clothing, others in normal street clothes. They're all carrying guns, and they're spreading out—it looks like they're trying to surround the house."

"But . . . they can't do that! Why?"

"I have to think Mother Blessing is behind it somehow," Season replied.

"I got that much."

"Then you know as much as me," Season snapped. "Sorry," she said a second later. "I'm just trying to figure this out. It's a new tactic, but it's still part of the same war, I'm sure."

Kerry was quiet for a moment, listening hard. Outside she could hear soft voices and the occasional snap of a twig or rustle of leaves, but for the most part the movements of their hunters were masked by the patter of the rain, which now blew inside through the shattered window. They could have been closing on the house, for all she could tell—about to burst in at any moment.

"She's controlling them," Season ventured. "I don't know where she found them, maybe just around the community. They don't look like men who know they're engaged in a life-or-death task—their faces are kind of blank, so I'm sure she's taken them over. But still, they won't be as easy to deal with as simulacra."

"Why not?" Kerry wondered out loud. "They're just humans, right? And if they're not altogether there, they should be—"

"That's exactly why," Season explained. "Their humanity. They can think, they can reason, and they can communicate. Mother Blessing may be behind them, controlling them, but she left them enough of their own personalities to allow them to become an effective unit."

"Great," Kerry said. "Then what do we do?" A horrible thought struck her. "Do we have to kill them?"

"I'm thinking," Season said, her tone bordering on impatience again. "If they were simulacra, I wouldn't hesitate to blast them. But they're human— we can't just kill them. Not only would it be wrong, but it would negate all the purification rituals we've just put ourselves through. We'd have to start over, and there's no way we'd be ready for the Convocation."

Another sound from outside, a footstep on gravel. The men were closer now. Neither Season nor Kerry had shown themselves at the window, so no more shots had been fired, but Kerry was convinced that wouldn't last long. As soon as the men were inside, she and Season would be the proverbial sitting ducks.

"Can we disable them in some way?" Kerry asked. "Immobilize them, paralyze them, something?"

"If they were acting of their own volition, we could," Season said. "Since they're not, it would mean trying to counter Mother Blessing's influence. I don't know if it'll work."

"It's worth a try, though, right?"

"At this point, anything's worth a try," Season said. She started to add something, but was interrupted by the sound of breaking glass from elsewhere in the house.

"They're coming in!" Kerry breathed.

"Then we have to get out," Season replied. "Kitchen!"

Both women scrambled on hands and knees toward the kitchen entry. From the back door there, a couple of steps led to the small yard, which was overrun by thick shrubbery and low-hanging tree branches. More noise inside the house told Kerry that someone had entered through the bedroom Season slept in, which also had a door facing off to the side of the house. They had no doubt broken one of the panes out of the door and reached in to open it. If they hadn't completely surrounded the house yet, the kitchen door might still be safe.

That was, as Kerry's mother used to say, a pretty big if.

In the kitchen at last, Season once again took the lead. While Kerry hugged the floor, Season looked outside. Not seeing any of the men from her vantage point, she laid out her plan. "I'm going to open this door," she said. "And then I'm going to run like hell for the trees. You give me a couple of seconds, to draw their fire if they're watching, and then follow. We'll meet up at that cliff you climbed."

"All I heard was the run like hell part," Kerry admitted. "And don't worry, that's exactly what I had in mind."

"If they hit me—"

Kerry cut her off. "They won't. Don't even go there."

"I'm just saying—"

The scuff of a foot on the floorboards. "Would you just go, already?" Kerry was afraid she'd have to shove Season out the door.

But Season was already in motion. With a single smooth move, she swung the door open and launched herself into the darkness outside. Kerry held her breath, expecting the roar of gunfire. Instead she heard the crash of underbrush, and then silence. Fearing the worst—that Season's exit would have alerted the hunters to this way out, even though they had previously been unaware of it—she swallowed once and charged out the door. A patch of light from inside the house floated between her and welcoming darkness, like a wall she would have to penetrate, but she was through it quickly enough and embraced by shadows. Behind her, she heard voices calling out, and then the report of a gun. Leaves not far from her flew as a bullet tore through them, but she kept her head down and ran.

The ground was wet and slick, and branches whipped against Kerry's face and limbs as she ran, snagging fabric and ripping flesh. Not as bad as bullets would, though. She kept running, full out, trying to breathe easily.

She knew she was in the best shape of her life—her legs pumped beneath her, each long stride carrying her away from the hunters and the deathtrap their borrowed house had become. As long as she didn't slam herself into a tree trunk in the dark, she would be okay.

Fifteen minutes later she had reached the end of the world.

It might as well have been, at any rate. Of the black Pacific she could see nothing. There were no stars, no moon to be reflected in the water—the clouds overhead blotted out all light. All she could see on the cliff's edge was Season, trying to keep her balance on the rain-slick rocks. Kerry joined her friend there and found cover behind an upthrust boulder, so she couldn't be observed from inland.

Season sat down beside her. Both of them were soaked to the skin, but alive and unhurt. Pneumonia was far easier to fight off than bullets, at least for Kerry.

"Now what?" Kerry asked.

"I hadn't thought that far ahead," Season said. "I just wanted us out of there. Now I guess we hope they give up when they find out the house is empty."

"But they know we were in there," Kerry countered. "They saw us through the window. One of them shot at me when I was running away."

Season shrugged. "I didn't say it was a good plan. Just the best I could come up with at the moment."

"You really think they'll give up?"

"I wouldn't want to count on it," Season admitted, wiping back the hair plastered to her face by the rain. "I guess it depends on how determined Mother Blessing is, and how much control she has over them."

"I have a feeling she's pretty determined."

"I put more hope in the second part, myself," Season said. "If her control over them slips, they'll probably wonder what on Earth they were ever doing out here and head for home."

"That would be good," Kerry said. She allowed herself a flash of optimism, but it didn't last long. "But what if they don't go home? Then we're pretty much trapped here on the cliff."

"Except for one thing," Season pointed out. "We know we can climb down. In this rain they probably can't—especially since they don't have complete control of their own bodies. I'm not saying it would be easy, in this weather, but we could do it. They'll fall for sure."

"And then we'd be killing them anyway," Kerry observed. "Not directly, maybe, but just as dead."

Season contemplated that for a moment. "Yes, that's true. We would be killing them, if you look at it like that."

"So it's not a very good option, is it?"

"I guess not."

They both fell silent then. Kerry tried to think of some other plan, some way to get out of this position. Nothing came to her. They were stuck on a cliff's edge in a driving rain, and armed men were looking for them. Even if they stayed out here all night, there was no guarantee the men would give up. Maybe they'd never give up.

"Kerry . . . ," Season whispered after a time. "I see one of them."

She was peeking around the edge of the sheltering boulder, looking back in the direction of the house.

"Has he seen us?" Kerry asked quietly.

"Not yet," Season answered. "And so far, it's just one of them."

Kerry hazarded a glance of her own. The hunter had broken out of the tree line and was walking toward the cliff, cradling his rifle in his arms and scanning the horizon with every step. Safe behind their boulder, they would be hidden until he was right on top of them. But then it would be a matter of kill or be killed, Kerry was convinced.

"We've got to try something before any more come," she suggested. "Maybe if we pick them off one by one—"

"That's what I was thinking," Season interrupted. "Wait here." She broke from cover and ran toward the man. He reacted to her charge, shouldering the rifle and sighting down it. He moved more slowly than Kerry expected—she guessed that Mother Blessing's remote automation included a built-in time delay, as if some electronic signal had to travel back to her, wherever she was, so she could give the appropriate order.

But Season moved fast, weaving as she ran to make it harder for the sluggish man to draw a bead on her. As he tried, she threw up her hands and shouted, *"Takilata!"*

The man stopped dead, as if he'd been struck by a hammer or walked into a brick wall. A look of confusion swept across his face. Season's spell was working!

Kerry's celebration was short-lived, however. The man lowered his gun for a moment, shook off the spell like a man stepping out of a shower, and then raised his weapon again, aiming it right at Season. Kerry stifled a scream as he pulled the trigger. Season hurled herself to the ground, and the bullet whizzed over her head and off to sea.

Hardly losing a moment, Season lunged to her feet and closed the remaining distance between her and the gunman with a fast, zigzag dash. He brought the gun around again, trying to get her in his sights, but his reaction time was too slow. Before he could get off another shot, Season was there. She ducked under the rifle's barrel and slammed it toward the sky with one hand. He managed to squeeze the trigger, but his shot sailed harmlessly toward the clouds. Season braced herself on her left foot and kicked out with her right, catching the man in the gut. He doubled over, and she twisted the rifle from his hands, swinging it around as she did. The rifle's wooden stock collided with the man's jaw, and he crumpled like an empty paper bag.

Season motioned for Kerry to leave cover and join her. Nervously, afraid to abandon the sheltering rocks, she did so. The man on the ground hadn't moved, and as she approached him, Kerry could see the gleam of dark liquid around his nose and mouth. Blood.

"He's . . . ?"

"He's alive," Season assured her. "But it'll be a little while before he's a problem again. He's just one of them, though, and those two shots will have alerted the others. I think we need to get out of here. This is going to be tougher than I had hoped."

11

Season led Kerry back toward the house by a different, and more round-about, route than they had taken going out. This was a path Kerry had never seen—didn't even know was here—and it seemed to confirm her guess that while she had been holed up in the house reading, Season had been out scouting something. She should have known it would be escape routes, since they were one of Season's specialties.

"The spell I tried should have paralyzed him," Season whispered as they hurried through the trees. "But it barely slowed him down. Mother Blessing's spell is too deeply embedded for me to break. Our best bet is to deal with them one by one, if they're spread out enough, and make our way to the car. Chances are she's already overextending herself, so they probably won't be able to follow us any great distance."

"That's encouraging," Kerry replied softly.

"We do the best we can." Season tossed her a wry smile and kept going through the woods.

They met the second of the hunters as they rounded a bend on the trail. He was coming in their direction, shuffling along like a sleepwalker. When he saw the women, though, he seemed to wake up a little. "Over here!" he shouted, bringing his gun up at the same time.

"*Takilata!*" Season tried, making the appropriate hand gestures.

Once again, the man was affected only momentarily. He was so close, however, that Season was able to reach him before he recovered. She cupped both hands over his ears and brought them together hard. The sensation seemed to stun him for another moment, and she followed up with a precisely aimed elbow to his windpipe. He dropped to his knees, choking. Season pushed him over and he fell on the ground, writhing and gasping for breath. She knelt beside him, touching his neck. She looked up at Kerry as she did. "Dislocated his windpipe for a second," she said. "I've fixed it. He'll be fine. But he won't be shouting again soon."

"How did you learn all this stuff?" Kerry inquired.

"Here and there," Season said vaguely. Kerry took the hint and let it drop.

Leaving him moaning softly on the wet path, they continued toward the house. Rustling nearby indicated that the man's initial cry had not gone unheard. Season gestured to Kerry and they both left the path, taking to the trees and waiting, as still as possible, a couple of feet back.

Less than a minute later, two of the hunters came down the path, stiff-legged and awkward. Their guns were at the ready, but their eyes were only on the trail. They walked right past Season and Kerry without ever noticing them standing among the trees. The women waited another couple of minutes, until they could no longer hear the two men, and then took to the path again.

They were almost back to the house when they encountered yet another of the hunters. Season braced herself for action, but Kerry put a restraining hand on her arm. "Let me try something," she said.

Season looked surprised, but then smiled. "Be my guest."

Kerry waited until the guy had spotted them and prepared to sound the alarm, and then she folded the fingers of her right hand until the fingertips touched the palm, and extended her thumb. With her left hand, she made a lifting motion. *"Kenesep!"* she exclaimed.

The man's cry died in his throat as a plume of earth rose up and hurled itself into his face. He backpedaled away from it, but his impaired control over his own limbs got in the way and he fell over backward, smacking his head against a tree stump with an audible crack. He rolled to the ground and lay still.

"You don't think I broke anything, do you?" Kerry asked, suddenly worried that she'd taken it too far.

"I doubt it," Season answered. Dropping to one knee beside the man, she examined the back of his head briefly. "I think he just got knocked out. Come on."

The 4x4 they had bought in San Francisco was parked within view, and there were no hunters readily apparent. They broke into a sprint. Kerry knew they'd left their purses, driver's licenses and all, back in the house, and probably their keys as well.

She also knew that wouldn't matter—such inconveniences were easily fixed with the help of a little witchcraft.

Season hit the driver's side door and yanked it open. Kerry ran around to the passenger side, and by the time she was in her seat, Season was already backing out of the gravel driveway. Kerry buckled in just as Season straightened out on the dirt road and stomped on the gas.

Some of the hunters heard the sounds of the vehicle and came running—running, at least, to the extent that their slow-moving bodies would allow. A couple of them raised their rifles, and Kerry heard shots fired behind them. No bullets impacted the Raider, however. Within minutes she and Season had left them far behind, cutting through the rain toward the highway out of Bolinas.

Mother Blessing knew when her targets were out of range. During the search and battle, she had taken refuge in a cheap motel room on the San Francisco peninsula, directing the action from there since she couldn't both drive and participate. Trucks rumbling past threatened to disturb her concentration, but she tuned the room's TV to a channel it didn't receive and cranked the volume, letting the white noise drown out traffic sounds from outside. Watching through multiple pairs of eyes—and eyes she had not manufactured, but only enchanted—was a strain in itself; doing that and controlling muscles, planning and executing strategy, took a lot out of a person. And now she knew that Season and Kerry were headed north— toward the Convocation site, no doubt—and that her plan had not worked.

Still, she'd had to try. The Convocation was upon them. Season could have decided to leave at any minute. Since she couldn't make it to Bolinas herself in a timely enough fashion, she had stopped in this motel and used its telephone book to locate a gun shop in Marin County, not too far from Bolinas. She then constructed a simulacrum and sent it into the shop, watching through its eyes to see who was inside. There were half a dozen men, some dressed like they were ready for the hunt, others engaged in conversation, shopping, or just browsing.

She didn't care why they had gone in, only that they were there.

It was brutally difficult—almost impossible, really—to cast spells over long distances. But the distance in this case wasn't too extreme, less than fifty miles, and she had the help of the simulacrum, whose hands could be sculpted into the precise necessary shapes for limited durations. She cast an overall spell on the men in the shop, freezing them where they stood, and then spent more time enchanting each one individually. She drilled the address of Rebecca's friends, the Morgans, into them, showed them their targets, and sent them on their way.

If that first shot had hit Kerry, she'd have had them both. Season wouldn't have abandoned the girl. She would have been so angry that she would have waited for Mother Blessing to arrive, just so she could have it out with her. Mother Blessing chuckled dryly. Human emotion could be so counterproductive, and Season had never been able to completely shake that handicap.

As it turned out, though the man she had used for the first attack had been the most seasoned hunter of the lot, her own manipulation of him had affected his ability to aim cleanly and to squeeze off a good shot.

Not for the first time, she wished she could have been there in person.

All the distance Season kept between them had kept her alive too many times. Mother Blessing was grimly aware that she had not been able to best Season the last time they'd been face-to-face, but that was then.

This was now. She was ready this time. She was primed. She had been preparing, training, learning.

All she needed was to meet up with Season Howe, one-on-one.

It peeved her royally to realize that it probably wasn't going to happen. Season had too much of a start. She was already racing toward the Convocation, while Mother Blessing tried to recover from a difficult, and ultimately futile, exercise. Perhaps she had, in fact, compounded her earlier mistake by going with surrogates yet again. If she had just driven straight to Bolinas, it was possible that Season and Kerry would have still been there, would have waited until morning to make the drive north.

But now she had flushed them out, and they were on the wing again. Even if Mother Blessing got on the road right now, Season had a couple of hours' head start. Mother Blessing's only hope was to drive through San Francisco, over the Golden Gate Bridge, and onto Interstate 80. From where Season was, she'd have a long haul to get to the Interstate, looping over the north end of the San Francisco Bay. Their way would be slow. It was remotely possible that Mother Blessing would be able to intercept them before they reached the Convocation, if she hurried. Maybe in Sacramento.

Leaving the TV blaring its noisy signal, Mother Blessing dragged herself wearily to her car.

Season pulled the car to a stop outside a twenty-four-hour family restaurant near Richmond. She had watched the mirror constantly since leaving Bolinas, and there had been no pursuit. She and Kerry were both hungry, and if they were going to drive all night they'd need some nourishment, and probably caffeine. This place would be quiet at this time of night, she explained. They'd be able to scrutinize all the diners at a glance as soon as they went in, and if anyone looked suspicious or made a move against them, they could immediately retreat or fight back.

Before they went in, Kerry pulled her cell phone from the purse that Season had magically arranged to be inside the car. *Either that,* Kerry thought, *or the purse is an exact duplicate of my old one, right down to the last stick of gum in its wrapper and the programming on the phone.* Only the names on her driver's license and credit cards were changed—now, as far as the public was concerned, she was Brenda Peterson, and Season was Amanda Cowles.

"I need to call Beck," she said. "I've been really worried about her."

"That's fine," Season said. "I think we're safe for the moment."

Season punched up Rebecca's home number. The phone rang only once before someone snatched it from the cradle on the other end. "Hello?" the voice asked breathlessly. Kerry recognized it at once, but it wasn't who she wanted to talk to.

"Erin?" Kerry said. "It's Kerry. Is Rebecca there?"

"God, no," Erin said. She sounded distraught. "I was hoping you were her."

"No, sorry. Where is she?"

"That's the thing, Kerry. I don't know. Scott and, what's her name, Brandy, were calling and calling, like, all night last night. They stopped for a while this morning, but they've been back at it now and then. I'm really worried about her. She left me a note saying she was leaving for a day or so, and that's the last anyone seems to have heard from her."

Kerry's heart sank. The bad feeling she'd had about Rebecca was accurate, and then some. Unfortunately, it didn't take an advanced degree in mathematics to put the puzzle pieces together. *Rebecca knew where we were,* she thought. *Rebecca vanishes, Mother Blessing turns up. Not a complicated pattern.*

"Okay, Erin," she said. "If you hear from her, please have her call me right away. I'll have her check in with you if I can reach her."

"Thanks, Kerry," Erin said. She sniffled, and Kerry guessed that she had started to weep. Sometimes the two housemates seemed barely aware of one another's existence, but that arrangement had worked for them. Rebecca even seemed to prefer it, since it made it easier to keep important aspects of her life private. But Erin genuinely liked Rebecca, in her own way. Of course she'd be worried and upset.

Kerry ended the call and turned to Season. "Rebecca's missing," she said. "Since last night sometime."

"Plenty of time for Mother Blessing to have found us," Season said, catching on instantly.

The ease with which Season jumped to the same conclusion that she had chilled Kerry to the bone. "That's what I was thinking."

"Try the others," Season urged. "Make sure they're okay."

Kerry was already scrolling for Scott's number. She prepared to call it, but at the last second changed her mind and chose Brandy's instead. She knew those two had had their troubles, and she knew that she was at the root of at least some of it. Why make things worse by always calling Scott first, instead of Brandy?

"Kerry?" Brandy answered a moment later.

"Hi, Brandy." Kerry didn't have time for pleasantries. "Have you heard from Rebecca?"

"No, we haven't been able to reach her all day," Brandy said. "Have you?"

"I just now talked to Erin and found out she was missing. I didn't know. Erin said she was going out of town for a while but didn't seem to know much more than that."

"It gets worse," Brandy told her. Kerry almost pulled the phone away from her head, afraid to hear what Brandy might have to say now.

"What?" she asked, almost against her own will.

"Adam was attacked," Brandy said. "By a simulacrum. Scott and I managed to fight it off—well, Scott did really. It was like some kind of miracle, Kerry—the thing just fell apart in his hands. But that was yesterday. We wanted to let you know Mother Blessing was on the move again, so we tried to call you. But when we couldn't get you, we called Rebecca. She said she would go to wherever you are and find you, warn you that something was up."

"Oh, no," Kerry said, as the weight of Brandy's words sank in.

"Yeah."

"Brandy, Rebecca never showed up, but some goons under Mother Blessing's control did."

"And Rebecca's the only one who knew where you were."

"Yeah," Kerry echoed Brandy. "I didn't want to tell Erin, but I'm really worried about her."

"Sounds like you have reason to be," Brandy said. "I kept hoping maybe she was with you, and you were all out of cell range or something."

"No such luck," Kerry said. "I wish."

"Me too."

Both were silent for a moment. Kerry thought she was going to cry, like Erin had. Only with more reason.

"I should tell Scott," Brandy said.

"Is he with you?"

"Yeah," Brandy said. "We're in a rental car, on our way to Santa Cruz. We landed at the airport in San Jose about a half hour ago—first flight out of Boston we were able to get."

"You guys be careful," Kerry urged, surprised to learn that they were already in California. "Chances are Mother Blessing is on her way up here, heading for the Convocation. But if she is still in Santa Cruz, I don't need to tell you she's very dangerous."

"I know, Kerry," Brandy said. "We won't take any stupid chances. But what if Rebecca is, I don't know, trapped someplace and needs our help? We have to look for her."

"You do that. I'll see if Season knows a way to search for her remotely. When you've found her, or . . . or when you're ready, head north, to Oregon." She drew the phone away from her mouth. "Where should they meet us, Season? After?"

"Have them wait in Klamath Falls," Season said. "That's not too far, and there are motels they can stay at."

"Klamath Falls, Season says," Kerry spoke into the phone. "I'll call you when I can to find out where you are. The Witches' Convocation is about to start, but we'll hook up with you after that. And everything will be different then, I can guarantee it."

"Everything's already different," Brandy said. "That doesn't mean I have to like it."

"Yeah," Kerry agreed. "That's a really good point."

12

It felt to Kerry as if they'd left the world behind.

She had never been anywhere so desolate, so isolated. Even the Great Dismal Swamp had been teeming with life, and there had been people around, towns all around it.

Not here, though. None of that.

She and Season had traded off at the wheel of the Dodge Raider through the night. They had bisected California on Interstate 80, leaving city and suburbs behind, entering agricultural areas, then the soupy region of the Sacramento Delta. Sacramento came and went in the dark, and once again they could smell rich and fertile farmlands surrounding them. Then the road started to climb. Flat fields turned to foothills, alfalfa and sugar beets to pines and firs and towering redwoods that blotted out the stars.

They had stopped for a few hours in Truckee, checking into a motel and grabbing some much-needed sleep on top of matching twin beds without even bothering to pull down the bedding. Breakfast was had at lunchtime in a nearby café, and then they were back in the car. The highway left California behind as it wove down from the mountains—the same Sierra Nevadas, Kerry reflected, that Season had mentioned earlier in her diatribe about global warming. That had been an eon ago, though, another age, before people had started shooting at them.

Coming down out of the mountains, they drove into Reno, which jutted up from the relative flatland like a child's toy forgotten on a lawn. Soon enough, even Reno vanished in the rearview mirror, and with it anything that smacked of population. The highway turned to the north and sliced through a state that seemed utterly abandoned. Every now and then there would be a roadside gas station/store/restaurant, or the buildings of some distant ranch, and then nothing again but mile after mile of rolling plains of sagebrush.

Then Winnemucca, a blink of the eye, and Season, who refused to reveal their destination except as the site of the Convocation, surprised Kerry by turning off Interstate 80 altogether.

Now she drove due north on Highway 95, a narrow strip of roadway that barely deserved the dignity of being numbered. It was paved, Kerry reflected, but that was about all it had going for it. With the setting sun on Season's side of the car, they drove up and up. There were mountains looming in the distance—this was basin and range country, Season had explained, which meant relatively parallel mountain ranges separated by deep valleys, like the wales of corduroy, cutting across the landscape. They followed the roadway through one of the valleys. Then the sun dropped behind the mountains to the west, and Season pulled over to let Kerry take the wheel for a stretch.

"Where are we?" Kerry wanted to know.

"Right here." This was about the extent that Season had been willing to reveal for hours.

"And where are we going?"

Season ticked her head north, on up the road. "That way."

Kerry blew out a frustrated sigh. "Okay. Will I know when we get there?"

"You'll know," Season promised her. "You will definitely know."

Kerry drove on, into the gathering dusk. There were no lights to be seen anywhere. If anyone actually lived out here, she couldn't tell. The idea suddenly struck her that this would be an awfully remote place to run out of gas, but then she smiled at her own naïveté—they hadn't stopped for gas since they'd bought the vehicle, and they wouldn't have to.

Finally, as stars began to wink into sight in the darkening sky, Season touched her right arm.

"Slow down," she said.

"Okay." Kerry complied. "Are we looking for something?"

"We are," Season confirmed. Kerry continued up the road for a couple of miles, with Season eyeing the left shoulder. Finally, she touched Kerry's arm once again. "We're looking for that."

Kerry followed her pointing hand. Season seemed to be pointing to a narrow, rutted track that led away from the highway. "That . . . that little path?"

"That's right," Season said. "Take that."

"This thing will be okay on that road? Is that really a road?"

Season showed her how to shift the Raider into its four-wheel drive mode. "This thing can go anywhere," she promised. "Just don't go too fast if you don't have to. Slow and easy."

Kerry almost asked why she might have to go fast, if slow was preferred, but then decided she'd rather not know. With Rebecca missing and Mother Blessing on the warpath, she had enough troubles weighing on her mind as it was. She turned onto the little track. The Raider chewed up the road easily, and she increased its pace a little, learning to slow down when approaching bumps or hollows. The headlights illuminated bugs flitting past, occasional clumps of sagebrush, dirt, and not much else. Once a pair of pronghorns dashed across a hill, limned against the rising moon.

A couple of hours later, Kerry yawned and stretched, gripping the wheel with one hand while she pushed the other against the ceiling, then trading off. "We're almost there," Season assured her. "Not much farther."

Kerry looked out into the distance and realized that beyond the headlights she couldn't see anything at all. The moon seemed to shine down on absolute nothingness.

"Are we still in Nevada?" she asked. "Are we still on Earth?"

"We may have passed into Oregon," Season told her. "I'm not a hundred percent sure about that. But don't worry, we're just about there."

Kerry brought the 4X4 to a shuddering stop and stared at Season as if the woman had gone insane. "Almost where? We're nowhere! There's nothing here. No one. Nada." She shut off the headlights and got out of the vehicle. She hadn't realized it, so focused was she on the narrow cone that the headlights illuminated, but they had been driving for some time on a perfectly flat, perfectly empty stretch of land. Beneath her feet, the hardpan was baked solid, the dirt cracked in hexagonal shapes. It looked like brownies left in the oven too long. She spun around, indicating the field of nothingness with her hands.

With the headlights gone, the moon shone down on the vast, empty space, which seemed to glow whitely of its own volition. Overhead, against the black backdrop of night, Kerry thought she could see every star there had ever been. The white sweep of the Milky Way had never been so distinct.

Season walked over to her, her boots crunching on the crusted earth. "Feel better?" she asked sympathetically.

"I'll feel better when I know where we are," Kerry groused.

"We're in the Owyhee Desert," Season told her. "It crosses between northern Nevada and southern Oregon. A lot of maps don't bother to name it, because what's the point? There's nothing here."

"A whole lot of nothing," Kerry said. "I can see that much."

"I mean, real nothing," Season said. "This is one of the emptiest spots in the United States. The population density of Humboldt County, Nevada, which we just passed through, is somewhere less than two people per square mile, and most of those live back down in Winnemucca. Here it's probably figured in negative numbers."

"Meaning what?"

"Meaning there are more dead people than living, around here."

"That's a comforting thought," Kerry said.

"It's just empty," Season said. "Nothing wrong with that. It's what we're looking for."

"It is?"

"I'll show you," Season offered. "Get back in."

Kerry grudgingly complied. She had come to trust Season, but she didn't like how secretive her mentor had been about this whole thing. She could probably backtrack and return to civilization if she needed to, but only because there were so few roads that it would be hard to get genuinely lost.

But she got in and buckled up, with Season taking the wheel again. The older witch started the engine, flicked on the headlights, and began driving up the dirt trail, faster than Kerry had done.

"We're really someplace?" Kerry asked. "This is like some kind of weird hallucination."

Season chuckled. "That's it exactly," she said. "Don't see what your eyes tell you to see."

"Sometimes you are so opaque," Kerry commented. "Why don't you just say what you mean?"

"Don't see dark, flat, empty land," Season pressed. "Close your eyes and see the Convocation."

"How can I? I don't even know what it looks like. But if it looks like this, I'm going to be seriously bummed."

"It looks like a carnival," Season told her. "Not a modern one. Maybe a medieval one. Look at the peaked tents—blue, white, red, yellow, green. Look at the banners and pennants fluttering from their points, at the bright piping wrapped around their guy lines, like garlands around the staircase at Christmas. Look at the little wooden buildings where people serve food and drink, and the fires roaring in the wind, sprays of sparks dancing up into the sky, where they cook the beef and ham and turkey, and the smaller fires where they grill the vegetables. Smell the aromatic smoke that funnels up like dust devils. Look at the people walking between the tents and the buildings, chatting and laughing and enjoying being in one another's company again, safe and at home. See the dance floor, encircled by glowing paper lanterns, where couples in their most elegant finery twirl to the music provided by the band in the little frame gazebo."

Kerry realized that she *could* see the things Season described as the Raider bounced its way across the blank lunar landscape. It was just because her eyes were shut, and Season's words were so hypnotic, so evocative, she knew.

But no! Her eyes were wide open. Somehow, as if they had passed through an invisible curtain, they were now driving toward something, instead of toward more of the same nothing. It was just as Season had described it—she hadn't been imagining it after all, she had been stating what she was seeing, right in front of her. The tall tents with fluttering flags, the fires, the crowded dance floor.

And most of all, the people.

The witches.

Kerry Profitt's diary, March 21

I'm home.

I've never been home before. Not really. Well, okay, maybe when I was a little kid and both of my parents were alive, back in Cairo where I was born and bred. But not since then. Certainly not since Mom passed on and I had to move in with my aunt and uncle.

But I'm home now. I felt it as soon as I could truly see the Convocation, as soon as Season's words turned into reality for me.

If you weren't meant to be here, you would never see it. If for some bizarre reason you were driving on that goddess-awful dirt road and you weren't a witch, you'd just keep driving right through, never realizing that you had just missed the greatest celebration you could ever have imagined.

I'm meant to be here, then, because I can see it, and smell it, and hear it. Season and I are staying inside one of the little wooden caravans, and every now and then I just have to get up and go to the door and stare outside at everyone and everything. Kind of like pinching myself to make sure I'm not dreaming, only without the pinch part.

It's amazing. Everyone is so happy, so friendly. Smiling. Laughing. Shouting to people they haven't seen in . . . well, in five hundred years. Calling to each other, running together, hugging. Lots of hugging.

And the sounds are so musical, so enchanting. The smells are heavenly. The clothes are . . . everything. Outfits from every time period in the last five centuries, and from every part of the world, but they all mesh together, they all blend perfectly, and they are all beautiful—the finest fabrics, the most skilled workmanship. I felt like a grunge in my dirty T-shirt and jeans and red-checked tennies, but then I looked down at myself, and my clothes seemed to have a glow to them. Same clothes, but somehow they had become fitting and appropriate and perfect, just like everyone else's. Every skin color on Earth is represented, too, and just like the clothes, it all makes a glorious visual display.

It's the world's biggest, best party. That's the only real way to describe it. A party where everybody likes each other, and no one is obnoxiously drunk or hitting on someone who doesn't want to be hit on.

It's a celebration of witchiness. It's a gala. It's a convention. It's a business meeting. It's a dream.

It's the Convocation.

It's home.

Somebody pinch me after all. Or don't, on second thought, because I don't want to wake up from this.

More later.

K.

13

When Brandy and Scott got to Rebecca's house in Santa Cruz, the place was crawling with police. Rebecca's VW was parked across the street, with yellow police tape surrounding it and the area immediately around it. Arc lights on tall stanchions gave a surreally bright glow to jumpsuited officers with cameras and evidence kits. It looked like a CSI episode come horribly to life, since it brought home with cruel bluntness the fact that Rebecca was truly missing.

At the door to the house, they had to introduce themselves to a sympathetic but terse female officer, who then announced them to Erin. Erin immediately rushed to the door to let them in. They had never met her, but Brandy recognized her from Rebecca's descriptions and a couple of photos. She was the archetypal California blonde—petite, button-cute, hair pulled back into a bouncy ponytail. But her red nose and the dark circles around her puffy eyes showed that she was not always the epitome of perky.

She led them into the kitchen. Brandy could hear cops moving in other parts of the house, and the static and buzz of their two-way radios. The kitchen was mercifully empty of them, and Erin sat down at a vintage Formica-topped table, in front of a cup of tea that looked like it had been there awhile.

"I'm so sorry I, you know, hung up on you guys," she said sadly. "I . . . you know, I thought she was just out or whatever, and you were just getting on my nerves. But if I had known . . ."

"How could you?" Brandy asked, pulling out a chair of her own and joining Erin at the table. "Her note said that she was going away for some indefinite period of time. So when she did just that, you had no reason to think there was anything wrong."

"Yeah, I guess so," Erin agreed as tears began to roll down her cheeks. "But still . . . there must have been something I missed. Some clue. I should have noticed sooner that her car was still there."

"You can't beat yourself up too much," Scott told her. He had remained standing, scanning the kitchen as if there might be a clue everyone else had missed. "Whatever happened to her is not your fault, I know that."

Brandy reflected that he couldn't tell Erin why he knew it. Erin had no inkling, she was certain, of the existence of Season Howe and Mother Blessing and the whole long war between them. Rebecca had sworn that she would never tell anyone outside of their circle—those who had been living in the La Jolla house the night they found Daniel Blessing, half dead, in the shrubbery outside. The night it all began. Brandy had never had occasion to think Rebecca anything less than scrupulously honest—if she made a promise, she kept it.

She almost wished she could say something now. If Erin could know what her housemate was really caught up in, it would lessen any feelings of guilt she might have over Rebecca's disappearance. But Brandy held her tongue. Erin was so emotionally vulnerable right now, so close to the edge, that she would either think Brandy was a complete, unabashed liar, or she would believe the story, realize that the entire framework of knowledge she had about the world was wrong, and go totally insane.

The La Jolla housemates had at least had some time to get used to the existence of witches, and the knowledge had been thrust on them at a time when they were relatively happy, secure, and comfortable with each other. Erin had no such advantages. She would be knocked over at her weakest point, and her grip on reality might not survive it.

So instead of telling her the only thing that might really ease her pain,

Brandy took Erin's hand and gently rubbed the back of it. "He's right," she said. "It's not your fault, Erin. We'll look for her. She's probably fine."

Only, of course, she probably wasn't. Mother Blessing had located Kerry and Season. Only Rebecca could have told her where to look. Unless she had come across the information some other way, Rebecca was certainly in serious trouble.

Behind her, Brandy heard Scott walking around, and then he left the kitchen altogether. She glanced at Erin and they both fell silent, listening as he addressed a police officer they couldn't see.

"Can you tell me anything about the investigation?" he asked. "We're close friends of Rebecca's—we actually just flew in from Boston to see her, and if there's anything we can do to help we'd really like to know."

"The best I can tell you is to keep out of the way and let us handle it," the police officer replied, his tone sympathetic but firm. "We can do our jobs."

"I know," Scott pressed. "But have you, you know, checked the hospitals and stuff? In case she's been in an accident or something?"

"We're working on it, son," the officer said. "Like I said—"

"I didn't mean to imply that you weren't," Scott said, cutting him off. "I just figured, if there was something we could do that would take some of the pressure off you, we'd be happy to."

"If I think of anything, I'll let you know," the officer said. Brandy heard the jangle of equipment on his belt as he walked away, and then Scott came back into the kitchen.

"They've got nothing," he said. "They're never going to find her."

The cops had nothing, but Brandy and Scott had no clue where to look for her either. The reality of it loomed over Brandy like a falling piano. Soon enough, the piano would hit.

"I've been missin' y'all."

Kerry was not surprised to hear Mother Blessing's voice, or to see her when she spun around at the sound of it. Season had assured her that their enemy would be in attendance. She also swore that Mother Blessing would be polite, even friendly, on the grounds of the Convocation, but Kerry tensed just the same, ready to run or fight.

Mother Blessing stood a dozen feet behind them, supporting her weight on a black metal cane. Even her usual polyester stretch pants and tentlike top seemed enhanced by their presence here, looking more like the garb of some weird kind of royalty than like the discount store specials they usually resembled.

"*Barely* missing," Season added.

Mother Blessing's smile broadened. "Well, a lady has to try, right? I thought maybe I'd run into y'all in Sacramento, but somehow you got past me."

"Imagine that," Season replied, returning the woman's ghastly grin. "I hope you didn't injure any innocent civilians while you were looking for us."

Mother Blessing laughed uproariously, as if Season had just told the best joke ever. Kerry couldn't quite get over these mortal enemies acting like old friends. She was reminded of politicians shaking hands before a debate, calling each other liars and cheats for an hour, and then shaking again when it was all over.

Then the old witch focused her gaze on Kerry, who twitched uncertainly beneath it. "Hope y'all are well, Kerry," she said. "It's been awful lonely at home since you left."

"Yeah, I bet you really wish I was back there," Kerry said, not bothering to hide the sarcastic edge. She was no politician, and she didn't intend to behave like one.

Season poked Kerry in the ribs, covering the action by laughing and grabbing Kerry's arm. "Kerry's told me all about how much she's learned from you, daughter," she said. It freaked Kerry out to be reminded that the

youthful Season Howe was, in fact, Mother Blessing's mother. "I'm surprised that you turned out to be such a good teacher."

"Kerry's a good pupil," Mother Blessing answered. "A natural."

"That's true," Season said. "I guess you have an eye for them."

"I like to think so."

"We were just on our way to get some breakfast," Season said, bringing
the uncomfortable conversation to a diplomatic close. "Would you like to
join us?"

Kerry wanted to poke Season this time, but her friend had moved out of
reach. Fortunately, Mother Blessing politely declined the offer.

Walking through the golden sunshine toward a tent from which wafted
a glorious assortment of aromas, Kerry fixed Season with a curious glare.
"What was all that about?"

"It won't do us any good to get into a brawl here," Season answered
reasonably. "We're at the Convocation. No one's getting hurt now. Nothing's going to happen until Witches' Tribunal, and then it'll be under the
procedures that have been in place for centuries. If she was going to kill us,
she needed to do it before we got here. Now we're perfectly safe from her."

Kerry couldn't quite wrap her mind around that idea. Perfectly safe?
There had been a time in her life when she had felt safe, but not in the last
year or so. She had been on edge virtually every minute, starting at every
unusual noise, eyeing strangers with suspicion. She supposed that maybe
she would be able to fully relax again someday.

It would take a while, though.

Regardless of Season's assurances, she would not trust Mother Blessing
until after the Witches' Tribunal had dealt out its justice.

The breakfast offered in the tent was every bit as delicious as its odors
promised. A crew of chefs in restaurant whites with tall hats—but all
decorated with a wide assortment of cheerful buttons, braids, tassels,
patches, and other additions, and all working with uniform good cheer—

turned out an equally wide assortment of dishes. There were omelets and eggs of every style, various meats and sausages, pancakes and waffles, cereals, pastries, fruits. . . . Kerry could barely bring herself to pick anything, because it all looked so good.

"No wonder you cook so well," she said to Season as they examined their options. "Do witches always eat like this?"

"Sometimes its gruel and hardtack," Season teased. "But what's the point of having a party if you can't indulge yourself?"

They filled plates and then sat down at long tables. The benches were filled with witches chatting, laughing, and seeming to have a good time. There were more women than men, but not by a huge margin. Kerry and Season squeezed in at the end of one of the benches, where a couple of people moved over to make space for them. Season hugged them both, a man and a woman.

"It's so good to see you," she gushed. "Kerry, this is Horace and Mae. They're witches from—Wisconsin, is it?"

"Madison," Horace said, beaming at Kerry like they were long-lost pals. He was as lean as a greyhound, with thinning silver hair combed over a bald spot, and small-lensed wire-rim glasses perched on a prominent nose. He could have been sixty or, Kerry knew, six hundred. Mae was rounder, more heavyset, with grandmotherly gray curls and a pearl chain attached to her horn-rims. Both were dressed like the grandparents in one of those black-and-white TV sitcoms from the fifties that ran on TV late at night.

"I've been to Madison!" Kerry said excitedly. The giddy mood of the other diners was infecting her. "Last fall, on my way down . . . down south."

"You've got to be pretty far north for Madison to be on the way south," Mae observed with a giggle.

"I figured that out," Kerry replied. She had realized that she didn't want to get carried away and reveal that she'd been on her way to stay with Mother Blessing. Everybody acted friendly here, but that didn't mean there weren't factions, and she wanted to be cautious about saying too much to the wrong person. At least until she could get the lay of the land, or find out from Season who to trust. "I didn't exactly take the most direct route."

"Did you like it, Kerry?" Horace asked.

"I really didn't stay long," Kerry admitted. "It was cold, mostly. That's what I remember."

"Well, you should come back this time of year. Between now and early summer. It's a real nice place."

"It looked like it," Kerry said. "I'd like to go back sometime."

"I met Horace and Mae in . . . what was it, 1890?" Season asked.

"Ninety-one, I think," Mae corrected. "That winter."

"They helped me out of a tight spot," Season continued. "They're good folks." Kerry waited for her to elaborate further, but she didn't. Instead she dug into her breakfast with gusto. Kerry followed her lead and did the same, not wanting to let it get cold.

After breakfast Season introduced her to another dozen or so old friends as they wandered through the lanes between tents, pavilions, and small wooden buildings. In these, every kind of witchy activity Kerry could imagine took place. Some held demonstrations of spells or potions. Some were shops where magical implements—swords, daggers, wands, cauldrons, herbs, censers, brooms, crystals, and more—were displayed and traded. Everything within the Convocation grounds seemed to be bathed in a soft, gentle glow. Kerry had thought at first it was just early morning light slanting down on things, but as the day wore on, it didn't dissipate or change. Finally, she asked Season about it.

"It's the light of magic," Season said. "Sometimes you'll hear late afternoon, just a little before sunset, when the sun is at an angle and the light has a golden tinge, referred to as the 'magic hour.' And that's by civilians. They don't know how close they are to the truth, but somehow the truth has filtered down to them."

Kerry didn't understand. "But . . ." She couldn't even come up with the question.

Season got it, though. "It's all around us. This whole thing, the Convocation. Remember the desert outside here? Flat, dry, hot, empty? We are here, we're not an illusion. But to an outsider, we wouldn't be. It's magic. We are bathed in it here, suffused in it. Those pavilions, those chairs, those trailers . . . they weren't here two days ago, and they won't be here next week. Not in the sense that one typically thinks of as 'here.' The molecules that make them up will be returned to where they came from—around here, pretty much dirt, and maybe a few scrubby sage-brush bushes for texture."

"But I don't see a glow like that when I cast a spell," Kerry pressed.

"Because a spell is an isolated instance of magic," Season explained. "Transitory, only there for the moment. Here there's nothing isolated about it. It's as much a part of our environment as the air itself. It would be strange if there *wasn't* an optical manifestation of it."

Good enough for me, Kerry thought. *That explains why my cruddy jeans and T-shirts look so spiff, and Mother Blessing's nightmare wardrobe too. Probably why everyone's in such a good mood, too.* For her part, Kerry felt better than she had in ages—years, maybe. Not just physically, but emotionally. She felt like she was in the bosom of a large, extended family, surrounded by people who cared about her, even though in fact most of them had never met or heard about her. But everyone Season introduced her to greeted her happily. She had never been made so welcome anywhere in her life.

For the morning, she and Season had no particular schedule, no appointments to keep. They just wandered, taking in the sights and sounds. Kerry tried to estimate the size of the Convocation, or the atten-dance, but found that it was impossible. Sometimes she thought they were almost at the end of a row, but then they would go into a tent or a shop, and when they emerged the row would stretch out toward the horizon, the empty desert she thought she had glimpsed totally eclipsed by light and color and activity. Every now and then she got the feeling that things were changing right behind them—like if they went into one stall, the one they had just left would metamorphose into something entirely different, so that one could never experience the whole array.

An astonishing variety of blooming flowers edged the paths and filled in spaces between the tents and buildings, a carpet of reds, whites, oranges, pinks, yellows, violets, and greens. Considering what she knew the "real" landscape around her looked like, Kerry was especially delighted to see the displays of poppies and daisies, lupines and lilacs, sunflowers and sacred datura.

Only one thing nagged at her, keeping her happiness from being complete. She remembered how much Daniel had looked forward to his first Convocation. He had told her stories of past ones—like Season and her daughter, he'd never been but he was full of the tales that witches handed down to one another. She couldn't help wishing it was Daniel walking beside her now. Maybe even him and Season, both having learned that they weren't one another's real enemy. Daniel's large, warm hand enveloping hers, his ready smile, his clear gray eyes crinkling in the golden magic-light. That would have made this experience perfect.

That afternoon she and Season took part in a ritual with about a thousand other witches.

With no verbal communication of which Kerry was aware, no printed schedule or loudspeaker announcement or anything like that, everyone seemed to just filter toward a vast, empty, grassy meadow that she would have sworn hadn't been there before.

Kerry wore a simple white shift that she'd picked up in one of the shops, which she learned were "shops" only in name, since they accepted no payment for the merchandise they provided. Her feet were bare. On her head was a wreath of fresh spring flowers: greens, whites, pale yellows. Ribbons streamed down her back, entwining with her long, silken black hair. She had no makeup on, but she felt beautiful without it. Not that she had done more than glance into a mirror to make sure the wreath was on straight since she had arrived at the Convocation—the beauty she felt was of the spirit, not the flesh. It was a sense of peace, of belonging.

With Season at her side, and with hundreds of other witches joining them, she walked down a gentle slope toward the meadow, as if she just knew it was where she was supposed to be. Some of the witches spoke in hushed, almost reverent tones, but here the mood seemed different than it had up on the hill. This was a special place, a sacred place, and the sometimes rowdy, raucous good humor of the Convocation's public spaces was left behind. In its place was a more spiritual, but equally comfortable, atmosphere.

In the meadow, the witches formed naturally into a great circle. Three witches, two women and a man, stood at the center of the circle, gathered about an altar of upthrust stones that looked like it had been there for a thousand years. On the ancient altar were a spray of flowers and branches, a cauldron also filled with flowers, a fat red candle, a knife, and a censer. When all the witches were gathered—and Kerry didn't know how the ones at the center knew that no more were coming, but they seemed to—one of them lit incense in the censer, and then lit the candle. Flame leaped up from each, then settled to a steady glow.

One of the women at the front lifted the knife and held it in the smoke from the censer for a second. Her hair was waist length and silver, hanging in thick braids around her, and her skin, though lined, looked as fresh as a child's. She smiled out at the gathering, turning in a slow circle so everyone could see the knife. Then she put its point down into the cauldron and said, "I consecrate and cleanse this water, that it may be purified and fit to dwell within this circle of our love. In the name of the Goddess and the God, the Mother and the Father, I consecrate this water."

That said, she lifted the knife from the cauldron, and Kerry saw that its blade was wet. There was water in the cauldron, then, with the flowers inside it sticking out as if from a vase. The man, tall and dark, with a heavy brow and huge hands, stepped to the cauldron next, and dipped his fingers into the water. He turned to the north and dribbled some of the water in that direction. Then he dipped his hand again, and repeated the process to the east, south, and west.

Preparations finished, the third witch took her place at the altar. This one was younger than the others, her blond hair almost white in the sunshine. She put her hands in the flowers, both the ones laying across the altar and the ones in the cauldron, and said, "O great Goddess, you have thrown off the icy grip of winter and embraced the warmth of spring. Now is the greening, the rebirth, the renewal. All things begin again, life takes root in all ways, in the germination and sprouting of every seed, in each breeze that bears warmth on its shoulders, in each ray of sunlight that falls upon your earth."

All three of the witches at the altar joined hands, and as one, the witches in attendance did as well. Everyone in the crowd, at least a thousand strong, was connected to everyone else. The witches at the altar began to speak, and the ones in the audience said the words along with them. Even Kerry knew what to say, as if reading from an invisible script.

"We walk the earth in kinship, in friendship, not in dominance. We are one with the trees and flowers in the field, one with the rocks and hills and mountains, one with each drop of water in the oceans and each grain of sand in the deserts. We are one with all the creatures on, beneath, and above the earth and her oceans. We ask not permission to use the earth but to exist with the earth, in harmony and cooperation with the Goddess and all she represents. We pledge in return to adore and appreciate her clean skies, her fresh rivers, the green and abundant bounty of her skin."

Even as she spoke the words, holding Season's hand in her left and a stranger's in her right, feeling the power of the thousand flowing through her like an electric charge, Kerry thought she could see minuscule green sparks rising up from the candle like motes of pollen. They rose until they were above the crowd, above the depression of the meadow, above the level of the rest of the Convocation, up the short slope, and then they spread in every direction.

That's magic, she thought with a growing sense of awe. *That's our magic, going out to touch every spot on the Earth. Spreading out to protect the air and water, to cleanse, to purify.*

A few moments later, the candle's flame changed, and the greenish dust was dissipating. The witches released hands, and the ones at the altar spoke the words that broke the circle. Season gave Kerry's hand an extra squeeze, and the beatific smile on her face, Kerry guessed, probably matched her own. She could barely believe that she had been part of something like that, something that gave back to the planet from which she had taken so much. They had celebrated nature, and spring, and themselves, all at once. But their celebration had not been an empty gesture, simple praise or lip service. It had included specific and concrete action designed to improve the world they lived in, or at least to help it withstand the ravages of their own kind.

As she walked back up the hill in the company of her fellows, the glow of witch-light was accompanied by the inner glow of deep, lasting satisfaction.

This, she thought happily, *completely rules!*

14

That first full day ended in one of the many tents set up for dinner. If anything, the mood at the evening meal was even rowdier than the earlier ones—the tables were full, and someone at any given table seemed to know people at one of the others. The laughter was loud and long, the stories told hilarious and often bawdy. After the dishes were cleared away, people stayed in the tent, although not necessarily in their seats. Old friendships were re-established and new ones struck. Kerry was treated like one of the gang. In general, the atmosphere was of a holiday meal with close family members, except that it was the biggest family Kerry had ever dreamed of.

The second day was much like the first. This time she felt more at ease, more familiar with her surroundings—ever-changing as they were—and a few times, she and Season split up to do different things. There was a lecture on growing herbs that Kerry wanted to attend, for instance, but Season wasn't that interested and said she had a business meeting that overlapped it. The Convocation wasn't just a fair and a celebration, it was a time of examining the past and planning for the future. This was the only area Kerry felt shut out of, but she figured that she was so new at the whole witch game that she wouldn't have much to offer that would be useful.

The whole thing was eye-opening. She had never imagined that witches came in such a vast assortment of shapes, sizes, colors, nationalities, and temperaments. Given her experience with Season and Mother Blessing, she had assumed that there would be a lot more infighting and treachery than what she had encountered here so far. Her perception, born of hard experience, was that witches were constantly at war with each other, which didn't seem to be the case at all.

The infighting didn't happen until the third day.

When that morning broke, it felt just like the one before. The golden light of magic filled the air, and Kerry's spirits felt lighter than ever, as if her very soul had been tethered to the earth but had now been set free. She woke up soaring.

Season's demeanor that day was different, however.

From the minute she got up, it seemed there was a weight on her. Her smiles were forced and artificial. Even her posture was a little slumped. She wore a conservative white blouse with black pants and boots and tied her hair back in a tight ponytail, a look that was a little formal and severe for her.

Kerry knew what the problem was, of course. Today was the Witches' Tribunal. Her case against Mother Blessing—or Mother Blessing's against Season—would be heard. She wasn't clear on which was the defendant and which the plaintiff. Then again, if it hadn't been for courtroom shows on TV, she wouldn't have known the difference anyway, her own life having been mercifully trial-free. She guessed it didn't much matter. The important thing was that Season would have her say, and justice would be meted out.

After breakfast she accompanied Season to the Tribunal—a vast open-air pavilion with several hundred seats set up in a configuration not unlike a TV courtroom's. They sat about halfway back and observed while several other cases came up on the docket. The Tribunal itself consisted of five witches, dour-faced, gray-haired eminences one and all, as opposed to the jovial group outside this pavilion. Season explained in hushed tones that it was deliberate—to sit on the Tribunal, one had to be a witch of considerable experience and wisdom, having attended at least three previous Convocations. Away from the Tribunal grounds, these justices might be as carefree as any other witch, but while they worked they kept serious demeanors to indicate the care with which they did the job and the respect they held for accusers and accused alike.

In this crowd, however, no one wore black robes, and that included the jurists of the Tribunal. They wore long, flowing robes, but two were of a deep forest green, one of darkest midnight blue, and two a rich wine color. The robe colors might have had some significance, but if so, Kerry wasn't told what it was.

The cases mostly involved matters that seemed minor to Kerry—the equivalent of small claims court or disputes over whose dog was using whose yard as a restroom. One male witch was accused of having counteracted the spell of a female for no reason except that he was angry because her dog had beat up his at a picnic. He claimed that her dog had been a vicious brute who should have been put down, but even so, that was not the reason he had counteracted her spell—it was because he had been asked to by the person her spell was directed at. Doing so, he declared, was perfectly legal under the witches' code of justice.

The judges agreed with his argument, but they still faulted him for not having communicated with her directly before countering her spell. Both witches were directed to do volunteer work in their community—nothing witchy about it, simply labor in the service of the people among whom they lived. All in all, Kerry decided, it was a lot like watching an extended episode of *Judge Judy*, except that the justices were less annoying and there were no commercial breaks.

By the time Season's case came up, however, she was having to stifle her yawns. Everything had been so orderly, so composed, that it was all a little dull. She knew that the dispute between Season and Mother Blessing was made of juicier stuff, and she guessed that many of the other spectators in the place were there to watch it unfold.

The justice at the far left of the bench, one of the two men, called Season

Howe and Myrtle Blessing—one of the few times Kerry had ever heard her referred to as anything but Mother Blessing—to the front. Both women rose and advanced, though Mother Blessing's legs seemed to have gotten worse—she relied more heavily on the cane, and she had a noticeable limp, accompanied by several winces and even a groan or two. Kerry thought the whole thing way over-the-top theatrical, and couldn't believe she was laying it on so thick. Surely the justices would see through it.

But instead, the one in the center—the oldest, judging from normal, non-witchy standards, which Kerry understood to be meaningless in this instance—tossed her a look of profound and genuine sympathy. "I'm sorry to put you through this, Mother Blessing," she said. "And I trust we will resolve this matter swiftly and to everyone's satisfaction."

"That's all I'm hopin' for too," Mother Blessing said. Even the cornpone Southern accent had been intensified for the occasion. Mother Blessing was obviously going to play every card at her disposal, and then some.

"I'm sure that's the result all of us will work toward," Season said. She sounded intelligent and articulate. Kerry hoped that didn't work against her—the city slicker trying to take advantage of the down-home gal. Both parties to the action were directed to sit at the front of the gallery, between the bench and the spectators. Season took her seat primly, with her legs crossed and her hands folded in her lap, while Mother Blessing practically sprawled into hers.

The center jurist, the one wearing the dark blue robe, glanced at a piece of paper, as if reminding herself of the nature of the case, and then addressed Mother Blessing. *Or Myrtle,* Kerry thought with a private smile.

"Mother Blessing, we are here to consider an event that occurred in the year 1704, in the place known as Slocumb, Virginia. Were you present at that event?"

"Durn tootin'," Mother Blessing said, provoking a raucous laugh from the audience, if not from the justices.

"And would you tell us what you remember about that event, including specifically the role that Season Howe played in it?"

"Yes," Mother Blessing said, more sober now. "I will."

She spent the next half hour telling the Tribunal pretty much the same story Kerry had read in Daniel's journals, adding some of the details that Daniel had apparently not known but that she had mentioned to Kerry. There were even a couple that Kerry hadn't heard before. For instance, when she described how Season had gone berserk and started magically blasting townsfolk, including her husband, Winthrop Blessing, she mentioned that Season had specifically singled Winthrop out, shouting, "You'll never live to spread your lies about me!" at him as she reversed his own musket ball into his brain.

With the exception of those embellishments, however, it was the same story Kerry had heard before. When witchcraft was determined to be the cause of the deaths of the Flinders children, both of the town's witches were suspected. Mother Blessing cooperated with the investigation, while Season Howe flew into an unreasonable fury, answering even the most innocuous questions with violence and death. The more she raged, the more furious she became, feeding on her own anger in some sort of escalating feedback loop. Finally, Mother Blessing, to save her own life and the lives of her unborn sons, had taken refuge deep in the Swamp. Season had continued her rampage even after everyone in town was dead, burning each house and starting a fire that burned for months, feeding off the peat that grew in the Swamp.

By the time she had finished her tale, tears streamed down Mother Blessing's face, smearing her eyeliner into twin black rivers. "I didn't dare come out of the Swamp for a month, maybe more, your honors," she declared. "When I finally did, and went to look at the town where I had lived, where my husband had died, where my sons had been conceived, the ground was still hot to the touch. Nothin' grows on that soil to this day, and you'll never convince me that anything will. It's cursed land, blasted and scorched by the explosive temper of . . ."—here she lowered her gaze, as if she was afraid to look directly at Season, and ticked her head toward her foe instead—". . . of Season Howe."

Kerry glanced around the pavilion. Faces were serious, reflective. Mother Blessing had told her story well, tossing in whatever theatrics she could to make sure it played to the room. People seemed to believe her. Kerry noticed a few spectators eyeing Season carefully, as if she might throw a murderous fit right here before the Tribunal.

"Is there anything else you would like to add?" one of the justices asked Mother Blessing.

"Only that both of my sons, blessed be their spirits, were later murdered by Season Howe for the crime of tryin' to find her and bring her to some kind of justice."

"Justice is why the Tribunal exists," another jurist pointed out. "It is not yours to deliver."

Mother Blessing sniffled and dabbed at her eyes with a formerly white handkerchief that had turned ash gray. "It's not so easy to tell a pair of grievin' boys that, your honor. Ones who never got the chance to know their daddy in this life."

"I'm sure that's true," the jurist replied.

"Season Howe," the justice in the center intoned. "You stand accused. How plead you?"

Season had sat quietly through Mother Blessing's entire monologue. Kerry thought it must have been difficult to resist rolling her eyes at some of the more obvious whoppers, or laughing out loud from time to time, but Season had managed. She maintained an air of dignity even as she turned in her seat to face the bench.

"I plead not guilty, your honor, and request the Tribunal's permission to state my case."

The justice nodded. "By all means," she said.

Season cleared her throat and began. "My daughter speaks the truth, up to a point," she said. "We did both live in Slocumb at that time. She did reside with her husband, Winthrop Blessing. What she didn't mention—what she apparently never mentions when she tells this tale—was that they had a first son, whom she named Darius. I had followed the tradition of giving my daughter a name from nature, but as you can see, that is but one of the many ways in which she chose to differentiate herself from me. When my former husband, Forest, heard about Darius, he came to Slocumb to meet his first grandchild. Forest was an evil witch, as I'm sure many of you will remember. Cruel, heartless, cold, and dedicated to dark pursuits."

There was a murmur of recognition and assent from the crowd—apparently Forest Howe's unpleasant reputation had not been forgotten.

"In Slocumb," Season continued, "Forest's influence over Myrtle grew quickly. I had tried to keep them separated from the time I first learned of Forest's true nature—sadly, only after Myrtle was born—but they were both adults now and I couldn't prevent them from being together. Myrtle, it turned out, was her father's daughter, much more than mine.

"Mother Blessing's version of events that followed is true again, up to a point. The widow Flinders did awaken to find her children brutally murdered. The townspeople did rouse the two of us, the two prominent witches in town—but not to question us. Instead, they wanted us both dead, right then and there, no questions asked. There had been earlier incidents, no doubt games Forest and Myrtle played, and the town had had enough.

"Both of us fought back," Season went on. "The townsfolk were prepared for resistance, and battle was joined. In the fight, the townspeople killed Forest and young Darius, and Myrtle simply became unhinged. From that point, everything she attributes to me was, in fact, her doing. She killed every living soul in town. She blasted the houses, ruined the land, started the fires. People from nearby towns saw the smoke and came to help, and Myrtle accused me, told them I was a witch—in itself, one of the most serious crimes with which this Tribunal has to contend. I ran, to save myself. Ran and hid. I had been injured in the battle, could barely escape with my life. But I left only after the town was razed by her magic. She claims to have run before the town was destroyed, yet she knows precisely the progression of events. How would she know? She never told a soul, including her other sons, Daniel and Abraham, about Darius and Forest. She didn't tell this Tribunal. But you all remember Forest. Do you recall any instance of him appearing after 1704? Do you know how he died, unless you've heard it from me? You certainly have never heard it from Myrtle, who has conveniently forgotten that she ever had a father."

She stopped then, regarded the audience impassively, and even let her gaze sweep across her daughter.

After a respectful period, the center justice spoke again. "Mother Blessing," she said. "You have now heard Season Howe's rebuttal to your testimony. Do you have anything you wish to add?"

"Durn—I mean, I sure do, your honor," Mother Blessing replied, garnering another laugh. Not as big as the first one, though. By now, the crowd was caught up in the drama of the moment. "No, I did not mention the fact that Season Howe is my mother—a fact I try hard to forget every day of my life. I didn't mention my father, either, because he wasn't there when all this happened. I don't have the first clue how he died—she made sure that I never really got to know him. Just like my boys never got to know Winthrop. Almost seems like she has somethin' against fathers and sons, doesn't it? As for this 'Darius,' I reckon she made him up out of whole cloth. Go ahead and examine the records—you won't find the birth of any Darius Blessing ever reported."

"We have inspected the records, in consideration of this account," one of the jurists who hadn't yet spoken announced. "And it is true, there has never been any report of the birth or death of Darius Blessing."

Mother Blessing gave a satisfied nod at that pronouncement, and a ripple of talk rushed through the pavilion.

"Season Howe?" the middle justice asked, raising her voice to be heard over the crowd.

"I'm sure the lack of responsibility Myrtle demonstrates by not having properly reported the birth and death of her first son will not be construed as evidence of anything but that simple fact," Season said.

"Very well," the center jurist said. "We will deliberate."

They left Season and Mother Blessing sitting in the front of the room while the justices put their heads together and spoke in low tones. They had done the same with the day's other cases, but Kerry thought this one probably deserved a more careful and spirited debate than those simple ones.

After only a few minutes, however, they broke their huddle and addressed the crowd. "We have been unable to arrive at a conclusion," the eldest announced. "Both stories have the ring of truth to them, although clearly both cannot be true. If there is more evidence to be presented, the Tribunal would be willing to hear it."

Mother Blessing spoke up first. "I really don't know what more y'all could possibly need," she said. "It's plain as day that she's lyin'. Just look at her."

The audience reacted with a surprised chuckle at her audacity. Horrifyingly, Kerry was afraid her pronouncement might have the desired effect. She saw some of the audience, as well as the Tribunal, examining Season as if looking for a big red L to appear on her forehead.

When the laughter faded, Season took her turn to address the Tribunal. "Myrtle's argument doesn't seem particularly compelling to me," she said. "I'd like to suggest a more definitive approach. I hereby request a Viewing."

Kerry didn't know what a Viewing was, but she could tell by the universal gasp of astonishment that it was not standard everyday Tribunal procedure.

"That's highly irregular, Season," the center justice declared. "Not without precedent, but unusual to say the least."

"I appreciate that," Season said.

"Not only is it unusual," the justice went on, "but I'm not certain we can accommodate the request. You are aware of the level of power and proficiency required for a Viewing?"

"I am," Season affirmed.

"You could not possibly accomplish it on your own," the justice said. "Mother Blessing could legitimately be a party to it, but the Tribunal can't force her to merge her power with yours, and given the circumstances—"

"Uh-uh. No way," Mother Blessing interrupted. "I ain't lettin' her get inside of me."

"As I suspected," the justice said. "The Tribunal itself cannot be a party to such an action, since we have to be free to see and interpret for ourselves. Unless you have some other suggestion—"

"I do," Season said, also interrupting. She turned her head, and her gaze caught Kerry's, bored into her. "I request that the Tribunal allow Kerry Profitt to participate."

15

Kerry felt her cheeks crimson as every eye in the pavilion fell on her. "Me?" she asked, fully aware that it was a cliché even as she said it. Surely there was no other Kerry Profitt around. And if there had been, just as surely Season would have mentioned the coincidence to her.

So the only out was if she had misheard altogether.

Since Season's gaze was fixed on her, and a slight smile curved her red lips, she didn't think that was the case. Kerry couldn't hear her voice over the buzz in the pavilion, but the word on her mouth was unmistakable. "You."

Kerry realized that her left hand was stupidly pointing at her own chest. "But—but I—" she stammered.

"Kerry Profitt," the center justice said, looking at Kerry as if she had only just crawled out from under something unsavory. The audience fell silent as she spoke. "She is . . . quite inexperienced, isn't she?"

"Maybe not as inexperienced as you might think," Season said.

"She does look very young," the male jurist on the end observed.

"She is young," Season admitted. "So were we all, once."

"A very good point."

Finally, Mother Blessing was able to do something with her mouth other than sit there with it hanging open. "I don't . . . I don't think that girl ought to be allowed to have anything to do with this," she declared.

"And why not, Mother Blessing?" one of the justices inquired.

"Because . . ." Kerry could see her trying to come up with some legitimate objection. "Because I taught her. I knew her before Season ever did."

"Well, then," the center justice noted, "you should be assured of her objectivity, isn't that right?"

Mother Blessing had opened her mouth and set her own trap. Kerry knew her well enough to recognize the look that crossed her face—the realization that she wasn't going to get her own way this time.

"All right," she said finally. "Let her try. We'll see if she has the stuff to pull it off."

The justices seemed satisfied by that. "Kerry Profitt," the eldest said, looking right at her. "Please approach the Tribunal."

As Kerry stood and made her way down her row of seats, various witches—some she had met over the past couple of days, others she had not—offered whispered encouragement. She was glad. Their confidence in her helped fight off the rubber knees, the dry throat, the quavering hands, as she stood before the bench.

"I'm Kerry Profitt."

"Do you know Season Howe?" the middle justice asked.

"I do."

"And do you know Mother Blessing?"

"Yes, I do."

"And do you have reason to believe one of them more than the other, in this case?"

"Definitely," Kerry said.

"Season Howe has asked for your assistance with a Viewing. It won't be easy. It will be a strain on you, physically, mentally, and emotionally. Your power will be linked with Season's. The two of you will be allied, for the duration of the Viewing, more closely than most people ever are with anyone—right down to the center of your being. This is necessary, however, because no witch lives who can manifest a Viewing by herself. Two very powerful witches can do it, three or more is better. Are you willing to participate in the way that I've described?"

Kerry swallowed. She still couldn't quite believe that Season had selected her for this. There must have been dozens of witches in this pavilion alone who were better suited for it.

But she asked for me.

"I am."

"And are you prepared to let this Tribunal see whatever there is to see, without trying to warp or alter the reality we are being shown?"

She hadn't even known she could alter any reality at all. But then, she still wasn't really clear on what the Viewing entailed. "I am."

"Very well," the jurist said. "This Tribunal calls for a Viewing."

Another buzz from the audience. Apparently a Viewing was a big deal, not something they experienced every day, or maybe even every Convocation. Kerry had the sense of having been swept up in something huge.

Season held out her hand to Kerry, who took it. Season gave hers a squeeze. "You'll be fine," she said quietly. "Don't worry about a thing."

"Just let me know what to do," Kerry said. "I'll give it my best shot."

"Just follow my lead," Season said. "We won't be alone for long."

Kerry wondered what she meant by that but didn't get a chance to ask her. Season took Kerry's other hand and held both tightly. She closed her eyes. Kerry did the same, but not before catching a glimpse of Mother Blessing watching them with a scowl, arms crossed over her expansive bosom. She looked like she wished they were both dead, which she no doubt did, having tried numerous times to achieve exactly that result.

As soon as Kerry's eyes were closed, though, she felt something like a powerful electrical current running through her hands and up her arms. The charge traveled into her shoulders, across her back, then down her spine, through her body, down her legs. She was aware of the fine hairs on her arms and legs standing on end, aware of the air brushing against her skin, aware of every inch of fabric that covered her and the weight of her hair against her back. The smells of the pavilion—the odors of people, flowers, soaps, perfumes, sweat, dirt, even the wood of the chairs—filled her senses. She thought she could hear the breathing and the beating heart of everyone in the place.

But then all those things fell away, as if she had shot up into the air and left everything behind. The sounds were replaced by a rushing noise, the smells by a coppery, electrical scent, and the sensations against her skin vanished completely, as if she had stepped out of her own body.

She was tempted to open her eyes and see what was going on. But Season had said to follow her lead, so she would not open her eyes until she was told to.

As it turned out, she didn't have to. Another moment of darkness passed. A dizzying feeling of vertigo struck her, a wave of nausea that was gone as quickly as it had come. Then her eyes were open of their own volition, and her vision filled with greens, every shade of green: the pale, almost yellow color of new leaves; the dark bluish tinge of fir trees by moonlight; the rich velvet of freshly cut grass, and everything in between. Gradually, shapes delineated themselves in the field of greens, and she realized she was looking at the Great Dismal Swamp, with its tall trees, its thick, almost impenetrable layers of underbrush, its stagnant pools, its hanging mosses.

More disconcerting still was the fact that *through* the Swamp she could see the Tribunal pavilion. It was as if she was looking into a window at night, with the light on the other side—one level of view showed the Swamp, but another one showed where her body stood, hands clasped with Season's. She could even turn her head and take in the bench, Mother Blessing, the audience, without affecting her view of the Swamp. The whole thing made her dizzy again.

When the eldest justice spoke, her voice was muffled as if by distance, but Kerry could still make out the words. For the first time she realized that the people attending the Tribunal could see what she was seeing—at least they could see the Swamp part of it. This, then, was the Viewing—

somehow, she and Season were projecting an image of the Swamp for them.

"You are showing us Slocumb, Virginia, on October twentieth of the year 1704?"

"We are." Season's voice, sounding closer than the justice's.

The image seemed still, static, and Kerry wondered how it could possibly be of any use to the Tribunal. But almost as soon as she thought it, as if in response, there was motion—a figure breaking through the trees, approaching them. A man. He was dressed in modern clothing, not the garb of the eighteenth century. A clean white shirt, sleeves rolled up over tanned forearms. Faded jeans. Brown hair swept away from his forehead. Gray eyes that twinkled as if he had just thought of a private joke. A smile that carved crags in his cheeks.

Daniel!

"Hello, Kerry," he said as he neared them. "It's so good to see you, even . . . even this way."

"I—I don't quite know what to say," Kerry confessed, her heart fluttering against her ribs like a bird in a delicate cage. "You're . . ."

He chuckled. "A sight for sore eyes? Dead? Both?"

In the pavilion, Season released Kerry's hands.

In the Swamp, Daniel took them, lifted one to his lips, pressed it there. Then he let it go and encircled Kerry with his arms. She moved into the hug, and she felt—really felt!—his body, the familiar solidity of his muscular form, the warmth. She could see Season standing beside her, watching with a happy smile.

"This is . . . kind of overwhelming, Daniel," she said. "I mean, I'm thrilled to see you, but . . ."

"I understand," Daniel said sympathetically. "It's not what you were expecting. The Viewing requires a Guide, and Season asked me if I would fill that role. Knowing I would get to see you, I happily agreed. And since my passing, I've come to learn the truth about Slocumb, so I'm happy to share that truth here."

Kerry risked a glance around the pavilion. Daniel wasn't there, so he existed only in the reality represented by the Swamp. "I guess I just don't get how all this stuff works," she admitted.

"No one expects you to yet. You will, in time. Just remember, death is a passage, not a destination."

"So you've told me," she said with a cheerful giggle. The realization that she was genuinely talking to Daniel filled her with a joy she could barely contain.

It took Season to remind her of the serious nature of their activity. "We should get to work," she said firmly.

"Right," Daniel agreed. He gestured behind Kerry, and she turned around.

As she did, the view shifted, and she knew the whole Tribunal audience was seeing what she did. Behind her stood the village of Slocumb as it had on that cold October day. A bitter wind rustled the trees and a rare dusting of snow powdered the ground and the rooftops. The houses were mostly wood-framed, although a few were built of stone or brick. Every one had a prominent chimney, and smoke leaked from most of those. Roofs were steeply pitched and interrupted by gables. Most of the houses were shallow, Kerry guessed only a single room deep.

Daniel led the way toward the village, Kerry and Season following right behind. None of them spoke now, and though Kerry thought she should be able to hear the sound of their feet crunching the frozen earth, their progress was silent. All she heard was the rush of the wind in the trees.

And then the quiet was split by a shattering scream from an open window of the nearest house.

The scene shifted, and they were inside that house. A woman—Kerry knew her at once as the widow Flinders—stared into her children's room, her hands clutching her cheeks in horror. Inside the room was a scene that Kerry didn't want to see. She knew what was there, had already caught a glimpse of blood, shockingly red on the hardwood floor. Kerry tried to keep her gaze riveted on the widow. As awful as the woman's horrified pose was, it wasn't as bad as what was inside the room. Her three children brutally savaged, torn apart with animal fury. The widow Flinders screamed again and ran through the room to the open window, as if whoever was responsible might still be standing outside.

The widow screamed again, louder. In the snow outside were the tracks of a large canine. A wolf, Kerry thought. But the children's room was on the second floor of the house, the window a gabled one set into the roof. How could a wolf have climbed up to that room to do this work?

The widow's screams roused the town. Soon people came running from every direction. Mostly men, many carrying weapons or tools that could be pressed into such service—axes, hoes, muskets. They called to her, and when she couldn't answer, having succumbed to great, wracking sobs and fallen into a heap on her floor, some of them rushed into her house.

Before Kerry had to look at the carnage again, the scene shifted once more. She had the sense that this was Daniel's doing, that his role as Guide was to lead them around, highlighting the most significant events for the benefit of the Tribunal. Now they were outside a house that Kerry knew was Mother Blessing's. Some of the townsfolk, led by a man who had to be Parson Coopersmith, rapped on the door of that house. They looked apprehensive, their weapons bristling toward the door as if they could hide behind them.

Mother Blessing opened the door, looking much as Kerry knew her. The wind fluttered her white cotton nightdress around her. She was a little younger, a little smaller than she was now, but still she dwarfed the man—Winthrop Blessing, no doubt—who tried to crowd into the doorway beside her. There was a brief, clearly antagonistic exchange between the Blessings and the parson, following which she closed the door. Barely a second later—Kerry understood that Daniel was compressing events to a certain degree—she reappeared at the door, this time dressed in a dark, high-collared dress and heavy black shoes. As soon as she stepped out, Parson Coopersmith grabbed one of her arms, and a burly man took hold of the other. Weapons were pointed at her. Winthrop looked on in horror as his wife was led away. Another man shoved Winthrop aside—a man with a ragged, wild look, an unkempt beard, and an infant in his arms. That was Forest Howe, Kerry knew. With young Darius. Forest stalked behind the group taking Mother Blessing away, shouting at them. Kerry was glad she couldn't hear the words.

Another whirlwind shift, and a similar scene played out at Season Howe's house. Season came out fully dressed, with a cap over her blond hair and a brown dress belted around her slender waist. As with Mother Blessing, she was taken captive immediately upon her emergence.

Shift again. Slocumb's town square. Witches being hauled in from two directions. Mother Blessing scowling, tugging, trying to free herself, while Season cooperated, chatting almost casually with those who led her.

Mother Blessing tore an arm free from her captors and pointed accusingly at Season. Parson Coopersmith flinched from her, and apparently that simple action ignited her fury. Now Daniel let them hear her words, screamed in rage. "So you believe that I am a witch, Parson? I'll show you what a witch can do! You should be glad I have suffered you for so long!"

Parson Coopersmith was almost blubbering as he replied. "M—Mother Blessing, there is no need f—for—"

But she cut him off with a simple gesture and a magical blast that Kerry had seen before. *"Hastamel!"* Mother Blessing shouted. A burst of energy expelled from her hands and struck Parson Coopersmith in the center of the chest, rolling through him like a cannonball.

The square was still for a moment, as bits of the parson pattered down on the cobblestones like a heavy rain. Then the townspeople turned on both Season and Mother Blessing, as if they had been equally responsible for the clergyman's demise. A pitchfork's tines drove into Season's ribs before she could even react. Musket balls flew. Axes were swung. Season defended herself magically, even as blood gushed from her initial wound. She drew back to a more defensible position, with the chimney of a nearby house at her back.

Mother Blessing, meanwhile, stood her ground in the center of the square, hurling spells in every direction. Bits of the parson still clung to her cheeks and dress. The townsfolk reacted in kind—trying to shoot her from a distance, prying cobblestones up from the square and throwing them at her. Forest and Darius were spotted at the edge of things, Forest tossing out spells of his own, and the attack was expanded to include him. A musket ball slammed into his shoulder, a cobblestone tore a gash in his forehead, and then he and the child both went down under a mob of townspeople wielding flashing blades and heavy objects. Mother Blessing saw this happen, and her fury visibly grew, her cheeks purpling, her mouth working in incoherent rage.

Season abandoned her position by the chimney and tried to approach Mother Blessing. Her posture and expression were consoling, as if she were trying to calm the other witch. But Mother Blessing wanted none of it, and she drove Season back with wave after wave of magical attacks that Season, injured and weakened, could barely withstand.

Kerry could see the intensity of Mother Blessing's frenzy spiraling out of control. She no longer cared where she aimed her attacks—Kerry wasn't sure she could even see anymore, or if she had been blinded by her own furor. Magical energy swirled around her in a kind of tornado that echoed what must have been going through her twisted mind. The power of her assault tore bricks from houses, ripped boards from their walls and sent them sailing into the Swamp, yanked shingles from their roofs. The dead in the square outnumbered the living now, and not even the people hiding in their own homes were safe from the onslaught.

Kerry looked away from the incredible scene and toward the Tribunal, where she saw faces in shock, aghast at what they were observing. It was obvious to everyone now, Kerry was sure, whose version of the day's events was more accurate.

And while she watched, unable to move or speak on that plane of reality, unable to do anything to intercede, she saw Mother Blessing leave her seat. Arms reached out to stop her but she deftly evaded them. She held something in her right hand—it took Kerry a moment to recognize it as a knife—and she raised it high as she lunged at Season.

Kerry felt the cold steel slicing into Season's breast as surely as if it had been her Mother Blessing had stabbed, felt the shock and pain as the knife's keen blade drove into Season's heart.

Connected to Season, she knew every bit of Season's agony as the life ebbed out of her.

16

In Slocumb the Season who stood with Kerry and Daniel opened her mouth in a surprised-looking O shape. A red spot blossomed on her white blouse, spreading like a rose opening its petals, and then a single drop trailed down the outside of the blouse.

In the Tribunal pavilion, Season made a small whimpering sound. Her eyes rolled back in her head and she collapsed to the floor as if all her muscles had failed her at once.

Kerry couldn't catch her breath. "She stabbed you," she said, but it came out as little more than a squeak.

"I know," Slocumb's Season said, more calmly but still with an edge of worry. She raised a hand to her blouse, touched her chest. The hand came away bloody.

"Season," Daniel said urgently, reaching for her.

"It's okay, Daniel," she assured him.

Kerry had been astonished by many things over the past few days—*make that several months,* she mentally amended—but few things surprised her like the sight of Daniel embracing Season and then drawing away with her blood staining his own crisp shirt. "I am sorry," he said. "For so much."

"You did what you believed was right," she assured him. "No one could expect more than that."

He glanced toward his mother, who in Slocumb was directing her power against what was left of the small town. Houses had been torn apart as if by hurricane winds. Most of the buildings were ablaze now. Nothing living still moved, as far as Kerry could see. "I was . . . I was wrong. We all were."

Season winced—she was still upright in this reality, but the pain she felt was evident. "Now you know. Now everybody does."

Kerry's own discomfort had lessened, becoming a deep, persistent ache instead of the sharp pain it had been at first. She guessed that she had felt it because she and Season were linked, but then as Season faded in the real world—at least, what she perceived as the real world—that connection was broken and the agony became less distinct.

But was Season dead, in that world? And if so, what did that mean for Kerry? Would she be able to get back there?

In that world Kerry could see that the other witches in the audience at the Tribunal had restrained Mother Blessing, wrenching the knife from her grasp and hauling her away from Season's fallen body. On that plane Kerry could only stand there watching Season bleed on the ground. Some witches had gathered around her body and were performing healing spells, and one of them helped move Kerry out of the way.

"Are you . . . are you dying, Season? That knife couldn't really hurt you, could it?" Kerry remembered Mother Blessing firing four bullets into Season's chest, and Season spitting them out into her hand.

"It's within the grounds of the Convocation," Season explained. "It's as infused with magic as everything else there. I'm afraid it was a very effective attack."

"But . . . how effective?" Kerry demanded. "You can't . . ."

Even as she spoke she could see the witches in the pavilion pulling back away from Season's lifeless form. One of them brought out a length of white linen from somewhere and laid it reverently over Season's body.

Once again Kerry's moorings had been yanked away from her. The deaths of her parents, then Daniel, now Season—it seemed that every time she became attached to someone, that someone was taken away. She didn't want to make Season's death be all about her, but it was a disturbing reality just the same.

Then she felt Daniel's comforting hand on her shoulders. "A passage, Kerry," he reminded her. "Not a destination."

"I'm standing here talking to you, right?" Season said.

"Yes, but . . . I'm confused," Kerry complained. Behind them Mother Blessing's Slocumb rampage continued, but no one was watching it—the witch was just as alone now as she had been on that fateful day.

"And you have every right to be." Season rubbed her arm, and with her and Daniel consoling Kerry, she realized she felt almost okay about it. "Life is a wonderful thing, Kerry," Season went on. "And you should embrace it every day. You should look at each new dawn as another opportunity, another promise of hope and love and miracles, and you should look at the stars at night the same way. But life—the kind of life you're thinking about—doesn't last forever. For anyone. Not even witches."

"She's right," Daniel added. "Which is why you need to make the most of every minute you do have."

"Do you understand how incredibly powerful you are, Kerry?" Season asked her. "Not one witch in a hundred could have worked with me to pull off a Viewing. But I had every faith in you, and you pulled it off. You've accomplished every task I've ever put before you. Now I'm asking you to do one more thing."

"What?"

"Go back into your world. Be the best witch you can be, and the best person you can be. Put your abilities to work in the service of something good, something lasting and true. I don't know what that should be, but you'll find it if you look."

"That's all?"

Season and Daniel both laughed. "A lot of people don't seem to be able to do that much," Daniel said. "If you can, you're ahead of the game. But I know you will."

"But . . . but I'll miss you guys so much," Kerry said. "Both of you are the most—"

"We'll be there when you need us, Kerry," Season interrupted.

"And you've been to this plane now," Daniel put in. "You can come back, you know. Drop in from time to time. We'd love to see you, and I know Rebecca, Josh, and Mace would as well. Your parents, too."

The awful reality of Rebecca's death struck Kerry with sickening certainty. Her head spun with the ideas and possibilities they were laying before her. "I guess I still have a whole lot to learn about this stuff."

"You do indeed," Season agreed. "And you can't do that here. You need to go back now."

Kerry glanced into the Tribunal pavilion. Season's body was being taken out, elevated over the shoulders of those carrying her. She could see tears there, but also smiles and laughter. She thought they were remembering Season as she had been, sparkling, full of life and good cheer.

"Go," Daniel urged. "Everything will be fine."

Kerry looked at them both, not wanting to leave them behind, but knowing she had to.

She closed her eyes and centered herself. Willed herself to feel the power that surged inside her.

A sharp drop, a moment's vertigo . . .

And then she was back in the pavilion, with its million aromas, its crush of people, its voices.

Its life.

"Welcome back, Kerry Profitt." That was the center jurist, the eldest one, smiling at her from the bench. "You performed admirably."

"But . . . Season . . ."

"Has moved on," the jurist confirmed, nodding.

Kerry looked around for Mother Blessing. As if guessing who she sought, the male justice on the end said, "She has been taken into custody. Thanks to you, Season, and Daniel, this Tribunal now knows the truth about what happened in Slocumb, and that the blame for all those deaths, all that destruction, rests with Myrtle Blessing. Further, we know of the crimes Myrtle Blessing has committed to cover that one up—the sacrifices of her sons and the many more deaths, over the intervening years, for which she is responsible. And, of course, her murder of Season Howe, right here in our own presence. She will be held accountable for all these crimes."

"What's going to happen to her?" Kerry wanted to know.

The justices looked at each other, as if not sure they wanted to tell her. Finally, the eldest spoke up. "She has committed crimes of the most grievous nature. She has shown no remorse, given no indication that she is willing to stop her criminal actions. She will be stripped of her power." The jurist paused for a second, then added, "All of it."

Kerry considered that for a moment, tried to imagine what it would mean. Mother Blessing unable to manipulate others, manipulate the very earth to do her bidding? She would be—

Wait a minute, Kerry thought, the true meaning of the justice's words becoming clear to her. "But she's hundreds of years old!"

The senior jurist nodded. Kerry thought maybe there was the briefest glimmer of a smile on her face. Just for a split second. "No one said she would enjoy the process."

Kerry stood before the bench, speechless for a moment, horrified at the possibility. Before she could fully compose her thoughts, the justice banged three times on the bench with the palm of her hand. "I declare this Witches' Tribunal adjourned until tomorrow!" she shouted. "And I further declare that it's time for dinner!"

This declaration was greeted by a loud whoop of approval from the crowd. Kerry started for the nearest exit but was caught by a few of the audience members, who offered congratulations and support. Each one held her hands or hugged her, and then more came over, and still more, and then there was a mob around her, and more hugs, and more, and more, and more.

And that was just the beginning of the fun.

17

Kerry had gone inside the little caravan to change clothes for dinner and the evening's celebration, and to grab a few quiet moments to herself after the drama of the Tribunal and its raucous aftermath. At one point she caught a glimpse of Season's bed and then looked around expectantly, remembering even as she did that the trailer would be empty. She didn't quite know how to react for a minute. She had been with Season every day since Christmas Eve, and even before that she couldn't recall a day in which Season hadn't been on her mind from waking until sleep finally captured her again. Suddenly all that was over, and Season wouldn't be greeting her as faithfully as the sun and stars did anymore.

Not only that, but the sun would never set again on Daniel Blessing, or Rebecca Levine, or Mace Winston, or Josh Quinn. She had lost so much—they all had, really. Kerry was becoming convinced that what Daniel and Season had insisted was true: Death was just a passage to another level of existence, and not necessarily something to be mourned. But that didn't keep her from mourning her friends just the same. She figured that ultimately none of them would regret the price they had paid, since the end result was keeping Mother Blessing from continuing her destructive rampage across the land. Certainly plenty of innocents had already fallen victim to her misguided quest, but now at least no more would have to worry about that.

So Kerry tried to smile and greet the evening with the cheerful outlook Season would have wanted her to have. She put on a fresh, pale green frock, slipped sandals on her feet—both things one of the "shopkeepers" had insisted on giving her after the Tribunal was over—and went outside to dinner.

The first morning she had entered the meal tent feeling like a stranger, grateful that she had Season to cling to.

This time, though, she was hailed by at least a dozen people as soon as she had filled her tray. Hands full, she smiled and nodded to several and then sat down next to Tamsinn, a young woman from Pensacola she had met the evening before. Tamsinn was blithesome, with close-cropped purple hair and a ready smile. She greeted Kerry with a grin and a squeeze.

"Are you okay?" she asked. "I know this afternoon was rough on you."

"I think so," Kerry answered, as honestly as she could. "I mean, I'm sure I have a way to go before I'm really back to normal, whatever that is. But I'm not as wrecked as I would have thought either."

"That's good," Tamsinn said. She took a sip of her herbal tea and squinted at Kerry through the steam. "I know this whole deal can seem all huge and complicated when it's new."

"Yeah," Kerry agreed. "I'm definitely still at that stage."

"It'll go by fast," Tamsinn assured her. "Seems like I was there just the other day."

"How long has it been for you?"

Tamsinn scrunched her face up while she did the math in her head. "I guess sixty-two years," she said finally.

Kerry was stunned, although she knew she shouldn't have been. She would have sworn Tamsinn was no more than a year or two older than her, if that. She had learned plenty of times that among the community of witches one couldn't guess age based on appearance. But she wondered, not for the first time, when she would reach the peak of her power, and where she would "freeze," in terms of appearance, as witches did.

"If there's anything you need, Kerry, any questions you have or anything like that, you just let me know, okay? I'll be happy to help. Me and about a thousand other witches, or more. We're here to help guide you, to teach you what we can, and to help you figure out what you're about."

"Thanks, Tamsinn," Kerry said. "That means a lot to me."

Both women resumed eating then, unable to resist the allure of the excellent meal. After dinner there would be a celebration, and then tomorrow, one more day of Convocation. There would be another day of Tribunal tomorrow as well, but she couldn't bring herself to go through that again. She had a feeling that she would cut out early tomorrow, go looking for Brandy and Scott. She needed to tell them about Rebecca, in case they didn't already know. And she found that she missed them a lot.

But before that, she had to finish her dinner.

And then there would be a party to remember.

Kerry lifted a forkful of fresh vegetables and tried to look at every spot in the tent, every face, every outfit, burning it all into her mind.

After all, five hundred years was a long time to wait until the next time.

She found Brandy and Scott at the While-a-Way Motel in Klamath Falls, Oregon, in a room on the second floor. A Harley Davidson convention seemed to have taken over the first, or at least the parking lot and swimming pool area. That didn't matter to Kerry—it wasn't hot enough for swimming yet anyway. The parking lot thing was a little more problematic, but she found street parking for the Raider and hiked in.

Scott threw the door open at her knock and dragged her inside, wrapped in his arms. Brandy joined him, and the three of them held each other for minutes before anyone was willing to break the hug. Kerry had always loved hugging, but her ribs were still a little sore after the lovefest that the last day and night of the Convocation had turned out to be. She had skipped the second day of the Tribunal in favor of trying to get acquainted with as many of her fellow witches as possible.

Finally, she was able to sit down on one of the beds. Brandy claimed the other, and Scott rolled over a wheeled chair from the little dining table. The room was motel basic, adequate for their needs but not much more than that. Kerry noted with a private grin that only one bed seemed to have been slept in. "So?" Scott began while she looked around. "We want to hear everything."

"So do I," Kerry replied. "But first, I should tell you about Rebecca. She's gone—Mother Blessing got her, as we feared. I don't suppose you found her body?"

Their faces fell instantly, so dramatically that they really didn't need to say any more. Brandy did anyway. "We looked all over Santa Cruz for two days, called every hospital up and down the coast, called the morgues, bugged the cops until I thought they'd arrest us. She never turned up. At this point, I have to say I don't think she's going to."

"I'm sorry, Kerry," Scott added. "I know what she meant to you. To all of us, really."

Even though she had already known, talking about their friend felt like a shaft in the heart for Kerry, but she remembered what Daniel and Season had told her. *Just a passage.* She would have to explain that to Brandy and Scott if she could, and she hoped they would understand it without the visual aid that she'd had.

"I'm sorry too," Kerry said, leaving it there for the moment. "Season's dead, too. Mother Blessing killed her at the Convocation. It was awful. But Mother Blessing is being . . . held accountable, finally. For everything she's done. Slocumb, Daniel and Abraham, us. Everything."

"So . . . it's all over?" Scott asked, his voice tinged with excitement. Kerry couldn't tell if he was pleased, or maybe a little disappointed, that their long adventure was coming to a close.

"That part of it's over," she confirmed. "There's no more struggle between

Season and Mother Blessing. No more looking over our shoulders, wondering who's coming for us next. We can finally relax, I guess."

"There's another part?" Brandy pressed. "What's left?"

"The part where I really am a witch now," Kerry said. "And remaining one, and working to develop my abilities."

She watched their faces carefully when she told them. Brandy's looked tentative, as if she was withholding judgment on Kerry's future plans. But Scott grinned like some kind of madman. "That's great!" he enthused. "I think you'll be such a good witch. Does that sound stupid? Kerry the good witch?"

"A little," Kerry said. "But I get what you mean, and thanks."

"I guess we should tell her our plans, too," Brandy said, leaning over to tap Scott's shoulder.

"I guess so," he agreed.

"'Our'? You guys have 'our' plans?"

"Well, we still have plenty of school to get through," Scott said. "Maybe even grad school, who knows? But the tentative plan is, as soon as we graduate, we get married. And then, as soon as we can, we start working on a family."

"I guess we're kind of used to having a lot of people around," Brandy said. "And a lot of excitement."

"And of course, Aunt Kerry is definitely a part of whatever family plans we make," Scott added.

Kerry laughed. "I'm an aunt already? The graduating part hasn't even happened yet."

"Well, when it does," Brandy clarified with a laugh. Kerry was thrilled to see the two of them looking so happy. Every time they glanced at each other, their gazes held. *They are definitely in love,* she thought.

Nothing wrong with that.

Kerry Profitt's diary, March 24

They kept telling me that death is a passage, and okay, I can buy that.

What they didn't say is that there are plenty of other passages too. Scott and Brandy, starting a family? Scott and Brandy sitting in one room speaking civilly to each other would have been a lot to ask four months ago. I don't know if they'll really do it—who ever knows what's going to happen next week or next month, let alone two years from now? There are a lot of passages ahead for them, and maybe they'll weather them together. Maybe not. They'll be okay either way.

Maybe that's what Daniel and Season have left me with. I'm going to be fine. Scott and Brandy too. Things work out if you let them, if you work at them, if you help them along. And if you open your eyes and your mind and your heart to whatever each day brings. Sounds like something out of one of Brandy's pop psychology books, but there it is.

Anyway, I hope they do start a family, because it's been a while since I've really had one I could call my own. Now I'll have two—theirs, and the family of witches. The members of the Convocation took me in, embraced me, really made me feel that I was welcome there, wanted there even without being under Season's wing.

Of course, it's a long time until the next Convocation. There's a movement under way to hold them more often, maybe every hundred years instead of every five hundred. Easier to keep track of old friends, and new ones, that way. I'm voting in favor of it.

After the Tribunal, and the celebration that followed, I made my way back to our trailer, a little sad that Season wasn't in it with me but also happy, happier than I can remember being, oh, pretty much ever. Because there was a new sensation I was carrying around with me, and it wasn't the love of any particular individual, I realized, and it wasn't even my new understanding of my own power.

It was peace.

That's all. That simple.

I don't know what Scott and Brandy's future holds, and I don't know what mine does. I'm the new witch on the block, the new pawn in a very, very old game. Chaos and entropy on one side, order on the other.

But that's the future. That's tomorrow, and all the tomorrows after that.

For now, for tonight, I cling to peace.

And that's all I really need.

More later.

K.

ACKNOWLEDGMENTS

I am greatly indebted to the many people who've had a hand in this, including (but by no means limited to) Lisa Clancy, Michelle Nagler, Amanda Berger, Annette Pollert, Nicole Ellul, Dianne Larson, Becca Lovatt, Alex Bennett, and my family.

ABOUT THE AUTHOR

JEFF MARIOTTE is the award-winning author of more than seventy novels, including thrillers *Empty Rooms* and *The Devil's Bait*; supernatural thrillers *Season of the Wolf*, *Missing White Girl*, *River Runs Red*, and *Cold Black Hearts*; and horror epic *The Slab*. With his wife, author Marsheila Rockwell, he wrote the science fiction, horror thriller *7 Sykos* and numerous shorter works. He also writes comic books, including the long-running horror, Western comic book series *Desperadoes* and graphic novels *Zombie Cop* and *Fade to Black*. He has worked in virtually every aspect of the book business, including bookselling, marketing, editing, and publishing. He lives in Arizona, in a home filled with books, art, music, toys, and love.